DISTURBANCE AT THE HOUSE OF LIES

EWIN GENGHIS

Published in Australia by Sid Harta Books & Print Pty Ltd,
ABN: 34632585293
23 Stirling Crescent, Glen Waverley, Victoria 3150 Australia
Telephone: +61 3 9560 9920, Facsimile: +61 3 9545 1742
E-mail: author@sidharta.com.au

First published in Australia 2023
This edition published 2023
Copyright © Ewin Genghis 2023
Cover design, typesetting: WorkingType (www.workingtype.com.au)

ISBN: 978-1-922958-46-4

For you, the Other
Through You we find Self
That symphony stalled—
Lost somewhere between death and madness

Know thyself

Oracle of Delphi, 7th century BCE

CONTENTS

DISCLAIMER

Readers who believe that mental health workers fully understand the human mind and/or always act in the best interests of clients are best to avoid this book if they wish to preserve peace of mind. Furthermore, the book should only be read if the reader accepts that the novel *Disturbance at The House of Lies* is likely, at some level, to provoke uncomfortable thoughts about the nature of mental health and mental health therapy.

Trigger warnings are given with regard to the following situations, which will all be encountered head on in the text: poor mental health, low education level, emotional distress, non-gratuitous educational explicit sex, body shaming, deprivation in childhood, step-motherhood, lesbian attraction, religious violence, police brutality, child abuse, sexual violence, PTSD, sexual perversion, suicide, infant loss, male-female relationship.

Readers seeking help to cope with these issues will not find the world's currently accepted solutions in this book.

This is a novel. The psychological and medical aspects of the text are literary in nature, not scientific. Many of the characters are intentionally portrayed as unreliable or mentally unwell or emotionally disturbed. Assertions are made for dramatic purposes and are often non-factual and cannot be relied upon.

All depictions are for illustrative purposes only and do not in any way represent the author's real opinion; neither are they intended towards any real person (child or adult), real institution, or real corporation.

Readers seeking reliable information or help with mental health issues need to engage with qualified and recognised real-life mental health professionals.
Lifeline is available in most countries if urgent help is needed.

PREFACE

Newly qualified counselling psychologist Alyssa Brown has been appointed as a staff member at an upmarket mental health clinic near where she lives in the centre of the city of Hubron. Alyssa is intelligent, physically attractive, and courageous, and hopes for a good life after the rigours of a difficult childhood.

She suffers a setback when Time starts to occur out of time. Her past, it would appear, is not done with her yet. Flashbacks increase, and soon they are truly frightening. Who is she really? And what is a person like *her* doing as a counsellor at the Donald Clinic?

The functional way of being that Alyssa has so carefully constructed over the past years is under attack. A war has begun, one that she does not understand. Yet, if she tells anyone what is happening, she will be labelled *mentally disturbed*. For the sake of her new job and her future, she must pretend that nothing is wrong.

Residual psychological issues are to be expected in all who survive childhood, she tells herself, and she is no different. As far back as she can remember, there have always been malevolent pressures at the back of her mind, and a need to resist giving in to madness. With her skills as a counsellor, if anyone can fight back, she can. After all, despite every bad thing in her life, she has managed to remain emotionally stable and achieve an independent life in the city.

Yes, she has always felt a little different to others, especially those in the city, but for her this has been the only remaining shadow from the dark days.

Until now.

Now that Time has started to mess with her head.

Seemingly out of nowhere, it has returned: the darkness of then. Like a beast waking somewhere inside her, a powerful force is rising.

The darkness of then.

One more death is required . . .

PART I

WHEN A MONSTER SPEAKS

CHAPTER ONE

1

A HEATWAVE WAS IN progress, made worse by the concrete canyons of the central city. While hot weather was not unexpected in Hubron—after all, beyond the mountains lay a desert—the heat outside was giving hot a new meaning. Alyssa checked the weather report on her phone. The temperature in the streets outside the gym had set a record. The entire country, it seemed, was burning up; not just Hubron but Astoria too.

Inside the gym, however, conditions were bearable. Fabio, the gym owner, was not a man to let his patrons down and the air-conditioning had been adjusted timeously. Fabio was good in that way, with his attention to detail. Alyssa liked him even though he was unduly obsessed with her body, but she often wondered what made him tick. What did old and obese Fabio think *she* would get out of having sex with him? She understood a great deal about men but not that.

Fabio's gym was a home from home for her. Indeed, it would be true to say that since leaving Ocean View for the city all those years ago, the place exerted an emotional hold over her. In a strange way, the gym felt like the small hometown Sunday school she used to go to as a child; somehow, it was significant.

Yes, that was a bit weird.

It was a Friday, approaching lunch hour, with the day so far uneventful except for the heat, but it didn't stay that way.

Everything became a bit weird.

When looking back on what happened, Alyssa wondered whether her mind had been a little more preoccupied than usual while getting changed in the gym's female change room. There had been her fears about the future, and the little voice saying, "not good enough", but in truth the thoughts had not been too concerning. Though negative, as always, they had seemed nothing more than a flare up of the background anxiety that normally followed her around.

No, it was only once she had emerged into the exercise hall in her gym gear that the strange thing happened.

When the terrible thoughts forced themselves into her mind against her will.

Death comes.

Out of nowhere, the dread crashed into her with the power of a collapsing wall and images of mutilated corpses began attacking her mind with sickening power.

Alyssa staggered in shock and clutched onto a nearby storage shelf for support.

Despair came at her in powerful waves and tried to carry her off, but grimly she focused on her breathing and held on.

This was not the first time it had happened, so she knew what to do: stand still, close her eyes tightly, and focus on the now. Use mindfulness to force down the flashback.

There had been a time, though, five years earlier, when she had not known what to do and had not won. But that seemed a lifetime away. During that admission to hospital, the feelings of awful badness had been so overwhelming that she had almost died. She had tried to jump out of an eleventh-floor window. To escape.

But she was fine now. And she had gone on to study psychology—to help others.

So, now, in the gym hall, she won in the end against the new intrusion.

She knew that she would win.

She had won before. And she was stronger now.

Too strong for anything from the past to be able to get the better of her. Which was not true, unfortunately, as it soon turned out.

The bad thoughts, though, initially appeared to have gone. Even so, they had been away for years, so it was worrying that they had attempted to return.

For the first time in a long while, it seemed evil again had its sights on her.

The dead were back.

Death had found her. The old familiar fear was back.

It was not going to be a normal Friday after all.

Her mind was playing tricks on her. She was being retraumatised. This was what those who had treated her in hospital would say if they saw her now. They would opine that she had post-traumatic stress disorder, a psychological condition where the victim was unable to distinguish between the present and the past. But, of course, what she had wasn't that at all.

Her truth had a different name.

One that she could not admit to anyone, including herself, without losing the will to live.

The air moves in; the air moves out.

After a few minutes of focused breathing, she looked around. Nobody was staring. The patrons at the health club were good that way: they did not stare. Thankfully, they knew her by now, knew that sometimes she behaved a little strangely.

Nevertheless, the unexpected episode of bad thoughts felt extremely embarrassing. And highly disappointing.

After all, she had studied Obermaaier's *"Gnomon Theory"* during counsellor training and should not have been caught out. According to the great professor's textbook, Gnomons were the rulers of Time. Conceptually—metaphysically—they existed in the unconscious mind and represented the mechanism for recording the exact time *Truth* became *A Lie*. At each such point, a gnomon froze and thereafter marked the error and continued to request the mind to return to it. Resistance to this requirement was futile. According to Obermaaier, far from being nonsensical creations, gnomons affected the destiny of everyone. The only way to unfreeze a frozen gnomon was to travel back to the time in question and deal with the true facts. To achieve healing from torment by gnomons, rearrangement of the mind was required.

Only now did she truly understand what she had read. Escape was not going to be easy. The past never failed to remember. Time did not heal. And, if anyone was going to be living proof of this unfortunate fact, it was going to be her. Obermaaier had said it well: she was still vulnerable. Despite her own best efforts, the passage of time had changed nothing.

The unwanted memories were stronger than time. Memory, so fickle, was the ruler of time. Parts of her mind were outside of time and seemed easily capable of turning the past into the future. Perhaps she would forever remain a bad person, seeing that she *was* a bad person. She was still that little girl, a part of her still irredeemably evil. This had to be why, after so many years, such a strong presence of evil had returned.

A wicked heart cannot be mended.

2

A movement at the corner of Alyssa's eye distracted her. It was the newcomer. She had noticed him earlier in passing when she was coming out of the change room. Now he was at the water fountain, directly across the exercise hall from her, where she could study him covertly. It was what he was doing that caught her attention. He was drinking water. He drank from the fountain swiftly, purposefully, and in powerful gulps. She watched in idle fascination. She liked young men, especially men who appeared strong and confident. She found them easy to deal with because they always wanted sex with her. In her hands, they came readily to heel.

When the young man at the fountain had slaked his thirst, he stood up, whipped a paper towel from a dispenser, and dried his hands. There was sweat on his face, and he wiped that away too. Strong hands, strong face, crumpled paper. Unexpectedly, as she watched the spectacle from a distance, it was arousing.

Nice.

At least feeling horny was better than feeling frightened, she thought. She continued staring until he moved away. She doubted she would ever tire of attractive young males.

Then she gave herself a mock slap in the face. She was not at the gym to stare at men but to keep in shape. She needed to concentrate on the job at hand. First, she had to put on her gym shoes. She was still in her socks. Blushing slightly, Alyssa extracted a pair of gym shoes from a plastic holder in her sports bag, which was sitting on one of the shelves she had been holding onto earlier. She had two pairs of shoes to choose from: newer or older. Today, she felt a need to look her best, so she chose the newer. Nothing like putting one's best foot forward, so to speak. The gym shoes were kept separated from her clothes by a plastic bag because she had studied bacteria as part of an extra course during training. What little she had learnt about germs in Sexology 101 had been enough to make her respect them. Germs were not something to take lightly.

While busy, she noticed that there was a new poster on the notice board above the shelves. When she tried to read it, though, she had difficulty focusing her eyes. For some reason, the poster kept going in and out of focus. She had to read it three times before it made any sense.

> Existence is the story you tell yourself
> You are the illusion you create
> Learn to get over yourself
> It begins today
> Write a new story
> *The Existentialists*

What an odd thing to have on a gym poster, she thought. She suspected it came from Fabio, who was forever trying to be inspirational. It was probably an attempt to encourage his patrons in the task of transforming themselves, physically at least. She was surprised Fabio knew about existentialism. Without the evidence on the wall in front of her, she would not have believed he knew anything at all about philosophy.

For some reason, the poster made her feel uneasy. Its words seemed to have a hidden meaning directed at her specifically. "You are the illusion you create". Did Fabio know too much about her? she wondered. The poster seemed too personal. It was as though he suspected something; as though Fabio knew she was an imposter; knew that her life was just a pretence; knew that even though she appeared to be alive, she was dead. Dead inside. Did Fabio *know* that she had killed everyone she had ever cared about? That she might do the same to someone else?

All dead.

It was impossible that he could know what she had done. No one did.

Perhaps it was hotter in the gym than she realised. Perhaps it was the excessive heat—perhaps it had given her a touch of heat stroke. The problem was that the poster on the wall wasn't really there. She had read something that wasn't there. She discovered that part later. That she had been hallucinating.

Not since second year.

Heat combined with anxiety made for an explosive combination. Whatever the explanation, something was going horribly wrong. Something had changed; the meaning of things had changed. She did not seem to know herself at all. She had no idea who she really was or even what anything really meant. All she could see was lies. Everything was a lie.

Did heat stroke do this to a person? Probably not. What then? Was it her illness trying to return. That seemed unlikely too. The weirdness happening in the gym was not like what happened in the past.

Back then, it felt quite different.

This was not insanity—not that she had ever been truly insane before.

Then something else happened—and yes, perhaps she should have told someone. Perhaps if she had not kept silent about what happened next, things may have turned out differently. Perhaps they would have stopped her in time. Perhaps the further deaths would have been avoided. Perhaps.

3

A strangeness came over her. It was a peculiar and drawn-out process, so it's exact beginning was unclear. It may in fact have begun with him drinking at the water fountain. The hands of the clock on the gym wall, the clock between the entrances to the male and female change rooms, began to shudder. It was the clock directly above the water fountain.

Its hands stopped moving. The clock stopped. Time stopped.

Was she imagining it, or had the hands of the clock stopped? She stared. The three hands had merged into one vertical hand. It was twelve noon, down to the exact second. And the hands stayed there.

Frozen.

A warp in the fabric of space-time had occurred. This was the only way she could describe it later; the way it had felt at the time. Something *warped*, not in her head, but outside of herself.

A mere coincidence? Nothing more significant than having looked up at exactly the right moment? Absolutely not. Twelve noon was when her mother was killed.

Alyssa stared at the clock with increasing alarm. To her horror, the hands of the clock remained motionless. Minutes passed. The clock was dead, just like her mother. She continued staring in hope, but nothing happened. It remained twelve noon. She was stuck back in another world.

Trapped.

Nothing was making any sense.

It had to be a warning. It had to be. The coincidence was too great. It was going to happen all over again. Her body began to shiver all on its own.

Something bad was going to happen.

She just knew it.

It was going to happen all over again.

Breathe.

She forced her eyelids closed with her fingers so that she could no longer stare at the dead clock.

Get over this crap, will you!

Swearing at herself was not going to help.

It's just anxiety.

Her new job was stressful. Work was stressful. The weirdness would soon pass.

She just needed to get a grip. Take charge.

Then she would become calm and functional again.

And nobody would be any the wiser.

4

Only then did she discover that she was blocking his access to the storage shelves. When she opened her eyes, the young man she had earlier been lusting over—at the water fountain—was standing right in front of her. It came as a shock.

'Oh!' she gasped.

He appeared to be talking. 'Excuse me,' he said, 'but I need to get to my keys.'

'What?' Up close, he was the most stunning creature she had ever seen. *Cripes, I'm in love!*

Was it possible to fall in love instantly? And was it love or just lust? 'Sorry,' she mumbled. She flicked her eyes back up to the clock. It read five minutes past twelve and was moving normally. It probably always had been.

Had this man just scrambled her mind?

What is wrong with me?

Not only had she lost part of her life, but she was in love with a stranger. She frowned. She was an expert in counselling, yet she did not seem to know anything at all about the human mind. She wondered how such a thing could be possible.

The outrageously attractive Adonis moved into her personal space. He spoke again, in a clear voice: 'My keys.'

She had not seen him before despite being a regular at the gym. He was not someone she would forget seeing. Clearly, he was new to the gym. He sounded irritated but seemed friendly. She stared at him, intrigued, but he did not step back. Instead, he returned her gaze with remarkable composure for someone of his age. Young men were not usually that bold with her—not in public. Despite the confident way he risked an accusation of sexual assault by standing an inch from her, he looked kind. His face spoke not only of strength but also of harmony and serenity. She felt weak inside.

What is going on!

He was tall and slim, had brown hair, and was wearing tattered navy track pants and a black track vest. The skin on his arms and chest was smooth and it glistened from exercise. It seemed he was about to depart. She, on the other hand, had only just arrived.

For the third time, he spoke. 'Excuse me. Is there something wrong with you?'

There was, but she did not know how to tell him.

He looked directly into her eyes, as though examining her, and as he did so she saw into his eyes too. She saw that he had a weakness. His weakness was that he needed a woman like her. The certainty of it flared in her like fire.

He wanted her.

He was just like her.

'Oh, I am sorry!' she said, finally able to move. 'Forgive me. I was away on another planet.' Hastily, she stepped out of his way. She felt her face reddening. 'Hi. I'm Alyssa, by the way. Welcome to the gym. You're new here, aren't you?'

He busied himself going down on one knee in search of his sports bag. 'Yes. I'm Mark. Nice to meet you.'

She had received many years of counselling over the events of her childhood and had even become a counselling psychologist in her own right in an attempt to fix herself, so she knew at least something about herself and about men. She knew perfectly well, for example, that she easily became obsessed with unobtainable men and that this was a weakness she needed to guard against. Despite this, blood continued to rush to her head—and to other parts. It was most disappointing.

The new man, whose name she now knew was Mark, continued to seem highly exciting. He was still on one knee, retrieving his bag and keys from a shelf low down and he brushed the side of her thigh with his shoulder as he did so. The contact seemed deliberate, even though she knew she was still partly in his way.

'Do I know you from somewhere?' he asked when he finally stood up. His voice sounded educated, though rural, and his teeth were perfect.

Like hers.

'No,' she said. 'It would be nice if I did, but I don't think so.' It seemed tragic that he was leaving. *What an absolute waste,* she thought. Wishes tumbled through her mind, bizarre wishes that spoke of making love immediately. She found herself hoping he would sweep her up in his arms and carry her off into one of the equipment cupboards. There, he would slam her up against a wall, pull down her pants and make fierce love to her. He would know what she wanted: masterful, forceful, passionate . . .

Fuck me good. Take me!

She almost said the words aloud, but she did not. She was not that mad. The man was a perfect stranger. It was just a thought.

'Are you sure?' he asked, peering into her face again. He was referring to her reply that they had never met before. 'You seem really familiar.'

'No. I'm sure we haven't met.' Alyssa heard her voice come out cold and hard and she felt disappointed. The ingrained protective reflex from childhood had sprung into action again, the tone of her voice guaranteed to discourage further attention of a male variety. She felt disappointed in herself, though not surprised. It was for the best. It was a way to protect them both. Besides, she already had a boyfriend. Wishes and fantasies aside, she was monogamous by nature, squeamish about strange bodies, and no fan of potentially harmful bacteria and viruses.

'Sorry to have bothered you,' he said. 'It's Alyssa, you say?'

'Yes. It's okay, Mark. See you around.'

'And you too.' The highly desirable young man seemed disappointed.

She did not encourage him. Instead, she stood and watched as he left.

I resisted, and then he was gone.

CHAPTER TWO

1

ALYSSA FELT A NEED to pinch herself. It seemed scarcely believable that she was sitting on the balcony of a luxury seaside apartment in the company of a professor of psychiatry handsome enough to weaken her knees.

Professor Summerfield was known to millions from his appearances on TV. He had also been one of her lecturers during her recent training as a counsellor, though at the time inaccessible to mere mortals like herself. Now, alone with him on his balcony, he was telling her about his failed love life.

He had had many wives. He explained how he lost his second one: 'We had our little problems of course, like all couples, but she took the time-honoured approach of the simple-minded and blamed everything on me. Towards the end, she concluded that what was wrong with me could be described in a single phrase: "You know too much". I mean, how ludicrous can a person get? That was it: the verdict. Seriously. I knew too much! And, because of that, I was incapable of a normal relationship with *anyone*, let alone a wife. I never stood a chance. She used to go on at me all day. "We will never be able to have a normal life". Yada, yada, yada. Then, one day, she said something different: she said "Goodbye". It was as simple as that in the end. Goodbye. And then she was gone; gone with all my money. Can you believe it, Alyssa? Women!'

The professor winked, as though he expected that she agreed that women were some sort of a joke. His wink reminded her of Fabio from the gym, who sometimes had the same mannerism. Alan Summerfield, though, was far younger, and genuinely attractive—in a Hollywood sort of way. He could have been a movie star. His broad, tanned face was handsome enough.

She gave him a little smile out of politeness but said nothing.

'Oh well, another one bites the dust.' The philosophising professor tried to sound nonchalant, but he was not very convincing.

Uncertain how to respond, Alyssa continued her silence. She wanted to put a hand on his knee in sympathy but restrained herself.

After a while, her host suddenly seemed to find the memory of his recent ex-wife extremely funny because he burst out laughing. The outburst soon sounded mildly hysterical, and when the mirth continued without end, she began to wonder if he could be choking. Just as she was about to slap him on his back, he abruptly recovered. Wiping tears from his eyes, he apologised.

'It's the money. The money.' Breathing seemed difficult for him. 'She's taken so much. It's so shitty unfair.'

To judge from his apartment and his car, Alan Summerfield was obviously well-off, so it must have been a lot of money, thought Alyssa. The second ex-wife may or may not have been morally entitled to it, but, whatever the case, it was hardly a laughing matter. She suspected that the professor's outburst concealed something more—deep hurt, or possibly emotional desperation. She knew enough about psychology to know that amusement and bravado were often nothing more than masks covering significant unresolved emotional issues. Even a famous psychiatrist could have emotional issues—especially when it came to matters of the heart.

They were sitting side by side on his apartment balcony, looking out over the ocean, which should have felt restful, but having the hero of her student life tell her about his personal problems was making her feel uncomfortable. Somehow, it was disturbing to experience Alan Summerfield as human, real, and no longer unreachable.

On the positive side, his confessions had the effect of drawing her closer to him. She knew now that he was a man who needed love, and that he was a man who probably had indeed done his inadequate best to love his ex-wife. Since the disaster of that marriage, he had tried to move on, tried to find someone he not only loved but who loved him in return. Or so he claimed. Now, he had a new wife, wife number three.

Alyssa silently wondered how things were getting on in that department.

She dared not ask. In the greater scheme of things, the professor's emotional life was no business of hers. Alan Summerfield, meanwhile, lowered the backrest of his recliner and stretched out like *a man relaxing*—even though, quite transparently, he was nothing of the sort.

Once settled in his new relaxed position on the recliner, he raised his head and spoke again: 'It's what we two have to watch out for in this job, Alyssa.' He looked directly up at her, his expression earnest. 'Like me, over time you will get to know too much. *That* is the danger. People do not like it. It's an occupational hazard. Soon, you'll be up against it too.' Then he abruptly sat up again and raised his glass. 'So, this is my advice to you, my words of wisdom after all my years of professional practice in mental health: stay human—at least when it comes to the ones you love.'

Stay human.

'Thanks for the tip,' said Alyssa respectfully. 'I'll bear it in mind.'

There was silence again as they enjoyed their wine. Stay human seemed an odd thing for her new boss to have said. It seemed like something a father might say to a daughter, yet Professor Summerfield was hardly the fatherly type. And besides, she had no idea what he meant. Perhaps, she thought, it was a stage of life thing, something said by older people. If she were to advise someone, she would say something different, something like: "be true to yourself". That would be her advice. As far as she was concerned, people were best advised to take the trouble to discover themselves before they made irreversible decisions in life, rather than worry about whether they were human or not.

Alan Summerfield, however, was a famous professor of psychiatry.

Compared with Alan, what do I know?

Not much.

From her deck chair on his balcony, Alyssa absorbed the view visible through the balustrade with a certain degree of wonderment. Like everything else about Alan, the vista from his seaside apartment was stunning. From where they were sitting, she had a panoramic view of the bay, the shimmering haze of ocean filling the entire arc of her vision. All she could see was water, which created the enchanting illusion that she was floating on the ocean. Instead of being in Alan's apartment she could just as well be drifting somewhere out on the iridescent seascape before her. Bobbing gaily over the deep blue sea, as it were. She noted with interest that the sea this day really *was* blue. Plain blue. No need for the ultramarines and aquamarines of romance novellas. No need for an attractive hero either. On this day, fantasy was not required—except to remove the inconvenient fact that she was hopelessly out of her financial league.

Like that time at the gym some weeks earlier—when the world had come over so odd—the weather was unusually hot. Yet, despite the heat, she seemed quite well. It could not have been the heat then, that had made everything go weird. She conceded this finally.

Something else had been responsible.

Best not to think about it.

Whatever the cause of her temporary mental dysfunction, Cy had driven the bad feelings away. She had felt better the moment she got home to him at their flat. Cy was good for her in that way. *His* head, at least, was screwed on straight. Also, being near the sea as she now was had its own soothing effect. She had grown up next to a beach and she loved the salty, cooling breeze always present at such places. High up, in Alan's luxury apartment, the ocean's gentle fanning of the fuming air felt like a lover's caress.

The familiar sensations made her mind float back to when she was a teenager. The family home had been three streets back from a beach—just a tiny welfare house, nothing like the professor's palace. Just a shitty little government house in a shitty little country town a hundred-and-fifty km away. They had been dirt poor, but she had not truly realised this until later. Instead, as a child, she had enjoyed the ocean. And now, at Alan Summerfield's apartment, the evocative sensations and smells contrived to emphasise her solidarity with him. She felt drawn to him, a feeling as languid and sensual as if he had spiked her drink.

He would never do anything like that, of course.

The professor was no ordinary middle-aged man. Because of the excellent tone of his physique and the enormous size of his brain, he looked and functioned like a man ten or fifteen years younger. Adding to the excitement of being in his company, was the fact that she was going to be working with him. Once she had been a student of his; now she was going to be a colleague of his.

2

Despite the outwardly relaxed atmosphere on the balcony, the prospect of life with Alan Summerfield as employer began to cause anxious feelings in Alyssa's stomach. It dawned on her that she was going to have to be sure to always do the right thing, which was going to be difficult. Not only that, but he seemed to have her mesmerised. She could not stop feeling fawning admiration for him even though she knew she was being childish. After all, nobody was *that* great. Yes, he was an associate professor of psychiatry, and yes, he had an enormous private practice, and yes, he had a great apartment, and yes, he was seriously handsome, but so what, she tried to tell herself. What did all that really mean? She had studied sociology as far as year two. The greatness aura of supposedly successful people was almost always nothing more than a cultivated illusion, a mechanism of subjugation. She had studied that sort of thing before . . . before . . . being put in hospital. It annoyed her to find that she still had a mental block when thinking about her past.

Talk about screwed up!

Although she was feeling much better than she had been on her Friday gym visit, the events at Fabio's gym had been a wake-up call. It was simply not good enough that she was having flashbacks again. And as for the hallucinations . . . she did not have the energy to think about them. Time did not seem to be on her side. Her training supervisor had warned that such a day would come. "The window will close when you least expect it, Alyssa." Wendy Greene had been like an annoying water drip.

The trouble with you, Alyssa, is that everything about you is a lie. I'm not saying it's deliberate, but you, of all people, should surely know that failing to acknowledge your true self is potentially very dangerous—not only to yourself but to others.

Yes, Wendy could be very annoying. And melodramatic. Nevertheless, Wendy was right. She needed to be a better person. In many ways, Wendy had been the mother she had never had.

Alan Summerfield adjusted his position on his recliner, breaking into her thoughts. She gave him a sidelong glance. Not a god, just a man, but close to a god. He was even more handsome than she was pretty. Somewhat reluctantly, she conceded this last point. It was easy to be jealous of someone who was not only highly intelligent, friendly, and tirelessly hard working, but also utterly good looking. He had achieved much of what she hoped for in her *own* life: the respect of others, skill at one's job, financial success, four children . . . that especially, although three would be enough for her.

He began to speak once more. 'I must apologise, Alyssa, for not introducing you very well when you arrived. It's an old failing of mine. I often assume too much, I'm afraid.'

'What do you mean, Professor Summerfield?'

'Alan. Please do call me Alan.' He then proceeded to explain what he had earlier not made clear.

She learnt to her surprise that the woman in her early thirties who had greeted her at the front door of the apartment when she first arrived off the tram, was actually his wife (the latest or third wife). The woman had said only that she was Kara, so Alyssa had not made the connection to Alan—understandably so, considering that Alan was over fifty. Instead, she had assumed that Kara was one of Alan's secretaries or nurses from the practice she was joining.

'So *that's* who Kara is. I was wondering. I never realised . . .'

'She's young, I know . . . that's Kara for you. Bless her.'

Alyssa now understood why Kara was so physically attractive and why she had appeared anxious when greeting the guests. For a third incumbent, the role of wife was almost impossible to play with any dignity in a formal social setting, especially with such a large age difference.

Alan was clearly in love with his new wife because he kept looking back over his shoulder at her whenever he mentioned her name. Alyssa turned and looked too. Kara was in the lounge, which was directly behind the balcony and separated from them by the soundproof glass of the wall-to-wall sliding doors, which were closed because of the air-conditioning. Kara waved at them from inside, where she was chatting to two other Saturday afternoon guests. Alyssa knew their names: Professor Douglas Barnes, head of the Donald Clinic, where she was going to be working, and Dr Jocelyn Goronowski, a psychiatrist employed there.

Kara's clothes intrigued her. She was wearing an elegant pastel sarong with a breathtakingly daring split down the side. Not only was she beautiful but also in excellent shape, something she clearly wanted the world to know. Without a doubt, Alan Summerfield was a man who appreciated the physical side of life.

She wondered if Alan and Kara went to a gym together.

'Kara's a dancer,' he said proudly, as if in answer to the silent question.

Alyssa thought it best not to ask what sort of dancer.

The guests in the lounge looked quite different. The psychiatrist, Dr Jocelyn Goronowski, she knew nothing about. She looked quite young, but seemed odd, disturbed even—more so than most psychiatrists. Donald Barnes, on the other hand, she had met at the job interview a month earlier, where he had come across as cheerless, predatory, forbidding, and altogether dried up—more vulture than human. Even now, on a Saturday afternoon at the seaside, he still managed to send a chill through her.

It was too late, though, for second thoughts. Effectively, she was already his clinic's new counselling psychologist. Wisely or unwisely, she had accepted his offer of a position at the boutique private institution called the Donald Clinic. Her colleagues at Public Hospital, where she had been completing her vocational training at the time, had been quick to remind her of the rumours about client financial exploitation at her intended place of work, but when she realised that the Donald Clinic was within walking distance of her rented flat in East Hubron, she had put in an application anyway, even though she was a new graduate with no work experience. She also had a lot of study debt and no car.

To her merit—and great surprise—it turned out that she was exactly the kind of counsellor that the Donald Clinic was looking for: someone young and fresh and with a new and radically different perspective on therapy. There were many applicants and Professor Barnes had wanted a quick decision. In a rush of blood to the head, she had signed on the dotted line.

In truth, she had felt rather proud of herself—and still did. At last, she had achieved something in life. Given the warmth of the welcome she was now receiving, it seemed she was of some value after all.

3

Once Alan Summerfield finally stopped talking about his new marriage, Alyssa took the opportunity to ask him some questions about work.

'What's it like working for Donald Barnes?' she asked.

The question made him laugh. 'I wouldn't work for that old bastard even if you paid me. Fortunately, I don't have to. As far as I'm concerned, he works for me.'

His words came as a surprise. 'How so?'

The answer was simple. Alan Summerfield and Donald Barnes co-owned the Donald Clinic in equal share. Dr Barnes was merely the spokesperson, administrator, and nominal chief.

Donald Barnes was also a part-time associate professor of forensic psychiatry in the public sector, while Alan was similarly a part-time associate professor in the public sector, in his case in clinical psychiatry. The Donald Clinic was merely a hobby for the two of them to indulge in.

And a cash cow.

'By mutual agreement, old Barnes here does the admin donkey work—thank God for that. But, beyond that, he does his thing and I do mine,' said Alan. 'My interest is in mainstream clinical psychiatry, so I'm far busier with actual clients.'

'Sounds like a good arrangement,' said Alyssa respectfully.

'It is. And I'm sure you'll enjoy working with us. It would be impossible to need anyone more than we need you now. The clinic has become too popular for its own good and our clients have begun to complain that they are not getting the empathy they require. Our sole clinical psychologist is overloaded. Besides, she's become increasingly limited by her advancing age and her fixation on using only cognitive behaviour therapy. And we can't help.'

Alyssa understood what he was saying. Supportive counselling fell outside the time constraints, interests, or expertise of the four psychiatrists currently working there, so having only one clinical psychologist on the staff was not adequate. 'I'll do my best to help,' she said.

At the job interview, her expected role had been made clear. "It will be nothing to do with money, Alyssa". Dr Barnes knew of the rumours. "Just counselling. Counselling of a sort that our clients actually *like*. That's all." Feedback had suggested that what was lacking at the Donald Clinic was kindness, so Dr Barnes wanted the defect corrected. "Unlike the rest of the mental health world, where interactions with clients have been turned into a sick joke by imbecilic funding agencies, at the Donald we aspire to unhurried, one-to-one interactions in a tasteful and calming environment. Our clients can pay for it, so why not?"

Why not indeed.

It was the same Donald Barnes who had sent her out onto the apartment balcony to be alone with Alan Summerfield that Saturday. The suggestion that she do so had come not long after she arrived at Alan's apartment, when Donald Barnes had come and spoken to her directly while she was busy admiring tastefully framed art prints in the hallway.

'Spend some time with Alan, Alyssa. You will find it most helpful. He's heading out to the balcony.'

It had not been a request but an order. She had tried to pretend it was not. 'These prints are really disturbing, aren't they? In a good way. What's with this one: *The Death of the Count of Orgaz*?'

Donald Barnes seemed surprised that she should be saying anything at all. 'Of course, all Alan's artworks have deeper meanings. Now, off you go. To the balcony. Get to know him. He sees half the well-heeled clients in Hubron, and he's out there waiting for you.'

'Righty-o.'

Get to know Alan.

So, there she was, next to him, with the late afternoon sun hot around them. They were well back from the rail, in some shade. With the cooling breeze, conditions were comfortable.

She asked Alan about the fourth psychiatrist at the clinic, the one who was not present at the welcoming party.

'That will be Simon Bristow,' he explained. 'Simon is doing a big push over at the magnet to keep his publication on schedule. You will get to meet him soon enough. At present, he's spending most of his time generating monkey puzzles on screens. The bad news, I hear, is that he doesn't know what they mean. It's all part of this new idea that collecting MRI images is going to be the way to understand the mind. Of course, for higher functions such as the conscious Self, this is complete bullshit. Simon, unfortunately, is incapable of understanding such basic logic. He's a clever guy, but I think you'll find him decidedly challenged in the upstairs department. Not that we don't all love him.'

Alyssa had not before heard anyone refer to MRI machines as "magnets", or functional MRI scans of the brain as monkey puzzles or bullshit, so she simply nodded and said nothing.

'Simon couldn't make it, but at least Jocelyn is here. You should have a chat to her later. I think you'll like her.'

Alyssa had not yet had a chance to talk to Dr Goronowski. She glanced back at the guests in the lounge once again. They were all standing and had drinks in their hands and the dark-haired female doctor was talking to Kara. She was smallish, and roundish, and had a noticeably energetic manner. Compared with Kara, she seemed physically restless, fidgety even. Alyssa found herself fascinated. Something about the woman was compelling. Possibly it was the wildness of her hair. Or the fact that in her loose-fitting grey dress she seemed to have no edges.

A woman with no edges.

The doctor could not be said to be slim, yet one could not say that she was fat either. Somehow, she succeeded in being hard to describe beyond the obvious: short, dark-haired, fidgety, not slim. And, though nothing like Alan's stunning Kara to look at, in a strange way Jocelyn Goronowski was not unattractive.

How very odd.

She became aware of Alan grinning at her. 'Jocelyn fascinates you, does she?'

Alyssa felt herself blushing. 'A little. She kind of draws the eye, doesn't she? And she never seems to stand still.'

'You won't be the first to be intrigued by our Jocelyn, believe me, but be warned, she has a sharp tongue. She's almost certainly going to give you a tongue lashing. She has a real thing about mental health support staff. She does tend to go on and on about what she calls the rise of stupidity—and without much tact. Even though I often agree with her, she can be a bit much.'

The rise of stupidity.

'She's very critical, is she?'

'Only superficially, don't get me wrong. Underneath lurks an absolute honey. Our Dr Goronowski will always surprise you in a good way. Jocelyn is like this weird mystery creature who will always cause you pain but never really hurt you. The pain comes mainly in the form of a headache. Speaking of which, I see she has attached herself to my Kara.'

The female psychiatrist had Alan's third wife crowded up against the back of a sofa. Kara's body language was defensive, bent backwards at the waist, while Dr Goronowski's was overly animated and pressurising. She was in too close. It seemed surprising that a psychiatrist could have such poor social skills. As for Dr Barnes, he was of no use to Kara. He looked bored. Drink in hand, he remained standing in the centre of the room, wooden and alone, aloof, failing miserably in his half-hearted attempt to not be the supremacist he so obviously was.

'Kara will cope,' said Alan, half to himself. He lowered his voice. 'Confidentially, Jocelyn is—how shall I put this—AC-DC—but Kara knows.' He winked. 'If you get my drift. As a female employee of ours, it's probably something you need to know. But don't worry, it's never been a problem.'

Alyssa assumed Dr Summerfield was telling her that Jocelyn was a lesbian. 'That's okay. Such things don't bother me. I quite like them.' She smiled at him. 'No hang ups.' Even as she said it, though, she knew it was a lie. She had plenty of hang ups. Fortunately, not about lesbians. It did not upset her in the slightest if people were gay or anything else because no one ever had any choice in what turned them on. At university she had studied the psychology of sexuality, including the non-heteronormative, as well as gender identification, which was different.

Alan was looking at her. 'You like them?'

'As the experts say: *everyone* is a lesbian at heart.'

He looked worried, as though wondering for a second if this meant that she too was cut from the same cloth. 'Everyone?' Then his expression cleared. 'Oh, I get it. You mean that psychologically, at a certain level, every one of us is a woman lover. It's how we all start in life. Good point.'

'Thank you.'

'Most excellent, in fact,' he said, looking pleased at the depth of her psychological insight. 'But now, Alyssa, why don't we focus on how the two of *us* are going to be working together in the future?'

'Whatever you say. I'm here to learn.'

4

'We'll be doing business together to such a degree, Alyssa, that I want us to minimise misunderstandings.' Again, the Hollywood smile.

'You mean with our shared clients?'

'That too.' He stood up and went into the sun at the balcony rail, where he appeared to be admiring the view. She watched from behind, wondering whether she may have upset him. They were four floors up and there was nothing between the top of his body and the sea. Framed against the water, he looked remarkably commanding, like a sea captain on the prow of his ship. He was physically powerful in an indefinably masculine way—and she liked that in him. She did not like men who thought they *should* be in command, but he was nothing like that.

He turned his head to talk to her. 'Jocelyn Goronowski may be a little odd but wait until you meet Greta. We have them all at the Donald.'

'You mean Greta McCreedy?'

'The same.'

Alyssa knew that Greta McCreedy was the Donald's clinical psychologist and as such her nominal boss. More highly trained than she was, Greta could perform functions that a counselling psychologist like herself with merely a bachelor's degree could not—not legally anyway. Tasks such as making a psychological diagnosis or interpreting a complex psychometric test. Like Dr Simon Bristow, Greta McCreedy had tendered her apologies and been unable to attend the welcoming gathering. 'I look forward to meeting her.'

'Understandably. However, I need to warn you that there are likely to be some initial difficulties between you and Greta. She's over sixty and rather set in her ways.'

Alyssa joined Alan at the balustrade. 'What does that mean?'

He seemed pleased by her presence next to him. He moved closer and looked into her eyes with an unfathomable expression. When he spoke, it seemed like an incidental activity. 'There is only one Greta.' He went on staring into her face. Finally, he made his eyebrows jump around.

She almost burst out laughing. 'Stop it!'

He did. 'I do like your laugh. Poor Greta. I shouldn't joke because, truth is, she's completely overloaded and almost at breaking point. Although, of course, she is her own worst enemy. It's a long story. We're really hoping that you'll be able to be of assistance to her.'

'I'll do my best.'

'Sadly, it won't be that simple. As you'll soon discover, she's strictly a cognitive behaviour therapy type, so she's going to resent what you bring to the table with your psychodynamic approach. At least, though, there shouldn't be a clash of interests between you two. Do you know them? The CBT types?'

Alyssa nodded in silence. Cognitive behaviour therapists were everywhere in clinical psychology, so it seemed a strange question to ask. What seemed of greater importance, though, was the answer to a different question: how had Alan Summerfield achieved such a flawless complexion? Even in the bright sunshine, the skin of his face was perfect. She wondered, too, about his language. He seemed to find it easy to mock people, Greta in particular, and CBT. Cognitive behaviour therapy was hardly something to make fun of, even though personally she was no fan of it either. 'I take it you have some reservations about CBT?'

'Cock-and-bull therapy, you mean? Yes, I don't like it. Personally, I regard it and most of its offshoots as pseudoscientific crap—like so much of counselling psychology these days. I mean, I know CBT is empirically validated as far as outcomes are concerned, but then so are all clinically permitted personal relationship talk-type therapies. They are all *valid*. But that's beside the point as far as I'm concerned. It's my considered view that any treatment approach where the therapist is largely unaware of his or her *own* mental dysfunction amounts to a form of client abuse. There are therapists out there who know less than nothing about what's really bothering their clients because they know less than nothing about themselves. Often, it's just about how much money they can engineer out of a duped funding agency.'

'Oh,' said Alyssa.

'You do know how the funding trick works, don't you?'

'Not really.'

He explained. 'A therapy professor takes a flea that has, during its earlier life, learnt the bad behaviour of jumping at the command *jump*, gives it some tomfool therapy, and then says he has proof he has cured it of its jumping problem by means of said tomfool therapy. So, how does he do it?'

Alyssa was not sure what he was getting at, or why he now seemed angry. 'Uh, no idea.'

'Well, it goes something like this: the professor *tells* the flea not to jump. "Little jumping flea," he says, "do *not* jump." However, the flea when it hears the word jump, jumps. Experimentally, the professor then removes two of the flea's six legs with a pair of tweezers. Again, he says "Do *not* jump." Failure; the flea jumps. Doggedly, he persists with his science and removes two more legs. The flea jumps. Not to be outdone, he removes two more legs. "Flea *do* not jump," he once again commands. At last, the flea does not jump. "Success!" cries the professor. "I have cured my flea." The professor's therapy has worked. His flea's behaviour has changed. Wonderful. One moment! Here comes the next act for the clown: he writes up his cure in a journal and publishes it. "Remove six legs from a flea and it will not jump" says his brilliant, empirically validated article. When people ask *why* a flea with no legs stops jumping, he says it is obviously because he has empowered the flea's system to respond to the new word *not*—as in do *not* jump—by using his now patented leg reduction method. The "New-Word Leg Reduction System" becomes the latest way to cure jumping fleas, and no one can dare to disagree. After all, it's backed up by a statistically validated study. Do you get my drift, Alyssa? We are dealing with an epidemic of shysters who haven't the faintest clue about the *why* of anything. They fail to understand that psychological treatments work for reasons unrelated to the reason they imagine. And the very worst part is that their publications always fail to state what their own personal views are. If you ever *do* get the opportunity to find out what these personal views really are—as I have done because some of these so-called experts go nuts themselves and get sent to me—you will find yourself appalled and disgusted. The notion of doing experimental studies on metaphysical aspects of the mind rather than observational studies is complete rubbish. The results will always be based entirely on the preconceived bias.'

She felt a little shaken by the vehemence of Alan Summerfield's long tirade, the logic of which was hard to follow. What was clear was that he had strong beliefs of his own. She tried to be diplomatic. 'They wouldn't agree with you, though, would they, the CBT people?'

'See if I care.' His voice had a defiant edge to it. 'That's why I'm so pleased to have someone like you joining us, Alyssa. Someone with a proper understanding of what the mind really is and how it needs to be approached.'

It seemed a tall order. 'I'm fairly new at this, I hope you realise.'

'Nonsense, Wendy Greene will have taught you well. Any other type of therapist would be useless in our setting at the Donald Clinic. I can't stand the hubris of the types who incessantly make moral judgements regarding clients yet can't even tell their own ass from their elbow. I certainly wouldn't want any patients of mine subjected to idiots whose morals come straight from their parents and social media. But then again, I am a psychiatrist. I keep forgetting this.'

'Why are you so against CBT in particular?' asked Alyssa, finding it difficult to understand what was upsetting him.

'It's their arrogance that gets to me; their deliberate blindness regarding their own motives; their lack of a functional model of the human mind. It's the result, of course, of their denial of the existence of an unconscious Self. They don't see it. They insist on telling clients that whatever they think about themselves is true and then insist on giving advice about what they should or should not be thinking in future based on what they themselves think. I strongly object to people who attempt to justify the odious personal garbage in their own head by claiming it to be scientific fact based on nonsensical experiments. It's gone beyond a joke.'

'Do you mean they don't have a *metaphysical* model of the mind?' It was a term she recalled him using in one of his lectures during the previous year—and in some of his journal articles.

He smiled, seeming to see her as a kindred spirit. 'Brilliantly put. Yes, that's exactly what's wrong with modern clinical psychology. It lacks a universally accepted master model of the mind. And, no, I'm not referring to the hopelessly grandiose and rightly defunct Grand Narrative of psychoanalysis. I'm referring to the fact that modern clinical psychology refuses to accept that the declarative mind—conscious and unconscious—exists *only* in the dimension of cyberspace. The declarative mind is a neurological *computation*. It simply isn't the equivalent of the physical brain, so it cannot be approached physically but only via congruence with another mind. We need to use *this* route, indirect as it is, because there *is* no other way. Give me the benevolent intersubjective *embrace* of transference-focused psychodynamic therapy any day and spare me the prescriptive intersubjective *impositions* of CBT—and the rest of them.'

'Right.'

It seemed the best thing to say.

He became calmer, and in the subsequent silence she wondered what it was like to have a jawbreaker of a mind. Whatever one's opinion of Alan Summerfield, without a doubt he existed on a rarefied plain.

5

Once the man with her on the balcony realised that she was not going to try to argue with him, he became more friendly. Side by side, they admired the view.

'Don't let me discourage you, Alyssa. Counsellors have their value. Just be sure to keep me away from a CBT one if *I* ever need help.'

'I think I understand where you are coming from,' she said politely, even though she did not. 'I just hope you aren't being too dismissive of clinical psychology in general, especially of us lesser counselling types. We aren't *all* bad, you know. At least, I hope not.' She smiled as disarmingly as possible, which made her feel even more like she was being his therapist.

'Maybe not. But certainly, some *are* bad: the ones determined to bray despite being lost in the wilderness of their own confusion. Unwittingly complicit with the psychopathology of their clients, these people pander to them. Which is hopeless. The only good they can ever do is assist with temporary symptom suppression. There is no long-term healing happening. Nothing.'

Alyssa nodded politely. In certain ways, she agreed with him. During her own illness she had experienced a wide variety of therapists and many of them had indeed been shockingly useless. In the end, a psychotherapist had turned out to be the most helpful type of therapist for her personally—which was why she had decided to train as one when she got better. Getting into a training course had not been easy, though. Psychotherapy had mostly ceased to be taught anywhere in the country and almost all training positions were in CBT—or IPT, which stood for time-limited interpersonal therapy. As far as she could discover, the reason for this approach related to nothing other than financial expediency. Non-psychodynamic courses were easier to teach, better suited to high workloads, and more usable by clients and practitioners with average or low intelligence.

Fortunately, the psychodynamic therapist who had treated her during her own illness—Norman Bullock—had known of her ambitions to become a counsellor herself and had managed to secure for her a rare training position in pure transference-focused psychodynamic therapy. He believed she was "gifted" in this field—whatever that meant. Even though the two-year vocational training course was only offered to one or two candidates per year in the entire city of Hubron—and via Public Hospital only—he had managed to secure a training position for her provided that she first successfully completed a degree in psychology, something that she had then done. The subsequent vocational training had placed a strong emphasis on advances in the field because many earlier Freudian-type ideas were widely considered to be wrong in the light of modern studies. What remained essential to psychotherapy, though, was Freud's understanding that all people were influenced by hidden parts of themselves and were *not* who or what they claimed to be. People were liars. They told untruths, and never more so than to themselves about themselves. Nothing in life could be more foolish—or dangerous—than to take people's claims about themselves at face value.

Alan Summerfield waved a professorial finger at the ocean. 'Some days, I despair at the current intellectual decay of the West. Perhaps I'm revealing my age, but the result—to quote Dickens—is almost certainly going to be misery. All we seem to have left is this fantasy of how great we are.'

His hands looked very attractive resting on the balustrade. After a while, he peered intently into her face. 'Am I imagining it, Alyssa, or have we met before? Personally, I mean. Not just at lectures and tutorials. Why do I feel that we've met before?'

'We haven't. Not personally.'

'Yet it's such a strong feeling. Like I *know* you.'

She shrugged, holding his gaze. 'Can't help you.' Many psychiatrists had crossed her path when she was a psychiatric inpatient during second year at university, but none of them had been Alan, of that she felt sure. She had been at Olympic Hospital, on the other side of the city, whereas Alan only taught and did sessions at nearby Public Hospital.

Though before that, I suppose I was on the front page of every Sunday newspaper for weeks . . .

If Alan ever discovered this, it would mean the end of her employment. She needed to keep her mouth shut and take care to avoid slip-ups.

She changed the subject.

'I liked your lectures,' she said. 'They were great, especially the ones about how it's a big mistake for therapists to think they have the ability to know what's troubling their clients.'

'Thank you. Yes, people need to understand that in the non-psychotic client, the journey is a *mutual* journey of discovery. There's certainly no place for pontificating by some or other prick of a therapist. It's predatory, that's what it is. There's something very wrong with any type of person-to-person relationship therapy where you treat your client as your inferior. The level of hubris involved in talking down to someone you barely know is mind-boggling, let alone then telling them what's wrong with their mind after half an hour. The last thing we want at the Donald is some or other tin-pot clown forcing our clients into meaningless journeys without end to nowhere.'

'It's actually because of your lectures that I came to understand what countertransference even is; that it even exists. And, of course, how relevant the countertransference of the therapist is. How even Freud didn't get that part right.'

'Yes, he was hopeless at recognising his own countertransference, especially at the beginning.'

Alan had criticised Freud many times in publications in respected journals and was widely quoted. The reminder of his status made her feel a little overawed. 'I'm looking forward to working at the Donald,' she gushed, 'but I know my limitations. I do know my place.' What she had *not* known until today, though, was that she was going to be used as a counterweight in an ideological war against Greta McCreedy.

'I'm pleased,' said Alan enigmatically. 'Enough sun, do you think? I'm going back to my recliner.'

She followed him.

'More wine?'

She had already had a large glass of New Zealand Sauvignon blanc.

'I'm not really a drinker, so I'm probably a bit affected already. Just a quarter of a glass.'

'Got you.' He went to an ice bucket on a table in the corner and poured the quarter exactly as she had asked.

She appreciated the way he respected her request. Once they resumed their positions on their recliners, she found herself relaxing in his company. Contrary to her initial suspicions, Alan Summerfield seemed a genuine and friendly man. Yes, he expressed his views frankly, but she felt honoured that he trusted her enough to speak his mind as freely as he did.

He put his head back on his recliner, placed his fingertips together, and closed his eyes. 'Has the world gone mad, Alyssa?' After a while, his eyes opened again. 'There is a question I ask myself every day. Have we given in to expediency? Healing a mind requires ability. At least that.'

'I promise to do my best to help.'

She hoped she was not making a fool of herself in front of her ex-professor. She felt juvenile and barely articulate compared with him. Trapped, too, because she was hardly in any position to disagree with him on anything. She wondered if he had had a bad personal experience with a counsellor or was just plain nuts, as most professors were. She tried to imagine how he would react if he himself went for counselling and the counsellor told him to "focus on the now" or told him to recite "I no longer give my shadow power". It made her smile.

'Enjoying it out here, are you?' he asked.

'Yes. Must be the company.'

The comment made him smile too.

'I'm on the same page as you, Alan. I refuse to simply agree with clients or conspire with them to avoid their real issues.'

'Thank God.' He stood up and began fiddling with his chair. 'I knew we were right to bring you in.'

6

'I've read your assessment, you know. The one from Wendy Greene, your training supervisor. Don't look so alarmed—it's not about you personally. Although that would be interesting.' He gave her an odd smile. 'It's just a business value assessment. It's a routine value report we obtain on all prospective staff. You'll be pleased to know that Wendy regards you as the most gifted psychodynamic therapist she has yet mentored.' Again, that smile from Alan. 'I wanted to tell you that.'

'That's very kind of you, although I doubt you are telling me the truth.'

Still grinning at each other, they both sat back and sipped their wine.

As she watched the sea through the railings, she could not help noticing how Alan Summerfield discreetly glanced at her chest from time to time. The light top that she had selected to match her short skirt was cut low and she knew it left little of her spray-tanned breasts to the imagination. She had wanted to take advantage of the good weather and be as attractive as possible, and in this she had obviously succeeded. Far from feeling offended by his attention, she found the sexual interest fascinating considering his age and position in life. His behaviour made him vulnerable to her—she could influence him—but she knew perfectly well that he was fully aware that he was being affected by her and that therefore she could be dangerous to him. That said, the two-year-old boy lurking just below the surface in all men, lurked in him too. Alan wanted her. And, fortunately, two-year-old boys were something she could handle. To her, his sexual interest felt reassuring. Validating. She found herself thinking it would be nice to be his friend.

Meanwhile, on the broad expanse of Santos Beach far below, huge crowds baked in the furnace air of the late afternoon heat haze, while on the horizon mirages of the Hubron CBD business towers danced a pitiless and unsteady jig. It felt curiously thrilling—decadent, even—to be sitting high above the sweating masses in absolute comfort, drinking wine and being appreciated by a handsome and successful man.

So, this is what success feels like.

She pulled her skirt well up to catch as much sun as possible on her legs even though they were already nicely bronzed from the fake tan she had applied the day before. Her legs could do with a bit of real sun. While she looked like a regular beachgoer, in truth she was too poor for that given that she lived in the centre of the city well away from any beach. However, the new position at the Donald Clinic was going to bring financial stability to her life. She was tired of struggling.

Something was definitely sparking between her and Alan. Maybe it was just the effect of the wine, but she had become aware of her underwear. A powerful unspoken sexual current was flowing, and it was flowing *both* ways, just beneath the polite veneer of their conversation. *Wow,* she thought. There was more to Alan than she had believed possible, and his presence was proving hard to resist. She was amazed at where her mind was taking her.

She was glad she had dressed casually. At first, she had not known what to wear when the invitation came from Dr Barnes to meet members of staff for a drink at Alan's place, but she had soon worked out what was best. Judging from the address Dr Barnes had given her, she knew the apartment was on the beach. So, when she woke to a hot Saturday, she went for a minimalist beach look: light, low-cut top, short at the waist, and an equally short flippy skirt, the entire skimpy look offset by stylish red sandals with delicate ankle straps. She loved the sun and the sea, and she knew that her chosen look would suit her. There had been a time, years back, when she had been familiar with the seaside.

When she saw Alan glancing at her again—this time at her upper legs—she wondered whether she should have worn something more concealing. She pushed the thought away.

It's the beach and it's midsummer.

Her clothes were definitely appropriate. Alan was casually dressed too. The others, though, Drs Barnes and Goronowski, were dressed more soberly, as though on their way to evening functions afterwards. She turned her eyes towards Alan again, only to be met by his, their mutual gazes of unspoken admiration trapping each another. She did not look away, and neither did he. He looked ridiculously attractive in his oversized, largely unbuttoned, white linen shirt with its half rolled-up sleeves, and he winked at her. He had on matching white slacks and sockless teal-blue boat shoes, and his excellent salt-and-pepper hair looked clean and healthy. He looked perfect in the heat.

She felt sure he dyed his hair. The colouring was too uniform. Same for his teeth. Too good to be true. The man holding her gaze and grinning at her was almost a caricature of the older, well-to-do beachside dweller with an eye for the girls. She had to give him credit, though. He still had the figure for it. She imagined him jogging along the esplanade in the evenings in tight lycra shorts. She tried not to blush at the thought of it, but it was enough to make her finally drop her eyes. Alan may have been old enough to be her father, but he still had what it took to excite her—and any other hot-blooded woman.

She was surprised at how much the man sitting next to her on the balcony differed from the stiff, business-suited lecturer she had known previously. In one life, Alan Summerfield was a great university professor. Yet, in another life, here he was sharing his psychological paranoias with her and having the hots for her. The situation began to make her feel slightly apprehensive. He was so much more intelligent than she was that she knew it was possible he was playing games with her.

7

Pity about his age. He would have to be at least in his late forties, probably older. Yet he was in much better condition than other men of such advanced age. Another unusual thing about him was that he appeared to value her opinion. Normally, most professional men of his seniority looked down on people like her and did not take anything they said seriously. Indeed, one of her less pleasant discoveries about the medical world—while training at the giant Public Hospital on the edge of the Hubron CBD—was that intellectual snobbery was almost guaranteed in senior medical staff. Yet Alan Summerfield showed none of that towards her.

Instinctively, despite her suspicions about his true intentions, she liked him as a man. She felt sure that he was astute enough to realise that when it came to young women the joke was on him. He would know it was hard for a handsome and virile man to age gracefully in relation to women and would realize that he would always desire any sexually interesting woman that he encountered.

But would he be able to get over it, as required by society?

That is the question, Alan.

'More wine?' He offered to top up her glass with more of the New Zealand Sauvignon blanc.

'It's lovely Alan, but no thanks. I'm at my limit. I'll definitely be tipsy after this.'

Being the gentleman that he was, he did not push her. Instead, he poured himself some more wine. He was clearly enjoying her company and seemed in no mind to re-join the others inside. 'It's a pity your partner couldn't make it today. I would have liked to have met him.'

'Cy's not really my partner.' As she said it, she felt guilty for having said such a thing. *What is wrong with me?* she thought. She corrected herself. 'Well, I suppose in a way he is. But I think of him more as a boyfriend. We've been together for almost a year now, but we haven't made any commitments yet.'

'Wise woman,' said Alan Summerfield.

He would almost certainly have read her resume and know her basic domestic arrangements. He would know that Cyrus Beauchamp was her partner and that he was an author. Having never heard of any author called Cyrus Beauchamp, he would have put two and two together and realised that Cy was penniless. He would be right.

Maybe he disapproves.

'Why did you say wise?' she asked him. 'Do you think people shouldn't commit to each other?'

'I think one shouldn't commit unless one is absolutely sure. Although I'm hardly the one to talk.' The husband of three wives found himself laughing at himself. 'You know,' he said suddenly, 'I don't think I've enjoyed a glass of wine so much with anyone.'

'Yes. It is nice out here.' She wasn't sure how else to respond to his compliment.

'You'll be a big help. I can see that.'

'Why thank you, Alan. I do want to be able to help people. That's my main interest: helping people.'

He moved his recliner closer to her. 'The thing is, Alyssa, in just a few minutes you've already got me wanting to spill my heart out to you. That is such a rare and wonderful gift. Never underestimate yourself as a counsellor.' Ever so casually, Alan Summerfield placed a hand on her bare knee. He looked directly into her eyes. 'If I may be brutally frank, you have this fantastic way about you, Alyssa, this ability to come across as totally non-threatening. Our clients are going to just love you.'

The warmth from his hand had travelled alarmingly far up the inside of her thigh. 'Oh.' She found herself stammering. 'I . . . I don't know what to say.' Despite her best efforts to resist his charm, she felt awestruck.

'Then don't say anything at all,' he smiled. 'Come, let's go in and re-join the others.'

Then he removed his hand.

CHAPTER THREE

1

IT WAS NOT THAT Cy had been unable to make it to the welcoming party. He had refused to go. "Hell no, I'm not going anywhere near those pricks." Those were the words he used.

He despised doctors. He was apologetic, but his decision was final. "They are just going to mock me. You know that. You know what they are like. Right up themselves. They'll convince themselves that I'm a complete shit compared to them."

Her attempts to reassure him had been futile. Cy's fears were real enough to him.

"Hell no, I won't go."

She had had to go alone.

Alyssa recalled the conversation with Cy with some annoyance while on the tram home after the visit to Alan Summerfield's Santos Beach apartment. It was already early evening, though still light, and the tram was full of chatting people. She was alone. It was mainly this that annoyed her. Being alone. It felt wrong, especially on a Saturday evening.

She tried to adopt a more positive attitude. Maybe Cy's concerns were valid, she reasoned. Especially when seen from his point of view. Doctors *could* be very condescending. Professor Barnes certainly took the cake in that regard, and Dr Goronowski hadn't been that far behind. Maybe she needed to accept that Cy was Cy.

Maybe.

After traversing the central business district, shedding patrons as it went, the tram finally reached East Hubron, where she lived. Although called East Hubron, the suburb wasn't really in the east—Hubron was over eighty km wide—just east of the CBD, and really part of it. She alighted at the Jowlett Street intersection. From there, it wasn't far to her flat, just over five minutes on foot. The sun was still up, and she had no concerns about safety. Walking swiftly, as she always did, she was soon at Jowlett Street's intersection with Alfonso Street, where she turned left. She lived only a few hundred metres further down the street in an aging and mildly dilapidated six storey apartment building, where she rented a flat. She loved walking, and she loved the area. If she went in the opposite direction, up Alfonso Street, the skyscrapers of the CBD were just under a kilometre away. Neither she nor Cy had a car, but in the middle of the city this had never been a problem for either of them.

While she walked, she thought about the three doctors she had met that afternoon. She wondered why they had gone to the trouble of inviting her out. She was only a junior counselling psychologist after all, hardly anyone of significance to their practice. Hopefully, it was simply an act of kindness, not something more complicated. Alan Summerfield, at least, had turned out to be surprisingly approachable—warm and open even. How wrong her past impression of him as cold and calculating had been when she attended his university lectures as a student. Now it seemed there was every chance they would become friends.

The dark-haired young psychiatrist called Jocelyn Goronowski had been difficult to fathom. After the compulsory stint on the balcony with Alan, she had been able to talk to the doctor for a while once back in the beachside apartment's lounge. It turned out that "Call me Jocelyn, for heaven's sake" lived in the suburb of Woodville, which was not far from her own flat. The coincidence was not as improbable as it seemed because Jocelyn worked at the Donald Clinic and the clinic was in East Hubron. Despite having a sharp tongue—as Alan had warned—the woman psychiatrist seemed pleasant enough despite the amount of alcohol she was consuming. One of the first things that Jocelyn Goronowski made clear was that she was single. Also, that she had a car. And was friendly. To top it off, at the conclusion of the afternoon, Jocelyn Goronowski offered her a lift home.

Rightly or wrongly, she had declined the woman's offer. She had done so politely of course, but now, in retrospect, it felt wrong. Why had she been so antisocial? she wondered. Probably because the psychiatrist had seemed in no fit state to drive a car. And been a bit too friendly, too. She had not forgotten Alan's bit of gossip about her. Though she had not feared the possibility of sexual attention during a ride home—after all, she was not afraid of any woman—she had not had any interest in what Jocelyn might wish to offer. She had not wanted to upset her by being forced to reject her. Nevertheless, the refusal to travel with Jocelyn now seemed particularly ungracious. She felt a twinge of guilt.

No wonder I have no friends.

She hoped Dr Goronowski would not hold a grudge against her in future. There was nothing she wanted more at her new place of work than to be approved of. Had she blown it? She found it hard to shake off a sense of disappointment in herself. After all, it had been fairly obvious to her that Jocelyn Goronowski was unwell; that she was struggling emotionally. Yet she had been unkind to her. Downright nasty, in fact— and all because of her *own* insecurities. Perhaps the truth was that she had been too proud and not wanted the medical specialist to see her very modest home—even though she knew she had no reason to be ashamed of it. Not everyone had money . . .

Like Cy, she was in no mood to be secretly mocked by anyone. The realisation of this bond with Cy made her smile to herself. The two of them were more alike than she had suspected. 'It won't be long,' she said, as much to him as to herself, 'before things begin to improve.' *Not long* until she could afford better things . . . *not long* until she could get her finances into a better place. Joining the Donald Clinic as a paid employee was going to enable her to turn the corner on her mountain of study debt. For the first time in her life, she would have a secure income. Yes, she could earn more if she went into private practice by herself, but that sort of venture, those risks, needed to wait until later. First had to come stability. And a family.

As she strode down Alfonso Street in the evening light in her short, flippy skirt, an animal vitality began to assert itself. Sensuous feelings began to arise. Warm air caressed her bare thighs high up under her skirt, and her skimpy underwear failed to blunt the pleasure of it, becoming instead complicit in an increasingly thrilling ride. She daydreamed about making love to Cy. As her mind floated along, thoughts appeared out of nowhere, in tune with her footsteps: *I want a baby, I need a baby; I want a baby, I need a baby.* Left, right. Left, right. The thoughts caught her by surprise and were mildly annoying. The timing was all wrong. Yes, she knew her clock was ticking, but it was not the time. Or was it? *I want a baby; I need a baby.*

That old incessant rhythm.

An afternoon at the beach was all it had taken.

2

Alyssa had little doubt that the young man she had sent away at the gym—Mark—desired her. For some reason, the memory flooded through her mind as she walked. Everything about it—about him— spoke of desire. She remembered his eyes. Despite his brown hair he had the same colour eyes as she had—blue-green. The odds of them having the same colour eyes by chance seemed vanishingly remote. She imagined looking into them while they kissed. It would be like making love with oneself.

Meeting him at the gym had not been by chance. Destiny had been at work. She wrinkled her forehead at the memory. Had she met and lost the man of her dreams?

Why am I thinking romantic rubbish about other men?

Cy awaited, and he was great too.

Despite years of counselling and training, her upbringing still left her confused about relationships. One thing she did know for sure, though, was that males were keen to have sex with her. Almost without exception, she was attractive to them in that way. She possessed that which they desired—even though what *that* was, apart from the obvious, she did not exactly know.

As a person, I'm a pretty shit person.

Wendy Greene, her one-time psychotherapy training mentor, was probably the only one who knew how negatively she felt about herself. Wendy knew, too, about how men had turned out to be her salvation in early adulthood; how, through them, she had found a way in which she could relate to others. Yes, it involved a bit of trickery, but by sexually enthralling men she blinded them to her otherwise scarcely tolerable emotional deficiencies. Though not the cure for feelings of worthlessness, sex equalled company.

Wendy wasn't fooled, though, and she never tired of pointing out the obvious.

Sure, you have this fabulous body, Alyssa, but you won't be able to hide behind it forever. There's no point in avoiding yourself. You are going to have to stop using sex as a crutch.

Wrong.

She was an invalid, and an invalid needed a crutch.

The truth was Wendy was jealous of her body.

Other women almost always were.

Even if what Wendy had said was true and she did use her body to obtain power over men to support a limping Self rather than in the service of egalitarian love, did this matter? Did anyone care? Did she care? Not at all. Only one thing mattered: that she got through one more day. She was damaged goods and a large part of her was missing.

Despite the efforts of many therapists to improve the situation, and despite every effort of her own, the precondition that in a relationship a man should desire her continued to run as strongly as ever in her psyche. No amount of navel-gazing made the slightest difference. She desired to be desired. That was her deepest wish—and need.

Desire me.

It was how she controlled men. She could not risk having a man have power over her. Not ever again. Maintaining control of the situation was how she stayed alive. And she had become a genius at it.

Yes, she had. The incident with the young man at the gym had provided further proof of her ability. In just a few seconds, an Adonis called Mark had come under her power.

3

The entrance to the aging apartment building where she lived came into view, prompting her to forget about babies and fantasy lovers and occupy her mind with more immediate problems. Like what to do if Dr Jocelyn Goronowski turned against her. Women had caused her nothing but grief for her entire life and she doubted she would be able to cope with yet another vindictive one. She could not cope with nastiness from women.

After checking for mail in the lobby of the building, Alyssa fretted about the alcoholic psychiatrist as she climbed the stairs. For some reason, the woman was continuing to trouble her. Women did not usually prey on her mind. Men yes, but not women. Generally, she just ignored other women. Froze them out. There had to be more to her worries than mere guilt over rejecting a lift home. Something deeper was at work—but what? Doctor Jocelyn from Santos Beach was evoking something deep; making her feel uneasy. But why? Her usually reliable psychological insight had abandoned her.

She became aware that she was not moving. She had frozen on the second-floor landing.

Like a Gnomon.

The thought intrusion seemed bizarre. No matter, she told herself. There was no hurry. She would take her time and get a grip on herself.

She focused her mind on Jocelyn Goronowski. The attack of butterflies she had experienced when talking to her at Santos Beach had not stemmed from envy, that much, at least, she did know. Jocelyn lived by herself and had no children. In the doctor's own words, she had no interest in "snotty brats"—husbands or kids. So, no, she did not envy her. So, then, why the butterflies? Had the unease been the result of feelings of professional inadequacy? After all, Jocelyn had declared to her face that ninety-nine per cent of talk therapists were bogus imbeciles. "Although not you, of course, Alyssa my dear." According to Jocelyn, bogus therapists were breeding out of control and had become a curse on the planet. Though obviously inebriated, she was still a psychiatrist, so the cruel comments had felt like a slap in the face.

Until that moment, she had never doubted—in keeping with the collective assumption of her counsellor colleagues—that she had professional worth. Yet, all it had taken was the loosened tongue of a medical specialist to leave her nursing a suspicion that there might be an element of truth to the damning words. Perhaps not only Jocelyn but *all* doctors secretly found her and other counsellors a bit of a joke. After all, no one at the party had shut Jocelyn up. So, was her sense of disquiet simply a case of anxiety about a possible lack of worth?

No, she decided. It was not that. During the tram ride home, once back in the familiar crush of ordinary humanity, she had seen enough reminders of society's desperate need for counsellors. No matter what Jocelyn said, she *did* have something to offer. She could help people. If anyone was wrong about counsellors, it was Jocelyn. Indeed, if anyone *needed* a counsellor it was Jocelyn herself. Her drinking problem was way out of control.

Perhaps, then, the strange anxiety assailing her had something to do with a repressed sexual attraction towards women. Surely not.

Yuk. How disturbing.

She had absolutely no wish to kiss the pink bits of another woman. She was not sexually attracted to Jocelyn, she told herself. Definitely not.

No. Something else was at work. A sense of longing. A feeling of . . . of remembrance past. At last, her true feelings seemed to be coming into focus. Yet it was not an entirely comforting longing. Fear was somehow mixed in with it too. Jocelyn was causing her to feel fear. It was as simple as that. She was feeling fear. Jocelyn frightened her. Jocelyn had an ability to force parts of her unconscious mind to the surface.

Jocelyn has the power to force the evil in me to rise to the surface.

Something about Jocelyn reminded her strongly of the horrors of her past. Technically, from a professional point of view, some sort of boundary issue occurred whenever Jocelyn spoke to her, some form of role reversal. In the weeks to come, Jocelyn was going to *force* her to relate to her, and it was the *knowing* of this that was causing her to feel fearful. The woman was going to start relentlessly seeking after her. Investigating. Interfering. There was not going to be a happy ending.

Shit!

At least the anxiety attack was now under control. Time to get moving again. But then a peevish little voice at the back of her mind insisted that she address one more possibility—the most important one of all, the one that she was still refusing to face. What if Jocelyn Goronowski, astute psychiatrist that she no doubt was, *knew* that she had done something bad? Had recognised that she was hiding something. Had seen on her face that she was guilty as hell. The thought was too frightening to hold. Alyssa placed her hands over her ears and ran.

Nobody can ever know . . .

She needed to anchor herself in the light.

'Cy, my darling, I'm safely home.' Heart thumping in her chest, she burst into her flat.

4

Cy was sprawled on the sofa, barefoot and in a black grandad T-shirt and old jeans, watching television. The living room windows were wide open, and music was blaring.

She always felt safe with him. As a couple, they had made remarkable progress in the year they had been together. He provided emotional stability for her, and she helped him too by getting him to straighten himself out. Cy needed that: straightening out. He was the sort of man who needed someone like her. She felt blessed that he was as kind as he was handsome. Sensitive too.

No one was perfect, of course, and Cy did have certain "issues". The most important of them was his career. As things stood, he did not earn enough money to stay alive without relying on others. If one wanted to be charitable, one could call him a penniless aspiring novelist, or, if one wanted to be brutally honest, one could say that he was a no-hoper. However, whatever one wished to believe about his writing talents, he had reached a time in his life when something needed to happen. And she was there to encourage him.

He looked up from the sofa. 'Hello sweetie.'

She smiled down at him. 'Hi. It's great to be back home again.'

Cy sat up properly, then stood up and switched the television off. She gave him a hug and they kissed lightly on the lips. She could tell he had been eating a bag of salt and vinegar chips.

'Well, how did it go?' he asked. 'Did you manage to find the old doc's apartment?'

'I did, and it was great. They were very kind. You could have come. It would have been okay. I missed you.' She went to the bedroom to put her bag down and take off her shoes. 'It went much better than I expected,' she said from the bedroom. 'I think I'll be able to work with them. Dr

Summerfield seems especially nice.'

'If you say so.'

She knew Cy did not believe that a medical doctor could be a nice person—no doubt because financial failure as an author had left him resentful of what he saw as an astonishingly overpaid profession. To some degree, she sympathised. After all, it was not as though Cy was lazy— even though he often appeared that way. He worked quite hard. When she arrived home, for example, he had been watching the soap opera *Away from Home* on television and not been relaxing—as most would think—but been busy studying dialogue. Authentic sounding dialogue was what he struggled with most in his writing. There was a notepad and a pen on the coffee table, and some scribblings. He worked constantly yet earnt next to nothing.

He was desperate to be a better author. His biggest problem— according to him—was that people understood almost nothing that he wrote. He needed to learn how to better communicate to others the genius that lay within him.

They had met at a small alternative bookshop in Troy—a quirky haven where she often browsed when out shopping and where he worked part-time as a sales assistant. Right from the beginning, she had been charmed by him. He had seemed full of what she herself badly lacked: self-assurance and self-belief. A confident, self-assured lover was exactly what she needed, and matters had progressed swiftly from there. But how things had changed.

The real Cy proved to be quite different from the man behind the bookstore counter. Deep down, he was desperately insecure, and an ongoing lack of financial success as a writer only made matters worse. She had always known that he was short of cash, but the ongoing failure to generate interest in his novels, and the consequent lack of funds had begun to weigh heavily on them both. More unfortunately, any attempt on her part to address the issue had become taboo.

Cy still worked at that same bookshop, and still one and a half days a week—just enough to keep himself alive—but the sad truth was that he was never going to be a success as a writer. What self-confidence he did manage to display from time to time was mere bravado. After thirteen years of intense effort, Cy had zero assets and just about zero income.

It had taken six months of living with him for these facts to begin to penetrate.

How attraction can blind.

Alyssa went to the bathroom to wash her hands. Germs she did not like, especially ones from the tram. While there, she studied her face in the mirror. Pretty good, she thought, even though she was not the most beautiful woman on the planet. Especially not to Cy: he too had progressed beyond the stage of blindness in their relationship. They had both matured. They had reached the stage of amicable equipoise where neither any longer made the other out to be something they were not. Which was a good thing—except for the fact that suggestions to Cy about what he needed to do about himself were off limits.

Back in the living room, music was still playing. The reedy strains emanated from Cy's budget Bluetooth soundbar, which sat on top of his bookshelf next to the balcony door. Even though the quality of the cheap speakers was terrible, he did not seem to mind. Fortunately, music meant little to her. She could not even recognise the artist, although she did know it was likely to be some version of underground dubstep because that was all Cy ever played. The track seemed pleasant enough. Though she knew next to nothing about music, she did at least like dancing. She liked that a lot.

'I feel bad about not having had the guts to go with you,' said Cy. 'I feel, somehow, that I've let you down.' He sat on the couch looking dispirited. She went and sat next to him and put an arm around him.

'I think you were right not to go. It was more of a work thing.' She gave him a playful hug. 'You would have been bored. Don't worry about it.'

Now that she was thinking about it properly, she realised that Cy had been right to refuse to attend. The welcoming party at Santos Beach may well have been disastrous for him—exactly as he had predicted. She tried not to imagine what the three hard-headed and successful psychiatrists would have made of him. Cy was better off not knowing. The drunken Goronowski might even have accused him of being a childish fool.

'So, tell me,' said Cy, 'was *everyone* there a psychoanalyst? Did you lot spend the afternoon seeing through each other? Please don't tell me you did.'

'You have the weirdest ideas, Cy. We simply had a few drinks and a bit of a chat to get to know each other, like normal people. That's all. They were all psychiatrists, by the way, not psychoanalysts—except for Dr Summerfield's wife, who's not even in the mental health field. Modern psychiatrists aren't analysts; they are just doctors. They treat mad people using drugs mainly, with a bit of environmental manipulation thrown in. I was the only vaguely psychoanalytical person there—although, as I've tried to explain to you before, I'm a psychodynamic therapist, not a psychoanalyst. The only other vaguely analytic person there was Professor Summerfield, who's mostly a mainstream psychiatrist anyway, but does dabble occasionally in psychodynamic therapy as a sort of conceited intellectual hobby.'

Cy frowned and stood up. She had upset him somehow, maybe with the tone of her voice. Perhaps he thought she was talking down to him. He went to his low-rent soundbar and fiddled with the base controls, his back to her.

He spoke over his shoulder: 'Do you seriously mean to tell me that these people of yours—who work every day with the mentally unwell—aren't analysts? Now, why do I find that hard to believe? Why has everyone got this all wrong?' His base adjustments proved futile, so he turned the volume of the music down until it was barely audible. Usually, he listened to his tracks on earphones anyway. 'Have I become fucking stupid, or what?'

So, that *was* his problem. His sense of intellectual omniscience had been dented. 'The mental health world is very complex, Cy. It's almost impossible for a layperson to understand it.'

'Is that so.' He changed to another track—more dubstep—and increased the volume slightly. Then he returned to the sofa.

She tried to humour him. 'What are you playing now?' Her knowledge of music was limited to whatever was currently on the hit parade.

'Guess.'

'Knife Party?'

He found the suggestion amusing. 'Nope. Try again.'

'D J Chef? Avicii?' She knew he had these tracks.

'Next you'll be telling me it's Birdy Nam Nam.'

'Is it?'

'No.'

'I give up.' Too much of her life had required attention to things other than music—things like surviving her mother and her father and her stepmother, and getting through her mental breakdown, and passing her university examinations. When it came to knowledge about music, Cy would always win.

He laughed at her. 'It's a new track by Infected Mushrooms. Don't worry, I'll spare you the details.'

'Well, it sounds cool anyway. I like it.'

5

Cy put his arm around her. 'Tell me more about these psychiatrist dudes of yours. Why aren't they psychoanalysts? Didn't they *invent* psychoanalysis?'

She tried to be gentle. 'It's really complicated, Cy. Yes, they did invent psychoanalysis, but that was back in the olden days, and it's no longer mainstream or even part of the medical world anymore. There's still a place for it, sure, but only in certain highly selected clients. Psychoanalysis is far too expensive, takes far too long, requires far too high a level of practitioner, and is far too vulnerable to client abuse by cranks. Today, the mental health treatment stream is much broader and more robust. Human behaviour and interpersonal relationships are now studied as a science, so understanding has advanced greatly. None of the psychiatrists at the Donald Clinic are psychoanalysts—certainly not in the original sense of the word.'

He looked unconvinced.

'It's true, Cy, really it is. The closest thing these days to Freud's old *psychical processes* is modern psychodynamic therapy, yet even that is nothing like the old psychoanalysis. It's far more advanced.'

'Psychiatrists don't do it, but you do?'

'They could, but they simply don't have the time. That's *my* job, Cy. They send their clients to me once they've made a diagnosis. If it's required. The subsequent talking and relating is what *I* do. It requires time. These things are not worth trying to get your head around.'

That made him angry all over again.

'Knowing what makes people tick is *my* job too in case you haven't noticed. You're not the only one, you know. And you still haven't told me what's *wrong* with psychoanalysis. What happened to the subconscious? Why is *that* wrong? I quite like the idea.'

'The subconscious is still there, Cy, but the word is so misunderstood by the general public that in my field we now refer to it as the Un-conscious. We do this to emphasise that, unlike the mythical subconscious of popular mythology, it is *not* easily accessible. And we also do it to indicate that the subconscious is not the same as the repetitive-task-mind, which is easily brought in or out of conscious awareness. Furthermore, by using the specific technical term *Un-conscious* we avoid the risk of confusion with the word "unconscious" as understood by neurophysiologists and the broader stream of health professionals.'

He frowned at her convoluted explanation. 'So then, what's not to like about psychoanalysis? You are not convincing me.'

'The problem is that metaphysical theories about the functional structure of the mind can't be verified experimentally.'

'You really are not making any sense tonight.'

'I only know what I've been taught.'

'That sounds childish.'

'It's not. I can give you some Obermaaier if you like. Maybe that will explain what happened to psychoanalysis.' She was able to quote most of her course textbook off by heart, and he knew it. She closed her eyes to assist concentration and reproduced a memorised passage:

> The modern view is that when one person interacts with another person, the relating of the *one* to the *another* is largely a matter of the Un-conscious "Self" of the one person *agreeing* with the Un-conscious "Self" of the other person that he or she "knows" unstated aspects of the other's Self. Somehow, in their interacting, they are recognising, i.e., sharing, the *same* consciously unknown aspects of their respective Self.

'Is that so, Little Miss Smartass?' Cy pinched her bottom playfully under her skirt.

'Yes, it is.' She squirmed out of harm's way. 'And in any case, theories don't appear to be all that important anyway when it comes to helping people with emotional problems. Whatever one believes about anything, it remains true that interacting with another person in a benign way is helpful to them. When you cut through the verbiage, it's *that* that helps.'

He interrupted. 'You are getting way too intense.'

'It's going to be my whole life in the future, Cy.'

'What? Being someone else's drug?'

'That's a weird way to put it.'

'But true.'

'Maybe. It's going to be a challenge, I agree. There are only three or four counselling schools left in the entire country that still think that the Un-conscious Self is central to any understanding of the conscious Self, but I count myself lucky I went to one. It's only through true Self-knowing that we can truly know the Self of another person.'

Where would I be today were it not for Wendy Greene.

Cy reached for his notepad. 'Dang, I can use this.' He scribbled some words: "intimacy is Self-to-Self congruence, conscious *and* Un-conscious". 'Great.'

What he meant was that it would look great in his latest manuscript, the writing of which seemed to have stalled. 'Just so long as you understand that relating needs to be a benevolent process,' she reminded him. 'People have strong defences. Now, aren't you hungry? Shouldn't we make dinner?'

'In a minute. One final question: why do people pay for counselling? From what you've been telling me, couldn't just *anyone* be someone else's drug?'

'Believe me, you can't pay someone enough to have to sit and listen with genuine care to what a random other person has to say. The skill is in the benevolence. It must be genuine, not muddled and self-serving.'

'Good point,' he said, and wrote it down as well.

6

'I love it when you get all irritated with me. It makes you really sexy.' He put a hand between her legs.

'Stop it.' Alyssa was feeling tired. 'Tell me, honey, have you eaten? I'm starving.'

'Stop worrying.' He smiled and put a finger on her lips as though to silence her. 'I've been busy. Not only have I written a few more pages of my new book this afternoon but I have also made us some pasta.'

'That's really thoughtful of you. Thank you.'

Cy went to the stove top of the open-plan kitchen and tilted a saucepan at her with a flourish. 'It's one we both like: salmon linguine. And I've made us some salsa verde—okay, mostly it's just parsley and olive oil, but we did have some garlic and I found some capers at the back of the cupboard.'

'Excellent.' He was a passable cook, so she knew the pasta would taste good. As for the fresh parsley, it almost certainly came from the next-door neighbour's balcony garden. Cy had sourced herbs this way before. With effort and not inconsiderable danger, he could reach parts of that garden from their own balcony. He had gone to a lot of trouble for her sake. She watched him with interest as he moved about in the kitchen. He was not tall for a man, only fractionally taller than she was, and, if truth be told, a little weedy, but to her at least, he seemed imbued with an indefinable masculine assurance that still weakened her knees even after almost a year of living with him. In keeping with this was his surprising physical strength. Though she went to the gym regularly and he never did, he was stronger than she was. This was something she discovered early on in their relationship, during lovemaking, and it still gave her a thrill every time he beat her at play wrestling. However, although he was strong, he was weak too. She soon discovered that he had no self-confidence when it came to the actual act of making love. When it came to that, she could overpower him without even trying. For some reason, that still seemed disappointing.

'How much do you want?' he asked. He was talking about the pasta.

'A lot.' She needed to keep her energy levels up. She planned another visit to Fabio's gym the following day.

They sat together at their round table, one of the items of furniture from Cy's previous rented cottage. 'Pity we can't afford to go out tonight,' he said.

'We could have some wine. Is there any left?'

'Nope.' He shrugged his shoulders.

Still drinking on the quiet, thought Alyssa. 'We'll have to amuse ourselves, then. Could be fun.'

'Just what I was thinking.' He gazed at her silently and with unmistakable intent—something she always found exciting when coming from a man she herself fancied. He broke into a grin. 'I think it's those beach clothes. You are looking incredibly hot sitting there.'

It still made her blush when people said this to her. She looked up from her food. Cy had brown eyes, matching his lanky hair and lean moustache, and she found herself gazing briefly right into them. Then his gaze shifted to take in her breasts. 'Stop it,' she said. 'You're making me go all red in the face. I'm trying to eat.'

'What's with the overpowering boobies today? What have you done to them?'

'It's just spray tan.'

'Eat up,' he said. 'I really need to do something.'

There was a good-natured truce. For a while, they ate in silence, listening to Cy's music in the dying heat of the day. Through the open lounge room window there was a pleasant view across their balcony to the small park across the road. Before long, reflecting off the tennis club sign, rays from the setting sun began to radiate silently over them. For a few enchanting minutes, the silvery light shimmered like flitting fairies. The effect was eerily romantic—as was the cooling breeze that suddenly began to stir the curtains. 'This is really lovely,' said Alyssa, her face bathed in silver.

'The food, the sun, the breeze, the music—or us?'

She smiled back at him. 'Everything.'

'Agreed.' They continued eating in intimate silence.

He ate well, she thought. Not only did he look good, but he was a good eater too. No noisy sucking and slurping, no food overboard, no ghastly blocked nose or open-mouthed chewing—none of the physical horrors so prevalent in other males.

I really am very lucky.

While thinking about how happy she was with his general habits, her gaze took in his three pot plants out on the balcony. Though green and healthy, they still had no flowers on them despite the recent heat wave and despite her regular watering efforts whenever they looked dry.

Maybe it was the fault of the romance in the air, but for some reason the continuing lack of flowers on Cy's plants bothered her. She wanted to see flowers.

He seemed aware that something was troubling her. 'A penny for your thoughts.'

'Oh. It's nothing,' she said. Then she was more honest: 'Actually, I'm just thinking how nice it would be if we could start a family. You know what I'm like. I know it's not practical.'

She saw him wince. They had discussed the baby issue a few times in the past, and he had made it clear that he had no interest in having children. None whatsoever. Yet she knew he could change—if he wanted to. It seemed the perfect night to change one's mind and have a baby.

Instead, Cy changed the subject.

'Tell me more about your new doctor friends,' he said. 'Were they as up themselves as I predicted?'

Clearly, he was going to be bloody minded. Angry, she stood up. 'Don't you worry yourself about doctors. I can handle them.'

'Where are you going? You're not cross, are you? Sorry.'

She did not answer his stupid question. 'I'm getting more food. A glass of wine would have been good with it.'

'You know I said sorry. And I'm sorry about the baby thing too, okay? I'm sorry about everything. Just give me a break, will you. Maybe someday I'll improve.'

'You won't.' She left the table. There was little more she could do.

From the kitchen she tried to be more pleasant as there seemed little point in provoking an argument that evening. 'I've worked with doctors before, remember,' she said. 'During my training. They are just people, so no need to fret about them.' She thought it best not to mention that Alan Summerfield had been one of her lecturers during training. That would have been hard to explain without fuelling paranoia about conspiracies. She mentioned Donald Barnes instead. 'Even old Barnes himself was there, the one the clinic is named after. He's a scary motherfucker, if ever there was one.' Normally, she never used swearwords, but with Cy she did because he used them a lot.

She returned to the table with more food and sat down. 'One wouldn't want to mess with a bastard like him. They call him the Dog, you know.

Apparently, it's a common nickname for Donald. It certainly suits him. There was a young woman psychiatrist there too, someone called Jocelyn Goronowski. She's so restless she makes a person tired just looking at her. And then there was the guy who owns the apartment. That's Alan.'

'Alan? Really. And how does *Alan* afford a home on the beach at Santos Beach? Whatshisface must be ripping off the mad people big time.'

She gave him her best schoolteacher stare. 'His name is Alan Summerfield. And it's not like that, Cy. Maybe he has a lot of debt, or maybe he inherited money or the apartment. We shouldn't judge. He's a nice guy. Really, he is.'

'People like that just make me feel jealous. You must think I'm an absolute nothing by comparison.'

So that's what this is all about.

'Don't be silly, Cy. You have your own unique value and I love you for it. Money has nothing to do with it.' Even as she said the words, she felt an inner sense of disquiet. She knew she was lying. Money *was* important. She pushed the thought away.

7

'What did you write today?'

Cy became defensive. 'This and that. You know I don't like to discuss it.'

'Come on.'

'It's still about that sadist chap. The man who thinks that because he's a man he has the option of being a sadist.'

'That's Chad, isn't it?' Alyssa already knew a little bit about "Chad", Cy's latest male character, and from what she knew so far, Chad sounded like a real swine. She looked at Cy expectantly, to encourage more sharing.

He kept his head down. 'There's not much more to say. As I've told you earlier, the whole point of my book is that sadism is the central problem of the male condition. Today, Chad's just continued doing exactly as he pleases.'

'I see,' she said politely. 'And do the women in your new book get a chance to object?'

He looked up with what seemed genuine surprise. 'Oh, no. It's part of life.'

And there I was thinking that sadism was something horrible.

He sensed her incredulity. 'That's all it is, honest. It's what the world calls life. Society puts up with it all the time, and the loser feels pain.'

'Has the parsley gone to your brain?'

'Not at all. And here's the clincher—this new book of mine is so brilliant—losers mostly internalise their pain. They either no longer notice when they are being screwed over, or simply accept it as their lot. So, luckily for us all, society exists in winner-loser matrixes that are generally stable.'

'With women mostly the losers and in pain?'

Cy seemed surprised by her reluctance to see his point. 'Well, yes, especially in the olden days. People are cruel things. Win or lose is the stuff of life and men will go to extremes if they can get away with it. That's what my book will claim, anyway.'

He was being grandiose, as he always was when discussing his art. 'Extremes like everyday life, you mean?'

'You said it.' Cy appeared very pleased with his fictional exposition of sadism despite his usual reluctance to talk about his writing.

'Sounds like your theory could be interesting.' She did not mean what she said. Cy was exclusively a writer of fiction, and she was not into fiction. There seemed no point to it. 'I'll make us some coffee, shall I?'

'Will you now? And what if I start behaving like Chad?'

Then I'll kick you in your balls.

No, she never actually said it.

He grabbed one of her wrists. The grip was powerful, and she found herself unable to move. He looked her in the face. 'I've never met anyone as fuckable as you. I mean it. You are looking really hot.'

Coming from you, that is saying a lot.

She glanced disapprovingly at her trapped wrist. Cy's hand did at least have beautiful olive skin—*like the rest of him,* she thought. The little black hairs on the back of his knuckles gave her a tingle in her lower belly. 'Patience,' she said. 'Coffee first.' For a tense moment, he kept her in his power, as though contemplating just getting on with things regardless of what she wanted, but then, as always, he yielded. His grip relaxed.

In the kitchen, she was conscious of his gaze as he admired her from behind. She liked being desired, and men always said her bottom was the best part of her. Or was it her tits?

She understood a great deal about men, but not certain details.

What exactly is it that makes him want me?

She had to confess that she did not know.

Instead, she held Cy's assertion that she was fuckable in her mind like a disembodied literary fragment. She turned it this way and that as she made the coffee. She felt sure the sentiment had applied to all his girlfriends—and still did to almost any woman he met. Heaven only knew how many women he had slept with. When she asked him the exact number, early on in their relationship, his answer had been evasive. Sometimes, she still worried that he may have given her a disease. There was no sign of any such thing, but she knew enough to know that often there wasn't.

The best approximation she had been able to achieve was nineteen.

Counting you, Alyssa.

Nineteen sexual partners. The worst of it was that, judging from what she had come to know about him over the months, it was almost certainly an underestimation. Even if true, nineteen still seemed a shocking and vaguely disgusting number. To her, it did not seem right that anyone should be intimate with that many people—even though for a thirty-three-year-old it was nothing unusual according to the course in sexology she had recently completed.

He was only her third.

How could he have allowed himself to be abused by so many women?

Women were not the innocent victims that society seemed determined to believe they were—certainly not in Cy's case. How could he have been *that* weak?

The first time they had sex, Cy had assured her that he was in search of a relationship and was not a believer in casual sex. She could still recall the words he used on the day he soothed the pants off her, words that had seemed romantic, like a quote from one of his books: "I want us to *keep* seeing each other. I want us to mean something *more* to each other." Earlier, he had said that sex where you intend never to see that person again was deeply demeaning and abusive—to *both* involved. "That's just not me."

So far, he had remained true to his word. They were still together, and she felt certain that he was faithful to her. They had dispensed with condoms within a month of living together, though sometimes that still worried her. Hadn't the sexology lecturer said that one should wait three months? She had not been irresponsible with contraception, though. Right from the beginning she had put herself on the pill.

She sensed him as he came up behind her to collect his mug of coffee. With one hand, he raised the back of her short skirt. It was a flippy skirt, so he flipped it up.

'Oh man,' he groaned, 'you should be illegal. I think I'm going to die.'

'Don't,' she said. 'I'm all sweaty. And I've only got a G on.' She pushed the back of her skirt down again. 'Just be patient.'

'Okay, I'll try. But I don't know why.' He went and sat on the sofa with his coffee. 'I can't believe you actually went to a work function dressed like that.'

'It's been a warm day. And besides, nobody can see under my skirt.'

'Yes, Alyssa. Whatever, Alyssa.'

That was rich coming from someone like Cy, she thought.

8

Nineteen fucked.

That's what he said.

These women, according to Cy, meant nothing to him when all was said and done. However, they had at least unlocked his mind. The by-product of getting to know so many women intimately had been an increased understanding of sex and life. Indeed, it had been the discoveries about the realities of women that had spurred him to become a writer of erotic fiction. Cy believed he had come to truly know women. He believed not only that but also that by the promotion of a more truthful understanding of all things erotic he was uniquely placed to save a humanity destined otherwise for self-destruction.

He wrote and wrote. "Not for the experts, who know it all anyway, but for the common herd."

He did not seem to suspect for even a minute that he may have weird ideas. Or—more to the point—that he may have taken up a vocation for which he had no talent. He had no training in writing. Although born in Hubron, he had later lived in a small provincial city in the north of Astoria, where he enrolled in law school. After a few years there, he dropped out and gave up completely on conventional life. According to him, this was because at university he discovered that most people were "absolutely fucking nauseating". Unable to let that remain as it was, he took to writing. He invented a more dashing name for himself and moved south to Hubron. He would have preferred Paris, he said, but at least in Hubron he could get welfare payments. The thing that had surprised her most about Cy was that his real name was not Cy at all, but Simon Page. Cy was short for Cyrus Beauchamp, his assumed literary name. What was even more strange was that despite knowing this, she never thought of him as Simon Page. Neither, it seemed, did he.

'What are your plans for tomorrow?' she asked.

'What?' Cy was impatient, and his hand was high on her thigh, making it difficult for her to concentrate. He seemed surprised by her question but remained civil. 'Nothing much. Just a lazy Sunday. Why, what do you have in mind?'

'I'm feeling very anxious for some reason, so I think I'm going to need to go to the gym. Will that be okay?' Exercising at Fabio's always made her feel better.

He laughed. 'You and the gym and your cock-breaker of a bum. When are you going to stop obsessing about it?'

She gave him a playful slap. 'Stop it.' His comment about her bottom was, of course, meant as a compliment. 'Maybe after that I'll go to church too. Or maybe not.' She toyed with the single small silver earring in his left ear as they spoke. He had only the one earring, but secretly she disapproved of it. It was the only thing about him, physically, that she did not like.

A real man does not wear an earring.

At least, that was what her father used to say. Shakespeare and pirates notwithstanding, the assessment still seemed right to her. One day, she would have to confront Cy about his earring. And his tattoo: no more of those. There was a fiery dragon in chain mail armour on his left forearm, stretching from his elbow to just above his wrist. Unlike the earring, she was in two minds about tattoos. While they seemed a bad idea in general, sometimes she found herself quite liking Cy's dragon—like tonight, when it looked masculine in a scary, bad boy sort of way. Maybe, she thought, she needed to try to see his earring that way too.

'Anything *else* on your private agenda for tomorrow?' Cy asked. He seemed irritated by her earring-fiddling because he stopped it by grasping her hand.

'No.'

He no doubt knew that she wanted to talk, but instead he kissed her on her lips to emphasise his own agenda. Then he relented. 'Okay, the gym I can understand, but what's with the church crap? You hardly ever go, so what's with the sudden religious fervour? You can't base your life on bullshit.'

'Maybe it's not bullshit. Not totally, anyway.'

'Oh, please. How can any good or sane person believe in the kind of god specified in your ancient texts?'

She knew—from books that Cy himself had written—that Cy believed religion to be morally unacceptable. It was nothing more than an unpleasant cultural tumour that had somehow metastasised off the deceased rumps of deluded primitives, as he put it, so she did not try to argue. Instead, she said, 'You know I like to go sometimes. I want to focus on getting myself back on track.'

'And you don't think you're just giving in to superstition?'

'Church still has me confused. I do think it helps sometimes.' Cy kept silent, indicating his disagreement. 'You know I used to go a lot with my dad when I was a kid,' she said finally. 'I'm not embarrassed to support Jesus.'

She could sense that Cy was itching to say something damning, but he managed to hold his tongue. He was being mindful of the tragedy she had experienced with her father, and it made her embrace him. She was grateful for how considerate he was of her needs. Though he saw churches as institutions inhabited by morbid cranks who had failed to grow up, he knew she had attended church regularly as a young child. Her father had taken her with him to services week after week. Now that her father was dead, cruelly killed when she was just thirteen years old, church reminded her of him.

Cy was wise enough to be patient. After all, in another of his books he had asserted that fathers always screwed with their daughter's heads. Which was undoubtedly true in her case. Doubly true, in fact.

That part, though, she preferred not to think about.

9

Instead of thinking about what had happened to her in the past, Alyssa had a dream at about four am in which she couldn't get her mind off a man. She was watching him as he walked away from her across a gym hall. Physically, he was everything she ever wanted.

He was leaving her. Why had she sent him packing? The fact that she already had a partner did not seem relevant. It was only a dream. Perhaps she had sent him away because she did not wish to harm him, a man so handsome and so innocent-looking. More than likely, she would just ruin his life. After all, she was not to be trusted.

And, of course, the moral question needed to be addressed. Certain things were definitely immoral. Surely. Besides, when it came to sex, she was not the sharing kind. There was no way that she was going to be participating in the ever-expanding culture of casual sex that seemed to characterise civilisation—or lack of it—in Hubron. Maybe she was old-fashioned, or maybe too much Sunday school as a child had resulted in moral rectitude, but she was never going to be having sex with a total stranger. No. Sex had to come *with* attachment. Relationships were otherwise too difficult.

For someone like me.

There were consequences to immorality; to doing the wrong thing. Unforeseen, unexpected, and lifelong consequences.

She saw him head for the change rooms. He walked well, with the grace of an angel and a neat little bottom to die for. When he reached the female entrance, he stopped.

At least he did not enter—that would have been a real surprise.

She had known then, finally, how it was going to play out.

She had had this dream before. Or was it even a dream?

A woman emerged. She was tall like him, but unlike him she was not a good-looker. She was overly skinny and had a prominent nose. A crucifix dangled on a gold chain around her neck. She had blonde hair, much like her own, and when she smiled at Mark, he took her by the hand.

She kissed him full on the lips.

Which was traumatic to witness.

There were situations that were natural and meant to be, and there were situations that were forced and nauseating, and this was the latter. There was normal body weight, and there was skinny, but the scene that played out across the gym hall was both hideous and ridiculous. The tall blonde was too thin by half. Also, her hair was fake blonde and in need of a wash, and her face was greasy. Her breasts were almost non-existent, and her nose far too long. Horrible. The kissing woman was like a predatory bird, like the ones that used to land on their lawn when she was a child and attempt to eat their cat.

In her dream, the nasally challenged woman was called "Beak Face". It made her feel better. Mocking the ugly always made her feel better. She wondered what Mark saw in her. Beak Face looked older than him, nearer to thirty than twenty-five. A stunning looker like him deserved something far better. She was in culottes. And she had blue spectacles. No dress sense. Too awful.

The dream got stranger. Adonis was leaving the building. He was going down, down the stairs. Then he turned and looked back at her. His eyes locked with hers and he smiled.

She was his and he was hers.

A bullet went through her brain and her head exploded.

She had blown apart.

He had blown her apart.

And yet she was still alive.

And stuck in a gym, with her mind crazily off track in a mixed-up dream that had become somehow terrifying.

CHAPTER FOUR

1

ONE OF THE JOYS of the new job was that it was within walking distance of their rented flat in lower Alfonso Street. On the first day of her first real job, Alyssa emerged from home early and headed for the Donald Clinic on foot. She was smartly dressed in a fitted, navy coloured, above-knee business skirt, crisp white shirt, and stylish black business shoes. She had washed her hair the night before and had it neatly styled. The weather was good, and she felt light-hearted. She knew the walk would take less than ten minutes because she had timed it previously, and all other preparations were in hand too. The bag over her shoulder contained her smartphone, two important books, and a packed lunch. She had decided to take her books, even though they were accessible online, because of the many useful notes in the margins from her time with Wendy Greene. The books formed the basis of everything she knew about transference-based psychodynamic therapy at counsellor level.

She started the journey to work by cutting diagonally across the small park in front of their apartment building and heading in the direction of the Yarradonga river. Walking was something she enjoyed, and she kept up a brisk pace. Going to the gym regularly had its benefits. She noticed some fellow pedestrians, mostly men, glancing at her appreciatively and it pleased her. The fact that people were finding her attractive confirmed that her appearance was in good taste. No doubt, having a good figure helped.

Cy had still been asleep when she left. She had given him a kiss on his forehead while applying a last-minute fragrance to herself, before heading out the front door. 'Wish me luck.'

He had responded, but with an incoherent, 'Mm,' then gone back to sleep.

'See you later, my sweet.'

At a local coffee shop, she turned right into Willow Street then headed past the library in the direction of the Troy Gardens. It was not yet eight o'clock but already the midsummer January sun was hot on her skin. Ahead, above the trees of the distant public garden, the skyscrapers of the central business district loomed, like lurking giants, and the sound of traffic hummed. As she got closer to the Donald Clinic, which was near to the Troy Gardens, the ceaseless rumbling of the traffic grew louder. Cars were pouring into the central business district from every direction it seemed—except one: hers. Where she was, in East Hubron near the residence of the archbishop, it remained peaceful. By a miracle of urban design, vehicular inundations were unable to penetrate this section of the suburb because of the barrier of the nearby public parklands. Despite its proximity to the CBD, Willow Street was peaceful, with the sound of traffic disembodied and scarcely real, as otherworldly as the sound of the sea. The contrived tranquillity reminded her of her childhood town, Ocean View. There too, had been the sound of a sea.

But no peace.

She had been extremely lucky to secure the rented flat in Alfonso Street. Once again, it had been Wendy Greene who had come to her aid. Wendy's previous trainee had just vacated the same flat and Wendy knew that her new student—someone called Alyssa Brown—had just broken up with boyfriend Aaron and would need a place to stay. Wendy had a good heart.

She continued to think about her old tutor as she strode along in the bright sunshine. Wendy had been a great teacher and she owed her a lot— probably even her life. There were times when Wendy had been the mother she had never had. It was sad to think that there was going to be no more of her. Student days were over. Professionally, she was on her own now.

In her mind, she rehearsed the "Four Understandings" of Wendy Greene, checking that she was still able to recall them word for word. It was hard, because there were twelve counselling facts to remember, not four:

Where do we hang our hat when modelling a mind? On four pegs and on four realisations. The pegs: seeing unconscious motive, countering countertransference, identifying the attachment splitting, and managing the death drive. Through attention to these factors, we see that people do things for reasons that are not what they say or think they are; we see that a counsellor's perception is unexpectedly and uncontrollably dependent on the client; we see that the mind interacts with any object—in the mind or external to it—by a mechanism that involves simultaneously splitting that object into the parts it loves and the parts it hates; and we see that to the parts it loves, the mind attaches life—in the form of desire—while to the parts it hates the mind attaches death—in the form of anger and aggression. What then of our consequent four realisations once we see that the mind is largely outside of the control of its owner? We realise that people are treacherous and irrational; that people hate or love with minimal objective validity; that stated motive is never true motive; and that people are not who they say they are. In doing so, we become good therapists.

Wise Wendy had taught her many valuable things.

She was close to the Donald Clinic now. Alyssa felt her anxiety increasing given that it was an extremely snooty place and that the staff there would be expecting a lot from her. Even the security of having had excellent vocational training under Wendy could not hold back the self-doubt that began to gnaw at her.

What if I'm not good enough?

She tried to force negative sentiments out of her head. Objectively, there was no reason to feel apprehensive about her professional abilities. On the other hand, she had not graduated from the best university in the country, unlike those up ahead. And neither had she progressed without a false start. She had wasted two years trying to do sociology and having a mental breakdown before having the sense to switch to a psychology degree. She could not afford any further false starts in life. Wendy, at least, knew how much she had had to struggle financially. Knew, too, something of the blackness and the accusations—what little she had told her—and had tried to be encouraging. "Turn everything into an opportunity to understand yourself better, Alyssa. It will make you a better counsellor."

Perhaps. After all, some things she *did* now understand better.

Such as what a bad person she was deep down. It was quite unbelievable, really. Especially in someone who appeared so innocent.

2

While she walked along the quiet street, the strange dream she had had involving a gym—which in retrospect was obviously Fabio's gym—came to mind. She had a bad feeling that it was some sort of warning; that some sort of emotional disaster was approaching. But a warning about what? About the need to stop enticing men to their doom? A warning to stop lusting over men?

Or what?

It made her cast her mind back to the time some weeks earlier when she had come over all strange at Fabio's for real, not just in a dream. On that day, she had tried to pretend that everything was okay and had simply continued with her normal routine. She had found an unoccupied elliptical trainer and begun her workout.

She tried to recall the details. As always, she had begun slowly on the machine, giving herself time to warm up properly. She remembered looking at herself in the wall mirrors—one of the perks of going there—and confirming that she was in excellent shape. As always, she only really liked herself when she was at her absolute best. Emotionally unwell in some way, she *needed* to exercise.

Her hair had been in a ponytail, which was a pity because her hair was one of her better features. However, with her hair pulled back, the structure of her face showed better, which had advantages of its own. According to most, she had an excellent bone structure. Aaron, her second boyfriend, used to insist that her face reminded him of Polly Alexander the supermodel, which used to make her laugh but also gave her a secret twinge of pride. However, unlike the supermodel, she herself was no model of perfection. Aaron was clearly wrong. Yet, from certain angles and in certain light, maybe there was some resemblance ... Not everyone saw it, of course. Ethan, another of her past lovers, saw only "natural harmony". That, at least, was *completely* wrong. Mentally, she was a basket case and always had been. Still, whatever the various opinions might be, the fact remained that in some way or other men seemed to find her greatly attractive.

Which did not mean that she was attractive *enough*. Given her past, that would always be a task beyond her—as Wendy Greene had pointed out with brutal honesty and not a little cruelty. Cy had not pulled any punches either. According to him, she looked "not like a beauty queen but like a sex machine". Those words—of a few months back now—still stung. The truth was that Cy did not think that she was truly beautiful.

It had damaged her confidence with him. At first, she had taken the sex part of his assessment as a compliment, but lately she was less sure about even that. Perhaps what Cy had really meant to say was that she had a hard face. The gym mirrors gave a different view. She did *not* have a hard face. Many women these days *did* have hard faces, though.

Not me.

Yes, she had studied the reflection of her bottom. The athletic tights left nothing to the imagination. Clearly, there was still room for improvement. Women were wrong to be complacent about the health of their body. Being in good shape was important, and tight and lifted was the gold standard. Yes, undoubtedly, she was genetically gifted, but it still angered her when women pretended that their physical side was not important. Everything she had learnt in life so far told her that a good figure was the key to attracting the right sort of man. Indeed, on some or other profound level, it was the passport to being wanted.

She liked exercising. She went to the gym regularly and was fit, so, as per routine, for fifteen minutes straight she strode strenuously. Imperceptibly, as the strain on her body increased, she began to zone out of the immediate surroundings and disappear into the world of her body, connecting to it in a heightened union.

The usual had happened, even on that day. The exertion began to become sensual. As her arms pumped in unison with her legs, her bra began to feel like it was caressing her breasts, and, as her legs scissored ceaselessly backwards and forwards, pleasing sensations started up below her waist. With increasing clarity, she had perceived the sexual pleasure inherent in movement.

And, as always, the more she relaxed into the rhythm of her body, the more she transcended the anaesthesia of the everyday. She had waxed herself recently, and the denuded areas of skin now seemed electrifyingly sensitive. Her gym underwear began to feel too tight. Before long, the ride on the elliptical trainer became fully arousing. Parts of her, one in particular, began to ache in a most insistent way and she knew that if she continued with what she was doing she would climax. She knew this because she had done so quite a few times before: orgasmed on gym equipment.

God, how I need this!

That was what she had felt. Even on that day.

As she walked along the street towards the Donald Clinic, Alyssa wondered if she could be oversexed. Was there even such a thing? The embarrassing side of it apart, her gym behaviour surely indicated that she had some sort of problem with her sexual appetite. So, perhaps what the gym was trying to tell her was that she was going to get herself into trouble if she wasn't more moral. Sex could get a person into a whole lot of trouble. If anyone should know this, she should. She needed to get herself under control. That was it. That, surely, was what the warnings were all about: the need to stay in control.

Do not lose control.

This had happened before, and there was every chance that it was going to happen again. She was in danger of causing yet another disaster.

It was entirely possible that more death was just around the corner.

I have to be more careful.

3

Unexpectedly, the Donald Clinic was right in front of her. On her left, really. A looming bulk. Becoming suddenly aware of her surroundings caused her quite a fright. Time to snap out of daydreaming and meet her destiny.

Alyssa stopped on the footpath. She needed to gather both her wits and her courage. She looked up at the restored double storey mansion. It had an attic with windows. She had not noticed that before during her earlier visit. She half-expected to see bats flying out of them. She had been there only once before, at the time of her job interview with Professor Barnes, but had not paid much attention to its architecture then. It was an impressive and sober building. Weighty.

Without warning, a dreadful feeling of emptiness came suddenly into her heart. She felt utterly alone, as though she did not exist. Her father was dead, her fault, and her mother was dead, her fault too. She had nobody. She had nothing. All entirely her own fault. She might just as well go ahead and die too. It would serve her right. Despite the bright sunshine, the sky above the clinic looked dark. So dark.

She knew it was just anxiety, so she let the feeling wash over her.

She remained standing. Anxiety attack aside, the truth was that she was going to struggle to fit in at the upper-class establishment. After all, she had a distinctive countrified accent—despite her conscious attempts to speak better—and her university degree was from what could best be described as a suburban bush college. The professional staff at the Donald, on the other hand, were all graduates of Olympic University, the premier university in not only Hubron but the entire country. Getting into a top university had not been possible for the likes of her. At high school, she had not thought of further study and not achieved anywhere near the required grades. People were almost certainly going to play the intellectual social snob card against her at some stage and she would have no defence.

Not quite up to the mark.

Wendy, who knew so much about her, knew too of her anxieties about being inadequate. Once again, she had tried to put a positive spin on it: "Stop beating yourself up, Alyssa. You are as intelligent as you need to be, no doubt about that." Wendy had said something else too, which had seemed more believable: "Besides, Alyssa, you are extremely attractive, so you have an advantage over others. There are people out there prepared to die for you simply for that reason alone."

Wendy always did like to exaggerate. Nevertheless, feeling more encouraged, Alyssa started walking again.

Her heart was beating in her throat when she announced herself at the reception desk. The clock on the wall read 8.05 am. She was early. Starting time was normally 8.30 am and first clients arrived at 8.45 am.

4

'Hi. I'm Alyssa,' she said. 'The new counselling psychologist.'

The receptionist, a youngish, plump brunette who was typing a letter behind a counter, gave a start and clutched theatrically at her throat. 'Oh!' Oh!' exclaimed the woman. 'You gave me quite a turn. There's no one else here yet. Not downstairs.'

Alyssa looked at her expectantly. She judged her to be about her own age. She looked friendly enough.

'Alyssa, you say?' said the overweight character, as though trying to recall the significance of the name. 'Oh, yes, *Alyssa*. How silly of me.' She stretched out her hand. 'Trish. Hi. I'm Trish. Welcome to the madhouse.' They shook hands. 'Would you like a cup of coffee?'

'Okay, thank you.'

'I'll show you our staff room. We can get a coffee there. Greta McCreedy, our other psychologist, should be along shortly. I know she's expecting you. She said to have you wait in the staff room if you arrived before she did.'

Trish the receptionist gave a brief and helpful tour of the facilities on the way to coffee. She started by heading back out to the front gate and then into the street.

'First, one has to get the big picture. As you can see, the clinic is a restored Victorian era mansion. It was built in the 1880s in the Italianate style. It's heritage-listed and worth a packet. So, don't damage or alter anything.'

'I won't.'

Next came a lesson on how to operate the lock on the heavy, wrought iron front gate. The building stood close to the street, evidently the custom when it was built, and was protected along its full street aspect by high wrought iron railings. While Trish fiddled with various key tags, Alyssa took in the surroundings in more detail. The ornate north-facing mansion had obviously once been a substantial private residence. Its location in a quiet, almost deserted street was a good thing, she realised, for those suffering from mental health issues—especially the ones undergoing inpatient care in the ward upstairs. She glanced at the upper story widows—not the attic this time—to see if there were any anxious, trapped faces staring down at her, but there were none. All appeared peaceful. A small brass plate on the front gate read *The Donald Clinic*. Nowhere was there a mention of the word "mental".

Neighbouring the clinic on its right was a 1950s-style, three storey, red brick apartment block built almost flush with the side of their building, while on the left side of Donald stood a row of connected double storey terrace houses. A narrow lane separated these from the clinic, and the entrance to the lane was unusual in that it was potentially concealable by the currently open door of a false garage-front, which was flush with the clinic front. One entered the lane through the garage door—provided the door was open.

Trish noticed the direction of her gaze. 'Neat, isn't it. Useful for parking. And, yes, we do close that door at night. It keeps the backyard secure.'

Trish continued to be friendly and helpful, and Alyssa found herself warming to her. After the demonstration of how to operate the gate lock, Trish led the way back through the front entrance and along the downstairs main corridor, which led straight across the building, past her reception desk and the staircase to upstairs, and across another corridor that intersected at ninety degrees.

Trish stopped them at this point and turned to face the way they had just come. 'A few things to know: those there are the stairs to the inpatient section—which luckily you shouldn't ever need to use—and down these side corridors are the consulting rooms of our four psychiatrists and Greta our clinical psychologist. There's also a waiting room for the clients along there, and a clinic room, and patient toilets—don't use them. The staff toilets are further back, near the staff room, and your key tag will work on them.'

'What exactly is upstairs?' asked Alyssa.

'As I said, nothing to bother yourself with. Just three inpatient suites, a clinic room, a nurse's office, another staff toilet, and a kitchen.' Trish explained further that the psychiatric nurse was Gail Wilson, and that Gail was the only nurse on the permanent staff. When more nurses were needed, for example at night, they used agency nurses.

They then continued down the main corridor towards the back of the building and finally arrived at the staff room, which lay on the right at the end of the corridor. The corridor itself ended at a sturdy looking back door, which marked the rear of the building. Opposite the entrance to the staff room were doors to other rooms, which Trish explained were for equipment, supplies, cleaning, catering, gardening, and the like. Trish used her key tag to open the staff room door, explaining that it always had to stay locked.

'For obvious reasons,' she said, lowering her voice.

The room was surprisingly large.

'This is a good place to take a break,' she continued. 'If you need one.' She gave Alyssa an uncertain look.

'I'm the kind that does,' said Alyssa. 'Clients can be very exhausting. We counsellors are advised to take both morning and afternoon tea breaks as well as proper lunch breaks. For our own sanity.'

Trish said no more and went to make them coffee at a well-equipped kitchen counter in the corner.

'Do the others use this place much?' asked Alyssa, strolling around the room. 'It seems very nice.' Besides the excellent-looking corner kitchen, there were two comfortable sofas in the room and a gas fireplace. Also, two large tables with four chairs ranged around each one. Victorian lattice windows looked out over a garden at the rear of the property, a garden not visible from the street and surprising to see. Pleasing too, considering that she liked gardens. She placed her bag on one of the sofas.

'I don't come in here much,' said Trish offhandedly. 'There's a kettle at the reception desk. Someone has to stay at reception.' She handed a mug of black coffee to Alyssa. 'Greta doesn't come here much either. She never rests. Milk and sugar are over there.' She pointed. 'Nurse Gail comes sometimes, but mostly she seems to prefer her own company upstairs and old Dr Barnes is too grand to bother, so you can imagine who's left. Mostly Professor Summerfield, Dr Bristow, and Dr Goronowski. That's who you'll get here.' She smiled sweetly at Alyssa. 'You'd be a brave person to be in here with them talking in riddles and making fun of you the whole time.'

So, that's what this is about.

. . . . **5** . . . .

The lock on the door to the staff room disengaged and a sinewy old woman in a crumpled dress opened the door. She stood in the doorway,

72

blinking in the bright light. Not only had she forgotten to iron her dress, but it looked to Alyssa as if she had forgotten to brush her hair as well. Incongruously, she sported glaring lipstick. Once able to stop blinking, the newcomer took a step and closed the door behind her. Then, from the distance, she studied Alyssa in silence.

There was an awkward pause.

Trish came to the rescue. 'Alyssa, meet Greta McCreedy. Greta, this is Alyssa Brown.'

'So, this *is* her, is it?' Greta came to life and moved forwards. She mechanically extended a hand for the required handshake. 'Pleased to meet you.' She barely made eye contact. 'Have you been photographed yet?'

Before Trish's introduction, Alyssa had been unsure whether the person in front of her was the senior clinical psychologist Greta McCreedy or an inpatient who had wandered in from upstairs. 'Do you mean, have I been photographed yet for an ID card?' she said this as politely as possible.

'Yes.'

'No,' said Trish, interrupting. 'I was just about to do that.'

'Very well. Welcome, Miss Brown. I trust you have mastered the general orientation documents we sent you in the mail? Fire drill. Evacuation. Resuscitation. The important things?'

'Err, yes,' said Alyssa, not entirely truthfully.

'Good. We can dispense with that, then. Tests may be conducted later.' She peered at some papers in her hand. 'I see that your professional insurance and professional registration are in order, so that's another thing already done. And I see you are already enrolled in a supervision program.'

'Yes. With Susan Lindow. She's going to be my resource person. Dr Barnes arranged it. He said I should see her every two weeks once my clinics are fully booked. Susan works on the other side of the CBD, near the Olympic Hospital, and she's an experienced psychodynamic therapist. Do you know her?'

'Of course.' Greta's voice softened slightly. 'She's famous enough. Probably somewhat effective too, though sadly that's not the usual correlation when it comes to psychotherapists.' She placed the documents in her hand onto a table and rolled them into a tube and gave them to Trish. Then she went over to the large staff room window and peered out of it.

Alyssa dutifully followed her.

'We might as well get down to business, Miss Brown. Your first clients are due this afternoon. Trish has the bookings. And, oh yes, the roster.' She pointed across the room. 'The roster for the clinical meetings. It's there above the bookcase. Your name will appear on it for presentations. Be sure to check. Now, come and stand next to me.'

Still trying to make sense of Greta's abrupt manner, Alyssa went and stood next to her as commanded. From there, as prompted, she looked out of the window.

'See that cottage over there in the corner of the garden?'

'Yes.' There was indeed a cottage to see. It was tiny, had a steeply sloped terracotta tile roof with moss growing on it, and stood at the very back of the property, on the right, behind a large, gnarled, and droopy tree, which partly shielded the little dwelling from the main house. The cottage looked out of scale and like something out of a Hansel and Gretel fairytale.

'See it?'

'Yes.'

'Is that all you have to say? Take a proper look.'

Alyssa looked more closely. She could see it was built into the clinic garden's eight-foot-high bluestone-block back wall and twelve-foot-high red brick right side wall and that the whole area was overrun with Boston ivy creeper. She wondered if the cottage was occupied by mice. 'It's derelict, isn't it? A garden folly. Is that what it is?'

'No, that is not what it is. It's where the caretaker used to live about seventy years ago. And it's where you live now. Or should I say, work. That, my dear, is your office.'

'My consulting room? Seriously? That's where I'll be seeing clients?'

'Oh, yes. Quite seriously, it is. Don't worry, it's been refurbished. It's a new idea that the practice is going to try out: the concept of a *cottage* approach to therapy. They are putting you to work out there.'

'I see.' Alyssa felt dismayed. It was the first she had heard of it. Donald Barnes and Alan Summerfield had mentioned nothing of the sort.

'Good luck to you is all I can say regarding the whole hair-brained idea. I hope you are not afraid of spiders.'

'Excuse me, but what exactly are you getting at?' She was not sure if she was being over-sensitive, but the woman next to her seemed to be trying her best to be obnoxious. She forced herself to remain calm as Greta McCreedy began to chuckle.

'Oh, don't worry. You look like a tough cookie. I'm sure you'll cope.'

The outburst of black humour made Alyssa wonder if her new boss might be unhinged. The possibility seemed increasingly likely. Not only that, but she wondered how many cigarettes Greta smoked each day and how often Greta took a shower. She tried to get some sense out of her: 'So, that's where I'll be seeing some of my clients? In the garden?'

'Not some, *all*. Those are the orders from the managing partners, Miss Brown. *Psychotherapy in a cottage*. That's the new buzz. Hard to swallow, isn't it? There was I thinking that psychotherapy was dead. Silly me.' Greta looked her straight in the face. 'Do you know that nobody asked me about you? Can you believe it? Or about the cottage. I'm really not happy about any of it.'

Greta was being shockingly unprofessional and unpleasant, but rather than be intimidated by her anger Alyssa ignored it. She was not afraid of women. Besides, she knew she had the support of Donald Barnes and Alan Summerfield. Greta could do nothing to her.

She decided to remain civil. No point in being assertive on one's first day. 'I'll do my best to fit in, Greta. Hopefully, there won't be any security issues out there. Oh, and do call me Alyssa. Nobody calls me Miss Brown.'

'Security has been taken care of.' Greta spurned the offer of friendship and turned away from the window. She consulted her phone to get the time. 'Let me give you my official assurance that I am pleased to welcome you on board as our psychodynamic therapist. Transference and all that. They say we need it, so I'm sure we do. And you seriously want me to call you Alyssa?' She headed for the door.

'Of course.'

Greta turned to face her. 'So, Alyssa, we have a real live one working for us, do we? A psychodynamic therapist. My goodness. Imagine that. You know what, you look like just the person for it.'

Greta McCreedy marched out and slammed the door behind her.

6

Far from being full of mice and spiders, the cottage was quite charming. Alyssa's initial fear that the Donald management did not value her dissipated as soon as Trish took her across the garden for a visit. Not only was the little building properly set up for conducting consultations, but it had a comforting atmosphere—something that Greta clearly did not understand or appreciate.

Even the route across the garden to the entrance of her new domain was charming. From the end of the main corridor in the grand old house one went down a small flight of steps at the back door and then along a winding, brick-paved pathway to the cottage. The path meandered through the garden and passed under the canopy of the solitary but spectacular old tree that formed the central feature of the backyard. There, the droopy branches formed a rudimentary tunnel into which one disappeared and then re-emerged to a new vista of lawn and stepping-stones leading to a flower-surrounded cottage porch. Up close, the cottage merged so artfully into the surrounding boundary walls that it seemed impossibly tiny. In fact, it barely seemed to exist at all.

The biggest surprise of all was the discovery that there was an alternative route to the cottage. One did not have to approach it through the main building. Trish explained that to get there one could, if one wished, arrive via the driveway at the side of the Donald—by going through the fake garage entrance on the street when the roller door was open. One then proceeded along the gravelled laneway to where there was a parking area for up to three cars at the side of the cottage. Initially the driveway went along straight, but at the rear boundary of the property it circled back on itself, coming close to the side of the cottage and the parking area as it returned to the exit.

Numerous flowerbeds and lawns complimented the landscaping. Some of the flowers, she suspected, were fuchsias and salvias, but she knew little about plants and was not sure. A plant she did recognise with certainty was the Boston ivy creeper that graced the high rear boundary wall, where it softened the solidity of it. There was a similar creeper at her childhood home in Ocean View. Roses she could recognise too. There were roses everywhere.

Trish pointed out that the entire area behind the Donald's main building was shielded from prying eyes. It had been a condition of the building permits for the surrounding properties over the years. Thus, while the clinic building itself still had windows facing the garden, the windows on the side of the terrace house adjoining the gravel driveway were bricked up, and the main windows of the apartment block on the opposite side faced away from the high boundary wall. By design, all windows visible to the garden on that side were small and glazed with frosted glass.

In deference to the evolution of social tastes, the managing partners of the Donald Clinic had recently decided to capitalise on the privacy feature of their garden and establish a therapy venue for high value clients that was not only super luxurious and super satisfying but also super private and super confidential: hence "The Cottage". Clients now had a place to have therapy in complete secrecy and comfort if they so wished—provided they could afford it.

The cottage had only three rooms. The front door, which opened off a small porch on the left side of the building, entered the first of these, a small waiting room. Clearly, the room had once been the living room and kitchen of the original home but was smaller now because a rest room had been built into it and formed its second room. The third and final room was more spacious as it had once been two small bedrooms. Now, it was a single professional consulting room—her new office. Its large lattice window faced the back of the clinic main building, which was partly obscured by the large intervening tree with the droopy branches. To the right of the tree, one was greeted by a peaceful vista of lawn and flowers.

Trish showed her how the office computer worked and gave her the login codes. The equipment was part of the secure main building system. Trish then pointed out the three CCTV cameras that monitored the entire premises for security purposes. They recorded everywhere, excluding the toilet but including the consulting room. None of them, of course, recorded sound. The cottage had a further special feature: panic buttons. One for each room, each artfully concealed. Trish showed them to Alyssa. 'Press one and all hell breaks loose,' she explained. 'It activates the alarms in the main building. Someone will come running to help.' It had been Dr Summerfield's idea.

Thank goodness for Alan, thought Alyssa. Another sign that he understood women.

She asked Trish about the plants growing in profusion around the cottage. 'Do you know what sort they are exactly, Trish? And the tree?'

'Afraid not. But you won't have to worry about that sort of thing. A gardener comes in every weekend. Some of them are sweet alyssums, I reckon, because I heard Greta making jokes about it when she heard you were coming to work here. I think she's got something against alyssums.'

'Alyssa's, you mean. She's certainly got something against me. What am I supposed to have done to offend her?'

'Um, who knows. She was a bit rude to you wasn't she. Personally, I think she's resentful about you joining the staff at the Donald. She definitely did seem to have it in for you. Usually, she's okay with colleagues.'

'But she's not okay with me, obviously. It's quite upsetting, you know.' It always seemed to happen to her: woman problems. Once again, and for no reason that she could understand, yet another one of them had decided to hate her. In joining the Donald Clinic, she had fallen into the clutches of one more vindictive old bat. What had ever-wise Wendy Greene had to say on the subject of vengeful women? "When the monster speaks, Alyssa, be always on the lookout for the knockout blow. And remember, it works both ways."

Yes, she really did say that.

But what did she mean by "works both ways"?

'What do you suggest I do to improve things with Greta?'

Trish, an airhead, had no idea. 'You can't do anything with Greta. Not once she has a bee in her bonnet. Perhaps you should just try to avoid her as much as you can. That's all I can suggest.'

'How very helpful.'

'At least *I'm* not avoiding you,' said Trish sweetly. 'I think you're lovely.'

Once Trish had left, Alyssa sat on the new swivel chair in front of her new desk and tried out the computer. She was pleased to find that she was able to access the afternoon's list of bookings without too much difficulty. There were three names on it, names that meant nothing to her yet, clients who had been assembled in advance by Trish according to instructions given by Greta McCreedy. Being new, Alyssa knew that she would have to put up with seeing clients in this way for a while, but she intended to gain personal control of her lists as soon as practicable. The first weeks in any new job were always going to be difficult, especially if Greta had anything to do with it.

Unpleasant lizard.

The employment contract specified that she see seven clients per day, four days a week, starting at 8.45 am and allowing fifty minutes for each plus ten minutes for dictation. There would be a client-free combined education and administration day each Wednesday, and weekends would be free. Effectively, given the odd extra emergency case, the duties amounted to thirty sessions of transference-based psychodynamic therapy per week, an enormous load. Dr Barnes had warned her at the job interview that she might be attempting too much by going full-time to start with, but she had insisted on it. She wanted full-time work.

She needed the money.

7

Now, she felt less certain of the wisdom of trying to work full-time. It was clear that an exceptionally high standard of practice was going to be expected. Perhaps she should have paid more attention to the warnings from her stepmother. When Diana heard about the new job, Diana had said that she was trying to be too big for her boots. "This is so typical of you, Alyssa, isn't it? Pig-headed. Given your history, you won't cope with full-time in a million years."

Alyssa swivelled idly in her new chair as she thought about her stepmother's cruel words. Normally, she had no regard for her stepmother's opinion on anything, but now she began to wonder.

What if she is right?

What if full-time proved too much for her? She was not a well person, after all. Still, it was important to remain positive. If others could do the job, so could she. It was going to be essential, though, to take the permitted breaks without fail every single day: the 10.30 am thirty-minute coffee break and the 1.00 pm sixty-minute lunch break. Thirty clients a week meant spending most of her life in the company of emotionally disturbed people. Which was a very long time to spend in a bad space.

She went to her shoulder bag and extracted a well-used 700-page paperback textbook—the prescribed main textbook of her recently completed course in transference-focused psychodynamic therapy—and placed it carefully on her new desk. The cover of the book read *Beyond Freud; Practice of Validated Transference-focused Psychodynamic Therapy* by Jorken Obermaaier. She fingered the pages reverently. The insights and advice within represented the holy grail for any modern psychotherapist wishing to practice effectively and safely. To reassure herself, she sat down and read a page of it at random to absorb once again some of its wisdom:

> . . . therefore, if, in all of us, aspects of our early childhood mind persist Un-consciously, beyond a veil, behind the shut gates of the realm of Glory, in that place in the mind where the river of adult mental life runs underground, it must follow that *there*—in our originating parts—we continue to relate to parental figures. It must follow, too, that the implications of an ongoing secret relationship are far reaching because then we are, all of us, unwitting tools of unperceived imperatives. Sexual desires, religious beliefs, and political opinions now become mere *secondary* outflows of a deeper stream. Precious so-called free-choice decisions regarding sexual taste, political viewpoint, and religious certainty become nothing more than accidents of childhood experience with no intrinsic value or objective significance.
>
> Impinge upon the sexual belief, religious belief, or political belief of any person and you impinge upon the very foundations of that Self. Apply pressure and you encounter resistance, for you are at the interface of conscious existence for that Self. Squeeze hard enough, and you will be eliminated—through your own death if needed. Consciousness of Self is compelled to protect itself against the destruction of its foundations by any means necessary, including lethal force because without its Un-conscious foundations a Self cannot find meaning. Without meaning, it is not possible for a Self to exist as a conscious being.

The solution to this curse of the human condition can only be as follows: we must, all of us, *accept* that we are but a tool of Un-conscious forces.

Unfortunately, there remains strong resistance to this obvious solution, even among counselling psychologists—a field sadly bedevilled by pseudointellectuals—because the Un-conscious continuation of early parental relationships remains strongly denied by most. Tragically, the Un-conscious—as described above—is rejected not on objective grounds but through the influence of precisely those Un-conscious processes that are being denied!

Sadly, however, denial will not make the *Un* go away any time soon. If we are to think more clearly, we need to be more Self-aware. The unafraid see with perfect clarity the blindness that arises when personal truth is experienced as uniquely unspeakable.

What the brave and unafraid see is this: they see that there continues to exist in us all a childish, parent-focused Un-conscious component to our adult mind—a continuing early mind, as it were— which, with development, becomes craftily cloaked in one or two degrees of separation and hides behind gates of Glory so it can persist endlessly in its original supremely powerful "Way of Being". There, though magical and irrational, this essence of us remains, safe from the limitations of language and time, and supplies us with the basic operating rules for our conscious logic circuits in later life. All sense of "meaning" thus derives ultimately from the Un-conscious component of the metaphysical mind. Without these foundational operating rules about "what means what", the superstructure that we know as self-consciousness simply is not possible. The mind must have ground rules to be able to interpret incoming data. For consciousness of Self to occur, there must exist an underpinning Un-conscious.

The Un-conscious mind does not disappear, and it cannot be wished away in adult life. Increased awareness of the "child within" remains critical for the future of humanity.

Professor Obermaaier made everything in life so much more understandable. His famous book had a long title, but usually it was referred to more simply as *Beyond Freud*, or as *Obermaaier*.

8

Alyssa closed her textbook by Professor Obermaaier reluctantly, aware that time was marching on.

In her bag was one further useful textbook, slim by contrast and more an idiot's guide. Its title was *Wallenstein's Short Neuroleptic Drugs: A Guide for the Non-Physician*. She placed it on the desk next to Obermaaier. With four psychiatrists in the practice and all of them potentially sending her clients, there were going to be many clients on medication. The little "Wallenstein" would be invaluable because she still found psychiatric drugs bewildering. They seemed to have many side effects, some of them quite serious, and she seemed to have a resistance to remembering too much about them. Long ago she had decided that she would not by choice take any of them. Wendy Greene told her that this was because she had a defective education and therefore did not truly understand neurophysiology or biochemistry.

Who does?

She arranged her two textbooks on the bookshelf above her desk. There were already some files there, and one other book. She had a brief look at them. The book was titled *DSM–V: The Diagnostic and Statistical Manual of Mental Disorders of the American Psychiatric Society*, 5th Edition. It was enough to give anyone a headache from just paging through it. It was out of date too. There was a current version that she could access online if she needed to, so she hid the old book in a drawer. Then she flipped through the files that had been pre-placed on her shelf, no doubt by Trish. One was labelled "Practice Protocols" and the other "Paper Forms". Both were surplus to requirement: the clinic was fully digital.

Bookshelf sorted.

She sat back in her swivel chair and paid more attention to her new consulting room. Whoever was responsible for it had done well, in her opinion. On one side of the original hearth stood a leather armchair for the therapist and on the other side, about five feet away, an overstuffed two-seater sofa for the client. The original fireplace had been preserved, adding a touch of class, even though the antique mantelpiece now enclosed a modern gas fire system. A mahogany bookcase filled with classical volumes and a few magazines stood next to the fireplace and there was a coffee table with two upmarket water glasses and a crystal jug full of water. Completing the homely touches were many pastel cushions, a box of tissues, and beautiful rugs. The wooden floor between the rugs gleamed, colourful curtains rippled, and two encouraging art prints on the walls—one of sunflowers by Van Gogh and the other of a horse and foal in a green field by Turner—sang of life and hope.

All very cheerful and tasteful.

The only feature of the room that disturbed the comforting illusion of emotional safety was the presence of a video surveillance camera. The CCTV camera was fixed high in the corner behind the therapist's chair, near the ceiling, and was focused on the sofa. For the protection of all, it was unavoidable.

Overall, the new surroundings were genuinely upmarket. The realisation brought her suddenly close to panic. Wealth and luxury were not what she was used to; such places were not *her*. She lacked experience as a counsellor and had third-rate university grades from a third-rate university. She was not going to be good enough.

What am I doing here?

She found herself longing for the familiar crowded shabbiness and chaos of Public Hospital, where she had trained under Wendy. There, at least, clients did not expect too much. She had been a fool to come to a place as grand as the Donald, unwise to try to rise above her station, and an idiot to attempt to achieve so much all at once . . .

She took a few deep breaths to arrest the impending panic attack and pulled herself together. 'No,' she said out loud. 'No negative thoughts. *This* is what I want. I *will* be a success.'

9

At her job interview, Donald Barnes had explained to her what success looked like. It took the form of a blue-ribbon boutique service for the niche market of the well-heeled. Not only did the rich deserve such a service, he had said, but they were happy to provide financial reward for those providing it. And, because the Donald Clinic operated at a level above normal private practice, the high fees were, of course, justifiable.

"While our ideas may seem a little unethical to the uninitiated, Miss Brown," he had explained, "you would do well to ignore any rumours you hear about us."

However, the practice *did* sound financially unethical, and she *had* heard the rumours.

He had not finished: "I am confident you will find that there is indeed a place in society for what we offer. We believe that our clients get value for their money at the Donald. We really do. I guarantee that as a therapeutic environment we are second to none."

In the end, she had believed him.

She had wanted to believe him.

The clients at the public hospital where she had just completed her training had depressed her. She was hungry for a better way, a better life. Many of her previous clients had been impoverished and in an awful mess and beyond hope. Some of them had even seemed to be nothing more than heavily medicated overgrown babies. She had kept such thoughts to herself, of course. For a naïve girl from Ocean View, the clients of the mental health department at the giant Public Hospital on the eastern edge of Hubron's CBD had come as a shock.

While her dream had always been to help people with mental problems get better, she had not initially realised that what she actually meant was that she wanted such people to be intelligent, and functional, and suffering from emotional rather than thinking problems; wanted them to be people who could truly improve with her help; wanted them to be people who could sometimes even be cured by her. She wanted to treat people who *wanted* to improve, people who *could* be helped—not people who were beyond help or simply seeking taxpayer benefits. She was tired of manipulative patients, tired of the need to suppress vast crowds by resorting to no-nonsense behaviour therapy in large groups. She took another deep breath, then stood up off her swivel chair. *Anxiety, self-doubt, and second thoughts be damned,* she told herself.

Here I can be free.

Yes, she was in the right place.

She caught sight of the time. It was time to focus on work. There was going to be a clinic after lunch. She looked again at the three clients on the clinic list for the afternoon session of "Ms Alyssa Brown, Counselling

Psychologist". The clinic was due to start at 2.00 pm. She wondered what Greta had concocted for her—who her first clients would be and what they would be like. She had a closer look at them.

1.   Benjamin Clayton, 24, Paranoid schizophrenia, Stable, AJS
2.   Ellen Goodman, 53, Anxiety/ Insomnia Meds, GP-GAM
3.   George, No further details

She frowned. Something was not right. Why would anyone send her a paranoid schizophrenic as her first client? As a psychotherapy-based counsellor, and an extremely junior one at that, she had almost no experience in dealing with schizophrenia. More alarming seemed the fact that the client, this Benjamin Clayton, not only had schizophrenia but was paranoid as well. She would be alone with him in an isolated garden cottage.

'For heaven's sake!' she said out loud.

The codes at the end of the names indicated case managers. AJS had to be Alan Summerfield. Alan would not have sent her Benjamin Clayton as her first client on her first day, of that she felt certain. There was another explanation, the only explanation, in fact. It had a different name, and that name was Greta McCreedy.

The silly old woman's sly hand was to be seen also in the final case that had been selected for the afternoon clinic. What was an *unknown* doing on her list? How could she be expected to cope with that? On her first day. As a supportive counsellor, she needed a *diagnosis* first.

She wondered whether she should speak to someone about the situation. After all, she had heard of instances where anonymous undiagnosed clients had turned out to be deadly. She did not trust Greta, and her instincts were ringing alarm bells. Perhaps, though, she was overreacting because of her anxiety. She did not know what to think. Perhaps it was wiser not to cause trouble on the first day. Wendy Greene always used to say that she lacked faith in the good intentions of others. Assertive behaviour was not a wise strategy on a first day at work.

The time on the screen of her new computer read 12.58 pm, so she decided that instead of causing trouble she would go for lunch. She might be lucky and find Alan in the staff room. In which case she would be able to raise her concerns without appearing too negative.

As she headed out the front door, she realised that something was missing from her new cottage. It needed something to bring it to life, a female touch. She looked for a suitable flower in the garden. There were numerous non-specific plants around, some of them no doubt sweet alyssums according to Greta. They had nice pink and purple flowers, but all were too small for her purposes. What she wanted was a single large flower with a lovely fragrance, so she headed for the rose bushes and there she found something that appealed to her. When she picked it, because she knew so little about gardening, she pricked her thumb. It was a minor setback, though. In triumph, she returned to the waiting room with her rose. She found a vase for it, added water, and then arranged the display on the magazine table.

'To the start of a wonderful life,' she said to the rose. Final touches completed, she collected her lunch box and headed for the staff room in the main building, making sure to lock the cottage door behind her.

Behind the locked door, a drop of blood slid silently down the stem of the rose until, finally, it tinged the water. Luckily, there was nobody there to witness the truly disturbing sight. The blood that flowed from the rose was not just any blood. It was exactly the same colour as the rose.

Black velvet.

Which was impossible.

An illusion. Or something monstrous.

PART II

THAT OF WHICH WE MAY NOT SPEAK

CHAPTER FIVE

1

LUNCH HOUR IN THE staff room at the Donald Clinic was not the sociable occasion Alyssa hoped it would be. There were two people present when she arrived, but soon she was the only one there.

The initial two were Donald Barnes—who supposedly never attended—and a woman of about forty, who turned out to be Gail Wilson, the psychiatric nurse from upstairs. Alyssa found them seated close together at one of the tables when she came in, and her entrance startled them, as though they had momentarily forgotten that she existed. They appeared to be engaged in an earnest discussion of some sort or other.

Dr Barnes looked up sharply. 'Alyssa Brown.' He said the name more as if to remind himself of who she was than to inform his companion. Once again, he resembled nothing so much as a vulture.

'Hi everyone,' she said to them.

The professor glanced at his wristwatch as he stood up. 'Of course. It's lunch hour. Alyssa, meet Gail. She's our psychiatric nurse specialist cum charge nurse. And Gail, Alyssa here is our new in-house counselling psychologist. She's just started.'

'Hi,' said Gail. She stuck out a disinterested hand while remaining seated and barely paid attention.

Alyssa politely shook the nurse's hand. It felt damp and sticky, and the fingernails were partly chewed. Gail Wilson looked to her more like a trollop than anything else: busty, perfumed, on the make, ill groomed, and running to fat. Perhaps her obvious unhappiness explained the look. The associated bad attitude, though, required something more—and she knew immediately what the *more* was because she had encountered it many times before in lower-level health workers, including some of her own counsellor colleagues. Gail Wilson, psychiatric nurse for the Donald Clinic, had a bad case of the head-swelling disorder present in many of her sort: dumb-aggressive inflated belief in her own importance.

'So, you are a nurse,' said Alyssa sweetly.

'Consultant psychiatric nurse-specialist,' countered Gail. 'I run the show upstairs.'

Is that so.

'Do you know where Gail fits in?' asked Donald.

'Yes. Trish told me the setup,' said Alyssa. Trish had also said that Dr Barnes and Gail hardly ever came to the staff room. Wrong.

'We were just on our way out when you came in. Pity we can't stay.' Dr Barnes made an upward motion with his hand and Gail stood up. 'We have some business to attend to. Sorry to leave you all by yourself.'

'I'll be fine. I know where everything is. I'm sure some of the others will be along shortly.'

'No chance,' said Gail. 'Everyone is busy.' She attempted unsuccessfully to conceal the extent of her rear end as she stood up. 'Busy, busy.'

Dr Barnes looked mildly embarrassed by her. 'What Gail means is that today is the day of the monthly grand audit over at the Public. All the psychiatrists from this part of town try to attend, including our own. There's nobody here at the Donald except me. I'm holding the fort for the next few hours.'

'You'll get used to it,' Gail assured her.

Alyssa tried to remain polite. 'Thanks for letting me know.' She remembered the grand audits from when she was a trainee at the Public. As a non-physician trainee, she had been too insignificant to be allowed to attend.

The professor and the nurse departed, and she was left to have lunch all by herself.

She found it difficult to relax, perhaps because of the size of the room. It caused her to feel out of place as its solitary occupant. Ignoring the advice of Wendy Greene—and countless others in the counselling world—she therefore ate lunch quickly and returned to her new consulting room prematurely. Back at the cottage, the atmosphere felt more friendly and restful. That wouldn't last, though, that much she did know. The atmosphere there would change as soon as it became busy.

2

Alyssa used the extra time to sit at the computer and scroll through the case notes of her first client, Benjamin Clayton. He would be arriving at 2.00 pm and he was going to be her first ever independently seen case—someone she was going to remember forever, according to Wendy Greene. *Pity he had to have paranoid schizophrenia,* she thought, because she had almost no expertise in providing psychotherapy in such cases—mainly because no one normally used psychotherapy in schizophrenia. Still, it was possible that some sessions with him might enable him to cope better. Perhaps that was all that the Donald wanted.

According to the notes, Ben was a strongly built twenty-three-year-old youth whose paranoid thoughts were minimal when on medication. The more she studied his clinical notes, though, the more obvious it seemed that Greta had behaved irresponsibly by sending him to her. Although medicated paranoid clients were usually harmless—despite what members of the public usually believed—if anyone *was* going to become dangerous it would be someone like Ben. Benjamin Clayton's problems were all about a deep-seated determination to kill bad people. What he required wasn't analysis of his transference; what he required was appropriate medication combined with behaviour supervision and integrative social support. By a team. Isolated visits to a place like the cottage were not appropriate for someone like him.

She began to feel apprehensive.

Why, exactly, am I seeing Benjamin Clayton out here all by myself?

The question swirled through her mind with increasing importance when, through the lattice window of her new office, she spotted a stocky young man heading towards her on the pathway leading from the back door of the main building. It had to be him: Ben.

He was ten minutes early for his appointment.

Her prospective first ever independently seen client paused for no apparent reason once hidden under the low hanging foliage of the big tree and only emerged some minutes later. He then marched in military fashion towards the porch at the side of the cottage, arms stiff and scissoring like two swords. He was dressed in a pair of overly short brown shorts, long black socks, oversized cheap white runners, a shirt buttoned up tight against his chin despite the hot weather, a multicoloured waistcoat, a clear plastic raincoat, and a trilby hat complete with a feather in the hatband. According to the file on the screen, there were two names she could use for him: to his family he was *Ben* and to his friends he was *Jabba*. It would be better, she decided, to stick to calling him Ben. She did not need to have him thinking she was his friend.

The hairy legs of stiffly marching paranoid Ben/Jabba Clayton rippled with muscles, and his shoulders looked equally thick and powerful under his numerous clothes. Finally, he disappeared from view once again as he reached the side of the cottage. She then heard him enter the waiting room and make himself comfortable there.

It was just her and him in the building. Fortunately, the door into her office was still locked as per Trish's general orientation advice. It was not yet two o'clock, so she continued skimming through Ben's notes.

His family was wealthy and lived in Baronbridge, just across the Yarradonga river, not far from the clinic. Ben still lived with them. He was an only child.

Jabba from Yarra.

His mother was a homemaker and his father a senior director in the banking sector, which explained how the family could afford to have their son managed long term at a ruinously expensive place like the Donald Clinic. In contrast to his wealthy father, Ben's occupation was recorded as "horticulturist". Alyssa assumed this to mean labourer, which it usually did in this context.

One good thing was that Ben Clayton was young. Younger than she was. She had two brothers, Greg, and Harry, who were also younger, and keeping *them* under control had never been a problem for her. Greg was twenty-five and Harry twenty-two. In her experience, young men were entirely predictable. Hopefully, with Ben being twenty-three, it would be the same. If anyone knew how to deal with young male creatures, she did. As a bonus, Ben still lived at home with his parents. He would be used to obeying instructions.

From what she could discern from the seemingly endless notes on the computer, his behaviour had been a cause for concern since the age of fifteen. It was then that he first began to show an unhealthy interest in blades and started to menace his parents with them. On more than one occasion while a teenager, his parents had needed to lock him in the basement of the family home for his and their safety. Finally, one night, at the tender age of seventeen, he went out and beat the pet donkey at his school unconscious with a crowbar and cut its heart out with a hunting knife when it tried to kill him with horns that had appeared on its head. As he had long suspected, during the hours of darkness the so-called donkey turned back into what it really was: a giant goat under the control of Satan. The horrifying incident got him arrested by the police, widely reported in the news media, expelled from school, and admitted into the mental health system, where a psychiatrist duly diagnosed paranoid schizophrenia. It soon became apparent that Benjamin Clayton's central preoccupation in life was a desire to "cut the root of iniquity". To accomplish this important task, he needed a blade, the larger and sharper the better. Which was why the Donald Clinic insisted on the use of a metal detector and a body search by nurse Wilson every time he attended.

This desire to "take the blade to evil" occupied most of Ben's waking life. Despite the best of treatments, he had not been able to make any progress in gaining therapeutic insight into the cause of this need. However, other than serious mental instability in relation to blades, he was pleasant enough. He was blessed with unusually high intelligence and was normally quiet and well behaved. He spent most of his time in his bedroom at his parents' house, where he researched human wickedness. The rest of his time he spent pulling out weeds in council parks.

'Great,' said Alyssa aloud to herself as she scrolled. 'This is just great.' She was being sarcastic. The notes were endless, and they began to give her a headache. Ben's mother, to make matters worse, wanted him off his medication. She wanted the Donald Clinic to attempt psychotherapy on him because she had heard of instances in America where this had helped. There were letters from her to Professor Summerfield pressuring him in this regard. Letters from Alan, in return, advised her that transference-type psychotherapy was of little use in schizophrenia in general terms, but conceded that in Ben's case there was no harm in trying given that he had an extremely high IQ. The words "There may be hope for him yet" featured in a recent reply to Ben's mother, referring to the possibility of him benefiting from psychotherapy and getting off his medication. Alan had added a rider for the case file:

Ben will need extremely cautious and high level initial psychodynamic assessment to determine feasibility. I won't have the time for this until mid-winter—so Greta could you please initiate. Thanks, Alan.

This explained Greta's involvement. Though Greta did not/could not do any form of true psychotherapy, she had been allocated the task of arranging to have Ben "farmed out" to an outside contracted practitioner. Alan had no doubt intended for Greta to behave responsibly in that regard.

There were also numerous notes regarding Ben's medication. He was on a high dose of the antipsychotic medicine called zasperidone, which he was receiving by injection because there had been compliance issues in the past. Nurse Gail Wilson administered the injections every two weeks. Gail also had the task of arranging regular lab tests so that Dr Summerfield could keep an eye on Ben's zasperidone levels and ensure that they remained within the therapeutic range.

Ben began coughing loudly in the waiting room. It was 14:01. She could not put off seeing Master "Cut the Root of Iniquity" for much longer.

She stole a final anxious look at his notes. Gail had seen Ben at her upstairs office in the main building less than ninety minutes earlier and all checks had been completed. Gail's note stated further that if there were any problems with his lab test results when they came through just after lunch, she would immediately phone.

There had been nothing mentioned in the staff room and no phone call.

She had been worrying for nothing.

She unlocked the door.

What could possibly go wrong?

3

'Hullo, Benjamin.'

Her first ever unsupervised client failed to respond. Instead, Benjamin Clayton remained seated, staring silently into the middle distance. She moved in front of him, but he avoided eye contact. Not to be discouraged, she went right up to him, squatted down, and took his hand in hers. She shook it as warmly as possible.

'Your name must be Benjamin. Come inside,' she said. 'My name is Alyssa. I'm going to be helping you over the next few months.'

He looked up sharply. 'Why did you say that? Say that?' He sounded annoyed.

'Say what?'

'Say that I need help. Could you stop that? Please. Please.'

'Sure.'

Slowly, as if reluctant to do so, he finally stood up. 'And it's Ben. I'm not Benjamin.'

He was quite short for a man, noticeably less than her own height of 177 cm, and still wearing his hat and clear plastic raincoat. That aside, he at least seemed well-groomed—a positive sign in relation to mental function—although he had overdone his deodorant. She recognised the overly pungent smell of *Homme Support*, a fragrance seemingly favoured by mothers for their teenage boys. Her own brothers and their friends had sometimes reeked of it too.

'Ben it is, then,' she said cheerily. Young men like Ben needed firmness. She held out her hand. 'Coat and hat, please. I'll put them on that hook in the corner for you.'

Meekly, he complied.

'Now, into the consulting room with you.' She herded him in. Instead of stopping at the client's couch, however, he went and examined the books on the bookshelf next to the fireplace. 'Take a seat, Ben,' she commanded.

He looked hurt but obeyed.

'We can't have you mucking about. We have an important task to accomplish. I want you to learn to trust me. That is going to be the focus of your visits: trust. And I want to learn to trust you too.'

He half-heartedly took a seat on the consulting room couch. There, he made a point of staring at the CCTV camera.

She let him stare.

'Dr Summerfield has one too,' he said finally.

'We all do, Ben. They are standard. You know that. Now, what's that letter you are hiding in your left hand? Is it something I need to know about?'

His eyes fell. 'It's from my mother. I'd prefer you didn't see it.'

'What does it say on the outside?'

He looked at it. It was a small envelope. 'Dr Alyssa Brown. New Psychologist.'

She held out her hand. 'Hand it over.'

He remained seated.

When she came over to him, though, he gave it to her. She observed that he had heavily chewed fingernails, but no hand tremors despite his long history of medication. Up close, she was able to detect the characteristic odour of antipsychotic drugs oozing out of his pores despite his deodorant. 'You know I'm not a doctor,' she said to him. 'Be sure to tell your mother that. I'm not Dr Brown. I am Alyssa Brown. A counselling psychologist.'

'Yes Miss.'

'You can call me Alyssa.'

'You are very pretty, Alyssa. Are you married?'

'That question is out of line, Ben. You know that. There are rules.' She said no more on the subject and instead busied herself opening the letter from his mother. 'Why don't you tell me what you know about the word *iniquity* in the meantime, Ben? I see from your file that it seems important to you, yet it's a really strange word for someone your age.'

'A leprechaun mentioned it to me.'

'You know I don't believe that. And neither do you. I'm not a fool.' She saw him stare at her with something akin to shock.

'Why did you say that? Say that?'

She ignored his question.

'Okay, I lied.' His voice had grown smaller.

'Try again. I want to know about *iniquity*.' Benjamin Clayton began to look uncomfortable. His face reddened and he became visibly physically agitated.

'I can't,' he blurted.

'Why not?'

'They have put a lock on my tongue.'

With some degree of alarm, Alyssa read the note from his mother:

> Dear Dr Alyssa,
> Please help Ben.
> If you can.

He is forgoing life's little luxuries.
To bring light into the world.
Yet, he is being given medication that is killing him.
It is time to set him free.
Please!
Sincerely, Marielise (the beloved mother).

Alyssa wondered what chance Ben had with a mother like that. 'Who has put a lock on your tongue?'

He refused to tell her. Instead, he stared at her, as though studying her.

She found his behaviour puzzling. He was behaving like someone partly off his head—off his medication, more correctly. She had seen such cases in the emergency department during training. She tried waiting for an answer from him, but after a while gave up. It was not going to be that easy. Once again, she recalled the wise words of Wendy Greene: "You cannot win against a schizophrenic".

Then Ben surprised her by talking.

'When I was young, they said I was maladjusted.'

'Did they? And are you?'

He appeared puzzled. 'You do know, don't you, that officially it's got worse? That now I've gone and become *completely* insane? Completely insane.' His voice died away, as though in disappointment.

She thought it best to be honest with him. 'Yes, I know your history, Ben.' She leant over and squeezed him affectionately on his knee. 'The main thing to remember is that all the bad stuff is in the past. We are all working to make things better for you.'

He seemed unconvinced.

4

'Do you think God gave me this life because he knows I'm strong enough?'

Ben Clayton's question surprised her, but Alyssa managed to catch herself before unthinkingly giving him her honest opinion, which was that no god had anything to do with his mental illness. It was likely that Ben was echoing his mother's words and it was not yet the time to destabilise such supports. Instead, she said: 'I wouldn't know. I'm not a theologian.'

He persisted. 'Do you go to church, Miss Alyssa?' The question came out slowly and gravely, as though of critical importance.

Normally, she did not answer clients' questions about her own private life, but this time she made an exception. The enquiry, though odd, seemed innocent.

'Sometimes,' she said, leaning back again in her own chair. 'I do know about church.'

A look of relief came over his face. 'Hallelujah! You see, they sin who cannot perceive the glory of Jesus.'

Hooh boy.

To avoid falling into the interminable morass that was theology, she avoided making a comment. Instead, she said 'So, you go to church, do you, Ben? Why don't you tell me a bit about it?'

'Whatever may be the surprises of the future, Jesus will never be surpassed. Yes, I used to go. Ernest Renan. But they have disappointed me, so I am reporting them to the authorities. It's a book.'

The jumble in his head was hard to follow. 'Reporting your church to the authorities?'

'Not them exactly.'

'Then who? And to whom?'

'The religionists.' He smiled smugly. 'I am compiling a report about them for the true authorities.'

She smiled back at him. 'It may surprise you, Ben, but I know a bit about religion.' Unlike most people of her age, she had been well trained in it as a child. Her father had made her go to Sunday school regularly—which meant that she was knowledgeable enough about the Bible to readily perceive the hollowness of the foundations of any crank who believed that his or her own selective interpretation of it was the infallible truth. 'You're saying that you don't like religious cranks, is that it?'

Plus, you want me to believe that you are not one yourself?

'Not exactly. The word is "fanatics", by the way.'

'Okay. So, exactly which authorities are you reporting these fanatics to?'

'I can't tell *you*, but *they* know.'

She tried a different track. 'Why did you want to know if I go to church? Why is that important to you?'

'I can't reveal that either. They are ruthless. Unforgiving…'

'You mean these enemies of yours are dangerous?'

'Supremacists who would lecture God? What else could they be?'

'Mm. Will you tell me more if I promise not to tell anyone else and try to understand?'

He remained silent.

She tried another line. 'You say you are writing a book about it? That's wonderful. Why don't you bring it along next time? I'd like to read it.'

'They do not love, except their own reflection. That, they confuse with God. Besides, it's not finished.'

'The book? Why don't you bring it anyway?'

'Maybe.'

'What's it called?'

'I can't reveal that.'

The hour with Ben Clayton turned out to be rather tedious, but she kept up a show of pleasant interest in him despite his reluctance to reveal anything. She knew enough about counselling to know that he would say nothing meaningful unless and until he felt he could trust her.

Finally, his time was up. When she stood, so did he. He had been to many treatment sessions and knew the procedure.

In a quaintly formal manner, he extended a hand, so she shook it for him. She felt the deep scars on his palm—from when he killed his school's pet donkey—and a chill passed over her. She remembered the newspaper reports at the time: he had also cut his own hands to shreds during that attack.

Despite the past injuries he had a strong grip.

'I like you,' he said shyly. 'You are totally tubular.'

Totally tubular?

He sounded like one of her brothers. 'I like you too, Ben. I'm sure we are going to make a good team.'

'You are not like Nurse Wilson.'

'How so?'

'I can't tell you.'

Alyssa accompanied him to the front door and handed him his plastic raincoat and his hat.

'I can say only one thing,' he said to her confidentially in the doorway. 'And what is that, Ben?

'They will that there will not.' He put on his hat without smiling.

'Will not what, Ben?'

'Will not be any more barking. No more barking. Of that, we can be sure. It may be the symptom of the disease, but it is not the disease itself.'

He had not sounded fully sane during the visit, but now he sounded even worse. However, she did not have enough experience with clients like him to know if she should be concerned. Though alarm bells were ringing somewhere in her mind, she felt reassured by the fact that there had been no phone call from Gail Wilson. Ben was appropriately medicated. She tried to smile. 'I'd like to hear all about this next time, Ben. Perhaps then we can discuss the barking. I'd like to help.'

'You can't because I have already been informed. The dogs will lose their bark. They *will*. Goodbye, Miss Alyssa.'

'Goodbye Ben.' She waved to him as he walked back to the main building looking a little like a troll in a fairytale. She felt sorry for him.

The dogs will lose their bark.

She had entered the world of the insane, where anything could be whatever it wanted. She was not unduly worried, though. There had been a time when she herself had not known what she was doing. The clients at the Donald Clinic would not frighten her.

If there was ever going to be a problem, it was more likely that it was going to be the other way around. After all, look what she herself had been capable of in the past.

CHAPTER SIX

1

THEY SAT SIDE BY side on the sofa in the flat in the stillness of early night, about to have sex. Cy had pulled her work skirt up around her waist. It was hot, and the windows over the balcony were wide open in the semi-darkness. They had sex almost every night.

Alyssa felt close to him tonight. It was how she used to feel with him at the beginning, when he used to tell her his literary dreams—innocent and doomed ones, as she now knew. The honest sharing had drawn her to him even though she had already seen the immaturity in him. What she had not known then, but now knew for certain, was that Cy was doomed. There was no place for him in the real world. He had written many books, mostly e-books, but not been able to sell more than a few hundred copies of any. There was no future in that; no future for him in writing. He would not be a success for that most incurable of reasons: a lack of talent.

At first, of course, she had dreamed with him. In the cold light of day, however, the man on the couch next to her was someone who had failed to grow up; someone who clutched in vain at the lost magic of childhood and lingered there in denial. Most of him was pretence. And yet she still felt drawn to him. In some way, he was like her. He needed help and she wanted to help him.

Love is a strange thing.

Cy was nothing if not persistent with his literary aspirations. A favourite excuse of his went as follows: "The problem I face as a writer, Alyssa, is that the great unwashed possess only bovine levels of understanding, so they stampede all too readily when shown a reflection of themselves in a mirror". To him, people were irredeemably stupid, self-centred, selfish, and gullible.

Talk about living in cuckoo land.

Yes, she had come to know a great deal about the real Cy. And, strangely, this had not alienated her. Knowing him more deeply had served only to bind her to him more deeply. The paradox was that the more she discovered of his weaknesses the more like her he seemed. Inadequate human beings they were, the two of them, in a strangely roundabout way indeed soulmates.

He kissed her tenderly at the apex of her thighs, over the top of her briefs. It was pure Cy. At first it used to embarrass her; now she quite enjoyed it. Soon, though, he was cheating. He had quietly rolled the top of her panties down and his tongue was on her bare skin. She needed a shower first. 'You are rushing ahead too fast, Cy. Just let me finish my drink. I need to have a shower.'

'Seems fine to me,' he said, kissing her there again.

In the bathroom, just before stepping into the shower, she stood as usual in front of the large mirror on the back of the bathroom door and once again examined the long vertical scar on her abdomen, a scar that ran down the middle of her, from her ribcage to her pubic bone. The scar had matured over the years into a thin white line flush with her skin, but it still retained its power to mortify. It made her feel imperfect. Ruined. If only . . . but it was too late for regrets.

She would never be whole.

After the shower she returned to the lounge naked. With Cy at least, she had long ago overcome her shyness about her scar. He had his pants off too and looked ready for action. She half expected—wished—that he would jump her there and then, over the side of the sofa or on the carpet, but she knew he would not. Cy never did anything like that. Still, he was obviously excited—and she was too. She never tired of seeing how much she affected men when she had her clothes off.

Cy became bashful. 'We have the whole evening,' he said tenderly. 'Let's go to the bedroom. I want us to be together properly. I want us to make love.'

The flat was in an old building, so the bedroom was spacious, which Alyssa liked. Somehow, it evoked pleasant childhood memories of her grandparents' house. The ceiling was high, like in all the rooms, and the bedroom had an enormous wood-framed window with aging red velvet curtains setting off the rich brown of the timber. Unlike in the rest of the flat, the original wooden flooring had been preserved too, and the ceiling also still had its cream-coloured art deco mouldings from when the building originated in the 1920s. Two of the bedroom walls even retained their original stucco plaster, though the other two were now bare red brick—which had a charm of its own. The faded elegance, the lingering wood fragrances, the creams, the reds, the dark browns, the richness of it all: this she loved.

The bed was hers. Aaron's actually, but he had given it to her when he left for Oxford. Aaron was her previous boyfriend. For some reason she always thought of him as Aaron the ass fucker. She never allowed him to do any such thing with her, but he did like to try his luck from time to time, hence the name. He was certainly fond of sex in the doggy position. With Cy, she sometimes missed the tension inherent in that.

Like now.

She wondered what had become of Aaron. The last she had heard was that he was still in England.

The bed was a good, modern, queen size bed, low to the ground and with a padded headboard and quality mattress. She pulled back the covers to allow her and Cy to lie on the sheets. It was too hot for covers. She knew what she was in for with Cy, and knew it was going to be nothing like what she got from Aaron. It seemed weird that such different kinds of sex could happen in the same bed.

2

They lay down, side by side, and embraced, she still completely naked and Cy in a T-shirt only. The concerns about Cy's failing career and his overly submissive sexual behaviour began to fade as she warmed to the occasion. Before long she began to ache for him. Perversely, though, she was not yet ready for him. There had been problems with her orgasms lately and she did not want to end up frustrated yet again. Not if it could be helped.

She needed to talk to Cy first. About anything. She liked that—talking to him. She needed to get into a better headspace. Perhaps, by doing that, she would recover her ability to climax when the time came.

Gently, she forced Cy back from the precipice of no return. 'Let's first cuddle more,' she whispered. Pausing things now was her only chance. Unlike her two previous lovers, Ethan and Aaron, Cy was not one for second time around; in fact, lately, he had started to become not one for even first time around.

The increasing failure of their love life had started to become upsetting.
She snuggled closer.

'What are you thinking?' he asked. He ran his finger gently down the scar in the middle of her body to indicate that he had guessed.

'About the accident. About my dad.'

'I thought so.'

By now, the night had finally closed around them. The darkness felt peaceful. It was just them and the distant roar of the unseen pressure of the giant city.

She felt guilty about holding Cy back but did so anyway. 'What do you want to do for lunch tomorrow?' she whispered. It would be a Wednesday, and on Wednesdays she had an administration day with no clients. She could nip out for lunch with him somewhere nearby.

He laughed. 'Stop worrying about me, will you. I'm happy to just be at home, but I'll see what I can do if you like. I'll probably be able to arrange something somewhere near the clinic. I'll send you a text. Probably it will be with Brian again. He's always keen to see you. If I hint, he'll probably even pay. You know he loves poor authors.'

What Brian really loves is to stare at me.

Brian was Cy's boss, owner of the small bookshop where Cy worked part-time, and a man fond of her bits—all of them, it seemed. He was fond of weird food too, like okonomiyaki with seaweed sauce, or creepy things like crickets and mealworms. 'Sounds cool,' she said, to keep the peace.

'Settled, then.' He began proceedings by giving her a passionate kiss.

.... **3** ....

Cy was about to make a move on her, so she felt mildly anxious. Already he was invading her throat with his tongue. It was all happening.

Despite her best efforts, she remained disconnected. Cy was trying to relate to her, but her mind kept wandering. There seemed to be a barrier building between them. None of her previous boyfriends kissed like he did, and she just could not warm to it. He loved deep tongue kissing, but the practice still felt unpleasantly invasive to her and not entirely wholesome. Nevertheless, there he was, sticking his tongue down her throat even though it was making her squirm. Maybe that was why he liked doing it . . .

What do I know?

She thought about Ethan, her first lover, to distract herself.

There had not been a cruel bone in dear Ethan's body. He was eighteen and she nineteen when they met at the local football club gym in Ocean View. She was still a virgin and still living with her stepmother. The gym, Ethan, and sex: that was how true love first began for her. They were both silly, small-town teenagers, yet there had been a magic to their sex life that she longed for now. She needed that elusive something, whatever it had been. Perhaps it had been that Ethan, in his ignorance, had not lacked confidence and showed no hesitancy when it came to the matter of how to deal with the female of the species. After all, once she became his girlfriend, he simply *did* sex to her, completely without shame or preamble. They coupled often, usually in the dunes beside the ocean, and always with him on top because they both assumed that this was the only way that sex was done. Although he always performed with kindness, he showed little regard for her fulfilment because he seemed to think that such a thing was entirely her own business. And, bizarrely, even though she seldom had an orgasm with him, she now thought of their lovemaking as profoundly healing. At least with him she had been able to relax.

Her second boyfriend, Aaron, had been quite different; more experienced and far more domineering. Unlike Ethan, he took great interest in her climaxes whenever they had sex and always required her to orgasm visibly before he would. Which had seemed a good idea at first, but, as she soon discovered, had nothing at all to do with any real concern on his part for her welfare and everything to do with him controlling her. When it came to lovemaking—and life in general—Aaron's main desire was always to control her. In the end, it became intolerable, and they had split up. Perhaps his youthful male virility had been the problem and maybe he would have improved with time, but she doubted it. Whatever the truth, she was not one for performing orgasms on demand.

Meanwhile, Cy was still kissing her, although he had progressed to other parts of her body. Passively, she let him amuse himself, moving as required. She had learnt after only a few months with him that he was very orally driven. Besides, away from her throat, the kissing felt quite pleasant. Unlike Ethan and Aaron, Cy had a submissive heart, and she knew he would never do anything against her will. With him, *she* controlled what happened.

It was something she had only come to perceive later in their relationship, and, at first, the realisation had made her feel guilty, as though it signified that there was something wrong with her. She had tried without success to get him to lead until a chance lecture during the sexology course at university informed her that sexual submission was common in men, even grown men—so much so that studies had shown that women were as likely as men to be "in command" during bedroom proceedings. The same gender balance also applied to the unrelated domain of being "in control". One could be in command but not in control or vice versa or all or none. The permutations were endless. The point being that it was perfectly acceptable in modern society for a woman to feel okay about taking charge sexually seeing that very often this was the reality of it anyway. In the past, women had needed to fool men and act with subtlety when it came to such matters, but in psychologically advanced urban societies hypocrisy was no longer required.

Whatever Cy might believe to the contrary, he belonged to that very large group of men—about half the men on the planet—who were incapable of taking the lead during sex with a woman.

Sometimes, this seemed a real pity. She missed the "being taken" side of life. Although she had no desire to be dominated in real life, when it came to sex within the safety of a trusting relationship, she missed being dominated sexually; missed *being taken*.

With Cy, she could not relax during sex. Cy expected her to do everything.

She had only herself to blame for losing Ethan. After all, she had been the one who had decided to end the relationship. After wasting a year after high school messing around with him in Ocean View, uncertain what to do with her life, she had sacrificed him for the promise of a sociology degree at a third-rate university in the city. Determined to escape her intolerable stepmother and their silly little town, she had been ruthless. Selfishly and without any concern for the potential consequences, she had engineered a clean and complete break from her old life. It had been cruel.

She felt ashamed of herself. Ethan was the first to go to pieces. Within weeks of their breakup, he began cruising bars, and it did not take long before he became involved in bar fights. His angry behaviour escalated and, within a few months, after a particularly unpleasant assault, he ended up with a short prison sentence. Yet, despite knowing of his troubles and evident distress, she had ignored him and blithely continued with her new life in the city. Nothing was going to hold her back from achieving her goals. Or so she had thought.

She discovered—too late—an unfortunate truth: tossing aside the one she loved was going to be more serious than she had bargained for. Her turn to go to pieces came next. She was tough, so it took more than a year for the wheels to come off completely, but come off they did, and in spectacular fashion. The collapse was as dramatic as it was sudden. One day, early in her second year at university, an abyss opened in her mind, a black hole, strange and frightening. It seemed to have come out of nowhere, and out of it came awful feelings. Then, in what seemed like a delayed form of divine retribution, there came accusations of evil. The voices paralysed her ability to concentrate. The abyss became more terrifying when she began to understand that it was going to suck her in. She was so evil that she had to die. She needed help but she had not known what to do. Instead, she became uncertain about where she was or what she was doing. This was what happened to evil people, the fate they deserved. Blackness.

Then death.

She held tightly onto Cy to block the increasing rush of recollections. Her mind was starting to frighten her again. She tried to focus on reality, on Cy, and on his skinny but surprisingly strong arms. If only he would just take her *away*. Fuck her senseless. That would be the best medicine. How good it would be to forget everything about the past. How *necessary* it seemed that evening to just *be* fucked . . .

Just fuck me!

4

Cy was still messing around, kissing her here and there. She could not connect with him in this way. He needed to take control of her for once. She thought of Alan Summerfield and his commanding presence on the balcony of his magnificent home, his physically powerful frame, the ocean, the strong wrists on the balustrade, and felt herself blushing. *He* would know how to fuck a woman. Somehow, she just knew this. Instead of Cy's dubstep there would be strains of something like *Love Me Harder* by Ariana Grande.

She had had more than enough of messing around. It was time to take charge.

'Right. Over you go. My turn.'

She steadied herself in the correct position and fixed her gaze on Cy's eyes. Using one hand to support herself on the headboard and the other to hold his shoulders down, she took control of the situation. She slipped into an assertive trance and let her body do what it had to do: fuck *him*. Cy smiled. He just loved her like this.

In the hushed peace of their bedroom, they made love like that, with her riding him without inhibition, controlling him, taking him. An exquisite velvety pressure filled her. There seemed no better feeling in the whole world, nothing else quite like it. She tried to keep her eyes fixed on Cy's, but everything started to go hazy. She felt herself losing control. Cy's eyes glazed over. She knew she had him. The situation began to become confusing as her imagination took over. Now *she* was the one who was being taken; Cy was behind her, screwing her, taking her . . . from behind. Intoxicated with lust, she went for the kill, thrusting as fast as she could, feeling the night air between her cheeks. She felt her face becoming warm with shame, and her back too. She was sweating, turning pink. The surroundings began to pause, as though time itself was stopping. The pattern on the stucco wall became inexplicably enchanting. Sound disappeared. The night air became haunting. Breathless expectation hovered.

Her aroused breasts bounced in intoxicating unison with her thrusting. Everything was ready, wanting, receiving. The tightness in her lower belly was growing tighter. A torrent was coming, coming, coming . . .

I am going to burst!

A rapturous eruption of almighty clenching was just . . . moments . . . away . . . when . . . it happened again. Cy began to lose it. He began to lose his erection.

No! No!

Trying to carry on was no use.

They went into their default side-on hug for a while.

'I'm really sorry,' he whispered.

'It's okay,' she said, as kindly as possible. She wanted to cry, but she fought back her tears. It was her fault, she told herself. Clearly, she was not very good at taking a man, but she did not know how else to achieve it. At that moment, she needed a real man more than ever, a man who could take charge and make things right for her.

After five minutes, there was still a problem.

'I could just lie here for you, you know,' she said. 'I don't mind.'

'You've said that before. You know it won't help. You'll get nothing out of it, so I won't be able to bring myself to do it to you.'

'I don't mind. I'll do it for you.'

'Stop it.'

'You can do whatever you want to me. Will that help?' She made the offer even though she had done so on previous occasions, and it had not helped.

'You are deliberately missing the point, aren't you?'

She persisted. 'Why not? We could try things. You could tie me up, or something. Or take me up my bum.'

'Can you be serious for a moment?'

'I am. Maybe you are missing what you really want. Maybe you want something a bit more . . . sadistic.'

'You just don't get this sex stuff, do you? In the first place, you don't like being tied up, you know that. In the second place, as far as your ass goes, that part of you is still a virgin in case you've forgotten. There's no way I can just screw you up your ass out of the blue. It doesn't work like that.'

'What do you mean?'

'What do you mean what do I mean? What planet are you from?'

'Okay, then.'

I suppose I need to be stretched, do I, and watch what I eat beforehand?

'I could never bring myself to hurt you and humiliate you. I'd feel absolutely terrible, and you'd burst into tears.'

Will I?

She tried again: 'So what about your books, then? Everyone is ass-fucking everyone else there. How come? What's going on there?'

'That's not real life. Jeez, what is *wrong* with you? I just can't.'

Can't keep it up, you mean.

'Don't worry. I understand,' she said instead.

'God, I'm useless.' He held his head in his hands. 'I don't know what's the matter with me.'

'It's okay, Cy.'

'It's not. And now I've hurt your feelings.' He gripped her. 'Please don't get me wrong. I *do* find you exiting. All of you.' He turned her over and gently spread her. 'Oh, God,' he groaned. 'You are so perfect that I think I'm going to die.'

'Well, why not just do a doggy then?'

'Oh, oh, oh. I'm such a failure, aren't I? I don't think I'm good enough for you. I think that's what it is.' His voice became small. 'I'm sorry.'

He was becoming tiresome.

She cuddled him. It was not the first time they had had this conversation after he had gone soft on her, and it probably would not be the last. Cy would not be solving their sexual impasse any time soon. She had mentioned Viagra once, but that had been a mistake. For a man of his age, it had only succeeded in being an insult and a slur on his manhood. He did not speak to her for a week afterwards. All of which meant that there was only one thing for it if she wanted to achieve any sort of satisfaction that night: once again, she would have to take charge.

'First, I want you to suck my boobs,' she said quietly.

Cy's mood instantly changed. They were back on track. 'I'd love that.' He knew what was coming.

'Good.'

Later, she got him to relax on his back with his head on a pillow and took him in her mouth. It was an activity that did little for her—although it was nice to have him to herself so to speak—but evidently it did a lot for him because it was not long before he came all over her.

Ooh, aah, aaah, was all he could say about his coming back to life.

He might be finished, but she was not. Facing him, she again straddled him, this time sitting well forwards, near his face, resting on her knees. She took care not to smother him.

She got into position, keeping both hands on the headboard this time.

She began to move across his eager and co-operative tongue, gingerly at first, but soon her inhibitions washed away. There was anger now, and she lost her polite ways. Bucking wildly, she abandoned all pretences. Lewdly, she squashed herself across Cy's tongue and face, growling as she did so. The end came quickly for her too. The whole world seemed to draw up into her insides, a whole world that seemed to be filling her up again . . . again . . . until . . . until . . . everything in her head exploded.

She saw nothing but stars and felt nothing but mind-bending clenching. Overcome, she curled down, mewing loudly. However, she could not help herself or stop. It would not end. Her body went into spasms. Again, she was onto him, again letting rip. Insatiably, she kept on coming, again and again. In a torrent of pelvic convulsions, she lost her mind and fucked herself senseless. She *took* Cy.

After that, she lay peacefully in his arms.

Later that night, it dawned on her that what in fact had happened was that she had fucked *herself.*

That was the truth of the matter.

Sex was a strange thing.

I fucked myself.

CHAPTER SEVEN

1

PROVIDING HELP TO MRS GOODMAN was straightforward in theory but not in practice. As soon as she set eyes on her new client, Alyssa had known deep in her heart that setting out to assist such a woman was going to be a waste of everyone's time. It was something she had realised instantly, but still, after many weeks, lacked the courage to admit—to Mrs Goodman or to anyone else. Mrs Goodman was one of her original "big three", i.e., one of the three *first ever* unsupervised clients of her career, so she wanted to avoid damaging her perceived usefulness to the Donald Clinic so early in her time there.

Men—of any age—she could handle with relative ease, but older women tended to leave her at sea when it came to trying to counsel them. She simply did not understand them. This was a major defect, of course, in her usefulness as a therapist. She hoped to overcome the flaw over time with more experience, but for now it seemed best to conceal the weakness as far as possible.

While some in her position would have run from Mrs Goodman after the first day, or at least sent her packing back to Greta across in the main building, she had elected to not do that. Bravely—or perhaps foolishly out of pride—she had pressed on regardless of any limitations. Now, it was too late.

To be fair, she had been trying her absolute best.

The first day with the woman was still etched in her mind. A sneak glance into the waiting room at the cottage had revealed a respectable-looking, elderly, nondescript, matronly woman. She was obviously well-heeled and appeared to be a prototype of the Baronbridge version of a housewife hypochondriac. She had smiled with relief. After the shock to the system that had been Benjamin Clayton, Mrs Goodman had looked harmless enough.

Monsters often did.

It was something she wished she had realised earlier on.

And now Mrs Goodman was here again. Smiling at the woman as warmly as she could, Alyssa ushered her client to the couch in her consulting room. As always, and as befitted a proper older lady from Baronbridge, Ellen Goodman was not too short and not too tall, not too thin and not too fat, not too attractive and not too ugly. Almost perfectly, she matched her place in society and filled the appropriate empty space on the canvas of humanity.

It was only when up close and personal that illusions evaporated. Something was not quite right with Mrs Goodman. For starters, her given age seemed wrong. Alyssa glanced once more at her notes to double check. The woman in the room with her was supposed to be fifty-three but, clearly, she had to be in her sixties at the very least. There was an air of worn-out seniority to her: ponderousness, shallow breathing, wrinkles, jaw sag, bullfrog neck, general gloom.

God, I hope I don't get like this when I'm only fifty-three.

An uncharitable thought popped into her mind: how were men like Alan Summerfield supposed to cohabit with women like Ellen Goodman? After all, they were about the same age. She knew the answer, of course: the typical man of fifty-three was nothing like Alan and exactly like Ellen. Even so, Ellen Goodman's poor physical condition was enough to make her feel angry.

She forced herself to try and be professional. She needed to stop falling victim to her own personal hang-ups, she told herself. She needed to focus on the positive in others. For all her faults, Mrs Goodman was at least well dressed, and this was more than merely the result of wealth. She showed evidence of genuine good taste. The shoes, pearl necklace, couturier dress, coiffure: they could not be faulted. Pity about the rest of her, though. She could not decide if she should think of her new client as fat or not. Like most modern middle-aged women, she had a heaviness to her and was overweight, but not more so than what was seen almost universally in women of her age. However, whether fat or not, she was in poor physical condition. Her footsteps came in tiny shuffles, as though she might overbalance at the tiniest hindrance.

Why am I just itching to give this woman a slap to wake her up?

Something about the client reminded her of someone she knew, yet she could not place the resonance. The countertransference, however, was powerful; negative enough to make her feel anxious. As always, Ellen generated unpleasant feelings.

Mrs Goodman's past visits to Greta McCreedy filled thirty computer screens of notes. From what Alyssa could discern, these past consultations had been futile and had achieved nothing except enormous financial cost. It seemed almost beyond belief that so much time and money could have been wasted by any client, let alone the unfortunate specimen sitting on the couch in front of her. No wonder Mrs Goodman spent most of her time glaring.

'I was not unhappy with Mrs McCreedy,' volunteered Ellen Goodman. 'And I certainly don't wish to be any trouble to anyone. So, I'm still not sure why I am here with you.'

Alyssa tried to warm to her. 'Everyone is trying to do their best for you, Ellen. I'm sure you understand this. It seems Ms McCreedy was unable to make much progress with your problem, so she felt that you might benefit from a fresh perspective on things. What do you think of that idea? A fresh perspective?'

'I miss counsellor McCreedy.'

You would.

Given the past thirty or more fruitless consultations with Greta, Mrs Goodman reluctantly agreed to continue attending at the cottage for a while.

Ellen's problem was that she could not get to sleep at night, a simple enough problem at face value. No one was able to cure her, though. That part was proving far from simple. Cure had remained beyond the reach of all previous caregivers. No matter what anyone did, she remained unable to get a good night's sleep. For the past few years, she had been sleeping at most two or three hours a night, with serious consequences for her functionality. Extensive investigations had been carried out, with no physical disease found, not even a neurological disease despite MRI brain scans and sleep laboratory monitoring. Also, there was no sleep apnoea present. Furthermore, all aspects of sleep hygiene practices were regarded as optimal or optimised. She knew to exercise daily in sunshine, watch only light comedy on TV near to bedtime, cease electronic screens after that, have a light snack of grapes or bananas or milk or oatmeal near bedtime but no alcohol or tea or coffee, have a hot bath, go to bed at a fixed hour every night (well before midnight and in a quiet and dark and cool room used for nothing except sleep), engage in stretching and or a massage in the bedroom, and then, finally, once in bed, engage in mindfulness exercises until asleep. However, still she did not sleep. Physically, though, her health remained surprisingly good. Her cholesterol level was slightly elevated, but everything else was normal; even her thyroid gland functioned normally. Needless to say, sleeping pills and antidepressants of various sorts had not helped in the slightest.

Ellen Goodman's problem had been determined to be entirely psychological.

2

Alyssa noted that at no stage previously had sex or sexual activity ever been mentioned or discussed with her client by anyone, which seemed odd to her for a case of psychological insomnia. This aspect of such a client's life was not something that could be ignored, in her opinion, and was going to need to be addressed at some stage—perhaps later once she had got to know Ellen better. She glanced at the work tablet resting on her lap and made a note to ask the client about her sex life at some stage.

While doing so, the official diagnosis on Mrs E Goodman, from Greta, was visible at the top of the page in front of her:

> Intractable insomnia despite full exclusion of organic disease and despite environmental and pharmacological optimisation. Even though non-responsive to CBT, presumed to be psychogenic.

The logic underlying Greta's transfer of her client to the cottage had seemed at first glance to be a suspicion on her part that something was bothering Mrs Goodman unconsciously to such a degree that her mind could not rest, but Alyssa now doubted that this was the real reason behind Greta's action. Greta almost certainly did not believe in the existence of a psychodynamic Un-conscious. No, the offload was a challenge; that was what it was. A test: CBT versus psychodynamic therapy. A dare to do better.

No problem, Greta old girl. I'm more than happy to go toe to toe with you.

To do this, she needed to get to know her client better than she already did. Some honest conversation was required.

Therefore, she redoubled her efforts to be pleasant and gentle with Ellen:

What was troubling her? "Nothing much".

Was she happy? "Yes and no".

Was she functioning adequately each day? "Mostly".

Why was she seeking counselling? "I don't really know".

How could she be of help to her? "I don't think anyone can help me".

And thus, it went. Interminably.

The senior matron from Baronbridge was not going to be giving a straight answer to any question any time soon. Indeed, in her special way, Mrs Goodman made it abundantly clear that she was not going to be opening up to any young snot *ever*.

Finally, Alyssa uttered a swear word under her breath. 'Fuck, I can't believe this.'

Trying to hold a conversation with Ellen was like sinking into a bog of quicksand. The more she tried to engage with her, the less traction she achieved. The levels of psychological resistance were astounding. Why, she wondered, had Greta not added "passive-aggressive personality disorder" to the diagnosis? Clearly, Mrs Goodman was diabolically oppositional.

It seemed obvious that the so-called insomnia problem was a cop out. There was something more going on. Nothing about Ellen was straightforward. In fact, the only thing that Greta had right about Ellen was that Ellen was not depressed. The endless psychometric evaluations done by her all showed the same frustrating result: no depression.

No. Ellen Goodman was concealing something. And that something was slowly killing her from within.

But *what*? After more than thirty circular sessions with Greta—and thousands upon thousands of dollars in fees—Ellen had made absolutely no progress. Greta had no idea what was going on.

Alysa decided on a new line of questioning: 'And how are things on the work front?' she asked, as innocently as possible.

'Fine. Despite the poor economy, we are still making over a million a year. US Dollars, that is.'

'You and your husband Steve?'

'Yes.'

Ellen's husband was called Steven. He was fifty-one years old and owned the family business, called *Better Buttons*. 'And it's all from selling buttons?'

'Yes. Not only selling. We make some of them too.'

'Right. And you have a child?'

'Yes. Paulina. She's twenty-five and lives with us.'

'I see. And when it comes to you and Steve, how are things between you?'

'We're good. Mostly good.'

They were still stuck in the quicksand of fake. Alyssa gazed silently at the nondescript figure fading into the couch in front of her, a person pretending to be sixty-three instead of the fifty-three that she really was. The woman's hair was expensive, yet also disturbing. She searched for the correct description of its colour: *mouse*. That was it. Ellen Goodman was a mouse. Not only that, but she had been sent to a counsellor who was about the same age as her daughter. For the first time, she found herself feeling sorry for the woman in front of her.

'I can understand how difficult it must be for you coming here,' she said. 'Believe me, I can.' She meant it. 'I know I'm young and inexperienced, and I know things are hell for you as far as sleeping goes. What I also know, though, is that nothing has helped so far, not even medication, so I think we need to try something new and different. What do you think?'

'Like what?'

'Honesty. Ellen, I want you to try to see past me. I want you try to disregard the person you see in front of you. Think of me only as a friendly and safe voice in the background of your own mind. Can you do that?'

'I don't want to be told what to do,' said Ellen in a small voice.

'Exactly. That's why, for the first time, you are in the right place. I don't work like that.' She almost added "unlike Greta" but resisted the temptation. 'With my kind of therapy—psychotherapy—you don't get ordered to do anything. Sure, I'll help you as much as possible, but ultimately it will be you who calls the shots. Which makes sense because the only person who can change you is you. So, I want you to feel free. Pretend I'm not even here and that this is *your* lounge room at home. Just talk aloud to yourself. Try to get in touch with what you are feeling. Everything you say is absolutely confidential, so I want to encourage you to be as open as you can.'

Ellen remained silent.

Alyssa allowed the silence to drag on, but Ellen Goodman was no pushover.

'As I said, whatever you say won't go anywhere. You know that. Remember, too, that nothing you say will shock me. Nothing can shock me. Try me.'

Ellen Goodman glared at her.

'What's on your mind, Ellen? What is it, Ellen?' Alyssa waited in silence in the peaceful room, allowing the discomfort to build, determined not to give in. She could play silly buggers with the best of them.

At last, she was rewarded. Emotion slowly began to fill Ellen Goodman's blank face while she struggled not to speak. Alyssa recognised what she was seeing: pain.

'I keep reading these sad stories,' she said in a low voice. 'These terrible tragedies. They are so awful.'

'Tell me about them.'

'You'll think I'm stupid.'

'No, I think I'll understand.'

3

And so it was that Mrs Ellen Goodman first began to unburden herself of her storehouse of sad stories:

> There was this duck, just a simple park duck. Life for the duck was hard. Then, one day, it fell pregnant and had three beautiful little ducklings. However, food was scarce, and she struggled to feed them. Then she learnt a trick. People in the park would

feed her if she went up close to them. At last, things looked up for the mother and her three ducklings.

One day, the duck went up to a teenager in the park with her three ducklings to see if she could get some food. For a reason that the mother duck could not understand, the teenager began to scream. Finally, he kicked her in the face. The kick smashed the duck's beak, and she ran away with her ducklings.

For two whole days, the mother duck walked resolutely around the park with her broken beak and her ducklings—there was nothing else she could do. She had to pretend that nothing had happened. Her actions were those of disbelief and desperation. Unable to eat or drink, she became increasingly unable to look after her ducklings. The little ducklings died in front of her, one by one. Her heart finally broke, and then she died too.

The worst part was that absolutely nobody came to help them.

Mrs Goodman dabbed her eyes with a tissue.

Alyssa needed a tissue for her own eyes, too. 'That is a very sad story, Ellen.'

'It is.'

'Do you have any idea what it means?'

'It's from the newspaper. Some ducks died. That's all it means. It's just life, just the truth. The stories mean nothing to me, but I keep seeing them everywhere. The sad stories.'

'Are you quite sure this story means nothing to you?'

'Nobody understands,' she said. Her voice was now hardly more than a whisper.

'I can try.'

'I am nothing,' said Ellen Goodman. 'I have nothing. I can offer nothing.' And with that, her body became wracked with silent tears.

Alyssa let her cry, even though it felt uncomfortable to watch.

I am nothing. I have nothing. I can offer nothing.

'I would be better off dead.'

It was clear that Ellen Goodman was oppressed by the weight of the hopelessness of her own existence. Although not officially authorised to make a diagnosis, Alyssa recognised Ellen's mental state for what it was:

Existential Dysphoria. It was a condition that lay beyond psychology. Ellen was not depressed. Ellen simply no longer wished to exist.

'What is it that makes you say these things?'

'It's pretty obvious, isn't it? I'm a useless person. A worthless piece of shit.'

She said the final words so softly that Alyssa was not sure if she had heard correctly. 'What was that, Ellen? I couldn't quite hear what you said.'

Her client, the second of the three who came originally from the horror very first day at the Donald some weeks ago, stood up suddenly.

She was leaving.

As she stormed out of the consulting room, Mrs Goodman turned, threw her shoulders back, and began to bellow. 'You stupid girl! You stupid, stupid girl!'

4

Silly old bag.

Except she wasn't that, and Alyssa knew it. The problem was that she was a hopeless counsellor when it came to older women. She was somehow not on their wavelength. She seemed to have wrong ideas about what went on in their heads.

Given her past, this was understandable, surely. So, why did she find it so hard to improve? She could not afford to have clients storming out of counselling sessions with her. She would soon get a bad name.

Now she had unused time to kill. Feeling stressed, she sat at her desk and tried to think of something positive and encouraging to recover her emotional equilibrium.

Positive thoughts seemed in short supply lately—even when thinking about the gym. There, Fabio, the gym's owner—whose real name was Carlo—had recently interrupted a sex dream she was having while exercising on one of the elliptical trainers. 'How are we going there, Alyssa?' He had been doing his rounds. He spoke loudly and hovered directly in front of her machine.

The timing was terrible.

Go away!

She couldn't say it, so instead she did her best to ignore him. The flamboyant elderly Italian often came and chatted to her, but she had hoped this time that if she said nothing he would go away.

He didn't.

She had had no choice but to speak to him. She slowed down on the machine but kept moving. 'I'm fine, Fabio. Just fine.'

Undeterred by her lack of interest, Fabio remained close, watching her with a show of professional insight. It was something he obviously liked doing because he often did it. He would wait until she was well into an exercise and physically compromised and then "arrive". It seemed to her, as a psychologist, that he liked his women at some sort of disadvantage, which was mildly disconcerting to say the least. Also disturbing was the barely disguised sexual interest he showed in her despite his advanced age. He was over seventy.

He offered some advice: 'The constant speed. I could not help noticing that. Too constant. Variation is better. It's all in the variation.'

His visit had nothing to do with professional advice, and she knew it. He fancied himself as a ladies' man—he was wealthy enough, divorced, and a snappy dresser—and the real reason he had come to her was to once again see if she had any interest in what he had to offer. Fortunately, he had not yet had the courage to directly proposition her, though it worried her that one day he might be brave enough. According to club rumours, it would begin with an offer of a free massage in the privacy of his office.

'Everything to your satisfaction?'

'As I said, Fabio, all fine.'

'You are looking a bit tense today. The shoulders, perhaps? Do they need a massage?'

'No. Definitely not!'

It made him smile. 'I hear you are now working just a few streets across from here,' said Fabio after a while. 'In East Hubron, they tell me. At that private madhouse near the archbishop's house. How are you finding that? Don't you get scared?'

She wished he would not refer to a mental health facility as a "madhouse". It showed just how lost in the past he was. 'It's fine, Fabio.' She slowed her pace again to catch her breath as he continued his chatting.

'You're with that Professor Summerfield fellow, aren't you? And Professor Donald. They were on TV again the other day. Personally, that sort of freaky stuff I just can't handle.'

'How come you know so much about my work?'

He grinned. 'I know everything about you. No, not really. Your partner told me the other day while he was waiting to pick you up. Cy, is it? Do I have his name right?'

'That's him. Trust him.' She was surprised that Cy had spoken to Fabio. Cy hated gyms.

'Handsome guy, your Cy. You're a lucky woman. He should join too.'

'He doesn't like exercise. He's too lazy.' He didn't have any money either. She knew Fabio did not really want Cy to join. He preferred his clients to be female. His top-floor gym was well known for not only its glamour but also for its preponderance of women. Situated as it was near the state parliament at the edge of the central business district, the gym's true advantage lay in also being near to Public Hospital—one of Hubron's four mega hospitals—where most of the staff were female. In a masterful application of reverse psychology, Fabio had achieved success with the modern female by changing the original name of his enterprise from City Health Club to the more macho and retro sounding *Fabio's Gym*.

He placed his head close to Alyssa's. 'At least we have you.'

'Sure.'

She did her best to ignore him and tried to return her attention to her exercise. Fabio, however, rested a proprietary hand on the control box of her machine and continued to lean in and loiter. He was so close that she could read the label *Giorgio Vincenzo* on the whistle lanyard around his wrinkled neck. Furthermore, given her elevation on the machine, her heaving chest was now at the level of his eyes.

'What do you think of the new doctor, Alyssa?' asked Fabio, as his gaze seamlessly alternated between her cleavage and her face. 'Do you two know each other from the hospital?'

By now, she was perspiring profusely. She could feel the dampness between her breasts. She tried to reply to Fabio's inane conversation while continuing to exercise. 'No, I don't know him. He's a doctor, is he? Looked pretty young to me.' Her legs felt like jelly as they moved relentlessly backwards and forwards in front of Fabio. It felt as though her crotch was in his face too. To her dismay, he took a step back, as though to get a better view.

'He's joined here with his fiancée,' confided Fabio. 'Another blonde. I like blondes.' He winked at her. 'She's a doctor too. I don't suppose you know her either. Mark and Ruby?'

'No, I do not. Good luck to them.' Fabio was making her angry now. She had no choice but to be blunt with him: 'Can you give me a break, Fabio? I need to concentrate.'

'Sure.' He had at last behaved like a gentleman and moved away— only to stop somewhere behind her. She did her best to ignore him. He had ruined her session on the machine. Ruined her desire to have yet another orgasm at the gym. Her chance of achieving that seemed to be diminishing everywhere.

Then Fabio had said something she now remembered with pride. "That's one impressive ass, Alyssa," he had said from somewhere behind her, as though giving a professional training opinion. She had turned to see a huge grin on his face. Then, finally, he did go away.

Alone in her consulting room at the cottage, Alyssa held her head in her hands. Maybe she was fucked in the head, but Fabio, at least, did like what she had to offer. And a whole lot of other men too. So, there was no need to be too negative about things. One could not please everybody. Besides, thinking about the gym had reminded her of the existence of Mark.

If she was unable to help Ellen Goodman, then so be it.

CHAPTER EIGHT

1

THE FIRST PERSON TO make use of the concealed driveway to attend at the cottage turned out to be the last of the three clients from her first day at work, a man called George. He was not really called George, of course—it was a fake name, as Alyssa subsequently discovered—but that had been his name during the initial consultations. He came always in the same powerful car, its arrival heralded by a deep engine throb that made the windows of the cottage tremble. The first day he came, Alyssa remembered wondering how he knew about the driveway. She thought Trish must have told him, but once again that had been a wrong assumption—as she also subsequently discovered, this time to her cost.

She did not know much about cars so, at first, she had suspected it was a Jaguar. In keeping with this, the man who emerged was richly dressed in an impressive, dark-coloured pin stripe business suit. He appeared to be in his forties, though he still had a full head of hair. Everything about his manner spoke of considerable education and wealth. She had hoped he was in fact rich because if not he was in for major bill shock, courtesy of the Donald Clinic.

'Hi,' she had said to him from the front porch as he approached in person. 'I'm Alyssa, counselling psychologist. Welcome.'

'George. Pleased to meet you.' He mumbled his words and did not extend a greeting hand. Instead, he studied her, as though uncertain whether to proceed. He appeared highly embarrassed by the situation.

She held his gaze and studied him in return. He appeared genuinely civilised—his voice was distinguished—and his face radiated a superior intelligence despite his crestfallen emotional state. Her instincts informed her that he was in serious need of psychological counselling, so she took charge.

'No need to be nervous. Come on in.'

He did, and after first getting him to loosen his tie and take off his jacket, she settled him in front of her at her desk in the consulting room. Before any counselling could begin there were administrative matters to deal with seeing that he had bypassed the main desk and absolutely nothing was known about him.

'I hope I'm not making a big mistake coming here,' he muttered.

'Relax, George. A little preliminary chat can't possibly hurt. Together, we can work out if you are in the right place for your needs. Firstly, I assume you know about our fee structure?'

'The daylight robbery, you mean. Yes, I'm aware of it. It will be okay.'

'Well, that's something positive, then. Next, why don't we get underway with a few administrative details? Do you have a referral letter?'

'No.'

'Some identification, then? Name, address, and occupation?'

'I assume you are joking.'

'No. It's a requirement—anywhere in the country. Otherwise, we can't register you.'

'With whom?'

She had not given the matter much thought before. 'I don't know. It's just an information screen that we are required to fill in. For the health department, I suppose. The government does pay part of your fees. The practice computer won't accept you without at least some basic details.'

'Is that so? The *computer* won't accept me. Are you telling me that the government is monitoring me even if I go totally private and pay the full shitload of fees in cash? That *nobody* will see me if I don't comply? Has everyone gone completely mad!'

She must have appeared startled by his anger because he immediately apologised.

'Sorry. I shouldn't have taken it out on you. And I shouldn't have used a swear word. It's just that I'm under so much stress. No matter where I turn, everyone I encounter seems to be a dickhead—not you of course but your system. I can't cope with all this nonsense anymore. You were my last hope. I had hoped that *you*, at least, would see reason.'

She did her best to soothe him. 'Believe me, I understand everything you are saying, but I'm only an employee here, so I can't register you with this practice without some details.'

'You want identifying details? How about George Roberts, car salesman? Will that do? It's not true, but will it do? What sorts of lies make you people happy?'

'Personally, I don't mind if you prefer to be careful with the truth, but unfortunately certain untruths don't satisfy the system. The authorities immediately recognise a fake identity. It's just the way it works.' There was a reason it worked that way, which she did not try to explain: any potential client who pretended to be George Roberts could just as well under his real name be a recognised drug addict, or have a history of violence, or be seriously deranged, or be a sex criminal—or even be a known case of *all* these rolled into one. 'If you refuse to give us your correct identity there is no way for us to receive information about your past.'

'Good grief. I can't believe humanity has sunk to this level. What if I assure you that I have no past of any interest to anyone but myself? Why is my word not good enough?'

'It's just a precaution. For your own good.'

'How about I give you at least *some* truth? I'm forty-six and I'm harmless. Surely that's enough. Sure, I've been having some emotional issues—that's why I'm here—but I've never been coded as a nut job. I've never even seen a mental health worker before and I'm perfectly respectable and perfectly sane. Your computer will throw up absolutely nothing negative about me, that I can guarantee. So, why involve the government?'

'As I say, I only work here.'

'Correct me if I'm wrong, but here's what I understand about your health department computer program: any person anywhere in the country who gets given a mental health code gets marked by it for life. The pejorative code is forwarded automatically to the state intelligence service as well as to any professional registration body or parastatal agency that requests it. Not so?'

She had no counter to his allegation because it was true. Mr George Roberts was no fool. Every client who attended the Donald Clinic, or any other mental health clinic in the country—for no matter how trivial a reason—ended up labelled as a *mental case* for life. It was probably the most scandalous of the many secrets and lies concealed within the industry she had just joined. Luckily for herself—thanks to her own careful concealments—Professor Barnes still seemed to be in the dark about the many negative secret government codes against her *own* name. It was only going to be a matter of time before he stumbled across them, but hopefully by then she would have proved her worth.

George smiled at her, as though he sensed that she was wavering.

She did not know what to do. The stranger in front of her seemed decent enough, in need of help, and able to pay his way. Why mark him for life with a code that would shut many future doors in his face without him even knowing? That seemed wrong.

However, if she did not register him on the official system he would not exist. There would never be any proof of who he really was. He had come to the cottage directly off the street—which meant that he could be anybody. Yet perhaps it was time to stop pandering to the fake morality of the faceless officials of uncaring bureaucracy. In the bigger scheme of things, secretive behaviour in clients, especially older men, was not unheard of. A wish for privacy did not necessarily have sinister implications.

She made her decision: 'Okay,' she said to the stranger at her desk. 'I'll agree to see you on your terms.' She felt confident in her ability to recognise fundamental decency—or lack thereof—in another human, and her instincts had assured her that she could trust him. 'I hope you understand, George, that I am making an exception to the rules. The matter of your true identity we can revisit later, once you realise that you can trust me with it. Happy?'

He was delighted. 'I will do my best to come clean at some stage. Promise. I really do appreciate the fact that you are not just another mindless idiot. Thank you. You have no idea how much this means to me . . . Alyssa.'

'I just hope I have done the right thing.'

She had. After that, the consultations with George Roberts went from strength to strength.

2

'I can hardly believe I'm actually here,' he would often say. 'I never thought I'd get over the embarrassment.'

'Well, it's just little old me, so there's hardly any reason to be embarrassed.'

'I was told I could talk honestly with someone here and they wouldn't throw an immediate fit. I'm so pleased to find that with you it's true.'

She smiled. 'Yes. Nothing you say will upset me.'

The man calling himself George smiled a lot initially, but within a week or two his smile began to falter. Her kindness towards him seemed too much for him because soon his lips began to quiver and then he grabbed his head in his hands. He tried his best to conceal his difficulty with his emotions.

He could not. One day, he became openly anxious and began to hyperventilate. 'Oh, oh, oh,' he groaned, 'this is so embarrassing.'

Alyssa stood up and came to him. She put a hand on his back. 'The breathing, George,' she said. 'Try to slow the breathing. Try to relax. Believe me, everything will be okay.'

'Oh, thank God there is at least one sane person left in the world.' He tried to breathe more normally. 'Sorry. I'm so sorry.'

She gave him a box of tissues.

'Let's focus on how you are feeling, shall we? How has your day been, George?' She kicked off her shoes and made herself comfortable on her counsellor's chair with her legs demurely folded to one side.

'My day?' he said in a strangled voice.

'Yes. How are things with you, George?'

To her surprise, he burst into a flood of tears and sobbed for a full five minutes before he could pull himself together. Luckily, the box of tissues had many tissues. Trish kept it well stocked.

'This is terribly embarrassing,' he said, at last. 'I can't believe this is happening to me. I haven't cried in front of someone since I was a child. I'm so sorry.'

'Don't worry about it,' said Alyssa kindly. 'Just stay with your feelings. What is it that is making you feel so sad?'

With this, the attractive, distinguished-looking middle-aged man with a Jaguar went to pieces. This time, it seemed his sobbing would never end.

In keeping with her training, Alyssa did not move off her armchair. She sat quietly and respectfully and let her client sob his heart out in front of her. It went on for a long time because every time he appeared to be recovering, he went off again in a renewed crying fit.

Finally, he appeared to be feeling better, although his eyes were now bloodshot. When he spoke, it was in a small voice. 'I need help. I don't know what to do. I've tried everything.'

'Help in what way? Tell me a little more.' Alyssa tried to be as gentle as possible.

'I can't.' He looked at the floor.

'Try.'

There was silence.

'Do you think you could be depressed?' asked Alyssa.

'No. It's nothing like that.'

Again silence.

'Have you discussed this with other people? Your wife, for example? I assume you're married. Are you?'

George nodded. His voice came in snatches. 'I love my children so much.'

She did not hurry him.

'I don't think I can go on like I am. That's really why I'm here.'

She reached out and placed a comforting hand on his knee. 'You've come to the right place. There are ways around this, George. I can definitely help you. First, though, you'll need to be completely honest with me. Have you ever tried to harm yourself before? What I mean is, why don't you think you are depressed?'

'No, no, it's not that. Quite the opposite. It's not like that at all. Sure, I did think it was that at first, of course, but it's not that. I did some psychometric tests on myself via the internet, and they were all negative. Highly negative.'

'You tested yourself?'

'Yes. The PHQ-9, the Beck Depression Inventory, that sort of thing. It seemed the logical thing to do. After all, I did first year psychology as part of my law degree . . .' He caught himself at this point. 'That wasn't very clever of me, was it? Now I've gone and given myself away. I wouldn't make a very good criminal, would I?'

'So, you're a lawyer?'

He seemed reluctant to confirm it. 'Sort of. Not really. Mostly, I do civil litigation.'

'And do you enjoy that? It sounds like a horrible job. There seem to be so many unfair outcomes in lawsuits.'

'It's a job,' he explained. 'People tend to get confused, but the legal system has absolutely nothing to do with truth or justice, just law. I've long ago stopped trying to be a hero. There's no such thing as justice, by the way. Not in Astoria, not in the world, not at any time in history.' He seemed quite certain about it.

'No such thing as justice? How depressing. What's the whole purpose of a lawyer's existence, then?'

'You don't want to know.'

Alyssa knew she needed to stop the inappropriate questioning and gain control of her sense of outrage. After all, she knew she hated the law, knew that her judgement was clouded by her past—yet she felt compelled to make one final protest: 'Sorry, but I *do* want to know. What *is* the law there for then, George? I want to know.'

He seemed taken aback. 'Perhaps I shouldn't have said anything.'

'Come on. I want to hear it from a real lawyer.' At that moment, she did not care about professional niceties. Her own experience of the legal system had been awful. She had found it unbridled, bloated with avarice, bottom-feeding off titillations from sex and violence, and infected with ignorance. Too easily did the accused fall prey to the deranged countertransferences of hell-bound prosecutors and judges riddled with immorality and ignorance, especially about sex. Desperate to conceal their own perversions, the self-righteous hypocrites relinquished objectivity and clutched for support at the overheated delusions of the general public, especially regarding female purity. She needed to know which side George was on.

She had become the client and he the therapist. He looked at her with an expression on his face that she had not seen on him before: command. Through her own emotional weakness, she had precipitated some sort of role reversal and made herself vulnerable to injury. From the way he now looked at her, she realised that George had discovered something about her. He now knew that the law had hurt her badly; realised that deep down she feared the law. He could have used her vulnerability against her, yet he was kind with his reply and gracious with his sudden surge of power over her. Whatever else George might turn out to be, he was at least a good person.

'If you must know, Alyssa,' he said gently, 'the law has nothing at all to do with the clients, or the victims, or the accused. Instead, it's all about the legal profession itself. That's all. It's just about us and nobody else—about how much we are paid and about how much our careers are advanced or impeded by any particular verdict. Truth or justice don't come into it at all other than for lip service. I include the police in this too, by the way. It's all part of the same self-serving crap. Lawyers, judges, police—we are all a law unto ourselves with little or no relation to anything else.' He smiled. 'It's what you've always suspected, isn't it? You've seen through all the schmaltzy bullshit.'

She reached out and squeezed his forearm. 'Thank you, George. Thank you for being so honest with me.'

At least, like me, he has no illusions about the true nature of the police.

'That's okay,' he said. 'You can see, though, why I didn't want you to know what I do for a living. It's too distracting.'

He was right, of course. He could hardly make himself emotionally vulnerable to a young woman and be a high-powered professional male at the same time. That was impossible and not fair on him. She had to pull herself together and restore the power dynamic.

George is not a dangerous prick but a troubled man.

She had to forget about her *own* problems and get back to dealing with *his* problems.

3

There was a good practical technique for getting through a client's defences, as set out in Obermaaier's textbook. It involved concentrating on the client's feelings, so Alyssa resorted to it.

'Let's get back to focusing on your feelings, shall we, George? Back to what you were telling me before I so selfishly interrupted you. Can you do that?'

'The feeling that I can't go on as I am?'

'Yes, that.'

'Okay. I'll try.' He began to look sombre as he collected his thoughts. 'I think I can do it. Here goes.' He closed his eyes. 'As I say, I've done tests on myself. The bottom line is I'm not anything at all, not psycho-pathological in any way. Not even slightly.' He opened his eyes again. 'So, what the hell is wrong with me? That's my problem. I'm lost. I don't know where to go from here.'

'Nothing abnormal to find at all? Maybe you haven't been doing the right tests. What about post-traumatic stress disorder? That can be very hard to diagnose.' She knew at least that much about psychometric testing.

'I haven't been in any wars.'

She smiled at his ignorance about things psychological. 'Has your family doctor put you on any sort of medication? And if so, has it helped?'

'I wouldn't trust my family doctor's opinion further than I can throw him, certainly not on anything serious. So, no. No pills. I wouldn't take head pills anyway. I mean, do they even work? Aren't most of them just part of some giant pharma conspiracy to make money?'

'As far as I know, they do work. At least a bit.'

'But once you take them you are not yourself, are you? For that reason alone, I wouldn't even give them to my dog. But maybe that's just me.'

'Has your doctor at least offered to give you some?'

'No. You don't understand. I haven't been to my doctor in twenty years. I'm incredibly healthy. I eat well, I exercise, I don't smoke, I work well, I get on with people. I even still have sex with my wife almost every day.'

It sounded too good to be true. 'Then why do you feel you can't go on?' Alyssa studied the figure on the couch in front of her, who had mysteriously metamorphosed from gracious and commanding lawyer back into crumpled wreck.

No answer.

She allowed the silence to build, but he kept his head down. 'Has something happened recently, George, to give you these bad feelings? What more can you tell me about that?'

'I really don't know.'

'What does your wife think?'

'Nikki? She doesn't know.'

'Nikki doesn't know that you can't go on even though you are having sex with her almost every night?'

'It's not that simple.' George held his head in his hands. 'Oh. Oh. Oh,' he said.

She tried another approach. 'Well then, what *sort* of a lawyer are you? Specifically, besides just being in the field of civil tort.'

'I prefer not to say. I should never have mentioned it the first place.'

'Why ever not?'

'In case it gets out that I'm here.'

'You, more than anybody, should know that these consultations are completely confidential.'

Again, silence. 'There's no such thing as confidential,' he said finally. 'And you, of all people, should know that. I feel I should just walk out and forget this place ever happened.' His voice became choked. 'But I can't, Alyssa.' The sobbing began again. 'I am so fucked.'

The situation became difficult to cope with. Her father used to cry in a similar way when he was drunk, and it used to frighten her when she was a child. Once again, it made her feel helpless. She did her best to put aside the uncomfortable feelings. George's tears were not something she needed to feel apprehensive about, she told herself. Wendy Greene had lectured often enough on the perils of countertransference.

The visit is not about you, *Alyssa.*

The counsellor in her knew that George needed to be encouraged to cry as much as possible in her presence—even though he was a grown man and she a young woman. Tears were an excellent sign. Tears meant that her client was accessing his mental pain—pain that was coming from the child within. A child who was in pain. According to the theories in Obermaaier's textbook, George's tears were a sure sign that he felt safe enough in her company to lower his defences and weaken himself by exposing his childhood inadequacies to her. Through her, he was channelling his childhood mother. She hoped this was because she was ticking all the right emotional boxes and was a good counsellor with rare psychological talents, and not merely because she was a young woman whom he regarded as physically open to him and therefore harmless. Whatever the truth, he clearly felt safe enough with her to confide in her. Perhaps for the first time ever as an adult, George was making contact with previously hidden parts of himself, something she herself enabled in him. Indeed, according to Obermaaier's chapter on "Catharsis", George's tears were the product of emotions discharging in response to re-established linkages to memories of his parents, with this reunification achieved by his Un-conscious resonance with Un-conscious aspects of *her* own Self. Through a process known as "Kairos", or Self-to-Self intimacy, George was able to share his childhood burdens and thereby face them. Indeed, he was displaying greater intimacy with her than he had ever achieved with anyone else in his adult life, including his wife.

Alyssa felt secretly pleased with herself. How easily she extracted tears from the alpha male in her office. Filled with professional pride, she watched as her relationship and interactions with the mysterious man calling himself George Roberts went from strength to strength as her twins *Kairos* and *Catharsis* soared in full flight.

4

They settled on a block booking for George to attend last up every Monday afternoon. Over the subsequent weeks Alyssa did her best to guide his healing process effectively and benevolently.

'These bad feelings that you've been having, George. How often do they make you feel like you might die? Have you been thinking that you might kill yourself?'

He glanced up at her with concern. 'Is it safe to even mention such things?'

'Talking about suicide doesn't make it any more likely to happen. Less likely, in fact.'

Her words seemed to come as a relief to him. 'They do and they don't make me want to die,' he confessed. 'I mean, I won't actually kill myself. Not yet anyway. I'm not ready for that.'

'If you do, how do you think you'll go about it?'

'I won't.' But then he gave the matter serious consideration. 'If I did, it would be away from my work, or my home, or my car I suppose—so as not to contaminate the memories for my family. Perhaps I'd fall off a cliff on a remote nature walk. Something like that. As I say, I wouldn't want to cause any undue negative associations. I'm not selfish. But don't worry, I'm not going to kill myself. Something *inside* me might kill me, though—that's a different story—but not me personally. I have kids.'

'I see,' said Alyssa. 'Something inside you.' She made a three-word note on the blank page of her work tablet: "Not personally suicidal". She took care not to add his name.

George's revelations had a calming effect on him. By the time consultations ended, he always looked brighter.

'By the way, George,' she asked, 'who was it who referred you here in the first place? I've always wondered. And how did you know about the concealed driveway? Don't worry, I won't write the answers down, but they do intrigue me. How did you know that this place exists, that I exist?'

'I have my methods.' He gave her a smile. 'No, it was my wife, actually. She told me all about the cottage. And about you.' He stood up to go.

'Your wife?'

'Yes. Nikki.'

The one he has sex with almost every day.

'Have I met her?'

'No. But someone told her about this place and said you were great.'

'But you don't know who?'

'Nope. And to be honest, it's probably better that way. For me.'

'Right.' It must have been Trish, she decided. After all, it had been Trish who had added George to the list for her first clinic afternoon at the cottage. Or had it been Greta?

When standing, George was well above 180 cm tall and had powerful shoulders. Overall, he was remarkably muscular for a supposed professional man. Despite his age, she knew he would be able to overpower her with relative ease if he felt so inclined. As with client Ben Clayton, she felt grateful for the three emergency buttons concealed within the cottage. That said, so-called Mr George Roberts always remained perfectly well behaved, even when walking close behind her to and from the waiting room.

On this occasion, she walked with him as far as the front door. It was already after five pm and she was keen to get away from work and back home to Cy.

George paused on the front porch and turned to face her. He looked amazingly distinguished with his jacket on. He wanted to thank her. 'You've been wonderful today,' he said graciously. 'For the first time, I feel there may be hope for me after all.'

'I know there is, George.'

'I just hope that in the future you're not going to start telling me what to do or start ordering me around.' He said this as though making a joke.

She knew enough about men of his gravitas to know that such types did not make jokes when it came to being monkeyed about with. His next words confirmed her assessment.

'The thing is, I really can't stand twerps,' he said. 'Especially people who try to tell me what or what not to think.'

He did not seem to consider that what he had just said was impolite, so she took it to mean that he did not consider her to be one of the twerps to whom he was referring. He was starting to remind her of Alan Summerfield. 'I promise I won't do that,' she said to him. 'It's not how we work.' She was referring to psychotherapists.

By now, they were standing on the cottage porch in beautiful late afternoon light, with the peaceful garden all around. He shook her hand, as though in partnership, but also, it seemed, to demonstrate that impressions of his strength were not exaggerated. His hand, though warm and gentle, was all too evidently able to crush hers without even trying. It was like steel.

'I'll be honest with you, Alyssa,' he said quietly, still holding onto her hand. 'You see,' he hesitated, 'the real problem. The real problem with me—it's a sexual thing. I'm afraid I'm going to have to put it bluntly. The thing is, I'm a pervert. A sexual pervert. There, I've said it. It's that bad.'

He must have sensed the sudden tension in her body because he immediately let go of her hand. 'Sorry. I wasn't thinking. Don't worry, I didn't mean to alarm you. I'm perfectly harmless. Honestly.' He seemed embarrassed. 'I'm not normally so gauche.'

Fortunately, female fear did not seem to turn him on.

Alyssa did her best to act professionally. 'I'll take your word on the harmless part, George.' She tried to sound as normal as possible: 'I look forward to our next meeting. Once we work out what's going on, I'll get you to see an expert.'

He gave her a pained look.

'Don't worry, I'll only send you away when you are ready. I'm not qualified to delve into the deeper aspects of sexual psychology, but, until then, just the two of us. Deal?'

'Deal.'

The self-styled and hopefully harmless pervert climbed into his car. As he did so, she discovered two more things about him: firstly, his car was not a Jaguar but a Maserati—she saw the name on its badge—and secondly, hiding under the formal trousers of middle-aged George lay a trim stomach and particularly well-shaped bottom. Physically, he was still desirable. She wondered what sort of pervert he was.

It was impossible to tell.

One thing she did know, though, was that George would have significantly incorrect ideas about what was wrong with himself, despite the doorstep revelation. People had the strangest ideas about sex. So-called sexual perversion was spectacularly wrongly understood by the general public. Anything to do with "abnormal" sex caused immediate muddle-headedness and hysteria, but the sobering truth of the matter was that *all* people were sexual perverts to some degree or other. Wendy Greene had been quite definite about this in her tutorials: sexual quirks and foibles were universally present in every person on the planet. Why? Because such variations were inevitable in view of the unique environmental and constitutional condition present at the time of each person's sexual imprinting in early childhood. Sexual psychological processes became set in stone well before the age of five years and before any possibility of conscious choice. The initial polymorphous perversity present in all humans became fixed early in life at a certain point. After imprinting, sexual wishes could not be altered, although obviously social behaviour still could.

George gave a friendly wave from his car as he slowly headed off down the driveway and back out into the street through the disguised entranceway to the Donald's secret garden. Behind the wheel of his magnificent car, he looked normal enough, but she had no illusions about the possibilities that lay ahead if she continued to see him. Some perverts amounted to *more* than just odd imprinting in an otherwise well-balanced person. And this was especially true of those who sought therapy. In these, the real problem often had little to do with sexual perversion and everything to do with serious mental illness, or even plain simple evil. George could well be extremely dangerous. She would need to discover as soon as possible just where he fitted in.

She did not know much about sexual psychology, but she did at least know what BDSM stood for—assuming that it was relevant. She tried to remember the details: bondage, discipline, domination, submission, sadism, masochism. Which looked more like BDDSSM. She knew a bit about LGBTQ+ too, including the fact that the "I" at the end had been dropped lately because it wasn't psychological like the rest. She tried to picture how all this potentially fitted in with her George. Was he non-LGBTQ+ but *with* a BDSM bent, was he indeed LGBTQ+ but *without* a BDSM flavouring to his sexuality, was he both—or was he something else entirely: an emotionally deranged person?

The field of sexual psychology seemed suddenly extremely confusing despite the lectures she had attended. She would not be the first therapist to have little real grasp of the subject—that much at least she did realise. Yet, with someone as physically powerful as George, a mistake on her part could well prove fatal.

After the handshake and the wave goodbye, she turned and headed back for the safety of the cottage interior. She felt anxious now, half-expecting to be grabbed from behind. Then something made her stop just before the doorway: another realisation. Not only was Georges' car a Maserati, but the small sticker fixed to the inside of its back window carried a message—one that she had not truly taken in before. Like the car's badge, she had seen the little advertising sticker low on the back window often enough but not realised what she was seeing. The words flooded into her mind now in a torrent: *Berkowitz Berkowitz Rockport.*

She remained frozen to the spot. The name was known to everyone in Hubron. It was the name of the city's premier law firm. And it was on the back window of George's car. Oh yes, it was. Berkowitz Berkowitz Rockport: her so-called George Roberts, lawyer, and sexual pervert, was none other than Gilbert Rockport, the multimillionaire owner of the firm. It had to be so. The coincidence in the initials was too great.

'Holy shit!'

It had to be him: the founding partner of the most famous law firm in the city. The great silk himself, Queen's Counsel Rockport. It was he who was coming to her for help.

Oh, God.

It did not make any sense or feel real. He could so easily go to the greatest experts in the country. Why come to her, a young woman newly qualified?

What am I missing here?

The anxiety she was feeling became tinged with fear.

Seeing Gilbert Rockport as a client had the potential to end up being professional suicide. His law firm had a dreadful reputation for ruthlessness and had ruined many lives. One wrong step and she would end up at the bottom of the Yarradonga river—and not necessarily only figuratively. She had far too little experience as a counsellor to be suited to someone like Gilbert Rockport. Not to mention the fact that she knew little about sexual psychology—and had personal psychological issues when it came to the law.

Wendy Greene would advise her to run.

She needed to run.

Unsure what to do next, she spoke to the little blue flowers crowding around the front porch of the cottage: 'Could one of you dears please tell me what is going on here? What is this man doing at my clinic?'

The little blue flowers did not reply because they could not talk. In fact, they did not even know what sort of flower they were. But they could respond. So, they did.

They laughed their heads off.

CHAPTER NINE

1

ALYSSA RECEIVED AN INVITATION to lunch from staff psychiatrist Dr Jocelyn Goronowski. The socially challenged doctor of dubious sexuality invited her to meet up at a nearby shopping precinct on the coming Saturday. Alyssa agreed, but more out of politeness than genuine interest, seeing that agreement was probably expected from someone like her. A boring lunch with a more senior member of staff was a chore to be endured with good grace when at a new place of employment. The other reason why she agreed was because the suggested venue was quite near to her flat anyway. The outing would not require much effort and if handled well would be the last time she would need to oblige the doctor socially. She had no interest in having Dr Goronowski as a friend; in fact, she had no interest whatsoever in having a female friend of any sort. In her experience, relating to a woman was more trouble than it was worth. With Jocelyn Goronowski it was likely to be the same old story, though perhaps with a new twist.

Everything about the psychiatrist was odd, including the way she made the invitation. The doctor came and sat down beside her during a coffee break in the staff room—a bit like the spider in the nursery rhyme—grabbed her by the shoulder, pulled her close, and began to whisper in her ear. She seemed excited because her breath was hot.

'Hey, Alyssa,' she said, 'I've booked a table for us. Saturday. At Little Critters. For a bite of lunch. That sort of thing. Know it? Want to come? Say yes.'

Alyssa knew of the restaurant. Little Critters was a trendy brasserie on Eastwick Street, within walking distance of her flat. She had been there before with Cy and his friend Brian. 'On Saturday, you say?'

'Yes. Do your shopping beforehand if you need to. Just think what a wonderful chat we'll be able to have. We can talk the whole afternoon away. It will be so nice to converse with someone who is not a *complete* idiot.'

Alyssa decided to take the ambiguous statement as a compliment. 'What about Cy?'

'Of course. He's invited too. Don't forget to bring your Cy along. I insist. I'd love to meet him.'

Despite the inclusion of Cy, Alyssa hesitated to accept. Socialising with someone of Jocelyn's reported tastes seemed a pointless waste of time.

Jocelyn, however, forced the issue. 'Don't worry, I'll pay. Think of it as a welcoming gift from me.'

There was no escape.

That Saturday, at around one pm, the social meetup with psychiatrist Dr Jocelyn Goronowski went ahead as planned.

Little Critters—a recycled warehouse—was busy, as expected, but Jocelyn was already there and had secured a good spot near the front windows. She handed Alyssa a menu as she arrived at the table. 'Hi. Read that,' she said. 'Where's Cy?'

Alyssa sat down opposite her. 'Cy's still at work, but don't worry, he's coming later.'

'Brilliant.'

The sight of Jocelyn sitting completely crooked in her chair—looking either disabled or oblivious to human physiology—caused a resurfacing of the same sense of disquiet she experienced at the welcoming party at Alan Summerfield's beachside apartment all those weeks earlier.

Why does this woman disturb me?

There was something psychological going on that she did not understand.

Warily, she continued to observe her dark-haired hostess over the top of her menu card. She had no intention of encouraging Jocelyn if it turned out that she had sexual designs on her. One thing she was not was someone with "tendencies" waiting to be discovered.

No way, Jose.

Meanwhile, the enigmatic doctor behaved as restlessly as ever, squirming constantly and intermittently throwing one arm over the back of her chair and then the other. Perhaps she was deliberately trying to project an image of carefree youthful relaxation, but if so, the efforts were futile. The flopping about lacked the required flexibility and sleekness of youth. She was in her mid-thirties at least and looked it too. Her body had thickened and there was a spinsterish air about her. Lounging at ridiculous angles in chairs was not going to fool anyone.

While they waited to be served by the waiter, Jocelyn seemed positively friendly towards her. But why the friendliness, Alyssa wondered. What possible reason could Jocelyn have for wanting her as a friend? There was an obvious age difference. Besides, Jocelyn was a psychiatrist and on a different social plane to her. In her considerable experience of such people at hospitals, medical specialists were generally an obnoxious lot when it came to relating to lesser mortals. They preferred to exist on their own rarefied plane and not waste their valuable time. Any potential friendship with Jocelyn would be an unbalanced one. Unless of course it was just about sex. This still seemed the most likely explanation for the lunch invitation. Why else would Jocelyn—or anyone—want to be with her?

The woman opposite was scaring her slightly. It had something to do with her eyes. Jocelyn Goronowski had uncanny eyes; eyes that seemed able to see through things: people, walls—her. It was as though Jocelyn *knew* things about her that she could not possibly know, things to do with her past. Secrets. Every time Jocelyn looked at her with those eyes, the gaze somehow touched a chord deeper than nascent friendship. There was a power there; something visceral was at work between them. And, most disturbing of all, it was *not* just to do with sex. Jocelyn's gaze had a way of awakening a past long buried. Was it the dark hair? Her mother had had dark hair. Was this how her mother's hair had been? Maybe, but the resonance was much richer than that. Darker. The dead mother she had never known was re-appearing in a quite frightening way.

How bizarre.

Alyssa tried to resist Jocelyn's mesmerising power, but it proved impossible. After twenty futile minutes of trying to fight it, she gave in. She had to accept the truth: yes, she did like Jocelyn. Even though the psychiatrist constantly caused previously unknown domains of her mind to present themselves for examination, she seemed nice enough and seemed to have a good heart. She also clearly had emotional problems and needed help.

Which seemed a good enough reason to persevere with her for a while.

Meanwhile, Jocelyn was bravely attempting to make small talk, which obviously she found difficult. 'I come here quite often over the weekends,' she said. 'I like the atmosphere.'

'It's a nice place,' Alyssa agreed politely. 'Especially in this heat. Nice and cool.' It was. The old warehouse had thick walls and a high ceiling with fans. Their table was also near a large open window overlooking the street, so they had an additional breeze at times. 'I reckon it's boiling hot out there in the sun by now.' Summer was certainly at its peak. 'The weather seems straight in off the desert today.'

'It's probably something to do with global warming,' said Jocelyn. 'Me, I don't mind the sun. Provided I can avoid the radiation. I don't like radiation.'

'Me neither.'

Her new friend came across as clean and fresh in the breeze, which surprised Alyssa—for some reason she had expected something different. She hoped she herself came across equally well in the heat. She had, at least, been sensible enough to dress appropriately. She had on a pair of light cotton shorts—ultra-blue in colour—and a lightweight pastel-yellow T-shirt complemented by a silver bracelet and matching silver stud earrings. The silver suited the blonde of her hair and set off the burgundy of her nails.

Jocelyn, by contrast, did not seem to care too much about her appearance. Even though pleasantly fragrant, she looked shabby. She had on a nondescript and obviously well-used grey dress and flat black shoes. Her hair, thick and black, stuck out in places, while jewellery was absent, and her fingernails were plain and soberly clipped. Her legs were untanned, and her upper arms, where they emerged from her dress, had a slight wobble.

Old lady's fat arms.

Alyssa felt sorry for her. Jocelyn needed to take more care of herself. Then she wondered why she even cared how Jocelyn looked or that she was getting too fat. It was none of her business, after all.

'There is too much on this menu,' said Jocelyn, frowning at it. 'I always find it hard to decide in this place.'

'Fortunately, there's no rush.'

'No.'

2

Cy was still not there. Supposedly, he was still busy, having earlier that morning taken his usual tram to the bookshop where he worked, a store which by coincidence was located quite nearby. She had come to the shopping strip later, on foot. Cy only worked two days a week, but it always included Saturday mornings. The last she had heard from him by text was that he was definitely not going to make it to *Critters* for lunch but would get there in time for coffee.

'I hope I do get to meet your Cy,' said Jocelyn, who continued to seem ill at ease. 'It would be nice if we could all become friends, don't you think? I don't have a lot of that, you know. Friends. I seem to struggle with that.'

The confession felt like too much information. They hardly knew each other, so Alyssa found it difficult to think of an appropriate reply. 'It's not easy, I know,' she said, finally.

'I always seem to say the wrong thing.'

'People can be sensitive.'

'I suppose.'

Indeed, they could, and if anyone knew how to wind them up Jocelyn Goronowski sure did. Curiously, though, she did not seem to suffer from any shortage of company from the male psychiatrists at work.

'No friends.' It was Jocelyn again, in a morbid tone.

It was hard to know if she was being serious. 'I assume you are talking about close friends?' Alyssa asked the question as kindly as possible, as if in a counselling session.

'I suppose that. Real friends. Cuddly. I don't seem to have those. I think it's the warmth thing that I miss. I don't like hard. I like cuddly.'

'I see.'

'And do you have many friends, Alyssa?'

She felt herself going on the defensive. 'Friends?'

'Yes, those.'

'Friend friends?'

'Those. Those non-sexual beings that one reads about.'

She realised that Jocelyn was toying with her. Jocelyn had seen right through her from the very beginning. Now, like a ruthless emotional assassin, she had placed her lance right on her weak spot: she had no friends.

I am the one with no friends. I have no friends.

With unfailing skill, the psychiatrist opposite had identified her vulnerability: no friends, only lovers, and those only male. When it came to true friends, female friends, she had no one, not even one. She had not had a single female friend since she was a child, and Jocelyn was forcing her to confront this truth. As a woman, she was utterly alone. It was something she had never truly realised or faced up to before. Ever since things had gone so horribly wrong with her as a child, she had not been able to feel close to women. She did not trust herself with them. Women were not safe with her.

There were dangers.

'I do have a few friends,' she lied. 'But not around here. Mostly in Ocean View. To be honest, it doesn't bother me much. I'm pretty happy with my own company. And there's Cy, of course. He's great. And he has heaps of friends. So, it all works out for the best.'

Jocelyn smiled. 'That is such a nice story.'

A waiter came and hovered yet again, so finally they ordered their lunch, having at last given up on Cy: a glass of Hillocks River Riesling for both, a gourmet teriyaki chicken salad for Alyssa, and an exotic deluxe kangaroo meat pie with steamed rice and greens of Arcadia for Jocelyn.

'No fries with your pie?' asked the waiter, a student, confused by Jocelyn's order, which was not strictly in accordance with the menu.

'No fries with my pie.'

That was the lunch order dealt with. Lunch for two.

Alyssa was disappointed with Cy's behaviour. Even though he had told her before leaving home that he was going to turn up only at the end of the lunch, a part of her had hoped he would change his mind. 'Cy often gets stuck at work having to sort things out,' she said, yet again, to Jocelyn. She hated making excuses for Cy. It seemed wrong of him not to cooperate with the genuine efforts of others to befriend them as a couple.

'Won't he be hungry?'

'He'll grab something to eat at work—a slice of toast or something—so don't worry. I'm confident he'll get here in time for coffee.' Listening to herself talk, she sounded just like the liar she was. She was no good at lying. Cy had never had any intention of eating lunch with them. His views on medical specialists remained unyielding: they were smug bastards best avoided. No doubt he was concerned he might lose his temper in such company. The fact that Jocelyn Goronowski was a woman seemed to have made no difference. "Female medical specialists are the worst", he had yelled that morning as he rushed out for his tram. "I have no interest in fat-bummed semi-dykes. They are just sociopathic money-grabbing total shitholes, the whole bloody lot of them!"

He was wrong about Jocelyn, at least, who appeared the very opposite of a smug criminal. Cy's real problem was that he feared people with money because they caused him to feel inadequate. Somehow, he had managed to convince himself that financially well-off people thought him their inferior, not merely monetarily but also intellectually and morally—in all dimensions of human existence, in fact. He was therefore extremely wary of people like Jocelyn, which now seemed a pity.

'You know, I'm quite excited at the prospect of meeting an author,' said Jocelyn between sips of wine. 'A real one, I mean. I don't think I've ever met a real one. I've met authors of scientific papers, of course, but that's not the same. They are just plain boring.'

'Cy is a bit different from a scientist. His books are entirely creative fiction.'

'That must be so liberating for the mind.'

'Yes and no. There isn't much money in it. Almost everyone seems to be into it these days.'

When their food arrived, Alyssa discovered that she had forgotten to specify no salad dressing.

She tried to scrape off the sticky sugary substance with little success.

'Oh, well,' smiled Jocelyn, 'I don't suppose a little so-called vinaigrette will hurt.'

'Probably not.' Jocelyn seemed to be finding her amusing. Alyssa observed, too, that her new-found friend's wine glass was already empty and that she was already ordering more from the waiter.

'You too? More *Hillocks*, Alyssa?'

She declined politely. 'Still happy with this one.'

Jocelyn's drinking at Alan Summerfield's Santos Beach apartment had clearly not been a one-off occurrence. Jocelyn had many problems, and one of them was called alcohol.

3

As they ate lunch without Cy, Jocelyn revealed her own attempts at novel writing. 'I suppose a lot of people try to write something,' she theorised. 'We all have a story to tell, of course we do. Yet, most of us can't write for toffee, so that's the big problem, isn't it? If I *could* write, I'd have the perfect book: "The Horrible Goings-on in Fuckwit Land". That's essentially what Shakespeare is on about, did you know that? Just because people decide not to "realise" that their motives are bad does *not* mean that they are not bad people or that they are not evil. Far from it. That's the essence of his message. Lying to oneself is no excuse.'

'Right.'

Jocelyn paused to eat a stalk of steamed broccolini with her fingers. 'The Bard did his best. However, it's too late for me to try stopping evil. No career in literature for me, sadly. To begin with, I know nothing about grammar. Besides, given what I *do* know about people, if I were able to write a proper book it would be just too scary. They say one always writes more than one knows, so that would be the problem, wouldn't it? Imagine what horrors might come out.' Jocelyn paused once again to dig into her salad with her fingers. She extracted a carrot stick and proceeded to chew on it rapidly, like a rabbit. 'I did once write—at school—when I was young and gullible, but at least I had the sense to get over myself early on. I have absolutely no talent.'

'Don't say that. What did you write about?'

'Nothing in the end, like most people. My book started out as some outlandish story about an abused child, but I never got anywhere with it. It was too mixed up.' Jocelyn stared across the table absent-mindedly. 'You know,' she said, 'the strange thing is I now treat people who were abused as kids—and so do you. There must be some unconscious process going on there. With both of us.'

Little prickles of ice began to creep down Alyssa's spine. Why had Jocelyn mentioned child abuse? Was it just coincidence or did she know more? What *did* she know?

How could she know?

Jocelyn was at it again, staring directly into her eyes, playing psychiatrist, fishing for something. Wary of her trickery, Alyssa avoided eye contact and replied as nonchalantly as possible to the speculations about her childhood. 'No doubt our childhood is significant in both our cases. It always is in all people. The Un-conscious is always at work.'

'No doubt about that, then.'

Alyssa resisted revealing anything about her own childhood and reflected Jocelyn's speculations straight back at her: 'If you don't mind me asking, Jocelyn, what do you think it was in your life that made you want to write about an abused child? Or is that too personal a question?'

Jocelyn speared a piece of pie with a single violent action of her fork and placed it in her mouth. After more strange chewing, she spoke with her mouth half-full, not a pretty sight. 'Sorry. Hungry. I suppose the truth is I did have an abusive childhood. We both did, sadly.'

'We both?'

'Yes, my brother Ricky and I. Mostly him. I managed to cope, but he didn't—even though he was older. Or maybe because he was older. Don't look so worried, I'm fine now. Ricky didn't make it, though. He had some bad experiences. Nobody saw it for what it was at the time, but it turned out to be, you know, schizophrenia.'

'Oh,' said Alyssa. 'I never knew. I'm sorry to hear it.'

'Yes. Sad business that. Full-blown ultimately. I was the only one who could get through to him in the end. The world became so traumatic to him that all he could do was escape into his own head. I should have done more. Done things differently. Poor Ricky.'

'What does he do these days?'

'Oh, nothing. He's dead. He's long been dead.' She drew a hand across her throat, presumably to indicate suicide. 'Like most of them. There's just me now.' She carried on eating as though everything she had just said was a perfectly everyday occurrence.

'Oh. I am sorry.'

A dead brother.

'It's okay. Understandably, though, I don't like to talk about it.'

'Of course.'

Jocelyn changed the subject. 'Enough of tragedies. Tell me more about this Cy of yours. What does he write? Thrillers?'

'Uh-uh.' Alyssa stalled. She was still trying to process Jocelyn's roundabout revelation that she too had had an abusive childhood. Not only that, but a dead brother. Not a dead mother, granted, but a dead brother. The news intrigued her. Another coincidence? Who exactly was the woman across the table, and what was she up to?

4

Jocelyn persisted with her line of questioning about Cy. 'Well, then, if not thrillers, what *does* he write?'

Alyssa tried to avoid the probing. 'Nothing special. I think it's just called e-book fiction. I don't think he's into genres, but then again, I don't know a whole lot about what he does.'

'Well, what about titles? Are there any of his titles you could give me? Maybe I know them.'

Alyssa felt herself blushing. 'It's not what you think.'

'What do you mean?'

'It's a bit embarrassing, actually.'

'There's no such thing as embarrassing. You of all people should know that. Is it right wing politics? Anti-gay stuff? Come on. You can tell me.'

'No, nothing like that. Mostly, he writes erotic fiction.' The embarrassment she felt was not from that but from the fact that he was a failure as a writer and sold very few books.

Jocelyn continued to misinterpret her blushes: 'You're joking!' she gasped in feigned horror, causing people to glance in their direction. Then she almost fell off her chair laughing as Alyssa's face reddened even further. 'This is absolutely fantastic news. And I'm just so amused at how embarrassed this is making you.'

It's you who is embarrassing.

Jocelyn tried to behave more seriously. 'These books of Cy's, are they pulp romances like *Mills and Boon*? Or are they—how shall I put it—the real deal? I've read some of the great French books. Calaferte, Bataille, Anais Nin, that sort of stuff, erotic literature. Is that more Cy's style?'

Alyssa had no idea who the people mentioned by Jocelyn were. 'I don't know what you've been reading, Jocelyn, but one thing, at least, I do know: Cy's books are not *Mills and Boon*. In fact, if you must know, they are not even *Shades of Grey*. Cy is way beyond any of that. He says he doesn't believe in fairy tales and refuses to write them. I, on the other hand, am quite partial to a good *Mills and Boon*.'

Jocelyn stared into her eyes again. 'You like fairy tales?'

Alyssa looked away.

'Sex embarrasses you, doesn't it, Alyssa?'

'You really like to push people's buttons, don't you? No, I don't find sex embarrassing, but I do find tactlessness hard to cope with. I come from a small country town. Cy's writing is too blunt for my taste. His books are too truthful—I think that's their problem. He doesn't pretend enough. People don't like to face reality, so he doesn't sell very well.'

'I get it. Too much in-your-face stuff and not enough neo-con baloney.' Jocelyn closed her eyes and tilted her head back. 'I'm trying to imagine it: no fake sex scenes, just real. Full in the face. Hooh boy.'

Alyssa tried not to feel alarmed by her perceptiveness. 'People are such hypocrites when it comes to sex.'

Jocelyn smiled. 'Of course, Alyssa, of course they are. It's because they feel so incredibly ashamed of their behaviour. You of all people should know this. Haven't you seen it in your work? The blatant dishonesty in all matters related to sex?'

'I suppose so.' She was being polite. She did not think her clients were dishonest, rather that they were self-centred and often ignorant.

'Believe me, people lie about themselves all the time, and never more than about sex. It seems to me that nobody has told them that there is no such thing as normal sex, so they go around terrified they will be found out for the inadequate deviants they always are. I never get an honest answer. What about you?'

'Probably people aren't honest with me about that either. You sound pretty authoritative on the subject by the way. Do you practice as a sexologist too?'

'Good heavens, no. It's just that my clients are frustrating the hell out of me. If anyone admits to even *having* sex, it's always whiter than snow. I can't understand where all the nastiness has gone. Why then, do they even bother?'

It was difficult to understand what Jocelyn was getting at. 'Are you referring to the actual sex act, or what exactly?'

Jocelyn nodded. 'That, yes. And everything else. There's a lot more that goes on. What has interested me lately—professionally—is the final mental release just prior to orgasm. I like to call it the psychology of the orgasm—or at least the female orgasm. It's what I'm currently researching for a paper because I need to present something at the upcoming conference. The more I investigate, the more I'm finding that it's not very nice at all, mental process wise. Big surprise: there's evidently meant to be lots of anger and aggression involved in sex. But you would know all this anyway.'

'I would?'

'Stop it. I hate it when psychotherapists get coy with me. Why is everyone in denial? The psychology of the orgasm clearly provides a highway into a client's Self psychology, so don't try to tell me that you people aren't using it. The rest of us need to stop ignoring this important mental process too. We need to clarify. Why continue to lie?'

'You want people to tell you the thoughts they have just before they climax?'

'Yes, Alyssa, yes. *That* of which we may not speak. That is what I want to hear. That which comes into the mind in the last moments, that part of us that we conceal from all others. The cruel thoughts; the perverse fantasies; the violence. The shocking truth. I have been astounded by what I have uncovered so far. All the violence and the lies, all the goings-on in the head. In the head.' She poked at her own head with a finger. 'Bizarrely, it seems sex is always had only *here*—talking psychologically again—no matter what is going on in a practical sense.'

'You can't be serious.'

'I am. It's all to do with this movie that apparently plays in each person's head in the final moments before the Big O. It's a scenario that's always uniquely the same in any individual. That's my big discovery. In each person, a specific fantasy is required to achieve release. It's the key to it, the essential component. And obviously, therefore, we have a potentially powerful analytic tool at our disposal.'

That of which we may not speak.

Alyssa smiled at the sight of Jocelyn Goronowski intensely waving her arms around and expounding ideas. A conversation between a psychiatrist and a psychodynamic therapist was always going to be a little unusual, but Jocelyn Goronowski certainly knew how to push things to the limit.

5

Jocelyn seemed to have no sense of social propriety, and to make it worse her voice continued to be a little too loud for a public restaurant. 'Secret movies in the head aside,' she said, 'what depresses me the most in my research into the psychology of the Big O is that it turns out it's a far from loving place. Did you know that, Alyssa? That the orgasm is *anti*social? Mentally, I'm talking about. Always mentally.'

'I'm hardly in a position to comment, Jocelyn. I'm no expert on sex. But what I do know is that professionally you are into incredibly difficult terrain. I hope you realise that you won't be able to state any of your assertions at any scientific meeting without being attacked by virtually everyone. People have strong beliefs when it comes to this sort of thing because it's so personally threatening. And besides, perhaps I need to point out that as a rule people do *not* usually have sex in accordance with their fantasies, as you are proposing. Generally, they stick to just the few generally accepted ways. And they usually do so lovingly. So, that's your entire theory blown away.'

She looked unperturbed. 'Not so. It's easy-peasy to get around people like you who try to deny the obvious. You see, Alyssa, when it comes to the psychology of things, sex always happens via the mechanism of proxy. Real-world sexual activity is just the stage upon which inner fantasy is enacted. Surely, given your training, you realise at least that much? Why are you finding this so hard to grasp? The key to orgasm lies in a subject's ability to sufficiently actualise his or her particular fantasy by tying it to a sufficient approximation in a real-world proxy situation. Proxy *helps* make the psychological fantasy *real*. Obviously, the mind can proceed regardless of reality—it's powerful enough—but some form of real-world

152

approximation does help produce a more satisfying experience.'

Alyssa frowned with concentration as she tried to work out what Jocelyn meant. 'You're proposing that a form of reverse mental activity is taking place, aren't you? Like when just thinking about lifting a weight makes a muscle grow stronger in the real world? The weight is in your head, but it affects your body. In the same way, you say, when someone has sex with another person, then what he or she is *thinking* at that time about foundational aspects of their own Self affects their body.'

'Exactly.'

'So, the lover in the bed with you in the real word is just a scene setter and secondary phenomenon. Is that what you mean?

'Clever girl.'

'Mm. It sounds too bleak to me.' She considered the implications of Jocelyn's theory while Jocelyn waited patiently for the cogs churning in her brain to click into place. If what Jocelyn was saying was true, then any sex act with another person always had *two* components, each fundamentally different. Firstly, there was the in-your-head part that related to those aspects of the psychologically primitive relationship with your parents that had been incorporated into your early Self and transformed unrecognisably into conscious fantasies, and secondly, there was a mature component that consisted of real interpersonal sex at an adult level. The first component of any real sex act with another person was full of perversions and anger and aggression, while the second component of a real sex act with another person was considerate and socially acceptable. However, at a deep level, the former always drove the latter. And orgasm was a deep level event.

'Exactly,' said Jocelyn. 'A bit dim, but got it now? Deep-seated. That is my exact point. The Big O is not a polite adult event. It isn't. So, why all the pretence about it?' Jocelyn seemed outraged. 'The primitive drives the mature and it's time we faced up to it. Therefore, this is going to be the punch line for my proposed conference paper i.e., the fact that only the primitive can climax. This *has* to be the truth of the matter. Why? Because climaxing is mammalian. It's almost vegetative. Got the point? Anyway, it's what I'm going to be proposing in my research paper. One has to get primitive to orgasm.'

'This is heavy stuff, Jocelyn. Too heavy for most.'

'Tell me I'm right.'

She had no idea whether Jocelyn was correct or not. Studying the psychology of climaxing seemed a bizarre thing to be doing. 'No point looking to me for validation,' she said. 'I'm no expert.' She did know, though, that while the universal occurrence of sexual fantasies was well-known to all properly educated persons in the field of sexual psychology, the same did not apply to the general public. Jocelyn was going to need to answer certain inevitable questions correctly every time she raised her theory in a public forum if she wanted to avoid getting herself into trouble. She pointed out the problem to her: 'In your proposed paper, Jocelyn, are you going to be dealing with fantasy with an "f" or phantasy with a "ph"?' The concept and the distinction were straight out of Freud, even though Alyssa knew that, officially, Freud was supposed to be obsolete.

Jocelyn appeared close to laughing at her. 'With an *f* of course, what do you think? Phantasy with a *ph* is a childhood thing and always stays unconscious, whereas fantasy with an *f* is what I will be talking about: fantasies transformed into consciousness. I'm sticking only to the transformed sort. No children here. Give me a break.'

'I'm relieved to hear it because I'd say that with this sort of stuff you need to take care that the uneducated don't mistake the normal unconscious link between adult sexuality and childhood as something to do with paedophilia.'

'I'm not a twit, Alyssa, so I'm fully aware of the dangers from uneducated windbags when it comes to matters of sex. But thanks for the warning. While I may know, and you may know, that people always have sex with unresolved aspects of their own formative years, try explaining that to the lay public.'

Jocelyn was blundering into wild territory now. There was little consensus on these matters among the experts. 'I still think you'll need to slow down with your theories, Jocelyn. I'm not sure you have things quite correct. These days you have to be extra careful when it comes to saying anything in the public domain about sex.'

'I know, don't tell me. It's the old "it doesn't apply to me, only to evil perverts" cop out of the masses, isn't it? Though often equally guilty, members of the general public blithely deny or project anything to do with themselves when it comes to sex. So, yes, I *am* careful. Saying "childhood" and "sex" in the same sentence is like yelling *witch* in the sixteenth century. I never do anything that foolish. I know the dangers. I only ever talk about this stuff to people who I know aren't shitheads.'

It was probably a compliment. 'I'm pleased you are being careful.'

'Relax, Alyssa. I'm staying well away from the unconscious in my investigations. I'll leave that sort of stuff to you. What I'm doing is handing out questionnaires and confining myself to the conscious private thoughts that adults have when they are about to climax. Forget phantasies and childhood. I'm only interested in present-day reality, especially the non-loving sentiments.'

'Questionnaires requesting deepest and most hidden thoughts? You don't do *easy* in your research projects, do you?'

'Apparently not—as people keep telling me.'

6

It seemed impossible to stop Jocelyn from talking about sex. Perhaps it was the only thing she was capable of talking about. Or maybe her idiotic choice of research project was making her anxious. Whatever the case, she had become very intense.

'You see, Alyssa,' she confided in a hoarse whisper, 'I want to be part of the cure. There's this pandemic of low libido to be dealt with and I'm convinced that most of the difficulties relate to an inability of us women to be honest about what we truly desire. I'm not yet sure, though, that I'm on the right track.'

'Steady on. What "low libido pandemic", exactly, are we talking about here?'

'Everyone's, of course. The global one. The whole of Western civilisation. That's why I need to pick your brains. Am I barking up the wrong tree? Give me your honest opinion.'

'You must be joking.'

'All this trouble people are having: could it be largely psychological? Have we failed to grasp that sex has very little to do with the partner in our bed and a whole lot more to do with connecting to unresolved aspects of our Self? In other words, should we be looking more at the *roots* of the conscious Self? Is *knowing* one's frustrations the real key to satisfaction? What do you think?'

'Steady on, Jocelyn. Give a girl time to think.'

Jocelyn, however, continued to rattle on at breakneck speed: 'The orgasm is a brain switch. It is, isn't it? It's the mechanism for returning the Self, however briefly, to default mode—which is to say to the state in which it was in at the dawn of consciousness—thereby enabling the brain to identify poorly purposed circuits for subsequent pruning, not so?'

Jocelyn was out of control. 'What? Slow down. Say that again.'

'Oh please. It's just a theory. Obviously, you don't agree, and I yak too much. You're supposed to be the expert. Why don't *you* tell me what it all means? The in-your-head stuff is what I want more information about. Tell me where I'm going wrong. With your knowledge of psychology and someone like Cy for a partner, you would have to be some sort of authority.'

'I think we need to pause here for some deep breaths, Jocelyn. For starters, you know I'm not a psychoanalyst, right? Also, Cy and I don't discuss his writing very much.' She gave a wry smile. 'Besides, if you really want to know, I'm no hot shot in the sex department. I'm probably the last person you should look to for advice.'

'Nonsense. Just tell me about threatening thoughts during sex. I still have some confusion there—you know, professional uncertainty. Throw me a bone.'

Jocelyn was pushing her luck.

Alyssa checked her phone. 'Maybe later, Jocelyn. I'll give the matter some thought. I just need to point out that Cy will be here any minute.'

Saved by the bell.

.... **7** ....

Cy had left the bookstore and was on his way.

'Quick,' said Jocelyn, suddenly anxious, 'tell me something about him. Quick, before he gets here. Something about his truthful erotic works, perhaps.' She emphasised "truthful". 'I want to read some of them. It would be really interesting to me.'

Alyssa tried not to blush. Somehow, Jocelyn easily provoked the response in her. 'His books have absolutely nothing to do with me,' she said as firmly as she could. 'Zero, zilch.'

'If you say so.'

'I do. And they're not about him either. He's nothing like the characters in his books. I have no idea where the stuff comes from that he writes about. What you do need to be aware of, though, is that a lot of it is disturbing. I honestly don't think you'd benefit from reading any of it. In fact, I think you'll be disappointed—although obviously I'd never tell him any of this.'

'I have an open mind, you know that.'

'Me too, but it's not that.' She became quiet. 'It's his actual writing that's the problem. I don't know much about grammar and style and those sorts of things, but even I can see that his books aren't very good. I'd hate you to be disappointed.' She knew Jocelyn was expecting far too much from Cy. Cy was not an intellectual writer—his work was amateurish in many ways. 'He's no Baudelaire.' She had no idea who Baudelaire was other than a Frenchman, but it was something that Cy often said about himself.

I'm no Baudelaire.

And he wasn't. Cy was merely a Beauchamp. Perhaps he had been right all along to be wary of lunch with the likes of Jocelyn.

'I'm getting it now,' said Jocelyn, gazing intently across the table. 'A protective sort. That's what you are. That's really good in a couple.'

For once, she held Jocelyn's gaze and to her amazement she saw something completely unexpected: tenderness escaping across Jocelyn's face as she said the words "protective sort". It came as a mere flicker, an unguarded moment, and the deep emotion was gone in a second, but it had been enough to lay her bare. In that privileged glimpse, Alyssa saw something primal, something that Jocelyn was doing her best to hide: her true feelings about her. Feelings of kindness and love. Jocelyn was close to being overcome with tenderness. Even more intriguingly, the feelings did not seem merely sexual.

They were somehow maternal.

The revelation caused Alyssa to catch her breath.

Who is *this woman?*

As if to prove her insight correct, Jocelyn kindly changed the conversation away from the painful subject of Cy's poor writing. 'Have you two been together long?' she asked instead.

Alyssa was not used to being treated gently by a woman. Wary of a trap, she took time to answer the question. 'Almost a year,' she said finally. 'It's still more boyfriend girlfriend. We're not committed.' She wondered why she felt compelled to say such a thing. She was actually very happy with Cy.

'I suppose time is always the best guide.'

'Yes,' she said, and then kept silent. Until she knew more about Jocelyn it would be better not to reveal too much about herself. Her instincts were warning her that, beneath the frenetic exterior, Jocelyn might in fact be mentally unwell—not just in a minor way, but seriously so.

8

There was an awkward silence, during which Jocelyn appeared anxious.

To help the conversation along, Alyssa asked Jocelyn a question of her own, one completely unrelated to sex: 'How was your food?'

Jocelyn brightened. 'The kangaroo pie? Pretty damn good. I often have it here. You should try it one day.'

'It's too exotic for me.' She almost said "unnatural" but managed to stay polite. 'I'm a bit like my dad. I'm very fussy about what I eat.'

Her new friend ceased the nervous fiddling with her napkin. 'Fussy good or fussy bad?' It was a professional question, and she was the expert on eating disorders for the Donald Clinic.

Alyssa laughed aloud. 'No,' she said. 'I definitely don't need your services. I eat like a horse.'

'With no . . .?' Jocelyn stuck a finger down her own throat and made alarming gargling noises.

'Stop it, Jocelyn!' No, she did not have bulimia.

Jocelyn was back in her element. 'So, your appetites are functioning well, it seems. I'm really pleased to hear that. How, then, do you manage to keep that figure of yours?'

'What figure?'

Jocelyn reached over the table and stuck a finger into Alyssa's solar plexus. 'That one, wasp waist. And as for those boobs, are they even real—or are you going to tell me it's just a fancy bra?'

'What?'

Jocelyn smiled slyly. 'What's your secret? All the guys back at the clinic are practically beside themselves lusting over you. Even old Barnes is making a fool of himself. Same with Alan. I've even caught Simon staring at you, and he's as gay as they come. You are incredibly attractive, Alyssa.' Jocelyn fluttered her eyelids comically. 'Please don't tell me you hadn't noticed.'

'Not really.' She did not know how else to respond to lesbian admiration. 'I haven't had any sort of plastic surgery if that's what you mean.' While it was true that most men—and some women, apparently— appeared interested in having sex with her, she did not think of herself as truly desirable. She wondered what the superficial admirers would think if they knew her mental history or saw the scar that ran down her middle from her solar plexus to her pubic bone or felt the metal plates holding her head together. She tried to change the subject. 'Is Dr Bristow really gay?'

'His name is Simon, Alyssa. Simple Simon. And yes, he is. And don't change the subject. Were you born like you are?'

From anyone else, the questions would have been completely inappropriate, but Alyssa knew Jocelyn meant well. Her constant struggle to contain her direct and abrupt manner was almost amusing. She humoured her: 'I was on the beach a lot growing up and did a lot of swimming. I'm sure that helped.'

'Tell me more. I also swam as child yet look at me now.' She poked a finger into the side of her bottom, making it sink in rather theatrically. 'Look at that. Got any tips?'

'You're not fat. Especially not for . . .' Alyssa bit her tongue.

'Especially not for what? My age?'

'I don't mean to be unkind, but yes. And your job. I know how busy you doctors are.'

'I'm only thirty-six for God's sake. I've tried the whole yoga-Pilates thing, you know, the atheist type. Maybe I should go back to that.'

'It wouldn't hurt. I go to the gym a lot. I find exercise helps. Also, I try to avoid too many carbs in my diet. I stick mostly to proteins and vegies.'

'What a commendable modern youth.'

'I'm not that young, you know that. I've just turned twenty-six. That's not young anymore.'

Jocelyn reached across the table and clasped the back of her hand. 'You know, you really do crack me up.' She kept Alyssa's hand in her grasp, pretending to notice her painted fingernails for the first time. 'Wow. You should take up erotic modelling on the side.'

'What!'

'No doubt you are a bit shy by nature, so you could just stick to closed-leg work.'

Jocelyn was being ridiculous. 'Not a good idea.'

'Mm, I suppose not.'

The hand on her hand lingered a little too long. Alyssa flicked off the physical contact by moving to deal with the stray leaves from her salad.

Jocelyn was not to be deterred. 'Your teeth, then. That killer top row when you smile. How do you do that? It's so gut wrenching to us mere mortals, so superior. How, how, how?'

'Stop it, Jocelyn! You are going to make me cross.'

The reprimand stopped the fooling around instantly and seemed to make Jocelyn lose confidence. She stopped talking and began to study the menu. The recent outburst of familiarity notwithstanding, she was ill at ease and Alyssa saw it clearly. As if to disguise what seemed like a crippling case of social anxiety, her new friend busied herself with summoning a waiter. She ordered a lemon tart dessert and another glass of wine, her third or fourth, then turned to Alyssa: 'More wine? Dessert?'

'No more wine thanks, Jocelyn, but I wouldn't mind a fresh fruit salad if that's okay with you. They're a bit expensive, but the mango and passionfruit one looks delicious. Or I could just wait for coffee when Cy comes.'

'Nonsense.' She nodded at the waiter. 'We'll have a fruit salad too. Now, Alyssa, what about the wine? Want to change your mind on that? This Hillocks River Riesling will go perfectly with your fruit salad.'

'I'm not a big drinker.'

'Really? How very odd.' She seemed puzzled.

Finally, the waiter departed, and Jocelyn continued to make attempts at small talk. 'Now tell me, Alyssa,' she said, 'did you buy anything at the shops this morning?' Her question sounded artificial, as though from a "how to have a conversation" textbook.

Alyssa smiled at her again, this time trying to conceal her teeth so as not to appear too condescending. 'No, I haven't bought a thing. I'm still watching my pennies. Boring, I know.'

Her amusement was lost on Jocelyn. 'Understand. We've all been there, Alyssa. Good news, though, is that I'm hearing good reports about your work. I have no doubt that you'll do well in the future from a financial point of view.'

'It's kind of you to say that.' Alyssa got up and went to a nearby counter to get herself an extra napkin for her dessert, during which she was conscious of Jocelyn watching her from behind. She handed a spare napkin to her lunch companion.

'Thanks. Nice pants, by the way. Am I allowed to say that?'

'They are a bit tight I know.'

Jocelyn smiled at her. 'I meant what I said. I like them. And not just because of that divine shade of blue. I'm serious about what I said earlier. You have a body to die for.'

'You are being too kind to me today.'

'That's not kind, it's true. I wish I had the motivation to get to the gym like you. I'd so love to get my own bum back.'

'Don't be so hard on yourself. You of all people should know that a person's shape has very little to do with their physical attractiveness.'

'That's the whole bimbo versus feminist thing, isn't it? I know I should just get over myself.'

'It's your value as a person that counts.'

'Right. Although, what does that mean?' She scratched her head. 'Body, tick, yes, we all have that—but is it only a decoy meant for the shorter term? Is there something that counts more when it comes to sex? The brain, perhaps? Is that what we really want to fuck—not the body but the brain? You're the expert, Alyssa. Is that it? Brain fucks brain. Is that tantric sex or something?'

Alyssa laughed.

9

Alyssa was forced to discuss tantric sex with Jocelyn for a while, but fortunately dessert arrived without too much delay.

'Looks fantastic,' she exclaimed.

Her mango was fresh and perfect, and her passionfruit natural and unsweetened.

'Yes, it's to die for,' said Jocelyn. 'I've had it before. But now, for me it's just the wine. This Hillock's River is just great. I'm so happy. This is such a lovely day, isn't it? Just a pity it's so hot.'

'Hot as the devil's bottom.'

'The devil's bottom?' Jocelyn raised an eyebrow.

Alyssa blushed. 'It's something my dad always used to say. Sorry.'

Jocelyn smiled at her strangely and asked her nothing about her father. It was as if she knew that anything about her father was off limits. Too painful.

It's like she knows.

'We're so glad you've joined the Donald.'

'Not Greta.'

'Yes, except, it seems, Greta. I still can't believe that she slipped you those curve balls on your first day. Everyone's heard about it, of course. I think it was despicable of her.'

'What do you mean?'

'Stop that. You know what I mean.'

'Not really.' Her smile was sweet, but she knew that her top teeth were showing and that she was lying. She was being exactly the kind of dishonest person that Jocelyn despised. Nevertheless, it felt safer to be misleading. She had no idea where Jocelyn's allegiances lay within the greater scheme of things and had no intention of jeopardising her employment. Of course, she knew what Jocelyn meant. She knew what Greta McCreedy had done.

Greta had personally seen to it that the initial referrals to the cottage clinic were as unsuitable as possible for a new graduate. In what had clearly been a fit of malicious spite, she had sent a dangerous madman, an incurable middle-aged disaster, and a sexual pervert to her as her first clients. It had been a blatant attempt at intimidation—no doubt in the hope that she would flee—but it had been a miscalculation. Greta had picked the wrong person to mess with, someone with no fear of women, especially not jealous old women.

Loser.

Greta may have spat the dummy, but in return Greta had bitten the dust. She had made sure of that. She had pretended to not even notice the woman's vicious attack on her and instead acted as though Greta's best efforts to hurt her had felt no more taxing than a pin prick.

Jocelyn was talking: 'Greta's been struggling with too much work for months, but I think she definitely went overboard with you. I heard she even sent you a nutcase who insisted on being anonymous. There's no excuse for toxic dumping. I wouldn't do that to a colleague.'

'That's good of you, Jocelyn. Luckily, though, I found that the clients Greta thought were toxic were actually quite nice—even down to the anonymous caller.'

'Now that is something that I really don't understand. How can any therapist say such a thing? How is it possible to find any client *nice?*' Jocelyn frowned. 'I don't get it. And I don't understand the shape of your ass either.'

Alyssa laughed again, politely, and tried to downplay Jocelyn's comment. 'My ass is just my ass.' She wondered if Jocelyn disapproved. Her shorts were an extremely close fit. It was the fashion, though, and besides, Jocelyn was hardly one to opine about the shape of people's bottoms. She was never going to be able to go out in a pair of shorts herself. Alyssa attempted to keep the conversation above the waist: 'I try to see clients in the best possible light. It's what we counsellors are supposed to do. I'm sure you psychiatrists do the same.'

'Oh please, spare me the crap.'

'Don't get me wrong. When it comes to non-clients, I'm no saint—in fact I know I'm often quite harsh—but I do think I'm different with clients. I'm much better with people if I feel they need my help.'

Jocelyn smiled and began to look like an indulgent cat playing with a mouse. 'What you mean is that provided you are with someone who is damaged you feel more at home. No doubt you see where that leads?'

To the fact that then I too must be damaged.

'Maybe. But I doubt it's that simple.'

'No point being defensive with a psychiatrist, Alyssa. Also, there's another component to your confession that you may not yet have realised. When it comes to the company of "normal" people, you feel ill at ease. Not so?'

'Mm. Not exactly, Jocelyn. You keep adding two plus two and coming up with five. It doesn't quite work like that.'

'Really. I thought you believed in psychotherapy.'

'And I thought you believed psychotherapy is junk.'

'Well, okay, I do. But not in your case. With you, you *need* to be a psychotherapist. It's seeping out of your pores. It's what is holding you together. This is so fantastic. You have this wonderfully contrived Self, and it fascinates me. I need to know all about it. About what's underneath.'

'Steady on, Jocelyn.' She was starting to sound intoxicated.

'No, I'm serious. Personally, as you have discerned, I'm well off the rails—so, I need to learn how you stay on track. You see, I've got big problems. So far, it's only the drinking that's been helping.' She raised her wine glass and gave a forlorn look. 'Just between me and you, of course.'

'Of course.' Alyssa half-expected a hiccup. It was far too much information. 'Still, if you want my opinion, Jocelyn, I'd say you are pretty together as it is. Take my word on that.' Her top teeth were showing again. 'And you are very astute as well, so you'll work out what to do. And as for me, whatever the underlying structure of my mind may be, I've always felt better through helping people. I have this need to help people. I don't think that's a bad thing.'

'Okay, then, if you say so.'

It was becoming easier to understand why Jocelyn caused potential friends to flee. There was a way to rattle her cage, however—and potentially help her. 'Without getting too personal, Jocelyn, are you seeing anyone?'

'You've got me there. I suppose I have no choice but to answer, don't I? Sorry about that hand thing, by the way. I didn't mean to embarrass you. Do I have a partner? Unfortunately, the answer is pretty pathetic. Yes and no. Actually, it's no. Nothing permanent. It's hard, you know . . . getting what you want. There is so much bad stuff out there. Despite what you may have been told, I'm not a complete dyke. Bi would be a better word. I can do the shoes, bag, and jewels thing, but that hasn't seemed to work either.'

'I never . . .'

'I'm adaptable, as they say. Sometimes I envy people like you and Cy. A good penis can be kind of nice, I suppose. Sometimes I think I'm slowly going crazy.'

Alyssa felt herself blushing again, partly out of regret at having upset her new friend and partly out of imagining having lesbian sex with her. 'I'm sorry.' She could not tell if Jocelyn was being serious or not and did not know whether to feel concerned or not. Her new friend had had far, far too much to drink. 'Have you not thought of settling down?'

'I wouldn't last a week with one person.'

You mean a person wouldn't last a week with you.

She never said it. This was not a therapy session. This was a free lunch.

CHAPTER TEN

1

'HELLO YOU TWO.' IT was Cy, late but still in time for a coffee.

'Cy!'

He sauntered around the table and gave Alyssa a long kiss. Then he pulled up a chair and sat down, pointing the forefinger of both his hands at Jocelyn like revolver barrels in acknowledgement of her.

He looked different to how he had looked when he left home that morning, causing Alyssa to look at him questioningly. He still had the languid, longish hair, the moustache, and the earring she did not approve of, but on his feet were a pair of comical pirate boots that looked like something from a bankrupt theatre company.

Comic-book man appeared to be in an upbeat mood. 'Like my new shoes? Sorry I'm a bit late.'

'Fascinating.' She wondered if he was determined to embarrass her in front of Jocelyn. She introduced Cy and her new friend to each other.

'Hi, Cy,' said Jocelyn, suddenly come over all coy.

'Hi. Pleased to meet you.' Cy informed her that he knew she was a medical specialist doctor psychiatrist sort of person. He said something else too: 'I never realised you were so young—or so attractive.'

Jocelyn took the compliment in her stride. 'Aw, thanks. Your name intrigues me, Cy. Is it short for something?'

'Cyrus. It's a stand in for my rather boring real name, Simon.'

'He writes under an assumed name,' explained Alyssa.

'I'm Cyrus Beauchamp when I write. No doubt Alyssa has been telling you stories about me.' He glanced accusingly at her.

'Actually, Alyssa has told me very little about you so far. Just enough to tantalise me, Cyrus. How exciting it all seems. Tell me more. I find published authors of fiction really interesting.'

'You do?'

Alyssa said nothing. She knew Jocelyn had never even met a fiction author before.

'What woman wouldn't find you interesting? Provided you are not a children's author. That would be a bit deflating. You're not one of those, are you?'

Jocelyn was playing poor Cy like a violin. It even looked like she was fluttering her eyelids at him. Alyssa had to resist a strong urge to kick the woman's shin under the table.

Cy brightened up visibly under the positive comments. 'Strictly adult,' he said. 'With a capital A. I find everything else complete crap.'

'You *know* what sort of a writer he is,' said Alyssa.

Jocelyn ignored her. 'Why, Cy,' she breathed, 'you are a man after my own heart. How has Alyssa managed to keep you hidden for so long?'

There appeared to be a bizarre spell developing between the two of them. Alyssa tried to break it. 'Where did you get your boots?' she asked. The unasked question was: where did you get the money for them?

'Great aren't they.' He talked to her as though she were his mother. 'They are second-hand. I got them for ten bucks at the junk shop. The original owner is probably dead.'

Not to be outdone in the juvenile imagination stakes, Jocelyn leant down and had a good look at them. 'The original owner was probably killed, I'd say.' She and Cy then burst into chortles of self-satisfied laughter for reasons only the two of them understood.

It wasn't funny.

'You know, you are not nearly as stuffy as I thought,' said Cy to Jocelyn when the giggling finally subsided.

Alyssa beckoned to the waiter, who had been hovering after the arrival of Cy. 'Do you want to order the coffees?' she asked Jocelyn.

'What? Yes, okay,' said Jocelyn. She consulted her two guests: 'What will it be?' It turned out to be one long macchiato for Cy, a small single-shot skinny latte for Alyssa, and a large regular cappuccino for Jocelyn.

Cy and Jocelyn continued their animated chatting and Alyssa was surprised to see how well they got on considering Cy's views on doctors. She felt more than a little annoyed. The meetup had been intended mainly for her, and Cy was not supposed to be stealing the show. Perhaps the fact that he and Jocelyn were about the same age explained some of it, but the rest of it looked like plain bad manners.

'I'm hopeless at writing fiction,' gushed Jocelyn. 'Scientific papers no problem, but I don't seem to have the restraint required for art. At school, they told me that my essays were too direct. Too blunt. Apparently, that is a big problem in fiction writing. Bluntness. Am I right, Cy?'

'You amaze me with your grasp of the central issue,' said Cy. 'Tactlessness is the problem of fiction exactly. One can't simply state something and expect people to swallow it. Being people, they will always refuse. No, you need to persuade them to swallow. Convince them. Good fiction is a bit like getting medicine into a domestic animal. It's all sleight of hand. Artful. What incredible insight you have, Dr Jocelyn. Instantly, you've arrived at the essence of it. Spooky, isn't it, Alyssa?'

She had hoped he was joking, but, clearly, he was not. It seemed best to say nothing.

Jocelyn talked instead. 'This adult erotic fiction that you write, Cy. Isn't it awfully hard to avoid calling a spade a spade? I know you aren't supposed to, but I've never been able to work out why. I mean, half the world has a penis. Why the pretence?'

'Or a vagina,' said Cy. 'You can't mention that either. People prefer to believe that such things don't exist, or, if they do, that they are really special.'

'I think it's the *yuk* factor,' said Alyssa, determined to participate in the conversation. 'And because of children.' It seemed obvious to her.

'So, what's yuk about a vagina?' asked Jocelyn.

'Of course, I'm not saying that,' said Alyssa. 'It's just that people are easily disgusted by unwanted intimacy—it's part of human nature . . . the sense of disgust.'

'Really? You know just as well as I do that *disgust* is only operative after early childhood and is nothing but a learnt behaviour, not so? Therefore, so what.'

'Adults are still disgusted. Besides, disgust is neurodevelopmental, not just psychological.'

'Disgust is not *real*, Alyssa. It's regularly overcome by both lust and true intimacy, so how can it be? It's just hysteria from half-wits too brain-dead to realise they are just pre-programmed robots. It's just people unable to face reality. It's just complete hypocrisy.'

Alyssa was determined not to be fobbed off so lightly, especially in front of Cy. 'I know what you are saying, Jocelyn, but I think I have a valid point. I think it's normal to feel disgust at intimacy one doesn't personally desire. It's hard wired into our brains. Getting up close and personal with someone you find distasteful *is* somehow disgusting. In fiction stories there *are* some things people just don't want to be forced to imagine. Not everyone is mentally toughened. Not everyone has an interest in some random old guy's ass, for example.'

'Good heavens,' breathed Jocelyn, 'what language.' She fanned herself mockingly.

'And don't forget the danger of children being exposed to this stuff,' said Alyssa, driving her point home.

'Don't!' said Jocelyn, becoming suddenly animated. 'Don't even start.' She began to make inverted comma signs on each side of her head with her fingers, as if to indicate that her brain was about to explode. 'I refuse to participate in *that* mass hysteria. Children *aren't* stupid, Alyssa, and not all children are children. And teenagers *aren't* asexual.'

'Hello. How about somebody asking *me* about erotic fiction writing?' suggested Cy diplomatically.

Jocelyn turned to him for support. 'Your Alyssa here thinks teenagers are children. Tell her that she is wrong.' Her voice developed a pleading tone. 'Tell her that they aren't.'

'I have to agree with Dr Jocelyn,' said Cy. 'I hate this nonsense that's been foisted on civilisation by bureaucrats.'

Jocelyn appeared elated. 'See. I'm right. Authority figures just pretend to have teenagers' interests at heart. In truth, they are mostly nothing but ignorant fascists.'

'And there are a lot of them around,' said Cy, egging her on.

'I have had them up to here!' Jocelyn ran a hand under her chin. 'These fuckwits bleat about family values and at the same time go around shagging one another and jerking off everywhere.' She looked to the ceiling for salvation while a large vein jumped in her neck. The wine was really talking now. 'There is too much hypocrisy in the world!' With that, she slammed her empty glass on the table.

2

People were looking in their direction.

'Calm down!' Alyssa hissed at Jocelyn.

Cy was no help. 'Dr Jocelyn has a point,' he said instead. 'Besides, another good example of the two-facedness of society is the vilification of pornography.'

Alyssa groaned. All the obsessing about sex at her table was starting to get very tedious.

Cy, however, seemed to be in his element with a drunk Jocelyn. 'Don't you just love the clowns they trot out on the TV? The ones that condemn porn and pronounce it to be *illicit*?'

'Yes, yes,' agreed Jocelyn enthusiastically, 'as though humanity's interest in sex could be abolished by the command of cranks too ignorant to understand even the words coming out of their own mouth. Sex is a physical need, like the need to breathe oxygen, so it can't be abolished, yet always we have some or other opinionated dog of a person demanding just that—without having the slightest clue about biology. Worst of all, they seem to have this bizarre narcissistic certainty that whatever *they* believe is true for everyone.'

'Exactly,' said Cy. 'And have you noticed how they always assume that the porn women have been forced into it and that it's all about the abuse of women?'

'That's their imbecility perfectly illustrated,' agreed Jocelyn. 'Sometimes I think the biggest offenders against female sexual enjoyment are other women, not men.' She turned to Alyssa. 'Why is there this bizarre view that we women have no independent sexuality—that everything sexual is male? I object! If you ask me, I think the sour pusses are angry because they can't get what they want.'

'And what is that?' asked Alyssa.

'It's pretty obvious, isn't it? Control of sex. They want to be in charge, but their personal limitations and failures cause their aspirations to collapse, so they try to spoil the party for everyone else. No porn. Simple.'

'That is so brilliant,' said Cy.

'I think you are both missing the point about pornography,' said Alyssa. 'The concern is not to do with who controls sexual excitement, it's to do with who the people in the images are. Did she—or he—have free agency? That is the question. Not to mention the ages of everyone. It's all to do with agency.'

'Agency? I'd say *that* was bleeding obvious,' said Jocelyn.

'Only to you.'

Cy cleared his throat. 'Let's assume free agency, shall we? This is Astoria after all, not Russia. As far as I'm concerned, opponents of porn aren't in the least bit concerned about agency because if they were, they'd go away. In Astoria it's perfectly clear to anyone prepared to be objective that with few exceptions the people who are there are there because they want to be there.'

'Agreed,' said Jocelyn. 'And I applaud those women because I believe they are making a statement. They are saying that they understand how sex works, which is that a man who desires sex with a woman needs to feel unthreatened to perform—which has been obvious since the dawn of time. It goes without saying, of course, that at all times we women still have total female governance of all proceedings.' She gave a toothy smile.

Alyssa had a disturbing suspicion that Jocelyn was trying to give her personal advice about how to have sex. Psychiatrist or no psychiatrist, her intoxicated lesbian new friend was digging a hole for herself. 'And how did you suddenly become an expert on men?' she asked, trying not to sound too sarcastic.

'I'm just dealing with the facts. Aren't I, Cy?'

Cy grinned sheepishly. 'I say nothing.'

There seemed no point in trying to have a sensible conversation with the two of them, so Alyssa kept silent.

Have these two just accused me of being inadequate in bed?

'You've suddenly gone very deep,' said Cy. He appeared concerned that he might have upset her.

'I'm fine.'

Fortunately, the coffee arrived.

3

Jocelyn wanted to know more about Cy's books. 'You must be very brave, Cy, to want to battle constantly against the ignorance of the average citizen.'

The unlikely pair were getting along a little too well. *What a bitch,* thought Alyssa.

Cy was in his element. She could almost see him puffing up. He was starting to resemble his delusional fantasy: great author of global significance.

Sipping on his coffee, he proceeded with one of his favourite pastimes: making derogatory pronouncements about readers who avoided his books. 'What I have come to realise,' he said, 'is that in the life of the public, reason plays no part at all. Instead, for the average Joe or Jill Soap, everything in the world outside is merely symbolic of some or other unresolved aspect of his or her own personal life.'

Jocelyn, who was listening with interest, had something to add: 'Implying that apart from being completely ignorant and irrational, the public is also totally immature and completely self-centred. Is that what you are saying?'

'Top of the class. Sadly, however, there's more. The average reader not only has no idea what's going on—especially when it comes to sex—but is also extremely defensive and aggressive when it comes to preserving the sexual imprint that occurred in his or her own early life, no matter how bizarre. These specific frissons are, of course, of supreme value to the individual but by no means are they the same as society's proclaimed universal gold standard. Unfortunately, it transpires that the greater one's ignorance, the greater is one's fear that there does indeed exist such a gold standard—the implication being that one has fallen mortifyingly short of it. Which brings us neatly to the central problem of erotic fiction: people have no idea that there is no such thing as "normal" sex and therefore are riddled with personal sexual guilt. The result, generally speaking, is that the public desperately *pretends* to be sexually "normal". People are terrified by the discovery that their own personal sexuality does not match up to "expectation", so they remain resolutely tight lipped on the subject. Offer one of my books to persons such as these, and they run. Quite literally. A mile is nothing. Most people simply don't want to know.'

'So perceptive,' enthused Jocelyn. She turned to Alyssa. 'See. There isn't a person alive who wouldn't be regarded as something of a pervert by somebody else. It's because of the inevitable oral, anal, or phallic hangovers intertwined within everyone's sexuality.'

Alyssa ignored her new friend's attempt to say something psychoanalytic.

'Exactly,' confirmed Cy. 'Everyone's sexuality is flavoured by some or other primordial throwback, yet everyone denies that this is so in their own case. Which leads us to the lamentable situation of total sexual hypocrisy. People will only engage publicly with sexual matters in accordance with the commonly received idealised nonsense of the day. Untrue nonsense is safe to parade openly precisely because it is not true, so nobody has any emotional investment in it. The phenomenon is well depicted in current mainstream TV or movie sex scenes, where the sex that is presented threatens no one because we all know it has nothing to do with reality—except of course those with minimal or no sexual experience, who don't know.'

Jocelyn began to giggle. 'Like left-wing university feminists?'

Cy glanced uncertainly at her. 'I was thinking more of teenagers, but sure. The point I'm trying to make is that confusion about sex is very widespread in society. The only thing about it that the average limp-wristed loser feels safe reading in public is fictional rubbish. Works of genuine erotic truth, like the ones I write, are too stressful. Thought-police vigilantes invariably get hold of a copy and when they do, they complain to the authorities without fail.'

'As though one can object to reality,' said Jocelyn, sounding oracular. 'Now, why don't such people surprise me? The public space is full to overflowing with these sadistic cowards. Any unsuspecting innocent person who lets his or her sexual defences down gets immediately destroyed. Don't believe me, anyone? Try publishing a *truthful* article about your own sex life and then standing for election to parliament and see how far you get.'

'Brilliantly put,' said Cy. 'That's exactly what I've found with the responses to my writing: the sniggering, the abusing, the demeaning, the mocking. Actually, it's universal whenever sex is written about, and it's disgraceful. You get it in even the largest publishing houses.'

'The response to the sexual activities of others is always hostile and juvenile in the hypocritical and the ignorant,' announced Jocelyn. 'That part of humanity is incurable.' Her words were perceptibly slurred but despite the large amount of alcohol she had taken in, she remained determined to continue to demonstrate the size of her brain. 'Unfortunately, the problem can't be fixed because it relates to unresolved childhood fears and rages caused by inadequate mothers and inadequate fathers. It's the "pathetic person" all over again. Which is the central problem of the world. The pathetic person. No cure.' She emphasised it with a burp.

Alyssa was beginning to find Jocelyn's inebriation annoying. 'Perhaps you could be more specific, Jocelyn?'

Or stop talking so much.

Jocelyn looked into her eyes. 'Oh, stop fussing. These problems are endemic in the chattering classes. These people have only a rudimentary grip on things. There is this mental fog, and out of it there emerges for only a short time a mindless, cruel lust. Then it soon tapers off inwardly and then, . . . and then it turns into whining self-mortification and dependency. But fortunately, most seem content to seethe with resentment and live shit lives. Biologically speaking, though, it's not appropriate for them to continue having sex. Like dead flowers, that soon goes. Puff.'

Jocelyn was seriously drunk and had now become seriously annoying. 'How can you say such things?' demanded Alyssa. 'What evidence have you got that your so-called chattering class is anything like you say?' She had done two years of university sociology—one of them while going insane, granted—and heard nothing of the sort.

'Because it's true. You can see it in their intolerant attitudes.' She wagged a finger. Everything had become a joke.

Cy was frowning. 'Good point,' he said, trying to be diplomatic. 'Daily, I get attacked by belligerent ignoramuses braying from wildernesses of confusion.'

The fact that he was attacked daily was an exaggeration. Alyssa knew he received only occasional emails.

'I get you, honestly I do,' enthused Jocelyn. 'If we have eroticism, then immediately we have hypocrisy, betrayal, and deception. It's all in Anais Nin.'

'Quite so.' Cy had read her *Delta of Venus* twice. 'It's my aim to fight sexual hypocrisy too, through my work. Always, I strive to encapsulate the spiteful sexual dumbass so that I can expose such people for the stain on the soul of humanity that they are. The creature I have uncovered so far is a disgusting one. It squats in the filth of its own hideous mind and asserts, nevertheless, that anything to do with sex is—wait for it—*filth*. The anti-sex espouser possesses no moral validity precisely because what underpins his or her morality is nothing more than the obscenity of his or her own mind.'

'I see these people every day,' confessed Jocelyn. 'All furtive, they are. And forcing us to accept the arrogance of their smugness.'

Alyssa helped her speak more sense: 'Surely you mean the arrogance of their *ignorance*. People are clueless about the unconscious motivations behind their sexual morality. People have no idea that sexually we are all in the same boat.'

'Oh, whatever floats your boat.'

Cy intervened. 'All I know is that whenever I try to write sense for the appreciative few, hysteria soon breaks out in the ranks of the vindictive and the creepy.'

'That's sex for you,' said Jocelyn. 'Creepy, creepy.'

More coffee was ordered, and Jocelyn went for an emergency toilet break.

4

Jocelyn took her time in the restroom.

'It's getting late,' said Alyssa to Cy as they waited. 'We should be on our way.'

'What's the rush?' he asked. 'It's a nice place and Jocelyn is paying.'

'She's drunk.'

'No, she's not. She's just feeling loose. She likes our company.'

Jocelyn returned from the ladies' room looking brighter. She smiled. 'Did you two lovebirds miss me?'

'We sure did,' said Cy.

The new coffees arrived, as well as more lemon tart.

'How's your media profile, Cy?' asked Jocelyn in her best conversational voice.

Alyssa suspected she had consulted a topic list on her phone while throwing up in the toilet.

'To be honest, I'm a bit of a phobic,' confessed Cy.

'Since when?' asked Alyssa. It was the first she had heard of this.

'I am. Social media has become just one more struggle with morons. I can't be bothered with it anymore. The advent of total digital surveillance has returned the world to the claustrophobic hypocrisy of small-village life centuries ago. Once again, permitted thought is being dragged down to the idiot level of the *official authorities*.'

'Oh, the rotten hopelessness of the human condition,' said Jocelyn.

'Oh, please,' said Alyssa.

'The fake pages,' said Cy, 'have become a place where you can only say what you are *supposed* to think and not what you *do* think.' He proceeded once again to give a speech: 'Do I know this place? Oh, yes. Nothing but crapulous people, sanitised pseudo-reality, and meaningless lies. Add pot calls the kettle black, and *voila*! you have the automated fabrication of scapegoats. Oh, how it crackles with jealousy, and resentment, and anger, and cruelty, and treachery, and . . .' He consulted his fingers, counting them. 'Hubris, and backwardness, and greed, and stupidity. . .' Words failed him further. 'Beware the new fake morality, that's what I say.'

'As in: do not submit to the jackboot of misguided societal gatekeepers?'

'Precisely that, Dr Jocelyn. Do not get caught in that fatal pincer grip. Do not suffer the moral judgement of others according to the rules of fake morality. Humankind has become trapped in this unforgiving illogic and finds itself disintegrating.'

Jocelyn's face lit up. 'All because of the fatal pincers of illogic, you say? How horrid. How many of these are there, Cy, how many fatal pincers? This must be Hegelian, surely.' She turned to Alyssa and began to imitate a crocodile's mouth with her hand. 'Look, here's one coming for you: Positive Psychology and . . . and . . . the Prosperity Heresy. Snap! That's yet another fatal combination—and *you* done for.'

'What!'

Cy tried to intervene: 'The prosperity heresy is from the Bible isn't it, so yes, just bullshit.'

'Pfft.' Jocelyn seemed no longer capable of holding a serious conversation.

'If you want my opinion,' said Alyssa, 'I think the social media platforms are a good thing. They've brought things out into the open.

For the first time in history, we can see that we are all essentially the same. Surely that's not a bad thing.'

'I think you are missing the whole point of why we need to be concerned,' said Jocelyn.

Cy tried to explain: 'The point is that the average inhabitant of the public space is too much of an idiot to know that they are an idiot. Or to put it even more simply, the public space is not without danger for the *insouciant*.'

At Cy's ongoing use of French words, Jocelyn became completely carried away: 'What he really means is that all that is left for the masses is to be abused or go mad. This fake morality thing is just terrible.' She turned to Alyssa and whispered, 'I will look after you, my darling.'

Alyssa did her best to ignore her.

Cy, meanwhile, continued to look extremely grave as he sipped the last of his coffee. 'Humanity's inability to face truth is truly tragic. I wrote a magazine piece on this topic once. People have many flaws, but some seemed to me particularly egregious at the time. What were they again, the main flaws? Spinelessness—that was one of them for sure. Ignorance too, of course. Then there was Self-centredness, Dishonesty, Superstition.' As he enumerated mankind's failings, he bent the fingers of his left hand. A change to the right produced Treachery and Herding. 'You know, as in cattle.' The eighth and final flaw proved more difficult to recall. 'I think it must have been Scapegoating. That rhymes with *scum*, doesn't it?' It did not, but it had to do. 'Not a pretty picture.'

'The Eight Flaws of Man,' cooed Jocelyn. 'How profound.'

Alyssa suppressed a yawn. As far as she was concerned, the real problem with people was that they were unconsciously driven. It was this that turned them into the irrational, self-centred, generally cruel creatures they undoubtedly were, a race of mental toddlers frustratingly unable to come to terms with their own cosmic insignificance, their biological inadequacies, or their fake mortality—or so according to Obermaaier. She had heard Cy's opinion on the problems of the world a thousand times, but sadly he had not yet worked out that nobody was particularly interested in hearing his opinion. Except, it seemed, Jocelyn Goronowski.

'You should write a whole book about it,' she said.

'No point. Publishers wouldn't touch it.'

'Oh, the dangerous, addled shithouse that is the commercial mind! Tell me, Cy, I'm dying to know, is there a *reason* why popular writing needs to be aimed at half-wits? I mean, *why* is this necessary?'

Jocelyn was sounding increasingly ridiculous.

Cy straightened his back and proceeded to deliver his well-practiced *coup de grace*. 'The secret to popular writing,' he said, 'is this: if you want to sell books, disregard worth, abandon reason, and pander to the societal delusion of the day. Even better, label your work non-fiction even if it's ninety-eight per cent total rubbish because then publishers will be more likely to be interested.'

'It might at least make you some money,' murmured Alyssa, rather unkindly.

Cy ignored her. 'If I wanted to write a best seller, I'd have to abandon my principles. Heaven knows, I've been tempted to go down that road often enough. But no, for the sake of my own sanity and self-respect, I have stuck to my principles. Truthful erotic fiction is where I need to be as an authentic artist.'

'Good man,' said Jocelyn. 'We need more people like you, given the nonsense that some people are writing in the field of erotica today. The tales have become absurd. All links between the sex act and anger and aggression are feverishly denied and heavily censored.' She was back on her hobby horse. 'People are such cowards. From what I see, the atmosphere of denial has become so toxic that people are no longer allowed to state the obvious when it comes to sex. Some writers, I know, have tried to correct the mythology, but even those with good intentions seem to have chickened out.'

'If it's any consolation, almost *all* writers seem unreadable to me when it comes to sex,' declared Cy. 'For me, it's due to their inherent unresolved sexism, one way or the other. In the case of the male writers, the Joe Ordinaries, they constantly fail to realise that the most fundamental thing about sex is that women also have a sex life. Sex is not something confined to men. The clowns still haven't worked out that the whole of sex hinges on what the *other* party will *permit*. Worse, they simply don't seem to understand that doing actual harm to a sex partner is criminal and nauseating, no matter how pseudo-psychologically it is "explained", or how artistically it is embellished. Even with sadomasochism, whatever happens must be mutually agreed and never truly harmful.'

'Agreed. It must be in the head,' explained Jocelyn. 'It's pretending. Violations and orgasms are in the *head*.'

'You don't say,' said Alyssa.

The two of them ignored her.

5

Jocelyn had Cy completely under her control with her pretence of deferring to him on things psychological. 'By violations we mean surrender, and loss of dignity, and coercion, and brutality, and that sort of thing, not so, Cy?'

'Whatever the participants desire,' declared Cy.

Jocelyn swivelled her gaze towards Alyssa. 'Relax. Pretend violation is okay; it's only actual violation that's not okay. It works the same for everyone, male or female.'

'Exactly,' said Cy. 'As Jocelyn says, it's all to do with what's going on in the head. It's *this* that the hack writer about "truthful" sex constantly fails to understand. They have no idea how sex works, so they depict "real" scenes involving coercive males, which ends up doing nothing but nauseate everyone except the disturbed. Some normal readers, hopefully, assume right from the start that the author is intending a nonsensical fantasy, but for most that's not the case and the depictions are taken seriously. The result is that sex becomes confusing to everybody.'

Jocelyn had something to say. 'People fail to understand that unless humankind is to revert to savagery and barbarism, *true* sexual desire can in our day only be carried out in the mind.'

Irritated by the newly loquacious psychiatrist's fixation on such ideas—and by her assumed expertise in such matters—Alyssa had a question for her: 'What if people decide to behave like barbarians anyway, Jocelyn? Because I'm sure that many do.'

'Then they need to be locked up,' said Cy.

Jocelyn smiled. 'No wonder women are not happy with their men or their sex lives. Men simply are not the way they are being portrayed in the books, are they? For starters, I doubt that in real life men give a damn

179

whether their woman has an orgasm or not. Nobody cares. Okay, maybe a few pretend to care, but deep down they don't. Someone needs to tell us ladies this. Let us know that we need to look after ourselves. Hullo.' She waved a hand in front of Alyssa's face.

Cy gave a polite cough. 'I know what you mean Dr Jocelyn. The trouble, though, with publishable erotic fiction is that it has rules, and the rules are pretty lame. For example, you can't portray a female as debased in relation to sex, no matter how complicit she may be in losing her dignity. Instead, publishable erotic fiction always must be about how sexually wonderful, dignified, and irresistible the heroine is. And then there's the whole nauseating, mawkish middle-American myth to be pandered to as well: slavish super-tough beefcake dotes on mildly flawed but amazingly pretty and hyper-competent protagonist. In this idiot world, anything any man ever does is done only to pleasure his one and only woman. She is his princess, so his own needs are completely unimportant compared to hers. Just perfect for him, he is enthralled by her and enslaved by his need for her. She dictates their physical relationship, and he cooks for her and does chores for her. In love, they are together forever. Finally— plot climax—to her utter amazement, and for the first time ever, she is "unlocked" and becomes properly orgasmic. At which point *everyone* has orgasms, reader included.'

'Well, I'd like to read a book like that,' said Alyssa.

'And I would not,' said Jocelyn. 'And stop trying to crush me with that smile! Put that smile *away*!'

'Ladies! Please.' Cy looked mystified. 'Let's not get carried away. The fact remains that I don't know what to do about readers who won't read my books. All they seem to do is swallow what the critics feed them and avoid me. Yet these self-same critics are capable only of juvenile sniggering and tiresomely predictable pejorative disparagements when it comes to looking at my work. It seems that even literary critics are too frightened of the deviancy in their own sexuality to be honest about sex. People are the biggest cowards ever.'

Alyssa felt the hairs at the back of her neck begin to tingle at Cy's use of the unusual word *coward*, one so favoured by Jocelyn. She realised that she was witnessing something bizarre: a mental bond between Cy and Jocelyn at a telepathic level.

The occurrence was not lost on Jocelyn either, even under the influence of alcohol. 'Now, that is the most truly incredible thing I have ever heard,' she mouthed.

'What is?' said Cy, once again unable to understand the interaction between the two women at the table.

'Someone who actually agrees with me,' said Jocelyn, who was still whispering for some reason. 'I *knew* there had to be someone.' Her upper lip quivered, and she held her head in her hands. 'People are *such* cowards.'

'What's with her?' asked Cy close to Alyssa's ear.

'Too much to drink.' In a louder voice, she added: 'She thinks you're great.'

'Yes, I do,' said Jocelyn, perking up. 'I can see that you are an author after my own heart. I'd like to get hold of your books. Which ones do you recommend I start with?'

God, this is going to be embarrassing.

Alyssa felt ashamed of her thoughts.

Cy, normally retiring and shy about his work, seemed genuinely pleased by her interest in his books and not at all concerned that she might be appalled by their quality. 'Well, there's *Dawn Rose Rising*,' he said. 'That's pretty good. And *Lost Harold Found*. That's a bit darker. Perhaps you should start with those two. They are under the name Cyrus Beauchamp. Some are still floating around in alternative bookshops, but of course you can just download them off Amazon.'

'Excellent. I have a Kindle. I'm so excited already.'

I don't believe this is happening.

Alyssa wondered if she was dreaming. She seemed to be in the company of two sex maniacs, and what was happening between them was turning into a nightmare. Suddenly, Jocelyn was no longer a lesbian. Which was ridiculous. The situation had gone beyond a joke.

It was time to do something about it, starting with taking control of the two downwardly spiralling figures at her table. She stood up. 'Come, people. Time for everyone to face reality. Time to head home. Come.'

PART III

DEAD MOTHER'S DAUGHTER

CHAPTER ELEVEN

1

ALYSSA MANAGED TO SETTLE into the rhythm of her new job as a psychodynamic counsellor at the Donald Clinic before long. Despite amateur dramatics from staff psychiatrist Jocelyn Goronowski in her efforts to become her friend—and increasing difficulties with boyfriend Cy—the days soon developed a familiar and manageable pattern. After the horror first day attempt by Greta McCreedy to scare her away with three extremely complex cases, the subsequent clients turned out to be more straightforward and more suited to her skills and training.

The legacy of the first day remained, however. Alyssa knew that she had survived Greta's heartless attack only because of her determination to not give in to her, but now she was stuck with having to continue to counsel dangerously paranoid Ben Clayton, intractably sleepless Ellen Goodman, and sexually perverted Gilbert Rockport alias George Roberts. She was going to have to go on seeing them on a regular basis— and all because she was too proud to admit defeat to someone like Greta and offload them.

Nothing like a challenge.

Mysterious George Roberts had been the hardest of the three to know what to do with initially. And then later, when he metamorphosed into Gilbert Rockport QC, multimillionaire owner of the city's premier law firm and notorious squasher of silly little people, it had taken her a further entire week to decide on how to proceed.

One option she had had was simply to refuse to go on seeing him. After all, it was obvious that severe transference and countertransference forces were inevitably going to develop between them and make counselling extremely challenging. Her youth and gender were undoubtedly powerful triggers for a sex maniac, while *his* older age and legal background were undoubtedly triggers for her own traumatic past. Simply walking away had been a real option. And yet she had not done that. Admitting defeat had seemed too much like capitulating to Greta McCreedy. The idea of *that* old witch crowing over her inadequacy had felt too much to bear.

Monster!

Sticking with Gilbert Rockport despite the potential difficulties had felt like the only realistic option—though not one that many would support. The risks were too great and her judgement too clouded. Both Wendy Greene and her stepmother had warned her often enough that pride was one of her weaknesses. Yet, even if true, there were ways to guard against such things. After all, there was nothing stopping her from getting advice from someone like Alan Summerfield if she felt out of her depth at any stage.

Which was what she had in fact done before making the final decision.

She had asked Trish to locate the professor for a phone consultation. According to the daily schedules, Alan was on site at the Donald that day.

Which was where Trish found him—in his consulting room between patients. Alan had only one minute to spare.

'Sorry to bother you, Dr Summerfield, it's Alyssa here,' she had said to him over the phone from the cottage. 'I just need a brief bit of advice.' She was disappointed to hear herself sounding nervous.

'Always a pleasure, Alyssa. Shoot.'

She had collected her thoughts before speaking because she knew that all the staff at the clinic had access to clients' names on the outpatient lists. Alan might see George Roberts, but he would not see Gilbert Rockport. Above all, she needed to avoid inadvertently betraying George's real identity. 'It's just this, Dr Summerfield,' she said. 'I'm finding that some of the clients that have been put onto my lists by Greta seem to have psychosexual issues. Do you think that as a new grad I should be seeing them? Some of them are quite old too, much older than me.'

'And the problem is?'

'Could I be in danger from some of them?'

'Be more specific.'

'Like, say, if they were serious perverts.'

There was a momentary pause. 'Most unlikely, I'd say, Alyssa. Not with all the CCTV around and the emergency call buttons and the like—and our high fees. Don't forget the fees. The truly deranged won't be here. They aren't functional enough to afford our fees.'

'Mm.'

'You don't sound convinced. Stop worrying. You'll discover soon enough in this job that perverts are everywhere.' There was a pause, as though he thought he had solved the problem.

'But what am I supposed to do about them?'

'Counsel them, then refer them on to a suitable expert if needed once the issues have been clarified. Provided other people aren't being harmed, it's much ado about nothing. So-called sexual perversion is nothing more than a regressive substitute for whatever type of incestuous pre-genital autoeroticism escaped repression. If it's causing the client emotional distress, which it rarely does, the distress is most likely the result of castration anxiety. Handling that shouldn't be a problem for someone with your background I shouldn't think. So, stop doubting yourself, Alyssa, and go for it. You've got the skills and nothing to lose. Being trained in psychotherapy gives you excellent leverage. Trish can forward you the list of our contracted sexual derangement therapists if needs be. Must go. Have a nice day.' He put the phone down on her.

'Right,' she had said to herself, as she slowly replaced the receiver. She wasn't sure she had understood exactly what Alan Summerfield had said about sexual perverts. It had seemed very glib. She would need to improve her understanding. It seemed, though, that because of her inexperience she had overreacted to Gilbert Rockport.

It was time to confront her own anxieties and put unwarranted concerns about her own safety to one side.

It's not all about you, Alyssa.

She could almost hear Wendy Greene's voice.

Gilbert Rockport had duly arrived that afternoon as planned, and she had seen him. Following that, he continued to arrive every Monday afternoon. Yes, he *was* indeed Gilbert Rockport and not George Roberts. And, yes, he was indeed *the* Gilbert Rockport QC. Not only that, but he was also secretly attending The House of Fantasy, a commercial BDSM establishment, for severe beatings on a regular basis.

That was what he meant when he said he was a sexual pervert. He had a thing about being flogged.

He went every three months or so and had been doing so for quite a few years. The beatings were carried out at his own direction and were truly severe. He explained that while he had always had a love-hate relationship with the school cane at a fantasy level, in recent times he had begun to have an overpowering desire to have real-life beatings inflicted upon his naked buttocks. The reason he was seeking professional help was not so much the fact that he was attending The House of Fantasy, which was a harmless enough place, but because he did not seem able to stop himself from overdoing things.

What he meant was that he was overdoing things "in the severity department".

'Overdoing *what* things and in *what way* exactly?'

'It hurts too much. Pathetic, I know. Sadly, it's become obvious even to me that there must be deep-seated and significant unresolved emotional issues in my life.'

His wife Nikki had begun to insist that he seek help, and he had decided that this was probably true. He *did* need to see someone. His wife had a point.

Alyssa had let him talk.

It turned out that every time Gilbert went for a visit to The House of Fantasy, which was in the nearby suburb of Troy, he arranged in advance to receive fifty strokes of corporal punishment upon his buttocks from a dominatrix while restrained and stark naked. He always specified this exact requirement in a phone booking a week beforehand. He also specified that the fifty strokes be applied as furiously as possible, half with a heavy wooden paddle and half with a heavy rattan cane, given in alternating sets of twelve, the whole package administered without recovery breaks and with the express purpose of being unbearable.

No, he was not exaggerating.

'You see, I need the terror of it. And Mistress does it so well. The visits need to terrify, and with her, they do. Somehow, she understands.' He became silent.

'With her, you feel *terrified*?'

He tried to explain.

'The thing is, I deliberately make the booking well in advance—a week is about as much anxiety as I can stand—so that as the punishment day gets closer and closer, I can get to feel more and more fear. As I said, for some reason I need that terror. My hands start to shake, and my heart pounds, and my mouth goes dry. The dry throat is sometimes a problem in court. I start to feel almost paralysed. In fact, I think my secretary is starting to suspect I may have Parkinson's. And, of course, then comes the big day. I take the day off work—and the following day too.'

'It's that bad, is it?'

'Oh yes. When I arrive, I'm a trembling wreck. Sometimes they have to put a paper bag over my head to treat me for hyperventilation before Mistress can even get started on me.'

'Shit, that sounds terrible. Sorry.'

Personally, I could never deliberately hurt anyone just for fun—not badly.

'Yes, it is bad.' He was fully aware that the level of brutality he insisted upon bordered on the insane, but it was what he needed. By trial and error, he had discovered that this was the recipe for him. Fifty hard strokes. Only "extremely severe" truly satisfied.

The rules of engagement at The House of Fantasy were what saved him from major injury despite all the savagery. Chief among them was that the paddle and cane be rotated every twelve strokes and that the target be confined to his buttocks. If this was done, it minimised his downtime to at most two days off work. He was a busy man after all. Indeed, if beaten to formula, the deeper layers of his skin remained intact after even the fiercest attack by his favourite mistress and recovery was fast. Of course, there was always gross bruising and swelling to contend with afterwards, and large, ridge-like welts across his haunches, but the damage always resolved completely over four or five weeks and never left any scars.

'Ultimately, no harm is done.'

With his clever plan he could achieve the most dreadful of beatings— severe enough to make him shriek from about halfway through and struggle unsuccessfully to break free—and afterwards, when it was all over, somehow feel wonderfully liberated. Which was good and well, he said, except for the fact that he was putting his life on the line each time with absolutely no idea why he felt compelled to do something so apparently idiotic. What he needed to find out was *why*—for him—getting beaten half to death was critically important to being able to go on living.

'You see, Alyssa, it seems it's the only way to *fix* whatever it is that's wrong me.'

Some fix.

'Every time I go to Troy, I get closer to where I need to go, but, frustratingly, I can't quite get there no matter how hard I try. I need your help badly.'

Fortunately, she knew how to help people see their truths.

So, he kept coming.

2

Clients of a more regular type came too, and in increasing numbers. Her reputation as a good counsellor began to increase, the cottage clinic lists filled up, and the weeks began to slip by.

While the spectrum of emotional disorders was different to what Alyssa had been used to in the public sector, the basics remained the same and her confidence increased. Also, the snobbery she had feared did not seem evident in the attitude of the clients towards her. Though generally cleaner, sleeker, better dressed, better behaved, and more intelligent than her previous ones, they appeared no less appreciative of her.

The staff, though, at the Donald upmarket boutique mental health clinic *were* different. Her new colleagues seemed more remote and calculating than the ones in public service. The fabled bonhomie of private practice was certainly nowhere to be found. Maybe, she speculated, it did not actually exist. There was an aloofness there—in the staff—an aloofness born of contempt for lesser humankind, which, somewhat alarmingly, seemed to include her. In some intangible way, they looked down on *her* too. Perhaps the small-town accent irritated them, or perhaps it was her financially and culturally stressed upbringing that did it, or her third-rate university background. Or maybe it was her inbred disapproval of profligacy and pretentiousness that caused them discomfort.

The psychiatric nurse Gail Wilson was the biggest offender—biggest snob—of all. No surprises there. She had encountered many nurses in her career and with surprising frequency found them prone to overestimating their worth to society. She assumed the rampant emotional defect was due to the way they were educated combined with their lack of psychological insight, but in Gail's case the fact that her husband was extremely wealthy probably added to the problem. Within a few weeks of commencing duties, the only way she was able to endure the patronising psychiatric nurse was to ignore her completely. Condescending clients, on the other hand, she had no difficulty with. If someone needed help and was prepared to pay the ridiculously high fee required to attend the Donald Clinic, she was happy to interact, no matter the attitude.

On the plus side of her new job at the Donald, the physical conditions were most pleasant. Rooms were clean and spacious, there was no crowding, and adequate time was allocated for sessions. Even though the flow of clients was relentless, she found she liked being at work. Before long, she even began to believe that her appointment at the clinic had been a lucky break.

Only Greta McCreedy's continuing negative attitude towards her remained difficult to get around. Greta obviously did not like her—had taken an instant personal dislike to her in fact—which was not ideal given that Greta was nominally in charge of her. Unfortunately, the reason for the silly old woman's strange behaviour was not immediately discernible and therefore hard to fix. She had done her best to calm the senior clinical psychologist, but despite her best efforts to be civil and work hard, Greta steadfastly refused to warm to her. Instead of any thawing in the relationship, Greta appeared increasingly determined not to like her.

Be that as it may, she had no intention of letting the Greta problem get her down. If anyone could weather the psychological warfare born of another woman's hostility, she could. To show this power of hers to Greta, she made a point of exhibiting abundant cheerfulness whenever the woman came near her. By always smiling at her, she hoped to indicate to the prune the futility of an unpleasant attitude. Perhaps if she smiled at her often enough it would shame Greta into showing her some respect. An attitude of respect towards a new member of staff was all that was required for the situation to improve. After all, being a therapist was not all about being like Greta McCreedy. Greta was not all that great, and neither was the Donald Clinic when all was said and done. It was important to maintain perspective.

Advertised claims about the therapeutic superiority of the clinic were misleading. The psychiatrist, Simon Bristow, to his credit, confirmed this to her one lunch hour. The truth was that the Donald Clinic achieved its excellent results only because it was able to avoid seeing clients of the "wrong kind". Which was cheating.

3

Dr Bristow was sitting at one of the tables in the staff room studying his phone when Alyssa arrived there one lunch hour. She knew who he was, of course, having seen him at the Donald in passing. He was by himself, and the room was otherwise unoccupied. There was no food or cup of coffee on his table, and it was the first time she had seen him there during a lunch hour. In his mid-forties, the doctor was tall and slim and wore noticeably high-tech spectacles. Unusually for an academic psychiatrist, he was quite handsome and immaculately dressed.

Seeing that she did not know him personally, Alyssa discretely proceeded to an unoccupied table with her lunch box. However, not long after that, while she was munching on a sandwich and reading a gossip magazine, he dropped suddenly into the empty chair opposite her.

It startled her. 'Dr Bristow!'

'Hello.'

Up close, he was even more attractive than she had given him credit for. The Montego-blue of his light linen jacket perfectly complimented the canary yellow of his shirt. Self-consciously, she returned her half-eaten sandwich to her lunch box. He had passed her many times in the corridors before, but without any greeting or acknowledgement. Perhaps until now he had not even realised it was her.

He shot out a hand. 'Simon Bristow. Welcome. I hear you have joined us.'

'Hi. Yes, I'm Alyssa, but I guess you already know that.' His hand felt clammy.

'I do know that, indeed. You are our new psychodynamic therapist.'

Although Dr Bristow had missed the welcoming party at Santos Beach, Alyssa already knew quite a lot about him from Jocelyn. According to her, he had a reputation for being too clever by half, so much so that those who knew him well tended to call him Simple Simon behind his back. "He sees zebras when others see horses", was how Jocelyn had tried to explain him to her. "He's lost contact. He's like, you know, life from another dimension." The assessment had sounded bizarre coming from Jocelyn.

Simple Simon spoke. 'Now,' he said, 'no doubt I'm here for a reason, but what was it again? Darn. I've forgotten.'

She looked at him with a deadpan expression. He was interfering with her lunch. She could see why he appeared to some to be a genius and to others simple-minded. It was a trick of his, a trick of his affected manner. To a psychodynamic therapist, it was all too boringly obvious: the man across the table used the deliberate and contrived strategy of appearing constantly flummoxed by the obvious to achieve secondary gain. Impersonating Einstein may once have pleased his parents, but it did not fool her. Instead, he seemed rather juvenile. Of more concern, though, was his attitude towards her. She saw immediately that he did not regard her as a colleague but merely as a subset of the genus "junior staff".

Somewhat irritated, she played his game and tried to help him out of his dilemma of not knowing why he was there. 'You've come to say hello to me. Is that it?'

'Aha! No. Not that. Nothing social. Policy! That's it. Deliver policy to the new fairytale artist. *That's* why I'm here.'

'I think you have the wrong person,' she said. 'I do supportive counselling, not fairytales.'

'That's the one. Metapsychology.'

'I do transference-focused talk therapy; emotional progress via a personal relationship.'

'So, everyone keeps telling me. And how are you finding that? I mean here, in a scientific organisation.'

She wondered what the real purpose of his visit was. 'I found it tough at first, but I think I'm settling in. It's a pleasant environment and the cottage is just brilliant.' She hoped she was saying the right things to maintain the peace.

He peered at her. 'This transference-focused personal interaction stuff that you do—you do *know* that it's just fairytales, don't you? I mean, you *do*, don't you?'

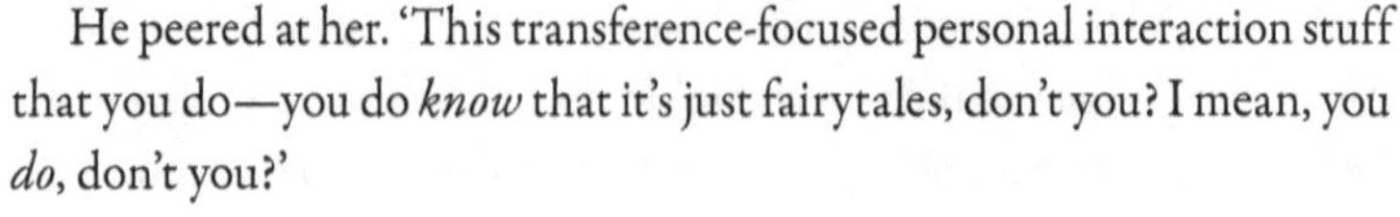

'Which part of what I do is a fairytale, Dr Bristow?'

'All of it. Anything to do with subjective psychotherapy.'

'It is?'

'Sure. No need to look mystified. I'm sure that by now enough people will have told you that it's impossible for any person to escape their own attribution bias. But that's the problem with this wishy-washy stuff, isn't it? Pointing out the obvious doesn't help because, at heart, it's always a personal belief founded on a personal delusion. Still, I suppose I shouldn't continue to be surprised. I mean, we all know that belief occurs *prior* to declarative cognition. I'm sure you won't change.'

'Change what?'

'Your idea that what you people do has any rational basis.'

Alyssa felt her face turning red, not with embarrassment but with anger. Under normal circumstances, she would have no difficulty in putting someone like him in his place, but circumstances were not normal. Potentially, he could get her fired, so she had to be careful. What angered her was that there was ample proof that her method of treatment, like the many other varieties of talk therapy licensed for clinical use, was effective. 'We seek merely to uncover that which is hurting emotionally because it is hidden. And I accept that the old "psychical theories" are not everyone's cup of tea,' she said, as evenly as possible. 'However, that's Freudian, which I'm not.'

Simon Bristow made a giggling sound. 'Really? Why don't I believe that? Oh, the old *psychical processes*. What a hoot. Freud was a major crank—you do know *that* I hope. His writings clearly show that just like all his contemporaries he was riddled with the most extraordinary of sexual hang-ups.' Dr Bristow became wistful. 'Yet I do think that I might have liked him as person. After all, he was the one who freed the LGBTQ+ world from the closet—a world that as you well know makes up twelve per cent of any population. At least, in the end, poor old Freddie did finally realise that every single person on the planet, without any exception, was at least as sexually screwed up as he was. But I digress. My question for you, Alyssa, is this: how can anyone do transference-focused psychotherapy without drive theory? After all, isn't that the source of your imagined unconscious component of the conscious mind? Where's the evidence for any of this? There's no biological evidence whatsoever for drive theory.'

He glanced at his smartwatch. 'Sadly, I don't have the time to explain to you how properly to integrate neuroscience, cognitive science, behavioural science, and developmental science into clinical science. However, here's a quick suggestion: how about you train your clients to apply discipline to their thoughts? Have you heard of that way of treating emotional difficulties? The discipline of intentional thought? Surely that would have to work better than benevolent intersubjective embracing, or whatever it is that you do.'

She stared at him in an attempt to work out why he wasn't going away and why he seemed to feel a need to goad her. Normally, she could read a man's intentions towards her easily, but the true Simon Bristow remained shielded from her. 'There are a lot of things out there,' she said cautiously. 'Why this upsets you, I don't know.'

'It doesn't upset me, believe me. Far from it. I'm perplexed by you, though. I don't understand what it is that you do here.'

She gave him a smile that she hoped did not appear too condescending even though she knew she was revealing her top teeth. 'I'm here because the clients need me and like me.' Her clinics at the cottage were fully booked for weeks ahead. 'I help people, Dr Bristow. That is what I do.'

Which, I suspect, is more than you do.

He was unmoved. She was never going to win any argument against him. Clearly, he had long ago decided to refuse to understand the basis of interpersonal therapy, which was "Self-growth via the tool of intimacy", or, to quote Obermaaier further, "improvement of a troubled Self through healthy Self-object acquisition via mutual congruence with a more developed Self, especially in the Un-conscious realm". Instead of arguing with Simon, she tried humouring him. 'I don't know much, Dr Bristow. You know that. I've just started, so I'm not an expert at anything.

I know there are other explanations for things, and I accept that things are complicated.'

'Mm. Rest assured that the theories you have been taught are bunkum. Take my word for it.'

'You are not a fan, I can see that,' she said, trying to maintain her cool.

'No, I am not. What's the point, anyway, of all these so-called empirically validated mind theories? We know for a fact that people *choose* what thoughts they have—and are therefore responsible for them— and we know for a fact that motivations arise from *external* stimuli. The evidence for these things is indisputable.'

The point is, Simon, nobody *knows all the answers.*

She dared not say it aloud. Instead, she repeated what she had said before: 'We just try to help people.' Despite the arrogance of the man at her table, she sensed in him an underlying misery, an endless searching...

'Help them?' He seemed disappointed that she was not rising to his bait, because he stared expectantly at her, seemingly waiting for her to engage in an academic argument with him about the origins of motivation. The gaze was strangely asexual, which, coming from a male, felt disconcerting. Clearly, instead of sex with her, what he wanted was debate.

Against her better judgement, she finally snapped and decided to fight fire with fire. She quoted again from another part of Obermaaier's textbook that she knew off by heart: "If you think that you are being rational when you think that you know people's motivations, what if there is an inherent design fault in your conscious mind that is secretly rendering it *irrational* because of hidden activity occurring in an Un-conscious part of your conscious Self?"

Simon Bristow laughed heartily. 'Old Jorken can't help you here. The design faults in the mind are not in the slightest bit mysterious. For your information, we are just like the great apes in the compulsion that we feel to attribute a causation to an outcome. We need to know the *cause* of something, regardless of the truth. This need is so strong that we will happily elevate authority to the equivalent of truth. There's nothing new or surprising here. People's logic circuits have long been a highly predictable joke. The issue is not one of how we are secretly influenced by a mythical unconscious part of the Self, the issue is that people like you think that you know how the mind is structured based on nothing other than the contemplation of your own navel. In my frank opinion, and I'm sure I'm right, psychodynamic theory is well demonstrated to be complete nonsense. We may as well believe that the ancient Egyptian god Osiris governs mental regeneration because, indeed, this is what some New Agers assert after examining their own navel.'

She said nothing further. It would be a waste of her time.

Even he could see that he had hurt her feelings. 'But enough of all that,' he said magnanimously. 'I am here for another reason.'

5

He was there for another reason.

'And what reason is that Dr Bristow? asked Alyssa. He had already revealed what she most needed to know, which was that he was nothing more than a stereotype of the classic intellectual snob found in every medical megaservice. Blinded by ferocious personal conceit, overconfident, and blind to real life, he was the product of his own megalomania and victim of himself. There would be others like him in the city, all bereft of genuine warmth. There would be no small talk about personal life. The Simon Bristows of the world did not socialise with what they regarded as lower forms of life.

'Policy orientation. That's why I'm here. I was allocated the task a good while back, by Professor Barnes, but I've been rather busy. Alan reminded me today. Therefore, even though I really don't have the time, I came to find you. I'll just run through the Donald's overall policy and be done with it.'

'You mean here and now? While I'm eating? I do have Wednesdays free for admin.'

'I don't have the same luxury.'

'Well, okay then.' She could hardly tell him to go away. 'Aren't you going to get something to eat while you're here?'

'No. I'll just say my piece, Alyssa, and be on my way.' He used her name after a slight hesitation, as though finding it difficult to recall—or as though Alexis or Alison would have been equally useful. 'First, I'll get to the heart of the matter: certain people we definitely do not allow in this place.'

For a horrible second, she thought he was referring to her being in the staff room, but he was not. He was talking about the type of client that the Donald Clinic management did not permit to attend for treatment. The clinic did not accept the "wrong sort".

'It's important that you know the ground rules because everything flows from there. In essence, we are not permitted to let the side down by letting in undesirables. It's this that we all need to understand and accept.'

'Yes, I do know the basics.' It was true. She already knew the rules in a broad sense through Jocelyn. However, she had not yet had any interest in wading through the official written protocols on the shelf in her cottage office. 'I know what our target market is supposed to be, and I know who needs to be excluded. In any case, I only do supportive counselling. I hardly ever get to see a client who doesn't already belong to someone else. I just do what I'm told, Dr Bristow.'

'I'll run you through the main headings of our policy, nevertheless.'

He was not going to be paying attention to anything she said. Instead, he was going to tell her what she was and was not going to be doing at the Donald, watch her eat her lunch, and not eat or drink anything himself. This was his plan for his lunch break, and he did not seem to think it unusual.

Are they all screwballs?

She wondered if social awkwardness was a quality required of all psychiatrists prior to admission for training. If so, Simon Bristow was a perfect fit. In fact, the only psychiatrist she had ever met who did not come across as obviously odd was Alan Summerfield. Perhaps occasional exceptions like him were used by the admission authorities to protect their profession from bad publicity.

Dr Bristow was talking: 'What you have said so far—that you actually know that there are policies located in your office—that sounds reassuring. Nevertheless, we have the driveway access issue to contend with, don't we? I was against that silly idea from the start. As you can well imagine, independent access to the Donald has the potential for enormous complications. Therefore, it's vital that there is no confusion regarding the rules.'

'I'm listening, but you'll have to understand that I need to finish my lunch at the same time. I have a long afternoon ahead of me.'

He giggled again. 'Busy?' Then he continued on his main train track: 'What we want here at the Donald is smooth sailing. That, and economic efficiency. Sound reasonable? So, how do we achieve this? As you will know—assuming you have actually read at least some of what's in your office—the way we achieve smooth sailing and good economics is by restricting access. This is our key point of difference—the deliberate policy of our founders, Drs Barnes and Summerfield—and we are all expected to work towards this goal. So, what does "restricted access" mean in practice?'

She began to eat the remains of her sandwich. 'I know all this.'

'It means we cut back on low-functioning hallucinating clients, especially the noisy ones, avoid children and adolescents entirely, and turn away dements. To further enhance economic efficiency, we similarly exclude criminal sex offenders and substance abusers—except, of course, food and tobacco abusers. And, needless to say, anyone unable to pay the going rate gets the chop. Got it so far?'

'This stuff isn't exactly news to me, Dr Bristow.'

'Probably not, but there is more, and it's this more that worries me. For various reasons I am unable to be more specific, but please listen carefully.'

Dutifully, she stopped eating and paid attention.

'New employees need to understand that because of the great economic benefits arising from our policies, we do not want potentially troublesome clients of any sort to attend here. Such a client will inevitably spell disaster.'

She had no idea what he was carrying on about and he was starting to be seriously annoying. 'Okay, I get the drift,' she said, to shut him up.

'Easy enough to say, but the question I feel compelled to ask is *do* you?'

'What is that supposed to mean?'

Simon Bristow lowered his impenetrable spectacles and peered at her in a way that made her feel like a scientific specimen. 'I think you know what I am talking about.'

'Not really. I'm not used to people talking in riddles.'

'It's not a riddle. Keep the wrong sort of people *away*. It's the policy.' He seemed hurt, as though she wasn't playing ball.

'Of course.'

'Excellent.' He pushed his spectacles back up.

She tried to finish her sandwich but found it increasingly difficult to swallow as it slowly dawned on her that the visit from the man opposite was occurring for only one real reason: he had come to warn her. He was trying to warn her without appearing to do so; without getting himself into trouble over it. But warn her about what? Was he referring to Gilbert Rockport? Or Benjamin Clayton?

Surely not.

Gilbert was not causing the clinic any trouble and Ben belonged ultimately to Alan Summerfield. Besides, Simon Bristow could not possibly even know about Gilbert because Gilbert was not registered on any clinic database. Yet, if he was not referring to Gilbert Rockport or Ben Clayton, then what *was* he talking about? Who else of her clients was she better off not seeing? Mrs Goodman? Impossible.

'Ruthlessness is what it will take,' continued the psychiatrist. 'I know that what I am saying sounds counterintuitive to you—much like scientific psychology—but selectivity is the key to survival here. We want the better client, yes, but not at any cost. Follow the rules but follow that one too. Only then will disaster be avoided.'

She frowned at him. 'Don't worry, I'll be sure to follow all the rules.'

Simon Bristow looked concerned. 'You still don't get it do you? Despite my efforts. What is *wrong* with people?'

His emergency pager suddenly went off loudly. 'Good Heavens!' He stood up with a jerk and fumbled under his jacket to stop the shattering noise. Then he studied a text message on his watch with annoyance. 'Damn these nurses!' He had to go. 'Another fitter. Sorry.' Without saying any more, he hurried away.

Someone had to be saved, somewhere upstairs. Someone had been mismanaged by lesser staff and was having convulsions.

6

With Simon Bristow gone, Alyssa was none the wiser about what he had been trying to tell her. She was now also the only one left in the staff room. The sudden abandonment felt anticlimactic. Clearly, he had been trying to suggest something to her that he knew was just an educated suspicion on his part. He had seemed convinced that something untoward was afoot. Now she might never know what it was that he suspected. It was most disappointing. If only he had had better people skills.

Paradoxically, in the empty room, she missed his quirky company. In fact, she felt slightly ashamed of herself for the way she had inwardly mocked him the whole time he tried to talk to her. People like Simon had a valuable place in the greater scheme of things. After all, she too had once suffered from convulsions and been saved many a time by doctors just like him.

For a long time after the road traffic accident that had killed her father and left her critically injured, she had suffered from seizures. The fits had caused her to fear that she would never be normal again, but after expert care from neurosurgeons and psychiatrists the problem had come under control after a few years.

You need to stop being so critical of everyone, Alyssa.

Being critical of others was nothing other than Self-criticism. Wendy Greene again.

Alyssa went to the corner kitchenette to fix herself a coffee. The interrupted lunch break had not been entirely a waste of time, she decided. After all, she had never actually read the Donald Clinic's attendance policy documents in her office, and was never likely to, and Simon Bristow had saved her the effort.

There had been another benefit from the visit too: Simon Bristow had reminded her of something valuable she had learnt a long way back, which was that brittle academics often knew little about the mental world of ordinary people. Those in ivory towers almost always failed to understand the most important thing about health care, which was that unwell clients wanted above all else to see someone who actually cared. Despite the sniggers of the Bristows of the world, there would always be a place for therapy that involved human warmth and kindness. People needed someone like her. People *needed* their so-called fairytales.

Professor Barnes—despite his age, or perhaps because of his age—had at last come to understand this inconvenient truth. Unlike most in similar positions, he had finally worked out that a good number of his clients wanted benevolent intersubjective embraces. Which, as he explained, was why he had appointed her to the clinic. It was for purely commercial reasons. He had even said as much at the appointment interview.

To make his clinic clients "feel better", she was to "comfort" the ones who needed this part too, such as those with poor self-esteem, grief, post-traumatic stress disorder, non-specific anxieties, insomnia, mild situational depressions, smoking addiction, general life stress, weight control, relationship stress, and so on, blah blah. The phobias, the more serious anxieties and depressions, the anger managements, and the domestic abuses would stay with Greta in view of her seniority and her use of cognitive behaviour tools.

The Barnes/Summerfield super-selective method appeared to work well. Some days, the clinic was so busy that it did indeed feel like the bedlam that Trish the receptionist jokingly liked to call it. And as far as Alyssa could make out, the clinic was not only popular but financially successful as well. To the Dog's credit, the administration was excellent, unlike at public hospitals where managers tended to be so incompetent as to be beneath contempt.

She sipped at her coffee and felt proud that she worked at the Donald Clinic. She could see herself having a long and successful career there. The only negative—besides Greta—was that the commodification of healthcare did not sit well with her spirit. The overt mixing of money and illness still felt wrong to her no matter how she juggled the matter in her mind. To be fair, though, no one was being duped. There were prominent panels in advertising pamphlets, as well as signs within the building itself, to the effect that the Donald Clinic had extremely high fees and was a place for only the exclusive few. Perhaps her own financially deprived upbringing had made her overly sensitive; certainly, the clients themselves seemed happy enough paying the absurd amounts of money involved. Not being a snob herself, it had taken her quite a few weeks to realise that snob clients felt personally honoured by the exclusivity of the Donald Clinic.

How little I know about business compared with Alan and the Dog.

She wondered where Alan was. Sometimes he did come to coffee or to lunch, but not nearly as often as she had thought he would. Instead, he was always in high demand somewhere else. She had not been able to see as much of him as she had hoped. They remained on good terms, though, so whenever he *did* happen to be in the staff room he always came and sat with her. Which was better than nothing.

She would always be grateful for the time they had spent together on the balcony of his luxury apartment. Now, whenever she saw him, it gave her a little thrill, as though Elvis himself had arrived. There was something special about Alan. Almost everyone agreed about that.

No doubt, given a little more time, they would be able to grow closer and become true friends.

CHAPTER TWELVE

IF THERE WAS ONE psychiatrist at the Donald Clinic who did indeed spend a lot of time in the staff room, it was Jocelyn Goronowski. There was no escaping her.

A few days after the bizarre Simon Bristow event, Alyssa's new female friend arrived once again, this time armed with a new lunch box and determined, it seemed, to be as irritating as possible. 'Psychotherapists aren't all *that* bad, I suppose,' she said, as she took a seat at Alyssa's table.

'I'm pleased to hear it.' Though she liked Jocelyn, Alyssa did not yet know her well enough to relax fully in her company despite previously spending an entire Saturday afternoon with her. She did not fully trust her. Something about the new friend continued to cause her to feel wary, and her instincts were seldom wrong.

Who, exactly, is this woman?

'See, new lunch box. Two compartments to facilitate weight control. There's chicken salad in this one,' said Jocelyn, 'and shredded capsicum in this one. See? And what are you eating?'

'Tofu and noodles and broccoli.'

'*Eeuw.* Well then, go on, carry on. Eat up.' Jocelyn peered into her own lunch and picked out a shred of capsicum. 'May I ask, Alyssa, what system you are using on our clients?'

'System?' It was supposed to be lunch break, not question time. 'What do you mean, *system*? Are you referring to computers or counselling?'

'Psychology.'

'You know counsellors don't work like that.' She quoted some Obermaaier at her to shut her up: 'Our approach is multimodal with an eclectic focus.'

'Yada, yada, yada, yes, fit for purpose, as you people say. But I want to know more about *you*, my dear. What is *your* chosen focus? Wait, don't tell me. I know you are not a complete thumb-sucker, so I'll see if I can guess.'

It seemed Jocelyn was determined to ruin her lunch. 'Supportive counselling is not an exact science in the way you are suggesting.'

'Shush.' Jocelyn closed her eyes. 'Let me think. Mm, I know you are not a wet or a creep or a gluten intolerant.'

'What?'

'Quiet, I'm calculating. Not into any sort of dialectics, and, like Alan, not a behaviourist, mmm, also not a bleeding heart. So, what *is* she?' Jocelyn's eyes popped open. She looked straight across the table for a minute, without blinking, then closed her eyes again. 'Not airy fairy enough to be a Jungian . . . but then again you do seem a little spiritual . . . so I would have to venture Assagiolian. I reckon you could be that. In broad terms.' Her eyes sprang open again. 'You are an Assagiolian.'

'A what? No, I'm not.'

'Yes, you are.'

It felt like a criticism. Alyssa tried to work out what Jocelyn was getting at. 'You're talking about psycho-synthesis, aren't you? From, like, before I was born?'

'Yes. Roberto Assagioli, your intellectual father.'

Alyssa felt her face reddening. She knew almost nothing about Roberto Assagioli except that he lived a long time ago and was supposedly too spiritual. As soon as Jocelyn became scholastic, she was out of her depth. 'I'm not in a position to argue with you about this, Jocelyn, you know that. Don't forget, I've only got a bachelor's degree. Mostly, I just follow our main textbook, and we certainly don't work according to any one person's theory. A lot of what we counsellors do is based simply on emotional IQ. On instinct.'

'Instinct?'

'Yes, and knowledge, too. I know Obermaaier's textbook pretty well. Almost backwards, in fact. A lot of it I've even managed to memorise verbatim.'

'Really?' It was pure sarcasm, but Alyssa knew she deserved it.

She tried to explain herself better to Jocelyn: 'Our role is to facilitate psychodynamic growth and provide safe support in times of emotional crisis.' It became evident, though, that Jocelyn knew that she was quoting directly from Obermaaier, so she stopped.

'I've read it, dummy.'

'You have?'

Jocelyn looked at her, puzzled. 'Let's put Jorken Obermaaier's bullshit to one side, shall we. What have we got left? Who are *you*? What *are* you? Are you an orchard rose or are you a cactus dandelion? What is your *own* professional world view? Surely you must have one.'

What did cactus dandelions have to do with anything? Jocelyn had her flustered. Did she have a world view? Not really. Mostly, she just read bits of books, so it was difficult to formulate an exact answer. 'I believe in some of Freud, I suppose, together with Anna Freud and the classical ego psychologists. With transference-focused therapy, those are a given. However, we also factor in the later schools of psychodynamic theory. I find value in people such as Melanie Klein, Jacques Lacan, Kohut, Ogden, Winnicott, Stern'—she ran out of names—'all those.' They were all quoted in Obermaaier's book. 'I agree with some parts of all those.'

'Impressive. Klein for her elaboration of the death drive, and Lacan for his views on the nature of sex?'

'You could sort of say that.'

Jocelyn looked at her suspiciously. 'What about the "Self-object" of Kohut? And the "Third Object" of Ogden? And the "Knowing" of Stern? Are you into *that* weird stuff too?'

'Pretty much. It's not weird Jocelyn, it's advanced. Unlike your friend, Freud, I am pretty much into embracing co-subjectivity.'

'Is that so. Co-subjectivity?'

'Yes.'

'And what?'

'What do you mean *and what*?'

'You still haven't told me how you see the world—what's really making it tick, us tick, what's *really* out there. Everybody knows we have the drive theorists, the ego psychologists, the object relations people, the Self psychologists, and—God help us—even dumbassed social psychologists, but I want more. I don't want a history lesson; I want to know how *you* believe I tick.'

'It's not that simple, Jocelyn, you know that. Like you, I believe in a bit of everything. And when it comes to the practical side of seeing clients, I probably just follow my instincts anyway. You could call it the unconditional positive regard approach of the humanists—the Carl Rogers stuff of the olden days. Although I don't, of course, follow the Rogerian school as such.'

'You are not making any sense.'

'What I'm trying to say is that we are all of us a combination of everything.'

'A combination?'

'Yes, all the people I mentioned are helpful. And, of course, Obermaaier's practical tips are what I rely upon most. There's that famous chapter at the end of his book called "Practical Tips".'

'Holy shit. So, that's it? No Gestalt? No Neuroplasticity? And not even *one* of the plagues of Mindfulness?

'Afraid so.'

2

Another interrogation by Jocelyn went as follows: 'So, then what about your stance on feminism? Where are your Karen Horneys and Juliet Mitchells? And what about your Nancy Chodorows? Where are they? Please don't tell me you've gone fully third wave.'

'I'm not unsympathetic to all that stuff, Jocelyn, it's just that I don't know enough. I'm not even sure I know what you mean by "third wave".' She knew there was a second wave of feminism, which was all about neo-Marxism and the rejection of male subjugation, but that was about all she remembered from Sociology 102, which was a bad year. Admitting her academic limitations to Jocelyn made her feel sheepish.

'Third wave feminist: the female who believes the struggle is over and no longer sees a *them* and an *us*. Have you waved us goodbye?'

'Of course not. But to be honest Jocelyn, male bashing doesn't appeal to me. I don't have a problem with men.'

'My people at the university will have a fit if they hear about you.'

'What people? You have no people.'

'I do so.'

'Who?'

'People. We collaborate. Stop avoiding the issue. Why are you letting the sisterhood down?'

She had a vision of Jocelyn cackling in a circle of lesbians. 'Obviously, I don't know anything about feminism. Sorry.'

'Much better answer.'

'The truth is, Jocelyn, I'm actually a bit of a twit. I can only do one thing properly at a time, so that is what I'm doing with my psychotherapy. I can't do feminism too. I'm new at all this, and I've come from a small, conservative town. I've started off with Unconditional Positive Regard, Kairos, and Catharsis, and that's about as much as I can cope with at present. I'm not as bright as you doctors are.'

Jocelyn reached across the table and took her hand, as was her habit. 'Rubbish. You are great. And you are just so sweet.' She lifted the hand into the air and held it there. It was not clear if she was even aware of what she was doing. 'Although how one could attempt to treat post-traumatic stress disorders with psychotherapy I'll never understand.' She kept Alyssa's hand in the air. 'I would never have the patience in a million years.'

'Dr Barnes thinks I should try.'

'He would. He lives on his own planet.' She stared absent-mindedly at Alyssa's hand. 'I think we two are going to fall in love.' Then she dropped the hand as though nothing had happened.

'I hope not,' said Alyssa, pulling her hand back out of harm's way.

'I can't believe you don't want to fight for us women.'

'I never said that. It's just that I'm, you know, not anti-men.'

'You aren't filled with implacable hostility towards males?'

Towards women, maybe, but not towards men.

'No. Not more than is necessary.' She laughed, trying to lighten the mood.

Jocelyn remained serious. 'So, you don't think heterosexuality is a male conspiracy?'

'No. I'm afraid not.'

'And you are happy to subject yourself to gendered hierarchical oppression and be ostracised by language?'

'Personally, I don't have a problem with gender.'

'Really? Then how about you answer me this question: if we can do everything a man can do, who will do the things that only a woman can do?'

It was an obvious trick question, and she knew the stock answer from her own time at university. The answer had to be women. This then proved that men were surplus to requirements and that men therefore felt compelled to spend all their days suppressing women in order to conceal this inconvenient truth. 'I'm not foolish enough to give you the answer you want. You know that.'

She smiled strangely. 'You are just such a little funny bunny, aren't you?'

'Wrong, Jocelyn. I'm nobody's bunny. And your problem is that you don't understand why not.'

'Mm. Maybe. Okay, I'll give you that.'

Following the bizarre attempt at light lunchtime conversation, Jocelyn seemed to run out of ideas and be unsure what to say next. She became silent and forlorn and began to stare into the middle distance. Alyssa had seen her do this before, so she let her be and resumed her interrupted meal. Jocelyn would soon enough snap out of herself. She always did. While Alyssa ate, she studied the psychiatrist, who for some reason looked younger than she had at the Little Critters brasserie. Perhaps the lighting had something to do with it. Jocelyn was reasonably attractive in her own way, she decided, but uncomfortable in her own skin. It was as though she had missed certain vital inputs during early development.

She had come across such women before. They professed to have no sexual interest in men whatsoever, yet they remained troubled by how clueless they were when it came to how to appeal to men. Despite what Jocelyn had just said about feminism, Jocelyn did not seem that much of an enthusiast to her. 'Why were you on at me about feminism?' she asked her, after a while, to break the silence. 'I'm astute enough to know that you are no activist. If it's any consolation, let me assure you that no man controls me. In fact, I'd say it's just the opposite.'

Jocelyn's head jerked in her direction. 'Shit! A victimisation eschewer too. And there I was thinking you couldn't get any dafter.'

Alyssa called her bluff and held her gaze and smiled at her. Jocelyn could not intimidate her on the issue of men. On this subject, at least, the tables were turned. She was able to see right through her. She saw the memorised phrases, the academic braggadocio, and, above all, the helplessness.

3

'You must admit that people are so confused that it's distressing,' a determined looking Jocelyn declared some days later in the same room and at the same table.

'In what way, Jocelyn?' Alyssa smiled at her, showing her teeth, but this time her new friend made a point of looking down so as not to be psychologically knocked out.

'I'm talking about *history*, dummy. Napoleon. I was reading about him last night. He thought nothing of killing hundreds of thousands of people, yet he threw the Marquis de Sade into prison for life for writing a book about the sexual thoughts that everyone has, including Napoleon himself. What's with that? I mean, kids can watch hundreds of people being killed on TV, but they can't even get to see one bare tit on TV— even though they've spent years sucking on them. Explain this to me. All of it.' Luckily, they were rhetorical questions because Jocelyn then stood up and went to the corner kitchen, where she began to busy herself with fixing a coffee.

'It sounds like you think a lot about what people think, Jocelyn. I thought you didn't have much time for psychotherapy.'

She replied over her shoulder from the kitchen top. 'Not your transference-focused stuff, no. No science in it, sadly. No verifiability, no predictability. And too inefficient by half. I mean, it's generally a complete waste of time—unless the client has the right mindset, a big bank balance, and an IQ above a hundred and twenty. Want coffee too?'

'Not yet. Thanks.'

Jocelyn returned with a single mug of coffee. 'Your stuff is not all bad news, I concede. The "way of being" paradigm—that's useful. You know: the "assumed rules of engagement".' She went to her chair and plonked herself down. 'The main lesson we are to take from you lot, I gather, is that people are never who or what they say they are. Not so?'

'What do you mean?'

'Not being who you say you are; transference and all that.' Jocelyn stirred her coffee noisily and stared into her face.

She was spooking her again. 'You do realise, don't you, Jocelyn, that you don't properly understand even one word of psychotherapy.'

'I do so. I do like the idea that there is badness in us all and that we are blind to it.'

'Really.'

'At least it's better than positive psychology. *That* stuff drives me crazy. "You are of great value; whatever you think about anything, including yourself, is true; forgive yourself; love yourself; everything is just great; you are just great". Those people drive me crazy. All the *lies*.'

Alyssa felt her heart beating in her throat. She knew, somehow, that Jocelyn's words were not random or innocent. Jocelyn was trying to worm her way in, trying to unsettle her, trying to force her to come clean. She defended herself: 'What if people can't improve, Jocelyn? What then? Surely, sometimes it's best to make the best of what one's got?'

'Oh please. What about others? The rest of us? Mind you, I suppose there is the reality of needing to make a crust, isn't there? People need to make a living. Oh God, I'm so tired of all the crap. I sense that the two of us, at least, can grow to be honest with each other, Alyssa. You see, personally, I don't believe most of the baloney I'm forced to swallow. I don't *need* to believe it either. I don't have any illusions.'

It seemed best to not respond. 'Me neither.' Alyssa tried to give a smile, but the result was too timid to be successful. She felt nervous. Was Jocelyn playing a cruel game with her, she wondered. Or was she imagining it? Surely Jocelyn could not know about her past—or did she?

'Do you mind if I pick your brains?' said Jocelyn.

The voice seemed far away. 'About what?'

'Stop looking like you've seen a ghost. It's just me, and I'm harmless, promise. I have this plan for us. You see, you are so sexy that I've realised you could be of help to me.'

The lunch break was going from bad to worse. 'Help with *what*?'

'Just with some *questions*, silly. I'm doing a survey. Client questionnaires. I have all these questions as part of my research project on the psychology of the Big O. Remember I told you about it?'

She could hardly forget.

'Well, it's all a bit delicate because the questions are all to do with sex. And the trouble is, I'm not getting proper answers from anyone.'

'You're doing a survey about sex, and you don't like the answers?'

'Yes.'

What next.

'Well, if it's just advice that you want, go ahead and shoot—for what it's worth. It's not a subject I know much about, as you well know, but at least I don't have any hang-ups.'

Well, not many, anyway.

'I knew I could count on you. So, here's the central sticking point in my understanding of the whole business: if people *don't* have sex, what happens to them?'

'Are you being serious?'

'You aren't deaf.'

'What do you mean by "don't have sex", Jocelyn? Be more specific. Completely nothing? Or just with others?' Luckily, there was no one else within earshot of their table.

Jocelyn nodded, possibly indicating both possibilities. Then she answered her own question: 'Boom! Anger! Slaughter! *That's* what happens, isn't it?' She punched her fist into her opposite hand, making a loud noise. 'You get angry, don't you? You kill!'

The sudden use of the word "kill"—said loudly—caught Alyssa by surprise and made her freeze. For a long second, fear telegraphed itself uncontrollably across her face.

'Don't you?' repeated Jocelyn, again loudly, and with something akin to glee in her voice.

Alyssa recovered herself almost immediately, but she knew that time had stopped for her and for no one else. As quickly as it had come, the bizarre sensation passed. She laughed to cover her confusion, but across the table Jocelyn was looking at her with psychiatrist's eyes. She had seen everything.

What does she know?

She forced herself to relax.

'I am right, aren't I?' said Jocelyn. Once again, the words seemed to float.

The woman at her table *was* playing some sort of sick game with her.

'No, Jocelyn, you are not right. If you ask me, it sounds like you are beginning to go a little crazy.'

Her words caused Jocelyn to burst into uncontrollable laughter. 'Ha-ha-ha,' she shrieked. 'Ha-ha-ha. You are so precious.'

4

Less than a week later, the great man himself, Alan Summerfield, came to the staff room during lunch hour. Alyssa had just finished setting out her food when he entered and because she was facing the door, she saw him immediately. He smiled the moment his eyes found her. She smiled too and raised her hand, an action he copied as he headed straight for her table.

He pulled up a chair opposite. 'Mind if I join you?'

'Not at all.' She had forgotten how tall he was, probably over 185 cm or six foot two in the old measurement. The impulsive and spontaneous exchange of affection between them had caused her to blush, and now, with him so close, she felt a tingle in her lower belly.

What is wrong *with me!*

It was ridiculous the way he affected her.

'Hi,' he said.

'Hi.'

Just then, the practice nurse, Gail Wilson, entered the room too, but after hesitating momentarily she proceeded to ignore them both and take a seat at another table.

Alan appeared to not even notice. 'Nice to see you again, Alyssa. Want a coffee? I'm going to make myself one.'

'Thanks for the offer, but not now. I'll get one after all this.' She pointed at her food.

He grinned. 'Very good.' After a few minutes at the kitchenette, he returned with his drink and sat down. 'How's life?'

'All good.' She smiled at him, aware that they were behaving like teenagers. He seemed impossibly handsome and well-groomed and had an uncanny way of making her feel bashful.

'Seeing you here has made my day,' he said.

She saw how he looked at her appreciatively and how he absorbed her physically, and it pleased her. Clearly, he valued the femaleness in her. In the same way, she liked the maleness in him. There was more to him, though, than just that. He also dressed amazingly well. Today, he had excelled himself in a pastel pink silk tie and magnificent rich-cloth blue-grey pinstripe suit cut in a modern Scandinavian style. Combined with his inherent good looks—which, despite his fuller stature and salt-and-pepper hair, somehow channelled Robert Pattinson of the vampire days—Alan Summerfield could just as well have been a movie star. For a mad second, she caught herself believing that secretly he was one.

He noticed her favourable response to his suit. 'Like it?' he asked.

She had forgotten how perceptive he was. 'Sorry to stare. You're looking very impressive, I must say.'

'There's a rather mundane reason for it, unfortunately. Today is "Meet the Relatives Day".' He took a sip of his coffee. 'I have the event every month or so. You'll get to recognise it.'

'Relatives day? What's that?'

'The other half of my psychosis clinic—the supposedly sane half, though some days I have my doubts.' He gave a boyish smile. 'As you will have realised by now, even though we try not to collect psychotics, we do have some—the non-substance abuse, non-geriatric sort. And for obvious reasons these individuals do unfortunately require financial support from a benefactor to be able to continue attending here. So, occasionally I discuss progress and management with the benefactors— just them and me.'

'Without the clients?'

'Exactly.'

'I see.' A benefactor's clinic. She had never heard of such a thing before and wondered how it could be ethical. She had much to learn. She finished a yoghurt and wiped her lips and fingers on a paper napkin. 'You do know I have one of your schizophrenia cases, don't you? Ben Clayton.'

'Yes, Greta told me. I sent Ben to *her*, of course, so her sending him on to you seems a bit of a cheek. Still, I suppose everyone is at their wit's end when it comes to Ben. I just wish he wasn't so inherently dangerous given his paranoid hallucinations about blades. His mother doesn't help either. She's excessively demanding, as I'm sure you'll discover. She's determined to have him cured by any means possible and won't accept that all we can do is keep him drugged.'

'I suppose she's encouraged by all the neurobiology research coming out in the media.'

'I doubt it. She's too intelligent to be conned by the charlatan side of neurobiology. She doesn't even like Simon Bristow—though, of course, *he's* anything but a quack.'

'Of course.'

He studied her. 'Looks like they've got to you, though, these neurobiologists. Have they? Don't worry. Stick around in this job and you'll soon enough discover that most of the so-called great advances in neuroscience are just overblown hype. They still don't have the slightest clue when it comes to explaining the conscious Self.'

'I don't really know enough to have a firm opinion.'

'It's all hype, believe me. Sure, the newer drugs are good, but it's glaringly obvious that consciousness of Self is a global computational function of the brain and non-existent in any real sense. That said, almost all neuroscientists who are looking into this make the fatal mistake of grievously misjudging the magnitude of the difference between lines of code and trains of thought. Doggedly, they persist in their delusional quest to "find" the conscious Self even though the answer exceeds their capacity. Science may one day master the brain, but it is inherently impossible for humans to master the conscious Self.'

'I suppose so,' said Alyssa diplomatically. Alan Summerfield sounded surprisingly like her textbook by Obermaaier, a book that almost all psychiatrists and certainly all neurobiologists usually laughed at, at least officially. The reason they laughed was because Obermaaier claimed that all "experiments" in search of the Self were logically meaningless. According to him, the most that any scientist could ever do regarding the mental computation we call "the Self" was use personal observation to formulate a theoretical model of its most likely basic operating principles.

Alan seemed to notice that she was perplexed by his unorthodox views. 'Not sounding much like a psychiatrist, am I? Sorry. That's enough of me ranting on about the need to return to some form of psychotherapy in our interactions with patients. It's my latest hobbyhorse, as you know. Now, what were you saying earlier about Ben Clayton?'

'To me, he seems rather unstable. I'm worried he's going to explode.'

'Mm. Sorry he got dumped on you, then. He can be a handful at times. On the positive side, though, I'll be interested to see if he improves under you. He's rather perfect for just such an attempt, you know. He's incredibly intelligent and may not be quite as deeply schizophrenic as previously thought—exactly as his mother has always insisted.'

'You mean that potentially he could be accessible?'

'Exactly.'

'Really?'

'Full of doubts, aren't we? I know schizophrenia has become all about genetics and organic impairment, but I'm still not fully convinced that psychology isn't central—despite the twin studies.'

'Even with his extreme history?'

'You mean the dead donkey thing?'

'Yes. And the rest.'

'Pure psychopathology, in my opinion. There's no family history and there's never been any evidence of illicit drugs or brain injury. Believe me, Ben's not your typical garbage head. I assume you know his IQ is genius level? We don't often see that. So, maybe we *can* help him. Funds are not a problem.'

'Okay. I'll do my best, then.'

5

Alan Summerfield glanced at his wristwatch. By now, he had drained his coffee cup. 'Have to fly. What are you and your boyfriend doing on Astoria Day?'

'You mean next week?'

'Yes. Astoria Day.'

Alyssa was not sure what she should say. It was a public holiday. 'I was going to take the train and visit my stepmother in Ocean View . . . it's nothing definite.'

'Brilliant. Kara and I are going down to the South Coast for the day. Ocean View is on the way, so we could give you a lift if you like.' He stood up to leave. 'Let me know for definite and we can arrange to pick you up.'

'I'll discuss it with Cy and let you know. It's very kind of you. Thank you.'

As Alan made for the door, Gail Wilson came to life and rushed after him. 'Dr Summerfield,' she cried. 'Dr Summerfield!'

The dramatic tone in Gail's voice was highly irritating.

'Can I have a moment of your time?' she asked. Alan paused with his hand on the door handle.

'What is it?'

'You know that patient who we started on *zasperidone* two weeks ago? I'm worried about him. Do you think he could be having muscarinic side effects?'

Alyssa saw Alan roll his eyes in disbelief at the nurse's question. 'Douglas upstairs?'

'Yes.'

'Come with me and we'll go past him.' Continuing on his way, Alan Summerfield siphoned Gail Wilson out of the room after him. His voice had had a steely edge to it—something Alyssa had not heard from him before.

She still had plenty of time to finish lunch, but suddenly she felt anxious. The strange feeling in her abdomen was back again, but this time it was not in her lower belly. It had nothing to do with desire. It was a sick feeling, and it had flooded into her stomach taking away her appetite. Alan Summerfield had commanded, and another had obeyed. Somehow, this was making her feel greatly disturbed.

The counsellor in her saw immediately that she had been triggered and that if she got emotionally involved with the man who had just left, he would hurt her. He was a man who got what he wanted; a man who did not take no for an answer.

The sudden "knowing" of it filled her with unexpected fear. Alan Summerfield's manner with Gail and the tone of his voice had aroused something in her—something secret that she had not yet come to terms with. It was something feral, something dangerous, something she knew she would not be able to resist if she needed to. Horrifyingly, when the time came, no matter what Alan might do to her she was always going to like him. There was nothing she could do that was going to be able to stand in the way of that.

Nothing.

He could do anything to her, and she would be powerless to stop him.

She knew then that the sudden feelings of helplessness towards Alan Summerfield had something to do with her father.

6

A few days later, Jocelyn turned up in the staff room once more and converted lunch break into yet another problem-solving session. The problem for Jocelyn this time was that her research project—the one due for presentation at the upcoming conference—was falling behind schedule. She explained it all to Alyssa once she had settled at her table, overripe banana in hand as an excuse.

'Lunch. Also, my project is turning to custard. Speak to me, oh mind expert.'

'For heaven's sake, what now?'

'Sex. It's completely inappropriate, I know, but pretty please'.

Fortunately, once again no one else was nearby.

Jocelyn explained that following on from their last conversation on the topic, she remained confused about the link, if any, between sexual feelings and aggressive feelings.

The topic was hardly suited to public conversation, let alone lunch, but Jocelyn did her best to be encouraging.

'You are my best resource when it comes to these matters.'

'Pull the other one.'

'No, I'm serious. There's this epidemic of gendered violence in society, and I need to get to the roots of it before I can start sprouting at the conference. Clearly—to me—sexual behaviour and aggressive behaviour are somehow linked, but how? And why? Above all, Alyssa dear, I need to know if a *lack* of sex leads to feelings of aggression strong enough to lead to outbursts of anger.'

'What about my lunch? Besides, you've already decided that if someone doesn't get sex, they kill people. What's the use of me saying anything to you?'

'Oh, don't worry about that. I was just speculating with ideas. But now the time for monkeying about is over. You won't mind me bugging you. You can still eat your lunch and relax. We can both eat.' She waved the banana. 'Giving me what I need will be like totally restful for you. Promise.'

Alyssa had been busy eating a bowl of tuna, Asian greens, and wholegrain noodles. She tried to discourage her newly arrived friend. 'I assume you realise, Jocelyn, that any answers I give to your problem of a lack of sex will depend on the definitions you propose to use in your research paper. Seeing that I have no idea what you mean when you say "sex" or "aggression", whatever I say isn't likely to be of much use.'

'Oh, stop being difficult. Is there a connection between sex and aggression or isn't there?'

'And you seriously want my opinion?'

'Of course.'

Alyssa tried to humour her. 'Psychodynamically, of course there is some sort of relationship between these elements, but the relationship is not simple or clear-cut, and you know it isn't.'

Jocelyn frowned at her. 'There are only three types of aggression, aren't there—or at least that's all I could find when I looked it up—so why the problem? I am talking about *all* the types—except maybe the civilised type we call assertiveness, which is too boring. The other two forms of aggression, then; overt in the form of violent anger and concealed in the form of sadism. And, yes, I do know that sadism can also go inward as masochism. My revised question for you, therefore, is this: does a lack of sex lead to angry violence and sadomasochism?'

Nothing too complex, eh Jocelyn.

'Will it help anyone to know?'

'A lot, I think. I'm sure that a lack of sex lies at the bottom of many of society's ills. Please tell me I'm right.'

The question from Jocelyn about violence was obviously loaded and far from innocent. Alyssa once again felt her appetite for the food in front of her diminishing. Potentially, all of Jocelyn's questions were going to be double-edged. Though the young doctor tried hard to appear merely a harmless troubled soul, Alyssa knew that this was not the truth of the matter. Jocelyn Goronowski was continuing to do her best to get into her mind.

Fortunately, she was able to see the other woman's sick game.

It felt ungracious, though, not to give her some sort of considered reply, so she tried. 'I don't think human behaviour is as cut and dried as you are making out, Jocelyn,' she said finally. 'People don't work like that.'

'They don't? Then why don't you tell me how they *do* work? In particular, tell me about violence. What's with that?'

Alyssa tried to appear unconcerned. 'Stop your silliness, Jocelyn.'

'This is serious. Do you not agree that death of some sort will occur if there is a lack of sex? The build-up of anger becomes dangerous when sex is infrequent, does it not? Then the aggression becomes lethal if it can't be safely expressed through sex. Isn't that how society works?'

She tried to humour her: 'There's the metaphoric little death if you *do* have sex, Jocelyn, but no real death if you don't. You know that.'

'Do I?'

'Yes, you do. People express emotion inwardly just as much as they do outwardly. More so, in fact, in modern civilisation. Frustrations are diverted mostly inwards. So, even if what you are proposing about sex and violence were true—which it isn't—then people who are sexually frustrated would be just as likely to kill or harm *themselves* as others. More likely, in fact.'

'Really? So, if no sex, then lots of inward sadism you say? Depressions, masochisms, and suicides? That sort of thing?'

'You are over-simplifying.'

'Why? There's lots of that, and lots of outward sadism in society too, not so? Cruelties and violence are everywhere. What's with all this stuff if it isn't all due to frustrated sex? Aren't you supposed to agree with Freud on this?'

'You know I'm not a Freudian. And I don't think Freud said anything like this, anyway.'

'I'm not so sure. People don't understand Freud. He's a bit like Einstein's physics.'

Forget Freud already!

'I don't know enough to give you a proper answer, Jocelyn.'

'Then what about Freud's whole *sex* thing?'

'You're being a bit single minded, don't you think, Jocelyn? And you obviously know a lot more about this than I do, so why keep asking me?'

'I can cover terrain, but I don't really know what's going on. You, on the other hand, are different. I'm convinced you know the deep stuff.'

'Are you serious?'

'Yes. And you still haven't answered my main question. *Why* do people become violent—internally or externally—if they don't get sex?'

'You've leapfrogged the first question: *do* they?'

'Don't they? When it comes to violence in society, why do you say it's *not* the result of sexual frustration? Or are you saying it's a chicken and egg thing?'

'Slow down, Jocelyn. Let me think.'

'Okay, then. Think.'

Out of kindness, Alyssa tried her best to formulate a plausible answer for her worried friend. 'Assuming we have a mature adult, frustrating an impulse will lead to anger, sure, but it *doesn't* result in violence—violence being the same as uncontrollable anger. The mind is more advanced than that. So, assuming I'm right, what then *does* result in violence? I'd say that what leads to uncontrollable anger is unconscious frustration stemming from an abusive childhood. So, I'd say violence results from emotional problems.'

'Double *duh*.'

Jocelyn seemed disappointed to hear that possibly violence was not the result of a lack of sex.

7

The hypothesis of Jocelyn's research paper was in jeopardy.

'What about Freud's libido theory, then?' she demanded. 'As far as I know, Freud believed that every impulse has a tension between physical life creation and physical death creation. There is always that tension. Which means it's not possible to have successful sex without expressing some degree of anger—although of course most people don't realise this.' She began to wag a finger in a way that mirrored Cy remarkably. 'Now, because the mental orgasm point lies somewhere in this spectrum, and because it gets permanently fixed there in early childhood, everyone has a fixed sexual release point.' Jocelyn seemed to have disappeared into her own world. 'Each individual gets his or her rocks off at a unique fantasy point in the spectrum between egalitarian love and sadistic cruelty.'

Alyssa tried to stay with her. 'Say that again, Jocelyn. Are you referring to the concept that there is a sexual key unique to every individual?'

'Yes, that. To the "special something" that each person requires to able to get off.' Jocelyn could not be stopped. 'It's closer the one way for some and closer the other way for others, this fusing of the split between love and hate during sex, but there must always be at least *some* aggression—inward or outward—for sex to be successful, by which I mean orgasmic sex, of course. It's Freud. You know what I'm talking about.'

'Is that so? Really.'

'Yes, you do. So, the question for you to answer is this: what happens to the death drive if there is no sex happening? Death as in the aggression a woman releases when she feels contempt either for herself or for the man fucking her. What happens to all that if it can't get out?'

Alyssa knew her new friend was poorly integrated socially, but this was getting ridiculous. 'One can't oversimplify psychodynamics in the way that you are doing, Jocelyn. People in healthy relationships simply don't have contempt for each other in the way that you are suggesting.'

'Now who is talking crap?'

'Okay, maybe sex isn't always loving. Maybe *within* a special, beautiful, and precious relationship—in other words, where there is safety and trust—mutually agreed aggressions may sometimes be permitted. But only within a loving context.'

'Still crap. Sexual truths have *no* option but to be expressed if orgasm is to occur. I've been reading Jung. The desire of an animus exists in a constant balancing act between hate and love, with the death wish, aka the emotion of aggression, always evoked by the rejected component of any object.'

'That is not Jung.'

'Someone, then. The point is that a death drive is required if we are to have a life drive. And the life drive, or the desire to possess the loved component of an object, is what enables us to move *out* of ourselves, so to speak.'

'Not so fast, Jocelyn. Your understanding of the so-called psychical drives looks all wrong to me, and not only because they are from the wrong century. What the hell is an "animus"?'

'Oh please. Use your brain.'

Alyssa ignored the insult. 'You need to realise that metaphysical psychodynamics are way too complex to make sense of in a few readings.'

'Is that so?'

'Yes, it is.'

Jocelyn was not impressed. 'Duh. You are totally missing the point of what I've been saying. I'm not talking about relationships between people, am I. I'm talking about sexual frustration and orgasms. Just that. Sexually frustrated people. Where does their anger go? How can you say people aren't dying?'

'Because they aren't.'

Jocelyn's face fell. 'Damn. Of course! You're right. I'm getting it now.' She began to slap her forehead. 'That's it! The link! The link between sex and aggression. It's at the fantasy level! It's only in the fantasies. It's in the fantasies . . . How stupid can one get!'

One of the cleaners, who was busy at the kitchenette, gave sidelong glances at Jocelyn as she continued to berate and slap herself.

Alyssa tried not to laugh. 'Yes, Jocelyn, she said, 'fantasy aggression is not rare, but real-life killing obviously is. Crossing the line as an adult involves the failure of almost every intrapsychic regulatory process.'

Jocelyn allowed her jaw to hang open. 'This is really great, Alyssa. I honestly never realised you were this profound.'

'You know you worked it out for yourself.'

'No. This is truly great. I'm learning things from you all the time. You have a wonderful gift.' She scratched her head. 'One more thing, Alyssa. It's just occurring to me. Can people do well on fantasy alone?'

It seemed an innocent enough question, but like everything else to do with Jocelyn, it had the potential to be something quite different.

'Hell, I don't know, Jocelyn. How should I know?' Jocelyn was frightening her yet again. Either she was taking after her dead brother and showing a schizoid tendency towards interminable theorisation, or she knew too much about her past. She tried to shut her up: 'I didn't realise there was so much frustration around, Jocelyn.'

Her friend looked suitably hurt. 'Yes, Alyssa, there is. Believe it or not, there are frustrated people out there. Unlike you, not everyone is able to be assertive.'

'I'm hardly assertive, surely.'

'You are. And it is *so* annoying.'

It felt like a put-down. 'I'm not. And in any case, what if I was? Would that be so bad? Assertiveness is a good thing, isn't it? Aggression properly channelled into non-violence. So there.'

'Damn! I give up.'

'Whatever do you mean?'

'I had my hopes, but it seems that sex is not an issue for you at all. This is so disappointing. You don't seem to have any problems with your fundamental drives.'

'My what! This drive theory stuff of yours went out the window years ago, Jocelyn. Besides, it's not the *sex* drive that's the drive, it's the *life* drive. Most people have that all wrong. Even Freud got confused about it early on in his career and at one stage he had about twenty different drives going all over the place. Later, those who still believed in drives boiled them down to just two: the life drive and the death drive. As in: "all nerve centres in nature seek pleasure and avoid pain: therefore, we *acquire* pleasure, and we *eliminate* pain". Obermaaier. As far as I know, there is currently no need for an isolated sex drive as such. Instead, the Self is better likened to an ancient despot. It dispenses life or death to everything it perceives. Yes-to-that and no-to-that. If you believe in drives, that's all there is to it.'

'Silly me. I should have known. Sorry. How stupid. It's not the sex drive, it's the life drive, except it's not that either. Yada, yada, yada. Now I have to forget all the Lacan I've been reading and toss Melanie Klein onto the scrap heap. God, you sound like a neurobiologist on acid.'

She had succeeded in making Jocelyn angry, but she was not sorry. 'You asked for this. You know you did.'

'You are being a right royal little shit, aren't you? You deny me a specific sex drive, yet you still refuse to tell me the *real* truth about the death drive.'

'Classical drive theory went out about seventy years ago.'

Jocelyn held her head in her hands. 'Jeez, who am I kidding? Why do I find it so hard to understand what is going on?'

It was impossible to work out whether Jocelyn was playing some sort of a game or not. 'There's no point carrying on like this, Jocelyn. I'm not going to be providing you with any oracular pronouncements. No one is.'

'Is that so?' Jocelyn sulked for a few minutes in silence.

Then she seemed to make a conscious decision to brighten up. Gushing with sweetness, she suddenly clapped her hands together like a small girl: 'This is so great, Alyssa, isn't it? We are on the same page.'

'We are?'

'Yes.' She finally peeled her banana. 'Unlike everybody else that I know, you are no run-of-the-mill bullshit artist. I see it all clearly now. This is so, so great. I see us getting to know each other *really* well.'

CHAPTER THIRTEEN

1

KARA, THE THIRD WIFE, insisted that Alyssa sit in front, next to Alan.

'You're our guest. And in any case, I'm sure you and Alan want to talk shop. I'm pretty useless when it comes to the academic world.'

The car was beautifully shaped and expensive looking, a white coupe. Alyssa strapped herself into the front passenger seat. 'Nice car, Alan.' It still felt wrong calling her one-time professor by his first name. 'What sort is it?'

He smiled at her from behind the wheel. 'It's an Audi RS5 Quattro. It's a bit old now, and a bit of a planet shredder, but I still like it because it's the V8 version.' He spoke indulgently, as though to a small child or to someone who should know better.

'I see.' Cars were generally Greek to her, but she knew what she liked. She liked his car. It seemed to suit him—manly, and sexy in an upmarket sort of way.

'I presume it's very fast?'

'The discs are ceramic with drilled rotors, and it has four hundred horsepower,' chimed Kara from the back seat.

'Four hundred and fifty, actually,' said Alan. 'Enough to give us all serious whiplash if I'm not careful. Still, the speed limit is only a hundred km max.' He added the last statement as though giving a reluctant reminder to himself. Then, with Alyssa safely buckled in, they pulled away from the kerb with an impressive jerk and merged into the traffic of Santos Beach.

'Now what's this about you finding your own way back?' he asked as they drove. He was referring to Alyssa's return-trip plans. 'It will be no trouble for us to pick you up again on our way home.'

Alyssa had already decided it would be kinder to everyone if she returned by train. 'Thank you so much for the offer,' she said, 'but getting back won't be a problem. I'm not sure exactly when I'll return anyway, and I'm quite used to the train trip.' She wanted to preserve the option of returning home early because sometimes her stepmother, Diana, became completely intolerable. Even at the best of times, Diana was unpleasant—so much so that Cy had long ago refused to continue seeing her. She had a further reason, too, for making her own way back. The trip to Ocean View involved a significant detour for Alan and Kara. Their destination was Quaytor, some thirty km further down the coast. It seemed heartless to inconvenience them twice.

'As long as you are sure,' said Alan. She was, and the matter was settled.

There was silence for a while as they negotiated the heavy traffic. Although it was only 8.30 am and a public holiday, the roads were close to gridlock. Originally, Alan had wanted to pick her up at her flat, but she had resisted this, citing the traffic issues. Instead, she had taken a tram to Grand Park at Santos Beach, from where the freeway system was readily accessible, and from where Alan had picked her up at the kerbside. She had her shoulder bag with her and in it were a towel, her one-piece bathing suit, dark glasses, purse, and suntan lotion. Apart from seeing her stepmother, she planned to have a swim at her childhood beach and indulge in some sunbathing. The weather appeared promising, and Kara and Alan were also dressed for a day at the seaside. She could smell suntan lotion on Kara as well as an expensive perfume. Clearly, Alan's new wife anticipated a fun day.

An impressive vista of skyscrapers swept past on their right as Alan manoeuvred onto the M1 towards the satellite city of Box Town and beyond. The powerful car felt comfortable, though stiff over bumps, and made frightening growling noises whenever Alan pressed the throttle. It was properly air-conditioned, and Alyssa noticed that the seats were made of real leather. She was not used to travelling in luxury cars—or cars of any sort since her accident—so the experience felt intoxicating, much as if she were a young child going on a family vacation. Exiting the city centre over the towering Yarradonga Bridge felt like an escape from a cage. On the other side, the air felt lighter. Even Alan seemed affected by their new-found liberation because he began to amuse himself by threading through gaps in the traffic with bursts of spectacular acceleration. Sitting next to him at the front of the car, his actions felt like a mad dash for freedom, and somehow this made her feel cheerful. Alan always seemed to have that effect on her. He was exciting. He was an expert driver, too. Before long, they had cleared the traffic and were heading at speed towards the shimmering heat of an endless horizon.

He drove confidently and well and stuck mostly to the speed limit except for the overtaking—even though, according to him, his car could reach three hundred km per hour. From her position next to him, she noticed that his arms and legs were more athletic than she had previously realised. Or was it just that the muscular car made him appear more physically powerful than he was?

Or is it because I'm so near to him?

'I do love the seaside,' said Kara from the back seat. 'It makes me feel so relaxed.'

She was sitting directly behind Alyssa, which made eye contact difficult. 'Do you plan to swim?' she asked Kara, half turning in her seat.

'Sure thing. Got my bikini in my bag. I don't know about Alan, though. We never know with you, do we darling?'

'I swim,' said Alan. 'But I have no intention of freezing or drowning or getting skin cancer. Or getting eaten by a shark.'

'There aren't any sharks,' said Kara.

'Oh please. That's what they always say.'

'Have the two of you got a place in Quaytor?' asked Alyssa diplomatically.

'Not us,' said Alan. 'But Doggy Barnes has, and he's lent it to us for the day. It's a nice house, near the beach. The Barnes clan have had it in the family for years and we often get to use it.'

'There are some good restaurants nearby, too,' said Kara.

'Sounds great. Are any of your children joining you for the day?'

'Good God, no,' said Alan. 'I've only just got rid of the last one. She's finally at university.'

'That's Harriet,' explained Kara. 'She's living in a share house with friends of hers.'

Probably to escape from you.

Alyssa knew how difficult it would be for Harriet to tolerate a stepmother, especially one as young as Kara. 'Have you got any children of your own?' She twisted in her seat and addressed the question to Kara directly.

'No. But we do have plans. Don't we, honey?'

'Sure.' Alan did not sound very positive.

'And you, Alyssa?' asked Kara in return. 'Any little ones?'

'No kids. But I'd love to have some. It's just a matter of finding the time.'

'I know the feeling.'

Alan seemed to have had an adequate amount of fun with his car because he set the cruise control, though not at one hundred but at one hundred and two km per hour. 'This way, I can talk more.'

He could, and the three of them chatted away pleasantly enough as they progressed down the highway.

2

'I'm really impressed with your car,' said Alyssa.

'Thank you,' said Alan.

'Looks can be deceiving,' said Kara. 'This one's really a monster, isn't it, honey?'

'I suppose it is,' said Alan. 'But it does have manners and it can be kept under control.' He seemed embarrassed by his wife.

Later, he selected some music from the car's extensive collection and played it in the background. The tracks reminded her of Cy's music, which both intrigued and surprised her.

'Am I hearing things?' she asked, 'or are you into this sort of music?'

He smiled at her. 'No. It's for you. Thought you might like it. It's my son's music, and he's not much older than you. Me, I know nothing about music. Spent too much time hitting the books when I was young.'

She felt her face reddening. 'Me too. Although I love music, of course.'

Alan turned up the music.

The fifth track on his playlist caught her attention and, when it was over, she asked him to play it again.

'Sure.'

Once again, the music struck an arresting chord in her emotions. 'It's so weird, isn't it, how music can affect a person. It's freaking me out in the strangest of ways.' When it was over, she asked Alan to play it yet again. 'Please, I know it's the third time, but I have to hear it just one more time.'

'Be my guest.' He fiddled with the replay switch on his steering wheel.

'What's it called?'

'Good question. Mm, let me think.' He winked at her. 'It's called *Chicago*. And it's from the album *Illinoise*.' He was reading from the screen where the name of the track was scrolling right in front of her. 'Like it, do you?' He turned up the volume yet again.

She listened to the track, motionless and emotionally frozen.

Why do I feel so anxious?

She knew she was being antisocial, so when the track ended, she indicated to Alan that she had had enough and that he could resume the normal playlist and lower the volume. 'Sorry. It's just that there was something about that track that I found really, really spooky. It made me feel frightened, though I have no idea why.'

He glanced at her oddly. 'Oh dear, that's not good, is it. Sorry. It says here that the track is from Sufjan Stevens. As far as I know, he's not officially scary.'

'It's not him who's the problem, it's me. I think sometimes I get reminded.'

'Of what?' asked Alan.

'Oh, nothing really. I can be a bit silly sometimes. Just aspects of my childhood, I suppose.'

'Right. Parent issues.' Kindly, he did not pursue the matter.

Alyssa looked again at the strong wrists and hands of the man next to her as they rested on the steering wheel and tried to imagine them as her father's. Fortunately, she could not. Alan was not her father. She needed to remember this. Alan, she could go to bed with. 'Luckily, I don't think of you as a parent figure at all,' she said. 'Quite the opposite.'

She had forgotten that his wife was in the car, which was a mistake seeing that in such circumstances the comment was inappropriate.

Almost instantly, the wife chimed in from the back seat. 'Yes, Alyssa, he *is* good for his age, isn't he? Married life suits him.'

She caught a glimpse of Kara's face in a windshield reflection. The proprietary glint in her eyes was unmistakable. A day at the beach with Alan was about more than just swimming.

For a while, in the bright sunshine, they drove along the six-lane highway in silence. Alyssa occupied herself with trying to work out why the music track had disturbed her so greatly. It had been about love and madness—or so it had seemed to her. So, why was that so frightening? Probably because when it came to love, there was no guarantee that she would not lose control yet again.

Love and death.

Her hands had begun to tremble and for the first time, the car felt too small. An anxiety attack was threatening. She tried to focus on the outside world to calm herself. Outside, in the lanes, the traffic was building again. They were nearing the coast.

'Something troubling you?' asked Alan. His tone was gentle, like that of a psychiatrist.

'Just that song. It's stirred up something within me.' She noticed that she was whispering.

'Any idea what?'

'I don't know. I think it reminds me of work. You know . . . clients. But I know it's deeper than that really.'

'Yes, I'm sure it's something deep. Unsettling echoes always are. To my way of thinking, such things are usually a resonance with an early childhood experience. I hope you didn't have too unhappy a childhood—did you?'

'Hey, can you guys speak up,' said Kara rather too loudly. 'You're giving me the creeps.'

'How about we all take a chill pill,' suggested her husband. He activated *The Best of Beethoven* and let it play softly. Then he continued his muted conversation with his front seat guest: 'Don't get me wrong, Alyssa—whatever it was that did happen to you, I'm sure you're the one best placed to judge the way forward. It hardly needs any input from me. You've probably forgotten more about psychotherapy than I've ever known.'

It was an outrageous compliment, coming from him, and she almost slapped his thigh. She managed to stop herself in time, but the spontaneous intention had made her arm come towards him. She knew

Alan had noticed, so she grinned at him self-consciously. 'You're a pure flatterer if ever I met one.'

The smile he gave her in return travelled straight to her lower belly.

'You have no idea how glad I am that you actually understand people,' he said. 'I don't know whether you realise it yet, but you are part of the beginning of the recovery of sanity in clinical psychology, counselling in particular.'

'I am? How so?' She wondered if he was joking.

'You are the future, believe me. Part of an emerging phenomenon, the first wave of resistance to the neglect of the Self. We need people who understand people. There's nothing out there at present, just a vacuum, just disaster. Most counsellors have become lost in a forest so thick with wood that they are no longer able to see the trees. They have no universally applicable model of the mind, nothing clinically useful. Surprise, surprise, the world has woken up to find that almost every so-called counsellor on the planet is nothing but a victim of his or her own countertransference. Some are downright dangerous. All I can say, Alyssa, is thank goodness our clinic has you.'

The professorial high opinion of her psychotherapy ability was nothing less than a sexual pass, of that she was certain. No one knew more about psychotherapy than Alan Summerfield himself, which meant that his words had to have a deeper meaning. Besides confirming that he knew nothing about her past, what he was really saying was that he valued her and cared about what she thought; that he was keen to get to know her better.

One did not need to be a psychologist to know what *that* meant.

The next track in Alan's music collection, *Fur Elise*, began to play, and the normally sweet music sounded inexplicably sexual. She was finding it difficult to control her feelings for him.

Why do I find such men irresistible?

'Pity we aren't all going to the beach together,' said Kara unexpectedly from behind the front seat. 'Just think what fun we could have as a threesome.'

The idea had never occurred to Alyssa, so she tried to imagine getting up close and personal with Kara. She wouldn't be able to do it.

Yuk.

'I think what Kara means is "as a group of three",' said Alan tactfully. 'A threesome means something different, honey.'

'Does it?' she said innocently. Kara then spoke directly to Alyssa: 'I'll get Alan to explain the difference to me later.'

It seemed safer to say nothing in return.

3

'Let me find us something more modern,' said Alan, referring to the music he was playing over the car's sound system. Dutifully, they listened and commented as he tried out various tracks. He had not exaggerated when he said he knew nothing about music.

They settled on Santana's greatest hits, and after a few minutes of this Alyssa thought it opportune to break the ice with Kara. After all, she was not really going to be having an affair with anyone's husband, let alone Kara's, not even if that husband was Alan Summerfield. She turned in her seat: 'How did you and Alan meet?' she asked.

Before Kara could say anything, Alan spoke. 'We were introduced to each other at a party,' he said, a little too quickly and too glibly.

'Yes. That was it,' agreed Kara. 'Alan was lonely after his divorce, and I was free at the time, and we met, and *bam!*'

'I see,' said Alyssa. 'That is such a lovely story. And you stopped . . . dancing . . . after that?'

'Not really. I don't have to anymore, of course, but I like to keep up my skills. I enjoy it. I like the exercise.'

'She's in fantastic shape,' said Alan.

'What sort of dancing do you do?'

'I'm not going to bullshit you on this, okay, because I'm proud of what I do. It's exotic dancing.' She appeared angry at the question. 'I'm quite famous for it.'

'Oh,' said Alyssa.

'She does modern dancing too. She teaches it. She has a studio,' said Alan.

'Yes,' said Kara. 'And you are welcome to come along for lessons. Can you dance, Alyssa? At all?'

Alyssa relented. 'No. Not really. I was never taught. And I don't know much about music.'

'God, you sound just like Alan. He can't dance either.'

There was more silence.

They turned off the M1 and began to thread their way through the seemingly endless sprawl of Box Town to get to Ocean View. The conversation turned to Alyssa's hometown and her childhood there, and it was Kara who had most of the questions.

'Are your folks still working?' she asked.

Alyssa noticed Alan cringe. 'No. My parents are both dead.' She said it matter-of-factly, as though it was a perfectly everyday occurrence. She knew that Alan knew—from her job application. Both her biological parents were deceased, but obviously Kara did not know. 'There's just my stepmom left. And she's too ill to work.'

'Oh. I am sorry. I never knew. Me and my big mouth.'

'I lost them when I was quite young.'

'That's amazing. What happened?' asked Kara.

'Honey, maybe she doesn't want to talk about it,' said Alan.

His new wife seemed determined not to take any orders from him. 'Do you mind me asking, Alyssa?'

'No, it's okay. Everyone asks me about it once they know. It's a long story, but no doubt it all began when my biological mother abandoned us. I was only five years old at the time.' Her voice broke: 'Too little. Which is probably why I'm so psychologically stuffed up.' She had no idea why the question had made her suddenly so emotional. There was an embarrassed silence in the car.

'Oh,' said Kara finally. 'I didn't realise.'

'Sorry. It's affected me badly. It was a big shock to all us kids. I'm the eldest, but I have two brothers and none of us took it well. My youngest brother, Harry, was only two. Our mum never even said goodbye to us. She told my dad, though, that she had had enough of us all. Three months later, she was dead.'

Kara seemed genuinely upset. 'That's really sad, Alyssa. I never knew . . . How did she die?'

'Honey!'

'It's okay, Alan,' said Alyssa. 'She was killed.'

Kara was relentless. 'Murdered?'

'Yes. Sort of. I can't explain.'

Alan intervened more strongly on her behalf. 'She was only a small child when it happened, honey. She won't want to discuss this.'

'I'm sorry,' said Alyssa. 'I know I'm not making much sense.' She was sounding weird, but she could hardly elaborate on who had killed her mother. There were some things best not revealed.

Kara was determined to be inquisitive. 'What about your father, then? Where does he fit into all of this? You say he's also passed. Did that have something to do with your mother?'

She could easily have put a stop to the interrogation, but she knew Alan was listening and she wanted him to know more. She humoured Kara: 'No. My dad was an absolute star after my mother left us,' she explained. 'He managed to look after us three little kids all by himself for about a year, even though it meant he had to take leave from his job at the smelter. Later, the government helped us move to a different place and got us a house in Ocean View. That was where my dad met my stepmother, Diana, and she moved in with us. After Dad died, we stayed with Diana at that same house until I went to university in the city.'

They had reached the main hospital in Box Town. The hospital was a familiar sight to Alyssa, and it always succeeded in stirring up negative feelings. As the car glided past, she paused the account and stared in silence at the hated buildings as they slowly receded behind them. Back came a flood of bad memories: operating theatres, evil nurses, pain, intensive care . . . and police interrogations . . .

Up ahead the road split into four different directions. 'You'll need to turn diagonal right, Alan.'

'The Marine Highway? Yes, thanks. I've got it on the GPS.'

'Then your dad died too?' It was Kara again.

She did not like talking about her past to people who could not possibly understand. 'Unfortunately, yes. That was when I was thirteen. We were involved in a road traffic accident on the highway near our church—just Dad and I were in our car. It wasn't his fault. He was distracted and a drunk hit our car side on. The other car was going much too fast. Dad was only forty-one. The man in the other car died too.'

Alan reached out and briefly squeezed her hand in sympathy.

Unexpectedly, Alyssa felt tears welling. She tried her best to suppress them. 'The police interrogated me afterwards. I hate them for that. I'll never forget how they betrayed me. When I finally made a formal statement about what exactly had happened, they decided they were not going to believe me. On principle.'

'That sounds terrible. Why did they do that?'

Because according to them I was a known barefaced liar.

She did not say it out loud. She had already said too much. 'It doesn't really matter anymore. It's all in the past. And my dad is dead.'

'But you've been left feeling betrayed by the police?'

'As I say, I'm over all that now.' That part was not true, but she wanted Kara to shut up.

'Don't press her, honey. It's obviously very difficult for her. The police are as thick as two planks and they can be absolutely awful.'

The warmth of Alan's concern made tears threaten to start up again. 'At least he died quickly,' she said softly.

'You must really miss him,' said Kara, ignoring Alan's advice.

'I loved him very much. He was all that I had. I never did get on with my . . . stepmother.' She hesitated because she remembered that Kara was a stepmother too. That aside, the truth was that she hated her own stepmother, Diana, with a passion. Without a doubt, Diana had been the cause of her father's drinking and subsequent bad behaviour. If anyone was to blame for what had happened, it was Diana.

'This stepmother thing seems really hard,' said Kara, more to Alan than to Alyssa.

Tactfully, Alan turned the conversation in a positive direction. 'You've done really well to survive these traumas so well,' he said to Alyssa. 'I think what you've been through would have destroyed most people.'

'I forget you were only thirteen.' Kara reached around the seat and squeezed her arm again, mimicking the psychiatrist behaviour of her husband.

The attempts at kindness from the couple in the car finally overcame Alyssa's defences and she could no longer stop herself from bursting into tears. As she quietly sobbed, Alan reached into the glove box and handed her a box of tissues. He kept a respectful silence, as did Kara.

Alyssa felt guilty about involving others in her problems and angry at the treachery of her emotions. Her feelings had once again shown themselves able to catch her out without warning. It was as though all her years of counselling had amounted to nothing. She was still unable to tell anyone the whole truth—not about her father, and not about her mother. Some things, she simply could not reveal. Indeed, some of the truths about the deaths of her mother and her father she could scarcely even begin to tell herself. Her mother's passing when she was five years old, for example, remained a blur in her mind. Exactly what had happened there remained shrouded from clarity by the great sense of fear she experienced every time she tried to think about it. With her father, the events surrounding his death were clearer, but even so, also not explainable to others. Instead of being unsure of the events associated with *his* death, she was faced with the need to remain economical with the truth in order to preserve his honour. Despite what he did to her towards the end, when he was drunk, she still loved him. Their love had been absolute and unconditional from the beginning, and it remained so. He was all she had, even though she had killed him—yes, she had. She would have to live with that for the rest of her life. Once too often, he had tried to touch her between her legs, under her dress, while holding her on his lap in the car on the way home from church when he was drunk. She had fought him off, not caring about the consequences, and was the cause of that loss of concentration . . .

4

Robert Brown had died because of her actions. Alyssa knew that. And she also knew that while Diana had undoubtedly caused his drinking and bad behaviour to worsen, the disintegration had begun well before, following the death of his true love, Grace, her biological mother—a woman whose death she herself had also caused. Tragically, when she had killed her biological mother, she had ultimately killed her father too.

Despite the platitudes of the mental health establishment over the subsequent years, there was only one possible explanation for it all: she was a bad person.

Which was sad.

The Quattro RS finally crested Lone Leon Hill, which marked the end of the urban sprawl, and they entered a country road leading to her old hometown. Out in the open, clear of traffic, Alan seemed to rediscover his car and his own childhood. He planted his foot on the car's accelerator and caused the high-performance vehicle to leap forward with a spine-tingling howl from its engine. G forces tugged at her face as he showed off, and the exhilarating antics put an end to her gloom. A few times, on the bendy road, the car's speedometer climbed to over two hundred km per hour.

The sudden power-driving caused her to utter a cry of pleasure. 'Wow!'

Kara, though, was not amused. 'Alan!'

His wife need not have worried. He began slowing before she had even finished yelling at him. 'Sorry. I couldn't resist.' They dropped back to under the speed limit. He seemed interested, though, in Alyssa's response to his demonstration of what his car could do. 'Liked that, did you? The imperial ton and *then* some?' He gave her a boyish grin.

'Yes,' she said. 'That was great. I've never even owned a car, let alone such a powerful one.'

'One day, I'd like you to experience what this baby can *really* do.'

'You are being very juvenile about the car again, and you know it.' It was Kara from the back seat.

Chastened by his wife, Alan proceeded towards Ocean View in silence and at a sedate speed. Alyssa felt like a co-conspirator and somehow it felt good. She liked the surrounding countryside too, which began to look familiar. There was nothing quite as invigorating as returning to the place of one's childhood. Despite the traumas, she felt afresh the unique energy of her early life. For her, Ocean View would always be a place of refuge for her spirit, no matter what. It was beautiful, and she had been a beautiful child.

'Would you like to get behind the wheel?' The masculine voice cut into her childhood like a dagger, causing her to flinch perceptibly.

Her own voice came out strangely timid. 'Drive? Drive the car?'

'Yes. If you want to. To get a true feel of it. As long as you promise to be responsible. It's a magnificent beast, but obviously very dangerous. You can drive, can't you?'

She hesitated because her mind still felt scrambled. Certainly, yes, she could drive a car. She had had plenty of practice driving her father around when he was dead drunk. 'Yes,' she said after a while. 'I can drive. But I shouldn't.'

'Come on. Have a go.'

'Leave her, Alan,' said Kara.

'I don't have a licence.'

That ended the matter.

The family home stood three streets back from the main beach, not far from the road they were on. As they got closer, she explained to Alan and Kara how best to proceed to their own destination of Quaytor. 'It's quickest to carry on through Nabrow Heads and then reconnect to the M1 that way. I assume you know?'

'The satnav does. Don't worry, we'll be fine. Besides, I've done this detour once before, when I came to this beach with the kids in another life. It's all coming back to me now.'

Again, that warm smile of his. He was such a nice man, she thought.

'I've never been here,' said Kara.

'It's been really nice seeing all this again,' he said. 'It reminds me so much of the kids.'

'You know what,' said Alyssa, 'I've just realised something.'

'What?'

'Your youngest daughter, Harriet, and my youngest brother, Harry. They have essentially the same name. That's amazing, don't you think?'

'I'd say. And look at our own names too, Alan and Alyssa. Both with an A. Similar parental tastes. How weird is that?'

'Maybe.' *This* coincidence, though, had nothing at all to do with parents with similar tastes. Her mother had not named her Alyssa and her father had not named her Alyssa either.

As they turned into the street where Alyssa had once lived, Kara had something of her own to say about names. 'Talking of weird and names, Alyssa, isn't it *you* who's the weird part? I mean, don't think I've ever encountered another Alyssa.'

'Kara!' said Alan, clearly embarrassed by her directness.

'It's not that rare, actually,' said Alyssa, who was not troubled by people like Kara. 'And it's no weirder than Kara. At least my name means something.'

'Is that so. What?'

'Truth.'

'As in *the truth?*' asked Alan.

'Yes. Alyssa means Truth. According to my father, it's to remind me of the need to always tell the truth if anyone asks for it. That's what I've been told, anyway.'

Which was true enough, but not the entire truth. She had come to realise later in life that the government clerk responsible must have intended the name as a cruel joke when applied to her. Officially, however, the name "Alyssa" was intended as a reminder of the words of the trial judge: "Perhaps, one day, we will get the *truth* about this whole sorry business out of these people".

'How fascinating,' said Kara.

Alyssa held her tongue.

Alan brought the car to a halt. They had reached their destination.

The house looked even smaller and shabbier than Alyssa remembered, and suddenly she felt ashamed. The gutters were sagging and their small front garden, previously benignly neglected, was now disgracefully dry and overgrown, with some plants even dead. As she gazed at the little house, a great sense of sadness came over her—as though her heart was about to break. There seemed nothing bleaker in the world than the infinite sadness of a bereft childhood. Innocent life ruined at its outset. The enthusiastic hopes of a small child inexorably destroyed by despair and want.

The family had not had much when she was growing up and she did not want Kara to come into the house. The threadbare interior would fill her with intolerable pity. 'No need to get out,' she said to the couple. 'It will only hold you up. I'll be fine from here.' She alighted from the car, clutching her belongings, and went and stood her bag up against the front fence. The sudden blast of heat from the summer sun caught her by surprise—she had forgotten that the car was air-conditioned—and the glare outside the car was fierce, so she rummaged in her bag until she located her dark glasses. While bending over, she was conscious of Alan's appreciative gaze. Finally, glasses on, she turned to face the car again. She adjusted her shorts, which had ridden right up her bottom.

I suppose half my ass was hanging out.

Kara, meanwhile, had moved to the front seat. Alyssa waved goodbye to them. 'Thank you so much for the lift. I really appreciate it.'

'Look after yourself.' Alan entered the driveway to execute a reverse turn, and, as his car approached her, she noticed once again how handsome it was. Gleaming white and bulging in all the right places, the powerful coupe appeared positively sensuous. With the engine almost nudging her, she was able to hear ominous mutters and wheezes emanating from its complex mechanicals. Undoubtedly, something truly monstrous lurked under the hood. And yet, despite the brute lurking underneath, the car had little fairy lights around its headlights, which twinkled at her in the sunshine. She suppressed a desire to stroke the car. There was Kara to think of. She had to try to be a good person.

Alan's turning manoeuvres completed, Kara opened the front window on her side as the car pulled away and waved. For the first time, she appeared cheerful. Her long brown hair streamed out in the wind and Alyssa noted how she too had put on a pair of dark glasses.

She had to concede that she was beautiful. Aging, but beautiful. 'Have a lovely day at the beach.'

'We sure will.' There was a triumphant note to Kara's voice as they turned a corner and disappeared from sight. For the first time, Alyssa saw that Alan's car had four exhaust pipes.

Somehow, the sight of them unsettled her. How easily things could be taken too far. She needed to be careful.

5

Alone now, Alyssa picked up her bag and headed slowly for the front door of her one-time home. She realised she was missing Cy. She had not thought of him even once during the entire trip and now she felt guilty because she needed him. She was going to be emotionally tested once she re-engaged with her past. The depressing house was already sending its familiar chill through her. During previous visits, Cy had provided a welcome shield against what lay within. He did not allow people to abuse him—not even stepmothers. More than ever, she felt a need for his reassuring grip on personal boundaries. Once she entered the front door, her stepmother would immediately begin to do her best to upset her.

The relationship with her had always been poor, made worse no doubt by the fact that by any objective standard Diana was an inherently annoying person. She was one of those unfortunates born with the uncanny knack of always being able to say the wrong thing at the wrong time. Tragically, though, even the possession of an objectionable personality was not Diana's main problem. As the increasingly unhappy years of childhood had crept by, it had become increasingly apparent to Alyssa and the rest of the family that stepmother Diana was also mentally unwell. By the time Alyssa became a young teenager, there remained no further doubt that what the family had acquired was a rotten imposter; not a real mother at all but a monster whose main interest in life lay not in mothering but in destroying the lives of others.

Once Alyssa had managed to escape Ocean View a year after completing high school, the relationship with Diana had improved slightly, though for no reason other than her own efforts. Wisely or unwisely, Alyssa had followed the advice of the mental health workers who had treated her during her breakdown in her second year at university and redoubled her efforts to make something positive out of the toxic relationship with her stepmother. It was for her own good—in the longer term—they said. The visits home had required effort and courage, but she had done her duty. And now she remained stuck in a familiar pattern of a visit home every few months or so. Nevertheless, it remained hard to stay polite in the presence of the person who had tried so hard to ruin her life. Some days, the resentment boiled to the surface with such vehemence that she wished her stepmother would hurry up and die, while on other days she was able to control the bitterness. Deep down, though, she realised that she was never going to be able to care much for the welfare of her father's nemesis. Her heart was simply not in it.

Yet, she persevered. She knew from her studies in psychology that one could not run away from an emotional problem because, unfortunately, it always tagged along. If she were ever to escape her past, she needed to get down to the root of her troubles and deal with it. For that reason alone—acceptance of the past—she needed to continue to interact with her stepmother. To date, though, she remained nowhere near getting to the root of anything. All attempts at rapprochement had so far been fruitless. Diana was not, and never would be, a warm-hearted person—especially not when it came to a stepchild whom she had never wanted in the first place and one whom she would have been perfectly happy to see die.

The feeling was mutual. Whether Diana lived or died felt of little concern to her either. She had discussed this predicament with Wendy Greene often enough, but unlike the run-of-the-mill mental health workers, Wendy had been uncharacteristically pessimistic about the prospects for improvement.

> You never had a mother who was there for you, Alyssa, so you never will. Painful as this is, it's a fact of your life, and you will need to come to terms with it. When you needed a woman to be truly there for you, there was nobody. So, now, all grown up, you do not experience women as truly there for you. Deep down, you do not trust any woman, including yourself.

Wendy Greene was never one to pull her punches.

Alyssa remained standing in her deserted driveway, out in the blazing sun, while she struggled with her memories. Objectively, the situation with her stepmother was close to hopeless. Harry, her youngest brother, had stormed out of the house at the age of sixteen after calling Diana a supercilious dog and never returned—currently, he lived with a friend—while her other brother, Greg, who was two years older than Harry and a year younger than herself, never visited despite having left home conventionally after completing school. She was the only person left from the original family who was still prepared to make contact—and that only because of professional advice. What a sad legacy for any stepmother.

Maybe she should turn around and head for the train station. It felt no small thing to have to enter once again the home that had denied her any importance or validity; a place where she had received not even one word of thanks for all the occasions when she had been forced to adopt the role of mother herself. The lack of acknowledgement still hurt. How many times had she fed her brothers with her father dead drunk and Diana totally unresponsive to their needs?

Countless times.

Diana had taken a once cheerful and empowering home and turned it into a place of degradation. What her stepmother had done to their family no person on earth could forgive.

6

The front door was ajar. Her stepmother had obviously heard them arrive yet not come out to greet her or anyone else. Alyssa pushed the door with her foot, and it swung open slowly. And there, as she half expected, ghost-like in the gloom and resembling a large frog, stood Diana. The motionless figure gave her a fright when it moved unexpectedly.

'Hello, my dear,' said her stepmother, coming to life. She extended a cheek for a kiss. 'Welcome home.'

The woman who failed to care properly for my dad.

'Hi,' said Alyssa. Her stepmother was as ugly as ever. She had never forgiven her for that insult to her real mother's attractiveness. She performed the obligatory kiss on the cheek, but even as she did so she could not fail to remember the devastation she had experienced in that exact same hallway some twenty years earlier when first she set eyes on Diana Penelope Croft.

Then, their positions had been reversed. She had been the one waiting in the house, a young girl barely seven years old, and Diana had been the visitor, a lady with no children of her own. Alyssa, then a little girl, had been over-excited, breathless with expectation, desperate to meet the new mother to be. How could any adult have expected her not to be excited? Torn between loyalty to an earlier mother and hope for the future, she had come face to face with the new woman at last. How earnestly had she jumped up and down in the hope that her daddy's new, blonde-haired girlfriend would take notice of her and be a kind and nurturing *Penny*.

Two blondes together.

Unfortunately, the new blonde was no friendly Penny, but a witch called *Di*.

What an ill-behaved child. Take her away.

How crushingly had the new woman turned out to be nothing like the sweet angel she had so earnestly asked for in her prayers. Instead, what the family acquired was their worst nightmare: a deadly and menacing oppressor. An evil stepmother.

Die-ana.

The memory of that unfortunate day was almost too much to bear and, as she stepped back from kissing her stepmother, she steadied herself by instinctively placing a hand on the hall stand, which was still in its familiar place. The overly elaborate structure, an heirloom of her father's, had been their one and only item of household pride and had served her childhood well. She missed her father.

'Nice to see you haven't forgotten about me,' said her stepmother. 'I was beginning to think that you had.'

'I've been busy. You know how it is.' They moved further into the house. 'First it was the final exams, and now it's the new job.'

'All these busy people. I know I don't rate very highly with you. It makes me sad.'

Her stepmother had never worked a day in her life and did not know what day of the week it was, let alone the meaning of busy. 'At least I'm here, so let's try and make the most of it, shall we?'

'I've been very unwell lately,' said Diana. 'It's been the same old problem. Some days I can hardly move because of the pain.'

'Yes, Di, I know. I'm sorry to hear it.' She felt no sympathy. Her stepmother was always sick, and her X-rays and blood tests were always normal. The endless whining had grown very tedious. Despite having severe abdominal pains for the past twenty years, she had succeeded in remaining very much alive and well fed.

Her stepmother developed a suspicious expression. 'Are those your swimming things I see in your bag?' She was peering into the bag inquisitively; her abdominal pains now seemingly forgotten. 'Don't tell me you are going to abandon me again?'

'You know I like to swim when I'm here. It won't take me long. I'll go later, once we've caught up. You can walk with me down to the beach if you like. It will do you good to get out.'

She gave a dismissive wave with her hand to indicate that she had no intention of going anywhere. 'You young people. Come and sit in the lounge room with me. I want to tell you all my news.'

Alyssa followed her stepmother to the lounge, observing her from behind with increasing dismay as they walked. As expected, Diana still had her pigeon toes, knock-knees, and drooping shoulders, but now for the first time two additional rolls of back-fat protruded out of her dress under her arms. The double rolls marked a new milestone in the steady physical disintegration she had been forced to observe over the years. Not once had Diana ever cared properly for herself; not once eaten healthily, done any exercise, or looked after her appearance. Even her hair, at one time as blonde as her own, was now neglected, lifeless, and grey. How could a woman she was supposed to love and admire allow herself to cut such a pathetic figure? She could not think of any reason to feel any approval. Even Di's steps, as she walked, came in tentative shuffles.

She's only fifty-six years old, for God's sake!

That was only four years older than Alan Summerfield.

Not content with merely allowing herself to become prematurely decrepit, her stepmother had wilfully continued with total self-absorption and remained steadfastly determined to be trapped in a fatal funk of hopelessness. Living away from her, in the city, Alyssa had forgotten just what a toxic and cloying person she was. It was all coming back to her now.

Die-ana, the toxic stepmother of yore, eased herself into an easy chair. 'Perhaps you could make us a little tea, dear.'

'Sure. I'll go to the kitchen in a minute.' Alyssa tried to look positively at the faded woman in the chair in front of her, but—as always—saw nothing but the disgruntled frog she always saw. The creature—who now had the gall to be grinning at her—had sinned against three helpless stepchildren beyond measure or possibility of forgiveness. Diana was no kin of hers. She was looking at a stranger; someone who filled her with anger and disgust, and she felt close to being sick. Therapy had changed nothing. Diana was a monster, someone who had entered their home and devoured four innocent lives. It seemed very wrong to be sitting there with her as though nothing had happened. Trying to obtain healing was tough. It felt more like capitulation than acceptance.

Yet, she knew that if she wanted to make emotional progress she would have to face up to the truth, which was that her stepmother was never going to be the woman she wanted her to be. Which left her with nothing. It was this last truth that she simply could *not* accept—that she was a nobody with nothing; that she meant nothing to anybody. The frustrating thing was that there was nothing she could do to change her childhood; nothing for it but to be brave and try to persevere all by herself without any secure foundations. It was not a recipe for a good life.

Wendy Greene had been pessimistic for good reason.

'I'm pleased you are doing so well these days,' said her stepmother.

'There was a time, you know, when I despaired that you would ever come good.'

'Really.'

'Oh, yes. You used to give me hell's delight. They warned me that you would be a difficult child, but I never knew the half of it. I never even knew what that meant. And just when I thought it couldn't get any worse, you went and became a teenager. The teenager from hell, I might add. Remember the joys of that?'

'Seriously. Someone once told you that I was a difficult child. At seven!'

'We've had our difficulties, I know, my dear. But I'm so glad you have matured. I suppose it was about time. You are all I have, you know.'

'Do you still believe the rubbish that I was a difficult child. Even now? Seriously?'

'You weren't easy. Even your own mother found that, you know. Grace used to say so to your father.'

Grace was her biological mother, the one who had abandoned the family, and Grace and Diana had never met—that much Alyssa did know. She knew, too, that half of what came out of Diana's mouth was a self-serving lie. Wendy had warned her often enough against trying to argue with someone like that. So-called facts from Diana were bound to be grotesquely self-centred distortions seeing that reason played no part in any of her thought processes. Alyssa knew she should ignore Diana's comments as far as possible, but the malicious slandering of her childhood made her blood boil. 'I'm sorry you think like that. Still, it doesn't matter now. Not anymore.'

'I know you like to imagine things, Alyssa. I suppose it keeps you happy. You look happier now.'

Alyssa kept silent. *What a sad woman,* she thought. Everything about her was sad. Sagging, protruding, grey, listless . . . she could go on. Diana could easily pass for seventy. The difference between the old crone sitting in front of her and Alan Summerfield was hard to get her head around. Alan was trim and toned, and he behaved and thought like a man half his age. Her stepmother, by contrast, appeared almost dead.

Is this what evil does to a person?

7

One terrible day, Diana Penelope Croft had become Diana Brown. Diana had married her father and taken their surname. However, even though Diana had harvested her father's soul with apparent ease, she soon discovered that she was not up to the task of stealing the souls of his three children. At no stage had the three of them ever regarded Diana Croft as anyone other than a witch. There had been no co-operation with her; the three of them had existed as three children without any parents at all—their remaining father having become a man bewitched. It became three brave children pitted against a malevolent female adversary.

What a disgrace of a human being.

'Tea?'

'Yes, okay. I'll make it.' Alyssa went to the kitchen, stopping off in her old bedroom to stow her bag on the way. The bedroom held little evidence of her past life there, and seemed bare, but the framed photograph of her father, Robert Brown, remained on the wall just inside the doorway where it had always been. Alyssa touched the photograph briefly with a fingertip. There was nobody in the world that she loved more, despite what he had started doing to her towards the end of his life. If only Diana had not destroyed him, she thought. She remembered taking the photograph herself. She had received a camera for her tenth birthday and tested it out on her father. He looked surprisingly young and healthy in the photo, considering how things finally turned out, and he was smiling. The smile warmed her heart yet again. She had forgotten how sweetly he used to smile. That was how things were supposed to be, that kind of special smile that only real fathers could give to real daughters. Not like later. He was wearing a fancy shirt because they were on their way to church, but his hair was tousled because it always was. She used to believe he looked like a blond version of Robert Pattinson, who at the time she thought was the handsomest man alive. Her father had been like that, like Adonis, who they had studied at school that year in a poem by Percy Shelly. Her own good looks had come from her father, not only her blonde hair. Her biological mother, Grace, had apparently been plain and dark-haired.

Away from Diana, it seemed easier to breathe, but the depressions of childhood soon intruded. The sensing of it made her want to scream. When Diana first invaded their house—when she was seven—the pot plants had been the first to go. One by one, they had died in a slow and miserable process of neglect. Bizarrely, she missed the plants, as though she had once loved them, because she now realised that their demise had signalled the end of her own cherished and nurtured existence and the beginning of a nightmare. It was not long afterwards that she and the family had finally realised that what they had invited into their home was not a new mother but a Diana. With *her*, they had acquired a stranger; someone who always complained of pain, always sprayed for insects, always got the grocery shopping wrong, always listened to the TV far too loudly, always froze the house when using the air-conditioner, always screamed at them, always boiled the house when using the heater, always threatened to "kick them out", always poisoned them with unhealthy cooking . . . there was no end to the havoc. Always, always, always, like a giant self-centred baby, the new stepmother sucked the life and air out of everybody and everything in sight.

Viewed in hindsight and with the benefit of a degree in psychology, the cause of it all seemed obvious now: Diana Croft suffered from a mental illness, a mental illness called Munchhausen by Proxy—which was a dangerous disorder. With it, the sufferer required someone under their care to always be sick. Innocent dupes that they were, the Brown family acquired a stepmother whose main interest in life—right from the outset—had been to ensure that someone under her care was always unwell. Initially, the person selected had been her father, and steadily, over the years, she had managed to render him helpless from depression and alcoholism. Then, of course, there were still his three children to get through . . .

It was always about Di Croft, and it always would be.

Everything is always about her.

There had never been a place in her stepmother's life for a child called Alyssa and there never would be. The renewed certainty of this descended over Alyssa like a heavy gloom. She had been too frightened to face this truth when young and vulnerable but by now it had become obvious and today it felt almost unbearably hurtful: her stepmother had never wanted her. Right from the very beginning, Diana had never wanted to be her stepmother. As a defenceless small child, she had had no choice but to accept such views. And now she was stuck with their deadly legacy: she was of no value and never would be.

There had been no escaping Diana Croft, a woman who deep down had wanted her dead, but even now, now that she was completely independent of this woman, the past treatment by her still felt unbearably unjust. Even though Diana had failed—so far—in her main task of making her eldest stepchild lose the will to live, she had indeed succeeded in achieving severe and permanent damage.

The awfulness of it all threatened to crush Alyssa into a little ball on the floor and she struggled to remain standing upright. There was nothing for it but to fight back. She knew she had to fight back.

Two can play at the same game.

It was the only way. If anyone was going to die, it was going to have to be Diana.

After all, so many of the others had already died . . .

The people at the hospital had said that death was not the way, but what if it was the only way?

Alyssa went and sat on her old bed and held her head in her hands. She knew she needed to stop having such thoughts.

Must try harder.

However, the walls and ceiling of the little bedroom seemed to press in on her. She could sense them moving; somehow feel their weight. And the pressure was making her feel alarmingly unwell.

A loud voice cut through her struggles. 'What's happening with that tea, Alyssa!' The yelling was remarkably loud for an invalid.

The spell in her old bedroom broken, Alyssa hurried to the kitchen.

While she was soaking the teabags, her stepmother joined her.

'I've got some black forest cake for us,' she said. 'I'll get it out. What's been taking you so long?'

'I went past my old room.'

'Not that picture again. Bob was such a weak man, Alyssa. Such a no good in the end. Even so, I suppose he didn't deserve to die. Not the way he did.'

'What would you know? And anyway, you don't miss him. At least I do.'

'Well! How *dare* you say that! You of all people. If it wasn't for you . . . I'll say no more.'

'If it wasn't for me, *what*? I think you'd better return to the lounge before I lose my temper with you.' The calmness of her voice surprised her because she was close to slapping Diana's ugly face. 'Go! I'll bring you your cake.'

The old lady fled. 'You know what the police said,' she yelled from the corridor.

'Fuck the police!' Alyssa yelled back at her.

Yes, fuck the police.

Her hands shook as she cut two slices of cake, a thin one for herself and a thick one for Diana. As a thirteen-year-old, she had gone to the town's police station in an extreme act of bravery—for her—and asked to speak to a lady police officer, only to be laughed out of the station and told to return in the company of an adult, if at all. She had then tried to get Diana to agree to take her there, but her stepmother had refused and instead demanded to know what it was that could be told to a policewoman and not to her. All complaints needed to go past parents first. Her stepmother had done nothing. There had been no one to turn to.

And the next thing that had happened was that her father was dead.

Which she did not want to think about.

After that tragedy, life got even worse for the family. Diana moved on to her next project in earnest. The aim was to achieve the final destruction of the stepchildren, so, to get matters underway, she redoubled her efforts with the oldest one, a child the government insisted on calling Alyssa, and one who was now associated with not only the death of Grace Brown but the death of Robert Brown too. This was a child clearly so wicked as to be beyond redemption. In recognition of this fact, Diana bestowed upon the child the ultimate warning title: "Possessed by the Devil".

Her incurably evil child.

It was enough to drive any child crazy.

Years of psychological therapy following the mental breakdown at university during second year sociology had not been able to achieve closure for her. That someone could take a young and vulnerable person and deliberately set about turning them into damaged goods still seemed unforgivable. No amount of psychological treatment would ever enable her to love someone so hateful.

As she walked down the corridor with Diana's cup of tea and large piece of cake, Alyssa could not work out why she even bothered with the woman. Fretting about someone like Diana was a complete waste of time. There were much easier ways to solve such problems. She smiled grimly as she approached the lounge. For example, she could ram the cake down the woman's throat. That would shut her up for good.

Corpse found choked on a large piece of black forest.

Most plausible in the greedy.

Perhaps it was time for one of life's little accidents . . .

Some come-uppance.

What a lovely feeling *that* would be.

CHAPTER FOURTEEN

1

'MAKE WAY. TRIGGER WARNING. Here to pick somebody's brains about sex. Again.'

Alyssa cringed inwardly at the spectacle approaching her in the staff room.

Oh, God.

Jocelyn progressed ponderously across the room while balancing a large and obviously heavy pile of questionnaires on her hip, clutched under an arm. She staggered past a table full of cleaning staff and came and stood next to Alyssa, who was seated at a still empty table. She beamed down magnanimously. 'Here is my study on the psychology of the orgasm. Sorry. Hope it doesn't give you indigestion. The conference is getting still closer and I'm still in all kinds of strife with it.'

Jocelyn pulled out a chair opposite Alyssa and sat down heavily, placing her stack of results on the vacant chair next to her. 'I have no idea why I agreed to present on such a tomfool subject.' She patted the pile. 'Next to me here, Alyssa, I have a whole world of supposedly true thoughts just prior to orgasm. Neat, isn't it? Not! I can't get over how much garbage this all is. It's come as a genuine shock to me. Seriously. Right here, beside me, big shock. It's got me scared witless. Lies, all lies.' Theatrically, she wiped her brow with a napkin she found on the table.

'Hello, Jocelyn. Yes, I was having a great day so far. Thanks for asking.'

'Oh, please, get over yourself. This is important.'

There was no point in resisting her. Fortunately, the staff room was relatively empty, with just the cleaners present—and Trish, who was sitting with them. They were some distance away, gossiping raucously and out of earshot of quiet conversation.

253

'What do you mean, all *lies*, Jocelyn? Nothing earthy in your reports? Is that what you mean?'

'No. We are not talking about that. We are talking about nothing. They have given me *nothing*. At least, not anything even vaguely threatening.'

'Threatening? Whatever do you mean?'

'Threat-eliminating. Threat-combating. That's what I need from them, but there's *nothing*. No masochistic or sadistic behaviours, not even aggressive *thoughts* directed inwards or outwards. Nothing. They are giving me absolutely nothing. Just vanilla bliss. No submission or assertiveness in any format whatsoever. All lies, therefore. Nothing truthful.' She paused. 'Sorry if this sort of deep sexual analysis is news to you, by the way.'

'I wasn't born yesterday.'

'Well, seems I was. And now I'm in trouble. My survey clients have been playing me like a violin. I need an expert's perspective on this pronto. You still seem the best choice. My only choice, in fact.'

'So, now you want me to save your dud research project?'

'Guilty as charged.'

Alyssa understood finally what Jocelyn was on about. 'The women in your survey have been telling you what they think you want to hear rather than the truth; is that it?'

'Afraid so. Very perceptive, as always. I'm ashamed of myself for having been so naïve. Even though I made them anonymous, my people have been telling me lies. This is my sad discovery.'

Alyssa tried not to laugh. 'You are being ridiculous. How do you know they are lying?'

Jocelyn lifted her document pile and slammed it onto the table. 'Because I know enough about sex to know that they are.'

'You do? I thought only a proper study design could do that. Sex is all about the Un-conscious, Jocelyn, something that you modern psychiatrists don't even believe in. Personally, I'd say you have zero chance of getting to the truth by means of your sort of survey.'

'Not so, little madam. Because you are going to empower me to sort this mess out.'

'No chance.'

'You have to. I'm desperate. You see, by now I've managed to read up enough to at least realise that sex probably *is* all jumbled up with unconscious early childhood resonances. Unfortunately, though, I still don't know enough about this unconscious stuff to make any sense of it. So, I don't understand *how* I've been fooled. That's where you come in.'

'Oh no. I'm not an expert on the psychology of sex. You know that.'

'You have what I need, I know you do. If anyone around here can sort out this pile of nonsense for me, it's you.' She jabbed at the questionnaires angrily with her index finger. 'What about *your* people's "Un-unconscious", Alyssa? Maybe *that* will help me to get at least *something* out of this drivel.' She attempted to perform a karate chop on her stack of documents but failed miserably when her hand skidded off sideways. 'Ow! Ow. Fuck these people.'

'There's no point throwing a tantrum and coming to me. I only know what Obermaaier says, and you've read his textbook anyway.'

'Humour me.'

'You have to be joking. I can't tell you anything you don't already know.'

'Don't be shy. Just quote me something.'

'I'm trying to drink my coffee.'

'Pretty pleease.'

'Oh, all right then. But I haven't got long.'

2

Jocelyn seemed genuinely in trouble with her research project, so Alyssa did her best to help. For that, she resorted to her main textbook, which she knew almost off by heart. 'Well, Jocelyn, maybe Obermaaier could be useful to you. As you know, he sees the mind as a metaphysical two-part whole-of-brain cyber-function that occurs on a plane higher than that of the physical matter of the brain itself. The critical insight, according to him, goes something like this:

> For a computational entity such as the mind to attain Self-consciousness, it needs to have two separate compartments: an initial unconscious early childhood part to provide the relevant

computational rules and ways of being, and a later conscious part that processes the environment using the pre-established fundamental rules of meaning in its unconscious store. The matured mind can only process the outside environment meaningfully if it has recourse to rules that successfully enable its own differentiation from it.'

'Mm', said Jocelyn, her eyes closed. 'So, he wants us to believe that consciousness of a Self has arisen from the evolutionary drive towards maximum adaptation to a relevant environment. That's just elementary neurobiology, isn't it? Stated in a completely muddle-headed way. And don't forget the vocal cords. They come into it somewhere. Language.'

'That's in Obermaaier too, Jocelyn. But the point is, without the use of basic operating rules, consciousness of a Self is logically impossible.'

'Enough already. No more quotes, please. Besides, that's not only Obermaaier, is it? You've had lectures from Alan, haven't you? During your training. You must have, because lately he's been talking the same sort of nonsense. I can't use any of this at the conference. The people there aren't idiots. This stuff is like some sort of gangrene or fungus or something on the psychology profession and it's absolutely discredited. Obermaaier and Alan are both regarded as big embarrassments by almost everyone, so the conference delegates are going to end up laughing at me too. Already my people at the university think Alan's finally cracked under the strain of all his failed marriages. You do know this, don't you? That Alan is all cracked up?'

Alyssa had heard no such thing from anybody else. 'I was taught not just by Alan. And we were taught that the conscious mind is nothing more than one of the many products of the brain, just as urine is one of many products of the kidney. Urine is not the kidney and consciousness of Self is not the brain.'

'Oh please!'

Alyssa felt hurt. 'In that case, why are you coming to me to ask me for help?'

'What help? What has any of what you have been saying got to do with my research project on the psychology of the orgasm?'

'It's not rocket science, Jocelyn. Once you understand the basics of how consciousness of the Self is structured, you begin to understand the orgasm. Orgasm is a deconstruction of the Self. From there, everything begins to make sense.'

'A *deconstruction* hey? Incredible.' Jocelyn rubbed her hands together as if possessed by renewed strength. 'Well then, I suppose all we need to do now is work out what the hell *that* means and then work out how to use it to prove that the answers to my survey questions are untruthful. Shouldn't be difficult, hey. It will need to be swallowable by the conference delegates, though.'

'This is insane. If your research has been done with a poor design nothing will save it.'

'Is that the best you can do for me?'

Alyssa relented, mostly out of pity. 'Well, I suppose you could examine the transference and countertransference occurring in the communication between y'all.' She grinned, knowing that it flashed her top teeth at Jocelyn.

'Y'all? Y'all? That's it?'

'Yes, it is. Un-conscious factors are important when it comes to making confessions about sexual activity, so obviously this is where your study has gone all wrong. Your own personality, who you are—their doctor— probably stuffed things up completely. Your clients always knew that it would be you who would be reading what they wrote, so it made them economical with the truth.'

'You mean they've been giving me what they think I expected to hear?'

'I suspect so. As I said before, it's in the unconscious early childhood mind—the Un-conscious—where we find the basic operating rules for any individual, so your research clients won't be any different. Socially acceptable sexual behaviour is quite different from true sexual thoughts. The real sexual thoughts of any individual depend on the unique events of that individual's early childhood, coloured by their biologically pre-enhanced possibilities, and these dark truths are always kept secret, both because of the guilt and shame they evoke and because they are so personally precious.'

'And how many textbooks, exactly, have you swallowed on this?'

'It's not just Obermaaier. I also did Sexology 101. At university—as an extra.'

'You don't say.'

'I did.'

'Alright then, let's believe you. For now. So, let's assume that there's a lot of unconscious stuff going down in this whole sex business. But remind me: we know that there *is* an unconscious component to the conscious mind because . . . *how*? I need to know something here because some smart alec at the conference is sure to ask me.'

Alyssa tried her best:

'We *know* there is an Un-conscious component to the conscious mind because, universally and reliably, a childhood Self can be inferred in oneself and in others by anyone suitably perceptive. More specifically, an Un-conscious childhood can be unmasked if one analyses the defences of the adult host. In skilled hands, it is even possible to arrive at a good approximation of what necessarily underpins any particular Self-construct.'

'And Obermaaier is serious about this?'

'Yes. Although, okay, it's something that can only be discovered by personal experience. But it's still true. One person's Un-conscious *can* mirror and sound another person's Un-conscious. It's how interactions between Self-constructs always occur. We always interact more deeply than we think. It goes on all the time.'

'Holy shit, you people really do take this stuff seriously, don't you? Going down in submarines and all.'

'And you people have no theory of the Self whatsoever.'

'Yes and no. Metaphysics, though, is out the window, to use your terminology. We prefer to stick with the more tangible.'

Trish and the cleaners had finished their drinks and began heading back to work. Coffee time was almost over. Trish came past their table to greet them, approaching from behind Jocelyn as she did so. Silently, she mouthed "good luck" to Alyssa. 'Hello Dr Goronowski,' she then said sweetly. 'Nice to see you both so happy.'

Jocelyn swung around. 'Oh, hello to you too.' She grabbed Alyssa's hand, which was resting on the table. 'My Alyssa here is busy solving all my problems. Aren't you, dearest?'

Alyssa grimaced and took her hand away. 'Probably not.'

There were smiles all round, and soon there were just her and Jocelyn left in the staff room. Jocelyn consulted her phone. 'Got to go too, soon. What now? What do I do with all this unreliable truthfulness?' She ran a finger up and down her pile of papers, creating a musical sound. 'How does one make a pile of junk sing?'

How indeed.

3

Summer continued hotter than ever, but Alyssa had no time to enjoy the sunshine because work occupied most of her attention. New clients continued to turn up at the Donald Clinic in large numbers, often in a state of emotional crisis, and the pressure of work was relentless. It did not take long for it to dawn on her that she was trapped on an endless merry-go-round, one that spun relentlessly morning to evening every single day of the working week. There was no respite.

After just a few months of it she was already starting to feel dizzy.

Weekends, fortunately, she still had free, but when these precious off days arrived, she felt little inclination to do anything other than rest. Unlike in the old days, she had no emotional energy left to expend on the needs of others, so the tradition of tagging along with Cy's plans over the weekends and going places with him began to lose its appeal. Cy, however, showed no interest in understanding her new needs or in being helpful. Instead, he became restless and distracted. To make matters worse, his latest manuscript—the one about Chad, the man who thought that because men were stronger it was mainly men who had the option of being sadistic—hit a serious case of writer's block.

The problem was that Cy had found an article in a book in Brian's bookshop that indicated that his ideas about sadism were all wrong. According to Brian's book, to view sadism as just sexual pleasure from inflicting imagined (or real) physical cruelty was to mistake the meaning of the word entirely. Sadism was not a male thing; it was not about men with whips and ropes. Instead, it was all about winners and losers of *any* gender; all about being okay with the level of cruelty required to get one's own way. For every winner there needed to be a loser. And the loser was not the sadist.

Sadism was a sentiment present in *all* transactions between people. In any interpersonal interaction, there was ultimately always true give or take, no matter how much prior reversed give and take went on or how finely balanced this was. The winning "take-transactor" was, by definition, always sadistic in relation to the ultimately losing "give-transactor". Therefore, when viewed in its larger context, sadism had nothing at all to do with gender as such. Or so according to the book in Brian's bookshop.

Which was a disaster, according to Cy, because, if true, the intended punch line of his yet to be completed manuscript was ruined. Up until now, Chad had believed that he had something over women. Now, it seemed he did not. Potentially, the hero, Chad the optionally sadistic man, was just as likely to be a complete loser with no option at all.

Cy had lost his way.

Whatever the case, Alyssa had little time to pander to his endless moping around.

She, at least, was earning good money. And, unlike Cy, she knew the value of money. While he would have gone on a financial splurge had he been in her situation, she had resisted such temptations and instead set up several debit orders and begun reducing her mountain of study debt. She mentioned none of it to Cy. Long ago she had learnt that he and money did not go well together. He had only one approach to it: spend it as fast as possible. Exciting as that might be at the time, the less Cy knew about her finances the better. They still had their own bank accounts, so it was easy to avoid the issue. He could continue with his irresponsible life, and she could stay out of the mess.

4

Summer should have waned by now, but the air remained stubbornly warm.

Perhaps it was the lateness of the night that made the heat harder to bear than usual. Alyssa was in bed next to Cy, and he was asleep, but she was still awake. She should have been asleep too by now, despite the warmth, and she felt angry with herself. She needed the rest. It was going to be yet another big day at work tomorrow. The lights were off, and it was quiet, but try as she might, she could not get to sleep. There seemed no explanation for it. Yes, the curtains to the window facing the bricks of the adjoining building were open, but that was to maximise ventilation; in the room itself it was dark—darker than usual in fact, the inky shadows the gift of a moonless sky. The only thing she could discern from where she lay was a faint background glow from the streetlights reflecting off the wall of the apartment block next door.

She was lying on her side on top of the sheets, naked, and she turned to lie flat on her back. Perhaps the air was keeping her awake, she thought. It was much more humid than usual.

Stifling.

But no, it couldn't be that. Cy was half covered with the sheet and was sleeping perfectly well. Besides, the heat wasn't nearly as bad as earlier that summer. She was just looking for excuses. It was time to face up to the truth: she had become a failure at sleeping—at everything, probably. Seldom had she felt so negative. She wasn't coping at work and despite her best efforts she could not get to sleep. It was all too much, really. And now it had gone one step further: she had become an actual insomniac. Another Ellen Goodman. How humiliating. She stared at where the ceiling should be and tried not to grind her teeth. Obviously, something was wrong with her, but what? She had no idea what it could be even though she was a psychologist. It was infuriating.

There was an electric fan in the cupboard, but she was reluctant to get up and get it out because she knew it would upset Cy. Fans irritated him. Frustrated, she turned onto her stomach to see if yet another change in position improved matters. It didn't, though the air did feel rather sexy on her bottom. A different approach was needed if she was to get to sleep. She tried to imagine herself in the northern hemisphere, where it would be winter. She had been there once, to Oxford, in winter, where it had been deliciously cold. That was her only time out of the country— paid for by Aaron, her second boyfriend. He had taken her with him when he went there for a job interview after graduation, probably in the hope that she would move to Oxford too. Before the trip, she had half-promised to repay him, but in the end she never did. They broke up a month later when he got the job and she decided to stay on in Astoria. Strictly speaking, she still owed him thousands.

Lying on her stomach with her rear end uncovered, she missed Aaron.

5

The following week, Alyssa approached the office of professional supervisor Susan Lindow feeling unusually anxious. She did not normally feel this nervous when meeting someone new, so she wondered why this was happening. The unease felt more severe than straightforward anxiety, more like fear. Deep down, somewhere, her mind was in an uproar. No doubt, it was her Un-conscious playing up, hard at work trying to conceal things because it suspected that the person whom she was about to see—a counselling psychologist—would uncover too much. Which meant that the trepidation she was feeling was a warning to flee. Her Un-conscious was not wrong to feel concerned: if Susan Lindow got to discover even the slightest bit of truth, the outcome would be extremely unfortunate. For everyone.

After all, Susan was more than just a sister counselling psychologist. Susan was a *supervising* psychologist—still a counsellor, but one widely respected and vastly experienced—and therefore not someone easily hoodwinked. Those in the field rated her even more highly than Wendy Greene, which was high praise indeed. Alyssa knew she had been lucky with Wendy. Usually, she found it impossible to come under the power of another woman, but with her it had been different. Somehow, Wendy had been able to cast herself as her imagined real mother, Grace, and been able to channel Grace effectively. Relating to Wendy had been a profoundly healing experience. She would not be so lucky twice. The prospect of being examined and judged by a strange woman felt unbearable.

She was in no mood to be abused. Nor was she comfortable with the idea of subjecting her counselling practice to expert assessment, even though it was a routine and mandatory requirement for ongoing professional registration. Professor Barnes himself had set up the timetable for the supervisory sessions on the day he appointed her, and compliance was a condition of ongoing employment and out of her hands.

Thoughtfully, the Dog had even arranged for her first months to be free of distraction, but now she had no choice but to attend as scheduled and have someone check on her. Inevitably, it would involve some degree of prying into her emotional life. And the snooping was not going to be as kind and beneficial as the average mealy-mouthed supervisor liked to pretend. Being forced to reveal aspects of herself to another woman seemed too much of a sacrifice to make—no matter how supposedly voluntary such personal disclosures were.

The venue for the session was Susan Lindow's consulting room, which was on the north-western edge of the CBD, in a side street off Olympic Parade. Nearby, loomed the familiar Olympic Hospital, where she had once been a patient, and across the road from there was the university medical school. To get to Susan's place from the Donald Clinic, which was on the eastern fringe of the city centre, was a simple enough task. All that was required was a straightforward tram ride across the city centre.

As she stood in front of Susan Lindow's office door, mildly nauseous, Alyssa continued to hesitate, even though she knew she was being unreasonable. She knew perfectly well that the regulatory authorities had a legitimate interest in the mental health of any therapist involved in person-to-person relationship therapy. While her mind was hardly the business of anyone else unless she wanted it to be, it was not possible to escape from the fact that she worked as a psychodynamic therapist and that therein lay a potential problem. Justifiably, others had a rightful interest in what went on in her own head. It was necessary for her, and all others providing psychological counselling, to submit to regular monitoring by an objective and experienced peer, who would search especially for two deadly defects: factual ignorance and personal bias— the red and green monsters of counselling. Such shortcomings needed constant searching for in all talk therapists, and, when found, eliminated. There was no risk to client welfare greater than the risk of unbridled ignorance and bias in a counsellor. Resistance to monitoring was futile.

All of which she knew.

Yet, she continued to hesitate, close to being sick.

What about all the dead people . . .

She checked her phone. There was still time. She had a few more minutes. She walked to the side of the house to warm herself in a splash of sunshine. From there, she could see more of the house and was surprised to see that it was in dire need of a coat of paint. Did this mean that Susan Lindow did not care, she wondered, or was she struggling financially? She had no wish to be unkind, but the place was nothing like the Donald Clinic. The word *pathetic* sprang to mind.

She was going to have to sit in the converted garage of this same house for one to two hours every alternate week and present cases from her previous two weeks at work, as randomly selected by Susan, and also discuss selected problems of her own. And, while doing all this, she was going to be expected to listen to Susan's insights about where she might be at fault and where she could do better. Susan's skills included not only transference-focused psychodynamic therapy but also something called body-focused therapy. The latter part seemed ridiculous, because from what she had seen of Susan before at a lecture, she was about to fall into the clutches of a fat old woman. Not to mention the crumbling house.

Pathetic or not, time was up.

Her hand hovered over the old-fashioned knocker.

But Susan Lindow was one step ahead of her. Before Alyssa could knock, the door opened, and a person filled its frame. It was a woman, a woman wider than she was tall and positively brimming with jolly-hockey-sticks bonhomie. But instead of "Ho, ho, ho" she said: 'Hello, my dear. I'm Susan. Welcome.'

'Oh.' Alyssa took a step backwards.

6

'You must be Alyssa. Come on in. Funny, but I just knew there was someone out there. Amazing how one knows these things, isn't it? I'm so glad to finally meet up with you at last.' Susan's body trembled with emotion. 'What a fine young woman you are.' She put an arm around Alyssa's shoulder once she was inside. 'I've heard such wonderful things about you from Wendy Greene. Bad trip? You look a little shell-shocked.'

Susan was performing the age-old trick of radiating positive regard and acceptance, and it did not fool her for a moment. She had been wrong, though, about her weight. In real life, Susan was even fatter than she remembered. Worse dressed, too, in a faded, calf-length frock that looked suspiciously like a discarded circus tent. 'Hello, Susan. Pleased to meet you.'

'Come on through, my dear. Come on through.'

She was ushered into Susan's counselling room, which was furnished like a lounge but seemed fake because it was in her garage. The furniture was shabby and had none of the class of her own consulting room at the Donald. In addition, the room smelt vaguely of unwashed humanity and misery. Still beaming, Susan plonked herself on a chair—the counsellor's chair—and motioned for Alyssa to take a seat on the client sofa. Discretely above Susan's head, in the corner of the ceiling, was a CCTV camera, and it pointed at the sofa.

This is so embarrassing.

'Not such fun being in the hot seat, is it?' said Susan with some sympathy. 'Now you know what our clients have to go through.'

'I'm intrigued by how much anxiety this visit is causing me,' said Alyssa.

'I can see that. You are a bit of an open book, you know. I'm tempted to ask you what your thoughts are right now, but first things first. We'll have plenty of time for that later. First, I want to get you to be able to trust me completely—not as a friend, but as a counsellor and peer. Professionally. So . . . would you like a cup of tea?'

'Thank you. That would be great. No sugar and just a drop of milk.' Alyssa noticed, as she was talking, that she was sitting upright on the edge of her seat. She made a conscious effort to relax and shifted back into the couch. As she did so, she noticed the little side table with its jug of water and box of tissues.

God.

Susan handed her a large mug of tea and made another mug for herself. Then she settled once again into her counsellor's chair. 'I see you have your bag with you, Alyssa. You have your client material, I assume?'

'Yes. And I've also selected four problem cases that we could discuss. I hope that's enough.'

'More than enough. In fact, we probably won't even get onto that today. Today we will need to go through the registration process and get our baselines sorted.'

'I see. Baselines.' It sounded very juvenile.

Susan looked at her oddly. 'Supervision is intended to *help* you, as you know—and also help protect your clients from any blind spots and factual and ethical errors that creep into your counselling.'

'Yes. I understand fully.' She was being treated like an idiot.

Susan busied herself for a moment looking at paperwork, probably from Greta or Dr Barnes. 'The first thing I notice here is your enormous workload.' She looked up with an unreadable expression. 'It's incredibly brave of you.'

'I enjoy it.'

Susan said nothing. In a monotone, she rattled through Alyssa's personal details, getting the answers from her as needed: Age, Sex, Home Address, Next of Kin, Current Partner, Qualifications, Professional Registration, Income, Telephone Number, email Address, Family Doctor, Medical Insurance, Friends.

Alyssa's answer to the Friends section caused Susan to lose her stride. 'Say that again, Alyssa. Did you say none? Is that what you said? None?'

'Yes. I can make things up for you if you like, but that's pretty much how it is with me. I don't really have any friends. I assume we are talking about same sex. Maybe there could be one, but she's more of a fellow worker, really.' She was thinking of Jocelyn, but she wasn't sure if she was a friend or not. 'I've never been any good with girlfriends. They don't seem to do much for me. Guys are a different story, but with them it's never been what I would call just friendship.'

'You are not socially isolated or lonely?'

'Good heavens, no.'

'Okay.' She made some notes.

Alyssa changed the subject for her. 'The Donald Clinic is paying for this, are they?' she asked. 'Do I have that part correct?' It was supposed to be one of the fringe benefits of her employment contact and she wished to make sure that she would not be receiving an unexpected bill.

'Yes,' said Susan. 'Don't worry. That side is all taken care of.'

'Excellent.' Alyssa wondered how much Susan charged. Judging from what she saw around her, she suspected it was about a third of what her own clients paid.

'The next part of this registration form is a bit more difficult,' said Susan, still in her deadpan monotone. 'Medical and Psychiatric history.

It's entirely voluntary, but it's obviously important that I get as much detail here as possible—I'm sure that you of all people understand this.'

'Yes. Provided we are going to be signing the standard confidentiality and disclosures agreement.' Alyssa no longer assumed anything on trust from any health professional into whose hands she placed herself—and for good reason. She noticed a flash of irritation pass over Susan's expression.

'Of course,' said Susan. 'I should have gone through the whole document with you at the beginning, but I'm sure you know it backwards.'

'I'm not trying to be difficult,' said Alyssa, 'but this supervision thing is new to me. I don't know how much of a client of yours I'm going to be and how much of a colleague of yours I'm going to be.'

'Very well put. It's mostly colleague of course, but there will have to be an element of client too if I am to be able to advise you on your blind spots and biases.'

'That's what I thought,' said Alyssa. 'Therefore, before we go any further, I would like us to sign the official contract that covers me for that.'

'You want to sign it now?'

'Before I disclose any personal medical history, yes.' She was not about to be talked down to by an older woman.

'Okay.' Susan extracted the lengthy document from her file. 'You want me to go through it?'

'No. It will be okay.'

'Very well.'

Alyssa knew the contract well and signed it. Afterwards, she was amazed at how quickly her anxiety dissipated. She realised then that her earlier fears had related to the possibility of Susan harming her by getting to know her. Now, with her medical and mental health confidentiality assured, power had passed back into her own hands. No longer could Susan destroy her career.

Susan, meanwhile, pointedly reassembled her notes, getting them back into their original order with a show of laborious effort.

7

Looking up finally, Susan Lindow put on a cheerful face. 'Right,' she said. 'Where were we?'

'Medical and Psychiatric history.' Already, Alyssa found the tone annoying.

'Thank you, Alyssa.' Susan read from the pre-printed page: 'Any chronic medical conditions?'

'No. I'm very healthy.'

'Any allergies?'

'No.'

'Vaccinations up to date?'

'As far as I know.'

'Your parents weren't anti?'

'No.'

'And you?'

'No.'

'Anything surgical?'

'A ruptured spleen from a car accident.' And a whole lot more besides, she almost said, but did not.

'That's unusual. Recent?'

'I was thirteen.'

'Driving?'

'No, passenger. I was not a juvenile delinquent.'

Susan looked up briefly, as though puzzled by her tone. 'Anything else about the accident I should know?'

'Nope.' She was lying, but she had no wish to be completely truthful to someone like Susan. Telling her about her spleen had been enough. The woman did not need to know about the severed intestines, the ruptured bladder, the broken ribs, the fractured skull, or the subsequent epileptic convulsions. As for who was driving the car, that was none of Susan's business either. It had been enough to find herself accused by the police afterwards of having been behind the wheel. The matter was not fully resolvable anyway because of her retrograde amnesia, so she had no intention of involving any supervisor in any of it. What she *did* remember from the moment before everything went black was that she had been on his lap. But this she had not told the police—or anyone.

The withholding caused the highly experienced Susan to gaze at her silently, as though instinctively aware that what had been said was not all that needed to be said. Clearly, the silence was aimed at encouraging more revelations.

Alyssa had her measure: 'Well, I did have to have special vaccinations because of my spleen.'

Susan knew when she was beaten. 'Right.' She gave a sigh and returned to her interrogation list.

'Any regular medications?'

'Only the birth control pill.'

'I don't mean to pry, but been on it long?'

'Since nineteen.' She almost added: so, no, Susan, despite what people like you think, I didn't engage in underage sex. She managed to keep silent, though.

Unless of course you want me to count the attempts that my father made to rape me as underage sex.

There would be no point in telling Susan about it. She would overreact completely and become hysterical—as all such people did. The attentions from her father had not been such a big deal. He only tried when he was blind drunk, and it was not as though he had ever succeeded.

'No side effects from being on it for so long?' Susan was referring to the pill.

'None. Obviously, I have the right build for it.'

Not fat.

Susan frowned. 'On the same sort of topic, what about cervical screening? I'm checking for *anti*-beliefs, you understand.'

More that was none of her business. 'I'm not anti that.'

She made a tick. '*Any* alternative health opinions, special needs, or strong beliefs? Any at all?'

'No.'

Susan smiled at her. 'I wish all my clients were as healthy and balanced as you are—but of course no one is.'

'I take after my dad.'

'Right.' She turned a page. 'Now—last bit—anything psychiatric in your history? Any mental difficulties of your own? There's nothing mentioned in your official training report that I have here from Dr Barnes, but I've found it's always best to check directly.'

Alyssa could tell that Susan suspected something and was testing her. 'That's because training reports are public documents even though they are marked confidential. With you, though, I can be honest. The truth is, Susan, there is a part of me that is not entirely straightforward. In fact, it's no exaggeration to say that you could write an entire book about my confidential psychiatric history.'

'Oh my. Now isn't that a big surprise?'

It was the tone of Susan Lindow's voice that gave her away. Alyssa realised suddenly—with absolute certainty—that Susan already knew. The voice had been too triumphant.

You know! Of course, you know.

She knew. And Alyssa knew that Susan knew that she knew. Susan had given the game away.

'Sorry,' the fat woman mouthed, but it was too late. She had underestimated the client in her room, who was no fool. Just like Susan, she too could spot a liar a mile off and had seen immediately that Susan already knew all about Alyssa Brown's mental health difficulties.

Susan knew of them because someone had already informed her about them.

Which was disgraceful.

'This is really disappointing,' said Alyssa, giving Susan her best humourless smile. 'Really good patient confidentiality, isn't it?' She wondered who the informant had been. Most likely one of the psychiatrists at the nearby Olympic Hospital where Susan currently lectured. Olympic Hospital was where she had been treated as an inpatient in the psychiatric ward after her breakdown during Sociology. 'So, now you think I'm some sort of menace. Really great for me going forward, isn't it?' She did her best to sound sarcastic.

Susan was ashen faced. 'Yes, unfortunately someone at the hospital has told me about you. I want to be honest about that. And yes, it is inexcusable, I agree. The only thing I can say in my defence is that it was completely accidental on my part. I happened to mention your name in passing when I told a colleague at the Olympic that I had a new client for supervision. I know I shouldn't have mentioned names, but it was just a slip of the tongue. It's not as if I did any digging, honest. Please believe me. Unfortunately, your name is well-known there, so I immediately got told certain things. You can take my word on that. I would never deliberately pry into your psychiatric history. And if it's any comfort to you, Alyssa, please rest assured that nobody there thinks that currently you are a danger to society. I was told that you wouldn't harm a fly. Not anymore.'

'Is that so, Susan. Now why would anyone in their right mind think that?'

Finally, the truth was out: yet another old woman sought to cause her grief. Not only was Susan Lindow an idiot, but she was determined to tell lies too.

PART IV

TROUBLED OF MIND

CHAPTER FIFTEEN

.... 1 ....

IT WAS THE MID-MORNING coffee break in the staff room at the Donald Clinic, not even lunch break, but Jocelyn Goronowski once again appeared at Alyssa's table. She looked unhappy and downcast. She had a problem. Many. To do with her research paper for the upcoming conference, what else? She would rather die than feed people rubbish.

Or so she said.

Solving the young psychiatrist's problems with her study on the female orgasm was becoming rather tedious and somewhat circular, but for some reason Alyssa once again felt obliged to try to be helpful. After all, Jocelyn was obviously upset at the prospect of making a fool of herself. Alyssa knew, though, that training supervisors—like Wendy Greene—would point out an obvious fact, which was that she was allowing herself to fall into the clutches of a closet schizophrenic. Yet, tolerating the never-ending questioning by Jocelyn amounted to more than just kindness towards a mentally unwell member of staff. Jocelyn meant more to her than that. Jocelyn was the closest thing to a friend she had ever known. Despite the strange woman's many faults, she actually liked her.

She needs all the help she can get.

And so it was that Alyssa did her best to be helpful. 'Now, let's see, Jocelyn,' she said in a calming voice, 'if I have this right, what's *still* upsetting you is that your research subjects have told you nothing but lies. Is that it?'

'Yes,' she sniffed. 'They have claimed that their thoughts match their actions, but according to my theory that remains impossible no matter how I've looked at it. I've tried *everything*. I've even taken your earlier advice and looked into Self psychology. I've been hitting all the old books.'

'And where exactly are you with your orgasm theory now? Remind me again.'

'Proposed theory. It's something new for the conference, remember. I've titled the paper *Elucidation of the Psychology of the Orgasm in Females* and my hypothesis proposes that people—men too—are, for psychological reasons, required to have Self-protective ideas just prior to climaxing. There is always an element of threat elimination required. Which means that thoughts usually need to get downright nasty—inwardly directed or outwardly directed—just prior to release. Trouble is, nobody seems to know if this really is the case or not, though I, for one, think it's true. As you know, I originally got the germ of the idea from Freud's work. According to that, any physical sex act always evokes sexual thoughts that are primitive and wish-related rather than adult and reality-related. Therefore, reality always threatens the Self. Not so?'

'What are you doing messing with such stuff? You don't properly understand a single word of metapsychology. And anyway, Freud is dead.'

There was a pause of disappointment. 'So?'

'So—what's the point of it all, Jocelyn?'

'Just accept that there are *supposed* to be fantasies, okay, to do with preservation of the Self and therefore protective and potentially downright nasty. The point is, I'm not getting any of this reported to me in the questionnaires. What the hell am I supposed to do with vanilla?'

Use better study design when you conduct research.

She tried to be kind. 'Are you saying in all seriousness that your survey participants aren't giving you the results that you *want*?'

'*Need.* Therefore, if I can prove that they are lying then maybe I can still save my theory.'

'A study like yours can't prove anything.'

'Yes, obviously, dummy, but if I can plausibly infer that the participants are lying then I still have a theory. It's not disproven. Help me. That's all I'm asking.'

'I honestly don't think I can. I mean, if your subjects are in fact telling you lies—and that's an if—it will be because they lie to themselves. I doubt there's much you can do about that at this late stage. I mean, how does one separate a truth from a half-truth born of self-deception?'

'Think.'

Alyssa tried: 'What if you were to do some retrospective reverse engineering on your data? Assuming you know the mental state of each of your study subjects seeing that they are already psychiatric clients of yours, then if their replies in your survey lack evidence of predicted Un-conscious P-phantasy, that could be used as evidence of unreliability.'

'*Phantasy*, hey? Brilliant. Except for one thing: the questionnaires are anonymous.'

'Oh, shit, yes.'

'Besides, then I'd be back to having to have orgasms rest on trigger points from unconscious childhood. Which is no good to me without objective data.'

'Why?'

'Because, according to everyone out there, there *is* no Un-conscious part to the conscious mind, dummy. How many more times do I have to drum this into your head? The brain is just circuitry, with most of it non-declarative, and that's all there is to it. It's really all too boring for me to explain it to you—or the extent of my problems in trying to talk about orgasms to brain experts.'

'You need to snap out of this funk you have gotten yourself into, Jocelyn. Just do the best with what you've got. Maybe you could present the *expected* spectrum of unconscious P-phantasy in your overall client sample and then compare this with the *reported* spectrum of conscious fantasies in the anonymised study. Then you would be able to suggest that your respondents almost certainly lied when reporting on their sexual thoughts. It won't be proof, but it will give you something to say.'

'I'll be attacked. I don't know any deep Freud—regardless of whether anybody still believes in him or not.'

'Just confine yourself to the statistical analysis.'

'Mm. Maybe it's a way. Maybe not. Oh, oh, oh, I'm sinking. Quick, say some Freud to me. All the literature I've been looking at insists that people release both lust and aggression during climax and that the two are inseparable and always heavily in disguise, but what does all that even *mean*? Tell me something I can use at Conference. Anything along those lines.'

'Sorry, no point looking at me. All I know is that Freud supposedly had enormous blindness to his own countertransference.'

'Don't be difficult. I need your help with my own blind spots. Why are these Freudian people saying that this sadism masochism thing is intrinsic to all sex acts?'

'They are?'

'That's what my sources are telling me. Is it true?'

'I've no idea. Maybe sex unmasks the love-hate splitting intrinsic to all object relations.'

'Way too advanced.'

'There's no point trying to get stuff out of me, Jocelyn. I've only just started out as a psychotherapist. I doubt whether I can tell you anything you don't already know, especially when it comes to the more arcane aspects of orgasms.'

Jocelyn looked at her intently. 'Don't be like that, Alyssa. Just tell me what you think about such things.' The gaze was disarmingly admiring.

'Really. And just what exactly do you want to know?'

'Anything.'

'About thoughts that occur at orgasm?'

'Those.'

'Well, you're not getting any of mine, that's for sure.'

Jocelyn raised an unsatisfied eyebrow at her. 'Then just say something scientific to me.'

'No.'

'Yes.'

Alyssa gave up. 'Well, I suppose that when a climax approaches, then whatever mentally most threatens the foundational integrity of the Self comes increasingly into focus. A re-connecting with these aspects of normally Un-conscious early childhood occurs, during which, as a by-product, the more mature inhibitions such as shame and disgust become lost. Finally, there is a collapse of mature-function love-hate splitting followed by a cataclysmic fusion, during which the primitive reunification explodes through the Self like a bomb and obliterates it for a timeless fraction of a second. Stop raising your eyebrows at me. These exact explosions are observed in functional MRI scans done during orgasm. There is always a flash of global neuronal activity at exactly the moment of climax.'

'Which proves nothing, I'm afraid to say. Not to conference delegates. Or maybe, mm, mm. Yes, yes, could be. I see it now: no more woes, time disappears, eternity arrives, God is touched.' Then she sighed sarcastically.

'Not everyone is as sceptical about metaphysical aspects of the brain as psychiatrists are.'

'Not to worry about that part, then. I'll make some enquiries at *Wishful Thinkers Incorporated* and find an expert to confirm your ideas.'

After all the trouble she had taken to help her friend, her cruelly dismissive words felt like a kick in the guts.

'Why don't you get back to work, Jocelyn? I've done my best with you, but I give up.'

2

Later, at lunch, Jocelyn said she was sorry for having been condescending. 'Sorry, Alyssa. It's just that I was annoyed with myself for having done such a bad piece of research.'

'Right.'

'I've tried to get help from other sources, but nobody wants to talk to me. Everyone tells me I'm in the wrong century and puts the phone down on me. The attitude from my colleagues is inexplicable considering that sex happens in the mind. Why the lack of professional interest?'

'As I said, just present a pseudoscientific statistical analysis at the conference and be done with it.'

'Sorry, can't. People are lying. There's this whole big, awful truth thing that I think I've uncovered, and I need to gain more traction. People are not having sex with their partner but with aspects of them*selves*. This is a *huge* discovery—if it's true. You see, what I seem to have uncovered is that sex is an entirely selfish process unrelated to love. I can't just let such an important discovery die. It's only superficially true that we have sex "with" another person; deeper down it's a thing "done" to us or something that we "do" to somebody else. *That's* what sex really is. Only trouble is I can't prove that my data is reliable.'

'You can't rush around sprouting your own fanciful half-baked theories as fact, Jocelyn.'

'People lying about sex is not very nice, is it?'

'This is all too much for me, Jocelyn. I'm just a twit from Ocean View.'

'Oh please.'

'Don't forget the importance of sharing, Jocelyn. Whatever fantasies people might be having, they still need the arms of another person.'

'Silly me, I forgot about the sharing stuff.' She developed a sarcastic smirk once again.

'What about love, then? Surely love remains the most important part of being human. Personally, I wouldn't downplay it.'

'Don't tell me you still believe in that rot.'

'Don't we all need love?'

'Sure, but only in childhood. There it exists as a mirror to confirm our own existence and anchor our mental connection to reality. But adult love is not real, Alyssa. It's just a resonance with childhood, just an illusion.'

'The whole second-hand emotion thing? Very psychoanalytic, but far from orthodox. Even you know that.'

'What about this Freudian stuff then, Alyssa?' She consulted her phone. 'It says here that by recognising *Self* in others is how we constantly reaffirm the validity of our own existence and that by failing to achieve intimacy is how the Self collapses.' Jocelyn's mind began to gallop as she speed-scrolled: 'According to how I read this stuff, at the core we are totally self-centred. The thing that causes us to *want* to move from inside to outside—to real life—is the frisson obtained when the Self is validated by the Self of another, the experience of said frisson being how we achieve the motivation to overcome the death drive. It is *this* that love is, not what you've been saying. Love is that feeling we get when we make a connection, and the connection is benevolent and rewarding to the Self. This is the only way to understand the concept of love: a Self *knows* another Self and in return *is known* by that other Self. It's through that process. It is the *process*. Got it? Love *is* the process.' She put her phone away.

Jocelyn could not be argued with, so Alyssa did not even try. 'If you say so, Jocelyn,' she said. She hoped it would be enough to put a stop to the endless theorisations: just agreeing with her.

3

'Don't you even feel sorry for me?'

'No. Why did you volunteer to give a talk on such an impossible topic in the first place?'

'Because I knew that nobody knows about this stuff, least of all me.'

'So, what exactly is your point? You don't even believe in psychoanalysis, Jocelyn. Who exactly are you trying to kid? I know you don't care about this stuff.'

'I do so. Besides, how else do you suggest I try to avoid being laughed out of the building at Conference?'

'I don't know whether to laugh or cry on your behalf.'

'You can make jokes, but this is not funny. This whole Big O thing is a big industry. It turns out that everyone in the world wants answers. Mostly, it's magic pills that researchers are looking into, but I'm convinced that people are barking up the wrong tree on this, especially in the case of us females. For us, it's what goes on in the mind that's the key.'

'Mm, okay then, I think I finally see where you are trying to go with this thing, Jocelyn. You need to please the conference, is that it? Some sort of quick fix for women's sex lives? Well then, why don't you speak to a sexologist? I'm sure Alan could get hold of a good one for you via his contacts at the university.'

'Talk to a sexologist about psychology? Duh.'

It was a stupid suggestion.

'The thing is, Alyssa, for us women, when it comes to a successful fuck, it's all in the head, isn't it? It's really all about us getting *ourselves* fucked. Isn't it?'

This woman is scary.

'I say nothing.'

Jocelyn pulled a face. 'Anyway, I need to get cracking, don't I? Get back to work. Get more references. Get to grips with all these new ideas.'

They had finished their lunch and were drinking coffee. Alyssa watched in silence as her now sombre dark-haired friend produced a water bottle and greedily began to drain it. The action reminded her so strongly of her father when he was an alcoholic that she realised something for the first time: Jocelyn was not drinking water.

Jocelyn was drinking vodka.

Without any doubt, Jocelyn's water bottle would be found to contain vodka if tested. The shock of the sudden realisation hit like a blow to the midriff. This was serious. Her new friend was in far bigger trouble psychologically than she had ever believed possible. Emotionally, Jocelyn Goronowski was a basket case.

Despite the brave front that she was putting on, Jocelyn was desperately lonely and extremely unwell mentally. The simple act of thirsty drinking had given it all away.

Seemingly so innocent, the woman opposite was once again dragging a fingernail across the chalkboard of her own past life in a way that frightened her. Everything about Jocelyn suddenly began to frighten her all over again.

The worst of it was that she did not know *why* she felt suddenly scared.

With her father it had not been like that. Her father had never frightened her; with him she had frightened herself. But now, for some reason, deeper stirrings were gaining some sort of foothold in her mind—emotions over which she had no control and whose identity remained hidden. The woman across the table had some way of bringing to the surface uncontrollable unconscious forces.

Something terrible was stirring; some evil was lurking just beneath the surface, something too frightening to face.

Who was Jocelyn Goronowski? Who was she *really*? Alyssa gazed intently at her so-called friend as she continued to suck on her drink bottle, eyes half closed, eerily resembling her father, Bob Brown. Jocelyn was hiding something. Some monstrous lie. As a psychotherapist, she had no business being blind to what that was.

Jocelyn always seemed to want to discuss sex, yet their meetups had nothing to do with sex at all. Always it was really about Jocelyn trying to stay functional; about Jocelyn using the power of her intellect to forestall imminent collapse into insanity.

Jocelyn was only just holding it together.

Jocelyn was hiding some terrible secret that made her a danger to others.

For the first time, Alyssa *knew* this. She knew Jocelyn. Something of her own Self was *in* Jocelyn too, and finally she had glimpsed it. Jocelyn was as big a liar as she herself was. The two of them were equally monstrous liars, and each had an equally monstrous secret.

Exactly what Jocelyn's secret was, remained to be discovered. Meanwhile, great care was required.

One wrong move and the whole house of cards would collapse. And when that happened, madness of a most dangerous kind would break free.

Of that, she was now certain.

Catastrophe awaited.

4

The next session with supervisor Susan Lindow lasted longer than Alyssa expected and by the end of it she felt emotionally drained. She had had enough of suspicion-filled eyes and endless apologies. Already it was past four pm. She closed the front gate at Susan's house and stepped back out into the street with relief. The session—and the woman—had given her a headache.

Throughout the meeting, the fallout from Susan's initial betrayal of confidentiality had continued to remain unsettling despite the ongoing attempt by them both to downplay it.

There seemed little point in returning to the Donald that day. Fortunately, with Wednesdays being an administration day for her, she did not *have* to return to the cottage. If she didn't, though, she would fall even further behind with her case dictations. The backlog was mounting up.

So what.

She was tired. It would be better for her if she simply ignored her responsibilities for the rest of the day and went straight home. Yet, strangely, she did not feel ready for that either. Not home. It was going to take more than a tram ride across the CBD to unwind enough to be pleasant to Cy.

What to do?

Her body decided the issue for her. When next she became aware of her surroundings, she had already passed the first tram stop home and was headed at a brisk walking pace, bag over her shoulder, down Olympic Parade in the direction of the Olympic Hospital and the university medical school. Both were just over a kilometre away. Although smartly dressed in a fitted skirt, she had wisely selected comfortable flat shoes, which made walking easy. There were plenty of shade trees along the route and the physical activity seemed the best remedy for her agitation.

She was not sure how much longer she was going to be able to tolerate Susan Lindow.

That woman seems to think that everything I say is a load of rubbish.

As she strode along, she worked out how best to use her precious free time. Crossing the road, she headed in the direction of the university medical library. She had been there before and knew where it was. She would spend an hour there improving her knowledge by reading the latest psychiatric journals. In the coming battles with Susan, knowledge was power.

Not all knowledge, though, was conscious, and neither was the border between fate and cunning as clear as she had once believed.

Just like the first time, though, it still seemed surprising.

5

'Hello there,' he said, his voice coming from behind her.

She was in the university medical library reading room, sitting at a desk with the *Annals of Psychiatry* open in front of her.

'I don't believe it,' he said. 'Alyssa? It *is* you, isn't it? From Fabio's gym. Don't tell me you're a medical student!'

She turned her head. She had been engrossed in an article titled *Re-traumatisation in Complex Post-traumatic Stress Disorder*—something that seemed to apply strongly to her. It was him, Mark from the gym. He came up beside her, on her left, and peered down at her with an enquiring frown. She had recognised his voice the instant he spoke. Looking up at him, he was still Mr Hot, still unbelievably attractive. It had to be fate. Even though he was a doctor, and she was in his medical library, the odds of meeting him again purely by luck seemed vanishingly small.

'Hi,' she said, unable to believe her eyes. 'What a pleasant surprise.' It was definitely him.

'What an amazing coincidence.'

'I'd say. How have you been?'

'Good.'

They were both speaking in soft voices appropriate for a library. 'Pull up a chair. How did you pick me out? This library is so huge.'

'This may sound crazy to you, but I *knew* it was you from right across the hall, from far away, even though I was behind you.' The strangely familiar figure from Fabio's gym pulled up a chair as told and sat down at the side of her desk. 'In case you don't remember, it's Mark. Mark Stanford.'

She turned her own chair towards his. 'Of course, I remember, silly. Whatever became of you?' He had vanished from Fabio's the day she first met him—that memorable day when everything went weird—and she had not seen him since. She had begun to think she may have imagined him. This time, though, he seemed real enough.

'You remembered my name? Really? I'm amazed. It was such a long time ago. I thought I'd never see you again.'

Alyssa squinted at him. 'What are you on about? I go to the gym all the time. *You* are the one who disappeared.'

He was not taking anything in. 'I knew it. I just knew you had to be a medical student. Where are you based? I've haven't seen you around until today.'

'Sorry to prick your bubble, but I'm actually not medical student.'

'You're not?' He seemed shocked. 'But . . .'

'What am I doing in this library? I'm a counselling psychologist. A qualified and practicing one. For your information, doctors aren't the only people involved in health care.'

'Oh shit.' Comically, the moment he realised she was an independent woman and not some student he could lord it over, his confidence melted away. His face fell.

'I'm just passing through on my way home,' she explained.

He became embarrassed. 'Oh dear. You must think I'm awfully forward approaching you like this.' His voice developed a slight stammer. 'It's just that I mistakenly thought you were part of my new intake of students.'

'*Your* students? You look like a student yourself. Don't tell me you have students.'

He seemed hurt. 'I do so. However, I seem to have made a fool of myself. That's very disappointing.' The handsome young man called Mark tried to stand up, but Alyssa put a hand on his shoulder and held him down in his chair.

'Wait,' she said. 'Anyone can make a mistake. Let's not miss each other for the second time. My name really is Alyssa, and I really would like to see you again—at the gym. Like you, I already have a partner. I hope you and your wife haven't given up on exercise—*that* would be most disappointing.'

He gave her a sidelong glance, his expression flustered. 'You mean Ruby?'

'Yes. The one I saw you with at the gym. Her.'

He seemed surprised that she knew so much about him. 'We're not married yet. That's later this year. But thanks for the reminder about the gym. We need to attend more. I'll be sure to look out for you when I manage to get back to Public Hospital. I'm one of the surgical trainees here at the Olympic.'

'Is that so? That's great.'

'What I mean is I'm pretty stuck here. I can't really get away. It's 24/7. Even now, I'm on call.' He tapped a pager attached to his belt. 'I was supposed to be up at your end of town for a three-month rotation—which is why I signed up at Fabio's—but someone back here bombed out at the last minute. They had to call me back here. I miss Fabio's, though. It's a great place, isn't it?'

'Yes, I like it.'

He made to get to his feet for the second time and this time she let him.

'It was really nice seeing you again,' he said. 'Sorry about accusing you of being a medical student.' He rested a hand on her upper back in the way that she had done to him earlier. 'I'll definitely get back to Fabio's and catch up with you again when I can.'

'You do that.' The heat from his touch felt like fire and radiated sparks of electricity into her bra strap. From her bra strap the heat seeped around into the front of her chest and from there it drove deeply into both her breasts and then down. She smiled up into his eyes. 'Let's not lose each other.'

He seemed lost for words. 'Yes.' Then, recovering his senses, he removed his hand. 'See you around.' He turned, then he was gone.

.... **6** ....

She had not given him her phone number or email address, and he hadn't given her any contact details either. If either of them had done so, it would have meant the end of life as they knew it—of that she felt certain. She was sure he sensed it too: Things between them were in danger of spinning rapidly out of control. If they got any closer there was going to be an explosion. People would get hurt.

She sat at the medical library desk trying to make sense of what had just happened. She had found her dream, only to lose it again, yet felt nothing but joy—so much so that her hands were shaking.

This is so weird.

She had not truly believed that she would ever find Mark again, her perfect man, but here he was, larger than life, walking around in a university medical library—probably not that unexpected for a doctor in training, she now realised. Nevertheless, the repeat encounter had been an incredible stroke of luck. It was more than just her mind playing tricks with her. Fate had to have something to do with it.

Her heart was thumping so badly that the *Annals of Psychiatry* refused to stay in focus. Wendy Greene used to laugh at her when she got the shakes over men and say she shouldn't let her imagination run away with her, but Wendy did not know everything about her past—certainly not about the possibility that maybe, after all, she did indeed suffer from a severe but heavily concealed form of complex post-traumatic stress disorder, as suggested by the journal article still open in front of her. There were triggers in that condition, as pointed out. Which was something that she knew anyway. And yes, in her case it was not inconceivable that certain men could trigger her.

Is the way that Mark affects me just me being triggered because I'm suffering from PTSD?

Thinking about it, she felt sure that this was not the case. With her and Mark, it was not this that lay behind their instant attraction to each other. Their feelings were undoubtedly mutual.

Or is it the mutuality *that is the trigger?*

The various possibilities were enough to drive a person crazy trying to work it out. Besides, there seemed no way of knowing for sure. In the

287

past, assertions to the effect that she probably *did* have PTSD had been made often enough by various psychiatrists after her inpatient stint at Olympic Hospital during second year Sociology, but she still doubted that any of that was true. The diagnosis got too casually and too easily attached to mental health clients by fake therapists of dubious ability. True PTSD on the other hand—as reinforced by the journal article in front of her—was not some throwaway catchphrase to apply to anyone with a troubled mind, but an insidious, deadly serious, and ruinous condition. Genuine sufferers were haunted by triggers with the power to destabilise existence. Triggered people reacted inappropriately to their environment and perceived things that were not there anymore.

Which did not apply to her and Mark.

Mark had not triggered her. With him, it was not like that. No. Mark was just hot. Objectively so. Seriously hot. There was nothing mentally unstable about that. People like Wendy Greene might urge less gullibility on her part when it came to men, but then again what did Wendy know about men. Not a lot. And certainly nothing when it came to men as superb as Mark.

Mark was hers. Of that she was now certain. He was meant for her and she for him. Mark was the key to ongoing existence.

CHAPTER SIXTEEN

1

WORKDAYS AT THE DONALD CLINIC remained busy and felt increasingly stressful. As a result, Alyssa found it more and more difficult to unwind back at the flat at night. Insomnia was becoming a real issue. Once again, it was late, and she was still awake. Cy, on the other hand, was asleep as usual.

She found her mind drifting back to boyfriend number two, Aaron the ass fucker. It made her feel guilty.

Funny that I should be thinking about him when I have Cy right here beside me.

Aaron used to like her ass. Sex with him was exciting in many ways, mostly positive and pleasant, and she had learnt a lot. Unfortunately, there had been a dark side to him too, but back then, when still young and ignorant and easily shocked, she had not known that *everyone* had a dark side and that it always had a sexual component as well. Long-term lovers inevitably discovered this, though often it took years of so-called "conventional" sexual relations before they got to the truth. In her younger days she had known nothing of such things but fortunately she was no longer naïve about sex—or people. Not after Sexology 101. Not after reading Obermaaier from cover to cover. Not after Cy and his books.

Aaron had probably just been insecure and sexually dependent but at the time she had believed he was too controlling. When she had pushed back against him, he had responded by becoming cruel, sometimes even trying to hurt her physically, especially if she denied him sex for a few nights. Strange how she missed him now. Maybe she should have let him have his way.

Maybe not.

Outside, in the street, nothing stirred. It was seriously late, probably close to three am. She had insomnia all right. She really did. Which was extremely humiliating considering that she treated clients at the Donald for the very same thing. She thought of the awful Mrs Goodman, member of the "big three" from her first day at the Donald, and the irony of her predicament did not escape her.

What to do?

There seemed nothing for it but to resign herself to the situation. Perhaps she should read a book. There was an unfinished Mills and Boon in her bedside drawer. Instead, she stood up in the dark and arranged the pillows so she could sit comfortably against the headboard. Cy remained asleep despite the activity. He had been asleep for hours. He was a good sleeper, that much she had to concede. Quiet; no sudden jerks, no farting, no snoring. His many past girlfriends had been right about one thing: he was good in bed—when it came to the sleeping part, that was.

But lately not in the sexual performance department.

She sat up straight in the bed, her back resting against the headboard pillows, and stared resolutely into nothingness. Earlier that night, he had once again failed her. His willy no longer worked when it had to, which was exasperating to say the least. And what was doubly exasperating— annoying, actually—was how his sensitive sausage packed it in whenever she tried to do with it what *she* wanted to do yet behaved perfectly normally whenever he did with it whatever *he* wanted to do.

Maybe it wasn't fair to blame only Cy for what was happening. Possibly she herself had something to do with it too and was somehow emasculating him. Perhaps. Still, she wasn't the one with the non-functioning appendage. That part was his responsibility, surely, so she felt justified in feeling disappointed. She had not encountered such difficulties with males before—not with Ethan and not with Aaron—quite the opposite, in fact. Perhaps she had not appreciated their virility enough.

The worst part of it was that despite everything, Cy had still achieved satisfaction and she not. Which meant that the one with the problem was really her. After all, people were supposed to be responsible for their own orgasms. This was rule number one in her sexology notes: no use blaming someone else for your own inability to climax. It was juvenile to expect someone else to perform some sort of magic trick on your behalf.

You had to own your own orgasm. After all, the source of your orgasm was ultimately always your own mind.

To be fair, Cy had at least *tried*. She could hardly blame him for losing patience with her—even though after that he had miraculously recovered enough of his virility to please at least himself with her. Apparently, that was a common habit of men. They liked to please just themselves when having sex with a partner, then pass out. Very unfair.

That said, she knew enough about psychology to suspect that in recent weeks she had become too tense to enjoy anything. Deep down, she knew it wouldn't have mattered *who* she was having sex with. She would still have felt numb. The pressure of work made it difficult to relax and she was finding it harder and harder to tune into her old orgasmic self. Worries—mostly about clients—kept on intruding.

Bizarrely, after all the previous numbness, she now felt physically needful as she sat in the warm darkness. Instead of fading away after failing to catch fire with Cy, the desire to be touched and taken had grown stronger. Every intimate part of her ached. The slightest movement of her naked breasts, the touch of the pillow on her skin, the coolness of the sheet under her: they all seemed determined to torment her. Even the languid air felt sensual as it slid around her bare body and busied itself with igniting innumerable flames of desire.

She wanted to scream.

Instead, she cupped both her breasts and gave a sad smile.

Just me and the girls.

At least she did have nice tits, she thought. There was no doubting that. Everyone was always mad about them. To see them lonely seemed unbearably tragic. She wondered if Cy was secretly turned off by her scar. Out of curiosity, she felt her left side. Apparently, that was where a person's spleen was supposed to be. There was nothing to feel, which was not surprising considering that hers was in a bottle in a laboratory somewhere, sacrificed in the crash that had killed her father. Could people who still *had* spleens feel them, she wondered. Probably not. Then she ran a finger along her scar, starting at her pubic bone and following it all the way up to her solar plexus. Then she followed it down again, finally resting her hand between her legs. Sometimes the scar still caused discomfort, especially low down, but not tonight. It seemed a real pity that she had been disfigured in this way. It spoilt an otherwise perfect body. The surgeons had accessed the whole of her insides through this one midline incision. They had had no choice. She had been that close to death. Now, though, it all seemed such a long time ago.

It would soon be morning and she was in no fit state to be going to work in just a few hours' time, not work of any sort let alone trying to counsel disturbed and emotionally dependent people.

2

Alyssa felt mildly nauseous. There were too many people depending on her and the weight of it felt more than she could bear. Only a few months into her first real job she was already struggling. Yet, what could she do? She could hardly complain to anyone at the Donald Clinic. She would lose her job. With their fancy university degrees, they would not understand that the amount of work was too much for her. They expected too much. They expected high performance from everyone.

I never get a chance to rest.

She tried to remember who she was due to see at the cottage later that day. It would be the same old merry-go-round as always: seven highly needful individuals paying high fees and expecting top service. Trish printed the clinic lists every afternoon before clocking off and some of the names on the latest list—the familiar ones—she could recall. First up that morning would come Jessica Delahunty. The endlessly unfortunate and tragic young woman suffered from both morbid obesity and a tiny head—victim of a disease called microcephaly—and led what seemed a hopeless life. The only good thing about it was that she had wealthy parents. However, the thought of having to face Jessica's tiny wobbling head yet again, as it babbled away about her miseries like a talkative orange atop the gigantic blancmange that was her body, felt too hard to bear. It was not that she did not like Jessica—she quite liked her—it was more that there was nothing that she could do to help her. The tragedy of Jessica's life had no solution, and somehow the hopelessness of her situation seemed to emphasise the hopelessness of her own situation.

292

After an hour of Jessica's company, she always felt like a complete failure as a therapist and an equally great failure as a human being.

God help us all, Jessica.

The day's difficulties would not end there, however.

Next would come Mrs Parker, who could only be described as a nasty piece of work. Officially, she had a diagnosis of chronic atypical depression—though most who encountered her suspected that what she really had was Munchhausen's Syndrome. However, because she was extremely wealthy—and continued to remain otherwise perfectly well—there had clearly been little incentive to determine the truth of the matter over her many years of attendance at the Donald. The only positive thing Alyssa had been able to find regarding the whole charade was that Munchhausen's Syndrome was at least something she was familiar with. It was very similar to Munchhausen's by Proxy. The only difference between her stepmother's condition and Mrs Parker's condition was that with Mrs Parker the "sick person" was the client herself and not someone under her care.

The visits from Mrs Parker always felt too much like visits from her stepmother. Once again—for an entire hour—she was going to have to allow herself to be tormented by a self-absorbed crank. Alyssa felt her spirits wilting. Just like her stepmother, Mrs Parker was completely incapable of meaningful human interaction. Completely caught up in herself, Mrs Parker was going to continue to believe whatever Mrs Parker believed—which included that she was "terminal" and in some sort of "holding pattern" before the end. According to her, Dr Bristow was soon to "feed her to his magnet" with fatal results. Alyssa had tried in vain to explain that focused transcranial magnetic brain stimulation was a perfectly safe procedure, but, just like Diana, Mrs Parker knew better. It was all too tedious for words.

After the tiresome Mrs Parker and the prior horror of Jessica Delahunty, would come paranoid Benjamin Clayton. More stress. She was fond of Ben but coping with his intensity was always a challenge. Like all good maniacs, he burned constantly with the zeal of his mission. Rooting out the evil that was the organised church was a big job, and it left her feeling exhausted already.

She could not recall who else was on the list for the coming day. There would be at least four more, that much she *did* know. Then she realised it was Monday—which meant that one of them would be Gilbert Rockport because he always came last thing on Mondays: Gilbert, her pet pervert; her one and only pervert, in fact. Or at least her only *overt* one. She let her mind dwell on him for a while. Intriguingly, unlike with the others, the thought of having to spend time with him later that day did not feel depressing at all. Instead, she found herself looking forward to seeing him again.

3

She knew the famous lawyer well because he attended without fail every Monday afternoon. By now, they had even become friends. However, it had taken her months to admit this to herself. At first, she had merely wondered why she enjoyed his company. She had no interest in people who self-harmed, and she certainly did not share his sexual release pathways. So, why like him, and why had their relationship progressed to something more than idle curiosity? Why *did* she like him? What box did he tick for *her*? Pain and degradation?

Heaven forbid.

For a long time, she had thought her weakness for him was the result of his intellect and his wealth—both of which she was a sucker for in handsome men—but thinking about it more she had realised that her congruence with him was more complex than that. Some or other unconscious sexual mischief was at work between them. Something about Gilbert *did* turn her on, obviously. In an intriguing way, Gilbert resembled Alan Summerfield, and she certainly did have the hots for *him*. Both men moved in the same way, with assurance, like panthers. And both effortlessly commanded others. They were archetypes of the kind of man she longed for but seemed destined never to obtain.

The two men even both had fabulously powerful cars. Alan had his white coupe and Gilbert had his grey Maserati. Alan had let his Audi reach an insane speed—though briefly—with her in the car on the road to Ocean View, while Gilbert had half-jokingly warned her never to let him drive her anywhere in his car because he loved to speed. Apart from all his other problems, Gilbert also had a problem with speeding in cars.

I've become uninsurable in a car. It's that bad, Alyssa.

She remembered Gilbert saying those exact words: that he was uninsurable. His need for intensity—speed—was *that* bad.

Undoubtedly, possessing a dangerous car was a sign of emotional unwellness, yet bizarrely, she was able to understand the attraction. The sound of their engines was thrilling to her too.

Her liking for Gilbert was not a one-way street. Something in her own psychological makeup undoubtedly attracted him too. Because he was a client, though, she had tried to resist facing up to this realisation. Nevertheless, it had become glaringly obvious, especially recently, once he began openly confessing that he found her extremely attractive. So, yes, she and Gilbert had become more than counsellor and client; they had become friends.

Which meant that she was no longer in any position to counsel him because with him she was no longer able to be truly objective. There was something in Gilbert that *she* needed. And wanted.

As she dozed naked and frustrated in bed in the early hours, Alyssa thought about Gilbert Rockport's sexual problems. It was now almost two months since his confession that he went and had himself punished from time to time. His need for this had always just been there, was what he had said. "It's something that lurks constantly in the shadows".

Strange how powerfully the mind can disguise the truth.

Gilbert's lifelong awareness that there was something deep inside of himself trying to come out had only crystalised into something tangible after many years of remaining elusive. In his case, it had taken a Mistress Veronica to lift the veil.

And then there were her own problems to think about—but she couldn't. She was too tired, and the whole business with Gilbert had become too perilous.

The counselling sessions with Mr Rockport, QC had reached a dangerous stage and needed to end. He needed moving on to a specialised centre. It was something that she knew that she needed to do. More than that, she needed to get around to doing it as soon as possible.

4

The months of counselling him had managed to uncover what, in all probability, was going on behind the scenes in Gilbert's head. Most likely, his getting himself beaten was some sort of pathway to a hidden truth about himself—the way for him to "find" himself. A way to his reality; to *the* truth.

It had taken him long enough to get there. Gilbert had reached his mid-forties before his suppressed truths at last managed to drive him into the clutches of someone able to validate his existence, namely Mistress Veronica. It had taken him all this time to get to her because his inner truth was not generally acceptable—not as simple, or as innocent as a need for the services of a professional spanker. It was about something far harder to achieve; something that only a Mistress Veronica had the power to do.

For Gilbert, getting beaten on his buttocks was not about just a bit of harmless spanking fun, not about some horsing around by the curious but emotionally well. No. It was about death; about being beaten to death. And about anal rape. The extreme nature of his need placed him firmly in the category of the mentally sick, while Veronica was that rare individual able to understand where he was coming from. What he got Veronica to agree to do to him—thrash him so severely that it risked putting him in hospital or killing him—went beyond the bounds of sane behaviour on both sides. Though Sexology 101 labelled the sexual interest in spanking as relatively harmless and common—given that the buttocks and anus were erogenous zones in the same way that the genitalia were—the interaction between Gilbert and Veronica represented something far deeper.

In technical language, the whippings were, in fact, an attempt on Gilbert's part to self-medicate a so-far incurable and potentially fatal destructive force deep within himself, one that was tearing him apart by preventing him from relating truthfully to others. As a result of the counselling sessions with him it had become clear to her that what Gilbert had wrong with him was best described as childhood-related chronic Post-Traumatic Stress Disorder. His diagnosis was C-PTSD. It was that simple—and that complicated.

Of course, as a lowly counselling psychologist she was not authorised to *make* diagnoses, at least not officially, so this was only her own idea. She had no doubt, though, that the future clinical psychologists or psychiatrists whom he would soon be seeing would arrive at the same conclusion.

Alyssa felt proud of herself as she dozed in the dark. Reaching this point of insight—C-PTSD—had been a long and arduous road for them both, but worth it. It represented a great professional achievement on her part.

Yes, it had been a dizzying run, but the time had come to say goodbye to him. She would end the sessions with Gilbert when she saw him later that day. It was going to be difficult and unpleasant, yes, and he would resist, yes, but him staying on was pointless. Dangerous levels of transference—and countertransference—had begun to develop and, besides, she had reached the end of what she could offer him. To ensure objectivity, and for the welfare and safety of all, Gilbert needed to accept referral to a specialised centre with proper expertise in the management of his condition. It was time now for strictness. Without any further delay, Gilbert needed to take the next step. Gilbert needed to go. He was ready. She knew he was ready.

She felt a glow of pride at what she had achieved with him. Even though she was newly qualified and he a famous silk, she had nevertheless been able to be of great help to him. Despite his age, his social seniority, his financial status, even his gender, she had managed to get him to discuss his sex life with her in intimate detail and seeming honesty without crossing any boundaries. This was no mean achievement. They had discussed his sexual thoughts, his childhood, his emotions, even his possible motives, and done so without prurience or prejudice. Which was a great professional triumph, no doubt about that. Perhaps she did have a future as a counsellor after all.

Had not the great Gilbert Rockport himself said that she was the only person in the entire world he had ever been able to be completely honest with? Surely there could be no higher praise for a therapist than that. Maybe being able to truly help people would, in time, give her the strength she needed to overcome the emotional exhaustion that threatened to get the better of her.

Alyssa got up and adjusted her pillows yet again in the dark. She needed to get to sleep. It was still too hot for the sheet, so, still naked, she lay down on top of it, flat on her back this time, and closed her eyes.

5

She could not stop thinking about Gilbert. Her mind went back to their first few times at the cottage. Initially, the then anonymous but attractive middle-aged man in her office had struggled to gain enough courage to be honest about why he was there. This first step was always the hardest for someone seeking help for an emotional problem. After a few false starts, she had managed to get him over the line, after which the disturbing details about his perverse masochistic sexual behaviour had begun. Because of her training—and Cy's books—sadomasochism did not frighten her. While incompetent professionals (and most laypersons) would have responded with shock and outrage to confessions about whippings upon naked buttocks, she had not flinched. Neither had she laughed at the preposterous images in her mind that his revelations conveyed. No; she had known what to do: listen attentively and not show any signs of panic.

Clients' revelations, even graphic ones, needed to be respectfully contained and kept safe: this was the most important service that a health professional could provide to a person seeking help. The emotionally troubled needed to unload onto someone trustworthy, someone guaranteed to be on their side as they unpacked the jumble in their head, someone benevolently disposed towards any ugliness that was uncovered. Having a partner in crime, so to speak, as well as someone knowledgeable enough to be able to optimise the required repackaging, was what gave clients the emotional strength they needed to improve themselves.

Even newly qualified, she had known at least this much—which was more, she suspected, than ninety per cent of counsellors of any age knew.

The effect of her skill as a counsellor had been transformative for the once uptight silk called Gilbert. The more he realised just how much he could trust her, the more he revealed. Before long, he was able to relax completely in her company and after that it had not taken her long to uncover how ill he really was. Indeed, she was still the only person in the world who knew how bad things were for him emotionally.

What had amazed her the most in her journey with Gilbert was her realisation during the counselling that she was just as sick as he was. The insight had stunned her initially but was undoubtedly correct. The two of them were equally sick; their sicknesses just showed differently to the outside world. The mental health workers during her own breakdown at university in second year sociology had been unanimous about one thing, which was that aside from other debatable issues, Alyssa Brown definitely suffered from a severe childhood-related chronic post-traumatic stress disorder. Which was the same as the diagnosis she had recently decided on for Gilbert. In her own case, however, the situation was not as clear-cut. Her own mental health team at Olympic Hospital had got it wrong. They had become confused. She had been severely unwell all right, but not because of childhood-related PTSD. Not that. No. It was because she was a bad person.

Plain bad.

It was not all that complicated. She was tired now, so she preferred not to think about it any further.

She was not wrong about the source of Gilbert's problems, though. He truly *had* been abused by both his parents.

What pleased her the most was the way she seemed able to understand people—men, at least—better than they understood themselves. She could control them. Even great men like Gilbert Rockport—and Alan Summerfield.

She thought back to the apartment balcony at Santos Beach. There, Alan had said he believed clients would find her non-threatening; that *he* found her non-threatening. Even he had fallen under her thrall.

She smiled to herself in the dark. If there was one thing that she did know for certain, it was that a person's external persona, especially their external *sexual* persona, was always a pretence.

Why are people so easily fooled?

6

The morning clinic at the cottage progressed according to expectation and routinely enough. As scheduled, third up on the list for a therapy session was Benjamin Clayton, the paranoid schizophrenic.

Ben's treatment plan, set up by Greta, called for twenty once-a-week visits for transference-focused psychotherapy. Though this was an unorthodox therapeutic approach for schizophrenia, it was hoped that in view of Ben's superior intelligence the addition of such non-regulation therapy would improve him enough for the clinic to be able to at least reduce his medication and thereby satisfy his mother. Whether it benefited him or not, subjecting him to psychotherapy was felt unlikely to cause him any harm.

Alyssa watched Ben through the lattice window of the cottage consulting room as he approached down the garden path. As usual, he was on time, but what was not usual was that he was accompanied by the Donald Clinic's psychiatric nurse, Gail Wilson. Most likely the two of them were coming from Gail's office, which was upstairs in the main building, because that was where laboratory samples to monitor his drug levels were taken. It was also where the security checks for concealed blades were conducted on Ben by Gail. The rule with Ben was that before he could meet any therapist, he had to submit to a body search, a task that always fell to Gail because she was a registered nurse.

As Alyssa idly watched the approach of the two, she noticed something unusual about their behaviour. While they were far off, Gail walked close to Ben, holding his hand, but when they got nearer, she let go of his hand and moved a full step away from him.

Hello, what is that all about?

Something else was unusual too: Once freed from Gail, Ben began to walk like someone who was severely mentally ill. As a student, she had seen psychiatric inpatients in locked wards walking that way, but she had not come across it otherwise. Not until now. To her amazement, Ben began to swing his arms in exaggerated stiff arcs, like a soldier in a banana republic. He was dressed in his customary too-short khaki shorts, and, as he got closer, she saw that with each of his odd marching steps, in addition to his stiff arms the muscles of his thighs rippled with peculiar irregular twitches, like the flanks of a racehorse. Perhaps the bareness of his thighs emphasised what was happening, but the muscular spasms in his legs looked like something to be concerned about. Technically, he *was* ill of course—at least mentally—and, yes, the quadriceps muscles of his thighs were hugely muscular anyway, but the scything of his arms and the rippling of his quadriceps seemed to her signs that he was not fully under control. Unfortunately, she knew too little about the side effects of schizophrenia medication to be sure. Gail seemed unconcerned, but the more Alyssa watched Ben the more frightened she felt.

God, he's powerful.

She hoped that what she was seeing represented nothing more than what was sometimes expected. She needed to ask Alan Summerfield about it.

She heard them as they entered the adjoining waiting room, but she stayed at the window for a while, gazing into the now restored calm of her garden. While doing so, she tried to recall what she knew about antipsychotic medication. Almost nothing, she realised.

After what seemed like less than two or three minutes, Gail yelled "Yooh hooh" from the waiting room, in a loud voice.

The behaviour did not seem at all professional, just like Gail's earlier cuddly handholding with her client. Alyssa disapproved of such professional casualness. For all Gail knew, she might still be busy with a previous client. Yooh hooing in her waiting room was not acceptable in a place like the Donald Clinic—in any professional place, in fact.

Mildly annoyed, she opened the door to her office and went out to meet them.

'Look Ben!' she heard Gail say as she emerged. 'Your Alyssa!' Gail pointed at her with exuberant jabbing motions, her voice high-pitched and artificially excited. Ben, though, appeared completely uninterested. He had seated himself on a waiting room chair and there he remained, unresponsive. Gail went and patted him on the back and spoke to him again as if he were intellectually handicapped or a small dog: 'See, Ben? See, she's not so scary.' Gail gave a patronising smile. 'He really likes you for some reason, Alyssa. Be kind to him, won't you.' She spoke to her in the same voice that she used with Ben.

I don't believe this.

Gail was not her favourite person. She had not warmed to the clinic's psychiatric nurse ever since their first disastrous meeting in the staff room when Gail had been there with Dr Barnes and as good as ignored her. The woman had continued to be rude towards her ever since and seemed also mildly stupid. The behaviour in the waiting room felt like a last straw.

No, she did not like Gail Wilson. She knew the type well: the puffed up *nobody*—despite the wealthy husband. People like her idiotically believed that they were of great significance. Gail seemed incapable of understanding that she was just a minor health care professional, one of hundreds of thousands in the country, and that in the greater scheme of things she amounted to absolutely nothing at all. The gross deficiency in psychological insight felt intolerable. Most irritating of all was the talking down to others off a high horse that simply did not exist.

Very stupid.

Ben, meanwhile, was not going anywhere. He continued to pretend not to hear Gail and instead peered at the ceiling. After a while, he began to hum "four-and-twenty blackbirds baked in a pie".

Alyssa went up to him and tried to make eye contact with him, but he resisted her efforts too, rolling his eyes around in a macabre impersonation of an insane person. She knew he was faking, so his actions made her smile at him with amusement. However, he did not smile back. Evidently, he was not going to be taking sides in any struggle between two women in a room.

'He's not good, is he?' wittered Gail. She sounded concerned and moved closer and used a finger to lift his chin. She stared into his face, but he closed his eyes. She gave a worried frown. 'Don't worry,' she said to Alyssa, her voice breathless now, 'I'll let you know if there are any problems with his test results.' Going down on her haunches, she addressed Ben directly, returning to fake bonhomie: 'We don't expect any bad behaviour from you, do we Ben?'

Ben produced an idiotic grin.

Alyssa saw a flash of anger appear across Gail's face, despite the contrived cheeriness. '*Do* we Ben?'

Again, no response.

Gail was not amused. She stood up. 'Disappointing, Ben!' She turned to Alyssa. 'Have him with my pleasure!' Thoroughly angry now, Nurse Wilson gathered herself for departure. At the cottage door, she delivered a passing shot. 'This is *your* doing, Alyssa. I have no doubt about it.' She stepped out into the garden and almost lost her footing. 'What is it with all these plants in my *way!*' she cursed. 'Your bloody madwort is everywhere. What are you *doing* to Ben's mind in this *place!*'

'Excuse me! Speak for yourself.' Alyssa slammed the door behind her. Madwort, indeed. The old cow couldn't even walk properly. Not only did she not like Gail, but she did not like what she had just seen of the interaction between her and Ben. There was a tension there that should not have been there.

After all, Gail had known Ben for many years. And besides, Ben was no invalid.

Ben had a perfectly adequate brain. She had no doubt that Dr Summerfield was correct in his assessment that his intelligence was very high. Only auditory hallucinations and paranoia limited his performance. With these under control via his medication, there was no reason for anyone to treat him like a fool—and there was no excuse, either, for him to behave like one.

Unless he is trying to protect himself.

The curious thought flitted across her mind, but she let it go.

'Come on in, Ben.'

During their regular sessions over the past month or two, Ben had never caused any trouble. In his own words, he had come to like the cottage—and her—and was comfortable in her presence. Much to her relief, as soon as Gail left, he stood up smartly, evidently back to normal.

Looking shamefaced, he removed his plastic raincoat and multicoloured waistcoat as required and walked normally to the client sofa and took his customary seat.

So much for Gail.

'What was that carry-on all about, Ben?'

He ran a finger across his lips to indicate that they were sealed.

He would not be telling her anything about it today.

'Maybe later, then?'

'It's like a bowl of rice. The Cockatrice.'

7

Ben was not the only one with mental health issues. Between clients, alone at her desk in the consulting room, Alyssa often felt that she herself was the one in need of counselling. Undoubtedly, she still had unresolved issues. And endless anxiety. And worry that she was not quite normal in her sexuality. She worried more about *that* side of herself than people realised, in fact.

With the ever-increasing pressure of work, she was going to need to get herself sorted. Under control and behaving normally.

It wasn't helping that she was finding it difficult to understand what was happening to her at Fabio's gym.

Especially in relation to the fabulous new man there called Mark.

Was she being utterly ridiculous in her obsession with so-called Mark? After all, who *was* "Mark"? And why had she experienced an unexpected outburst of outrage at the gym. Ridiculous, uncontrollable fury over the fact that an unsuitable woman had latched onto him.

Ruby.

That was her name.

Ruby aside, why did great-looking men doom themselves to wasting their lives on unsuitable women? Why could they not see through them? The exact same disaster had befallen her father, with tragic results. What was it with men and their bad choices in women?

At the gym, she had felt so upset about it that she had not been able to exercise properly. Which was not normal.

Same with the poster she had once "seen" when it wasn't even there.

And now, more recently, at the dumbbell section, there had been yet more unsettling behaviour on her part.

She had lost the plot *completely*.

Everything was going wrong at the gym. It had to stop.

She needed to pull herself together.

It was how her illness had started in the past. The uncontrollable anger. After which had come confusion. Then restlessness—and then the unravelling. It had happened at a different time and in another place, but sometimes at the gym it seemed that the gym wasn't really there. That it wasn't real.

Which was not good enough.

She had felt it strongly that day at the dumbbell section. She had felt that she was wrong about everything and that everything she believed was a lie.

The premonition had been as strong as death itself; a feeling that something terrible was going to happen—and soon.

She had picked up a 10 kg dumbbell and it had felt like it had no weight at all. She had performed twenty bicep curls with ease.

It had been weird.

So weird.

And at the start of the year, that business with the clock. Why had the gym clock stopped at noon? Where had the missing time gone?

At the dumbbells, her reflection in the mirrors had looked different. The lighting made her gym tights look the same colour as her skin. It had looked for all the world like she had no clothes on—like she was completely naked. And there had been a siren, an ambulance in the street below, loud. Too loud.

Or was that from the time when they put her away in the psychiatric ward at Olympic Hospital?

Was it about to happen all over again?

She would not survive losing the little she now had. She was still too weak. It could not be allowed to happen.

She needed to keep fighting. She had no option. She needed to go on pretending that nothing was wrong, that what had happened to her wasn't all that serious. She was just a girl after all, and he was completely drunk.

She needed to go on doing what she had always done ever since those days: act normal.

Which should not be too difficult.

After all, advising people on how to act normal was her job.

8

The sessions with Ben were never easy or straightforward, yet the two of them made good progress in the task of building trust. She had learnt when to ignore him and when to take him seriously, so today she ignored his previous reference to a bowl of rice. Eventually, they would get back to that. Meanwhile, it seemed best to go with the flow. Despite her misgivings after Ben Clayton's very first visit, he now spoke to her fairly freely. He had also learnt to respect the boundaries that she insisted he observed. He knew, for example, that questions about her personal life, or statements to the effect that he found her "sexy", were off limits. The counselling sessions were about *him*, not her. She was his counsellor and not his potential girlfriend.

In his case, definitely not.

Her goal with him was to be able to see the world as he saw it. Difficult as that was going to be, she knew that if she could do that then she would be able to get through to him. With mutual mental intimacy would come access to his secret inner world. There, possibly, she would be able to improve him—even though it would be a place of much damage and much danger. The task would be difficult, but she had the support of the clinic. The question Alan Summerfield—or more correctly, Ben's mother—wanted answered was whether some sort of relationship therapy could achieve enough healing to get him off his medication. The experiment did not seem unreasonable given the many potential side effects of the antipsychotic drugs he currently took, especially viewed in the long term. The downside of attempting psychotherapy, however, was that it was usually not much use in people like Ben.

Once comfortable on the sofa, Ben produced his customary pencil and notepad from a pocket in his shorts. On the notepad, she knew, would be further records of his endless displeasures with organised religion. Present also would be his recommendations regarding their fate. The notes represented important work to him, so important that he could not entrust them to any digital device. There, he believed, they would be hacked by the Vatican and secretly altered to suit official doctrine. Instead, he kept his many piles of completed handwritten notes safely stored in his bedroom at home, and the plan was that one day his mother was going to have them published in a book.

He had some new pages to show Alyssa.

'I'm considering progressing to chapter ninety-three—for which, at present, I am still pre-ambling. Ninety-three is still within the sweep of the main theme, of course. There are some sticking points that I wish to mop up today.' With his important work he always adopted a tone suited to the gravity of his task.

'Sounds good,' said Alyssa encouragingly. The main theme for him was the completion of the Reformation. 'Pleased to hear you are making progress, Ben.' She knew he worked at this task every day, evidently unconvinced that Martin Luther had finished the job. In this, he had few distractions—nothing other than a very part-time occupation as a special needs horticulturist for the city council, which amounted to hand-weeding in public parks on three mornings a week.

'The issues for today are actually part of a sub-encyclical. But still under the umbrella of the main theme; still within the scope of the projected book title. Got it?'

She understood. 'Sort of.' They had discussed his projected book title before, in tentative terms. She knew, for example, that Ben intended to use *The Cockatrice and the Fatling* as the title of his book—once his mother got around to publishing it. The title may, in fact, have been a suggestion of his mother.

A cockatrice, Alyssa had discovered, was a mythical monster that could kill you simply by looking at you.

When first she learnt this fact, she had foolishly believed that Ben's monster represented whatever it was that was tormenting him, and that the fatling represented Ben himself—the monster's succulent prey. The clever theory neatly explained everything. Especially the paranoia, which now seemed understandable.

How wrong she had been on that score.

Nothing about schizophrenia was that simple. It hadn't taken her long to discover that she did not know very much about schizophrenia at all and that in the initial engagements with Ben, she had fallen into the seduction of lay thinking. Indeed, for a while with him, at the beginning, due to her ignorance, she had even become the "smart-assed pseudo-therapist" that Wendy Greene so often warned about. Wiser now that she had got to know Ben better, she was able to see her old mentor's point only too clearly. What foolish conceit on her part it had been to think that she could know Ben better than Ben knew himself. In the modern therapist there was no place for professional delusions of grandeur. Maybe in the old days, but not anymore.

So, yes, initially she had been completely wrong about Ben Clayton.

The inconvenient truth was that Ben was not just another version of her brothers or her father or her lovers. Far from it. He really was insane, and his mind went beyond her intuitive understanding. Benjamin

Clayton was nobody's succulent fatling. On bad days, he was in fact the cockatrice. Ben Clayton was not only a monster on a chain, but he was also not an ordinary monster. He was a resolute monster; a monster determined to fly. While he had not yet worked out how to take off, success was not far away. In every way, Ben was far from harmless. People were always going to be in significant physical danger in his presence, herself included.

How wrong I was about him in the beginning.

She blamed Greta McCreedy for the fact that initially she had not understood that Ben Clayton was not just a pitiful lost soul—not some harmless victim of overbearing parents—but a cyclone of death searching for the launch code. Greta had always known this and known that there was nobody more inappropriate than Ben Clayton to send to a new and inexperienced therapist on her first day at work. And yet she had sent him—a physically powerful young male suffering from paranoid schizophrenia. Without any doubt, the Donald Clinic's elderly clinical psychologist had acted malevolently. Greta had deliberately placed her in danger. But by now, at least, she was on to Greta's sick schemes. She had survived. Both Ben and Greta no longer had her fooled.

Alyssa looked at Ben as he sat in obedient readiness upon his couch waiting for her to snap out of her daydreaming. He looked peaceable enough. His thighs had even stopped twitching. Was this how monsters behaved when they wished to trick their prey? They stopped twitching? Probably.

She no longer had any illusions about what she was up against.

'I'd love to see what you've written this week,' she said finally, to get the consultation underway. She had learnt over the preceding weeks that discussing the latest pages in his notebook was a useful way to start a session. He seemed to value her attention and asking him to read his notes to her seemed an easy way to get him to explore himself.

9

Ben was talking somewhere in the background: 'As I said before, I have some ideas here for chapter ninety-three, and I want to clarify my thoughts.' His voice sounded timid, as it often did for no apparent reason. 'This is where I deal with the manifestation of the Oedipus complex. The chapter is going to be titled *The Manifestation*.'

Alyssa forced herself to pay attention. His use of the technical psychoanalytic term "Oedipus complex" was a new addition to his vocabulary. Almost certainly he was parroting her from earlier sessions, where she had mentioned it once or twice. The development made her smile. 'That sounds awfully technical, Ben. The Oedipus complex, I mean.'

'I've been reading. About it.'

By now, she had made herself comfortable. Her shoes were off, and her legs were up on her chair, folded sideways. She needed to engage—especially emotionally—with disjointed ideas as genuinely as possible over the next forty-five minutes, and this was going to take a lot of effort. She needed to win Ben's trust. Wendy Greene had given many tutorials about the importance of unconditional positive regard. According to Wendy, all forms of relationship therapy—*every* one of them—failed when the therapist fell into the trap of toying with the client. Across the entire spectrum of available options, from cognitive behaviour therapy through to mindfulness, there was no place for the supercilious. This rule applied especially in transference-focused psychotherapy. Clients were not easily fooled. Fake emotions blocked healing. Counselling was *not* about being a smart ass.

Tell me about it.

Ben had become impatient with her distracted state of mind. 'It's okay,' he announced.

'What is?'

'The depth. I'm within my depth. I know how to use the terms. That part of psychology I find easy. Psychoanalysis I cracked a long time ago.'

'Pleased to hear it,' she reassured him. She assumed he was referring to the Oedipus complex and that he was worried that she thought he did not understand what he was talking about.

'I don't have a problem with mental theories,' he explained. 'I pretty much know them all by heart. It's just people that I don't seem to be able to understand. You know, as in humankind.'

She smiled. There was a boyish gallantry to him that made him charming in his own hopeless way.

'Because, you see, the cause of everything that's going on in the world seems obvious to me, whereas it doesn't seem obvious to them. I see the connections, but they don't. They don't seem capable, and I can't seem to work out why not.'

'Why don't you take one step back for me, Ben. What *connections* are you referring to?'

'The Oedipus complex, of course, what else? It's everywhere. It's manifesting in everything. I have it fully outlined in my new chapter—in The Manifestation. The Oedipus complex. It's connected to everything. Responsible for everything.'

'It is? As in?'

'As in its outworking; its consequences. As in its effects. As in its *manifestations*. Why is the Oedipus complex so hard for you?'

'I'm not following you.'

'Don't tell me you don't see how it all ties in.'

'With what?'

'With what we have been discussing the whole of last month! The scourge that I have been expounding on. The Religionist Phenomenon. What else?'

At last, he was beginning to make some sense. Sometimes he behaved as though he believed she could read his thoughts. 'Well, thank you, Ben. Yes, okay, I agree with you that religion probably does have a psychological basis, if that's what you mean. And remind me again about your use of the word *religionist*. Do you mean a religious person?'

'Oh *please*!' He adopted a condescending tone and recited a definition with his eyes closed, no doubt to emulate scholarly concentration: 'Religionism is a malignant mental condition that metastasises early and is characterised by wilful ignorance and malevolent intolerance.'

'Did you just make that up?'

'No. It's known. I've told you all this before. Religion is a symptom of a disease, but it's not the disease itself.'

'What disease?'

'The unresolved Oedipus complex, what else? How often does a person have to repeat himself around here?'

'Religion stems from an unresolved Oedipus complex?'

He nodded magnanimously. 'Finally, the penny drops.' Then a new thought occurred to him. 'Hey, I have a question for you, Alyssa: how does a Pope differ from an Ayatollah, differ from a High Lama, differ from a Guru?'

He seemed off on a different tack. 'Is this a riddle?'

'No. The answer is obvious. At least to me it is.'

'You want to know in what way they are different?'

'Let me give you a clue. How do their clothes differ?'

'Their clothes? I don't really know. They all look the same to me.'

'Exactly! That's the answer.' He seemed disappointed. 'How did you know so soon?'

She frowned at him. He was back to not making much sense.

'As you have so ably demonstrated, Miss Alyssa, there is of course absolutely no difference between them. The four entities are symptoms of the *same* disease. Exactly the same.'

'Oh.'

He chortled. 'As there is no difference, the question must be *why*. And the answer must be the Oedipus complex because that is the only common factor. Therefore, it is the only possibility. This is the *eureka* moment. Oedipus is the *cause* of the phenomenon. It has to be.'

'Are you sure about this?'

'Absolutely. From what I have discovered it's so obvious that even a child can follow the evidence.'

10

Alyssa nodded away as Ben Clayton rambled on about the urgent need for society to destroy organised religion. She commented as little as possible to avoid throwing him off track and instead occupied herself with her own thoughts.

Technically, Ben had it all wrong, that much she did know. She was no expert on Freud, but, as far as she knew, the term "Oedipus complex" referred to a belief that children under the age of five years universally desired to possess the parent of the opposite sex and eliminate the other, a wish that became unconscious and desexualised as the child developed and then finally extinguished itself during psychological maturation. The Oedipus complex did *not* persist in the later mind.

Nevertheless, she did understand the essence of what Ben was trying to convey despite his ignorance about psychoanalysis. What he was referring to, no doubt, was the *consequence* of extinguishing the Oedipus complex, which was guilt and the formation of an unconscious so-called Superego. To Freudians, it was *this*, the Superego, which was the source of the "holier than thou" *aspirations* seen in all people.

Nevertheless, to be fair, there was probably considerable validity to Ben's assertion that similar psychopathology was at work in all religious belief. According to some reasonably respected psychoanalysts, even though the perverted desires of the Oedipus complex finally became transformed, it was true that a variety of longings and hatreds towards parents continued to flow unconsciously in all people. Now in disguise, these hidden emotional forces retained their yearning for a higher power—a higher power just as supernatural and irrational as once the parents had seemed to the young child. In essence, religion was nothing more holy or sacred than unacknowledged parent worship by the unacknowledged small child still within the worshipper.

While in some individuals—mainly the constitutionally oppositional defiant—the ongoing parental attachment spawned religious mania, in the less stubborn majority it morphed into fairly harmless mainstream religious feelings, including the related pathologies of fanciful political beliefs and regressive sexual imperatives.

The childhood Un-conscious certainly was responsible for much havoc in the world. Therefore, it was not without justification that the unresolved Oedipus complex, the originator of many an unstable beast, was of great interest to Ben Clayton. She needed to give him credit for that.

Indeed, the great Obermaaier himself had once pointed out in a lecture the fact that belief lay deeper in the mind than the intellect. Which meant that intellectual arguments among theologians became devoid of meaning once it became evident that their specific beliefs were already present prior to their therefore bogus intellectual "proofs" of the validity of their beliefs. Furthermore, as Obermaaier pointed out, if being religious amounted to nothing more than associating unconsciously with a proxy parent, then religiosity was always going to be a bio-psycho-socially determined aspect of human behaviour and therefore universal and impossible to standardise or limit—as history well demonstrated. Furthermore, what small child did not believe in magic? As an aspect of persistent childhood, religiosity was always going to include an element of superstition. Of necessity, all hankerings after a Supreme Being contained elements of irrationality.

Belief lies deeper than the intellect.

Powerful stuff from Obermaaier.

But was it true?

Ben wanted her attention. 'My plan,' he said twice.

'Sorry. I'm listening.'

'My plan is to use a series of key questions to kick off an exposure of how the Oedipus complex has led humanity astray through the stalking horse of religion. Thus, under chapter ninety-three's heading, The Manifestation, I will outline how the Oedipus "disease" manifests itself, so to speak. To achieve my goal, I make use of a series of replies to critical questions that I put to a virtual religious representative, whom I have named *Blastus Bamboozelus*. Thereafter, these responses will be collated into a master compendium for the chapter.'

Ben beamed at her with the smile available only to geniuses. However, what he had just said sounded suspiciously like something his mother had suggested.

'No doubt, Miss Alyssa, Blastus will be suspected of being a pope, but of course such a pope doesn't exist. People will know that, so I shouldn't get into trouble over it. He's not Catholic, or from Geneva. Therefore, I refer to him as an antipope. I'm allowed to do that. Those did exist, and therefore could exist. It's true. Therefore I am. *Ergo et sum.* Neat, isn't it, the Latin? Do you follow?'

She did not speak Latin. 'Sort of.'

'I worked on it all last night. These are his answers to my questions. Included are my commentaries on his answers. I got the idea by adding Voltaire and Job to Nietzsche. Seem reasonable?'

'Possibly.'

'Excellent. Well then, let's get cracking.'

CHAPTER SEVENTEEN

1

DESPITE HER RESOLVE TO end Gilbert Rockport's visits to the cottage, Alyssa had not yet been able to pull it off. Even more worryingly, concerns about him kept crowding into her mind as she tried to sleep. Another week and a half had gone by, and she had still not offloaded him. The attempt to say goodbye the previous week had been half-baked; her heart had not been in it. There seemed to be too much that she still needed to learn from him. Besides, spending time with him made her feel good about herself and her abilities when so little else did. Her thoughts about him were many and varied. And even she could see that their relationship was no longer objective. His next visit needed to be his last one with her. On the coming Monday, Gilbert was going to *have* to go.

When she woke, it was still dark. After a minute's confusion she realised that she must have dozed off, which was a good thing. Any amount of sleep was a good thing at the present time. Cy was fast asleep next to her, on his side and facing away from her, so she reached for her phone on the nightstand and checked the time. It read 04:27—which was both good and bad. Good because she had had two hours sleep and bad because she now felt wide awake. There seemed little chance of getting more sleep. And yet there was still a big day to get through at the Donald. Every day there seemed to be a big day. And she was going to have to get through it.

Rats.

She tried to get back to sleep but failed, as predicted. So, to occupy her mind, she once again thought about Gilbert Rockport. She had been worrying about him a lot lately, especially over the last week. Recollections of snippets of his visits to the cottage earlier in the year swirled through her mind.

'What concerns me,' he had once said to her, 'is that things are probably going to end badly for me. There is just so much harm that one body can take.'

She found herself able to remember that conversation with surprising clarity.

'As in the self-harming?'

'Yes. I think my life is in danger.'

'Really?'

Yes really. He needed help. Or things were going to go pear shaped.

I need help.

It had been this confession that had put him on the path to salvation because up until then Gilbert Rockport QC had been politely avoiding any explanation as to why, exactly, he was at the cottage, and she had been struggling to cope with his stereotypical senior male persona. Once he revealed that he was broken inside, however, she had obtained better command of the situation.

She recalled the great sense of relief she had felt on reaching more familiar territory with him: a need for help. Now, at last, she had the tools to potentially help him. She *had* what he needed, which meant that at last there was some possibility of interpersonal intimacy. Without a genuine relationship, psychotherapy had no possibility of working. Later, in view of how difficult the initial few weeks of stalling had been for them both, she had asked him why he had persevered with her. The answer had been empowering, thrilling almost.

"I kept going because I liked you".

He has always liked me.

What Gilbert was really saying, of course, was that he found that he had something in common with her; that there was something between them; that there was a sexual dimension to the visits. Which was true. And even then, she had found him sexually attractive too without admitting it to herself.

Thinking back, she regretted that she had discovered right from the first session that he was an important lawyer. The knowing of this had inhibited them both at the beginning. The intrusion of the fact that he was someone of exalted status had made it much harder for him to get past the initial humiliation of having to confess to weakness and ask for help. After all, his high status in the eyes of society was not an idle conceit. Not only had Gilbert Rockport achieved peer selection to the rank of Queen's Counsel for his skills in civil tort, but he was also part owner of the city's premier law firm. The name on the back window of his car, *Berkowitz Berkowitz Rockport*, was the name of his own multimillion-dollar enterprise.

How bizarre it had seemed, at the beginning, to have Mr Rockport himself sitting on a couch in her office, he a man so senior and experienced and she a woman so junior and inexperienced. How hard it was, he had said, for a silk to out himself, and how great it was to find someone safe to confide in at last. It had been both scary and flattering at the same time. Flattering because he said he liked her, and felt safe confiding in her, and insisted that he saw no reason to go elsewhere, and scary because she knew he could snuff out her career in an instant if he put his mind to it.

She had been the one who had forced his confession, of course, the one who had enabled him to tell the truth about himself despite the utter debasement and humiliation it entailed. After the initial weeks of stalling, she had bravely risen to the occasion and ended the impasse. She had asked him to attend his next appointment (his third) dressed in a cheap casual shirt and budget chinos, not one of his expensive business suits. She had wanted to lessen the aura of authority he generated with his power dressing.

'I know you probably think it's laughable,' she had said to him, 'but maybe if you turn yourself into a nobody it may help us make progress. I want to see if I can reach the Gilbert hiding behind the five-thousand-dollar suits.'

'This one only cost me four thousand dollars.'

'Just do it, Gilbert.'

Fortunately, he followed her advice. Without further protest, he dutifully removed the myth from the man and returned that following Monday socially engineered into a faintly ridiculous-looking middle-aged nobody. Even his shoes seemed to have come from a two-dollar shop.

She almost laughed. 'Oh, Gilbert, this is just brilliant.' He did not find it a laughing matter, though. Even in his funny clothes he resolutely kept his mouth shut except for meaningless pleasantries. Gilbert Rockport was not going to be overcoming his shame at being a sexual pervert any time soon and spill the beans. Even with him masquerading as a nobody, they were back to the old awkward silences.

She had been sitting on the edge of her counsellor's chair, perched upright in frustration, and Gilbert had been sitting in a sunken state on his sofa, looking diminished, when at last she had seen the way forward. The clue came from the way they were sitting.

Everything suddenly became obvious to her. In a flash of insight, she had realised that she was looking down at him and feeling dominant over him and that he was cringing in front of her. The situation between them had become highly sexual. The dynamics of the interaction were so evident that she had hesitated to believe that what she was seeing was really happening. Gilbert Rockport was acting towards her like a sexual bottom and, clearly, she was functioning towards him like a sexual top.

Usually, Gilbert was a strongly dominant person, probably even sexually in most situations, but now, it seemed, she had discovered that when he fell under the power of someone whom he truly wanted sexually, he collapsed internally into the supplicatory bottom he had suddenly become.

Somehow, sexually, she was controlling him to a ridiculous degree.

She was his key, she, as in her sexual self. His vulnerability to what she potentially offered him sexually was overpowering him.

The behaviour was clearly pathological—or at least highly unusual—and she was bringing it to the surface.

Sexy psychologist with emotional issues meets sexual pervert with emotional issues.

It seemed impossible to believe that earlier she had not recognised the sexual transference and countertransference that had been going on between them. The stark truth of the matter was that as a female of the correct sort, she was able to trigger his sexual perversion. It was the reason he came to her; the reason he liked her; the reason he trusted her. She wielded a lightning rod into his unconscious, so to speak. It was enough to do her head in.

She knew then that what happened next would depend on her. It was a case of now or never with regard to reaching the real Gilbert. Everything had depended on her remaining in control at that point. Provided she exerted sexual command over him, she *herself* had the capacity to conjure up whatever it was that was troubling him. She could force his sexuality out into the open. Potentially, she could fix him. If anyone could help him, she could.

The sudden *knowing* of all this had flooded over her as she gazed at the suddenly revealed alternate version of Gilbert Rockport, a shrunken man who stared nervously at the cottage floor, no longer attractive, strongly built, wealthy, or successful but a snivelling worm. The QC everyone feared was now revealed to be severely handicapped. After weeks of struggle, finally, she had channelled the transference.

2

'You are extremely anxious, aren't you?' she remembered saying to her shrunken Gilbert in a stern voice. 'Well, you are right to be worried because I have worked you out.' Magically, he had not resisted her but remained under her spell. 'I know exactly what you have been getting up to, Gilbert, and there are going to be consequences.' She had no idea what his sexual problems were, of course, but she knew that she needed to act as though somehow it was obvious.

Everything unravelled from there.

He looked up and the blood drained out of his face. 'If this gets out,' he breathed. 'The consequences . . .' His voice died away into a sad whisper.

'Let me assure you that only I know. Not even my computer knows. But I know.'

'How? How do you know? How much do you know, Alyssa?'

'Talk!'

'Can't we just forget this whole business?' His expression became imploring.

She counteracted the risk of losing the moment by appearing as disapproving and controlling as possible. She glared down at him, arching her back slightly to emphasise her breasts. 'My lips are sealed, Gilbert. However, I want no more whining from you. The time for the truth has come. Today, you must confess. I have a completely open mind, so nothing you say will shock me.' She drummed her fingers. 'I'm waiting.'

He stared at her, horrified.

'Come. Exact details. Speak. I can help.'

He hesitated.

She took a final gamble: 'Confess. Or you *will* face punishment.'

'What? Jeez,' he said, staring at her in amazement. 'You *do* know after all! You are just so amazing.'

'Out with it.'

'Will you be okay with it? All the graphic details? The sick stuff?'

She had no idea what he was talking about at that stage. 'Especially with that.'

'How did you guess?'

'A woman can. Stop messing around, Gilbert. This is not a courtroom. We deal with actual truth here, not convenient lies.'

He hid his face in his hands. 'I wish you didn't know who I am. It makes it so hard for me. People are supposed to be frightened of me.'

'Not in this room.'

Not under my thumb.

Sitting low in his couch, Gilbert stared up at her for a long time. He seemed to be trying to convince himself of something.

Using her new understanding of how she was triggering him, she had made a point of holding his gaze.

He was the one to break. Lowering his eyes finally, he spoke to the floor. 'I don't wish to be personal or impertinent, Alyssa,' he mumbled, 'but have you ever had sex before? I mean, do you have sex? I know you are only young.'

He appeared to be trying to make sure that she was not going to try to accuse him of sexual abuse of a young woman or some such thing and seemed to have no idea how idiotic his question was. Normally, she did not answer personal questions about herself from clients, but she knew he was not trying to be offensive. She had learnt from experience that law people were notoriously ignorant and out of touch when it came to sexual matters. In fact, with sex, the law had absolutely no idea what was going on. They were almost as bad as the church. One need look no further than their many ill-informed judgements to realise that.

'Yes, Gilbert, I do have sex. You know you are being silly. Everyone has sex. Even you.' She emphasised that last bit for him. 'So, why don't you tell me about it? It's obviously troubling you greatly. I'm sure I can help you.'

He looked like a rabbit caught in a car's headlights.

'It's too pathetic.'

'What is?'

'Me.' And with that, he burst into tears.

She watched silently as Gilbert Rockport QC sobbed his heart out. He used up five tissues from the tissue box. Therapy was finally underway.

In simplest terms, when it came to obtaining what he wanted sexually, Gilbert was terrified of being hurt.

How surprising that had turned out to be—that all his troubles were nothing more complicated than that.

And most astounding of all had been the innate sureness of her grasp in relation to the sexual needs of men like him. With remarkable prescience, she had managed to reach behind the defences of someone with complete power over her and find the road to an inner space where she was able to be in control. Through some sort of mutual trust, she had breached his defences and they had managed to achieve mental intimacy regarding sex. It was now safe to examine his true sexual needs and associated emotional difficulties. His problems could be discussed with complete honesty.

There was no point in Gilbert Rockport pretending anymore to be someone he wasn't.

3

Alyssa remained stubbornly in bed, waiting for the "get up" alarm on her phone to go off. Despite the occasional dozing off, her mind continued to wander on through her maze of recollections about Gilbert. Why had she arrived at her suspicion that he suffered from childhood-related PTSD? That was the question. There was much that she needed to learn. And, though she knew she was nodding off at times and that there had to be some factual uncertainty, this did not seem an impediment to her quest. Even if some of what she remembered was nothing more than the stuff of dreams, the objection was theoretical. There was no way to find out. With Gilbert, there were no written notes, only a few anonymous cryptic jottings on her tablet at work. Everything else about Gilbert Rockport existed entirely in her own head.

And yet it did not seem to matter. Nothing seemed to matter other than getting to the truth about why things had gone so wrong for Gilbert Rockport.

'It's just that I've been finding myself forced to visit people. You know, professionals.'

She took an educated guess: 'You mean sex workers?'

'Well, no, I wouldn't exactly call them that. Not prostitutes. Although I suppose they are in a way. But I don't have sex with them. I never would. You know I'm married.'

She was on the right track.

'You visit sex workers?'

'Nikki knows,' he whined. 'Besides, it is not illegal. Not in this state, anyway.'

She knew enough about Gilbert's domestic details to know that, like Alan Summerfield, Gilbert Rockport was married to a third wife, and that this wife was called Nikki. Nikki was someone she had neither seen nor met. Unlike Alan's third wife Kara, who was young, Nikki was older. Nikki was forty-seven to Gilbert's forty-six.

'I'm not here to judge you, Gilbert.' She wasn't. Besides, he was correct about the legalities. Sex work had long ago been decriminalised and become properly regulated in all but the most backward states in Astoria. 'But tell me this: if you don't have sex with your sex workers, then what exactly *do* you do with them?'

'You don't understand. It's not what I do with them. It's what they do with me.'

He had stopped talking at that point.

Feeling a tingle of vindication, she let the silence grow. She needed to force the struggling Gilbert to talk more.

'Hell, Alyssa,' he exclaimed finally. 'You're an attractive, sexual young woman just like them. You'll understand.'

That was Gilbert's final hurdle crossed. He was going to equate her with "one of them". She saw the final tumblers dropping in his brain. She was about to witness the unlocking of his soul.

'They beat the hell out of me,' he blurted. 'I get them to beat the hell out of me. There, I've said it. I like to get a good hiding on my bottom from time to time.'

Gilbert Rockport's shameful secret was out.

He liked a good whipping.

He was a sexual pervert all right. Despite his outward persona of pillar of society, he regularly visited prostitutes and got them to beat him.

The gruesome details unfolded over subsequent Monday afternoon sessions at the cottage, and it turned out to be no laughing matter. It was not a case of Gilbert attending a few ladies for a bit of light relief, but something far more serious. What went on when *he* visited amounted to life-threatening torture.

There was something very, very wrong with him deep down.

His explanation went as follows: 'Yes, it's true they whip me, and yes, I know I get them to do it too hard, but it's the only thing that keeps me alive. I was totally suicidal before that. Now, I really need it. Obviously, I'm sick.'

Obviously.

She tried to be non-judgemental. 'Why don't we begin at the beginning? Perhaps you could explain how it all started. And later, maybe you could outline a typical visit to your lady friends.'

'Yes. Of course.' He seemed relieved to be talking to someone about it. 'You see, I reached the stage where I was so suicidal that I didn't even know if I was going to make it to the next day—don't ask me why because I don't know—and I had to do *something*, anything. Believe me, it was that bad. I didn't want doctors and medication—probably because I'm pig-headed—although I told myself at the time that it was because they weren't going to be able to fix me anyway and would just turn me into a zombie. I didn't want that. Also, of course, being Gilbert Rockport, I was ashamed of what I had become, scared it would get out, scared of what everyone would think. So, I thought *what the hell* and walked out of my building in Willow Street—proper, logical, manly stuff. I was going to find an instant cure for myself or die. I knew I was walking out on my life, knew it was an act of madness, but anything seemed better than the way I felt. I think it was some sort of nervous breakdown. Whatever was going to happen was going to happen and I didn't care. I was too far gone. Vaguely, I had some muddled intention of ending up under a train as the final solution, but first I wanted to try something else.'

'You poor man.' She meant it.

'Do you believe in miracles Alyssa? Well, I had a miracle happen to me that day, although God knows I didn't deserve one. Quite by chance, in my desperate trek up and down nameless streets, I stumbled upon a place I never knew about. In fact, I would not even have known it existed had I not seen a woman enter a suspicious-looking door up ahead of me. It was the woman who caught my eye. There was something different about her; something that was everything that I wasn't. So, I went in after her at the same door. As I say, I was lost and desperate and probably half out of my mind. The woman had disappeared by then, but I found I had entered a business establishment called "The House of Fantasy". It's in a back street in Troy, and apparently legendary to those who know of such things. Have you heard of it?'

'No.'

'Most haven't. Anyway, when I finally managed to get admitted, I found this woman again. My saving angel. I was saved on a day when I barely knew *what* I was doing.'

And you do now?

'It was a miracle. She's called Mistress Veronica. She's so wonderful that I think I must have been trying to find someone like her for the whole of my life. By an incredible stroke of luck, she was free to talk to me.'

'You're talking about a woman at a brothel?'

He looked hurt. 'Yes. Except it's not a brothel, it's something else. If you'll listen, perhaps you'll understand.'

'Sorry.'

For once in her life, she needed to shut up and listen.

4

'As you can imagine, I was an absolute hyperventilating mess by the time I got to seeing this woman. I could barely speak—me, a QC. Somehow, though, I managed to explain what I needed. It was the hardest thing I have ever done in my entire life.' Gilbert wiped his eyes. 'Luckily, Mistress Veronica turned out to be just brilliant. Wonderful beyond my wildest hopes. She never once laughed or even smirked. Instead, she was as patient and kind as a saint. When I had quite finished falling through the floorboards with anxiety and embarrassment, she took my hand and told me that I had come to the right place. She said I was just the kind of man that she liked and that nothing would please her more than to whip me very severely. On that wonderful day I at last found someone who could handle my truth.'

'I see.' His story sounded a bit too good to be true. 'And you don't think you could be embellishing things just a little in your recollections?'

'No. That's the whole wonderful thing about it. That's exactly how it happened. We bonded at first sight. It was incredible.'

'Mm. Tell me more, then.'

'I'm so glad this is not grossing you out. You see, at this place in Troy you can get things done to yourself—anything. It's an amazing place, really. It's owned by a woman called Agnes and she has no men on the staff. You pay cash and remain anonymous. They've got some great people working there, women who are always pleasant and helpful. With them, I know I am not alone. They've stabilised me, as it were. Enabled me to go on. And Veronica, of course, is special. She's who I see. She's become my soulmate. And the weird thing is this, Alyssa: somehow you remind me of her. Of Veronica.'

Great.

'In what way, Gilbert?'

He looked up, as though trying to extract the essence of Mistress Veronica from her eyes. 'Mm, yes, it's definitely there. I'm not imagining it, but I can't quite put my finger on what it is exactly. You look kind of similar, I suppose, but it's more than that. Maybe it's a wavelength thing— us all being on the same wavelength, something like that. Silly, I know. Whatever it is, it's something deep—if you don't mind me saying so.'

Alyssa forced herself to remain neutral. As a therapist, it was her duty. 'Let's stick to Veronica, shall we? What is it that you most like about her? And I mean which personality feature.'

Not her tits or her ass.

He smiled. 'Sorry. Yes, I see where you are coming from. What do I like most about Mistress Veronica as a person? What indeed? I've often thought about it. It's her kindness, I'd say. Veronica is the kindest woman I have ever met.'

Alyssa was surprised. 'Her kindness?'

'Yes.'

Clearly, Gilbert was confused about women. According to him, she and Mistress Veronica were similar people, yet she knew for a fact that she herself was not in the least bit a kind person—though probably neither was Mistress Veronica in reality. No doubt Gilbert, like most men, mistook real women for creations from their fantasy life.

Gilbert was not entirely lacking in insight, though. 'I know, of course, that there is a paradox there, with this Veronica business. I'm not that far gone. She may be kind, but she does give the most painful of beatings. In fact, she's the expert in the field for The House of Fantasy. Sometimes she gives it to me so bad that it seems I really am going to die. Once, I couldn't sit for a full three days afterwards.'

Alyssa frowned at him. 'You know, Gilbert, none of this is making much sense to me. Nevertheless, I am here to learn. Let's start with the basics. When you say that Mistress Veronica *gives it to you,* what exactly do you mean by that?'

His face fell. 'You mean with the beatings? You want to know about that?'

'Yes. What exactly happens there?'

There were no more smiles from Gilbert Rockport. It was as if he finally realised that the game was up; that he had been deluding himself for the whole of his life and was in serious trouble emotionally. He sighed. 'She gives me what I deserve. That's what she does. No more and no less. It's what I deserve. God, I feel so ashamed telling you this.'

Only being punished—severely—truly satisfied.

He *needed* to be punished.

She could feel the arteries in her neck pulsing, yet she remained outwardly calm. 'Well then, tell me about it, Gilbert. You need to tell someone.' Bizarrely, even her voice sounded calm. Her voice sounded kind too, even to herself.

At this point, emotion overcame him. His manly frame began to tremble violently. Then, like a torrent of pus gushing out of a giant festering abscess, the truth about his inner life began to flow.

The volcanic outpourings did not surprise her. It was how the truth always came out: in a torrent. Like pus.

5

Gilbert left nothing to the imagination.

It was now that he told her of his overpowering desire to have beatings inflicted upon his bared buttocks. And about what exactly it was that he had done to himself in that regard; the exact details of what went on when he attended The House of Fantasy in Troy. And about how frightening it had become to discover that he was unable to stop himself from overdoing things. His life had become consumed by a desperate need to be punished.

'Overdoing things?'

'On the severity front. I know you think the whole business is crazy, but it's not. What *is* of concern, though, is that it has become obvious even to me that there are deep-seated and significant unresolved emotional issues in my life.'

There certainly were.

He had outlined the events of a typical punishment session with Veronica: the fifty strokes, the fierceness of them, the lack of respite, the restraint, the nakedness, the screaming, and the deliberately arranged savage brutality and awfulness of it all. Not to mention the gross bruising and swelling afterwards and the ridge-like welts across his haunches. And, most surprisingly, the fact that there were no long-term physical consequences involved. No scars.

No scars.

Subjecting himself to such tortures, he had discovered, was a sure way to fix himself, even if for only a few months at a time. It was the only way for him to keep going, in fact.

Being beaten half to death brought him as close as he could get to reaching the sickness that he knew was hiding within him. And, while this *thing* that he was trying to reach remained frustratingly elusive—he didn't yet know what it was exactly—he was almost there. If only he could reach it, then at last he would be able to rip it out.

Alyssa knew enough about sexology to realise that her client's self-punishment activities were not merely the result of some sort of constitutional BDSM bent. With Gilbert it was different. It seemed obvious to her, as a person trained in psychology, that with him he was instead instinctively trying to access troublesome unconscious memories through a process of re-traumatisation. By re-distressing himself he was attempting to revisit similar previous experiences so that he could re-process them in his mind. In his own strange way, Gilbert had a good understanding of what he needed to do to save himself.

The same method—re-traumatisation—formed part of proven therapy for PTSD, albeit in more controlled and less brutal ways. The goal was to reconnect the sufferer from PTSD with the causative catastrophic event that remained hidden from them in their unconscious mind. Gilbert, though, had gone overboard and was acting without guidance or insight or safeguards. His actions were those of a desperate man and he was putting his life at risk.

Alyssa had known, from this time onwards, that Gilbert's problems related to his early childhood, and that the correct name for it was C-PTSD, and that he needed to be referred on to a specialist treatment centre. She had not acted, though. She had not done anything except endlessly seek more information. She had wanted to be surer of her facts. She had needed to know more. At the same time, she had emphasised the importance of him taking care with his health.

'I don't want to appear critical, Gilbert, but don't you think that what you are doing could be dangerous to your health? It sounds to me like there must be definite medical risks involved, so why not at least stop going to extremes?'

Always, he had the same lame excuse: "I'm pretty tough. Besides, it's not that bad".

He was not being honest with himself. 'You know that that is not an adequate answer.'

Yes, deep down, he did know that. 'Okay, the truth. The truth is, Alyssa, I need what I need. And, obviously, I accept the consequences of my actions. Veronica has already explained the dangers to me. I could get a fatal heart arrhythmia from the pain, or I could go into kidney failure from muscle trauma. But, of course, none of that has happened. The risks are up to me really, is how she put it. Which is not true from a legal point of view, but then she doesn't know I'm a lawyer, does she. Legally, in this state, you aren't allowed to injure another person severely even with his or her express consent—did you know that? But I don't care.

The essential thing is she's prepared to help me. Which is why I like her so much. She does what I want.'

'Even though, as you have just pointed out, what she is doing is technically illegal?'

'So is speeding in a car. People still do it. I still do it. I *need* what she gives me. It's the only thing that keeps me functioning at work. Besides, what else was I supposed to do?'

As he explained, he hadn't been able to consider going to a run-of-the-mill counsellor; that simply had never been a realistic option. As a legal man, he knew the pitfalls, and they were too damaging. 'Psychological counselling has been ruined by all the hangers-on and the stupidities. *Anything* any client says in so-called complete confidence is in fact reportable to the police. It depends entirely on the counsellor—on their level of ignorance and bias. Clients have absolutely no rights at all. Anything sexual is almost always leaked to the police—and the police, of course, always take the allegations as fact and proceed to label and process the client accordingly. Go for counselling to the wrong counsellor and mention anything to do with sex and you are almost guaranteed to end up getting someone sent to jail, very often yourself. Believe me, Alyssa, it is no longer possible to discuss anything meaningful with a counsellor except on a ludicrously superficial and dishonest level.'

Seeing someone like Veronica was a far better bet when it came to anything meaningful.

"Dreadfulness" was the vital ingredient that he craved. It was what satisfied—even though he could not work out *why* it satisfied, or even what exactly it was that was being satisfied. All he knew was that it was important that he not be able to escape his fate and that his pain be truly awful. To be able to go on working as Queen's Counsel, what he required from time to time was to have his buttocks exposed and then thrashed mercilessly until he lost his mind. And yes, it did excite him sexually.

'That's me in a nutshell,' he said earnestly, without appreciating his pun.

She recalled how, at that stage in proceedings, she had formed her hands into a steeple under her chin, elbows resting on her chair's armrests, and stared at him like a dispassionate philosopher for many a long minute, as though in possession of full understanding, and asked the key question: why? 'Surely, you must have some idea *why* you do such things to yourself,

Gilbert. What do you think is going on in your head?'

His unconscious defences were one step ahead of them both. 'I really don't have any idea,' he said. 'You have to believe me. That's why I'm here, isn't it? I've wracked my brains day and night for years, but I can't work it out. I need someone to tell me.'

Now why did I think you were going to say that?

She did not know the answer. She had her suspicions, though.

Great sensitivity on her part was now required. Critical to Gilbert's future welfare was that nothing in her attitude towards him should inhibit his ability to be truly honest with her—and therefore with himself. His entire career was at stake. A barrister, like a health professional, was required to be a so-called "fit and proper person" to remain in practice. The consequences for Gilbert Rockport QC if he ended up in hospital as a result of a beating and word of his activities got out, did not bear thinking about. For reasons related to the law's own hypocrisy and abject ignorance of human biology, any discovered sex acts beyond very occasional vanilla intercourse with a spouse automatically excluded one from the mythical league of proper people. Certainly, being discovered to have an "interest" in sex of any sort was utterly unacceptable. And as for having oneself spanked by a prostitute, especially while married—well, that was a definite non-starter.

6

Alyssa knew from the events of her own life how quick the public was to condemn. Cy knew it too because he often objected to society's deliberate cruelness in his books. According to him, society preyed ceaselessly upon itself, searching out the vulnerable and shredding them with sadistic glee. Which was true. The destruction of the exposed was merciless, especially if their "offence" went against whatever "righteousness" was currently in vogue—the more salacious the offence the better. The worst of it was that the condemnation arose not from moral virtue—the public had none—but from the pathological cowardice of the craven hearted. As a psychologist this seemed all too obvious. Mob judgements were nothing but the inherent and persistent desire of certain humans to be cruel. And sadly, this blood lust was never more easily slaked than by denouncing sexual behaviour different from the pretended norm of the time. The *real* perversity, as Cy kept trying to point out to deaf ears, resided not so much in the scapegoats of society but in the feigned nature of the public's moral outrage.

Philosophies and injustices aside, however, and whether one liked it or not, Gilbert's career teetered on a knife edge.

What made matters particularly dire for him was that he did not fit into the mega-city potentially tolerated category of "just another run-of-the-mill BDSM tragic". He was not engaging in regulation BDSM behaviour, not anything that conformed even vaguely to some urbanite-approved ritual. His offence was not that of harmless kinkiness. No, his offence was that he was trying to stay alive—which made him vulnerable. His ideas and activities were not those of an emotionally well person. He was defenceless. The press would love nothing more than to devour and destroy him.

She had studied BDSM in Sexology 101. It stood for Bondage, Discipline, Domination, Submission, and Sadomasochism. While elements of the entire spectrum were undoubtedly present in Gilbert, he did not otherwise fit the bill. Genuine BDSM practitioners were not mentally sick. According to Freudian theory, *all* people without exception had a sexual key that was kinky in some way or other, certainly in fantasy life, but while such matters were generally nothing more than a question of degree, there were limits. With Gilbert, his behaviour was too intense to be considered normal. Emotionally well people who felt like receiving a beating usually settled for a harmless spanking, not for getting themselves beaten half to death. The mentally healthy stuck to the common-sense rules of acted-out BDSM, which were that the activity be safe, sane, and consensual. The real-life acting out of fantasy desires— desires that were always primitive and therefore dangerous—required the filter of adult judgement. Most people remained in command of their fantasy life and, generally, BDSM remained invisible in society. Mostly, it occurred in the heads of lovers or between couples in private as part of their mainstream lovemaking. Overt BDSM activities, as in clubs or commercial establishments such as The House of Fantasy, were far less common. Gilbert Rockport, however, was not indulging in BDSM. There was nothing safe or sane about the savagery he felt compelled to have inflicted upon himself—although obviously he did consent to it.

With him, something was seriously wrong. Something to do with the formative experiences of his mind. Something to do with his childhood.

Early on, she had already begun to suspect that this was what lay behind his behaviour. Later, once she felt more certain that it related to childhood trauma, she had asked him about it directly. 'You mentioned that you get beaten while naked. Correct?'

'Oh, yes. As I explained, there would be little point otherwise.'

'Exactly. Now, based on that, I have another question for you. What about Mistress? Is she without her pants too?'

He looked taken aback. 'Good heavens, no. As I said, it's not a brothel. There's no sex.'

'No sex. Mm.' It seemed obvious to her as a psychologist that corporal punishment *was* a sexual activity. Anything to do with a combination of sadism and the buttocks—bared or not—had to be sexual. As a schoolgirl in Ocean View, long before attending university, she had already seen through the detestable humbug of those who claimed that beating a child in a ritualised setting was not a sex act. Perhaps, she thought, the answer to her school-time perplexity lay in the fact that in those days the exponents of the paedophilic activity of beating school children's buttocks rested secure in their belief that nobody was able to detect the deep sexual satisfaction they experienced every time they applied their punishments. Fortunately, society was no longer that naïve and most people now realised that for many impressionable young recipients, ritualised severe corporal punishment was as damaging as anal rape from a mental point of view.

Right from when Gilbert had first begun to tell her the truth about himself, she had already known that his problems were the result of sexual abuse as a child. With him, she had always *just known* this. But how? How had she *known?*

In the silent darkness of the bedroom, her heart pounded with anxiety.

Then the alarm on her phone was ringing and her hand was resting between her legs, as though trying to guard her. She sat up feeling confused. Then she realised that she must have been asleep again.

Her head was groggy, but it was time to get up for work.

CHAPTER EIGHTEEN

1

THE HEAVILY MEDICATED AND officially insane paranoid schizophrenic, Benjamin Clayton, leant forwards and held out his notepad, half-sideways, so she could see the results of his scrawling. He pointed with a finger: 'You can see here what Blastus Bamboozelus says. It's their typical codswallop. Can I read it to you?'

'Of course. I would be most interested in what you have to say.' She wasn't, really. Many pages had been filled with his characteristic microscopic back-sloping longhand and she felt just plain tired.

Alyssa saw that Ben had written his questions to Bamboozelus with a blue pen and indicated them with a "Q"; his answers with a red pen and indicated them with an "A"; and his commentaries with a lead pencil and indicated them with a "C".

Wisely or unwisely, she let him read to her. Considering it to be her duty as a therapist, she listened as attentively and respectfully as possible and tried to understand what it all really meant.

Which was not easy.

Ben began to read aloud his exposure of religion for the codswallop he believed it was:

**The collected Codswallop Sayings of
the religionist Blastus Bamboozelus:**

Q: Why, Blastus, do you continue to deny that religion, no matter how well intentioned, is fatally weakened when it resorts to intellectual dishonesty? Why not accept what is known to all objective scholars today and perceived by all unbiased educated people, namely that most of your texts are not what they are made out to be by you people? The truth you continue to deny is that your so-called infallible ancient texts are nothing of the sort. The truth is finally out there, and the truth is that they are largely a deplorable confidence trick. The texts are in fact from much later in time and are often nothing more than highly embellished nationalistic political compilations engineered out of historical and legendary kernels. Written in Phoenician, the so-called facts vary in a most ungodly fashion according to the ruler and state capital at the time of composition. Indeed, most of it is clearly a peri-Babylonian production, not from ancient days at all. Eclectic fragments are retrofitted to show divine purpose, prophesies are made retrospectively, and folk heroes are constructed out of expediency—all entirely without shame. Confabulations obvious to those with proper education abound to such an alarming degree that only people determined to continue perverting logic can continue to take any of it at face value. Why, then, do you continue to deny the obvious fact that the use of antiquity is an authenticity trick? Why should we accept that deception is acceptable because it is ancient? Why continue to cover up the undeniable truth, which is that what underpins you is nothing more than a hellish version of wishful thinking? Why! Why! Why?

<u>A:</u> *I do not believe in your denials, only in our truth.*

<u>C:</u> How dare you! Because it is true what I have been saying. The small giant inconvenience for you is that your diabolical fraud has become common knowledge. Most now perceive that your fantasy documents massage what really happened into something that never did, and that it's done for reasons no nobler than a will to power. This is the joke you have played on us gullible dupes over the centuries, isn't it? Admit it! Admit that your ancient texts are nothing more than a compilation of selected archival works that have been suitably edited and tweaked by politically savvy later-year priests. If you bothered to read anything objectively, it would be impossible for you to believe that God wrote a great deal of it. No. A whole lot of it is all too horribly human, too immoral, too full of vindictive spite. There is just too much self-deception and plain

crap. How do we know that part for sure? For starters, we have a Nile, but we don't have a Mohenjo-Daro. Did God forget about the Indus valley and Mesa Verde? Can God forget? And what about where it says that men get created first while women only get to be created later? A woman can be anything a man can be, but it takes a woman to be a woman—so it is the female who is the default human form. It's the male who is the sub-specialisation. Go figure.

He broke off reading at this point and looked up. 'These facts about the male of the species are true, by the way. I have done a lot of scientific research into it. It's a requirement. Part of my work.'

'Part of horticulture?'

'Yes, reproduction. We have to know it all.'

'Pleased to hear it. Now why don't you continue.' She did not want him discussing reproduction with her—not even plant reproduction.

He grinned, then continued reading his commentary section with intense concentration:

The function of the male is that of assistant to the female. Not to mention assisting the offspring. So, Blastus, it seems you have gone and gotten the whole of human creation back to front! Why must we go on believing concocted *exact words of God*? What is it with your need for an authoritative text? Is this some sort of disease? Look at what happened with Aristotle. His medical writings, based on sucking his thumb, were followed verbatim for two thousand years. Disrespect often led to execution. Yet belief in infallibility is clearly childish. So, what about God's *laws*? Which of them, exactly, are from God, and which are merely the lore of primitive patriarchal society? Why is it that some of these texts can no longer be read in respectable gatherings today? What about the ones that demand the execution of drunkards, or the ones that demand the execution of non-virgins? And those that demand the extermination of entire populations? How are we to avoid throwing up? Besides, there's an entire ancient world, from the Sumerian-Akkadian empire of Mesopotamia onwards, full of similar texts. End of your claims about the exact words spoken by God.

'People are so far gone on these topics that sometimes I think our education system has failed us,' said Ben virtuously.

Alyssa thought it best not to interrupt his reading or encourage his ramblings, so she made no comment. Besides, she had no idea who or what Mohenjo-Daro was, or if there really had been an Akkadian Empire, or whether the old texts really were a gigantic later-year confidence trick or not. What *was* clear, though, was that Ben was being critical of texts held to be infallible and sacred, which placed him on dangerous ground. Outside of a therapist's office, only private doubts were safe when it came to religion. Public denunciations were out of order, especially in the form of derogatory comments made to strangers. She hoped Ben retained enough judgement to keep himself out of trouble in the real world. Someone might just punch him in the face—or worse.

2

Alyssa thought it fortunate that she did not personally have strong feelings about religion one way or the other, despite having gone to Sunday school as a child—or maybe because of that. She was fairly neutral on the subject. Had she been an unschooled gullible and pious believer, she may well have found it difficult to tolerate Ben Clayton's vituperative diatribe. Luckily, though, when it came to religion, she was no babe in the woods. She had attended Sunday school regularly as a child at her father's insistence, even though by then almost nobody else did anymore. She knew at least the basics of middle-of-the-road Protestant theology. While much of it now seemed juvenile, she did at least still agree with Mr Johnson, her Sunday school teacher, that "monkeying around with texts ain't never gonna save your bacon". Dangerous, enslaving cranks were everywhere, so resorting to faith needed to be based in the first instance on proper, untwisted information and personal revelation, not on unhinged orders barked by others. Unlike most modern people, she, at least, had sufficient knowledge to perceive the feet of clay upon which all dogma stood. Nobody could get away with telling her self-serving untruths about God.

At least I'm bullshit proof in that *regard.*

She knew, for example, that even in the hands of honest, well-meaning theologians, many interpretations of any given Holy Text were possible, and that this therefore meant that no single religious view could logically be held to be sacrosanct. There *was* no one certain form of the "truth" extractable out of the ancient texts. Indeed, by means of selective quotation from such texts, one could "prove" that whatever view of life one *already* possessed was "correct", no matter how emotionally deranged, immature, ignorant, plain untrue, or patently absurd this view happened to be. There was something deeply *unchristian* about the "certainties" of Christian fundamentalists—about all fundamentalists, in fact, most of whom were so stupid that they had no idea how stupid they were. She felt sure that an underlying cautious scepticism prevailed in the minds of the less fervent. Instinctively, most mentally balanced people tended to throttle back from the abyss of taking inchoate yearnings too seriously.

Cy, though, was opposed to even religious moderates. To him, *all* Christians were "certain" and therefore obnoxious. She recalled a line from one of his books on the topic: "To be cocksure about *anything* is evidence that one suffers from suboptimal mental function". In his view, certainty was a mental state that belonged in the same category as emotional immaturity, ignorance, low intelligence, and emotional unwellness. The worst part of it, according to him, was that certainty always existed in malignant combination with at least one and usually all four of its related defects. In another of his books, Cy had written: "Can any present-day person with an educated mind in its normal state of order—i.e., one able to recognise logical absurdities—continue to fail to see the glaringly obvious fact that religion is bunkum? To those nervous about the metaphysically correct fifty per cent possibility that some form of metaphysical God does actually exist, the correct answer is still *yes*, religion is bunkum. Why? Because the probability that the god of philosophical possibility is the *same* as the God that you are worshipping is so low as to be effectively zero".

What was strange though, was that despite Cy's negative opinions and her own misgivings, she still attended church services occasionally. The paradox no doubt stemmed from her upbringing; also, from a vague and un-thought-through notion that God worked not entirely through human logic but by personal revelation. However, the churches in Hubron continued to disappoint. None of them felt like the church she had attended in Ocean View as a child. No matter which one she tried, the congregation always seemed simple-minded and deeply ignorant. All she had encountered so far—to her increasing dismay—had been superstition, intolerance, vengefulness, and, above all, intellectual dishonesty. The need of churchgoers was clearly not a need for the truth but a need for "certainty"—even one that was obviously fraudulent. Once satisfied with their chosen brand of fraud, all those in the same boat sailed along happily, blithely playing at a mutually agreed game of pretence. Unfortunately, floating away into mythical sunsets was not for her. Believing honestly in something had seemed so much less complicated at Sunday school.

3

In the background, Ben Clayton continued to rant.

She was finding it hard to concentrate. It seemed a pity to reject the old texts entirely, as Ben was recommending. *Perhaps,* Alyssa thought, *they could still be valued as a record of humanity's duplicity and depravity. Perhaps in* that *way the texts could be useful: spiritually. As a "Book of Warnings".*

Perhaps.

Perhaps not. She saw the downside of that idea immediately. If the old texts were to continue to be taken seriously, then people would continue to use them to justify bad behaviour. Perverse souls would continue to believe that texts randomly assembled and edited by any number of Iron Age priests were literally written down by God on pieces of parchment in inerrant factual form. People with suspect motives and dubious mental and emotional function would continue to believe that every word, comma, and period present in the modern collection of the Old Text was there because God himself placed it there—even though punctuation never existed in the original texts. Wilful abusers of logic and knowledge in the service of the perpetuation of personally held primitive ethics would continue to remain incapable of functioning ethically in the real world—or of being tolerated by it.

Meanwhile, it seemed that Ben was not going to be running out of steam any time soon. She needed to pay attention. His notes on the Codswallop Sayings of religionists were still in his hand, and he was still questioning the non-existent cleric, Blastus Bamboozelus:

Q: You the clerics say we surely will not die forever, yet how can you know this? Similarly, you declare that everything that happens is God's will. Sure about that too, are you? Here is your cardinal error: you assume that *your* understanding of God is the same as God. In other words, you assume that God agrees with you—even though this must mean that you yourself are the equivalent of God, which obviously you are not. So, why talk gibberish?

A: *I decide what is or is not gibberish.*

C: And we need to accept this? Seriously? When are you people ever going to open your mouths except to tell a lie? It is clear to us now, after so many centuries, that the answers to existence are not as definite as you pretend them to be. Even in the case of your own scriptures, there is no one correct way to extract their meaning, no one way to interpret them. Nevertheless, on that very topic, you have thought nothing of manufacturing something as utterly ludicrous as the divine right of kings. Can we ever hope that you will stop indulging in such self-enhancing puffery? I doubt it. Take for example your laughably predictable extraction that the Elect of God is *you*. Why such ongoing tedium? Why the "Infallible" versus the "Inerrant". Why kill for the sake of the absurd drivel of your own particular soteriology? How can you claim to be living examples of people of God when all we see are little devils running around waving little gods stuffed in their own little bottles? Why are patronising nonentities odious with superstition ministering to us? Are your heads entirely fried? Your Holy Writ, I am sad to announce, provides us with no reason for hope. Demons love to quote the ancient texts when they engage in evil. Indeed, even the Devil himself does "quotes".

Ben looked up triumphantly, but Alyssa said nothing. She thought it best not to get into a discussion about demons because they scared her, especially *the* Devil. Even the word scared her. Her Sunday school teacher—no doubt at the prompting of her father—had often warned her about him. "Remember, Alyssa", Mr Johnson used to say, "the Devil is stronger than you are".

Without a doubt, he was.

She found it interesting that Ben's use of the name still made her anxious.

"But the demons are going down, Alyssa. Remember *that*". Mr Johnson assured her that Christ could not be overcome. "Jesus has rendered you defeated". As a small child, she had presumed the statement applied to whatever local invisible demons were hovering over her, but later she had come to realise that the Sunday school words had been directed at *her*. The teacher had not been talking to imaginary demons at all but to her.

Captured by evil and in serious need of salvaging.

He had not been talking to a small lost child without a mother. No. In his mind, it had been nothing as simple to understand as that.

4

Benjamin Clayton was becoming impatient with her inattentiveness. 'Do you have any questions for me, Miss Alyssa? I can provide you with all the evidence you require.'

She had a question for him. One unrelated to demons: 'What's "soteriology", Ben?' It had struck her as an odd word when he used it earlier. 'It seems a big word.'

He swelled with self-importance. 'It's really very basic to the theology field. I'll try to simplify it for you if I can.'

'Please do. It sounds important.'

'Mm. Okay then. It's something like a speedometer, I'd say. That's probably the best way to describe it. The speedometer of salvation. It's what a crank uses to measure you. It tells them whether you are going to avoid hell or not—a sort of *save-o-metre*.'

'Could you be more specific?' She almost added "or are you making this up?", but she managed to catch herself in time. She was not there to doubt him but to build up his confidence.

'This is very basic knowledge, you know. Oh, very well then. I'll explain it to you in full. Soteriology: it's a word. It means stuff to do with how you get yourself saved. What you must do to stay out of hell.'

'I see. Thank you.'

He had more. 'It's all to do with where you are on a specific save-o-metre when its owners come to measure you. The point is, if your needle is off the dial then you get your head chopped off. Mostly it's chopped off, although sometimes you could get strangled or fried or even boiled. That can be pretty bad. Once your reading is off the dial, all bets are off. All that is known for sure is that you need to die horribly. Even off-the-dial children get executed. Obedience is a must if they are to avoid this. I've read about it. You don't want to get into soteriology, believe me. It's too disturbing. Even for me.'

'Thanks for all that, Ben. Now read on, please.'

He had to have a last word: 'Even though it's all over their texts, it seems nobody told these soteriology people that salvation is not based on a reading on a jerkoff's metre.'

'Read!'

Q: Why, Blastus, do you condemn sex as *filth*? What's with taking non-procreative sexual acts—contraception, genital kissing, masturbation, pornography, and so forth—and turning them into "the Mortal Sins of the Sodomites"? What is *wrong* with you people! Why say that "sex" is a mortal sin unless performed in wedlock as a sacred and beautiful act for the sole purpose of reproduction? Excuse me, what childish fantasy world are we inhabiting here? How about we stick to real people and real sex. Have you even studied human anatomy and physiology? Do you even *know* that the nerves supplying those parts of the body are all *connected* to each other? Why say that lust is indecent? Why stoop to oxymorons? How can sex occur without lust, and how can lust be anything *but* indecent? How can a bowel motion not pass through an anus? Why do facts of nature upset you? Why do you feel the need to *purify* us of lustful indecency? How can such a thing ever be achieved. Just because *you* aren't aware of your own sexual feelings doesn't mean you aren't *having* them in some hellish alternative way. Why is a man *defiled* by a woman? Why is our flesh impure? Why call normal sexual activity deviant? Why is *everything* to do with sex a "sin"? Who put the Devil into sex? Why the *condemnation*! Why the *preoccupation*! Is this why you are *unable* to address the *real* moral evils out there, such as superstition, and poverty, and war, and intolerance of innate difference, and planetary destruction, and ongoing torture of the terminally ill, and exploitation of the vulnerable, and grotesque greed, and rank hypocrisy, and intellectual dishonesty, and God knows what else that you happily sweep under your carpet?!

Ben had been shouting towards the end and was breathing heavily by now. He had become so outraged by the religionists that he had to pause to control his emotions. 'I can get a bit scary, I know, but they make me so very, very cross. And I know all this information about sex is a bit rude. But these things *do* need to be looked at. We must face the *facts*. There is no other way. Face the facts. That's what *she* says too. She showed me a book about it that proves it.'

'She? Who do you mean, Ben?' She doubted he was referring to his mother.

'I mustn't say. The cat must stay in the bag. But I have it on authority.'

'Who and what are you referring to?'

'The facts.' He punched his notes with a finger. 'Right down to the *nervi erigenti*. Such are the *facts!*'

And what the hell are the nervi erigenti?

It seemed best not to ask him any questions. 'Sounds good to me,' she said. 'I don't have any problems with all that you have said. I'm not a religious crank.'

'Good. There's still some more embarrassing stuff to come, though.'

'I don't get embarrassed,' she said.

Which wasn't true because her face slowly turned red as she finally remembered from Sexology 101 what the "nervi erigenti" were. They were the excitatory nerves that supplied both the genitalia and the anus indistinguishably, as though the same organ. Which was why both areas were regarded as erogenous zones and why interfering with either area in another person amounted to sexual assault.

However, it hadn't been any part of the human body that had embarrassed her. What had caused her to feel ashamed—and blush—was her recollection of how ignorant she had once been about sex. As a child she had not known anything. If only she had known better. The embarrassment of what had happened to her back then made her block out any further thoughts about it. The events were too personal, too emotionally traumatic. Too shameful, in fact. And unfortunately, nothing could be done about it. Not at this late stage.

5

Mrs Ellen Goodman remained stubbornly unable to sleep. However, the root cause of her insomnia remained elusive despite the best efforts on Alyssa's part.

The situation was not helped by the fact that the aging woman seemed to have almost no introspective ability. Partly, of course, such personality types were constitutional in nature, but something important about Ellen Goodman still escaped her. Ellen was concealing a secret about herself—and it was slowly killing her. It caused her anger that she could not express. As her counsellor, Alyssa knew that she should at least be able to help her with that; at least be able to safely draw out the anger.

This was what counsellors were supposed to be there for. How many times had Wendy Greene not rammed this essential point down her throat? A counsellor's main role was that of a safe pair of hands for the client's anger. Being able to deal safely with the inevitable aggression from one's client was the central pillar of the art of psychotherapy. And unfortunately, all too often in the modern dysfunctional, anti-intellectual, non-rational, emotionally clouded counselling world devoid of any understanding of transference or countertransference, this essential function had become non-existent. In the hands of an incompetent and emotionally defective counsellor, any expression of aggression by a client was likely to lead not to safe professional containment but to instant termination of therapy and a complaint to the police. Yet true emotional healing in a client was impossible without the help of a therapist capable of receiving a client's aggression safely and containing it safely.

Fine words from Wendy Greene, but when it came to Ellen Goodman nothing seemed to be following any rules. Emotionally, she remained a stone wall, unwilling to let go. It was almost as if Ellen was a complete fake and was attending sessions at the cottage for reasons unrelated to any wish to be helped. But why?

Fronting as a slow-moving, overweight, middle-aged woman who denied responsibility for, or knowledge of, *anything* was bad enough, but if the underlying reason for it related to a genuine passive-aggressive personality disorder, then Mrs Goodman was incurable given her age. As it was, she seemed to positively delight in pressing buttons for frustration and stress in others. It was as though, subliminally, the woman sensed that she held an emotional whip hand over anyone trying to help her and relished the experience. Alyssa realised, as she looked at the matronly Mrs Goodman sitting perched upright on the couch in front of her, that she despaired of ever being able to feel any empathy with her. The woman came across as completely unlovable. All she saw was a pitiless soul.

I hate these people.

Earlier, before she had run out of empathy completely, she and Ellen had been making some progress despite the disastrous first meeting. It had been extremely tedious, but Ellen had navigated at least some of the feelings that were blocked by her disabling anger. Now, though, she seemed to have relapsed into disgruntled toad mode. What to do with such a challenging figure? Alyssa felt unsure. Right from the beginning, it had been as clear as daylight to her that Ellen's problems related to Ellen's relationship with her husband, but there still seemed no way to get her to consider the possibility.

She looked at the list of key phrases used regularly by Mrs Goodman, which were recorded in the therapy notes on her work tablet. Among them was the phrase *sad stories*. Throughout therapy, Ellen had recounted what she called her sad stories. These mostly fictional events always crowded into her mind last thing at night and, according to her, prevented her from sleeping. The vignettes were always interesting, but seemed to mean little, and Ellen seemed to have an endless supply of them.

They all seemed to go down the same path: nowhere. And, in someone like Ellen, they were likely to go on forever unless someone intervened. She was a master at avoiding the issue. It was part of her life strategy: denial. And denial was, after all, a key component of passive aggression.

'Ellen, I've been looking at your notes, and I see that you are troubled by much sadness. There are so many sad stories. Can you think why?'

'You are quite wrong there, about the sadness. I am not at all sad. The stories are sad, not me. They seem to find me, as though I channel them, somehow.'

'You channel them?'

'Perhaps I am more sensitive than others.'

I don't believe this!

'Right. Well, then, what about you tell me more about life at home. You haven't told me very much so far, except that you are at home a lot by yourself. How do you fill your days when your husband is at work, and you don't need to go in and help?'

'I used to go in almost every day,' Ellen whined. 'However, lately I've been too tired. From lack of sleep, you understand. Because of lack of sleep, I find I can't really do very much at all. Steven has even had to arrange for someone to help me run the home.'

'Domestic help?'

'No. Not that. Steven and my daughter tend to sort that out in the evenings and on the weekends. No. I have help with the garden and the pool. Someone comes in twice a week for that.'

'Are they much company?'

'What is that supposed to mean?'

'Well, do you talk to them?'

'For heaven's sake! What do you take me for? The workers are mostly boarders from the art college down the road from us. Youngsters. They come for the money. Steven pays well. They are no company at all.'

'How old are we talking?'

'Fresh out of high school. Eighteen or nineteen, I suppose. Why?'

'And you don't talk to them?'

'No.'

'Are they male or female?'

'They are all young men. Youths.'

'Men only?'

'What are you trying to suggest? It's Steven who insists on only men. He does it to avoid getting himself accused of anything. You of all people should know just what gold diggers young women have become these days.'

Ellen appeared extremely defensive, and Alyssa wondered why. 'I'm not suggesting anything untoward. I'm just trying to see the world from your point of view. Personally, I would talk to young men if they were at my house, but I accept that you may feel differently.'

'Of course, I feel differently. I'm not a child like you. Why am I not surprised that you don't understand even that much about me?'

'You're not making it easy, Ellen. I'm trying to build a picture of your world. The more complete it is, the more likely I am to see a pattern and get to the bottom of what it is that is troubling you.'

'Nothing is troubling me, except that I can't get to sleep.'

'This is what we need to investigate, this *nothing*. You need to trust me on this.'

Ellen stared at her suspiciously.

'To try and make some progress, Mrs Goodman, I want to steer us onto a slightly delicate subject, namely that of your relationship with your husband. How about we discuss that? How did you and Steven first meet, for example?'

Ellen seemed somewhat taken aback. 'I've told you before, we're good together. My husband doesn't have any problems. I'm the one with problem.'

'How old were you when you met?'

She answered in surprising detail. 'I was twenty. We met at a college dance when I was in third year. Steve was in his first year. It was the mid-year dance. I was older than him, but we got on. Anyway, we had an accident shortly after that and I fell pregnant. That's how we married.'

'You got married because you were pregnant?'

'No. We married a few years later. Steve had to finish his studies first. What's with all the *questions,* Alyssa?'

Mrs Goodman had at last become angry.

However, it was the wrong sort of anger and Alyssa was unable to be of any help.

Fifty minutes of counselling time had gone by and once again she had succeeded in achieving nothing. It was all too much to bear, really.

She had had just about as much as she could tolerate from this sort of woman. Something was going to snap—and if it did there were going to be serious consequences. Another death could occur. It was a real possibility, no doubt about that.

6

The merry-go-round of work continued its relentless spin and Benjamin Clayton, the dangerous young schizophrenic, was in the counselling room at the cottage once again. As always, he was going on and on about the dangers and evils of organised religion. Alyssa allowed him to continue extolling from his notes because this required the least amount of effort on her part. She promised not to interrupt his flow unnecessarily.

Today, he was still stuck on the section of his proposed book that related to the attitude of religionists towards sexual matters. According to Ben, the imagined evils of sex occupied ninety-nine per cent of the world of sin in which all religionists existed. Intense preoccupation with sex provided a justifiable way for them to fail to get around to addressing other "moral" issues, most of which were far more important and pressing.

Despite Ben's blunt and tactless way of writing, the message he was attempting to convey did have a certain validity. His outrage was sincere. Without a doubt, she was making good progress in her therapeutic goal with him, which was to build a relationship of trust.

'You are doing important work, Ben. I'm finding your notes very interesting.'

'It's the start, isn't it? Of something. I'm really working old Bamboozelus's case for him, aren't I?'

'Go for it.'

Encouraged, Ben read on, picking up directly from the corpus of Codswallop Sayings in his possession:

> Q. (Continued). Why, then, all the taboos, Blastus? What is
> it with this "fear-of-the-body" business, old chap? Women are
> sexual beings just as much as men are and have just as much right

to autonomy in this regard—or do you disagree? Really? Why the Madonna-or-whore attitude? Surely you know by now, as everyone else on the planet knows, that all this is just emotional immaturity at work. It's your Oedipus complex out of whack, man. What sort of moral blowhard are you? And as for men, they have erections every ninety minutes while they sleep. How, then, can you continue to declare that the male erection is a revolt against God? Surely, you must be preaching to yourself for it is clear now that what you have been asserting about sex is nothing more than an assertion of an unpleasantness that lies within *yourself*. Luckily, we are no longer fooled. Is the God of the mountain not also the God of the valley?

Ben giggled, but Alyssa maintained a serious expression to keep him on track. 'Keep going.' Even though his command of the subject was breathtakingly mature, she did not want him side-tracked while talking about sex. With him, it could easily spin out of control. Her stern expression was enough. Obediently, he continued with his denunciation of the fake morality involved in the church's obsession with sexual sin, reading from the microscopic handwriting of his notes with apparent ease.

<u>A</u> (from Bamboozelus): *It is written.*
<u>C:</u> Really? "Written"? Is that all you have to say about your attitude to sex? After all, the propagating of drivel has serious consequences. So, first, I request clarification: what, exactly, are we discussing here? Are we talking about the morality of the mechanics of the sex act or are we talking about the morality of the interpersonal relationship between the practitioners thereof? This is important, is it not, because a moment of reflection will surely inform us that in your sin-soaked world, ninety-nine per cent of what you call sin is nothing more than the intense feeling of guilt you experience when you contemplate certain physical sex acts. The feeling of guilt has no "holy" basis; instead, it relates to your persisting childhood perception that the mechanics of the sex act are evil and disgusting. Can you not see how primitive

and ignorant this is? Do you not see that in the process of pretending to yourself that you are "holier than thou", you have no concern for the involved *people* themselves? Why do your own discomforting thoughts about the sex act blind you to real ethics? The *fear* of sex and of women simply can't be holy, can it, because we are to fear only God. Therefore, O Blastus, a clue for you: could the source of your "it is writtens" about sex be *not* God after all but instead simply a succession of sexually ignorant morbid cranks with gigantic Oedipus complexes?

Ben broke off reading at this point and looked up. 'People think I'm stealing from Ludwig Andreas, but I'm not, am I?'

'Be more specific, Ben. Who is Ludwig Andreas?'

He looked surprised that she did not know. 'Von Feuerbach. Ludwig Andreas von Feuerbach. I thought you said you went to church.'

She had no idea what he was talking about. 'Yes, I have been to churches, and no, I have never heard of Ludwig von Feuerbach.'

'My mother said you would know if I cheated.'

'It's not important, Ben. Carry on reading.'

'Ludwig said it's wrong for churches to say that God is *not* mostly a human fancy. But I'm not saying that, am I? He didn't know about the Oedipus complex, but I do.'

'Correct.' It seemed the only way to shut him up. 'Now read.'

He did:

Have morbid cranks mixed up their own immature and ludicrous assumptions about women and sex with the words of God? Exactly. This is my point entirely. To wit: does your flesh miraculously become pure because you are a fanatic of some sort and prefer pickled onions to women? Or could it be that sexual purity is a matter of the heart and not a matter of the flesh at all? Furthermore, could it be that because *all* fanaticisms claim sexual purity as normative, so-called bodily purity has nothing at all to do with any god and has instead a whole lot to do with loving the *wrong* thing? Is that why fanatics who worship "text" rail against sex and have the vilest of hearts? Is that why preachers of sexual purity see no *impurity* in the slaughtering of others? Could it be that hatred of the flesh, far from being commendable, is instead sure evidence that a cold, vile, and dead heart sits in the centre of your chest? Flunked school biology, didn't you, Blastus? Didn't realise that you can't turn sex off, did you? Didn't realise that no one is *less* likely to have a pure mind than someone who is *not* having sex. There is no one with *less* understanding of the morality of sex than a religious celibate. So, who has the dirty mind now? Why do fanatics, without exception, lie about their own sex life? Why do they have constant prurient thoughts but say they are not vulgar? If the inside of a cup is clean, surely the outside takes care of itself. True or false? If you, the religionists, refuse to be honest, then how can you claim to be people of God and not people of the Devil? These are my questions for you, Blastus. Answer!

Alyssa wondered how an unschooled youth like Ben managed to think so deeply. Furthermore, judging from his scribblings, he was no stranger to sex. But how, and with whom? According to the clinical notes of his previous therapists, he had lived at home with his parents under close supervision for the whole of his life.

Ben had made some seemingly valid points about the church and sex, but she wondered if he realised that contraception was a modern development. Sexual intercourse would have been viewed very differently in the absence of this luxury, even by perfectly reasonable and emotionally mature individuals. In a world without contraception, it may well have been justifiable to attempt to regulate sexual activity by religious means. The so-called "unbridled fornication" of the old texts always assumed the possibility of unwanted pregnancy, and, with it, the possibility of an unwanted child. The life sentence of being unwanted as a child following a purely sexual act clearly meant that in retrospect such a sex act could be viewed as amounting to a supreme act of selfishness. Even in modern times, sexual intercourse without due regard to the possibility of pregnancy had to be wrong. Surely.

Unwanted child, broken spirit.

Without a doubt, in some situations unregulated sex could well amount to a great moral crime. After all, as a small child she herself had fallen into the hands of a stepmother incapable of wanting her. She shuddered at the thought. Without the saving love of her father, had she been completely unwanted, she doubted she would still be alive.

She would have liked to discuss Ben's ideas further with him, but she kept herself in check. Discussions were not helpful in his situation. Indeed, to attempt to do so would be to make the age-old mistake of the layperson, which was to think that one could have a successful two-way conversation with a schizophrenic. It would be a waste of time. Nothing she could say would alter his opinion on anything—much like some of the professors she had encountered during training.

Never get into a discussion with a schizophrenic. There is absolutely no point.

7

Another counselling day and yet more spouting from Ben Clayton's notebook to contend with.

It was difficult to concentrate.

'What's with all this thinking of yours, Miss Alyssa? Are there flaws in my logic?'

Ben was becoming impatient with her declining interest. She needed to pay more attention to her job. 'No issues so far', she assured him with fake enthusiasm. 'All good.' She rubbed her hands together. 'Proceed.'

She did not have the heart to tell him that his logic *was* flawed. He was showing occasional "knight's move" patterns in his thought processes, a feature often seen in active schizophrenia. It was not a good sign in someone on medication.

'What's up with you?' demanded Ben.

'Nothing. Read on. It's just that I'm amazed by your work, that's all. The maturity of your understanding is truly exceptional.'

The suspiciousness that had started to cloud his face eased visibly with the reassurances, as did the mounting tension in his body. Clearly relieved by her apparent approval, he now appeared pleased. 'That's what my mum says, too,' he confided. 'Exceptional. That's why she's collecting my work.'

'Let's hear more of it, then. Still doing Blastus Bamboozelus?'

'Yes. The cleric in the woodpile.'

'Extol away.' She smiled at him, though she knew he could see it was a fake smile.

'Righty-o then, for he's a jolly good fellow.' He massaged his throat.

<u>Q</u>: You want us to obey you, don't you, Blastus. Why do you want this? Why, oh why?

<u>A</u>: *You are called to obedience.*

<u>C</u>: Hang on. *Who* exactly are we talking about here? Who is it who is doing this calling? It can't be God using your voice, can it, because God could not possibly be as ignorant as you say he is. So, no, when you insist on our obedience, it's obedience to *you* that you are wanting, isn't it? It's you, Blastus, who wants this sort of obedience and nobody else. Got you there, haven't I? That's the truth of it finally unravelled, isn't it?

What you demand has nothing at all to do with God. God could not possibly demand such naïve and backward things. There is nothing holy about *your* demands. Oh no. Instead, we see a deadly preoccupation with maintaining control and crushing dissent. It's all about personal aggrandisement. "*I bind your conscience*": the breathtaking cheek of it—that you could even contemplate such megalomania. Given half a chance, you would happily continue with your hangings, and your burnings, and your garrottings. This you would do—as you once did—to all who do not obey you. And afterwards you will absolve yourself by calling your evil crimes the "just rewards for blasphemy". Can any person who knows your history feel anything but utter revulsion?

You people tore up the Magna Carta and burnt little children who uttered the Lord's Prayer in English. Why are there tears in my eyes? And then you went and gave one Hemisphere to Portugal and the other to Spain. How dare you! Clearly, for you, following God has nothing at all to do with doing what is right. Instead, it has everything to do with being self-important. Yet, is there anything more obnoxious than the bullshit of another's certainty about things that cannot be known?

Unfortunately for you, we now see clearly that you are a ventriloquist and that your texts are nothing but the dummy through which you yourself speak. You make them say whatever it is that *you* want to say. Countless times, you highlight the words you are predisposed to find and pretend not to see the words you are not predisposed to find. Then you proceed to emit fanciful and unjustifiable edicts in keeping with your own warped mind and lily-livered heart. Your own psychopathology you pass off to your gullible flock as being from God himself—as if someone like you could know the mind of God! Your theories are pure make-believe.

Yes, this is so! For every crank, there is a Word of God. First, you become encased in your own psychopathology, then, once you have that buttoned down, you select your "Word of God" of choice. The utter absurdity of the whole business has to stop!

But do you care? No. You *will* have your ignorant and superstitious puppets. But why? Why this authoritarian and implacable spirit? What hostile spirit is this that you dispense? What evil? And from whom exactly? Which devil? Tell us, Blastus. Tell us!

If you claim otherwise, why continue to torture us with a devil's canon? Why place a cruel and irrational elephant in our room, an elephant that is nothing but an excretion from the barrel of your own gun? Why place monkeys on our back? Why this tendency to personify? Why be inhuman with your hermeneutics? How does this differ from totalitarianism? And why the dietary absurdities? Why not eschew baloney? Should we not *demand* that you leave our fucking animals alone? And the dickybirds too!

Why, why, why? Surely, we cannot put this down to phenomenology any *longer*!

It was time to put the brakes on Ben, remarkable as his work was in parts. Gently, she interrupted him. 'Let's pause here for a moment, shall we, Ben. Your ideas are very impressive, but maybe, if your book is going to be about religious people, we should leave out the swear words. What do you think about that? You wouldn't want to end up offending people.'

He was breathing heavily. 'You think so?'

'You know what people are like. Just about everything upsets at least somebody.'

'Right. I know the score.' He took his pencil and laboriously began obliterating the offending words. While he did so, he began lecturing on the words he was expunging: '*Fucking*: a word damnable for its impiety; repugnant to morality; condemned by reason; hostile to welfare; demoralising to character. That's a quote from somewhere.'

'Stop it, Ben.'

He smiled at her. It was the smile of a small child, a child pleasing its mother.

The real elephant in the room is that the monkey on your back is the parent in your head.

The thought, Freud-based and probably incorrect, caused her to smile too.

Removal of swear words completed, Ben continued reading. He was on the final page of his attack on Blastus Bamboozelus and clearly heading for some sort of emotional crisis about him:

Q: Why not come out and confess, Blastus, that you are bogus and that your god is *you*? Why continue to peddle your own twisted mind as the mind of God? Why continue to irritate us?

A: *Be still, my child. You are my family. We are all family.*

C: Do you really mean this? Or do you mean to say that therefore I am under your jackboot and that you are my superior? Sadly, I suspect the latter. Herein the cardinal error of the cloth: you proclaim ignorant, self-serving, homespun, make-believe pseudo-psychology as religious truth.

Part of *your* family, my ass, Bamboozelus! It has become all too obvious that your so-called God-derived morality is nothing more than the nonsense issuing from your own personal unresolved Oedipus complex. Why use the word "family" when what you really mean is fascist cabal? All we see in your sort are growths of one-upmanship and swellings of smugness. Then you peer down at the rest of us and claim to see only pigs. However, what do *we* see of you? We see wallowing too, a wallowing in pseudo-certainty and superiority. We see implacable turds. We see jingoisms, ejaculations, superstitions, compliances, and God alone knows what else. Why do we have to follow you when the only purpose you have for us is to make *your* boat go faster?

Should you remain convinced that what you have captured in your own particular bottle is the *correct* Supreme Being, let me point out to you your obvious point of confusion: the only type of supreme being we *can* know is the parent still in our head from when we were little. It's basic psychology. Go away and compute. The truth of this will surely shock us all. In fact, this is my main point, is it not? The obvious explanation for *all* of this—for *all* your crap—is the Oedipus complex. Awe and guilt. That is all that religion is. It's all you have: the Oedipus complex. No mystery there.

All that has happened is that you have failed to mature psychologically. You remain clinging on to your parents psychologically, with nothing left for you but a preoccupation with your own genitals. This needs to stop *now*! Leave them alone. Leave your fucking parents *alone!*

'I know, I know. More swearwords. Sorry.' Ben struck out "implacable turds", put a line through "my ass", and rubbed out "crap" and "fucking". Then he continued reading:

Could this not be so? What are we to do with your dirty, dirty hands?

At that point, he paused.

Then, after a while, Ben spoke again. 'Sorry, Miss Alyssa, but someone is going to have to die'.

That said, he stopped talking altogether and started staring at his own hands for the longest time in a way that was truly disturbing.

Luckily, it was time for him to go. Standing up, she informed him in no uncertain terms that he needed to get a grip on himself. 'Come on, on your way, Ben. Threatening to harm people is not allowed.'

Definitely not.

8

Mrs Goodman was being as difficult as possible. Her sleeplessness was no better, and she wanted something *done* about it.

It was time to consider yet another approach.

Alyssa had an idea. 'I have this hunch, Ellen, about how to move forward. Just try and stick with me for now. I want you to consider the answer to this question: how would you rate your sex life with Steven?'

'I beg your pardon!'

'You needn't look so shocked. Everyone has sex. These days we know this to be the case. So, try and stick with the question.'

'I thought I was here because I can't sleep at night.'

'The question, Ellen.'

'It's a non-question. This is starting to get stupid. Of course, Steven and I don't have sex. We don't do *that* anymore, for heaven's sake. We're not youngsters. Not *everyone* is part of the modern sick culture.' Mrs Goodman glared straight at her in a rare display of self-assertion.

'How long has it been now?'

'You're determined, aren't you? What if I said over ten years?'

'Has Steven ever said anything?'

'He's grateful for what he's had. We are both perfectly happy. *Thank you.*'

'That's okay. I'll leave it at that for the time being. And I'm sorry if I seem to have upset you. However, I do think that these sorts of questions are necessary in your case.'

'This is ridiculous. Are you trying to tell me I can't get to sleep at night because I'm sexually frustrated? Is this some sort of a joke?' She raised her voice in anger. 'Is this all that young people ever think about? Sex? Is this all that is on your mind?'

'I'm just asking you to think about your sex life. We need to explore every angle in our attempt to help you sleep better.'

'I want you to change the subject, please.' Mrs Goodman was by now shaking with tension.

Alyssa moved to safer ground. 'As you wish.' She looked again at the notes on her work tablet. 'I know, why don't we move on to the dreams that are plaguing you at night? Why don't we hear more about those?'

The middle-aged woman on the couch became agitated again. 'They are not dreams,' she corrected, 'they are thoughts. I'm awake. They come in the form of stories. They keep me awake.'

'Yes, sorry, I worded that badly. Stories. What's been happening lately in your stories?'

'That's what *you* are supposed to be telling *me*, isn't it?'

Hooh boy.

Perhaps hearing another sad story would be a safe way to proceed with Ellen. More fairytales from the unforthcoming woman seemed appropriate, given her own distracted mood. 'Ellen,' she said as kindly as possible and with conscious effort, 'I think it may be useful at this stage if I talked less and instead, we spent time accessing further valuable clues from you about what is happening during the night. Is there a new sad story? Do you have one for us?'

She did.

A woman owned a rabbit given to her as a pet. She kept it in an old cage in the garden, where the pet dog used to bark at it. One day, to her surprise, the rabbit gave birth to four kits—babies. Unknown to anyone, it had been pregnant all along.

Ellen stopped. 'A baby rabbit is called a kit, but I think of them as babies. I believe I am entitled to that.'

'Of course. I would think of them as babies too.'

Instead of being angry, the woman was delighted. A few days later the rabbit managed to force its way out of the old cage through a rusted part of the wire. Its innocent intention was to go and eat some of the garden plants for the benefit of her offspring. Unfortunately, the mother rabbit was then discovered by the pet dog, which chased it around the garden. The pet rabbit dashed for the safety of the cage, but once there it found it could not enter the forced out opening quickly enough in the reverse direction. To make matters worse, three of her four babies had tried to follow her into the garden and were outside the cage. The pet dog did not attack the mother rabbit, but nevertheless managed to kill all three escaped babies by accidentally standing on them in its excitement. The mother rabbit thereupon died of shock and a broken heart at the cage opening. When the woman went out to investigate the commotion in the garden, she found that she only had one tiny baby rabbit left. She became very sad. Her friends told her that the baby was too young to survive without its mother, but she believed differently. She brought the baby inside and kept it warm in her jumper and bought rabbit milk at great expense. She fed it and it grew bigger. She knew the baby rabbit loved her dearly because it used to snuggle up to her.

Ellen paused, greatly moved, to dab at her eyes.
'It's certainly very touching,' said Alyssa.
'Believe me, it gets worse.'

The baby rabbit had to be kept safe from the dog. Therefore, the woman bought a new, smaller cage and placed it in her bedroom. To give the baby somewhere to snuggle down, she lined the bottom of the cage with straw from a bale in the garden. Despite her best efforts, though, her friends finally proved correct. The baby rabbit slowly weakened and finally it died. To her absolute horror, the woman then discovered from the vet that what had killed the baby rabbit was a gut infection from bacteria in the garden straw. The baby had sucked on the contaminated straw that she herself had unwittingly placed in its cage. She had as good as killed the baby rabbit. In fact, she had as good as killed the entire rabbit family. The woman felt her heart break.

By now, Ellen Goodman was weeping. She tried to conceal her emotions behind a handful of tissues, but long bouts of nose blowing gave her away. 'No wonder I can't sleep at night,' she said, trying her best to cover up her emotions.

The missing pieces of the Ellen puzzle fell into place for Alyssa. Suddenly, she knew what it was that was slowly killing her client. Elated, she then did something extremely bold based on blinding professional conviction—after all, the truth about the past had to be faced. Something needed to be done or Ellen Goodman was going to self-destruct.

In a quiet and solemn voice, Alyssa said: 'Ellen, why don't you tell me about your secret abortion.'

The blood drained from Ellen Goodman's face in shock.

And Alyssa realised with disappointment that she had just done it again: failed to understand the sensibilities of older women.

She might just as well have kicked Ellen in the guts, so alarming was the old woman's response to this latest outrage. 'How dare you!' she mouthed, aghast. 'Yes, how dare you! You horrible, horrible girl.'

Which was not an encouraging thing to hear a client say.

Maybe Ellen Goodman was right. Maybe she was indeed a horrible person. Quite possibly, in fact, given what she had done in the past—and was in danger of doing again—it was exactly what she was.

Horrible. Truly horrible.

PART V

STRONG MEDICINE

CHAPTER NINETEEN

1

THE SITUATION WITH PARANOID schizophrenic Ben Jabba Clayton, long term client of the Donald Clinic, grew steadily worse. He no longer seemed interested in further literary endeavours with his pet project, the *Codswallop Sayings of Blastus Bamboozelus*—in fact, he seemed uninterested in writing or saying anything very much at all. Which was a pity. The writing had, at least, seemed to help him greatly in his struggles to express himself.

'So, no more sayings?' Alyssa asked him finally, after a long silence during a later counselling session at the cottage.

'I have nothing more to say, Miss Alyssa. Sorry, but I am done with extolling.'

'I see.' She said it in a non-committal way to avoid upsetting him. It was clear that he was sulking. No doubt the unhappiness stemmed from an earlier visit, when she had told him off for suggesting that it was necessary to terminate the existence of people who exhibited strong religious belief.

Killing people was definitely a step too far. Nevertheless, she did at least agree with him to a large extent that religious belief—of any persuasion—had a psychological origin. As far as she had been able to determine during her own reading on the subject as a student, the stock conclusion of most psychoanalysts was that religious feelings were nothing more mysterious than deflections of unconscious parental veneration.

Awe and guilt certainties somewhere in the dark of the mind.

Not that she believed personally that all expressions of religious feeling were misguided, or that religious behaviour was necessarily

361

a bad thing. After all, most parents did a reasonably adequate job of raising their young and left a psychological legacy that was positive and comforting. It could hardly be wrong for grateful offspring to want to honour and preserve this in later life by means of benign religiosity. In that sense, religion played a positive role—the awe part more than the guilt part. Nevertheless, the irrational emotions and ill-formed logic characteristic of the Un-conscious world of early childhood—and therefore intrinsic to religion—remained just that: childish, and therefore potentially dangerous.

Perhaps giving Ben some feedback on his apparently completed collection of "Codswallop Sayings" by religious people would bring him out of his shell. 'If you want my opinion on your writing,' she said, 'I think the work is excellent.' She was being honest: the depth of his scholarship was surprising. 'I think your thoughts are wonderfully deep and worth exploring. If there's no new writing, then maybe we could discuss some of the points you made. What about your use of the term antipope? Why did you use that word, specifically, do you think?'

'Why? Why do you want to know *why*?'

'Well, why use a politically loaded title like "antipope" for Bamboozelus? Why, in your opinion, did you politicise the issue?'

'Politicise?'

'Yes. Why didn't you simply refer to him generically. As some sort of cleric.'

'Politicise?' Ben's face fell as he struggled with the concept. 'I *knew* you would criticise! If you are so clever, then why don't *you* tell me why it's a mistake?'

'I'm not trying to criticise, just trying to provide you with some insight. Political words can result in people getting angry with you. They can cause harm.'

This seemed to upset him even more. '*Harm*! Really? Clue: I said antipope. *Anti*-pope. Why? What is my reason for doing *that*? I must have had one. Tell me what it is, seeing that you know everything.'

She attempted to soothe him. 'Okay, I get it. You are not referring to a truly religious person. This antipope of yours, this Blastus Bamboozelus, represents the generic religious con artist. Is that what you really meant by the term?'

'Yes and no. More no.'

'Mm. What then? Clearly, he's an anti-version of something. He's not the person you think he ought to be, is he? Is that it?'

'He's all lies.'

He was not making much sense. Also, he had begun to make rocking movements with his head. In some way, she was having a powerful effect on his emotions, and he appeared to be having difficulty controlling himself. He was trying to tell her something of great importance and it was causing him to struggle with feelings of anxiety and fear.

She needed to act, so she tried to think of a way forward. She noticed that he had his notepad out again, this time holding it awkwardly, as though trying to conceal something. Perhaps the *real* ending of the Bamboozelus scribblings?

It was worth exploring.

'I need to learn Ben. I need you to teach me. You ask fascinating questions and I think you are very special. Believe me, I can see that you are much more profound than people realise. Now tell me, am I wrong, or have you kept the best for last? Are you hiding the deepest truth about the antipope right there under your hand?'

Ben went red in the face.

Bingo.

'It's not the deepest.'

For some reason, in that moment she saw her youngest brother, Harry, in him, and it filled her with compassion. 'Show me.' Her voice came out sounding very kind.

Against her expectation, he calmed down, then slowly and shyly uncovered his latest paragraphs for her to see. There was not much there, but it outlined the solution to the Oedipus complex, that force that was busy destroying the world through the agency of religionists.

Though nobody was interested in listening to a certified madman, the answer to the number one problem of the world lay at his fingertips.

He allowed her to read with him his final solution to the curse of the out-of-control Oedipus complex:

Q: What, O Blastus, are we to do with you? There needs to be some sort of payback, obviously. One that is painful. Fatal too, unfortunately. Any suggestions? You have been pretty good yourself at such things over the centuries. What form of farewell do you think you most richly deserve? Noose or match? Or could I interest you in a blade?

A: *It is you—not us—who is headed for the fire.*

C: Mm, yes, old boy, I can see that you remain pig-headed on this point. Still, whatever weasel words you currently emit, you are headed for an unfortunate ending. There is bad, bad news ahead for you. Your lies have escaped your concealment box. Now it's *you* who is going to be doing the departing and not us any longer. Tears must flow. Go! Go with that flow as we make it so. Depart! *Away* with you.

'There needs to be consequences,' he informed her. Then Ben stood up from the sofa and waved his notepad in the air and began shouting, as though acting in a Shakespearean stage play.

Your sentence, O Transgressor: *Severe*! The consequences: *Fatal*! Enough endured. *Calumny*! And thus yawns the pit.

The alarming gibberish uttered, Ben Clayton's mouth snapped shut and he sat down again. Then he carried on reading from his notes in a normal voice as though nothing unusual had happened.

Enough. Enough is enough. Quite so, yes. Believe me, we have our methods. Harm is assured and elimination is on the cards. And what about the good part? Do not forget the good part. They mean *us* no harm.

Benjamin Clayton's frame sagged after his final revelation. Slumped on the couch, he looked just like the Jabba he was at heart: a frightened child.

They mean us *no harm.*

The words clanged in Alyssa's brain. It was payback time, with the assistance of *others*. Alarming as the words were, they elated her. Ben had just revealed a genuine part of his secret world to her for the first time.

She was making progress. It was an astounding achievement in her therapy. The instant she heard the long-hidden words, she knew she had reached him. He had revealed his truth to her. At the core of him existed "they", and the purpose of his life was to exact payback with the help of these enablers, the "they", who had been sent to him to guide and empower him in his duties. He believed that by following the instructions of his *others*, he would finally succeed in visiting revenge upon persons antisocial enough to express their childish fantasies in the form of religionism.

"*They* say cut the root of iniquity" was the recurring expression at the heart of Ben's hallucinations. He had been recorded in the past screaming the words during paranoid rages. The end game was all to do with *they*. With sufficient counselling skill, there was every chance she would be able to get Benjamin Clayton to reveal more.

She encouraged him with a loaded question. '*They* say they don't mean us any harm, Ben, but how do we know this for sure? How are we to have certainty?'

He barely looked up. 'It's very special. You wouldn't understand.'

'Are they very great? Important?'

'Huh?' He became suddenly alert and seemed shocked that she knew. 'How did you know?'

'I know. I've been there myself.' It was true. In the past, she too had experienced voices.

He stared at her.

She had, and somehow, he knew it.

'It's the Lords,' he whispered, looking fearfully around the room. 'They are trying to tell me who must go. But I can't make it out.'

Alyssa held her breath.

The Lords of Sacrifice.

They were in her office. Whispering.

There was a frightening silence as he listened to hear what they were saying. These were those who told Ben what he needed to do: which root of iniquity to cut.

Which person to sacrifice.

All that was keeping her and the outside world safe from Benjamin Clayton's advisors was his medication.

He began to stare at her blankly, and, in the sudden silence, she observed changes in him with rising fear. His head began to nod, then his entire body began to rock backwards and forwards even as he sat. Shortly afterwards, his thighs began twitching, and finally, macabrely, and strangely horrifyingly, the muscles of his powerful arms began to ripple.

Physically, he was much stronger than she was. If he lost control, she would be in great danger.

Entranced, he intoned: 'Yes, I hear.'

Alyssa felt her mind racing as she tried to find a way to defuse the situation. It looked like Ben was about to get to his feet, so she had only seconds in which to abort his hallucinations and save herself. There was only one thing for it: alter his emotions. How often had Wendy Greene not hammered this into her skull? And to do this, she needed to alter her *own* perception of Ben. Doing so would simultaneously alter how he perceived her. She needed to stop thinking that he was dangerous and about to hurt *her*. Instead, she needed to reach out to the hurt in *him*. By changing one's own emotions, the emotions of the intimate other were changed too.

She tried. 'Believe me, Ben,' she said in a normal voice and with a deliberate calmness that came out sounding surprisingly authentic, 'I do understand. I know how hard it is to tolerate all the evil around us. I agree with you that something needs to be done about it.'

To her great relief, the atmosphere in the room changed almost immediately. Ben's state of panic receded, and he began to regain control.

The wisdom of Wendy Greene had saved her.

The effect of the intervention had been dramatic.

She had bought herself some time.

However, it seemed almost impossible to believe how quickly Ben had earlier flipped into dangerous insanity. He was definitely mentally unstable. Whatever else was wrong with Ben Clayton, he was undoubtedly deteriorating. He was fast becoming extremely dangerous.

But why?

2

Alyssa was sufficiently worried about Ben Clayton's state of mind to insist that Trish book him in for a further session sooner rather than later—which was how she ended up seeing him only a few days later.

On that day—the Monday when everything changed—Ben Clayton appeared peaceable enough. The demeanour seemed somewhat paradoxical given what had gone on the last time, so to try and quieten her apprehensions and make sense of him, she let him sit idly on the couch with a consulting room *Astoria Geographic* magazine in his hands while she reviewed his case notes in search of clues.

She knew—with the benefit of hindsight—that it was possible that something in her own attitude towards him during the last visit had caused him to feel threatened. But what? Was it something in her manner? Or had it been something she had said—or failed to say? Or was it that she was failing to understand something of great importance despite his best efforts to communicate it to her?

She wracked her brains. It seemed possible that Ben's hallucination episode related somehow to the way she had responded to his writing that day. After all, his whole existence seemed to revolve around his "notepad". Therefore, what was it about Ben's enormous "opus magnus" that she so egregiously still failed to grasp?

She closed her eyes and massaged them for a while, an old trick of hers. True to form, she did not have to do this for long. As so often happened with her and psychotherapy, the answer soon came to her out of nowhere. And when it did, she knew it was correct. The key to Ben's hurt, she realised, lay in the fact that despite his best efforts she persisted in failing to understand that his book was really about something *else*. She was failing to understand this, failing to understand *him*. In Ben's mind, she was refusing to acknowledge his reality, failing to see the *real* Ben.

What, then, *were* the endless notepad scribblings really about? What was he writing about? What lay beneath the smokescreen? The ideas he had raised so far seemed genuine enough—even though clearly amateurish—so there had to be something else that she was failing to grasp, some other aspect of his writing. But what? What part of all that he had written so far did not ring true?

While Ben sat immersed in his magazine, she thought further about his writing, but continued to draw a blank. Nothing about it seemed merely a pretence. Even the title seemed authentic enough. The *Codswallop Sayings* were pure Ben, quite true to form. Then she remembered that this part of his work was a sub-section and not the overall title of his efforts. The main title was *The Cockatrice and the Fatling*. Yes, it was. The case notes confirmed it. Surely it was here that the answer to her question lay. The overall title was so odd and out of character that it had to be a ruse. Almost certainly it was a contrivance Ben had used to protect himself from her and test her bona fides before opening up to her. The title simply did not fit with the rest of his work. More than likely, his book was not called *The Cockatrice and the Fatling* at all. It was no fairytale. No, its real title had to be something else, something that Ben did not want untrusted persons to know in case they used the information to get to the real him and harm him.

There was more to Ben's "truth" than she had given him credit for, and she needed to find out what it was, and fast. Up until now, her ongoing blindness to the reality of his situation had been driving him crazy.

It was time to correct her deficiencies and take command of the situation.

'Time to put your magazine down, Ben,' she said authoritatively but cheerfully. 'Let's focus and get back to the last time you were here. Remember what happened then, Ben? When the Lords came.'

'Yes.' He became alert.

'I'm not going to ask you what they said because I know that would be unwise, but what I do want to ask you to do today is tell me about your book. Not your notes, but your book. You see, I have come to understand that it has a secret.'

Ben's eyes fixed on hers, but his face remained inscrutable.

'The secret is one that I am permitted to know, I assure you. Therefore, why don't you tell me what it is? It's quite safe here. Between us. Whatever you reveal will go no further. Nobody else needs to know.'

Benjamin Clayton continued to stare, and his face now became suspicious.

She smiled back kindly. 'Your book is far greater than what you have let on, isn't it? That's the secret, isn't it?'

His entire body became tense. 'Are you mocking me? Is that it!' Filling suddenly and unexpectedly with rage, he stood up and began to shout. 'Is *that* what this is all about? Mocking!' His paranoia was flaring. 'You won't mock, will you, will you, or . . . or . . .' He did not complete the sentence, but the implication was clear.

Or I'll rip your head off.

He continued yelling: 'Is *this* what I have to put up with? I won't take it. I don't take *that*. Take that.' His voice died away.

She remained sitting and looking calm. 'You know me, Ben.'

Uncertain about her, he glared at her from a height, his nostrils huffing. For some reason, his eyes were focused on her feet, probably her painted toenails. Earlier, she had taken her shoes off and her feet were on her chair.

'Why don't you sit back down, Ben?'

To her relief, he complied, sitting down as abruptly as he had stood up.

'It's just that I know your book is not what you say it is, Ben. It's not as straightforward as the cover title suggests; it's far deeper. You need to trust someone with it. Why not tell me its secret?'

He remained silent.

For a moment, she thought she may have overplayed her hand because his eyes settled now on her chest. Although her shirt was partly unbuttoned, she doubted he was looking at her cleavage. Around her neck was a silver chain—the one from her real mother—and on it a small heart-shaped pendant. Sometimes, in the light, the pendant flashed.

Like a blade.

She shivered.

Ben remained seated but continued to stare. The staring went beyond anything socially acceptable, but she tolerated it because she knew it was his way of soothing a rising sense of panic. He was making an important decision about whether he could trust her.

Her judgement proved correct: he meant her no harm. After a while, his eyes began to flick between her neck and her face, and then finally he behaved normally and spoke.

'It's all about Jesus,' he said at last, in a quiet voice. 'That is the secret. My book is really all about Jesus. It's actually called *The Rape of the Name of Jesus by the Religionists*. That is what is really going *on*.' He jumped to his feet again and raised his notepad in a shaking hand and crushed it in front of her. 'Fanatics are raping the name of Jesus. *That* is what is going *on*!'

The Rape of the Name of Jesus.

The concept shocked her, which came as a surprise because she was only nominally Christian. She tried to put the unexpected feeling of outrage to one side. 'Is it a good book, or a bad book?' she asked. Even as she enquired, she realised that if his book insulted Jesus, she would not be able to maintain her objectivity.

She need not have worried.

'It's a good book.' He smiled down at her angelically. 'I love Jesus. It's a really good book. It reveals how everyone is trying to hurt Him. People will do anything except one thing: they will not *listen*. You have to confess the evil in your heart. That is the only way for God's glory to enter. The *only* way. But nobody will listen!' His voice became resolute. 'I have to put a stop to it. I have to stop the hurting. *Make* it stop.' Then he fell silent once more. A single tear ran down his cheek. He stretched out an imploring hand, which was visibly trembling. 'She must be stopped.'

'She?' Alyssa sat up straight, nerves jangling. 'Whatever do you mean, Ben? What "she" are we talking about here? What has this person done to deserve anything?'

He stared at her feet again, tears streaming down. 'Your feet are back on the ground. How did that happen? Did Jesus put them there? What are you going to do when Jesus comes for you?'

'Sit down, Ben.'

'You don't understand, do you? She is bad. She is so very bad. You see, when the pie was opened, the birds were singing. They were *singing*!'

'They were?'

'Yes, they *were*. And that is just plain wrong. It is so wrong that it can no longer be allowed. Sorry, but this is where it *ends!*'

3

Alyssa needed a coffee badly, so the mid-morning break came not a moment too soon. It had been a difficult morning and she knew she was floundering—professionally—with the more complex cases. Her own insomnia certainly was not helping. With a bit of luck, she might find someone in the staff room able to offer advice.

With Ben safely gone, she had located an apple. Once out on the porch, she locked the front door of the cottage. It was time to head down the garden path to the staff room in the main building and find some

370

relatively sane company. For a minute, though, she paused to admire the view. Perhaps it was a trick of the light, but today the pathway she was about to go down looked especially enchanting, winding as it did through the garden and disappearing under the drooping boughs of the ancient tree only to re-emerge on the far side and proceed to the stairs at the rear entrance of the main clinic building. Despite the stresses of the new job, she loved everything about her cottage and its garden.

Out among the plants, the air felt fresh and invigorating, so she stopped again to savour the atmosphere. After the dreams about Gilbert Rockport, and the sleepless nights à la Mrs Goodman, and the increasing madness of Ben Clayton, she needed the tranquillity of garden plants like never before. She wished she knew more about them. Some, she knew the names of—the roses, the fuchsias, the ivy, and her new favourites, the sweet alyssums—but others were a mystery. Weeping catkins, jonquils, snapdragons—did she have any of those? And what about helianthuses, and hellebores, and hollyhocks? Just names to her. There was so much about flowers that she knew nothing about. She wished she knew more, including what sort of tree it was that sheltered her section of the garden from the main building. Like the cottage, the tree extended all the way to the high red brick wall on that side of the property. She had seldom encountered such an attractive living thing. It seemed to want to be touched. She went in under its drooping boughs and once again stopped to rub its woody surfaces. The tree felt friendly and sheltering, like no tree she had ever encountered. Its trunk was thick and gnarled, ancient, yet irresistibly inviting. Spontaneously, she gave it a hug. The droopy branches formed a canopy around her that seemed filled with tenderness. It was a kind tree, her kind of tree. After a while, she realised that she was wasting valuable time, so she jogged the rest of the way to the staff room, including up the back stairs.

I must remember to find out what sort of tree I have.

She felt pleased that she had been brave enough not to activate the emergency alarm during the latest showdown with Ben. Had she done so, the rest of the staff at the Donald would have known that she was out of her depth. For her own future job security, it was important that she maintain a good impression, and fortunately her instinctive ability with men, especially young men, had won the day. Still, she did need to speak to someone about Ben. His response to his medication was not as effective as it needed to be. Even though she had been able to keep him under control by not panicking and by using stern words, this was scarcely a recipe for the longer term—despite his tearful promise that he would never hurt her.

"Don't worry, Miss Alyssa, I won't harm *you*".

Not yet anyway.

4

To her dismay, the staff room was empty except for Dr Simon Bristow—who on this occasion was reading a newspaper at one of the tables. He ignored her completely when she came in, so she hesitated, unsure whether to join him or not. She was not the only member of staff who found the prospect of Simple Simon's company unappealing. She could hardly forget the previous encounter with him during a lunch hour. Even putting the unpleasant awkwardness of that to one side, the fact remained that she did not know the doctor well enough to feel comfortable inviting herself to his table. And yet . . . and yet she still needed a professional opinion from an experienced member of staff about what to do regarding Ben.

After hovering just inside the entrance for a while, she decided to be brave and do what had to be done. First, though, she would head for the corner kitchen and fix herself the much-needed coffee. With a bit of luck, more people would arrive, and she would then be able to sit with them after getting a few words of wisdom from Dr Bristow. While at the kitchen counter, she took her time washing her apple, but nobody else arrived.

Rats.

Coffee and apple in hand, and acutely conscious of Trish's explicit warning to never ever do any such thing, she approached the newspaper-reading psychiatrist's table.

Do not ever *attempt to have coffee with Simon Bristow.*

She sat down at the unpleasant man's table, diagonally opposite him but far away enough to be polite. As predicted, he continued to ignore her. 'Hi,' she said cheerfully after a while.

He glanced up briefly. 'Oh, hi.' Then he continued reading his paper as before.

She was not used to being ignored and it upset her. As she forlornly sat there, she became acutely aware that the man across the table from her had a double doctorate and was vastly superior to her in terms of intellect. The magnitude of his achievements seemed impossible to ignore when close to him; the enigma of it so great as to be overpowering. How could any person be *that* clever?

Jocelyn had an explanation for it, of course. In one of her many jokes about Simon Bristow she said that he was *such* a genius that the only thing he could not understand was psychiatry. Of course, Jocelyn—being Jocelyn—failed to see that the joke applied to her as well. Jokes aside, Simon Bristow, MD, PhD, was not a man to suffer academic fools lightly, and this included counsellors, who were, by his definition, academic fools. He was indeed a true intellectual snob. Alyssa had little doubt, as she sat munching on her apple, that he was experiencing her presence in much the same way that a normal person might experience a small dog.

Cute but harmless.

Despite everything, he would still be wrong about the cute bit. Dr Bristow did not understand *her*. That much she did know about him.

Fascinated, she studied him over the top of her coffee cup as he continued reading. He was definitely attractive in her opinion, despite his sexual orientation. Some things about him, though, were unusual. For one, he looked remarkably clean—for a man—as though he scrubbed himself twice a day from head to toe. Also, his grooming was flawless: hair perfect, eyebrows perfect, skin perfect. Not all *that* surprising, she supposed. Gay men were often perfect, especially close-up.

He knew how to dress too. She remembered his stunning blue jacket from their previous encounter. This time, he was in a brown coloured one—not any old colour brown but a rich chocolate brown. Clearly, he liked eye-catching casual jackets. And even though the current one was frayed and tweedy, somehow, on him, it seemed highly fashionable. The same intriguing quality emanated from his red-and-cream checked shirt. Inexplicably, it had style. He had style.

5

Alyssa polished the uneaten part of her apple on a paper napkin for a while. 'Dr Bristow,' she said finally. 'Sorry to interrupt, but do you know if Dr Summerfield is coming for coffee this morning?'

He sat back and folded his newspaper. 'Alan is doing a lumbar puncture upstairs.'

She assumed this meant he was not coming.

Talking to Dr Bristow was not easy. When one tried to make eye contact with him, all one saw was one's own face reflected off his space-age spectacles. It was happening now, and the effect was disconcerting. It felt as though she was talking to someone with no interest in the needs of others.

'Are there any more apples?' he asked from behind his impenetrable façade.

'Oh,' she said, glancing self-consciously at the half-eaten Royal Gala in her hand. 'No, I'm afraid not. It's the only one. I bring them in from home.'

'I see. Not to worry, then. Hey, on the subject of jokes, I've got a joke for you. What's the definition of a counselling psychologist?'

She froze at his mention of jokes. 'The definition?'

'Yes. As in a joke. You know a lot about jokes, I hear.'

Plainly, he knew that Jocelyn was friendly with her, and that Jocelyn made fun of him behind his back. She tried to placate him: 'I'm sure that whatever I have to say about anything will be wrong.'

He looked puzzled. 'That's it, the answer. You have the answer to my joke: a counselling psychologist is always wrong.' His voice trailed off. 'How did you know?'

'You've lost me.'

'Counselling psychologists say they know how the human mind works, whereas the truth is that they don't have the faintest clue. Logically, therefore, they are always wrong. Get it? Always wrong: that's the definition of a counselling psychologist.'

She tried to stay polite. 'I get what you mean, Dr Bristow, but from my point of view I must say it doesn't sound very positive.'

He ignored her point of view. 'I explained all this to you last time, didn't I? That the whole mental illness racket has gotten way out of hand.'

'What do you mean, Dr Bristow?' She knew she should not have said it even as she said it, because she knew he was spoiling for an academic argument, one that she was never going to win.

He was immediately in his element. 'There is an abyss of difference between mere mental distress—which almost everyone seems to have these days—and true mental illness. The term mental illness needs to be confined to physical disease—which includes genetically based aberrant biochemistry, by the way. In other words, *organic* pathology. That's what I mean. The term should be restricted to only such manageably uncommon phenomena, with the treatment chemical or physical only. I'm talking about drugs, direct neural stimulation, surgery, that sort of thing. As far I am concerned, everything else, this avalanche of mental service hangers-on that we are seeing today, this has nothing at all to do with actual mental illness or its treatment.'

He was forcing her to engage in futile conversation with him, but foolishly—out of pride—she responded: 'But what about all the people out there with emotional difficulties? It's a really big problem, surely.'

He became more animated. 'The people you are referring to are not ill. Sure, they may be having a reaction to adverse life events, or they may *feel* disturbed for reasons they don't understand, but that doesn't mean they are mentally ill. A failed life, ignorance, these are not illnesses. Claiming that they are is an abuse of the English language. All that *these* people need is a re-jig of their mostly self-inflicted aberrant neural patterns. Virtually all of them have sufficient neuroplasticity to enable them to carry out the required repair job themselves—perhaps with a little downtime support. We can't babysit *everyone*. I mean, who's going to do it?'

It would not be the first time a psychiatrist had talked to her in this way. 'Is it the numbers that worry you?' she asked.

'What else?' He lowered his spectacles in one of his favourite affected mannerisms and peered at her as though needing to get an unimpeded view of her to reassure himself that she was not intellectually handicapped. Then he pushed his spectacles up again. 'Suddenly everyone has a mental illness. I mean, *please*! Give me a break. Biologically impossible.'

His level of exasperation perplexed her. Slowly, she took another bite of her apple, a large bite that exposed her top teeth and crunched audibly.

'Fortunately, it's not something I have to worry about,' she said smugly. 'I don't make the decisions. I just help people who want help.'

She had managed to irritate him. 'There you go,' he bristled. 'Perfect illustration of the problem. What do your transference psychotherapy crowd say again? Every mental problem has its roots in the events of childhood or, failing that, it's caused by a lack of sex. Which means, of course, that everybody is mad. Well, they're not, and those aren't the causes. It's time the authorities clamped down on this sort of nonsense. Mental illness is organic and rare. Or at least it should be.'

'We don't say every disturbance is due to a lack of sex. You know we don't.'

'Okay, then. Lack of connectedness. A lack of psycho-social connectedness, not as the *result* of mental illness, but as it's *cause*. Surely, that must be wrong. Surely, you need to concede that biology comes into it. What I say is that it's the biology that's the critical factor. The *bio* in the bio-psycho-social. Mental illness must reside in the neurobiology because that is the only fixed point in what is otherwise a limitless continuum. It is the only rational route to take. The rest of the saga, the blah blah—or the intimacy, as you people like to call it—logically that must be a waste of time. It's too variable. In fact, as far as I'm aware, scientifically, there are no cures available for an inability to connect with others other than medication or direct brain stimulation. Poseurs in the trade might tell you otherwise, but if people are *not* organically diseased then they always succeed in forging a path to intimacy; even without treatment, they can, and they must. Like speech, intimacy is a universal process, and in this case, it's based on the nervous system's requirement to be mirrored. The solution to your peoples' emotional problems is for them to grow into adults.'

She found the stylish psychiatrist's level of outrage at the world's reluctance to follow his instructions amusing, but she tried to limit the evidence of her mirth because she knew that deep down, he was angry. Her skill in understanding people informed her, further, that the man called Simon Bristow was very lonely. Despite his self-assured ranting, she found herself sensing an emptiness in him so profound that it left her feeling concerned for his welfare.

She tried to humour him. 'I see your point, Dr Bristow,' she said. 'People need to help themselves. I agree with you on that one.'

Even a psychotherapist knows that ultimately, we help ourselves.

Once he realised that she was not going to challenge his intellectual superiority, his attitude softened. He relaxed and straightened out his newspaper as if to start reading it again, but instead continued to make conversation with her. 'How are you settling in, Alyssa? I have heard some good reports about you.'

She felt herself blushing at his unexpected compliment, and she wished she could control the embarrassing weakness better. 'It's been good,' she said, bringing her hand to her face as casually as possible to try to hide the redness. 'I really like my new position.'

'I know I haven't sent you any of my own patients yet, but you do seem pretty sensible. Maybe I'll change my mind, even though I'm not a follower of the whole psychotherapy carry-on. From what I've been hearing from others about these transference-focused ideas of yours— well—at least our patients seem to like it.'

'Thank you, Dr Bristow. Yes, the approach is extremely user-friendly. Not only that, but I think you would be pleasantly surprised if you saw the results. There's no doubt that we do help people to stop fooling themselves. At least that.'

'If you say so. I've never understood that claim though, considering that all you people have to work with is memory and self-consciousness, both of which are notoriously unreliable and don't even exist in any stable form.'

'I am aware of the findings of neuroscience, but I still think that certain meta-psychological formulations of so-called temporary brain functions are useful in the understanding of human relationships.' She was quoting part of her textbook by heart again but did not tell him that.

She could not fool him; he knew. 'Most interesting. You mean to say that Obermaaier actually *knows* that self-consciousness is just a neural trick, and that memory is nothing but a creative narrative with the sole purpose of preparing us for our tomorrow? He *knows* this, yet he persists with his imaginary embellishments thereof?'

She tried not to laugh. 'Sort of, yes.'

'How fascinating.'

She wondered if he was mocking her. She knew from what Jocelyn had told her—and from what Simon himself said at staff meetings—that he believed that all forms of psychotherapy were iterations of mumbo jumbo. In his view, every counselling method in clinical use worked in the same idiotic way, which was by arranging for a client to experience interpersonal contact. Counsellors were just friends by a different name.

Despite the psychiatrist's disparaging views, she knew he was wrong. With clients who were not seriously mentally ill, the clever doctor did not have answers any more helpful than her own. This truth—that in the presence of an organically normal brain, even the greatest of experts had no greater understanding of the mind than she had—was something she had discovered early on in her time of vocational training with Wendy Greene at Public Hospital. Yes, the mind was a machine, but at a higher level it had a life of its own that was hard to grasp. When she first saw Simon Bristow at staff meetings near the start of the year and saw how confused he was, it had reinforced her belief that her own view of the mind was the more useful. She was very much like Alan Summerfield in that respect. She had sensed immediately and instinctively that Simon was a man of many clever theories but no answers. For all his education and brains, he was just a fool when it came to clinical psychology, and he was lost. Despite his grandstanding and his MD and his PhD, Simon Bristow had no idea how self-consciousness occurred. He did not even possess a useful model of the higher human mind. He had nothing, just a few enzymes.

6

The reason why Simon Bristow knew nothing much about the mind—as opposed to the brain—was because nobody did. However, because of his personal arrogance—something he had no insight into—instead of acknowledging his defective people skills, he kept pretending that he knew the answers to human psychology. Conceit, though, had blocked any chance he had of understanding others. All that he *did* know, down to the minutest degree, were details of the brain's anatomy, physiology, and pharmacology. And unfortunately, the inevitable consequence of approaching the conscious mind in this way was ongoing bafflement. There was no way he was ever going to be able to grasp real psychological truth. The mind was something he would never find.

Alyssa saw all this easily enough through the prism of her own mental modelling system, yet Simon Bristow, a man in full denial of the unconscious elements present in his concept of himself, was always going to refuse to accept that the declarative mind, his included, was just a minor sub-function of the brain and nothing more substantial than a cyberspace neurological computation. Whereas it took a trained scientist to know a brain, it required something else entirely to "know" the less concrete declarative mind—conscious and unconscious. And the "something else entirely" was, of course, true intimacy i.e., the objective and non-toxic *Self-to-Self intimacy* of transference-focused psychotherapy.

However, true intimacy with others—as opposed to "make do" intimacy—was difficult to achieve and required aptitude and training. The first requirement of the fully matured mind was that it know itself, and this, in turn required the courage to face up to oneself. It was only by seeing one's own truth that one could safely and truly sense the mind of anyone else with any prospect of being a successful therapist.

Self-to-Self intimacy was, however, a concept that some—if not most—modern therapists, including the man across the table, found too personally threatening and therefore point blank refused to even think about.

But at least Simon Bristow was talking to her. So, given the ongoing absence of Alan Summerfield and Jocelyn, Alyssa decided to be brave and ask him for some professional advice about managing the escalating risk of violence from Ben Clayton.

'There is something I have been wanting to ask someone about for a long time, Dr Bristow. It's to do with one of my clients. Do you mind if I mention work?'

'Be my guest.'

'What do you know about the monitoring of zasperidone levels in schizophrenia?'

'That is a very non-psychotherapy question.'

'I do see some schizophrenia follow-ups.'

'Really? Anyway, you shouldn't be bothering yourself with monitoring levels and the like. It's hardly ever necessary in practice once a client is stable, and I would assume his or her psychiatrist has a handle on things. It's not one of mine, is it?'

'No, Dr Summerfield's.' She almost added that her clients weren't "its" but decided against starting yet another argument.

'Mm. If he's doing levels, then it will be for research purposes I suspect. Or maybe there's been an issue with non-compliance. Therapeutic level can be tricky with zasperidone because it varies such a lot. It's heavily dependent on individual cytochrome expression. Normally, we just run such patients clinically.'

'You mean on their symptoms?'

'Symptoms and signs. Functional level of control. Side effects. And psychometrics if you've got nothing better to do.'

'I see. I was just wondering. I don't really have much experience with schizophrenia.'

'I should hope not.' He gave her an indulgent smile. Then he turned to his newspaper again and proceeded to forget all about her.

She thought it best to leave the matter there and try to speak to Alan about Ben. Silently, she sipped the last of her coffee. She needed to get back to the cottage. She had gone way over time and people would be waiting.

The lack of ongoing interest in her by Simon felt unnerving. Usually, men went out of their way to talk to her as much as possible, but the man across the table appeared to be Alyssa-proof. The lack of interpersonal interaction between them felt strangely depersonalising, almost as though her mind was being forced over a cliff.

Nobody else came for coffee.

She felt hurt by the way he completely devalued her as a professional person in her own right. After all, she was doing her best to be a good employee. Surely, she deserved at least *some* respect, especially considering her enormous workload and difficult clients. Being unsupported and undervalued did not feel right. It did not make her feel very good at all.

No, she really did not feel very well at all. Not at all.

Simon Bristow reached the last page of his newspaper. He had read it amazingly fast, considering how thick it was. 'What a load of crap.' He tossed it aside. 'Nothing in it, as usual. Time for work.' He stood up and pushed the paper towards her. 'You might want to have a look at it. I see some idiot crashed his car this morning and blocked the entire inbound Shamon freeway for hours. These constant traffic jams are turning life in the city into hell.'

'Luckily, where I live, I miss all the traffic,' she said pretentiously.

Where she lived was of no interest to him. 'Seems the poor sod went and killed himself as well. In a Maserati. Can you believe that? What a waste of money. What sort of idiot goes and does that?' He lowered his spectacles to look into her eyes. 'But then again, you went ahead and refused to heed my advice last time, didn't you? So, I think you'll know exactly who the idiot is. Was.'

Dr Bristow departed for his lab without another word. Unlike most humans, he neither waved nor said goodbye.

CHAPTER TWENTY

1

ALYSSA DID NOT MANAGE to complete the day at work after hearing of the fatal road traffic accident that involved a Maserati. The clients who attended at the cottage following her morning coffee break with Simon Bristow did so from within what seemed to be a dream. She heard herself talking to the Mrs Bunions and Mr Birdstocks of the world, but nothing felt real. It was as if her mind had floated free from her body and her body was acting independently. The true Alyssa had departed and returned to another place, another time: to another death in a car accident.

They were going to blame her for this one too.

She felt doomed. After the spine-chilling news in the staff room, she had immediately checked the news feed on her phone only to see that it was all true. Screaming at her was a photograph of a crashed Maserati on a freeway. The car was grey, just like Gilbert Rockport's car. There seemed little doubt that the man who had died was going to turn out to be Gilbert Rockport. In which case, there was little doubt either that she would carry some blame for what had happened. The therapy sessions with him must have spiralled out of control more than she realised. It was what everybody was going to think. And maybe they were right. Maybe she even bore *full* responsibility. Maybe it was *she* who had killed him. After all, her head was not in a good place, and it hadn't been ever since the beginning of the year. The pressure . . .

There had been others . . .

Assuming of course, that it *was* Gilbert who was dead.

She kept checking the news feed on her phone. The name of the dead driver was yet to be released, but, as the minutes went by, more photographs of the scene became available. The car responsible for the morning mayhem lay wrecked and upside down in the middle of five inbound lanes. It was clearly a Maserati and undoubtedly the same colour as Gilbert's car. She zoomed in on its back window. A sticker with three words on it was clearly present. Though they were illegible on the image, she knew then, for sure, that the words would turn out to be *Berkowitz Berkowitz Rockport*. Gilbert was dead. There was no other possibility.

From that time onwards her heart began to thump in her chest, and it became increasingly difficult to breath. By the time it came to take a break for lunch, she was too unwell to go on working.

She felt too out of sorts even to leave the cottage. The world began to spin every time she tried. So, sitting at her desk, she kept checking her phone. A headline above yet another photograph telegraphed *Shamon Freeway Trashed. Suicide Suspected*, while another headline had *Driver thought to be prominent city identity*. This report stated further that the accident involved a single vehicle and had no obvious explanation. Inexplicably, the Maserati had exited a perfectly straight section of the inbound Shamon freeway and passed through an access gap in the roadside barrier at what police calculate must have been an extremely high speed. The vehicle then mounted the side of the steep embankment—while shedding speed furiously to judge from the tyre marks—but had inevitably overturned given the increasing angle of the embankment. Upside down, the Maserati careened into the leading edge of the resumed roadside barrier. However, instead of the driver surviving, as was normally the case in bollard strikes, the driver had died instantly. With the car upside down, the roadside barrier had come through the windscreen. According to a police spokesperson, going off the freeway at speed at this particular spot was almost certain to result in fatality given the angle of the embankment.

Fortunately, because the incident had occurred in the early hours of the morning, nobody else had been harmed. However, this also meant that there had been few, if any, witnesses. Police were appealing for more information. There were a number of unusual circumstances involved, including an anonymous tip-off to the effect that the driver was known to be actively suicidal, implying that the fatality may have resulted from the deliberate intention of the driver. The police spokesperson stated further that in view of the unusual identity of the deceased, they would be investigating *all* possibilities, not only those of accidental death or suicide by vehicle, but also that of deliberate and planned homicide.

'Please God, no,' said Alyssa.

Ashen faced, she phoned Trish and asked her to cancel everything. She said she was unwell and would be away for at least two days. When Trish wanted to know more, she put the phone down on her. Then, grabbing her bag, she hurried through the cottage garden, up the back stairs of the Donald, and straight down the main corridor towards the open front door, barely able to contain her anxiety any longer. She ignored Trish, who stood up behind the reception desk as she approached and tried to say something. 'Later,' she mouthed back at the busybody and kept walking. At the building's entrance, as she was about to head out of the open front door, a figure appeared out of nowhere and blocked her path. She jolted to a halt. Standing directly in front of her was Benjamin Clayton.

She smelled him seconds before he surprised her, the sharp and distinctive fragrance of his deodorant, *Homme Support*, giving him away. He had been sitting on a chair in the foyer, in the shadows, partly hidden by a large pot plant, and had leapt up determined to halt her progress. His response to her flight—a feral, stooping rush with arms out wide in capturing mode—felt highly disturbing. Doubly so considering that officially he was off his head. The actions were those of a hunter grasping at a cornered animal. His evocation of a predator did not end there, though. Having forced her to a halt, he remained far too close to her.

'Hello, Miss Alyssa,' he said, touching his feathered hat respectfully, 'and where might you be heading in such a hurry?'

'Ben! You gave me quite a turn.' Close-up, he reeked of insanity but not of danger.

Why is he still here?

He was looking for a lift home. 'My mum is late,' he announced.

He was just an abandoned young man in a crazy hat seeking help, but despite herself she shuddered. The whiteness of his cheap runners contrasted strongly with the darkness of his hairy legs, and his too-short khaki shorts did nothing but emphasise his frightening muscularity. In anyone's book he cut a sinister figure, especially after springing out of a shadow.

'I don't have a car, Ben. Have you spoken to Trish?'

'I think Mum has forgotten all about me.'

She had had enough of him by now. With a single agile side-step, she evaded him and hurried down the front steps. 'Good luck,' she said to him over her shoulder as she rushed down the street. At that moment, Benjamin Clayton was the last person she needed in her life.

2

The flight home seemed to take only a minute, and she was thankful and relieved when she reached the haven of her own front door without further incident. Home was where she desperately needed to be. It offered her the best chance of pulling herself together. She needed to regroup. She had no idea how she had managed to get there that quickly, but she did not care. She had reached a place of safety.

Gilbert was dead. And he may have been killed. And once again, she may have been the cause of it.

She closed the door of the flat and locked herself in. Then she leant back against the locked door. There was no one in the flat. Cy was away at his bookshop. She was alone. The room spun around her.

She closed her eyes.

As a psychologist, she knew enough to know that the terrible anxiety she was feeling stemmed mostly from her past mental injuries rather than anything objective. To understand what was happening, a person needed to be "trauma informed", to use the technical term. Gilbert's car accident had reawakened the confused terror she had experienced at the time of her own father's death. Then too, there had been a car accident. On a highway . . . Almost certainly, the past was aggravating the panicky fear she was now feeling in relation to Gilbert's death. However, equally certainly, it was not only the memories of a car crash when she was a young teenager that had been reawakened.

Something dreadful was happening somewhere deeper in her mind, stirrings much more frightening than the death of her father. It was a nameless dread, and it was starting to resemble the terrors she experienced during her second year at university. At that time, the doctors at Olympic Hospital had said that she was temporarily off her head—had been driven to madness—and that it was something to do with her mother's death when she was five years old. They had been wrong to label her as mad, though. It was not madness. She was never mad. She had been sick, yes, but she had not been mad.

But now that same fear was back, and it was as strong as death itself. Something was trying to take control of her once again. The feeling was strong. So strong . . . Maybe she *was* mad.

There had been too much death in her life. Her father had died, her mother had . . . died, and now Gilbert, too, had died. All had died . . . yet not just died. Been killed. By her. Gilbert, too, had had to go. The problem was getting out of control. There was too much killing . . .

She stared at her hands, just like Ben Clayton had done at his, half-expecting to see blood. It might be happening all over again: the not knowing. It had started like that . . . with not knowing. And after that had come the full-blown panic attacks. Nothing had been able to stop them then. They told her afterwards that she had been having psychotic delusions, but she had no recollection of that. All she knew was that she could not remember what she had done to her mother. She had never been able to face up to that—to what had really happened—and still could not.

Her mind blacked it out.

She had recovered after treatment at Olympic Hospital. She had moved on with her life. Until now, it seemed. Still propping herself up against her front door, Alyssa forced herself to control her breathing. She was stronger now that she was older, she told herself. This time, she would cope. She was in her own home.

Unfortunately, she no longer had any anti-anxiety pills. She had not needed her *vorazepams* for many years. She would have to get some.

Later.

Not knowing what else to do, she went and lay face down on her bed. *Poor Gilbert.*

The anxiety seemed to improve once she buried her face in her pillow, so she remained motionless in that position until the world stopped threatening to spin. She focused all her attention on her body, as taught to do during mindfulness training. Curiously, the part of her that became most present turned out to be her bottom, maybe because it was exposed by how she lay. Or maybe it was out of sympathy for Gilbert. The mind was a strange thing. After an hour of lying motionless face down with her eyes closed, concentrating on only the physical sensations coming from her body, she felt herself regaining control of her emotions.

3

Finally, Alyssa felt able to think rationally, so she sat up on the edge of the bed. It struck her then that she had often lain sleepless in that exact same bed thinking about Gilbert during the time when he was still alive. Perhaps there was something to the psychic world after all. The coincidence of it—of her thinking about him before he was about to die—seemed too great.

Did I always suspect that with him something bad was just around the corner?

Now that she had calmed down, she doubted that she had done anything as crazy as killing Gilbert without knowing about it. It was most unlikely. Although . . . why the tiredness in the mornings? Was her insomnia even real? Or had she taken to wandering around outside at night without knowing?

No, she had not. The idea was too ridiculous for further consideration.

That sorted, a further realisation struck her: if Gilbert's death hadn't been from homicide—or a straightforward traffic accident—and Gilbert really had committed vehicular suicide, then, as his therapist, she would be held responsible for his death. Her own career—which had hardly begun—would be over. Given Gilbert's prominence, she would be destroyed, both professionally and financially.

All my sacrifices for nothing.

For now, though, it was not about her, but Gilbert. She tried not to think of him crushed to death in the driver's seat of his car because the idea of it left her feeling nauseous. She had known him too well for the pain of it not to feel all too real. More than anyone, she knew what a wonderful and brave person he had been.

She flopped back onto the bed, back onto her stomach, silent and shaking. This time, her skirt pulled up even worse than before. Also, her hair became a complete mess. But she did not care. Instead, she tried to recall what Gilbert had said to her at his last visit. In the absence of any meaningful case notes, any proof that he had not committed suicide hinged on what she could remember. Had she missed important clues at his final visit, she wondered, clues that should have warned her that he was about to end it all. She was not sure.

What she *was* sure about was that she had always known that she was playing a dangerous game by agreeing to see him. It had meant pushing her professional ability to the limit, giving unsanctioned leeway by ignoring clinic protocols, and getting into dangerous countertransference terrain. Yet, in all the weeks of therapy with him, she had never thought for even a moment that he was a suicide risk. Not even at his last visit, which was where he had expressed for the first time a hair-brained intention to leave his wife, Nikki. Had that been something she should have been more concerned about? Impulsive, irresponsible, high stakes ideation in a client; thoughts new and not evident before? Maybe it had been a warning sign that she should have picked up on. Maybe.

And yet the fact remained that her overriding impression of Gilbert had always been that he was a man full of hope, courage, and action—a man always in command of himself. If he had indeed committed suicide, how could she have got him so wrong? How could she have been *that* incompetent? She wracked her brain. As far as she was able to remember, he had been in good spirits when she last saw him.

She wondered who had anonymously suggested to the police that the accident was the result of vehicular suicide. The tipster would have to be someone who had known Gilbert in the past, when he had indeed been openly suicidal, or be someone with an ulterior motive, such as an insurance company anxious to avoid a massive payout. Then she remembered something that Gilbert had said about insurance companies. He had been joking about his love of speeding in his car and had made a throwaway comment: "The speeding has been so bad that I've become uninsurable". Gilbert *had* no insurance cover when driving his car. He was an incorrigible speedster. Almost certainly, Gilbert had died uninsured. So, no, the anonymous phone call had not come from any insurance company.

Who, then, had phoned the police?

Head now under her pillow, Alyssa tried to work out a rational way forward. She knew she had to try and be positive. After all, perhaps Gilbert's death was nothing more mysterious than a case of a speed freak crashing his car by accident. Surely, this was the most likely possibility. Gilbert had a history with cars. Despite this, though, she had a bad feeling that the answer was not going to be that simple. And, if it was not, then why, really, was he dead?

The more she thought about it, the more frightening the possibilities became.

No matter what, there were going to be questions asked of her. Given Gilbert's social prominence, the investigating authorities were going to go into overdrive. The Board of Psychologists was going to place her under a microscope. And the police, of course, would be wanting their pound of flesh; a whole slice of her, if at all possible. As in the past, they would be making every effort to accuse her of a crime.

Damn them!

She removed her head from under her pillow. She would get advice from Doggy Barnes, that's what she would do. He was a hard man and he had good lawyers. The unlovable vulture who masqueraded as some sort of psychiatrist had his uses. He would do his best to protect her—if only to protect the reputation of his clinic.

Plan of action decided, she rose from her bed. She knew she had turned a corner. Though she would remain anxious, there would be no breakdown.

Not this time.

She went to make herself a cup of tea and while doing so she checked the time. It was just past five pm. Cy would not be home until closer to seven pm.

She missed Cy's presence; needed him. She felt a strong desire to be with a familiar face, someone who could reassure her that she was all right. Her vulnerability during the earlier uncontrollable anxiety attack had left her feeling ashamed and a little angry with herself.

This nonsense really needs to stop.

Unfortunately, it seemed it was not ever going to stop. Someone was knocking loudly on her front door, and it wasn't Cy.

4

The knocking on her front door became insistent and authoritative, causing Alyssa to freeze in panic.

'Shit!'

She was in no condition to see anyone. With her hair and clothes all askew she looked like something the cat had dragged in. Cup of tea in hand, she peered nervously through the peephole, half-expecting to see the police. Then she relaxed. It was just Jocelyn Goronowski.

Double shit.

'Hello Alyssa,' said Jocelyn cheerfully when Alyssa opened the door for her. 'So, this is where you live, is it?'

Jocelyn wandered in, took a look to the left and to the right with interest, then plonked herself on the couch. Alyssa, meanwhile, remained standing near the door. It appeared that Jocelyn had come there straight after work because she was still dressed in one of her usual business pants-suits, a beige one today. The pants strained across her rump, doing nothing to enhance her figure.

'Now, what is this about you being sick?' she demanded. 'How sick? Where sick?' Jocelyn touched her head. 'Here? Are you bugging out? You've managed to scare the life out of Trish, so I've come to see if I can do anything to help. Is Cy here?'

'How did you know where we live?'

'I know stuff.' Seeing the concerned look on Alyssa's face, she softened. 'Don't worry. Nobody at work told me. Cy told me in one of his emails. He said I was welcome to pop in anytime.'

'In one of his emails!'

'I hope you don't mind. I thought you knew.'

Jocelyn and Cy had been exchanging emails about his books.

'Well, Cy isn't here,' said Alyssa, who remained standing. 'He's still at work. He doesn't get home till late.'

'Well then, that's just perfect because I really came to see you.'

'About what?'

'Don't be so defensive. I know what has happened.'

'You do? Already?'

'Alan phoned me.'

'You're joking.'

'I'm not. The Summerfields know the Rockports socially. Gilbert's wife phoned Alan's wife about it earlier today.'

'You mean these people all *know* each other?'

'Of course. How else do you think Gilbert Rockport came to see you in the first place? How do you think he found you? Hello.'

Alyssa was truly taken aback, shocked even, because she had never considered such a possibility for even a moment. The Gilbert Rockport saga was turning into a nightmare. She saw her career ending all over again and began to tremble.

All that study debt . . .

'Are you feverish?' asked Jocelyn.

'No,' said Alyssa. 'It's nothing. Just nerves.'

Jocelyn stood up, came over to her, and gave her a hug. The embrace happened before Alyssa could prevent it. 'Don't be a Silly Billy.' Jocelyn squeezed her warmly.

Alyssa felt motherly breasts squashing against her own chest and sensed a perfume. The heat of the enveloping fragrance surprised her. Up close, Jocelyn came across as sexy and exotic. She could swear she was wearing *Michel Gersohn*, one of her own favourite perfumes. Discovering that Jocelyn had an alluring side was extremely disconcerting. She thought that Jocelyn did not even use perfume. The woman never ceased to surprise her.

She disentangled herself from Jocelyn's over-enthusiastic arms and moved away to the kitchen area. 'Would you like some tea or coffee? I've just boiled the kettle.'

Jocelyn resumed her seat on the couch, sitting in the centre of it. 'A coffee would be good. White with one sugar. And stop getting your knickers into a knot over Gilbert Rockport. People die all the time.'

'I've never had a client die on me.'

'Believe me, it happens. And it's almost never the therapist's fault.'

'I really liked Gilbert. That's what's so sad about it. Not only that, but he was starting to make progress. I was just about to get him referred on—I think he was finally ready for that.'

'It may not even be suicide. Maybe he just fell asleep behind the wheel.'

'I'd love to know who suggested it was.'

'It'll turn out to be one of his legal enemies. Or someone who has something against Donald Barnes and the clinic. I wouldn't take it too seriously.'

'I'll try.' Her voice did not sound very convincing to herself. 'I'd be devastated if I *did* contribute to his death in any way.'

'I know you, and I'm sure you did no such thing. Though, of course, there is going to be an enquiry of some sort. I'm sure you realise that much. Someone from your registration board will want to see your prior professional assessment of Gilbert's suicide risk. I assume you have something like that available for them in your notes?'

'Something like what?'

'A completed "risk of suicide tool" from your association would be best.'

Alyssa felt her heart sink. At Gilbert's specific request, she had made almost no notes. All she had done was record a few key phrases on the work tablet to jog her memory.

Perceptive as ever, Jocelyn had a suggestion: 'Of course, if you can't find such a completed tool in Gilbert's notes, I'm sure the clinic will be able to help you locate where you must have misfiled it. Provided the investigators find it relocated to his notes before they check them, it will probably do the trick.'

You mean, maybe I should just add one retrospectively.

Jocelyn meant well, but Alyssa knew that tampering with notes was not a good idea. There were ways of finding out, especially in electronic systems. 'I *know* he wasn't suicidal,' she said. 'We counselling psychologists instinctively check for it all the time. He was fine.'

Jocelyn was insistent. 'Believe me, showing is better than knowing. Besides, just between the two of us, Alyssa, did Gilbert Rockport really never talk of killing himself?'

She was about to answer—about to explain that yes, he often talked about it, like most psychotherapy clients—when she regained enough of her senses to bite her lip. For all she knew, the Donald Clinic had sent Jocelyn to her flat specifically to gather information against her. She became defensive. 'Good question, Jocelyn. But you know I can't tell you his private details.'

'Shit, you *are* a little stick in the mud, aren't you? I'm only trying to help.'

Alyssa handed Jocelyn her coffee but said nothing.

'Okay, okay. I suppose you are right. The less anyone knows about this matter the better. You and the Dog make a right pair, I can see that.' Jocelyn patted the couch seat next to her. 'Now, come and sit here next to me, Alyssa, and talk to me. I want to get to know you better.'

It was a strangely bossy request from the socially challenged psychiatrist, yet one that she found hard to refuse under the circumstances. As commanded, she gingerly sat down next to Jocelyn. She did not want to appear ungrateful. She knew Jocelyn was doing her best, in her own way, to be helpful and supportive irrespective of anything to do with Doggy Barnes.

It was a small couch, but Jocelyn, who was still plonked in the centre of it, made no attempt to move. Alyssa found herself squeezed up against the armrest on one side and Jocelyn's hip on the other. She tried to remain polite and drink her tea, but the close physical presence of Jocelyn was very distracting. The only person who normally sat that close to her on the couch was Cy—and then only when what he intended was a hand or a tongue between her legs. The association was difficult to get out of her mind. She half-expected Jocelyn to attempt something similar, so she tried to imagine what it might be like. It would not necessarily be too horrible, she decided. Though she would have absolutely no interest in doing anything sexual to Jocelyn in return.

She just about jumped off the couch when Jocelyn placed a hand on her bare knee.

'You really are very jumpy today, aren't you? You are going to spill all our drinks if you're not careful.'

Jocelyn did not remove the hand from her leg; in fact, she used it to keep her pinned down sitting where she was. She could feel the heat from the psychiatrist's hand just above her knee, and the warmth of it began to creep up the inside of her thigh.

'I know I keep saying this,' said Jocelyn brightly, seemingly oblivious of where her hand was, 'but I can't get over how beautiful you are.' She peered into Alyssa's eyes. 'I hate to see you looking so distressed. If there is anything that I can do to help you, please let me know.'

'Thank you,' said Alyssa, looking away and down. 'I appreciate that. I know I've been overreacting to this Gilbert thing. I do have some past emotional issues which don't help.'

'Yes,' said Jocelyn. 'Me too. I understand.' She removed her hand to drink her coffee. 'I would suggest that you take something mild for anxiety over the next few days. At least until you know where you stand regarding the death. It's often the not knowing that's the worst.'

'I know you're right. I have taken medication before, and it did help. I'll get a script from my GP. There's one nearby that I go to occasionally.'

'I could give you one or two tablets. Unofficially, of course. But that's probably not very wise.'

'No, I'd hate to get you into trouble. It's okay, Jocelyn. I'll be fine. Thanks for the offer, though. I do appreciate it.' She finished her tea.

Jocelyn had finished her coffee too, but Jocelyn did not go home after that.

Jocelyn found an excuse to linger.

5

'Those books in that bookshelf over there,' said Jocelyn as she stood up to leave, 'there, next to your balcony door—are they Cy's? I think I can see some of his titles.'

'Yes. That's his work bookshelf. All the stuff there is his.'

Instead of heading home, Jocelyn went over to the bookshelf with ill-concealed excitement and began to inspect the books. 'Well, I never,' she said in amazement. 'The actual paperbacks. They are so hard to find. I'm busy with two of his e-books at the moment. Look, here's the actual *Lost Harold Found*. Real books are so much more exciting than e-books, aren't they? May I?' Jocelyn wanted to take the paperback off the shelf and inspect it.

Alyssa went and stood beside her. 'Help yourself. It should be okay with Cy as long as you don't disturb anything.' She was a good fifteen cm taller than Jocelyn and their height difference seemed noticeable to her for the first time. Jocelyn really was quite short. Then she remembered that Cy had bits of paper stuck all over the place inside his books. 'I'd better just check the book first in case he has notes in it. Cy doesn't like people fiddling with his notes.' Usually, in fact, he had a fit if they tried. She extracted *Lost Harold Found,* fanned through the pages and then shook the book with its pages facing down. No embarrassing notes. 'All good.' She handed the paperback to Jocelyn. She herself had already read it some months ago and regarded it as poorly written and naïve, though she had not told Cy this because she had not wanted to hurt his feelings. 'I've read it of course,' she confessed to Jocelyn. 'To be honest, I think it's a bit too blunt. But feel free to have a look at it. If you want to take it home, I'm afraid we'll need to ask Cy first.'

'Not to worry. I just want to see it.' Book in hand, Jocelyn almost skipped for joy and returned to the couch. She waved the book at Alyssa, who remained standing. 'Non-commercial and no bullshit. Do you realise just what a treasure of creation this is?' She located the photograph of Cy on the back cover. 'Gosh, he's hot, isn't he? You are so lucky to have such a sexy boyfriend.'

Jocelyn was supposed to be a lesbian, so Alyssa, said nothing.

'I've been through his e-book,' said Jocelyn, continuing to enthuse. 'Believe me, this is an incredible book.'

'What do you like about it, exactly?'

'Harold's list, of course. I've never seen anything like it. So brilliant. You know what I'm talking about, don't you? Harold's wonderful final formulation of humankind's universal sex myths. The one he codifies at the end of his sexual journey once he's finally found himself.'

'Huh?'

'Yes, yes.' Jocelyn read aloud from the advertising blurb on the book's back cover:

Harold has lost his way when it comes to sex. He is finding that more and more women are extremely tedious to be with and not at all worth interacting with sexually. Why? As he staggers from sexual loss of interest to sexual loss of interest in his desperate quest to discover what has gone wrong with modern society, he makes a ground-breaking discovery: modern society has been duped about the nature and purpose of sex. Present-day theorists have gone and got it all wrong. They have been too simple-minded to perceive that what people *say* about sex is anything but the truth. Finally, and fortunately for the rest of us, Harold has seen through the lies.

In *Lost Harold Found*, he bravely takes it upon himself to expose the hypocrisy, dishonesty, and mythology intrinsic to sex, a task he accomplishes through a series of personal engagements in which he confronts sexual lie after sexual lie with truly astonishing results.

The must-read exposé culminates with Harold's final, famous manifesto, in which he lists all the untruths about sex that he has uncovered. Guided by Harold's List we find ourselves sexually re-empowered, with the only remaining problem being that of the ignorance of the rest of the world. Will the world at large ever come to its senses regarding sex and embrace Harold's revelations? Here's hoping that by reading this book they will.

'It's fiction,' said Alyssa, tiredly, 'and Cy wrote that blurb *himself.* Also, in case you haven't noticed, he blames women for everything.'

'I don't think it's as simple as that,' said Jocelyn excitedly. 'That's what I find so astounding. Cy means his assertions to be taken *mutatis mutandis* for whatever sex one happens to be—that is the brilliance of it. Therefore, I find myself agreeing with everything that Harold/Cy says. It's not just fiction.'

'You can't be serious.'

'I am. Cy is a great writer. Here, Alyssa, have another look at Harold's list.' Jocelyn located it for her towards the end of the book. 'Look at this. Tell me what part of it you *don't* agree with. Which of these things here isn't the total myth that he says it is?' She shoved the opened book up under Alyssa's nose. 'Come and sit next to me again and read this part.'

Alyssa gave up. Taking the proffered book, she sat down next to Jocelyn. She knew the list that Cy had concocted. 'I've read it before,' she said.

'Read.'

To please her visitor, Alyssa read it again, all fifty-five myths, out loud. To shut Jocelyn up.

HAROLD'S LIST OF COMMON IDIOTIC FALSE BELIEFS ABOUT SEX

Fifty-Five Myths:

- Complete faithfulness and monogamy are what is biologically normal.
- Once "in love", sexual thoughts about others are abnormal and evil.
- Men and women do not crave variety in partners.
- Old men are the people best suited to telling women what to think about sex.
- Sex is a male thing.
- Women do not have much interest in sex.
- Women never have sex just for the sake of sex.

- Women only tolerate sex so that they can obtain a relationship.
- Sexual desire is not biologically innate; we acquire desire culturally—men especially.
- Overwhelmingly, men are the unfaithful ones in relationships.
- Women have higher sexual morals than men and are more virtuous.
- Men often say disrespectful things about women, but women never do this about men.
- If two people have sex, they are each other's equal in all aspects of life achievement.
- Women never voluntarily participate in demeaning sexual practices.
- It is acceptable to stop having sex with one's partner at about age forty-five.
- Sex is only morally acceptable if there is procreative intent.
- Pornography is all about the abuse of women.
- Inappropriate sexual thoughts are the same as inappropriate sexual deeds.
- No normal person has inappropriate sexual thoughts.
- Interaction with strangers of the opposite sex never includes a sexual assessment.
- A normal married person thinks only of sex with his or her spouse.
- Normal sex is a sacred act and involves only feelings of love.
- Normal sex never involves non-procreative sex acts.
- Respectable women and men do not masturbate.
- Respectable people do not have sexual thoughts of any kind outside their bedrooms.
- Fetishes are abhorrent and sick.
- Sexual deviancy is extremely rare and seen only in the darkest minds.
- No normal person finds an anus sexually interesting.
- Normal sex never involves feelings of assertiveness or submissiveness.
- It is incorrect to say that everybody has sexual fantasies.
- No normal sexual fantasy involves abnormal sex acts.

- ➤ Sexual deviants must receive severe punishment.
- ➤ It is impossible to be normal and have a fetish.
- ➤ Publicly divulged sexual fantasies speaking only of love are reliable and truthful.
- ➤ It is rare for women to be cruel.
- ➤ Sexual giving and sexual taking have nothing at all to do with sadomasochism.
- ➤ In a normal sexual encounter, there is no giver and there is no taker.
- ➤ Sex is never assertive near and at orgasm.
- ➤ Sadism and masochism are not versions of the same thing.
- ➤ Fantasies are not normal if they involve thoughts about pain or non-consent.
- ➤ Almost no women or men have fantasies about submission, violence, or rape.
- ➤ Sex is not a need and one's partner has no moral obligation to care about it.
- ➤ Sex is not important.
- ➤ Not having sex has no effect on a person's behaviour.
- ➤ Sexual taste has nothing at all to do with the events of one's early childhood.
- ➤ A person's childhood has no effect on their later sexual life.
- ➤ Orgasm is all about one's partner, not about evoked memories and emotions in oneself.
- ➤ Sex has nothing to do with a recurring fantasy that always plays in one's head.
- ➤ Love is not just a parental resonance; it is not just a second-hand emotion.
- ➤ There is no such thing as the unconscious.
- ➤ There is no such thing as unconscious penis envy. Freud is wrong.
- ➤ Women never feel hard done by.
- ➤ Women never feel unfairly treated.
- ➤ Sex is all about one's partner's needs. It's not about one's own sexual needs.
- ➤ Regularly refusing sex to a partner is absolutely no reason for them to be unfaithful.

'So, there you have it, Jocelyn. Satisfied?' It was hard to believe, but she had just read Cy's exhausting and somewhat tedious list of sexual myths to another person. 'Fictional Harold and his pseudo-philosophies in all its glory. Drawn entirely from Cy's own imaginary conquests of a disturbingly graphic nature.'

Jocelyn's eyes remained closed. 'Sooh great,' she marvelled. 'Sooh great. What an intellect.'

What was equally disturbing, Alyssa realised, was that reading Cy's *Fifty-Five Myths* out loud had reminded her of Ben Clayton reading his *Codswallop Sayings* of Blastus Bamboozelus at her clinic. Both Cy's rantings via Harold and Ben Clayton's rantings via Blastus rested on nothing more substantial than creative navel gazing.

Worse still, it now became apparent to her that in all probability Jocelyn was using Harold's fictional list of sexual lies as a resource in her acceptance or rejection of the answers she received in the "sexual thoughts" questionnaires of her research project for Conference. Almost certainly, Jocelyn was using Cy's work, and using it as if it were authoritative. There was a high chance that the woman in her flat was a person without a single moral bone in her body.

It was a realisation that left her reeling.

This woman is a fake.

But was she really that? Alyssa felt suddenly frightened because the real Jocelyn remained hidden from her. Cloaked. For a few confusing seconds, Jocelyn's presence caused her the same disconcerting feeling that she got with her in the beginning, that same familiar twinge of fear, the inner misgiving. She was not sure what was going on, but one thing she did know: Jocelyn Goronowski wasn't telling her everything.

Something was seriously wrong. With Jocelyn.

6

The new friend, the one who now seemed determined to remain in her flat forever, looked completely innocent and inordinately pleased with herself as she lolled next to her on the couch.

Alyssa thought it best not to say anything. It was not up to her to prick the bubble of a crazy person. Instead, she returned Cy's book back into Jocelyn's hands. 'Remember,' she told her as she did so, 'Cy only half studied law and has no knowledge of science. His claims are not factual. You can't rely on anything he says.'

Jocelyn, however, just grinned—which was annoying—and said, 'Nonsense, it's good stuff. But you don't agree with all of what's on Cy's list, do you? I can see it on your face.'

What part of "it's pure fiction" *am I missing here?*

'As I said, Jocelyn, Cy is not a scientist. He just sucks his thumb.'

'So?' she said. 'Which of his "Wrongs" *isn't* wrong? What on his list of statements about sex *isn't* the crap that Harold thinks it is?'

Jocelyn was being impossible, so Alyssa thought it best to leave her be. 'Okay, let's forget about whether the list is wrong or right. The other problem is that it's too much at once. It's the same problem with all of Cy's writing. Too much in-your-face, too much in one serving. I don't think people can take this sort of stuff in like this. Harold's list is exactly why Cy is unable to sell anything.'

'Too much information, do you mean? Is that it? Too much for a dickhead to absorb? I suppose they would lose track, wouldn't they? But is that Cy's fault? After all, the shit is out there and all he is doing is shovelling it up.' Her expression softened. 'Okay, okay, I confess that when I first read that list in Cy's e-book it upset me. Not because it offended me, or because I didn't agree with him, but because up until then I had not fully realised just how stuffed-up society really is. I mean, so *many* myths. No wonder everyone is so unhappy and so confused. Everyone is living a lie, Alyssa. We've all been duped in this male versus female carry-on. I mean, good God, what crap!'

'People have believed myths about sex ever since the start of history,' said Alyssa. 'You only need to look at the Bible to realise that. I don't think people are going to be changing any time soon. Besides, they don't even buy Cy's books.'

'The thing is,' said Jocelyn, 'I've worked it out. I know why.'

'You do? You have?'

'Cy's problem? Sure. It's pretty clear. All this myth stuff is actually to do with the control of us women. There's this mutually agreed societal conspiracy of untruth. That's why nobody wants to know about Cy's ideas—his ideas are too dangerous. I mean, the average Joe's biggest personal fear is that he won't get access to sex or, if he does, that he will find himself impotent because his woman is too threatening for him to handle. The result, therefore, is that everything in the public sexual domain is set up to protect these average Joe men and stop their partners from being stolen or getting out of hand. It's all done for the benefit of the *beta* male—which, of course, is almost every guy. All the sexual nonsense out there is just there to protect your average plonking semi-impotent Joe.'

'I don't follow,' said Alyssa.

While sitting next to her, Jocelyn leant over and tickled her under her chin with a finger. 'I just love it when you wrinkle up your nose like that. Think about it, Alyssa. Can't you grasp it? Men need to believe that they are in control of their women because otherwise their little doodle thing doesn't work. It's because we are mammals.'

Alyssa tried to ignore the tickling finger of the woman in her flat who seemed to know too much about her sex life. Finally, mildly angered, she arrested the tickly finger in an iron grip and spoke: 'Men and women are *equally* dominant from a psychological point of view, Jocelyn. That is a fact of life and it's perfectly normal. Surely you, of all people, know this.'

'Of course. But are you *sure* this still applies when it comes to having sex? After all, sex is a childhood throwback. Think Uncle Freddy and all that.'

'Of course, it still applies. A lot of Freud is outdated.' Alyssa maintained her control of Jocelyn's finger. 'Equivalent dominance is a well-established fact. And you've just proved it.'

'Is that so? How?'

'You see Harold's list as though it portrays females as unoppressed. What does *that* show?'

'That you are a bit dense? I'm not in the least bit dominating. It's obvious that the Freudian view is correct here. You see, the trick is that, yes, we are at least as powerful as men psychologically.' Jocelyn tapped her head. 'But, as Harold correctly points out, when it comes to sex we generally need to pretend otherwise. Being female is all about bluff. And it's about bluff precisely because the male needs to feel in control. Without that, they have nothing. Are nothing.'

'It's definitely *not* that simple, Jocelyn. Females *are* generally oppressed in society. *You* might run the sexual show while pretending that you don't, but this does not mean that others have the luxury.'

'And you really think that?'

'Yes. So, for most, it would be no different during sex, *would* it, Jocelyn?' She let her finger go.

'You really do talk horseradish. Women can be as deprived or as privileged as they want to be. Harold is correct.'

'What exactly is the point of your visit, Jocelyn, if you don't mind me asking?'

'Oh, I just love it when you get all worked up. Yes, okay, I confess. Sometimes I do have secret motives. Today, however, on this one occasion, I do not. So, you can relax. I just came past to cheer you up. Honest.' She became philosophical. 'I suppose the main thing I wanted to tell you is that you are very lucky to have someone like Cy to care for you and share his life with you. With him by your side, there's no doubt that you'll get through this Rockport carry-on. So, take courage.'

Jocelyn then sprang to her feet with surprising agility and headed for the bookshelf to return the book. There, she slipped Cy's book back into its correct position while bending over in a most unladylike way. Her posterior looked even broader than before. Then she straightened up and spoke. 'For the record, Alyssa, dominance is *not* the same as control. Women can be in command yet still allow men to be in control. As I said before, men must feel in control; without that, nothing works. *That* is the message of *Lost Harold Found*, in case it's escaped you. Cy's book is absolutely bloody brilliant.'

Alyssa did not care for the direction of Jocelyn's conversation, which seemed to be about Cy's impotence problem. The woman was being her usual extremely blunt and tactless self and over-indulging her mouth. Yes, she might be a genius, but she was clearly also a nosey parker. 'I think you are taking Cy's book far too seriously,' she said to her. 'It's not a textbook. There are no scientific references. It's just a collection of invented encounters that he's listed for dramatic effect. And for your information, they are not even Cy's own beliefs.'

'They aren't?'

'No,' said Alyssa, closing the subject. 'If anyone should know, I should know.' Jocelyn could have no answer to that.

'Oh. That is a bit disappointing.' Jocelyn looked at her suspiciously. 'I don't believe you, you know.' She moved from the bookshelf towards the front door, looking at her watch. 'I suppose I'd better get back to work. I've still got a ton of dictating to do. Thanks for the coffee.'

'That's okay, Jocelyn. And thanks for popping in.' Alyssa went to the front door with her.

7

Alyssa stood at the front door with Jocelyn, but Jocelyn seemed reluctant to depart. Then Jocelyn brushed against her and instead of apologising, embraced her in a hug.

'I've got to give you a big hug before I go,' she said. 'You smell too nice.' She squeezed sensuously. 'I'm so pleased that you are so much better than when I first got here. I do think I have succeeded in getting your mind off Gilbert Rockport and back onto the real purpose of your life.'

'And what is that?' She could hardly breathe because of the arms around her chest.

Jocelyn released her grip, then clasped Alyssa's head in her hands. 'Psychotherapy, dummy. That's why you exist. See, now we at least have some colour back in your cheeks. There's nothing quite like a little female companionship to get one back on track, is there?'

'I suppose.' It was a murmur, but in truth, until now, she had not fully appreciated how much her unexpected new female friend had helped her regain her equilibrium. The new insight amazed her. Also amazing was that she was meekly allowing Jocelyn to keep touching her.

Jocelyn looked into her eyes. 'So, this Rockport thing. You won't let it get to you, promise? And remember, it's going to get worse before it gets better—I want you to understand that. Much worse. These things always get really, really bad. But then you get through it. You will get through this. Meanwhile, get some vorazepams and use them if you have to.'

'Thank you, Jocelyn. I will. And thanks again for coming by.'

Jocelyn released her. 'You know, you are the only person I know who I can just be myself with. That is something special. There must be something wonderful going on between us. I feel sure of it.'

Alyssa smiled at her, but not with amusement this time. Instead, her voice came out soft and shy. 'Same for me,' she confessed. Jocelyn did something to her brain, something that resembled having it mashed by an eggbeater. Yet somehow it did not feel unpleasant.

'You are so beautiful. Look after yourself, Alyssa. There is so much ugliness out there.'

'Thank you.'

Jocelyn hesitated, then seemed to come to a decision. 'Let me show you something,' she said suddenly. 'Before I go. It's only right that I do.' She marched back to Cy's bookcase, dragging Alyssa along with her by the hand, and stood her there, next to the glass door leading out to the flat's tiny balcony. 'Look out there and tell me what you see.'

Alyssa looked through the window above the bookcase, as directed. 'What do you mean?'

'Oh please.' Jocelyn reached to the window ledge behind the open curtain in front of them, took the key, and unlocked the glass door. 'I do need to show you this. You have to see this.' They went out onto the balcony, where the two of them could hardly fit together. 'I'm not a judgemental person, Alyssa, but I have this horrible feeling that you don't know, and I don't want to see you hurt any further.'

'What on earth are you talking about?'

'An innocent fool, as I suspected. What is this growing here?' She pointed accusingly at the three pot plants on the balcony.

'Oh. Those. Those are Cy's. He's a bit of a gardener, although sometimes he forgets to water them, so I do.'

'A gardener?' Jocelyn stepped back into the lounge and marched back to the front door in her fancy pants.

Alyssa followed, unsure of what Jocelyn was up to. 'So?'

'My dear, you will need to be more careful.' Jocelyn spoke softly, and in an adult, psychiatrist's voice. 'Those out there are cannabis plants.' She opened the front door. 'Be a darling and deal with it. Oh, and by the way, nobody at work knows I've been talking to you. Best to keep it that way.'

With a cheerful wave, Dr Jocelyn Goronowski disappeared.

Cannabis plants!

8

Alyssa went back to the balcony of her flat and stared at the pot plants and their serrated lush green leaves.

Shit.

To think that she had been that stupid. She had even been watering them for Cy. If a law enforcement official ever found them in her flat, the Board of Psychologists would strike her off the practice register.

What is Cy thinking!

She had never seen Cy stoned, or even using the plants, but the plants would have to go. Even if they were only intended for a friend—maybe for his boss Brian from the bookshop—they still placed her career in jeopardy. Bookshop Brian was just the sort of person who *would* take drugs. He often talked to Cy behind her back in a way that demonstrated just what sort of a person he was. She had overheard him and Cy once and knew he referred to her as "your one with the hot pussy". What sort of person talked to one's boyfriend like that? If anyone was using cannabis, it would be Brian.

She went and sat on the couch again. While Jocelyn's visit had been helpful, now that she was gone her mind threatened to start spinning again. There was too much to worry about. She needed to plan strategies. Make plans about how to face tribunals and cope with endless investigations. Things had to be sorted. Tactics devised. Decisions made. Work stuff . . . and now Cy stuff too. She needed to have time, time to think about what to say about Gilbert Rockport, time to deal with whatever it was that Cy was up to behind her back. Time.

Unfortunately, she did not have much time left. The anxiety was returning, and it was going to get worse. Much worse.

She wished she could phone Cy, but she knew his mobile was out of money because it lay on the kitchen counter where he had temporarily abandoned it. It had been there, dormant, for the past few days.

She switched on the television to watch the news. The dramatic death of the prominent barrister Gilbert Rockport QC, who was now named, was headline news. It was Gilbert all right, and, yes, he was dead. Gory images of the crumpled wreck of his car were shown from every conceivable angle, interspersed with long-range aerial views of the subsequent mother of all traffic jams.

The TV images of Gilbert's smashed up Maserati burned themselves into her brain. The damage felt personal. After all, the same car had parked faithfully next to her cottage front door every Monday afternoon. From what she could see, Gilbert never stood a chance. As stated in the earlier internet reports, the end of a metal crash barrier had come through the upside-down windscreen.

Though she always knew that the TV news was likely to trigger her own past road accident traumas, the intensity of the sudden rush of emotion caught her by surprise. Her heart began to pound, and, as pulses hammered in her neck and in her head, she began to perspire and feel unwell and short of breath. Unstoppably, images of her *own* car accident took control of her mind briefly. They flooded in, together with unwelcome memories of intensive care, and police, and the death of her father. Death. And with that, a deadly despondency. Despair came over her, pushing down from the ceiling of the apartment, heavy, like a suffocating blanket. Inexorable pressure. Crushing her down. The old demons were back with a vengeance, and she was too tired to fight them. She had nothing to fight with. All she had was nausea. Waves of it welled up from the badness that was in her.

Unconcerned for her welfare, the television news continued. On a perfectly straight section of freeway, Barrister Rockport's car had exited the road at high speed through a known service gap in the roadside barrier. Because of its speed, the car travelled up the side of the steep embankment and consequently overturned. Because of the funnelling effect of the embankment, the car then almost inevitably struck the end of the resumed roadside barrier, but in this case upside-down. The car then ricocheted into the centre of the freeway in a shower of debris, on its roof, and resulted in closure of three of the five inbound lanes of the freeway for over three hours. Because of the early hour of the morning— and only because of that—no one else had died, although some vehicles had subsequently sustained damage from the debris.

Footage of the earlier police statement about a tip-off regarding the possibility of vehicular suicide then played, followed by a further report to the effect that no eyewitnesses had yet come forward. Freeway CCTV footage was being analysed, and dashcam footages awaited, but unfortunately fixed cameras were few because the Shamon was not a turnpike. There was no coverage of the specific area of the incident. Accident investigators had recovered the car's stability control computer and would be sending it to Italy for analysis. Information from this source was likely to be the key to what was otherwise a complex and puzzling case. Later, there would be a coronial inquest.

The news then moved on to an item about rioting in France.

Freed at last from her trance, Alyssa switched the TV off.

But, even with the TV off, she felt far from well. She was feeling too hot. Not knowing what else to do, she stood up and went to the window and removed her shirt and took off her bra to cool down. Her scar was aching, so she ran her fingers up and down it nervously as she stared idly at the little park across the road.

Have I killed Gilbert too?

She forced herself to take deliberately slow breaths and calm down. She knew she needed to be more rational. After all, the reality of the situation was that it was more than likely that Gilbert had *not* committed suicide, or at least that she had not *caused* Gilbert to commit suicide. The police had no idea what was going on. Judging from the tone of the latest reports, the death did not seem to be to them as obvious a case of vehicular suicide as it had earlier, when the news first broke. In the cold light of day, Gilbert was a known speedster.

However, Gilbert was still dead—and she had been his therapist. She began to pace up and down in the lounge. As she did so, images of Gilbert's body forced themselves into her mind against her will—pieces of body butchered by chunks of metal—except... except that the butchered body wasn't Gilbert's. And it wasn't her father either. The images refused to stop, bringing her close to panic. She walked faster and tried to think only of her own body. The butchered body was not that of a man at all. It was that of a woman. There was a woman in the Maserati, horribly injured, dying. A woman who looked like somebody she knew. Jocelyn? Yet it wasn't her.

What is wrong *with me!*

She wished Cy would hurry up and come home.

9

She was perilously close to the edge of some sort of mental abyss, and she knew it. Alyssa stopped pacing and went and stood still in front of the lounge window, supporting herself on the windowsill, and tried to focus on the trees across the road. She needed to anchor herself in the now. It took time, but finally the graphic images of death stopped. She had been well trained.

Next step: phone her doctor for a prescription for the anti-anxiety medication vorazepam. Still naked from the waist up, she made the call.

The practice receptionist answered. 'Right,' she said snootily to Alyssa, 'I'll just get your details.' However, when the receptionist discovered that she attended infrequently yet wanted tranquillisers, she became less than co-operative. 'Nothing available this week, I'm afraid.'

A pathetic pettifogger standing in her way was the last thing Alyssa needed. She suspected she was talking to the pimple-faced school dropout she sometimes encountered there. Naysayers of that sort somehow always seemed to manage to pop up at the most inconvenient of times, and always with hellish glee. And the ones prejudiced specifically against mental illness were always the worst.

The annoyance at the other end of the phone needed short-circuiting. 'Listen', she told the receptionist, 'it's Alyssa Brown here.' Her voice sounded surprisingly strong and calm. 'I'm registered there. And the *real* reason I need to attend is for a cervical screening test.' It wasn't, but she knew enough about psychology to know that mentioning intimate female body parts would put the juvenile idiot at the other end into panic mode.

It did. 'Oh,' gasped the dropout. 'Oh dear.'

'Yes,' said Alyssa. 'I was a bit too embarrassed to mention it earlier, but seeing that you needed to know, I've mentioned it. I'm really worried because I'm overdue.' At least that part was not an outright lie. The earlier history-taking encounter with professional supervisor Susan Lindow had reminded her that it was a good five years since her first screening test. She was more than due but had become distracted by exams and work.

Miraculously, the receptionist found an appointment space. Alyssa Brown would be able to see her doctor after all—at 9.30 am the next day.

'Thank you. Much appreciated.' Objective achieved she ended the call.

She hated it when employees in the so-called health sector failed to understand that mental health issues were urgent. However, by playing them at their own game she had made progress. She would have some vorazepams by morning. She had used the tablets before—after her breakdown—and knew that they did work in her case, at least in the short term. She would cope better with Gilbert's death once she had a few of the pills on board. Hopefully, as in the past, they would stop her mind from spinning so easily out of control and allow her to plan the way forward more clearly.

Buoyed by her success with the GP's receptionist, Alyssa went to the kitchen and began to organise dinner. There was just enough time before Cy got back. While thinking of him, she occasionally glanced out at the three balcony pot plants.

Such a mischievous imp.

Cannabis. Who would have thought? Then she checked for food supplies in the kitchen cupboard. There was nothing useful, nothing that sprang out. With the nipples of her still bare breasts squashing uncomfortably against the edge of the top shelf, she stretched right in to confirm that there really wasn't much there. Dinner would have to involve eggs. They could have an omelette with parsley, or they could have French toast. Cy wouldn't mind either way. He was very accommodating.

She was still deliberating absent-mindedly about culinary possibilities, empty frying pan in hand, when, pitiless as the summer sun, the truth about Jocelyn Goronowski burst through the fog in her mind.

Her new so-called friend was playing her for a fool.

There had been too many coincidences lately.

Far too many.

No person could know as much as Jocelyn seemed to know about her without there being some sort of underhand treachery going on. She should have realised this a long time back, especially given the ongoing hinting about remedies for impotent males. She hadn't forgotten the most recent hurtful words, something along the lines of: "Men need to feel in control during sex, Alyssa. Without that, they have nothing, so nothing works". Blah blah. As if Jocelyn had the slightest idea about anything to do with men. She obviously didn't. Which could mean only one thing…

Jocelyn and Cy were sharing information. Way too much information. But why? And more importantly, how?

That's it! The balcony door.

Her hand froze on the handle of the frying pan as she confronted the full implications of her realisation about the balcony door: if Jocelyn knew where the key to the door was kept—which she had—then the truth of what was *really* going on went beyond terrible. Jocelyn had been in her apartment before.

Alone with Cy.

It had to be so. There was no other way that Jocelyn could have known how to unlock the balcony door when she took her out to look at Cy's not-so-innocent pot plants.

Jocelyn was seeing Cy behind her back.

Jocelyn was visiting Cy under her nose in her own apartment.

You bastard!

Rage welled up suddenly and uncontrollably and hit like a bus, knocking all rational thought out of her head. She sank to her knees with a piercing shriek of pain, then jumped into the air and disintegrated into a rage worthy of a toddler. Screaming, she broke the handle of the frying pan clean off and hurled the stricken remnants across the room.

'Bastards all of you!'

The shrieking was so loud that it could be heard in the street. Then, after screaming her head off, Alyssa rushed to the toilet and vomited.

CHAPTER TWENTY-ONE

1

IT WAS STILL EARLY in the morning, probably between five and six am to judge from the faintness of the sunrise glow on the neighbouring apartment wall. Alyssa lay motionless for a while as she gained her bearings. It had been a sleepless night full of restless thoughts. Were her recollections entirely factual, she wondered, or was some of what she remembered the product of dreaming? As far as she knew, she had not slept at all, but obviously she had—for a few hours at least. The crick in her neck was proof enough of that.

When she stretched out an arm, the bed was empty. Then she remembered. Cy was on the couch in the lounge. Despite protestations of innocence the previous evening, he had accepted the marching orders out of the bedroom with docility, a sure sign of a guilty man. Later in the day, she would get the truth out of him about Jocelyn—and then tell him what had happened to Gilbert, and about the trouble she was potentially in regarding that, and about why she was off work on sick leave. She had never kicked anyone out of her bedroom before, so she hoped to see him back that night.

For now, though, she had Gilbert on her mind. Not the traumatic images of the day before, but her memories of him alive. She pictured him sitting in the consulting room at the cottage, co-operating with her in his attempt to gain control of his life. Like any good counsellor, she was encouraging him to concentrate on his feelings. It was what they had spent many weeks doing: examining feelings. Looking at the *why* of things, looking at what it was that he *really* wanted in life, exploring the possibilities. They had both had no greater wish than to get his future back on track.

She realised, as she lay there semi-awake, that she had spent the whole night sifting through memories of Gilbert Rockport's visits to the cottage—no doubt with the aim of assembling the salient points into some sort of coherent narrative. When it came to any enquiry into his death, there was going to be nothing findable in writing. With Gilbert Rockport, there *were* no notes. Everything about him existed only in her head. Which was going to be a problem because the recollections seemed to have become muddled. It had been a strange night. Consultations and fanciful imaginings had swirled and intermingled, and now they seem to have seamlessly fused. How was she ever going to be able to tell them apart? What in her memories was what Gilbert had really said, and what was just her—her filling in the gaps?

Of even more concern was the awareness now forming in her mind, a *knowing*, a conviction that somewhere in the middle of Gilbert's struggles had lain something relevant to her own life. Something that belonged also to her *own* lost Self had been in Gilbert; something of her had been in him. Frustratingly, though she had always sensed this, she had not been able to further clarify it—and now he was gone. Whatever it was of herself that had been lost remained lost. Hiding and biding its time, something relevant to life and death remained still unfindable. Some important truth waited to surface; something so awful that her mind still refused to accept it.

It was going to be important to think more clearly about Gilbert; about what she remembered. It was going to be the only way forward for her *own* peace of mind.

From a practical point of view too, certain other facts were also going to be critical, especially those related to her future employment prospects. There were going to be questions—such as "You say, Ms Brown, that you were counselling Gilbert Rockport QC about the possibility that he had PTSD, but what made you think this was his problem"? The authorities were going to want an acceptable answer. After all, as a counselling psychologist she was not qualified to make diagnoses; not officially. The board was going to want to be reassured that she had known what she was doing; that she had not contributed to his death in any way through incompetent counselling. It was also going to be important that the board not discover that she *knew* that what Gilbert was having done to himself by Veronica was illegal. "Why then did you not report him to the police, Ms Brown"? All of which meant that she needed to manufacture plausible explanations out of the nebulous fog that constituted what she knew about Gilbert. She was going to have to produce "data", even if it came almost entirely out of her own head.

What had been the QC's key psychological issues?

Good question. What indeed? There were no easy answers. Gilbert had been a complex man. It had taken months to gain even a rudimentary understanding of his problems. Yet progress had been made. The more she thought about it, the more convinced of it she became. Yes, towards the end, shortly before his death, the essence of Gilbert had indeed crystalised to a reportable extent. The way to a better life for him *had* opened. The possibility of healing *had* begun. In the weeks prior to his death, Gilbert had been on the mend. That would be the narrative to insist upon. Besides, it really was true.

Yet, instead of getting better, he died.

Why the paradox?

That part about Gilbert did not make any sense at all. As a victor, he should still have been very much alive. After all, she and he had finally got to the root cause of his psychological distress. His demons had become visible and could now be fought rationally. He had found new hope.

The simple incontestable fact of the matter was that as a child, Gilbert had been sexually abused. It was this that had been the driver behind all his psychological issues. Behind everything to do with Gilbert Rockport lurked this single demon. And until the visits to her at the cottage, they had proven unconquerable.

She recalled them getting to the truth, to that point of no return. It had not been easy because it had involved asking him about sex and about why his Mistress Veronica excited him. Sex was always a delicate subject for a counsellor to broach—not least of all because sexual *abuse* was potentially lethal to a client in the wrong hands—but there had been no way around it. To lessen the embarrassment for them both—given their age difference—she had asked the questions as matter-of-factly as possible.

'Tell me, Gilbert,' she had said, 'do you get sexually excited in relation to your beatings by Mistress Veronica?'

'Huh? What does *that* mean?'

'You know what it means; what I mean.'

'Maybe.'

This was evasive. She needed him to face up to himself, humiliating as the truth might be to him. '*Maybe*? What sort of an answer is that? It's just me you are talking to. This is completely confidential. With me, you know that's true.'

Nevertheless, he was unable to maintain eye contact. 'Do I get excited? What do you think?' he muttered. 'Use your imagination.'

'So, it's a yes?'

'Okay then.'

'Hugely?'

'You are a little nosy parker, aren't you? Okay, yes. Hugely. I get hugely excited.'

It was as she had thought. Sex was central to what was troubling him. Which had confirmed her developing theory that whatever was wrong with Gilbert stemmed from trauma in early childhood. This was the only time when sexuality was polymorphous. Gilbert had to have been sexually awakened during the immaturity of childhood. There was no other explanation for the bizarreness of what excited him sexually. It had been at that point in counselling that she had begun to feel certain that he had been a victim of sexual abuse in his childhood.

2

She kept thinking about him. The hunch that Gilbert Rockport had been sexually abused as a child seemed to meld perfectly with his compulsive sexual wish to have his buttocks traumatised by Mistress Veronica. It also explained his belief that getting such a thing done to himself somehow connected him to others. Clearly, thought Alyssa, he was expressing an important foundational aspect of his self-construct through such sexual actions—to those who understood.

True connection—intimacy—was essential to the will to live. Without a sharing of one's deepest secrets and wishes with *another* similar being who *understood*—if one's reality remained denied—then, effectively, at core, one became cut off from existing. In such circumstances, over time, life itself became impossible. A person could pretend for only so long before the need to reflect one's authentic Self off another *validating* Self became overwhelming. And therein lay the mesmerising power of Mistress Veronica. Without a doubt, if analysed, she too would be found to have early childhood issues related to cruelty and physical violence.

Yet, somehow, relating to Veronica also necessitated Gilbert destroying himself. In his attempts to stay alive, Gilbert had reached a point where he believed he had no option but to share the neglected part of his Self with the likes of someone destructive; someone like Mistress Veronica.

Fortunately, thanks to his sessions at the cottage, he had finally realised that he did have another option: instead of resorting to Veronica, he could share his neglected parts with a therapist. He had found that doing this rather than relying on The House of Fantasy was more likely to be helpful in the long run—and vastly more benevolent.

To get to the hidden core of Gilbert, Alyssa had needed to get truly close to him and get him to be fully honest with her about his sex life— and in this she had largely succeeded. Slowly, he had softened to her, and finally he had come to trust her enough to tell her the truth. While the initial revelations about his sex life had flowed from the request by her to know if Veronica's beatings were sexually exciting to him, they had also flowed later from her questions about his sexual relationship with his official sexual partner, third wife Nikki.

'What about your wife, Nikki. How does *she* feel about your need to receive beatings?'

'It doesn't really matter what she thinks, does it? Not at this stage of my life. Don't look so surprised. She can hardly complain. We still have sex regularly—normal sex—and she gets truckloads of money out of me. But, of course, none of that counts because the sad truth of the matter is that she despises me. She cares only about herself and doesn't care at all about what I need.' His face once again disappeared into his hands, as it so often did. 'I've tried so hard. None of my wives has ever truly loved me. Even you think I'm some sort of joke! Oh, Alyssa, in the name of Holy Christ, I am fucked beyond measure.'

He was. Deep down, he was damaged goods.

His body heaved with his sobbing.

Like a small child.

'There is a sickness in me. It's so serious that I think I may be close to death. I don't know what to do. Help me, please. I'm so lost. All I have is Veronica.'

That had been enough to bring tears to her eyes. He had nothing. Nothing except a broken childhood.

His bizarre sexual behaviour was just a secondary phenomenon.

'Veronica is so lovely. Really, she is.'

No, she had not dozed off into a dream. It was Gilbert who was talking, and he was talking nonsense.

'Lovely? Lovely in what way exactly?'

'Well, for one, with her there's no bullshit. She enjoys what she does and she's not labouring under any illusions. It's a clean transaction. In exchange for money, Veronica does exactly what I want and how I want it. I could use a safe word with her, but I don't. If I did, the experience wouldn't be real for me. With Veronica, things are real. The other great thing is that she has a truly fabulous body. No bullshit there either. The entire experience is just wonderful. No one has any idea who I am, and I can relax completely.'

'Why am I not seeing love here?'

He seemed taken aback. 'I don't know. It's there, believe me.'

What sort of a person are you?

'Okay, maybe I wouldn't call our relationship *love* in the normal sense of the word. I'm not that stupid. But without using the word I can't really explain it. It's not love in the usual sense, but it is still love. In fact, it's deeper than that.' A revelation seemed to dawn on him: 'Yes, in a way that I can't explain, what we have is deeper than that.'

'Deeper than love?'

'Yes. It's a life and death thing that we have.'

'Isn't *all* love supposed to be like that? Life and death.'

'Maybe, but I would never marry Veronica. Perhaps that clarifies the matter. We love each other, but not in the conventional way. What we have is not realistic. After all, we could never live like that. I'd be dead within a month—or at least in intensive care.'

'Exactly, Gilbert. Therefore, how about we add the concept of violence to the mix and change your idea of love to something else. What would you like to call it? *Extreme* violence?' She tried not to sound too sarcastic.

'Hell, I don't know Alyssa. Not that. What about weird love?

Something like that. Veronica is not violent. I think you've got that part all wrong. She's always kind. Calm and soothing. Strict, of course, but that's to be expected. She knows what needs to be done and she does not step back from her duties.'

'How lucky for you.'

'Once she gets going, she does rather get into it, I suppose. I mean, there is a definite brutality to her. She does have a mean arm. She goes to the gym for her arms, you know.'

'I'm trying to imagine it. It's hard for me.'

'The severity of it, that rush of fury from her—*that* is what I need. She's a real pro. I know it's supposed to be just a job for her, but it does excite her too. She gets aroused. I see the evidence. You know what I mean: the panting, the dilated pupils—and the other things.'

And what would they be, Gilbert?

He was unable to maintain eye contact. 'She enjoys it all right. Especially once I begin to struggle to get free and start to scream. She hits faster and harder once that happens, as though heading for a climax.'

Great.

'What do you think about all this, Gilbert?'

'Okay. Maybe it is a bit violent.'

'What I see, Gilbert, frankly, is more than that. What I see is a picture of abuse. What do you think of that word? *Abuse.* Were you ever abused as a child?'

The question seemed to startle him. 'You mean the whole child sexual abuse thing?'

'That.'

'You want me to tell you about that sort of thing? Seriously?'

'You need to face up to it.'

'What if I've not had it?'

'You have. I *know* you have. Are you saying you were *not* abused as a child?'

He did not protest. 'Well, not exactly sexually.' There was silence. 'I suppose I did have some trouble with my father. He meant well.'

'Well then, tell me about it. You can't keep bottling it up forever. You need to tell someone, otherwise you will never heal.'

He considered the matter for a while. 'This is definitely

confidential—even with you? No recordings going?'

'No. Nothing. Just the CCTV, but there's no sound on that. I'm not even taking any notes, as you can see.' She showed him her empty palms and smiled at him kindly.

'Mm. Okay then. I'll tell you something about my parents if that will satisfy you—mainly, though, because they are both dead. You won't be able to get them into trouble even if you do betray me and rush off to the police like the rest of you dreadful people. Besides, I very much doubt that my dead parents are in any way relevant to my current situation.'

'Relax, Gilbert, I'm not going to the police. I hate the police.'

'Good.'

3

The account that followed was extremely relevant to Gilbert's situation, despite his attempts at denial, because it explained everything.

'My father did have a bit of a violent streak, I suppose. He was a good man, and I loved him, and he meant well, but it wouldn't be an exaggeration to say that he was a strict disciplinarian.' Gilbert spoke in a strangely matter-of fact voice. 'There are benefits to that of course, as you can see. I wouldn't have been as successful as I am today without him. Nevertheless, I probably did receive a few too many beatings as a small boy. Legally, some of them would today probably be regarded as so excessive as to constitute child abuse—after all, small children have died from that sort of thing. But these are today's sentiments. And I am a lawyer. Back then, it wasn't the case. Also, I'm relying on my own memories from when I was a child, so the situation may not have been as bad as I'm making out. In those days, everyone got hidings, often bad ones. It never seemed to bother any of my friends, so I've never thought it has anything to do with what's troubling me now. I don't see any obvious connection. I'm not a small kid anymore.'

She remembered looking at him with something akin to frank disbelief on her face. It had seemed impossible to her that anyone could say anything more absurd.

It was when Gilbert Rockport QC saw this response to his cherished false narrative that his own face began to crumble. 'Oh shit, Alyssa,' he cried. 'Who am I trying to kid? You're right, of course. Yes, you are right. There is something there from my childhood, isn't there? It's all part of this endlessly stuffed-up-me business, isn't it? It's all connected. It must be. I've tried so hard to block it out. I've been trying to pretend that it was nothing, that I'm imagining things. But you are right. I *was* abused. There's no other word for it. And I have been refusing to believe it.' Tears began to fall. 'I love both my parents dearly, but my childhood was too much for me. It nearly destroyed me. I was totally alone.' He was sobbing now. 'I've been trying so hard to stay alive ever since. I've had nobody to turn to. Nobody to confide in. Until now. You are the first person who knows, the first person I've ever told.' He looked completely shattered by the new reality that had dawned over him. 'I should have faced up to this earlier. Reported it. I am an abused child. I am.'

This confirmation of the suspicions that had been building in her mind over many weeks had enabled her, at long last, to make her tentative diagnosis, namely that of a childhood-related post-traumatic stress disorder. It also marked the turning point in her management of Gilbert's therapy, for it was from this time onwards—a referrable diagnosis finally made—that she had begun to try to get him to move away from her supportive counselling at the Donald Clinic's cottage and on to a more appropriate specialist PTSD therapist.

'Yes, I should have gone to the police about that business in Tabralla.'

'What business? What's Tabralla got to do with all this?' Tabralla was a town about a hundred km away in the direction of the desert.

Going to the police, Gilbert, would not have made any difference. That much she did know.

He tried to explain about Tabralla, the place where matters had gone from bad to worse. 'I was only three or four years old when the beatings began—probably they began well before that, but I can't remember for sure. My father used to use a wooden paddle. It even had a name painted on it: "Mr Sorry".' Gilbert grimaced at the memory. 'My father was a large, strong man and I don't think he knew his own strength because he used to hit very, very hard.' Gilbert stopped for a while and stared into the middle distance. 'I used to believe I was just weak.' His voice trailed off. 'Sometimes I still do.'

She knew there was more to what he was trying to tell her, so she prompted him with an important question: 'Where was your mother in all of this?'

'There in the house with us. But no use at all. Looking back, I have no doubt that she was complicit in what went on. She was funny that way. She used to watch, and she used to encourage my father to beat me. Once, she even insisted that my father continue thrashing me until she saw blood. Looking back on those years, I think I feared her even more than my father. Mainly because there was no pleasing her. She *wanted* me punished. I remember how she used to grab hold of me and tell me how sorry she was for me, even though she was the one who minutes earlier had sent my father off to his office to get out the paddle. While we waited for the command to "come", she would cuddle me to comfort me until the time came. Then, with poorly disguised glee, she used to frog march me off to get *done*—which at the time always seemed to me a shocking act of betrayal.' He blew his nose. 'Sorry. As you can imagine, I never stood a chance. The beatings were dreadful. I remember how much I used to scream. And I remember how much she used to watch. My own mother . . .'

Gilbert's "recollections" were starting to sound suspiciously like his current sexual fantasies, so she began to wonder how much of it was true. The memory sounded a little too convenient, a little too glib. Though undoubtedly sincere, she wondered if it was a false memory, brought on perhaps by her questions and her counselling style and her sexuality. False memories were not lies, but genuinely believed imagined events. She hoped that some of what he remembered fell into that category because the alternative, the literal historical truth, was potentially fatal. If his account of his early childhood *was* literally true, it meant that Gilbert had been "visiting Veronica" ever since he was four years old. In which case he was doomed.

Unfortunately, he never wavered in his recollections.

'I remember it now,' he said. 'I remember how afterwards I used to need to lie face down on my bed for a few hours to recover. My mother used to come in and close the curtains to keep the room dim and cool and quiet. She used to be very soothing. She used to lower my underpants to check on me and apply antiseptic cream that used to sting a lot. I remember it all now for the first time.' Gilbert seemed hardly able to breathe. 'I remember.'

Things got worse for him. He lost his parents—they divorced—and he was sent to board at a church school in Tabralla, an hour's drive out of the city. Although by then a twelve-year-old boy, physical punishments continued.

Physically abusive institutions were not exactly rare in those days, and neither was the closely associated practice of sexual abuse. She knew of the many shocking reports.

'Looking back,' said Gilbert, 'I can see now that I was prime game. I was sensitive and vulnerable, fresh from a broken home and with a history of many previous beatings. To make matters worse, I looked young for my age. The teachers were almost all church brothers, mostly celibate or otherwise sexually screwed up, and for some reason they seemed to find me particularly sexually desirable. Why, I still don't know for sure.'

Maybe it's about making use of the assuredly obedient.

'Maybe you were an escape from their impotent existence.'

'Maybe. The guaranteed acquiescence . . . the fear—it certainly *did* something for them. It seemed to slake some thirst in their bent souls. It was obvious to everybody that they enjoyed the whole punishment experience immensely, especially the whippings. They used to seek me out in the most sick, sadistic way, knowing how compliant I would be. It wasn't long before I was being caned on a weekly basis.'

The never-ending story: child sexual abuse masquerading as corporal punishment.

4

'A single boy talking during silent time in a dormitory or classroom could get every student in that room caned. In such cases of guilt by association, they used to cane the entire group. The worst thing about that was that the tariff for group misdemeanours was always six of the best—maximum severity—meaning that we had to lower our trousers too. Not only that, but in group canings we had to leave our underpants down at our knees while waiting to be done, and afterwards too. The brothers said this was necessary to minimise holdups and ensure that no one inadvertently escaped punishment. It seems impossible to believe this now, but we believed them. We were innocent. Every bottom needed to be seen by them to have its stripes before a group could dress. The mass canings were a highly efficient process, but you can imagine how degrading it all was.'

She could.

'Something finally broke inside my head.' At this stage, his breathing was coming too fast. 'I think that's why I became a lawyer.' Then there were tears again. 'I did it to protect myself. I've tried so hard. So hard.'

He was deeply traumatised.

'I understand. You are so brave. I'm really proud of you.'

There was much weeping when Gilbert finally realised that he would never be able to escape the cognitive and affective injuries done to the fabric of his brain during his childhood—injuries that were in some way even more devastating than cerebral palsy. The best he would ever be able to do was live safely within his disability. It was time to grieve over the deliberate ruination of his childhood and permanent warping of his brain. Up until now, he had limped on bravely through life on a set of mental crutches, hoping always for a cure. There was no cure. There was nothing.

Just great poignancy.

Despite every great thing that he had achieved in life in the field of law, there was no way out for him, no way to escape—not even as a great barrister. Even the law had no way to protect him from the sadists who had twisted his mind. His parents had messed with his developing brain by connecting love and cruelty, sensuality, and pain, and then, in an unfortunate unfolding of fate, those intent on sexually abusing children under their care had identified him as conflicted and seized upon him as prey. Assaulted by such powerful adverse events in his early life, Gilbert Rockport had stood no chance. He had tried to fix himself later in life only to discover tragically that it was too late for that. The offenders had escaped into his head and re-screwed the wiring. They were unreachable now, and with macabre glee continued to abuse him with impunity. To the dismay of Gilbert Rockport QC, nothing in the Astoria legal system—or any legal system in any country—had the ability to save him. The law provided no cure for mental health problems. Perhaps rightly, it was time to realise and accept that he was beyond cure.

But not beyond salvation. Not if properly counselled on how to live safely alongside his disability and special needs.

According to Gilbert, each time he visited Mistress Veronica the goal was to induce a state of mental collapse in himself similar to how it had felt to him in childhood. And, heroically, most of the time this was indeed what he managed to achieve—by the end of proceedings.

More correctly, he achieved collapse about three quarters of the way through, which was usually the point where he truly could no longer cope. Once he "lost it", so to speak, all his resistance ended. His screams stopped, and his body became limp and fully receptive to its punishment from the ongoing assault by Mistress Veronica, who, as pre-arranged, never paused or slackened in her inexorable progress to stroke number fifty.

Receptiveness while being flogged was what was required.

Why? As far as he could tell, it was so that he could reach the place in his mind that he needed to reach in order to fix himself. By trial and error in his quest to reach maximum receptiveness, he had found that fifty continuous strokes worked a treat. Not only that, but the mental and emotional effects were enhanced if his buttocks were exposed during the ordeal. His mind imploded best with such a combination because then he had the added humiliation of having his naked body splay open helplessly as he struggled with his agonies.

In other words, to achieve an altered state in his case, not only was severe pain important, but also utter humiliation. "The truth is, Alyssa, it's only in a state of abject receptiveness that I can open some gate in my mind".

His words, not hers.

The gate to the Un-conscious.

Which all seemed rather over the top, quite sick, and hard to understand or believe.

5

No doubt Gilbert achieved some sort of orgasmic state during his visits to Veronica—a mental one at least. But why go to all that trouble to have an orgasm?

She had gone so far as to ask him that. 'Why?'

Why? To escape the agony that was his mental life, said Gilbert. Yes, it was only a few minutes of surrender, but it was an eternity too. During a Veronica experience, time lost its meaning, and he became immune to the pain of the real word. In his new world there was magic. Everything was bright and shimmering. Rest and peace stretched out endlessly. There was no way he could describe the wonder of it.

Yes, he knew that potentially Veronica could do anything she wished to him once he collapsed into full compliance. Fully restrained and mentally defenceless as he then was, she could sexually abuse him or even kill him. The important thing was that she never did anything of the sort. Though his body became fully hers, Veronica never took advantage of him. Fully in control and fully empowered, Veronica transformed into the sweetest of women.

Really?

She had blinked at him.

'You think I'm crazy, don't you?'

'No, just damaged.' Gilbert was not crazy. Far from it.

'Veronica is why I'm still alive today.' What reached to him out of her, so to speak, was kindness. She was the kindest person he had ever known. In his altered state he was able to see her for who she really was, an angel. 'She's some sort of angel. I'm sure she is.'

'Brilliant.' She was being sarcastic. 'So, you think Veronica is an angel even though she beats you half to death?'

'It's not what I think. It's what I *know*. What I can *see*. There is another world, and I see into it.'

Yes, Gilbert. The Un-conscious.

'It's all about love, isn't it?' he said. 'It's that, isn't it? Is it?'

In relation to Veronica, it seemed a ridiculous suggestion. 'Whatever do you mean, Gilbert?'

'Well, I think the beatings have made Veronica and me fall in love with each other. That's what I feel most strongly when I'm with her: love. It's not just coming from me. It's a two-way force. It's from her too. It's mutual. I have absolutely no doubt about that.'

'Are you telling me in all seriousness that you think a commercial prostitute is in love with you?'

Her incredulity did not deter him. 'I know it sounds absurd, Alyssa, but that's exactly what I'm telling you. With her, for the first time in my life, I don't feel alone with a woman. With her, I am not alone. What more can I say? My most wonderful discovery is that she needs to punish me just as much as I need to be punished. When she is flogging me, when it becomes truly severe, our two existences inexplicably fuse into one. We enter some sort of magic bubble with just the two of us in it. As I've been trying to explain, we create a world that does not exist except for the two of us, a place where there is nobody else. It's our own special place. The magic descends out of nowhere, out of the air above us, like a sphere, and takes us both in. I don't know how to describe it better than that, like a bubble in a fairytale, because that's how it seems at the time. Once we are inside, we rise, and then we float along with sparkles all around us, in a ring of light, perfectly safe. I know it sounds hard to believe, but everything feels right and authentic. Pure, yet incandescent with desire. Nothing can touch us. Nothing. And then, finally, flames. Flames burst through in a giant fireball, melting us. We fuse completely into one.'

'Mm. Sounds to me like sex. Are you sure it's not just that? You and Veronica having great sex?'

'Believe me, it's not sex. Veronica keeps her clothes on, and I certainly don't physically come. I'm in too much pain. But now that you mention it, I suspect that Veronica does.'

'While on the job?'

'Yes. And I'm not just fantasising. What we have between us is way better than the most intense conventional sex imaginable. It's love in its purest form. You have to believe me.'

Incandescent love.

With no consummation, it sounded like a pointless exercise. 'I'm trying to understand. Tell me more.'

He seemed pleased to find that he could discuss such intimate matters without shocking her. 'Look, Alyssa,' he confessed, 'I'm no fool, so I do realise that I'm unwell in some way. But honestly, I do believe that what Veronica and I have *is* love. I've never been as alive as I am with her. Once she's given me my beating, we give each other a good hug. The world seems fresh again, like the air after a rain shower. It's the most thrilling sensation. There seems to be so much space. My mind feels washed clean and I can think again. Everything is back in focus, razor sharp, and I am back to my younger, normal self. It's like my brain has had shock therapy and, at least for a while, I can go on living.'

'I see.'

'You *do* think I'm crazy, don't you?'

'No, Gilbert, not crazy. Just confused. But that's why I'm here. To help you unravel this mess. And the first comment I'd make is that it's hardly likely, is it, that Veronica is getting orgasms. Perhaps you are seeing things in Veronica that aren't really there.'

He fell silent.

'Have I upset you?' she asked after a while.

'Not really, I suppose.'

Clearly, he *was* upset.

'It's just that part of me feels like you are trying to belittle me,' he continued after a while. 'Go ahead. Mock me with your fancy smile and your superior attitude if you want, but I'm proud of what I've achieved all by myself with Veronica. I am!' Then, outburst completed, he held his head in his hands to apologise. 'Yeah, yeah, who am I kidding, right? I'm a total emotional mess and it's about time I faced up to it.'

She tried to be kind to him. 'Don't get me wrong, Gilbert. I accept that your visits to The House of Fantasy in Troy mean a lot to you and that they have been helpful to you in a certain way, so I'm not criticising you for going to Veronica or saying that your needs have no validity. What I am trying to point out is that your behaviour is so abnormal that you can't go on as you are.'

'Right.' He remained morose, probably in the hope that he could indeed end up going on as he was.

She had to insist that he be truthful with her. For example, how could it be that he was as physically resilient as he claimed? Despite the potentially deadly ordeals he described, he invariably got back to work at the High Court within two days.

'How is that possible?'

'It's not that difficult,' was his glib answer. 'My only residual difficulty afterwards, besides the ongoing pain—which at least keeps me awake in court—is an inability to sit properly. So, I say I have a bad back and I stand a lot. Easy.'

At that point, there had seemed two possible responses to what Gilbert had revealed to her so far: either Gilbert was exaggerating or everything that Gilbert said was true.

The trouble was that the recollections about Gilbert Rockport were curiously fuzzy. She had never really decided one way or the other where the real truth lay. And it was too late now to gather any more evidence.

Far too late.

6

How to get the muddled jigsaw in her head that was Gilbert Rockport into some semblance of order: this was the task ahead. Especially in view of the fact that there was more to it than she had mentioned so far; elements not yet examined. Memories of a different flavour.

Memories that began to intrude.

'You look depressed, Alyssa,' Gilbert had said to her. This had been during yet another consultation.

'*Me*? Depressed? You think so?'

'Yes. And what is more, I think I know why. What you are missing is a good whipping of your own. Some punishment for the bad things that *you* have done.'

'What!'

Did he really say that, or was she back dreaming?

'Seriously, Alyssa. You should try it. Don't look at me like that. I'm convinced you'll like it. Then you will understand me better. You should go and get yourself done.'

'Is that so?'

Field research.

'I'm not joking. Go out and get someone professional to do it for you. I can give you some names. I guarantee that a good hiding will make you feel better. Once the pain becomes more than you can bear, you will find yourself transcending your current unsatisfactory existence. You will cease to struggle and instead you will *accept*. The world will cease to be a burden and all your troubles will float away. Provided, of course, that the pain is severe enough.'

She did not like pain, so she did not smile at his pathetic attempt to cheer her up.

He continued to tug her chain: 'Obviously, yes, the pain part is highly unpleasant, especially at the beginning, but it *is* liberating, especially with your pants off. The experience would be eye opening for you and great fun for somebody else too.'

What eye, exactly, are we talking about here?

The reconstructions of the conversations with Gilbert were getting out of hand.

She was not the one with the problem. 'I am not the one with a problem, Gilbert. No, you are the one with the problem.' That made the smile leave his face. 'Very few people share your taste for pain, and I can assure you that I am not one of them.' She had no desire whatsoever to be spanked, not even on her bare bottom.

He looked suitably ashamed of himself for even suggesting such a thing.

'I forgive you, Gilbert. But please bear in mind that even though I remind you of Veronica, I am not Veronica. I am not like her at all.'

I have no need to punish or be punished.

'I don't know what came over me. God, I'm so embarrassed.'

'What do you think women think of people like you, Gilbert?'

'Okay, look, I know I crossed the line.'

'I'm not talking about me. I'm talking about women in general. What do *women* think about your self-obsessed needs once they know about them?'

He looked at first taken aback by the bluntness of her words, but then appeared relieved at the invitation to get the matter off his chest. 'Women? Oh, that?' Despite his general attitude that such things were of little importance to him, he had obviously given the matter some thought in the past because his answer was unusually insightful for a lawyer. 'It might surprise you to hear this, Alyssa, but I'm actually quite good with women. Provided, of course, that I keep my weird side hidden. What I mean is that I like female company and I'm perfectly capable of normal sex—you know, the missionary stuff and all that sort of thing. In normal life I'm not some sort of weirdo, except maybe that I am a bit controlling. Maybe I have a little bit too much of a need to be the one in charge in the bedroom. I've tried, but I can't let go of that, even though I know many women these days find such behaviour in men difficult to tolerate. But not all women, fortunately. It's only when the control equation flips that everything goes haywire for me. If I am to remain normal, I can't allow myself to flip. I need to remain in control at all times.'

Tell me about it.

'Trouble is, it's not possible to pretend forever. The truth catches up with you in the end.'

'What truth, Gilbert? What truth has caught up with you? Focus on that.'

Amazingly, he did. 'If you must know, it's like some sort of force, and it seems finally to have escaped my ability to suppress it. It's forcing me to pay attention to it. It's there.'

'Yes, but what does that *mean*?'

'It means I just know it's there. I don't yet know what it is, but I do know that it's behind all this Veronica business. There's something lurking somewhere underneath in my mind, deep down, in the shadows, waiting. But for *what* I don't really know. Yet it's always there—always just been there—a something. Some truth about me. I've tried my best to ignore it, but instead of fading away it's grown steadily stronger and more insistent. In more recent times, there's been this pressure, always getting stronger, scaring me. It got to the point where I was sure it was going to kill me. That's where I finally realised how deeply in trouble I was. That's when I got saved by Veronica.' He wiped a tear from his eyes.

'But now, fortunately, I have you, Alyssa. You have given me a glimmer of hope. In some mysterious way, you are someone I can truly relate to.'

A kindred spirit.

'You have no idea how much you have helped me. It's so incredibly encouraging to be able to talk to a sexy woman about my issues without having them freak out on me.'

In a sense, he was quite right, she realised. He *was* able to relate to her as a benevolent true "other", and she *was*—or had been—able to reach him and therefore help him. Veronica, too, had been able to reach him, but only in a way that had serious drawbacks and limitations. Veronica was hardly likely to be helpful in the long run. It was only through the prism of humanistic transference-focused psychotherapy, through her counselling skills, that truly beneficial communication was achievable—and had in fact been achieved.

"At last, I have hope".

Gilbert had used those exact words.

He had hope. Except that he was dead.

7

Gilbert Rockport's voice from yet another occasion cut into her thoughts: 'Do you know, Alyssa, I've never been back to my old school in Tabralla. I've just realised this.'

The school was where he had suffered years of physical and sexual abuse.

'Not even once?'

'Not even once.' His voice trailed off.

'And the police? Have you at least reported the brothers?'

'Gone to the police? You must be joking. Think what good that would have done. And think what it would have done for my reputation earlier in my career.'

'You should at least report them now. Besides, strictly speaking there's a statutory requirement on my part to make a report to the authorities if there is any possibility that boys there are still being flogged, especially if it's on their naked buttocks.' Though she hated dealing with the police because of her own negative experiences with them, it was her duty as a registered psychodynamic therapist to cooperate with the law in the fight against child abuse.

'Take it from me, there's no more corporal punishment going on there. That sort of thing is completely banned these days, as you know. However, in this state it's not a requirement to report child molestation if the person reporting it was the victim and is now an adult, and they request it not be reported. Obviously, it's different if they are still underage when you become aware. I can give you chapter and verse if you like. How's that for free legal advice? So, no, I don't want you mentioning my name to anyone.'

'As long as you are sure about this.'

'I am. Don't drag my name into anything. Besides, the brothers *were* reported to the police years ago by other ex-pupils. Two of the worst abusers got locked up for a couple of years, though they are free today as far as I know. The police aren't much use in these matters, Alyssa. I know this only too well through my work. Generally, the cops are just a lazy, prejudiced waste of space. But don't worry, I have decided to deal with this issue now that I am facing up to it. I'm going to bankrupt the school with a civil action. That's been my decision in these last few days. And you'll be pleased to know that I have already set the wheels into motion. They are about to be wiped off the face of the earth. That, I think, will be the most appropriate ending for them.'

She was amazed by the news. And by the sweep of his abilities. 'You're not planning any physical harm to any of the brothers, are you?'

He smiled. 'Me? I'm a tort specialist. I just break people in two financially. What they do to themselves after that, of course, is a different matter.' The smile disappeared without a trace.

Gilbert Rockport was a dangerous man.

'What does your wife Nikki think about the whole abuse situation?'

'Nikki? What has *she* got to do with anything?'

Everything, Gilbert.

'Doesn't your enormous psychological burden affect your relationship with her? What I mean is, doesn't she ever complain that somehow you are not *connecting* with her properly? Psychologically, or spiritually, or however else you want to put it.'

'She complains about it all the time—the things you just mentioned. She keeps saying I'm away in another place. But then so is she, so we get by. We do enough to get by.'

'Have you tried speaking to her about it?'

'I've tried, of course, but she refuses to engage. She doesn't want to think about it. She says spanking does nothing for her and she can't handle the idea of a man being weak. She knows I go somewhere for it, of course, but she has no idea where and certainly doesn't want to know. She accepts it as just one of the things she needs to put up with to be married to me. She knew about it before we got married. We've both been married before.'

'Her sex life doesn't sound ideal.'

'I tolerate a lot from her, too. Financially, she's a real menace. She spends everything she can lay her hands on. Talk about financial incontinence. I hate to have to tell you this, but she was a registered bankrupt when I married her.'

'Nikki? Really?'

'Yes, but don't get me wrong. There's a lot about her that I do love. She's very attractive and cultured, and in many ways she's what I need. And she looks after me pretty well. The money downside to her doesn't worry me unduly. I have life insurance that will look after her welfare, while my business is excluded in the prenup, so the rest doesn't really matter much to me. As far as the beatings are concerned, officially they're okay with Nikki. I'm permitted to occasionally go to Mistress Veronica—provided there's no actual sex involved. That's where she draws the line. Me too, I suppose. Although, I must say I do have to wank a lot afterwards. Am I allowed to say that?'

He was.

'Everyone masturbates, Gilbert. You know that. Even married people.'

'You mean even judges? I've always wondered.'

'You've got it. Especially judges.'

Gilbert had made remarkable progress in his understanding of things sexual. He even had some understanding of fantasies: that they were of a certain type and did not change. Although he might be able to modify his behaviour in the future, his specific sexual wishes would never die.

Fortunately for him—and for all people—they did not have to change. All that had to change was his behaviour. It had taken him forty-six years to work out the obvious.

8

'Yes, I get it. The problem is my behaviour—which is related to my emotional state. I can stay who I am sexually—because I will anyway, no matter what I pretend—but I need to express myself differently, behaviour-wise.'

'Brilliant man.'

Once he had crossed this insight Rubicon, Gilbert quickly appreciated the seismic corollary of his new understanding of himself.

'This will affect Nikki, won't it?'

'Yes.'

It would. Possibly badly.

His old, false behaviour—his life—was going to have to change. Abuse was going to have to be recognised for what it was and managed head on. Among other things in his new future, there was going to be less place for ongoing financial abuse by third wife Nikki.

'Coming to terms with this doesn't necessarily mean a threat to your marriage. With good will and perseverance, you and Nikki should be able to grow together. That will be the key: working together. For the best chance of success, Nikki will need some counselling too.'

Gilbert remained unconvinced. 'Unfortunately, Alyssa, the truth is that Nikki has absolutely zero interest in my true needs. All she wants from me—and ever wanted—is a money tree. To be brutally honest, if I could find someone more suited to the new real me—the person I have now finally come to terms with—I'd be happy to dump Nikki. In future, I'm going to need to be with someone who is more genuine. Someone less inclined to use me. I see that now. I need real love. For the first time, I see it all clearly.'

If there was a point in Gilbert's counselling where things had gone haywire, it was probably right here, towards the end of his sessions with her, just as he was starting to assert himself in preparation for his departure from her and the journey down a new path to sustainable existence. He was only at the beginning of what was going to be a very long road, with much professional assistance required, but the often-lethal combination of the curse of being a middle-aged male and insufficient knowledge of psychology appeared to have caused him to overestimate his decision-making abilities.

Wendy Greene would no doubt be horrified by the speed with which she had deconstructed Gilbert. Good counsellors were not supposed to end up with half-unravelled clients unwisely refusing to heed the dangers ahead. Perhaps she had been lulled into a false sense of security by Gilbert's prodigious intelligence. Or perhaps her own aspirations and pride in her psychological abilities had clouded her judgement.

That said, she had always known that Gilbert was moving ahead at a furious pace in his understanding of himself but had judged this safe in someone like him. The sudden and unexpected development of rash intentions by him towards his wife had come as a complete shock. The unforeseen revelation of her counselling inexperience had been a major wake-up call. Some members of the psychology board—those inclined to the high horse of hindsight—were, without a doubt, going to label her time with Gilbert Rockport as an example of complete therapeutic incompetence.

Unruly behaviour from him had characterised their last ever session together. 'Look, Alyssa,' he had said to her near the end, 'I've finally realised that it's not possible to cure this thing that I have. It's taken me long enough to see the light, I know, but it's all become clear to me. It's a sexual thing—this problem that I have—so it means that I'm pretty well stuck with it forever. It's not just PTSD, so it's not possible for me to get over it. It's so deep in me that it's become part of my identity. Not ideal, I know, but a fact of life, nevertheless. So, I've accepted it. Really, I have. Which means that now I know what needs to be done. The news is that I'm going to go out from here and do what needs to be done.'

'And what is that?' Yes, she had still been a smart alec, still attempted to talk down to him.

But he was no longer accepting guidance from anyone. 'I need to accept myself. Learn to live with myself in a more rational and responsible way. I've been looking at all this LGBTQ stuff that's out there now and I've come to see that I could well be one of them. Maybe. If they will have me. I don't think I'm homosexual or that I've got gender issues, but without a doubt, from a sexual perspective, I'm as queer as fruitcake. I never thought the day would come when I would be happy to say such a thing openly, but there, I've said it. Sexually, I'm queer. I'm a different person to most other people. And I have always felt that way. Deep down, I can't relate to others in a so-called normal way when it comes to sex.'

He had gone too far with his attempt at self-analysis, but how to tell him this without causing damage? Though his insight into himself at that point had in some ways been remarkably brilliant, and even though it was blindingly obvious to anyone else that he was sexually twisted and, in that sense, non-normative, she had her doubts about him being LGBTQ. But his sudden decision-making about himself had not prepared her for what he said next.

'I'm finally over all the childish nonsense about sex. I have no need to be ashamed of what I am through absolutely no fault of my own. There is no need to hide. I can come out. So, Alyssa, this is my plan: I'm going to embrace the bit of mad sexual masochism that's in me and take it as a positive attribute. It will give me my life back. I'll live out my needs openly but keep them sane and just part of my sex life. That will take the heat out of them, so to speak. At last, I know what I need and what I don't need. And, needless to say, the first thing I *don't* need is someone like Nikki.'

All the alarm bells in her head had begun to ring by then. But it was too late.

She had succumbed to the flattery of her own supposed brilliance and created a bull in a china shop.

She had loved the feeling of being a success, but had she ever really had any business messing with the head of the likes of Gilbert Rockport? The ghost of Wendy Greene put the boot in once again: "As a therapist, Alyssa, you know you've blown it when your client jumps the shark".

She had blown it all right.

Normally, she was able to control men—provided they needed her help, and respected her professional skills, and desired her body—but Gilbert had escaped her control. Yes, he still desired her, but he had begun to think he knew best and could now help himself. There was no future in that.

She cast her mind to the *end* of his last visit, back to the last time she spoke to Gilbert Rockport. Shamefully, out of desperation, she had begun pleading with him. 'I know a woman in Box Town,' she had said. 'Someone who is a clinical psychologist. Shirley has a PhD in the treatment of childhood-related post-traumatic stress disorder. She'd be ideal. What is more, I know her, and I know you'll like her. And Box Town is well away from the CBD, so there'll be no prying eyes. It's part of a specialist centre where they cater for *sexual* PTSD too.' EMDR therapy was available there. *Eye Movement Desensitisation & Reprogramming* had the potential to be helpful for all causes of PTSD. 'Pretty please.'

But he had argued against going there, calling the idea laughable. He had no faith in the conventional counselling world and was not for being sent away to some strange woman and being subjected to what he referred to as "futile circular dreck".

Her attempts to offload him were so professionally inept, so pathetic, that he had started to laugh at *her*. 'You look really pretty when you're trying to be serious.'

'This is not a joking matter.'

'I'll think about it.'

'You must stick to the boundaries.'

'Stop panicking. I'm still being a dutiful client, aren't I? I'm even going to discuss things with Nikki, as you've been telling me to do. Fat lot of good that will do, though. She's going to do her nut big time if anything in our relationship changes.'

Do her nut?

She had frowned at him to indicate her disapproval at his use of language.

'Sorry, Alyssa. I apologise. I should not have used the word nut in a nuthouse.'

In the end, Gilbert had started to treat everything at the Donald Clinic as a joke.

Big joke.

He had gotten the better of her, mentally, and become able to see her for what she really was.

Some sort of joke.

Sick joke.

The alarm on her phone woke her.

It was 6.30 am, time to get ready for work. Which meant that she must have been asleep, at least then. She had no way of telling how long she had slept. Not long because definitely she had been awake earlier.

Then she remembered. She wasn't going to work. She had the day off.

She was going to the doctor.

Gilbert was dead.

And she had nothing. No explanation. No clinical notes. No future. All she had was the jumble in her head. Everything she knew about Gilbert existed entirely in her own head. All jumbled up.

What a disaster!

PART VI

BROKEN CHILD

CHAPTER TWENTY-TWO

1

AFTER TWO DAYS OFF work on sick leave following the unexpected death of her client Gilbert Rockport, Alyssa resumed work as a psychodynamic counsellor at the prestigious Donald Clinic. Back in her office, situated in a cottage at the back of the garden of the main clinic building, things were as she had left them. Indeed, on a superficial level, everything at "the Donald" appeared to be the same as before—except perhaps that some members of staff, especially Trish from reception, nurse Gail Wilson from the ward upstairs, the cleaners, and the senior clinical psychologist Greta McCreedy now tended to stare at her with odd looks on their faces.

It seemed everyone at the clinic knew that Gilbert Rockport, the most prominent lawyer in the city, had been seeing her at the cottage. Initially she had found this hard to understand, seeing that supposedly she was the only person who knew it was him. However, it soon became clear that Trish had known all along and was the source of everyone's knowledge. The viewing screen for all the CCTV feeds at the Donald Clinic ran in a console under her counter at front reception. Supposedly, the screen remained covered behind its little locked wooden door unless someone triggered an emergency bell in one of the consulting areas. Trish had been spying on her.

The bloody little sneak!

She should not have expected anything less from Trish—or from any of them. The predictable odd looks aside, however, nothing else was really the same as before either. Deep down, something was fundamentally different. And it had nothing to do with a dead Gilbert or gawking simpletons. It was far more serious than that.

A change had occurred in her head.

Somehow, in the past two days she had lost her grip on some unknown part of her mind. It was something that she could sense but not articulate, yet it was quite clear. The building felt different. Its centre of gravity had shifted. The world had tilted ever so slightly on its axis, and she was no longer the person that she used to be. She knew the signs, and they meant only one thing: danger. She was starting to lose control. Again. And should it continue, the consequences were potentially serious. If she lost control *completely*, she would lose her balance. Then she would fall. She would topple, crash, and burn.

More could die. Would die.

What to do?

Good question. There seemed only one thing for it: try harder.

So, this was what she did. And, aided by good fortune, the plan seemed to work. The four psychiatrists remained sympathetic towards her, and the police, lawyers, and psychology board authorities remained nowhere to be seen. Investigations were doubtless underway behind the scenes, but at the Donald an atmosphere of contrived calm soon settled. It remained obvious, though, that secretly everyone knew that before long every authority in the land was going to be coming for her blood. The fact that she had been eminent QC Rockport's psychotherapist seemed known by truly everyone, though how even those *outside* the clinic knew about it remained a mystery. In time, she was going to be required to make formal statements to the police, to the lawyers, and to her professional board about the dead QC's state of mind prior to his death. More to the point, she was going to be required to provide proof that professional incompetence had not contributed to the unfortunate turn of events.

Which was where her problems were likely to begin.

Furthermore—as if the impending investigations were not enough—she was also going to have to stare down the secret friendship between Cy and Jocelyn that she had uncovered; and cope with Cy's lying too. He could hardly be innocent, even though he continued to deny ever having met up alone with Jocelyn at the flat. He was now claiming that she had become delusional, but she knew when a man was lying. Unfortunately, though, she lacked watertight proof. And Cy, being Cy, cleverly twisted the matter onto its head and was accusing her of hurting *his* feelings. As far as Cy was concerned, nothing improper had happened and he now refused to allow her to speak another word on the subject. Which left her feeling emotionally drained and deflated and unable to confront Jocelyn.

And all the while, Gilbert Rockport remained stubbornly dead.

The tranquillisers she had obtained from the GP during her days off got her through the remainder of that week. Cy was mildly helpful too once he learnt about her potential professional problems in relation to Gilbert's death. He even had the good grace to remove his cannabis plants from the flat, although, in keeping with his new truculence, he refused to tell her where they had gone.

Probably to his friend Brian.

She did not much care anymore, either about him or anything else.

Despite all that, she had at least taken the trouble to have a shower before seeing the GP during the time that she was off sick. Before leaving the flat for that, she had done a final last-minute check in the mirror to reassure herself that she was in a fit state to have someone peer between her legs. She was, despite being not at all well in the head.

Still perfect down below at least.

The doctor, on the other hand, had not seemed to care much about that part of her—or even about her as a person. The female GP's manner was brusque and unsympathetic. After performing a disappointingly perfunctory cervical screening test, she had handed over the requested script for anti-anxiety medication without discussion and with some annoyance and lingering reluctance—and only once all payments for the visit had been completed.

However, the most troubling thing about the two days off work had not been any of that. It had been how Fabio's gym had once again had a bizarre effect on her mind.

2

After the disappointing visit to the uninterested GP in the morning, she had gone to the gym next; to Fabio's. Mainly because she had felt too dispirited to return directly to the flat. There was nothing much for her at the flat seeing that Cy was still away at work. She needed to feel better about herself, and attending the gym usually did the trick. So, yes, she had gone to the gym.

Once there, though, she had once again come over all strange.

She had seen him, even though he wasn't there.

It wasn't an actual hallucination, but she obviously hadn't been well. She could have sworn it *was* him and not just her imagination. Mark. Mark gazing down at her from above while she was doing sit-ups on an inflatable Swiss ball. Undoubtedly, it had been him.

Only, it wasn't. When next she looked up, it was just Fabio. Watching her, as he always did, while she repeatedly leant back over the ball and came up again.

Not for the first time, she had seen something at Fabio's gym that wasn't there.

'Sweating nicely,' said the figure watching over her.

'Fabio? Oh. Hello Fabio.'

'My favourite girl.' He seemed barely able to control his glee.

I'm a woman not a girl.

'Day off? We don't usually see you here during weekday mornings.'

'Yes, day off.' She continued trying to exercise, conscious of how her tights were straining high up against the insides of her thighs.

Fabio did not seem to mind. 'Go further back, Alyssa,' he advised. 'Further. Get right over. Not so much for the stomach, but for the spine.' He supported her shoulders for a moment while she was upright and placed his other hand very low down on her lower back. 'Here. Feel the hand *here.*' The hand was resting on the beginning of her butt crack. 'Always, it is the lower spine that is vital.' Fabio's hand was trembling. 'This is what we must target. There is nothing better for a young lady than a good lower spine.'

With that he wandered off.

'Thank you, Fabio.'

Not.

She remained seated upright on the exercise ball and surveyed the patrons in the gym hall. There was no sign of him. No Dr Mark, surgical trainee. He was not there. She had been imagining things. The reality was that she had not seen him since the fatefully fortuitous meetup across town in the medical library at Olympic Hospital.

For some reason, the fact that he wasn't at the gym despite her initial belief that he *was* there, caused her to feel disappointed in herself.

The only person with any interest in her seemed to be Fabio. Sadly, she had reached a point in life where she half-appreciated *his* attentions, even though he was a creep. At least he had not rejected her.

Even failures at life—like her—needed someone who wanted them.

Later that morning, once undressed in the gym changeroom and with nobody else there, she had stopped briefly in front of a wall mirror before stepping into a shower cubicle. The mirrors were everywhere, one between each of the many windows; in fact, the way tall wall mirrors complemented the tall wall windows could be said to be the main feature of the changeroom. Each towering low-set legacy sash window in the outside wall of the room had an equally impressive wall mirror next to it. The windows themselves had armoured frosted glass and were permanently closed to ensure privacy from the surrounding skyscrapers and proper functioning of the air conditioning.

She studied herself. Were it not for the long scar on her abdomen, would she have had more success with her relationships? she wondered. Would Cy have valued her more? She was not entirely unattractive, but the scar really did spoil her looks. It was such a pity, really.

Suitably depressed, she turned and headed for the nearest shower cubicle, stepping right over one of the changeroom's narrow centre benches in the process—something she would not normally do without any clothes on if others were present. The benches could be annoying at times. Five or six of the low, slatted structures were fixed at regular intervals down the centre of the long room, while the shower cubicles were along the room's inner wall, well away from the mirrors. Often it was easier and quicker to step over a bench—as she had just done—than go around one to get from mirror to shower. Besides, doing so while naked always felt a little wicked.

Following a long hot shower, she began to feel better.

Then, while heading down the three flights of stairs to the street-level lobby below, she decided once again to not go straight home. Cy would be back home by now, and Cy would be in a bad mood. Home had become depressing. Losing herself for a while among the city skyscrapers would be a better option. She liked window shopping, and she liked walking. A good, long walk in the central business district of the city would give her time to think about how to solve her increasing problems.

3

Alyssa adjusted her shoulder bag, which contained her gym clothes, and set off in a westerly direction towards the centre of the CBD and freedom—not East Hubron and Alfonso Street. She still had the rest of the day off work. The best way to use it would be for her to work out how to get her life back on track.

She knew some parts of the city reasonably well, so she decided to make for Fondsdale Street, where there was a tiny but beautiful park surrounded by a fine selection of cafes, brasseries, and patisseries. She could do with some cheering up, and a coffee and a cake would be just the thing. Decision made, she began to move at a good speed, threading through clumps of pedestrians with practiced deftness and enjoying the patches of sunlight as they came and went between the skyscrapers. Above all, she felt encouraged by the power of her body.

She had been walking for perhaps ten minutes when she first began to develop a suspicion that she was being followed. The conviction seemed bizarre given the throngs of people all around her, but she could not shake it off even though she knew it was highly unlikely. There was no reason why anyone would want to tail her. Unless, of course, it was a potential rapist. However, each time she looked behind her she saw no one who looked even remotely suspicious.

Was her sense of alarm nothing more than anxiety getting the better of her once again? She wondered about that. Maybe. Perhaps she should have gone to the pharmacy straight after seeing the GP and obtained her medication there and then, as originally intended.

Am I losing the plot?

However, her sixth sense was seldom wrong, so maybe she was not imagining things after all. Maybe a potential rapist did indeed have his sights on her. Such a thing *was* possible. She knew she needed to remain vigilant.

Rape frightened her more than most for good reason. The reason, however, was not something to dwell upon right now. Instead, she kept walking at speed, trying to work out what to do. That seemed the best approach.

Escape. The story of my life.

That strange thought—or was it an insight—flitted through her mind, but then it went right out again for good reason: constantly running away implied a need to turn and confront. But confrontation was out of the question for her because there was a high chance that she would emerge as the loser. And then she would die.

As she finally turned the corner into Fondsdale Street, her destination, Alyssa saw a potential solution to the increasingly distressing certainty that she was about to be raped. Ahead was the church where years earlier, when first in Hubron, she had once attended on and off. It was how she knew the area. More to the point, she knew the layout of the church. Here, she could disappear.

After yet another glance over her shoulder to confirm that nobody else had yet turned the corner into the street, she swiftly opened the church's ancient wrought iron pedestrian gate, slipped through, closed it, and hid behind one of the nearby buttressing pillars of the church building. If she remained there for a few minutes anyone following her would not be able to see what had become of her.

The church grounds were dead quiet, which was understandable seeing that it was the middle of the day and a weekday, and the church's main gates were shut. No one approached, so after a while she began to relax.

Emotionally, she was in a bad way, and she knew it. Not only was she seeing people at the gym who simply were not there, she was also running away from imaginary rapists. She could not go on as she was. Something had to change. She had to do something. She wished she had someone to advise her, someone to at least discuss things with—a real mother for example. She knew it was futile to wish for her mother back, given what had happened, but she could not help having such thoughts. She needed Grace. Had Grace lived, she would no doubt have been someone she could trust.

Grace was dead, however, very dead—cut in half, in fact—so nothing could change that. Excluding real mothers, the next best person to talk to would have been Wendy Greene. Wendy had been a wonderful surrogate mother to her, but sadly Wendy was no longer a possibility. She was no longer her training advisor and there were rules about such things. Training was over. The regulations forbade further contact even as a friend. Wendy had many other trainees and Wendy could not be "mother to the whole fucking world"—as Wendy herself had once explained. So, no mother and no Wendy. In fact, no one of the female variety. Nobody close. Nobody whom she could trust. Not even Jocelyn, who was now, it seemed, kiddie-fiddling with Cy. Jocelyn had always seemed to her a bit of a sneak anyway. And as for previous acquaintances and ex-colleagues from the Public Hospital, they were of no use either. Essentially, they were all complete idiots. There was nobody she could trust—not even Cy. Realistically, she was on her own.

While hiding behind a pillar of the church, Alyssa realised that it—and the entire church—was made with stone remarkably similar to that used in the back wall of her cottage at the clinic. The church and parts of her mental health clinic were built of the same stuff, both about 150 years ago. Yet somehow the clinic had secured for itself heritage building status and the church obviously not. In contrast to the Donald, the Fondsdale Street church looked sad, tired, consumed, dying, fading into bankruptcy. No doubt it too had once had a garden, though there was no longer any sign of one. The entire surrounds consisted of a sea of cobblestones to facilitate car parking at service times. Apart from the lost garden, there would also once have been a graveyard, but even that was no longer there. The church she was sheltering behind had lost every bit of humanity it had ever had.

Worse still, impossibly tall business towers squeezed on every side, as though intent on burying the ancient aberration for good. And yet, as it mouldered away in the bleak remains of its yard, the dogged church appeared to her to be dozing peacefully even as it crumbled, as though indifferent to its impending doom.

4

Alyssa felt a little sorry for the church. Bizarrely, she quite liked churches—the buildings at least—even though most people seemed to see them as little more than hellish relics of a brutish and superstitious past, symbols not of good but of evil. And not in the past only. According to Cy, the few churches that remained were *still* hotbeds of theological jingoism and rife with completely intolerable levels of misogyny, homophobia, lies, greed, child abuse, censorship, racism, genocide, torture, war, homicide, animal abuse, fanaticism, corporal punishment, heartlessness, planetary abuse, and the rest—there were at least ten more horrors that had escaped her, but which Cy could name with ease.

Maybe the church *was* best forgotten about. She peered out from behind its pillar. It seemed safe to return to the world. The little greenspace park she had in mind for coffee and cake was only another three hundred metres or so further along. Yet, for some reason she hesitated. The ancient building where she had once attended for a few services felt strangely like an old friend—and she had precious few of those. None, in fact. Besides, just being there again made her curious about what had become of the place. As a child, through innocent eyes, her experience of church had been good. Perhaps, if she could find her way inside, she would be able to collect her thoughts in a helpful way. At least it would be more private than a coffee shop. The closed main doors at the front of the church would be locked at this time of day. However, she had attended there often enough in the past to recall that there was a small door around the back for visiting parishioners. It was unlikely to be locked except at night. With luck, she would be able to get in and take a seat inside once again.

She tried to remember what had caused her to stop attending there in the past but couldn't think of anything specific. After all, she had stopped attending at *every* church she had tried since attempting for the first time—during second year at university—to resume churchgoing after her father's death seven years earlier. She had tried many different places in the city without success. Usually, she gave up after only a few weeks. And almost always it was because she found that she had nothing in common with the parishioners who were there. Invariably, she found them too wilfully gullible, too ridiculously superstitious, too offensively vindictive, too intolerably self-righteous, or too obviously nothing more than social club attendees. There was nothing commendable about claiming certainty on matters that were, in fact, not certain, neither was there anything morally superior about believing in one's own moral supremacy.

So, why, she wondered, was she thinking of revisiting the church in front of her instead of heading straight out the gate? Maybe it was because she knew she needed help and did not know where else to turn. Her career, and her mind, and her relationship with Cy were under attack. As a little girl she had loved going to church with her father. She had felt love there. She did not need reason to get in the way. Not now. That could come later. What she needed now was comfort, no matter how irrational.

With her mind made up, Alyssa hoisted her gym bag over her shoulder and made for the door at the back of the church, conscious of the fact that she was now visible from the street. After only a few steps out in the open, the uncanny sensation that somebody was watching her—not people in general but a single individual—returned. Frighteningly, the sixth sense became so strong that she felt compelled to glance repeatedly over both shoulders for signs of danger. There was nothing to see that looked suspicious. Nobody was loitering at the railings on the street, the pedestrian gate remained shut, and the vehicular gate remained padlocked. Grimly, she pressed on towards the rear of the building. It was not the first time that she feared being attacked by a rapist, and it would not be the last. The fear of it was tied up with her general anxiety state. She needed to take control. 'No one is watching me, okay!'

Except about a million people up in those skyscrapers.

It occurred to her then that being at the church was making things worse—that a lot of her fear had something to do with churches. Being back at one was bringing something to a head in her mind, dragging something closer to conscious awareness. Maybe, she thought, without her realising it at the time, her decision to head for Fondsdale Steet had always been about the fact that she knew that there was a church there. Maybe she was forcing herself to confront some truth that was related in some way to churchgoing. After all, she had spent enough time in church as a child. But, if so, *what* truth was she trying to confront?

There had to be something to this latest insight because the compulsion to linger felt really strong. Something unconscious in her mind was demanding answers from a place where it knew answers lay. For example: had her real mother, Grace, been to church with her when she was a small child? She had absolutely no conscious memory of that. The attendances with her father, on the other hand, she remembered well from when she was older. Bob Brown used to think it of critical importance that his daughter attended regularly with him. She did remember that—though by now even those memories seemed vague.

She couldn't remember *why* he had thought going to church was so important. After all, he was certainly no Christian. Not considering what he constantly tried to do to her later in life. So, why the church? The understanding of that—of Bob Brown's *why*—still eluded her. More information of a conscious nature was required.

Perhaps by entering an empty church and absorbing its atmosphere without distraction—by jogging her unconscious, as it were—she would succeed in gaining further clarity about the lost early years. The later memories of church—once Diana had arrived on the scene—were clear by contrast. The new mother never attended—she refused right from the start—and her brothers had stopped soon after. For many years—right up until the car accident when she was thirteen—it had been just her and her father off to church each Sunday. That part, too, she remembered perfectly well, especially the pride she had felt at the beginning. Towards the end, of course, Bob had ruined it all by becoming an overt alcoholic and going to church in a drunken state. And then, of course, the drunken molestations in the car on the way home after church services had begun. She had no doubts or difficulties with *those* memories at all. Just the early ones.

Why had her father always gone to church and always taken her with him?

What exactly *had* happened in the time before clear memory; in the time when she was too young to remember? What indeed. She needed to find out. Somehow, she was beginning to understand that unless she uncovered the truth about her, Bob, and the church, there was going to be little prospect that she would ever be able to be a well person.

5

The visiting parishioners' door was set in a recess near the back of the church and was sturdy, narrow, and armoured against vagrants. Camouflaged with a paint job the same colour as the surrounding stonework, the door was indeed unlocked, though it did require a hefty push from her to make it budge. From what she could determine, the weighty door had sagged in its frame over time and become partially jammed. Once inside, she closed the door carefully behind her, lifting it by its doorknob to make it latch.

She was in some sort of office and there was no sign of life. She felt greatly pleased with herself. The rest of the church was now accessible. She stood still for a few minutes to get her bearings.

With the heavy outside door closed, it was eerily quiet even though she was in the centre of the city. Also, despite a lack of any visible air conditioning system, the air was pleasantly cool compared to the late summer heat outside. It felt like she was in a surrealistic oasis, a refuge from reality. But a sad one. The surroundings looked tired, the furnishings speaking of advanced age and impending bankruptcy. Given the unlocked door to outside, the most surprising feature of all was that the office had not yet been trashed by vagrants. She peeked out of the room's only inner door and discovered that it opened directly into the church proper, in front of the altar but behind the pulpit and communion rail. There was nobody out there either. As far as she could tell, she had the entire building to herself. She took a final look around the office. There was a single solid-looking wooden desk, a few wooden chairs, a stack of what looked like room dividers in storage in one corner, a bookshelf full of dated popular books on how to believe better or be a better person, and, on the wall above the bookshelf, a faded exhortation on a banner:

Seeing Jesus
None can lift the Gate to Glory but One.
Yet the Glory of God,
Inexpressible except in tears,
Only to the lost does Jesus show.
For see, that crown upon Christ Jesus' head,
See, it is a crown of thorns
And know that as God,
In His great Glory,
Only to the lost will Jesus ever show.

She wondered what Cy would think of the poetry. It looked amateurish to her, and pretty morbid too. Who would have written it, she wondered, and when? Someone from a bygone era, no doubt. There was not much else to see in the room. She examined the storage pile. The wooden sightscreens, probably once used in now extinct Sunday school classes, looked like antiques. Her father had known a lot about antiques. She lifted the top one to feel the weight of the wood as a test of its age—like he used to do—but part of it came away in her hand.

'Oh shit,' she said out loud. She had managed to dislodge what looked like an already damaged crosspiece support, about half a metre long. It was the brace between two bottom feet of the screen and one end had obviously broken off in the past. The dislodged brace felt heavy, a valuable hardwood just as she had suspected. She tried to return it to its position, but no matter how hard she tried she could not get it to stay in place.

'Mm.' It was time to get out of the crumbling office before anything else broke. The broken piece of wood, though, she decided to keep with her until she left the building later. If she happened to come across any members of staff, she would be able to show it to them and apologise. The solid piece of timber would also be useful as a weapon should an interloper attempt to interfere with her.

With her gym bag over her shoulder and a weapon in her hand, Alyssa went through the inner door of the office and out into the church proper. There, she tiptoed respectfully past the altar, and took the two steps down into the nave. About halfway down the centre aisle, she selected a pew and sat down.

The fact that she had now, however temporarily, become a pew Christian—a type of person she so easily dismissed as misguided—was not lost on her. Still, she had found a quiet place where she could focus on re-gathering herself, so she continued to feel quite pleased with herself. She waved her improvised club around to get a feel for it. If there *was* a malevolent interloper lurking around watching her, he would certainly get more than he bargained for. There was nothing like an unexpected blow to the genitals from a heavy piece of wood to discourage unchristian intentions.

Whack!

Big surprise.

6

It was time to work out how best to approach the coming fallout from Gilbert dying under her care and think about how best to repair the crumbling relationship with Cy. Alyssa closed her eyes and tried to concentrate. Within a few minutes, however, so many competing thoughts and ideas clamoured for attention that it felt like her head was going to spin on her shoulders like in a cartoon. Who was she kidding? she asked herself, holding her head in her hands. She was never going to be able to work her way through the muddle that was her life.

Familiar feelings of panic returned with a vengeance. Always, it was the same: the deep sense of despair whenever she tried to think about herself. Her stepmother had been the first to point out the problem when she was a child. Diana's opinion of her mental ability had been damning: the stepchild called Alyssa was too degenerate to grasp the implications of her actions and too stupid for complex thought. Case closed.

Only later, at university, had she discovered the treachery and sickness behind her stepmother's words. There was nothing wrong with her brain, and there never had been. Many at university admired her intelligence. The damnations in childhood were nothing more than products of Diana's *own* sickness. Her stepmother had been determined to make her stepchildren ill. And unfortunately, as was becoming increasingly clear, in that, she had partly succeeded. Evil had a way of succeeding. When pressure was applied, behold, stepdaughter Alyssa had trouble thinking.

I can't think properly at the moment. I just can't.

Maybe she was indeed some sort of degenerate. Perhaps she *was* stupid. After all, there was good evidence for this in the way she had mishandled Gilbert. It had been incredibly foolish of her to get involved with him. Diana had been right about her all along: she could not think properly. It explained a lot, including her real mother's death and the death of her father. And maybe the deaths would not end with Gilbert. Maybe, when all was said and done, the deaths of those near to her would never end—as some past therapists had claimed. Maybe she would always be a menace to society.

But what if that was just a lie? After all, Diana was nothing *but* lies. How much of what the woman said was true and how much of it just a lie? How could anyone know?

How can I know?

Nobody she knew could be trusted to tell her the truth about anything.

She had no choice but to try to make progress in life entirely on her own strength, weighed down by the terrible certainty that if this failed then there was nothing. Just complete mental disintegration. Yet, to keep on functioning, the only things she had on her side were a good body, and a licence to practice as a counsellor. That was it. All she had.

Becoming a counsellor did not seem to have done much good, though. To judge from the way in which she had botched Gilbert's therapy, she obviously understood almost nothing about counselling. Yet, how could things have gone so wrong with him when she had tried so hard? She even knew large sections of Obermaaier's textbook off by heart.

To prove the point to herself, she sat and recited *"Preamble to the Self"* to herself, off by heart—surely a prodigious intellectual achievement by any measure.

Self-awareness—or more correctly, *the declarative mind, conscious and Un-conscious*—is nothing more than a neurological computation and but a small sub-function of the brain, occupying less than ten per cent of its processing time. It (awareness of Self) has no purpose other than to provide a survival advantage by assisting the human physical host to cope with "meaning" changes in the environment (as opposed to unambiguous physical changes). Such an "awareness of the bigger picture" mandates in the first instance a consciousness of Self as reference point. It is this Self-reference that enables the brain to better decide what any ambiguous change in the environment might mean in relation to ongoing physical existence. Current sensory input is referenced against "beliefs" stored in the summary of existence to date (i.e., the Self).

Relevant incoming data is processed in the form of verbalised discussion with the Self (one talks to oneself). Thus: *What do I think of this? What should I do now?* The "Me" talks to the "Self", mostly in word thought but not always in this way e.g., during input from the Un-conscious elements of the Self.

Note the special nature of the Un-conscious part of the aware mind function of the brain: contrary to popular perception, the Un-conscious mind cannot normally be accessed except through special techniques, even though it is declarative and not vegetative. The reason for this is that the Un-conscious mind is the computational rule-setting domain for consciousness. To avoid confusion, the data processing rules appropriate to the environment existing around any particular mind during its formative years are finalised and then "lost" during early childhood.

Note further that repetitive tasks, such as driving a car, which seem un-conscious, *are* still conscious in that they can readily be made so with concentration. The "tasking" mind is not part of the Un-conscious mind. Note also that most brain-controlled *bodily functions* are unconscious in a non-declarative way. Though these are often referred to as "unconscious" functions by others, in our discipline we use the term "vegetative" function. When talking about the unconscious, the Un-conscious mind is not to be confused with either the supposedly "unconscious" repetitive task mind or the never-declarative vegetative mind.

Note furthermore that the neurological computations required for Self-awareness are many terabytes in size and note also that the aware Self does not "exist" other than mathematically, so it cannot be physically "found". The brain—which *can* be fully found and elucidated—is not the same thing as the Self.

The only way any "Self" can "understand" his or her own Self is by means of congruence with the "Self" of another mind. Congruence is what draws us OUT of ourselves, e.g., as in interpersonal love, hate, language, etc. Congruence is how I know you. The more I know Self, the more I know You, and the more I know You, the more I know Self. With perseverance, in the suitably gifted, there comes CERTAINTY that there exists in all humanity a basic and universal Self, a universal Self that CAN be known.

We, the few, in the tradition of Freud (even though modern psychodynamic therapists see the many blind spots in Freud's mind), find the human Self a most deceiving, treacherous, and dangerous thing. And, of course, from the dawn of history onwards, humanity has always known this to be the case simply by gut feeling: we the people have never doubted for even a minute that people are extremely lethal, intemperate creatures.

We need only look to the "Fall of Adam" myth and "Total Depravity" theology for evidence of such misgivings.

Is there any hope for improved behaviour? Not much, given the slowness of biology. Does anything MEAN anything? Not really. In the bigger scheme of things, nothing MEANS anything. Meaning is a relative concept in that it depends on choice. Each aware Self *chooses* what he or she believes anything to Mean. The sense of Meaning is nothing more than a mandatory outcome for the small sub-function of the brain assigned to the task of Self-awareness. There is no Self-awareness without a simultaneous sense of Meaning—and vice versa.

Does this mean that we should despair? Of course not. For existential peace of mind, all that an individual Self needs to do (and does, in fact, do) is engage his or her mind on the issue of ultimate Meaning and arrive at a solution that best aligns his or her specific Self-identity with the afterlife options offered by his or her specific environment. Furthermore, given that all "Meaning" is entirely Self-defined and personal, all attempts to force "final solutions" onto others need to be resisted, for obvious reasons.

Obermaaier's ideas were certainly impressive. Yet, reminding herself of them and of her ability to memorise them did not now seem all that helpful in resolving the anxiety she continued to feel.

Her heart was racing.

Something more practical was required. Besides, what *was* life all about, anyway? Was Obermaaier really correct to assert that nothing amounted to anything? More to the point, what was *she* all about? Nothing? But if not that, then what? Who was she? What was she? A sheep or a wolf in sheep's clothing?

Was she the food of wolves or the wolf itself?

She could not tell. No wonder she felt anxious.

7

Alyssa realised that she would need to resort once again to mindfulness to push her anxiety back down to a tolerable level. However, resorting to the technique made her feel guilty, as it always did. Both Obermaaier and Wendy Greene were against it. Obermaaier believed that mindfulness was nothing but "a prime example of that very large class of fruitless circular activities inflicted upon hapless clients by clown psychologists". And Wendy Greene refused to use the technique on her own clients, believing it to be just another way of avoiding the real issues. "It's just a form of temporary symptom suppression, Alyssa, not a long-term cure for anything". By contrast, the tutor in her course on mindfulness—not Wendy—had believed it to be a "sure-fire way for the client to become fully in the present and restore control". Whatever the truth, mindfulness usually helped with controlling anxiety attacks in her case.

Alone in a deserted and bankrupt church at midday, with anxiety threatening to overwhelm, mindfulness seemed the only realistic option. Alyssa did her best to focus on her body as required and establish the correct, slow breathing pattern—seven seconds in and eleven seconds out. The air was cool, the pew she was sitting on was hard, and surrounding her was silence. As she took all this in, her body, always powerful, began to feel extra powerful, no doubt aided by the recent visit to the gym and brisk walk to the city centre. Physically, she had always been an extremely healthy person—which was a blessing not often enough appreciated. She became aware of her breasts as she breathed—such fine breasts—and aware also of the movement of the air through her lungs and nose. The breathing felt effortless, as though her air passages were made of crystal, or Teflon, or something equally marvellous. Sitting, too, felt restful, if a little cool. Her bottom could hardly be faulted. Yet, as heavenly as her body was, it had two major flaws. One, really—the breastbone to pubic bone scar was just a vanity issue. The truly serious flaw was her head. Sadly, it was well and truly broken.

Best to face up to reality.

That said, under the influence of mindfulness the clamour in her head did slowly die down.

However, instead of nothingness rising to fill the empty space in her mind, as was supposed to happen, a growing awareness of sacredness seeped instead into the vacuum she was trying to create.

It was the church doing it to her. She wondered why. The place where she was sitting was nothing more than a corpse waiting to be buried.

The Fondsdale Street church was not long for this world. Yet, curiously, and unexpectedly, she began to perceive that around her lay a spiritual dimension. She tried to resist the fanciful drift of her mind but failed. What if there was more to the universe than just the four known dimensions (including time)? It was an important question because sometimes—like now—she could swear that she detected something more; more than what was known for sure. What if there *was* a fifth dimension? Maybe it was here that a spiritual aspect to life existed. Or, if that was too far-fetched, then maybe the Un-conscious part of the neurological cyberspace computation known as the mind *acted* like an extra dimension to existence. A fifth dimension could just as well be psychological as spiritual. Unless of course, in an extra-weird sense, the spirit world dimension *was* psychological, hidden in plain sight in the Unconscious mind.

The concept of spirits was very confusing. Alyssa tried to keep her mind focused on her physical surroundings in the church, but in the distance, beyond the communion rail and pulpit, a small silver crucifix on the altar twinkled distractingly in sunlight. She tried not to look at it and looked higher instead, at the semicircle of narrow stained-glass windows above the curved rear wall of the sanctuary, where the light was streaming in. The view, classically religious, was strangely comforting. It was as though she were once again a small child.

What do I really believe about all of this?

There was only one thing that she *was* sure of, and that was that she was not sure what she believed—though paradoxically she knew that she was not a non-believer in God. She knew she held some beliefs which, though impossible to justify logically, she found impossible to abandon. She had never been able to take the final step and become a *complete* non-believer in the possibility of God. Atheism had always remained, for her, a step too far. While non-believers might believe in anything but God, she was not yet willing to believe in *them*.

She knew, though, that those without religion showed no evidence of being any the worse off for not having it. Being a good person had nothing at all to do with being a believer in God. Anyone who had completed Psychology 101 knew at least that much. Atheists were no more or less wicked than anyone else and did perfectly well in life—albeit not without still having illogical beliefs of other sorts.

She felt a headache coming on.

Even though she had often thought about what she believed, she had never felt a compulsion to make a final decision. However, it seemed important now, alone in an empty church, to reach a conclusion.

She thought of Ben Clayton and his hatred of the religionist bureaucrats of the institutional churches. Like Ben, she too had no desire to support religionists and go around misrepresenting Jesus and insulting him daily. She would not be able to bring herself to believe in conventional religion. As far as she had been able to determine, its four pillars consisted of hypocrisy, bureaucracy, factual lies, and greed. Also, there was too much in church history that was truly horrible. While she might feel at home and at peace sitting in a crumbling church, she would never be able to descend to the level required for actual membership, namely gullible piety.

What she wanted, and what she missed, was the Jesus she had known at Sunday school as a child. Her Jesus from then had said that people should be honest about everything, especially themselves, and care about others. She *had* believed in *that* Jesus. On the other hand, the canons of organised religion, those products of the nightmares of sociopaths and psychopaths, did nothing for her. Perhaps, therefore, now that she was an adult, atheism was indeed the answer. If religion *was* merely man-made, then becoming an atheist would cure her seemingly endless mental anguish over the matter.

She closed her eyes and tried to take the required mental steps to life as an atheist. But then she realised it was a lost cause and gave up. She would never be able to embrace atheism wholeheartedly. The lines of an unofficial, rude verse came back to her from her Sunday school days: *Song of the Atheist*. She had had friends back then, at Sunday school, children who used to sing it, innocently, but with enthusiastic sarcasm. And she had joined in:

Here I come
Your atheist chum
I'll show the world my bum
It's where the sun shines from

The dirty ditty may have been just a bit of jingoistic childhood fun, but its message was clear: the idea that the world revolved around oneself was distasteful to others because on a cosmic scale the claim was patently ridiculous. Try as she might, she was unable to let go of the idea that there was *something* to life. Some inner part of her refused to allow that little spark of something that had been kindled in her childhood to die. She *wanted* there to be a greater good. She *wanted* there to be consequences for evil.

Her favourite teacher at Sunday school, Mr Johnson the used car salesman, once explained how *he* thought it all worked. According to him, there existed a spiritual dimension to the cosmos, a dimension knowable only through one's own spirit, but not intellectually. In this mode of existence, known as the Spirit, one persisted eternally. What was more, within this dimension existed a universal law, like gravity, to the effect that every act of evil done in the mortal dimensions stayed spiritually attached to the perpetrator, affected the cosmos negatively, and had spirit world consequences. The ideas of Mr Johnson had seemed plausible to her as a young child, although she had been too frightened—given her own extreme wickedness—to ask how, in that case, forgiveness by Jesus worked. Once an adult, she had of course realised that such teachings about the spirit world had been unofficial and no more than fanciful nonsense.

8

The absurd thing was that now, sitting in a church by herself, she found it impossible to reject a sneaking conviction that an extra dimension to the universe might just be a possibility after all. In which case, solving the problem of belief boiled down to whether she accepted or rejected the conclusion of most advanced people today, which was that any so-called spiritual dimension resided only in the Un-conscious mind and amounted to nothing more than a lost aspect of one's own childhood.

Which meant that whether she believed in a real external God or not amounted to deciding on whether the spirit world was merely an echo of early childhood or was something entirely different, something external and real.

God was a decision.

One had to *decide*.

Which seemed crazy.

And yet she had to believe *something* because otherwise she was going to go mad.

How crazy is that!

Fortunately, Obermaaier had it all fully explained. According to him, one had no option but to have a truth to believe in. Everyone always believed in something. The *Ultimate Truth* rule applied even to non-believers in theology. They still believed in something. They still sought to be part of a greater truth in the same way that the formally religious did. Fortunately, heaven-like premonitions and helpful ultimate hopes were obtainable in *many* spiritual ways. Transcendence, i.e., the experience of a higher presence, was a state of mind that was available no matter what one believed in. Moving up to this higher plane was instinctive and relatively easy to achieve. Explained psychologically, all that a practitioner of transcendence needed to do was make a connection with the unspeaking existence of early childhood, conceptualised as the "Greater Whole".

There were *many* ways to connect to the Greater Whole. Stock-in-trade favourites included zoning out to music (seen also in churches) and communing with Nature. These connecting modes—"Through Music I Touch Eternity" and "Nature is My Religion"—were extremely widespread. All varieties of unconscious memory of early childhood—all of them suffused with similar levels of blind certainty, flawed logic, glorious awe, and lack of words—had the ability to supply heaven. Heaven existed in one's head. And, most importantly, it existed in a largely preverbal space inaccessible to cognition. Heaven could only be reached through emotional resonance with the Greater Whole—in other words, through the "spirit" because the other name for the Universal You/Us was the *spirit*.

And Obermaaier had more on the subject too. According to him, the *only* way to find *any* god was through the spirit. God could not be reached by reason. The soaring of the spirit required a relinquishing of adult control and a yielding to primitive sensations—such as smell, and touch, and rhythm. Certainly, the existence of God could not be proved using reason—despite the misguided apologetics and grotesque logic fraud of innumerable misguided religionists who claimed not only that they could "prove" that God existed but also that they knew God's exact specifications. They even knew that He was in agreement with their own wishes, not realising that this turned God into an Ultimate Personal Servant and was an absurdity that consigned Him to zero cosmic meaning.

Thinking about God could not solve anything because one could never *know* Him in this way. God could only be known by being *experienced* in the spirit.

Alyssa held her head in her hands, close to despair. Ever since encountering the disturbing ideas of Benjamin Clayton during his therapy sessions, she had become more unsettled than ever about religion. Discussions over Ben's proposed book *The Rape of the Name of Jesus by the Religionists* always left her feeling uneasy. The title seemed to her disrespectful. It had surprised her how much it hurt whenever Ben talked about Jesus in that way. She knew what rape was. She realised then that she had an emotional bond with Jesus. She had never grasped how deep it ran.

She noticed that she was trembling.

What is that all about?

She was hardly a Jesus freak.

And, anyway, officially Ben was mad.

She was avoiding the issue. She knew she was. Could she place her trust in Jesus? Could she *believe* in Him; believe that everyone deserved a chance; believe that everyone was *equally* human?

The scars on her head felt tender to the touch, but she fought the distraction. She was determined to settle the matter. What exactly had Obermaaier said on the subject of Jesus? She tried to recall the famous so-called "Obermaaier Jesus" in as much detail as possible:

As we have seen earlier, God is nothing more than a transmuted parent figure from unconscious childhood that is collectively experienced by a social group. Furthermore, ANY transcendent spiritual figure emanating from the collective Un-conscious of ANY social group is infinitely precious. ALL gods are god-like to their believers. It is precisely through this tortuous mental mechanism that humanity comforts itself, reminds itself that all are in this life together, and keeps itself safe from others.

A figure like Jesus is significant in that he represents the prototype of the modern revision of humanity's "God experience". Seen for the first time in Jesus is transmutation of the unconscious aspirational *Self* (as opposed to the primitive parent). Representing a breakthrough in human mental development, Jesus embodies the endlessly wounded beating heart of the emerging universal *child*. With Jesus specifically, in a God-equalling way the unconscious *Self*-transmutation paradoxically enables the matured adult to be "saved" *from* the older, more primitive, ogre-like versions of God (i.e., the unconscious parent). The Self has freed itself from oppression by the unconscious Parent through feeling assured of the God-equalling power of Jesus. In certain mentally advanced societies, Jesus succeeds in becoming the word of God himself.

What it meant, of course, was that Obermaaiers's Jesus was just another mental mechanism, albeit an advanced one. But could Obermaaier be trusted when it came to religion? Alyssa felt her sadness increasing. She had no one, really, in the whole world, that she truly trusted. All she had was ideas about psychology—and now, somehow, they felt as empty and as silly as she suspected that she herself was. Gilbert was dead. There was a high probability that her career as a counselling psychologist was over. She would probably lose everything. There seemed little doubt, she told herself, that she was an even bigger fool than she sometimes feared she was.

It was entirely conceivable that she was confused about *everything*. Not only about Gilbert and PTSD, but about Ellen Goodman and insomnia, and about Ben Clayton and religion. Why, otherwise, she wondered, was Gilbert dead, and she unable to sleep? And why was she in agreement with many of the religious views of a certified psychotic? *Was* she, after all, too stupid to think properly? Was she indeed a worthless piece of shit, as her stepmother had always insisted? Was there something about life and about people that she failed to grasp?

9

Alyssa continued to hold her head in her hands. She could not work out what she truly believed about God. It appeared to be above her mental capacity. The earnest Mr Johnson from Sunday school, the man who had assured her that there was no truth greater than Jesus, would have been greatly disappointed. He had had no difficulty in resolving the matter.

There is nothing greater and there is nothing more than Jesus.

Mr Johnson had assured her that when she was older, she would come to know this; that it would become clear to her in a spiritual way.

Yet it hadn't. She had failed in even that.

She had no problem with her Sunday school Jesus, but she did have a problem with the versions of Jesus that were being proclaimed to adults in churches. The philosopher Nietzsche expressed the hindrance of the churches well: "Show me your redeemed and I will believe in your Redeemer". Nietzsche had a point. Hypocrites had gained control. Those in control of the established churches had long ago lost contact with their redeemer.

Her good version of Jesus had ended, however, with the accident that killed her father, and she had not gone back. Not with her father dead, the subsequent suspicions, the police accusations, and a disinterested stepmother. She had not attempted to return to any church at all, in fact, until the move to independent life in the city.

She felt her headache getting worse. Gilbert's death seemed to be having a powerful effect on her, much more so than was healthy or normal. There had been so much death in her life that her mind felt in danger of collapsing under the strain. Was she harmful to everyone who came near her? she wondered. Her own life was one big lie—that much, at least, she knew—but was *everything* a lie? The pain in her head increased to the point where every one of the old scars on her scalp was throbbing. Her skull had once been badly fractured, but something more was wrong. Something was trying to take control of her—just like before. The breakdown at university during sociology had been terrifying, and she knew it could happen again. She had a weakness. And it was here again, deep down. She could sense it, the *presence*. The presence of evil. It frightened her, this darkness in her. It was trying to emerge once again. It was something unholy, and it had always been with her, ever since she could remember.

She tried to pull herself together. She had to stay rational. She wondered if the way she was feeling was just an aura, a sign that she might be about to have another of her epileptic fits. It was possible, but she doubted it. The fits had ceased long ago, within a few years of her head injury. She had not had one since. And even then, during the time of the fits, the sense of foreboding had not been as bad as it was now. What was happening was no aura.

Her hands would not stop shaking. She tried to calm them by sitting on them. More than ever, she needed help. Yet she had no one to turn to.

The joke was that she knew how to be saved by Jesus. Sunday school had taught her well. All she had to do was say certain words truthfully:

I *know* you are Alive, and I *know* who you Are.

But did she really know any such thing?

One had to be telling the truth.

Taking a deep breath, she said the words from Sunday school anyway.

But afterwards, she felt no different.

Perplexed, she looked up at the image of Christ the Redeemer featured in the centre of the stained-glass window above and behind the altar, arms outstretched and crowned with thorns. She tried to make sense of the reverence she always felt when contemplating the age-old portrayal. The sense of awe seemed unusually present; very strong. Christ's arms seemed meant for her.

Silently and softly, the familiar sacred image radiated transmitted sunlight over her and over the interior of the church, as it had done during the whole time she had been there. The effect was strangely comforting, as though proof that the cosmos powered on despite her troubles. From girlhood, she knew that God lived in unapproachable light, and that this light burned the eyes of non-believers but not believers. Her eyes were not burning, so, childishly encouraged, she kept on looking.

Slowly, the cascade of gentle light diffusing through the Christ image began to coalesce, much like light through a magnifying glass coming together in a focused beam. The evolving effect fascinated her. The light grew stronger until, finally, visible sunbeams appeared in the dusty atmosphere of the church, like solid rays on a flag, somehow taking on weight and power. Part of her knew that the wonderful effect was merely the result of the shift in the angle of the sun as it moved across the sky behind the stained-glass window, but she felt overawed by the coincidence of it and unable to divert her eyes.

The majesty of the image of Christ before her continued to grow. Such a thing had never happened to her before. The sensation of truly seeing became so overwhelming that she wondered if she was about to have a fit after all. The image in the window became utterly glorious. The crown on the head of Christ began to sparkle, drawing her attention. Then everything intensified into pure white and flared into a pulse that burst through her like a celestial supernova, throwing her back in her seat. For the briefest instant she saw in the crown of Christ a beauty greater than anything she could describe—as though she had seen the glory of heaven. And embedded in her retina was Christ himself, arms outstretched and face too bright to see. He had passed through her body in an instant, leaving her blinded, the ripples feeling as precious as life itself.

Next thing she knew, she found herself coming to her senses collapsed on the floor, unable to see properly.

She slowly got back onto her seat, feeling confused. Had she had a fit? She really did not know. She checked herself. She had not bitten her tongue and she had not wet herself. Had the Jesus of her girlhood come to her? Tears began to slide down her cheeks.

The divine in Him we seek in vain to kill.

That was Mr Johnson again, from a hymn.

10

After a while, Alyssa felt better, and her eyes recovered their focus. She looked around to make sure nobody had seen her collapsing. The church was still empty. The sun had moved, though, so a good while had passed—at least fifteen minutes. That did not seem possible. She felt sure that she had not been unconscious.

Her mind was playing tricks again. The psychiatrist at her hospital admission during sociology had said something about that, about the absences.

Time passes but it will not give you healing no matter how long you give it.

No amount of time was ever going to cure her. But maybe Jesus could. Maybe with Him she would be safe. It was time to pull herself together. She wiped her eyes with the back of her hand. Jesus could shield her from whatever evil it was that was stirring inside her.

She began to think about her mother—her real mother, not her stepmother. Thinking about Grace almost always made her feel unwell, but she knew she had to be strong for her sake.

I'm so sorry. Please forgive me for being such a failure as a human being.

Nausea rose in her stomach as the infinite amount of badness that lived somewhere inside her tried to force its way to the surface. This time, she was able to hold it back. She could still remember her mother, although not well because she was only five years old when she died. Her mother used to comb her hair and she could still smell the sweet garden flower fragrance of her mother's perfume. She had thought her very beautiful. She wiped more tears from her eyes, but they kept falling. She remembered the look on her mother's face, her last look, her look of disbelief as her own daughter betrayed her and let her die . . . made her die. It was too much to bear . . .

In the past, psychologists had assured her that there was no evil left in her, that it had left her, and that she was well again. What had happened had happened, they said, and nothing could change the past. Her father had said much the same thing, and more besides. He had said that evil could not touch her inside a church. He had emphasised this whenever he took her with him to services, Sunday after Sunday.

A noise in the church office shattered her spiritual voyage and forced her back into the real world. She had heard the unmistakable sound of a door closing.

Ashamed of her tears for the first time, she quickly blew her nose on a tissue from her bag and dried her eyes on her gym towel. Then she picked up the wooden batten she had brought with her and held it firmly in her right hand. If the person or persons who had entered the church turned out to have sinister intent, they would find her more than ready to defend herself. She waited, alert, for the new person or persons to emerge into the chancel.

No one entered and there were no further noises.

'Rats,' she said aloud in exasperation. She was going to need to go and investigate. Weapon in hand and bag over her shoulder, she quietly approached the office.

'Hullo,' she said loudly. 'Anybody there?'

There was no answer. She entered warily, but soon relaxed. There was nobody there. And the outside door was closed, just as she had left it. Yet the noise she had heard earlier was not something she had imagined. Someone *had* recently been there. She could still smell their deodorant. Not only that, but the fragrance was one that she knew: *Homme Support.* Her brothers used to use it when they were younger and Ben Clayton's mother still used it on Ben Clayton.

It was probably a young person.

It seemed odd that they had not come into the church proper. If they had been teenagers, possibly her presence had spooked them. Taking care to keep a foot against the bottom of the outside door, and with the wooden club in her right hand, she opened the door a few centimetres and peered into the car park. There was no one there. She closed the door again and warily took a seat at the desk in the office, making sure to keep her back to the wall. There was no further sign of another person. She knew it had been stupid of her to make herself so vulnerable. Isolating oneself in a deserted building with free public access in the middle of a city was not exactly the wisest of moves.

I'm just such an idiot.

She was relieved to see that the wall poster with the verse about Jesus was still there, unlike the time at the gym when the poster had turned out to be some sort of hallucination. She had not understood the words on the wall poster in the church office when she arrived, but now she did.

Now it made perfect sense.

Only to the lost does Jesus show.

Her Sunday school teacher had said it would be like that: "Only when your heart truly seeks Him, will Jesus come to you, Alyssa, because once you *meet* Him, you will be born again and not be able to unknow Him. Thereafter, there will be nothing that you can do except believe".

Seeing Jesus
None can lift the Gate to Glory but One.
Yet the Glory of God,
Inexpressible except in tears,
Only to the lost does Jesus show.
For see, that crown upon Christ Jesus' head,
See, it is a crown of thorns

And know that as God,
In His great Glory,
Only to the lost will Jesus ever show.

What more could she—or anyone—say? Jesus existed and she loved Him. He was real and inexpressibly and infinitely glorious. Jesus was greater than any Bible text, greater than any intellectual theory, greater than any psychological phenomenon. He was in the world, and He was all-powerful, and He was suffering.

In meeting Jesus, she had been in the presence of God. She knew so with absolute certainty. In Jesus had been the presence of God.

Jesus *was* the presence of God.
For the first time ever, she *knew* Jesus.
He had come to her.
She needed to have a good cry and go home.
It was Friday when the police came for her.

CHAPTER TWENTY-THREE

1

THE ARRIVAL OF POLICE officers at the Donald Clinic came as a shock to everyone. Alyssa had expected that enquiries about her treatment of Gilbert Rockport would come via letters or phone calls from her professional board or a lawyer, not the police. She hated the police. They triggered some sort of bad reaction in her, an irrational response that therapists in the past had said was yet more evidence of severe PTSD. Whatever the truth of the matter, when Trish announced over the phone—while she was in the middle of a counselling session at the cottage—that two police officers were at the clinic's front reception desk looking for her, the news caused her heart to begin racing. Her first thought was that the police had somehow discovered what she had done to either her mother or her father, and her first instinct was to run as fast as she could. Luckily, she knew herself well enough by now to stop herself from doing anything that stupid.

'The police!' she echoed to Trish in disbelief.

Trish seemed perfectly calm about it. 'It's just a routine visit. They are gathering information. About the accident.'

'About Gilbert Rockport?'

'Yes. His road traffic accident.'

'*Gilbert's* accident?'

Trish seemed perplexed by her inability to understand what she was saying. 'Yes. They want to see you for about ten minutes. It's a male detective in a suit and a female copper in a blue uniform. Can I send them over to you at the cottage?' Trish lowered her voice to a whisper. 'They can't stay here in the main hallway. They are spooking our clients.'

'The police, you say? What do they want?'

'Good heavens, Alyssa, have you got a hangover or something? They simply want information about the accident. I need to send them over to you.'

'Does the Dog know? Has he given permission?' Trish was not supposed to interrupt counselling sessions. 'I'm in the middle of a client.' The client, Gwen Baxter, a compulsive shoplifter, was staring at her from the therapy couch, alarmed by the telephone conversation about police.

Alyssa heard Trish talking to the police officers. 'Yes, they say they have permission. And they say they can't be delayed because they have a busy schedule. You've got Mrs Baxter there at the moment, haven't you? I'll rebook her for you. Tell her it's an emergency. There's nothing seriously wrong with her anyway, from what I can see here. Just the shoplifting thing. She could safely wait a week or two.'

'Are you sure that Dr Barnes know about this?'

'He does.' Trish began to whisper again: 'And he wants to speak to you on the phone as soon as you get rid of Mrs Baxter. Before the police get to you.'

Mrs Baxter was duly dispatched and shortly afterwards the phone rang again. It was the Dog.

He was abrupt and to the point. 'You are going to have to see them, I'm afraid, Alyssa. Clowning around is going to be inevitable given that it's Gilbert Rockport who's dead. I work with the goons every day in forensics, so I understand them very well. Take my advice and be very careful with what you say. Though these people are generally just a self-perpetuating benefit scheme for lazy morons with violent tendencies it doesn't mean they don't like jumping to mind-boggling conclusions.'

The unexpected correspondence of the boss's opinion of the police with her own surprised her. There was nothing that Doggy Barnes had just said about them that she did not agree with from personal experience. Descriptions like lazy, violent, self-perpetuating, self-serving, and idiotic were no exaggeration in her opinion. Even Gilbert Rockport, another person who had had a lot to do with the police, had thought much the same.

The Dog continued talking on the phone. 'I've already spoken to the two you are going to see shortly. They seem harmless enough, just classic plodders. Their sense of their own importance has fried whatever is left of their brains, so I don't think they'll cause the business too much harm. Just say what you have to say and admit to nothing. Obviously, you need to remain outwardly polite and helpful, but be sure to reveal nothing that we can claim is confidential. Say *no comment* to as much as you can.'

'Understood. Shouldn't I have a lawyer? Or at least have you here with me?'

'Not at this stage. There are no charges, and we haven't had any civil claims yet. They say they simply want some information from you. They won't tell me what, exactly, except that it's of a highly sensitive nature, but they have assured me it has nothing to do with you personally. My advice, therefore, is for you to appear to cooperate. Play the game. However, don't talk a lot. They will misrepresent everything you do say. And, of course, make no written statements. And sign nothing. Got it?'

'Yes, Dr Barnes.'

'Good. I know I can rely on you.' Dr Barnes put the phone down.

Alyssa picked up her official work tablet and quickly punched in Gilbert Rockport's code name to refresh her memory from the scanty keyword case notes she had made about him. They were filed under the false name George Roberts—Gilbert Rockport's original alias.

The tablet told her that there was no person called George Roberts on file. Foolishly, she tried Roberts, G and then Gilbert Rockport, but the result was always the same: nothing. Perplexed, she turned to the computer terminal on her desk and did the same. An error message appeared on the screen. *Error: these clients do not exist.* No persons called George Roberts or Gilbert Rockport had ever attended the Donald Clinic. Not according to the official records.

The Dog was already hard at work. He knew far too much and was far too clever for her.

As far as the Donald Clinic was concerned, Gilbert Rockport did not exist, not in any form. All responsibility for his death, if any, rested entirely upon a non-compliant counsellor.

Someone called Alyssa Brown.

2

The young male plainclothes detective did the talking while the middle-aged woman in blue, a police constable, spent most of the time scowling suspiciously. She reminded Alyssa of a boiled frog. An old one.

Yet another stretched tit.

Staring at her was a reincarnation of bad memories. Any love she might have had for the police was lost when they not only traumatised her as a small child but later repeated the feat when she was a young teenager. Though she knew it was wrong, she felt justified in taking exception to the two who now crowded into her office: an old, fat policewoman and a young, swaggering male detective. The detective was exactly as she expected: leery and fidgety, uncomfortable in her presence, distracted by desire for her body.

Another beta male, if ever there was one.

'Thank you for giving us your time, Ms Brown,' said the detective. 'We are part of a team investigating the unexpected death of Queen's Counsel Rockport. Traffic are doing their routine processes, but I can reveal that from a crime perspective we have certain concerns about the event. What happened may not be as simple as a mere road traffic accident.'

'Is that so?' said Alyssa. She tried to keep a neural tone.

'Indeed, yes.' Though the detective who was talking to her was much younger than the police constable, he was clearly the senior officer. Despite this, he continued to appear anxious. It seemed he feared that because she was a psychologist, she was able to see right through him. In that, he was not entirely wrong. She knew the hidden identities of men just like him: pugilist, pornography viewer, drinker, traffic hooligan, general idiot. And, like them, if psychologically examined, the young man in her office would be found to be dependent on a mother figure, fixated on breasts, have poor coping skills, and be troubled by psychosexual and psychomotor instability.

'What I have to say is highly confidential,' said the detective as he struggled with his eye contact. 'As a professional person, I trust you will respect that.'

'Of course.'

'I can't reveal my sources, but we have reason to suspect that Mr Rockport's accident was no accident.'

'Really?' said Alyssa.

'Yes. Furthermore, we have information to the effect that he was a client of yours.'

'You do?'

'We do. And the nub of the problem is this: we need help regarding an extremely delicate matter. I'll be blunt. Do you know if Mr Rockport had any enemies? Someone who might have wanted to do him harm. For a man in his position, it is not unreasonable to suspect that he may have had problems of that sort. Dangerous adversaries. Criminal types.'

She was genuinely surprised by the question. 'No,' she said. 'Nothing like that.'

'So, you *have* been seeing him, then,' said the middle-aged police constable, speaking suddenly for the first time.

'I prefer not to make any direct comments,' said Alyssa. 'However, I can answer your question for you. I am not aware that Gilbert Rockport had any enemies.'

Both the official visitors looked at her wordlessly for a while, as though expecting her to say much more.

'And you have nothing more to say?' asked the detective finally, in a tone meant to convey that not saying more might be a very serious mistake to make.

'No.'

'No? In which case we have more questions. Many.'

The police interrogation continued relentlessly in her consulting room. 'What about the church school of St Alpheus in Tabralla?' asked the detective. 'What do you know about *that*? Any enemies there?'

'Huh?' Once again, the police question caught her by surprise. She had not thought that the paedophile church brothers in Tabralla from thirty years earlier were in any way relevant to Gilbert's death. As far as she knew, Gilbert had not yet taken any concrete action against his old school. He'd had plans, yes, but they'd been nothing more than intentions for the future. It seemed strange that the police knew about his time there. 'What about St Alpheus?' she asked cautiously.

'That school received a letter recently from the law firm Berkowitz, Berkowitz, and Rockport. To the effect that this firm of lawyers intends to "break them in half". The headmaster has complained to the police about it.'

'Which was a mistake on the headmaster's part,' said the police constable in her emotionless voice. 'There have been ongoing whispers about St Alpheus for years, and now, at last, we will be able to go in legitimately and start turning the place over once again. If there are still child abusers there waiting to be caught, we are going to catch them.'

That part, at least, was excellent news, but Alyssa still thought it best to preserve Gilbert's reputation for his family's sake and say nothing about his experiences there. After all, it was what Gilbert had specifically requested regarding the matter. 'As far as I know, Gilbert Rockport was not silenced by the church,' she said, choosing her words carefully.

The two investigating officers did not find this funny. 'Do not try to protect Mr Rockport—or the church—Ms Brown. It is too late for that.'

'Sorry, I didn't mean to sound flippant. The point is, I really don't think that Gilbert Rockport had any concerns about his security. So, besides the complaint from St Alpheus, are there any *other* reasons to suspect that Gilbert Rockport had *enemies*? Do you seriously believe it was a factor in his death?' She was genuinely puzzled.

'We know for a fact that he had enemies, Ms Brown. It is for us to know and for you to tell us what *you* know about the matter.'

'I've told you all that I know. I don't know of any enemies.'

The two police officials looked at each other. Then they came to a decision.

3

The young male detective reached into his pocket and removed a brown envelope. 'I had hoped it wouldn't have to come to this,' he said. 'These are photographs. From the autopsy on Mr Rockport. They are extremely graphic and distressing.' He placed the envelope on Alyssa's desk.

'We've already been to his wife and his doctor with these,' said the police constable.

'And they are mystified,' said the plainclothes detective. 'You are our last hope.'

'I honestly don't understand what you two are talking about,' said Alyssa.

'Open the envelope,' said the detective in a sombre tone. 'But first, prepare yourself for the worst. Perhaps the photographs will jog your memory. These bastards must be caught.'

In the envelope were two close-up photographs of parts of Gilbert's naked corpse, taken at autopsy. The pictures were of his buttocks. They were covered in injuries. There were rows of angry horizontal welts and extensive bruises.

Seeing Gilbert again, now as a dead piece of meat, felt sickening. She clutched at her throat at the ghoulish horror of it. She came close to being sick.

Oh Gilbert, what have I done to you, my darling!

The detective turned the photographs upside down to spare her any further distress. 'The pathologist says that there is absolutely no doubt that these injuries occurred before the accident, well before he died—at least six hours beforehand, maybe twelve. There is therefore no doubt in our mind, Ms Brown, that Gilbert Rockport was severely tortured before he died. He had enemies alright. We think he was trying to escape.'

'Therefore, tell us what you know,' said the police constable in her deadpan voice.

The police were barking up the wrong tree. Alyssa knew this the moment she saw the photographs. The parallel tramline welts clearly visible within the generalised deep bruising on Gilbert's buttocks were undoubtedly the result of one of his visits to Veronica. The autopsy findings were not evidence of torture. They were evidence of something Gilbert had arranged to have done to himself, something he had actually paid to have done.

'Do you find the situation funny?' asked the officer who resembled a frog.

'No, no. Not at all. Of course not. The whole business of Mr Rockport's death is extremely tragic.'

'You do know *something*,' insisted the woman. 'I can see it on your face.'

Alyssa knew she was in a difficult position. Gilbert's reputation rested in her hands. She thought of his wife and children. Nikki had obviously pretended to know nothing about the injuries when interviewed by the police, so she must have felt it best for all concerned to keep her husband's unusual behaviour private. Nikki would have realised that her deceased husband—and she as his wife—would become the laughingstock of the entire nation if the truth did come out, so she had obviously acted to protect Gilbert's secret double life.

As his trusted counselling psychologist, Alyssa knew that she needed to do the same. 'There is only one way in which I *can* help you,' she said to the police delegation. 'I can give you the absolute assurance that Mr Rockport never mentioned to me that he was either concerned about enemies or had enemies.'

The young male detective resigned himself to picking up the photographs and slowly fitting them back into their envelope, one by one.

'Is this really the best that you can do for us, counsellor Brown?' said the constable.

'For the moment, yes. But I would like to talk to the police pathologist who took the autopsy photographs. Could you get him to phone me later today?'

'We don't control the pathologist,' they said together, dismissively. The two then went into a huddle, speaking to each other in whispers. Alyssa heard enough to know that they had now given up on her and were deciding to visit certain "narks" next.

'We're off,' said the detective. 'Thank you for your time.'

Alyssa was left standing in her office all by herself.

It was not the first time she had failed to be completely honest with the police, and she realised this now. Always, though, her reason had been the same: to protect someone she cared about. The sudden insight left her feeling strangely numb.

She felt unsettled. She hoped she was doing the right thing.

Or have I just gone and harmed everyone all over again?

The photographs of parts of Gilbert's mangled body remained stuck in her mind, where they continued to have a bad effect on her. The images felt even more distressing than the recent presence of two police officers. The injuries from Mistress Veronica were worse than she had imagined. Judging from the photographs, Gilbert had been sicker than she had realised. With the benefit of hindsight, it seemed clear that Gilbert had needed more help than she had given him. He may well have driven into the end of the freeway barrier deliberately, out of sheer desperation at the hopelessness of his life.

She felt her confidence in her ability as a counsellor wilting. It now seemed frighteningly probable that vehicular suicide was indeed the explanation for the accident. The more she thought about it, the more definite this seemed. Viewed objectively, it was most likely that Gilbert Rockport had died because of her own pride and stupidity.

In her own special way, she had once again killed someone.

The new realisation, dreadful as it was, had a strange and paradoxical effect on her. For the first time since Gilbert's death, she felt quite calm. The new certainty—that she was guilty—felt better than the old uncertainty, even though it added a floating quality to the world.

The floating only began to recede after the second vorazepam tablet. After that, she was able to feel her heart beating in her chest again, not her throat. Though almost certainly responsible for Gilbert's death, this was not too serious, she told herself. No one would ever find out. After all, she had killed both her parents and nothing much had happened over that.

Still going strong.

God was going to have no choice but to give up on her.

Not only that. Her career was doomed.

4

The rest of the consultations on that Friday were a blur, but Alyssa got through them knowing that the weekend was ahead. Soon, she would have some free time and be able to restore her emotional strength.

Five o'clock came but—as befitted a bad person—the day turned out to be far from over. Before she was able to make her getaway, Trish phoned the cottage in a tearful state. The receptionist insisted on coming across to the cottage for help. She was in a giant muddle over client re-bookings following the recent two days of sick leave that Alyssa had taken. An hour of direct assistance was required.

Babysitting Trish was the last thing she needed. Precious free time was ticking away. Yet, she could hardly refuse to help. 'Oh well, come across then, Trish, but let's be quick about it.'

Trish must have sensed her irritation over the phone because as soon as she arrived, she apologised for taking up her time. 'So sorry about all this, Alyssa, but I've had a really bad day. People have been shouting at me over the phone over the bookings. I just can't think straight anymore.'

'Not to worry, Trish, just show me the lists and let's get these bookings sorted.'

'I'm so thankful for your help.'

While they worked and chatted, Alyssa apologised in turn for her earlier behaviour regarding the police. 'Sorry I was so dilly about them, Trish. It's just that cops always freak me out. It's something to do with my childhood.'

'Sure,' said Trish, adopting the soothing tone that she no doubt thought was used by therapists. 'Want to talk about it?'

And tell the whole world?

'Not today, thanks, Trish. Too tired. Let's just get out of here as soon as possible.' Alyssa was resigned to people's pity regarding her problem with the police. She had tried her best in therapy for it in the past and failed. She still hated the police. People would have to live with it.

Once she finally managed to get rid of Trish, she realised, as she was leaving the cottage for home, that Gilbert's pathologist had not yet phoned. Wearily, she headed back into her office. Could a day get any more stressful? she wondered. More precious time down the tubes. She would have to phone the pathologist herself. It was the least she owed Gilbert. After a frustrating half hour of futile calls, she finally tracked down the relevant doctor—and then only after insisting to the duty clerk at the central mortuary that she was a very senior health professional (which she wasn't) and that it was urgent. The pathologist, a Dr Herman Kreef, was already at home—it being Friday evening. And no, he had not received any message from any police official.

She explained to him, with as little detail as possible, the nature of QC Gilbert Rockport's pre-mortem injuries.

For a while there was silence at the other end of the telephone. 'Well now,' said Dr Kreef finally, 'this is a turn up for the books, isn't it? Convenient, though, isn't it? Miss . . . what was your name again?'

'Alyssa Brown, registered professional counselling psychologist.'

'Gilbert Rockport's *psychologist*. What next.'

She ignored the man's ignorance and intolerance. 'Given my knowledge of Mr Rockport's behaviour,' she explained, 'his pre-accident injuries were undoubtedly self-inflicted. They do not warrant any further attention from the police.'

'Thank you for the information, Miss Brown. I doubt, though, that the injuries were self-inflicted, as you so confidently assert. Given their situation, it would be physically impossible. Another person, a culprit, is implicated. The forensic evidence is unequivocal.'

She felt like she was going to have a stroke. 'There is no *culprit*. He arranged it! What part of this don't you understand?' Alyssa felt very tired. She knew she was shouting.

She knew, too, that it had been wrong of her to say that Gilbert's injuries were self-inflicted. There *was* a culprit. Technically, according to the letter of the law, what Veronica did to Gilbert—cause him severe injuries—was illegal despite his assent. Veronica was guilty of some sort of crime—and so was she herself for not having reported Veronica to the police as soon as she found out about the extent of Gilbert's whippings.

Dr Kreef was not for turning. 'It won't help to raise your voice. I will be making my own conclusions about this matter. It's what we do here. I decide what is or is not relevant. Me, not you.'

'This is ridiculous. How can you possibly place something completely unrelated to Mr Rockport's death into the hands of the police?'

'I can. And what is more, I'm busy writing your name down,' said Dr Kreef.

'Yes, you do that. And I work for Professor Donald Barnes, so I'll be getting *him* to explain things to you in a way that you *will* understand.' Her hand was shaking with anger.

'The Dog? You work for Doggy Barnes? Why didn't you say so earlier?'

'Sorry, I didn't think it was relevant.'

It was to Herman Kreef. There was a reflective pause. 'Barnes, you say? This is going to be a big case, isn't it?' Another pause. 'Ooh boy.'

She rattled his chain: 'Yes, very, very big. External pathology reviews. Lots of lawyers. And the Dog.'

'I think I am beginning to understand.'

Beginning to shit yourself, you mean.

'Thank you.' She put the phone down.

She had had just about enough of fucking idiots.

CHAPTER TWENTY-FOUR

1

BACK HOME AT THE flat, Alyssa tried to be nice to Cy.

'Why don't we go out for a change this weekend, Cy, and try and relax and be more normal, like in the old days? I'll pay, so don't worry about that.'

He seemed mildly surprised. 'Robbed a bank, have you?'

'No, but I think I haven't been good company lately. I think I have my priorities all wrong. We need to live too.'

'Well, I'm game. What do you have in mind?'

'I was thinking of that Italian place off Jones Street, *Umberto Ponti*.' It was a restaurant she knew well, and it was fairly nearby. Though small and unassuming, Umberto's was one of Hubron's unsung treasures, with even the occasional movie star dining there when in need of honest food. Fabio from the gym was the one who had told her about it. However, unlike Fabio, Mr Ponti was a recent immigrant with the indefinable civility of the true European. The Italian District of the city was a good three city blocks farther away, around Leonorte Street, so Mr Ponti always liked to explain in private whispers that his restaurant was deliberately not situated on Leonorte because his wife—but not he himself—was frightened of the Mafia. Alyssa suspected this was just a marketing pitch, but nevertheless the idea of being in danger from the Mafia somehow added to the zeitgeist of his restaurant.

'We could go there for dinner tomorrow night. And then somewhere afterwards. How does that sound to you?' Cy knew the place because they had been there a few times before.

'For a good feed? Sounds great. Count me in.'

She knew Cy would suggest that they invited friends as well, so she had already budgeted for that.

'We really should invite Brian along,' he duly said. 'We owe him. I could get him to bring a partner. That would make it a real hoot.'

'Okay, then, invite him and a partner,' she said. 'But only invite him if he *can* bring someone. I can only tolerate Brian if he has someone with him.' Unaccompanied, Brian tended to stare fixedly at various parts of her anatomy, whereas with a date his attention got diverted. Also, his dates were often interesting to talk to. From what she had seen of Brian's love life over the past year, it was certainly never boring. He endlessly attempted to have relationships but always seemed to choose bizarrely unsuited people with whom he had no prospect of long-term success.

'I'll go and get my phone,' said Cy.

'Good.' With Brian involved, the evening would be financially manageable. If there was one thing she and Brian *did* have in common, it was aversion to being ripped off financially. With him, outings were always good value for money.

Cy managed to get a reply from Brian. 'Done,' he enthused. 'Brian will find someone to bring along. He likes Umberto's. And, if we want, he'll be happy to advise us on where we can all go afterwards for some excitement. He's good like that. So cool.'

The plan was that they would meet at the restaurant.

The evening turned out clear and pleasantly warm, so she and Cy decided to go on foot rather than take a taxi. It was only a ten-minute walk, a pleasant journey in good weather, and one that they could undertake hand in hand. Cy looked particularly attractive in the gunmetal-grey St Goliath dress shirt she had bought him for his birthday the previous year, while she wore her stylish, well-fitting skinny-leg navy-blue pants, dainty mid-heeled brown ankle boots, and a crisp white sleeveless shirt that she kept half unbuttoned. At first, she had wanted to show off her figure by wearing her micro miniskirt, with stockings and drop-dead-sexy mid-heeled black pumps, but she decided against this because the combination was a little too confronting for a night walk in public. A light coat would have solved the problem, but the only one that she had—a gift from ex-boyfriend Aaron—was also unsuitable for walking in public. Its beautiful motifs looked for all the world like real gold.

Still, she was satisfied with her final decision. Cy was fond of her blue pants—he had often said as much. And Brian liked them too. The pants, together with the revealing white top, would be sufficient to capture the men's attention. To counter any potential chill in the night air, she added a light, three-quarter length cotton jacket in rich brown for the walking. The jacket ended in the small of her back, emphasising her excellent shape, and its dark colour set off perfectly the blonde of her freshly washed hair.

She wondered who Brian was bringing and how his latest attempt at female conquest would look. His previous date had been someone with orange hair and a ring in her nose. 'Any idea who Brian is bringing?' she asked.

Cy's grip on her hand tightened. 'Oh shit, I forgot to mention that didn't I?'

'What do you mean? Mention what?' They were already well up Jones Street by then, more than halfway to Umberto's.

'It's that doctor of yours that he's bringing, Dr Jocelyn. The lady psych. She's coming. Brian asked me to arrange it. I know you said you thought she was a lesbian, but Brian says he'd like to have a crack at getting her to be his girlfriend.'

'What!' She withdrew her hand. 'Jocelyn Goronowski? You've done what!'

Cy looked hurt. 'It's not all bad, is it? Dr Jocelyn was more than game. She more than jumped at the chance of meeting Brian.'

'Are you out of your mind!'

He failed to understand her anger. 'Brian and I did it as a sort of surprise for you. We thought you liked her. Besides, don't you want your new friend to be happy? And Brian too?'

'Jocelyn happy with Brian? What fucking planet are you living on, Cy? Brian is a complete creep. You *know* he is. And Jocelyn *is* a lesbian. I've *told* you!'

'She is? She seemed very keen to join us and meet Brian.'

'You are more of a fool than I believed possible.'

Cy looked hurt. 'Well, all I can say is that Dr Jocelyn agreed to everything.'

'Yes. She bloody well would, wouldn't she? She bloody well *would*!'

2

When they entered the Italian restaurant called Umberto Ponti, Alyssa saw immediately that everything that Cy had said was true and that horrors were about to unfold. Someone who looked suspiciously like Jocelyn Goronowski was sitting next to a hooded figure at a table near the window.

The woman immediately jumped to her feet with excitement and came towards them. It was Jocelyn Goronowski all right, but not any Jocelyn she had ever seen before. It was no fish out of water either. Jocelyn was dressed in a surprisingly glamorous emerald-green frock, complete with stylish black highlights matching the raven of her hair. The dress looked brand new. And topping off the surprise version of Jocelyn Goronowski was a sparkly necklace, purple eyeliner, and glaring red lipstick.

It got worse. Jocelyn's date, the motionless, shrouded figure sitting at her table, moved. He looked up, revealing himself. It was indeed none other than the nerd extraordinaire, Brian—creep of the highest order and owner of the bookstore where Cy worked two half days per week.

God help us!

He stood up to greet them. He was taller than Cy, but even skinnier, and a few years older. Despite his age, he had on a bright red hooded jacket—bizarrely matching Jocelyn's lipstick. From within the hood, his eyes gleamed with enthusiasm. He looked like nothing so much as an insane monk.

'My friends!' he cried. 'Welcome. Alyssa—my, my.' He made clucking noises, distracted by her desirable appearance. 'Have you met Jocelyn?'

It was an idiotic question. 'Yes. We both work at the same place.'

'They both work at the Donald Clinic,' echoed Cy lamely.

'Of course, how silly of me.'

'Sit down, Brian.' Alyssa greeted Jocelyn with a flick of her hand. 'Hi. You're looking very glamorous, I must say.'

'How exciting this all is,' said Jocelyn wickedly.

Exciting all right. Wait until Brian gets his hands on you.

She knew from previous experience exactly what occupied most of Brian's mind most of the time. On one forgettable occasion, he had even stared at her so intently that afterwards she had had to get Cy to assure her that he was not dangerous. "No, Brian is anything but dangerous" had been the answer. According to Cy, his friend Brian was actually "a jolly fine chap, just a bit sexually deprived". But not to worry about that part because Brian was actively working to fix the problem. Which hardly bode well for the welfare of the lost soul in the green dress.

Getting through an evening with Brian was always going to be a challenge, but with Jocelyn now tossed into the mix, the prospects for disaster had moved into a whole new league. Alyssa removed her jacket and tried not to shudder. She took care to sit opposite Jocelyn and let Cy sit opposite Brian. Already, Brian was irritating her. 'How about taking your hoodie off, Brian,' she suggested. 'We can hardly see you. Besides, you must be boiling.'

'Yes, that.' He took off his hooded jacket. 'Much better.'

Underneath the ridiculous red hoodie, Brian wore a surprisingly well-cut black T-shirt. His skinny arms were shockingly pale against the black, yet they looked unexpectedly healthy. She had never thought of him as potentially in good physical condition. His hair was clean, and his teeth and fingernails passable. Not bad for a total nerd.

How did I miss all this before?

Nevertheless, what she—or anyone else—could *not* miss was the large silver logo "Basher" emblazoned on the front of Brian's T-shirt. Basher was the name of a magazine, that much she did know, but writing Basher all over oneself on a first date—a blind one, at that—seemed to her an insensitive thing to do. Clearly, Brian was determined to be Brian.

Umberto arrived in person with the menus.

'My dear Alyssa,' he said, in his charming Italian accent. 'Beautiful as ever, I see. It is such an honour to see you here again. Welcome. And welcome to all your lovely friends. Tonight, nothing is too much trouble for me. Whatever you wish, you can have.'

'Thank you, Umberto.'

They ordered a bottle of wine between them, as well as a shared platter of antipasti for an appetiser, while for the main course they all went with the pasta—the restaurant's specialty—each choosing a different variety. Umberto initially suggested something Italian for the wine, but Jocelyn persuaded them to go with a wine from New Zealand because she had once been there for a holiday. 'You will like it, guaranteed. Later, we can get something Italian. Believe me, if anyone knows about wine, it's me.'

She grinned at them.

Talk about too much information.

Umberto had the good grace not to take offence. 'You want the Pinot Noir from Otago in New Zealand? Very well, madam.'

'Only way to go for wine,' declared Jocelyn. The Italian, who was already on his way, pretended not to have heard.

Fortunately, the wine was excellent.

Brian particularly liked it. 'I probably drink too much,' he confessed, 'but this kind of stuff is the reason why. Damn! You know, I'm glad I came tonight. Jocelyn here seems my kind of girl. We came early, so we've got to know each other really well.'

'Have you now, said Alyssa.'

'Oh yes, it's been amazing. Did you know that we don't know why we believe things or why we do things? Jocelyn here has told me all about it. It's how psychiatry works. Everybody is running around blind. It explains such a lot about my own life.'

Alyssa rolled her eyes at Jocelyn, who giggled, making her wonder just how much alcohol the woman had already consumed.

Cy inflamed the situation. 'You do know, don't you, Brian,' he said, 'that our Dr Jocelyn here has x-ray eyes too? She is able to see right through people, you included.'

'Through our clothes? Ha, ha, ha.'

Whereupon the two men fell about laughing. Jocelyn seemed to find it funny too because she winked furiously from across the table. Alyssa, however, failed to find any of the juvenile behaviour even vaguely amusing.

'He was scared to come tonight, you know,' said Cy to Jocelyn. He was referring to Brian.

Brian grinned. 'We all have our little problems. But I do declare myself cured.'

Cy seemed unable to stop putting his foot into things. 'Brian was convinced that you would turn out to be like his previous dates, Jocelyn. He's had these total disasters one after the other. I had to keep reassuring him that you were nothing like that.'

'God, I hope you're right,' said Jocelyn, looking nervous despite the alcohol—or because of the alcohol. 'What was wrong with these other women?'

Brian seemed to think he knew. 'It's a certain type of them that's the problem, I think—and of course the fact that I always seem to end up getting involved with them. They are like, you know, obnoxious. Generally awful. Demanding that I be a male feminist yet still grease their path with shekels. Horrible.'

'Brian is incapable of coming under the control of a female,' Cy explained further. 'It's a human nature thing he has. He can't do female governance, can you, Brian?'

'No. The pussy hound-dog thing that they all expect these days, I just can't do. I've tried and tried, but it seems I'm just not a pussy hound. I can't subserve the female. I seem to have a quirk in my nature.'

Jocelyn gave him a challenging smirk of disbelief, and the two men fell about laughing again.

3

Alyssa was finding the company very tedious. Everyone seemed determined to drink too much and talk nonsense.

'Believe me,' said Cy to Jocelyn, 'your Brian here has his problems.'

Brian looked hurt. 'I'm *not* just someone who obsesses over body parts,' he said defensively. 'I like them of course, but there's more to me than that. The criticisms have been most unfair.'

'Seems like you boys urgently need assessment by a psychiatrist,' said Jocelyn, who had become less nervous in her manner and looked more comfortable with the situation.

'Oh, doctor,' purred Brian. 'Life troubles me. I have so many things that need to be discovered.'

Not a moment too soon did the antipasti *giant share platter* arrive and return everyone to their senses. The nibbles looked good: Kalamata olives, baby bocconcini, assorted mushrooms, pepperoncini, prosciutto, carpaccio, anchovies, Jerusalem artichoke hearts, and various cheeses: Camembert, Blue, Cheddar, Emmental, Asiago. To help it go down, Jocelyn ordered a second bottle of wine. Alyssa, who had not yet progressed to even a third of the way through her first drink, felt irritated. 'How much are you planning to drink, Jocelyn?' she asked, as politely as she could. Her colleague had already drained two glasses in front of her—and many more beforehand, no doubt.

Jocelyn held up the first bottle to show it was empty. She seemed unperturbed. 'It's all good stuff. Don't worry, we won't waste any. No one's driving, are they?'

'No,' said Cy. 'I can happily do two or three glasses more.'

'Me too,' echoed Brian.

'There you go, Mr Ponti,' tittered Jocelyn. 'Another bottle. This time we'll take your advice. Bring us an Italian.'

Mr Ponti glanced at Alyssa with a look that requested she provide further clarification. It was as if he regarded her as the only adult at their table, and she smiled at him. 'It will be okay Umberto, do what they say. An Italian red. You decide what will be best, but not more than thirty dollars.'

'Very well, Miss Alyssa.'

'Hey,' said Jocelyn, 'don't worry about the cost. I'll pay.' However, Umberto Ponti, who was already walking away, once again pretended not to hear.

Fortunately, there was food to distract them. It was time to sample the shared antipasti.

'So, Brian, how are things going in the book industry?' asked Jocelyn, between mouthfuls of artichokes and carpaccio.

'It would be okay if it wasn't for the fucking government.'

'How so?'

'Harassment. I'm constantly harassed. Bureaucrats, it seems, are fascists, and fascists, it seems, have this need to harass people.'

'Oh dear. What have they been doing to you, Brian?'

'They want me to pay some sort of back tax. It's a ludicrous situation where they've just made things up.'

'Back tax?'

'Bastards.'

'It's just an attempt to get at him,' explained Cy. 'Politically, they don't approve of him.'

'Of the books in his store?'

'That. And of me in general,' stated Brian. 'I'm hated because I promote free thought.'

'Do you seriously think so, Brian?' Alyssa spoke for the first time in a while. She knew bureaucrats better than most, so she knew that what Brian was saying was not that far-fetched. She had a suggestion for him: 'Maybe you should make a complaint to the Human Rights Commissioner or someone like that.'

'No point,' he shrugged, 'it will be just another government stooge. Another fascist, this time cleverly in disguise.'

'What does the government dislike about the thoughts you promote?' demanded Jocelyn.

Brian tried to explain. 'You know I'm a small, stand-alone, independent, self-owned bookstore, right?'

'Yes, sort of. But why is that a problem?'

'It's complicated. The point is.' Brian stopped to flick a fragment of anchovy off his baby bocconcini. 'The point is, I don't fit into the Goebbels apparatus. The machine refuses to close when they feed me into it. I'm not an approved kind of anything. For the government, that is the worst thing possible.'

'He sells only proper books,' explained Cy again. 'That's been his problem the whole of his life.'

'Yes. I refuse to do mainstream commercial crap. I only sell proper books.'

But not bookkeeping books.

Alyssa knew her thought was uncharitable.

'Actual books,' said Cy, who was starting to be annoying again.

'Join the club. I too have always despaired for humanity's infantile mind,' announced Jocelyn.

Why was everyone being so indulgent of the truth, Alyssa wondered. 'Have you thought about why the authorities are after you, Brian?' she asked. 'Isn't it true that most of your books are rather antisocial and that quite a few of them are in favour of violence?'

Like domestic violence, for example.

With "Basher" still irritating her on his T-shirt, she felt she had to get at least that much out in the open.

He looked perplexed. 'The point is, *I'm* not violent, am I? Please. Thank you. However, violence may well have its place and we need to be able to think about it. There's always the bigger picture to consider, namely: who decides? Who is to decide what I may or may not think?

What gives anyone the right to decide? Ever since I can remember, I've always objected to thought censorship of any kind. I've always been able to see where it leads, so I'm completely against random turds determining what I'm allowed to think. I mean, where does that *end*? George Orwell and 1984 and Animal Farm?'

'The thought-police goons have been rifling through his shop recently,' explained Cy.

'Yes. And I don't know where they get such idiots from.' Brian rolled two olives in a strip of prosciutto. 'Is this stuff properly cooked, by the way?'

'Eat it, Brian.'

He did. 'Hey, not bad.' Then he continued complaining. 'As Cy says, a goon came right into my shop recently, ever so Harry-casual-like. To seize stock, he said. Bloody hell. Then he went and impounded ten of my books. I mean, can you believe it? I said it was harassment and illegal, and he said no it wasn't because he was acting on a complaint—I mean, fuck, that was a lie. Who makes a complaint about a book in an alternative bookshop? Anyway, he collected all the copies in the shop of the so-called complained-about item, put them in a sack and went off with them. Ten fucking books in all! My property.'

'Where have they ended up?' asked Alyssa. 'Do you know?'

'God knows. Book prison.'

'What sort of books were they?' asked Jocelyn.

'Coffee tables—you know, illustrated something or others. In this case, it was photographs of erect penises.'

'Books with photographs of erect penises?'

'Sure. We are known for them. They're part of a popular range of ours. The sex organ range. We have the whole range. Male unaroused. Male aroused. Female unaroused. Female aroused. That sort of thing. All the possibilities. We have them all—had them all. Quite tasteful. We get them in from Germany.'

'But the government only went off with your excited penises, right?'

'Yes, doc, they confiscated only those. As he closed his sack, the inspector said he could see why the complainant was disgusted.'

Jocelyn appeared perplexed. 'He didn't realise that female parts get aroused too?'

'No. He didn't take any of those.'

'Typical. So, what exactly *was* the problem with your penises, then, according to this official?'

'The fact that they were erect. The government is happy with flaccid but not erect. Erect equals titillation, which, apparently, is some sort of crime unless I have a licence.'

'But aren't all penises erect for at least some part of every day and every night?' asked Jocelyn, looking even more perplexed. 'Why aren't we allowed to face reality? I mean, half the people in the world have an erect penis every day. What's to hide?'

'I was assured it's pornography.'

'Anything can be pornography,' explained Cy. 'The concept depends entirely on the mind of the beholder: the sicker the mind the more it sees pornography in everything.'

'Very psychoanalytic,' said Jocelyn.

'You probably just needed a permit,' said Alyssa. 'That's probably what they were on about. They want you to pay a fee. Generally, one can't bring sex out into the open without some sort of regulation. Sex needs to be secretive to some degree if society is to function.' She remembered that from sociology.

Jocelyn burped. 'What! How can you say that? How can anyone say that?'

'Are you saying that sex is like drugs?' asked Cy.

Three pairs of eyes looked at her accusingly, but she stood her ground. 'You all know exactly what I mean, especially you Jocelyn. Sex and work don't go together. They are opposites. And the world needs to work. And there are children.'

Brian, of all people, came to her rescue before an argument could develop: 'Actually,' he said, 'the real point here is that there was only trouble at my shop because some wowser or other went and blew his or her peanut brain when they couldn't handle the truth. The prig was obviously so immature that he or she felt convinced that their meaningless opinion was of great significance. If only schools would do the right thing and explain to children that their shitty little lives and opinions are completely irrelevant, then maybe, when they grow up, they'll stop interfering with everyone else.'

Cy had his reservations. 'Good point, Brian. But have you considered that because almost all people are complete losers, maybe they *need* to be told lies—right from birth—or else there'd be no way for them to go on? Without lies about their own importance they'd lose the will to live.'

'Okay, maybe. But I still say—to whoever complained about my penises—so what if they are bigger than yours. Fuck you. Get over it.' Brian looked upset. 'It hurts.'

Jocelyn drained her fourth or fifth glass of wine and put her arm around him. 'Don't worry, Brian. As far as I'm concerned, anyone who complains about such an irrelevance is a fool.'

Alyssa felt her spirits wilting even more than they had been doing the previous day at work. It was going to be long evening and a complete waste of time.

4

By now, both Brian and Jocelyn were looking rather pleased with themselves. Brian had snuggled up close and Jocelyn seemed relaxed. 'All your knowledge is from psychoanalysis, isn't it,' Brian asked her.

'It is,' said Jocelyn wisely but untruthfully.

'Brian also knows quite a bit about psychology,' revealed Cy. 'He's read most of the books on the subject in his shop. Tell them some of what you know, Brian. Go on, I'm sure they'd be amazed. Don't be shy. Summarise the mind for us, like you did for me a few days back at the shop. The mind in a nutshell. He can do that, you know.'

'In a nutshell?'

'In a nutshell.'

Jocelyn appeared interested. 'Come, Brian, tell us what you know. I'd love to hear your ideas and I'm sure Alyssa would too. Wouldn't we, Alyssa?' Jocelyn winked from across the table again, her arm around Brian's middle but her eyes disconcertingly hungry for female breasts.

Brian explained the human mind to them: 'According to the books in my shop, it's actually pretty simple to understand the mind,' he said. 'Self-conscious *awareness* is there so we can decide in advance whether anything that we are *about* to encounter is likely to be good for us or bad for us, and *Self-consciousness* is there to provide us with a summary of the past to assist us in this decision-making. Clear so far? Then, of course, there is *neuro-evolution* in there too. That proves to us that the way our brain works—as just described—is best for us. It's the way to remain alive in any given environment. And that, folks, is all there is to it. The human mind in a nutshell.'

Cy looked conspiratorial as he listened. Then he enlightened them further, giving himself away in the process. 'In other words, we are just apex environment-surviving machines.'

Silence followed.

'What?' Brian looked hurt as the two women stared at him accusingly. 'That's all there is to know. It's according to the books in my bookshop. Honest.'

Finally, Jocelyn spoke, but to Alyssa, not Brian. 'That's straight out of Obermaaier.'

Alyssa nodded. It was. Somehow, Brian had obtained access to Obermaaier's textbook. But how? Had Cy given him her textbook to read without asking? If so, she would kill him. Its margins were full of personal notes by her, including comments about sex.

The two bookstore men grinned triumphantly at the perplexed psychiatrist and outraged counselling psychologist at their table and tried their best not to laugh.

'Actually, I'm impressed,' said Jocelyn. 'You are very sharp, Brian. I can see that.' She appeared intrigued.

'You mean good for someone who has no idea what anything he just said actually means,' said Alyssa, who felt less charitable. She was not fooled by the outburst of pseudo-academic loquaciousness. 'Who put you up to this, Brian? Cy?' She knew she sounded angry, but it was because she *was* angry. Brian turned pale under her glare and nervously pointed to Cy with his eyes. She should have known. 'This is not funny, Cy.'

'Aw, come on. Brian just wanted to impress. Are you impressed, Jocelyn?'

'Very.'

Alyssa had the good grace to shut up.

Everything was irritating her, especially Jocelyn. Even as her friend chatted away to Brian and Cy, her gaze from across the table kept centring on her chest. Jocelyn could not keep her eyes off her tits. The eyes might flick around for a while, but always they returned to linger on her body. Despite the desperate Brian-hugging that was going on, Jocelyn was losing the struggle against the disinhibition that was occurring because of her drinking. Her intense longing for the breasts of another woman were by now so transparent that they were embarrassing. It was sad to see that even though she was a psychiatrist she could not help herself in her hour of need. And Brian, of course, was blind to it all. She felt sorry for him too, but not half as sorry as she felt for Jocelyn.

5

Dimly, Alyssa realised that Jocelyn was speaking. She was speaking to the men. 'Cy,' she was saying in her artificial voice, 'tell us more about your writing.'

Jocelyn wanted to know more about the erotic e-book called *Dawn Rose Rising*, which, apparently, she had just finished reading. 'I was impressed Cy,' she said. 'I've never come across any other author with the guts to put things quite so bluntly. Or anyone with such insight. How did you manage to gain so much insight into the female psyche?'

Alyssa felt like throwing up. Cy had a weakness for being the centre of attention. And what Jocelyn was now saying to him was that not only did she understand his book perfectly—which was impossible seeing that his book bore no relationship to reality—but that according to her he was some sort of an expert on women. What Cy was not saying was that nobody else believed anything of the sort. *Dawn Rose Rising* had been a big disappointment commercially and had sold less than four hundred copies, the explanation for which—when she had once asked—was that he had written it for cognoscenti and not ignoramuses. And this despite the numerical superiority of ignoramuses.

Now he was telling Jocelyn about women. 'I've met quite a few in my time,' he assured her. 'So, I can probably be relied upon to know a thing or two about them.' He paused for effect. 'My biggest discovery, I'd say, is that the female psyche is pretty much the same in every case. Women are strangely similar. In a way, they are a bit like cats.'

Alyssa kicked his ankle under the table, hard. 'It's okay,' she said to the others, without smiling, 'I've given him the kick he deserves.'

'Yes, Cy,' said Jocelyn, unperturbed by the interruption, 'I did notice that your book makes Dawn Rose amazingly predictable—if one has the eye to see it, of course. Have I understood Dawn Rose correctly as archetypal woman? She has only one basic need. Is that right?'

'Sort of. And, importantly, it's not like the one in men.'

'Why not just *say* the word "sex"?' asked Alyssa.

'Because in women it's not that,' said Jocelyn. 'If we are to believe Cy, or rather, his protagonist, Dawn Rose, then what drives a woman in life is the wish to prove that she is of value. Every woman has this one big fear, which is that she is not valued—or less valued than a man.'

Brian was listening to the conversation with a perplexed look on his face. 'You mean, all I have to do is convince some chick that she's of great value and she'll jump into bed with me?'

'More or less, yes,' said Cy.

Alyssa made a face at Jocelyn, but Jocelyn winked back at her. She seemed to be playing some sort of game with the men.

Idiots!

'But what if I get accused of sexism?' asked Brian. 'If I jump this person's bones won't it be sexual harassment, or something? People are getting into so much trouble over sex these days. Some days I'm too scared to even go near a chick in case I get arrested.'

'No one is going to arrest you, Brian.'

'They might,' said Alyssa, 'especially if you keep calling them "chicks".'
And if you don't stop leering at women.

'Why is everyone confused about the meaning of the word sexism?' demanded Jocelyn.

'Because as soon as they see or hear the word "sex" their brain freezes with anxiety, and they become irrational?' suggested Cy.

Brian looked concerned. 'Are you guys saying I'm irrational?'

Nobody gave him a direct answer, but Jocelyn tried to help him: 'You see, Brian, like racism or ageism, the word sexism means "to discriminate on the basis of sex", doesn't it? You're a sexist if you don't treat a member of another sex the *same* as you would treat your own sex.'

Brian interrupted again. 'But how can that be so? We *always* view—and therefore treat—*differently* those of the sex that we desire. Otherwise, why would we bother to have sex with them?'

'If you'll let me finish, I'll tell you how it works,' said Jocelyn.

But Cy interrupted her in turn. 'It's easy to understand, Brian.' He wagged the finger of the expert on words: 'The problem with the word *sexism* is that people have no idea what it means. That is its problem. Take the classical heterosexual interaction, for example: if a man sees a woman and mentally makes a sexual assessment—which occurs always—it is said in the current idiom to be *sexism* because he does not do the same to men.'

Jocelyn was determined to confuse everyone: 'What Cy is *really* saying, Brian, is that a woman's sexual dimension may *not* be assessed unless she permits it.'

'Oh, please,' said Alyssa. Jocelyn was really getting under her skin. 'So, now all human sexuality is to be female controlled?'

'Of course,' said Jocelyn. 'It must always be so. Besides, in case you hadn't noticed, it always *has* been so. When, precisely, did you get out of bed this morning?'

Cy was still wagging his finger. He had the answer to all the confusion on the subject. 'The reason for the *apparent* conflict of standards is simple,' he announced. 'Society's judgement about what amounts to "sexism" is based on criteria that are *different* from those where society judges the interaction to be one of sexual attraction. Sexism is a hostile prejudice, whereas sexual attraction is a mutual celebration. In sexism, the emphasis is on hostility, while in sexual attraction, the emphasis is on mutuality. The key to it all is the word *mutual*. It's that simple.'

'And what is all that supposed to mean?' demanded Brian.

'It means that for the average Joe Soap the wheels have fallen off,' said Jocelyn darkly. 'That guy next to you is brilliant, Alyssa, believe me.' Then she turned her attention back to Brian. 'What Cy means, dearest, is that nothing that he said actually matters. When it comes to the business-end of life, all the intellectual crap flies out of the window. Just listen to your woman.'

Just listen?

It was embarrassing to hear Jocelyn talk about sex in this way. Alyssa felt compelled to say something. 'Don't let Jocelyn trivialise the issue for you, Brian. Sexism *is* very real, and these days you *can* get into trouble if you are not wide awake. Workplaces must never be assumed to be an appropriate place for anything to do with sex. And even in appropriate settings, attempts at sexual interaction need to be immediately abandoned if not reciprocated.'

'Yeah, yeah, I've heard all that,' he said morosely. 'Sex must be mutual. But surely that applies only to grannies? That idea really doesn't grab me.' He frowned at her across the table while his eyes darted hungrily around her body.

'The world has changed, Brian.'

Cy seemed annoyed by her attitude towards Brian. 'Actually Brian,' he said, 'the point to be made in this whole discussion is that an inconvenient truth lies at the heart of the current confusion about sex. Men simply aren't women. It's absurd to insist that we are, but that's currently where we're at. While what men want from women is *different* to what women want from men, currently men don't have a say. And it's this that is behind the current confusion over the meaning of the word *sexism*.'

'All we want is for the same rules to apply on each side,' said Alyssa. 'Is that really a problem?'

Jocelyn smirked at her: 'If I were a guy, I would discriminate against men, and at the same time, while I was a guy, if you were a lesbian, you would discriminate against me. Why? Explain.'

Why don't you instead try explaining how one person can drink so much alcohol without passing out?

'What's this about lesbians?'

'Nothing Brian,' said Alyssa.

Jocelyn reached across the table and grabbed hold of her hand. Holding it firmly, she proceeded to examine it.

'You know, you have the softest cuticles.'

Alyssa signalled to Umberto, and he came nearer. 'We need food.' He understood. Almost immediately, their four large bowls of pasta arrived, together with a large shaker of Parmesan cheese and a peppercorn grinder.

The one with fettuccine and shredded spanner crab, obviously non-kosher, was for Jocelyn, and it did not take her long to have bits of it stuck between her teeth. 'Hey, guys,' she announced. 'See how mine has lots of capsicum in it? That's the way to lose weight while you eat.'

'Luckily, you don't have any to lose,' burbled her new admirer in the black T-shirt.

'Aww . . .'

Alyssa was the last to finish her meal. Nausea made swallowing difficult.

CHAPTER TWENTY-FIVE

1

'WHY DON'T WE ALL have dessert and coffee at my place,' suggested Jocelyn brightly. 'I own a house just down the road.'

House?

Jocelyn had never mentioned before that she had a house.

She had one alright.

They walked there together in a group, Jocelyn in front to lead the way and Brian beside her. Alyssa could not help feeling concern at the sight of the two of them holding hands because at the start of the little journey back into the night her drunken friend had whispered in her ear that Brian "floated her boat". There could be nobody in the world less suited to Jocelyn than Brian, so what was happening had to be evidence of an impending major emotional crisis. At some point soon, Jocelyn's fake world was going to implode.

Brian certainly did not float her own boat. His physique was appalling for someone of his age. He had round shoulders, a hunched back, and a bizarre receding rocker-bottom backside. He was tall and skinny too, so walking next to Jocelyn, who was short and wide, the picture did not look right. To keep pace with her, his knees came up high as he walked, like those of a clown with overlong shoes, and the strangely absent buttocks and high-stepping gait reminded her of nothing so much as a giant spider easing along beside an intended victim. Except that Jocelyn had no place being anybody's victim. She was supposed to be one of the most dangerous beings on the planet: a psychiatrist. Maybe—and it was just a thought—her friend was playing some sort of game; somehow fooling them all. Could it be that Jocelyn was toying with an innocent, misshapen male for no other reason than to amuse herself and be cruel to

497

spiders? Or was Jocelyn trying to be cruel to *her*? Was Jocelyn secretly a cruel person? Or was Jocelyn deliberately hurting *herself* in front of her? She hoped her friend was not so sick as to be doing anything *that* stupid.

It did not take them long to reach their destination. Jocelyn's place turned out to be a freestanding double storey town house, part of a group of four such redevelopments. They looked relatively new. The neighbourhood, by contrast, was very old, with many of the surrounding buildings in need of repair, as was usual for Woodville.

'Wow, Jocelyn,' said Cy admiringly. Up until then, during the walk, he had been strangely quiet. 'I'm impressed.'

'Thank you, Cy. I'm happy with it.'

The inside of Jocelyn's house was surprisingly neat and clean. Alyssa was not sure what exactly she had expected, but neat had not been on the list. 'You are full of surprises tonight, aren't you,' she said, startled by the bitter tone in her voice. She tried to be more gracious. 'I'm really quite envious.' She was and she wasn't. Despite its potential, the house was curiously sterile, devoid of theme or soul, as though it was part of a display in a museum, and no one really lived there. To her, it spoke of an inner emptiness.

Her ever-perceptive colleague seemed to read her mind: 'It's a bit sparse and functional, I know, but it suits me. I'm by myself, so what with all the pressure from the Donald and the Dog, I'm seldom home. It's so nice to have some guests for a change.'

Brian was studying a framed photograph of Melanie Klein on a table in the hallway. He had it in his hand. 'Your mother?' he asked Jocelyn.

'No Brian. It's a work thing,' hissed Alyssa. 'Put it back!' She felt deeply embarrassed over what Cy had done by involving Jocelyn with such an inappropriate person.

Brian, though, was not to be deterred. Calmly, he replaced the photograph and asked another question: 'What's this about a dog?' he asked Jocelyn. Clearly, he was determined to make progress with his new squeeze. 'What sort of a dog do you have? I really like dogs.'

'God, Brian,' said Alyssa again, through gritted teeth. 'It's not a real dog. It's our boss. Doggy Barnes is our boss at work.'

'You psycho people really crack me up.'

Not psycho people, Brian, psych people. Psych people.

2

They settled in the lounge, which was large and situated two steps lower than the adjoining kitchen, which went off in an L shape. Stepping onto a kitchen step, Jocelyn announced that she had a proper coffee machine and could make a coffee of choice for anyone who wanted one. True to form, Brian requested an affogato, which presupposed that she also had ice cream available, but equally true to form for that evening, Jocelyn agreed that this was a great idea. She had ice cream. She liked affogatos and could make them.

Jocelyn's behaviour with Brian was getting more and more alarming.

'Make everyone comfortable, Cy,' said Jocelyn with a flourish. 'And you, Alyssa, stay there. I'll bring the coffees out to you all in no time. And Cy, why don't you put some music on for us?'

'Will do.' There was an upmarket-looking sound system under the window and Cy went to investigate, with Brian close behind.

'Fantastic setup,' announced Cy. 'I see it can do vinyls too.' There was a pile of them nearby. He selected one and showed it to Brian. 'Here's one that looks like something for you, Brian: *The Dead Flowers of Nocypher.*'

He seemed hurt by the suggestion. 'Aw, thanks, but no. It looks too nineteenth century for me.'

'Twentieth, actually.'

'Still not me. You know I'm more *Rüfüs Du Sol.* Choose something from a playlist, Cy. Those speakers look really good.' He flopped onto an unoccupied sofa and stretched out. 'This is the life.'

Jocelyn reappeared on the stairs, hopped down lithely, and came up behind Cy. 'I forgot. You'll need the password.' She whispered it into his ear while rubbing his lower back for him, then leant over him, and pressed some keys to start a playlist that she chose for him. Grinning, she then headed back to the kitchen.

'Fan-cee,' exclaimed Cy.

Alyssa felt like pinching herself. Had what had just happened right in front of her eyes actually *happened*? The unguarded moment of comfortable physical familiarity between Jocelyn and Cy around the music player had elevated the evening from merely odd to truly shocking. What exactly *was* going on? What exactly *were* Jocelyn's intentions? Was everyone taking her for a fool? Was she the only person there who did not realise that Brian was a red herring for the evening and that Jocelyn's intentions were far more sinister and aimed at her via Cy? She felt anger rising. Evidently her home-owning supposed friend and Cy had a lot more in common than just their age. The touchy-feely spectacle around the music centre had just confirmed her worst suspicions: Jocelyn and Cy were up to something behind her back. Her so-called friend was far more predatory than she had ever realised and was deliberately forcing a response from her.

Or was she overreacting? For some reason, she felt unsure of herself and intensely vulnerable. Was she in the wrong? Why was she struggling to trust Cy? And why did she not trust Jocelyn? She really could not work it out, and this all-too-familiar emotional disability made her feel helpless. But then the music started—the playlist that Jocelyn had chosen—and the track hit her like a baseball bat to her head. Out of Jocelyn's speakers poured an unsettling tune and relentlessly haunting words that pummelled her mind. The heartbreaking song was about the bottomless grief felt by children once their parents were gone, which seemed like a direct attack on her sanity. The track was called *Mother & Father*, from the album Evergreen by Broods. On and on it went about the depth of the love that children had for their parents—love that no doubt she too should have had for her own parents instead of killing them. Jocelyn was sending her a message.

She knows!

It was impossible, but it was as though Jocelyn knew everything: knew what she had done; knew that she was a bad person; knew that she feared people would find out. Jocelyn knew things that she had no business knowing. And she was blasting this into her ears like a trumpet.

The unexpected reminder of the horrors of her childhood and of her failures as a human being were more than she could bear. Alyssa tried to block her ears, but still the haunting strains of *Mother & Father* stabbed into her like pitiless daggers.

It had been bad enough when Alan Summerfield inadvertently played *Chicago* in his car earlier in the year, but this took disturbing to a whole new level. She would never have believed that music could have such power over her. It was turning everything in her head upside down, forcing her towards the edge of an abyss.

'Stop it!' she cried, her hands pressing desperately against her ears. She was going to be sick. 'Make it stop!'

Cy glanced at her, bemused. 'What?'

'Make it stop!'

'Jeez, no need to shout.' He went and did as she requested. 'Can we play something else?' he yelled to Jocelyn, who was busy out of sight somewhere at the back of her kitchen. 'Alyssa doesn't like it.'

Jocelyn appeared briefly at the top of the steps and smiled down directly at Alyssa. 'Don't mind me. Suit yourself, guys.' Then she was gone again.

Cy managed to find a playlist featuring Infected Mushrooms in Jocelyn's collection. 'Unbelievable!' He danced around triumphantly. 'I thought I was the only one with taste.'

'For retro yuk, you mean,' mumbled Brian.

Cy ignored him and with an appreciative grin of glee towards the kitchen, got the Mushrooms playing.

What were the chances of the Infected Mushrooms being on a playlist of Jocelyn's by accident? Zero. Too many terrible coincidences were happening. Alyssa did not know how much more of it she could take. And yet . . . despite her worst fears, Cy had been kind enough to turn off the offending track about mothers and fathers when she had asked him to. Was Cy, like Brian, just the innocent plaything of an evil psychiatrist?

Or are they all laughing at me?

'Not a music fan, I see,' observed Brian, looking at her with disappointment heavy in his voice. He seemed oblivious to the tension in the air.

'It's not that.' Alyssa glared back at him with disapproval. He was spread across his couch at impossible angles, as though gaining strength for further meaningless statements.

Idiot.

'I think the drink has affected her,' said Cy to him in a loud whisper.

3

Feeling emotionally fragile, Alyssa kept silent, and after a while both Cy and Brian ignored her.

'Hey, Cy,' said Brian, 'this Jocelyn of yours, she seems a pretty sorted bird, doesn't she? And this is quite some place. Are you sure there aren't any kids lurking about somewhere? You know I don't want kids.'

'No kids, Brian. Promise.'

Alyssa had to say something. 'Have you gone fucking crazy, Brian?'

'No need to snap,' said Cy.

'You two make me sick.'

Jocelyn appeared at the top of the steps with four coffees on a tray and a bright smile. 'What's with the glum faces? Now, who is for the long macchiato? Oh, yes, that would be you, Cy.'

'It is.' He stood up to get it.

Once Jocelyn had delivered the correct coffee to each target, she took her own coffee and went and sat next to Brian, which placed her opposite where Alyssa was sitting with Cy. Then, after a few sips of her coffee, her psychiatrist friend resumed the same bizarre behaviour she had exhibited at Umberto's restaurant. Alyssa watched in disbelief as Jocelyn placed a hand on Brian's knee, an action so overtly inauthentic that she almost burst out laughing. Jocelyn was no lady. She had her legs apart—the way she normally sat—and was unwittingly betraying the fiction of her sudden heterosexuality. Either that, or she was deliberately flashing at *her*. Fat chance.

Brian, though, seemed enraptured by his new conquest. Determined to play his part in such august company, he tried to say something suitably intellectual: 'As I said earlier, I've been looking into psychology a lot lately,' he confided. 'Mainly to understand women. So, it's really great to have an expert here with me.'

'Experts,' said Jocelyn, with a nod towards Alyssa. 'I'm impressed, Brian. Why don't you tell us a bit more about your learnings?'

He turned red. 'Aw, it's lots of different stuff.'

'Like?'

'Come on, Brian, tell them about the needs of the sexes. That one. You can do it.' It was Cy talking.

He had been doing a lot of talking lately.

'Oh, all right then,' said Brian. 'The needs of the sexes.' He sat up on his couch and took a deep breath and concentrated. 'Apparently, deep down—deepest down—women are seeking "restoration". That's the thing that they all really want. They want to be restored to wholeness. We men, on the other hand, don't want any of that. What we want is "return". Sounds weird, right, but of course this is all unconscious. It's all deep psychoanalytic stuff. And then that's it. This is all that the whole business of sex amounts to. Restoration and return. Really, it is. Just that.'

The words of wisdom were greeted with silence. More clarification was anticipated, but Brian just smiled smugly. Finally, Jocelyn spoke. 'What *sort* of wholeness, Brian? And return to *where*?'

He appeared flustered by the sceptical gaze of the two women in his audience.

'It's true,' said Cy in support.

'Yes, we men return. You know, as in return to the mother of our early childhood.'

'It's all in his bookshop,' explained Cy.

'Yes,' said Brian. 'That's what the books definitely say. Men return to mother/vagina. To the time before guilt ruined it all. Sounds gross, but it's all there.'

'*Eeuw*,' said Alyssa.

'Not *eeuw*,' said Jocelyn, correcting her. 'Touch, taste, smell, sound, sight, mouth, breast, bum. Childhood. Why is this news to you?'

'Oh, please.'

Brian was not to be daunted from fully clarifying his wise words on the needs of the sexes. 'Of course, we are not to forget the women,' he said. 'It's the same with women,' he assured everyone, 'except that they have one, of course.' He pointed to his crotch, presumably to indicate a vagina. 'But no willy. So, what *they* want is restoration to what they *thought* they had before they turned six—before they had a properly functioning brain.'

'Stop making a fool of yourself, Brian,' said Alyssa.

'It's true,' said Brian. 'What *they* seek is an end to unfairness—restoration of their willy—and to achieve this, apparently, they have relationships. In fact, that's the main thing for them in life, relationships—that sort of stuff. It is. And that's about as much as I know about the whole business.'

'Clap, clap, Brian,' said Jocelyn in a non-committal voice. She leant closer to him. 'Just one question: are we talking about relationships with sex or without sex?'

He squirmed under her scrutiny. 'Umm. I don't know. And I think that is my main problem.'

.... 4 ....

Brian had difficulty understanding relationships. Cy tried to help him with a clue: 'Remember the relative weight of the orgasm on each side, Brian. That is the key to understanding and managing relationships. One needs always to be aware of the forces at work.'

'What the hell is that supposed to mean?' asked Alyssa. Cy was beginning to be truly annoying with his persistently childish tutoring behaviour towards Brian.

'He's just stating the obvious with delicacy,' said Jocelyn. 'Aren't you, Cy? He's such a cultured man.'

'What's this about orgasms?' asked Brian, looking towards Cy, as though seeking his advice.

Jocelyn intervened. 'Should we tell him, Cy?' Then she did anyway. She whispered into Brian's ear at some length and then, when finished, licked his ear for good measure.

Brian's face lit up with an idiotic smile.

'What did she say?' demanded Alyssa.

Jocelyn got in first: 'I told him that because we women have much better orgasms on our own, we don't need men for sex, only for company. Men don't do much for our orgasms, only our emotions.'

'Did she really say that?' asked Cy.

'Yes,' insisted Jocelyn, 'I did. And I also said that, for men, going with a woman is everything. So, naturally, they think that sex is what a relationship is.'

'She didn't quite put it that way,' confessed Brian. 'Mostly, she said she likes me. But she did say you are only right about the weight thing from a male perspective, Cy.'

The weight thing.

Alyssa felt compelled to say something sensible. 'Can we please get over all this pseudo-psychology nonsense and just relax and be normal?'

'No,' said Jocelyn, 'we can't because no one here is normal.'

'Speak for yourself.'

504

'She's a psychiatrist,' said Cy, 'so she should know.'

Idiotic discussions about the psychology of sex continued.

Cy was at it again: 'As I said to you before, Brian, women struggle endlessly—both with their innate sense of diminished self-worth and with their orgasms—so we men need to be aware of this. They are in a lifelong struggle that never ends. We men can never fix them.'

'Is this all because of Freud?' asked Brian, looking uncertain.

'Yes,' said Jocelyn with a mischievous smirk. 'Somebody stole our penis when we were little.'

'Really,' said Alyssa, 'how could you! You *know* that the old Freudian stuff is mostly junk. How about we look at men's problems instead? What about *their* constant need for sex and their constant threats of violence? What about that, Jocelyn? How Freudian is *that*?'

'Excuse me, but none of this actually makes any sense to me,' said Brian, diplomatically. 'All I do know for sure is that women need to be championed and revered—that much gets rammed down my throat every day. The trouble is, no matter how hard I try, I appear to be stuck on merely objectifying them.'

'As in finding certain parts of them interesting but not much else?' asked Cy. 'That is very common in men.' He turned to the two women. 'Actually, it's a real problem of his. He's had it ever since his teens.'

'I'm sure I can cure you of that, Brian,' said Jocelyn.

'Ha-ha.'

As the good-natured bantering flowed, Alyssa began to realise that her work colleague and possible friend was one step ahead in the game she was playing with the two half-joking men in her house. She felt ashamed that she had been so slow to realise it. She had thought the two men were being cruel to Jocelyn, but the opposite was the case. Jocelyn was perfectly in command of them and finding her powers amusing. It seemed that for Jocelyn everything to do with men was a joke.

'So, you are offering to cure me, are you?' ventured Brian with ill-concealed enthusiasm.

'Yes Brian. But first, you will need to understand that I am special. Maybe feeling hurt is part of being female in your bookshop, and maybe some women do indeed have a need for compensatory restorative adornment embellishments, but this does not apply to me.'

'What? What did she just say?'

Jocelyn did not so much as blush as she stood up and sat on his knee. She lifted Brian's chin with her finger. 'In my opinion, Brian, there's not much point in you trying to reform yourself. Essentially, I would say you can't. It's a brain programming thing.'

Cy looked impressed by her.

'My brain has been programmed?'

'Mal-programmed. But relax, Brian. Hope is not lost. What will help in your condition is for you to realise that women are not *special* in any way compared to men. We are neither weaklings nor creatures from outer space. If you can master that concept, then you should be able to start to understand that logically women cannot be *inferior*—or superior—to men in any way. So, here's what you need to do, Brian, to start making progress with women: you need to stop regarding us as aliens.' She smiled at him sweetly and kissed him on his cheek.

5

It was time for dessert. Jocelyn stood up. 'Anyone for ice cream? I've got heaps of flavours in the fridge.'

Everyone wanted ice cream.

Jocelyn disappeared into the kitchen once again.

Alyssa still felt ill at ease, so she did not offer to assist in the kitchen. She let the ice cream lady depart by herself. She felt annoyed at all the hypocrisy she had been forced to listen to. Jocelyn had told Brian that women were not some sort of alien, but this was no cure for either her or Brian. The chronic relationship problems plaguing the lives of both Brian and Jocelyn had nothing at all to do with creatures from outer space. The problem was that they were both unrepentant narcissists who were too selfish to relate properly to anyone. There wasn't any sociological or psychiatric rocket science involved in the matter.

How do you explain to someone that their problem is that they are just plain selfish?

Alone on his couch now, Brian was chuckling and making signs at Cy, hand signals that looked suspiciously suggestive of copulation.

'I wouldn't find objectifying women so funny if I were you,' Alyssa told

506

him. 'You are going to get yourself into a whole lot of trouble one day.'

'And what is that supposed to mean?' asked Cy on his behalf.

'Stop playing your silly games with Brian. Women are people, not objects, unlike in your fantasy lives. It's wrong to treat real women as if they're worth nothing more than their parts. You know it's wrong. You too, Brian. Stop it! Quite frankly, the two of you are behaving like fourteen-year-olds.'

Brian looked shocked by her outburst of anger. Mirth disappeared from his face. 'Gee whiz, okay. I do get it, you know.'

Cy did not say a word. Instead, he stood up and went to switch on the television. He was angry. He did not return to his seat next to her but instead remained in front of the television, where he kept fiddling with the channels.

Jocelyn spoke up from the kitchen. 'Do you still want the vanilla, Cy? I've found some caramel flavour. I know that's your favourite. Do you want some of that instead?'

So, now she knows his favourite fucking ice cream flavour.

'Caramel will be great, thanks,' he said pleasantly. 'Can we watch the football?'

'Of course. Alyssa dear, could you come up here and give me a hand?'

Alyssa went into the kitchen. It seemed as good a time as any to confront the woman who seemed to think she could play games with her too. She needed to know the truth from Jocelyn about how she knew so much about Cy and about her; the truth about what was going on behind her back. The carefully crafted pin pricks she had been enduring from her supposed friend the whole evening had gone beyond a joke.

Silently, she approached Jocelyn until she was right behind her. Jocelyn, meanwhile, remained oblivious of her presence as she busied herself with placing four dessert bowls onto the counter from an overhead cupboard. She was in the corner of the L-shaped kitchen, and they were out of sight of the two men. Out of earshot too, with the television playing in the lounge.

'Jocelyn, there is something I want to ask you,' said Alyssa, very calmly and very quietly from right behind her. 'And I want you to tell me the truth. It's going to be better for you this way. Better for all of us.'

Jocelyn froze, becoming suddenly tense, as though she had been expecting something like this all along. Still behind her, Alyssa looked at her as she stood there motionless and breathless in her expensive emerald dress minus shoes: short stature, flabby upper arms, broadening rump, pathetically wild hair. Somehow, she was unable to feel anger. Not at something so hopeless. She felt only pity. Jocelyn made her feel like she wanted to cry.

Finally, Jocelyn turned around, her face strangely fearful.

'What are you and Cy up to behind my back?' demanded Alyssa.

She might just as well have punched her breathless friend in the guts. For a moment, Jocelyn seemed unable to comprehend what had just been said to her. She seemed unwilling to hear the words spoken to her so clearly and so forcefully. Instead, she blinked and then slowly turned white. Her response was not that of guilt. Alyssa saw immediately that it was not that. Her response was that of pain. What she had said to Jocelyn had hurt her. It had hurt her so deeply that she staggered, as though she might collapse from a broken heart.

Alyssa caught Jocelyn in her arms. She realised that she had just attacked a woman who was utterly in love with her and completely innocent of any betrayal. Tears were cascading from Jocelyn's eyes, and when she saw them, she could no longer contain her own emotions. She enveloped Jocelyn in her strong gymnasium arms and hugged her tightly.

'I'm sorry,' she whispered. 'I never meant to hurt you. It's just that for some reason I was convinced . . . I've become confused. Sorry.'

'I thought you were going to say you loved me,' whispered Jocelyn. 'I was so hoping for that. Oh Alyssa, I love you so, so much.' Jocelyn clung onto her tightly, like a small, frightened child.

6

Somehow, they ended up in Jocelyn's bedroom.

Alyssa was sitting on the foot end of the bed, to one side, with her feet on the ground, and Jocelyn was lying crossways across the bottom of the bed, head on her lap. It had all been a dreadful misunderstanding. Jocelyn was in love with her and with nobody else.

But Alyssa was not in love with Jocelyn.

Her heartbroken friend had a suggestion: 'A kiss?'

Jocelyn's head was still on her lap, so Alyssa had a sudden concern about where exactly the kiss was intended. To forestall any misunderstanding, she leant down and gave Jocelyn a peck on her forehead. She did it out of kindness—and guilt. 'Remember, I'm not . . .' She had wanted to say "gay", but Jocelyn was too quick for her. She reached up and grabbed her by the neck and kissed her full on the lips. Alyssa had never kissed a woman sexually before but did not recoil. It turned out to be the longest kiss she had ever had with a woman.

Jocelyn melted into a trance as their lips remained locked.

Finally, Alyssa recovered her senses and gently broke away.

Jocelyn sat up, now in much better spirits. 'You are driving me crazy, you know, Alyssa. Every time I spend more than fifteen minutes in your company, I get this throbbing feeling. What's a girl to do?'

Jocelyn was trying to take control and Alyssa could see this clearly. For a while, she tolerated it. It felt like some sort of experiment. A test. And she was enormously relieved to find that her body was not responding to Jocelyn. Lip gloss was not her thing, and neither were Jocelyn's breasts. The smell of another woman's hair was also not doing anything for her. Kissing Jocelyn had felt like it used to feel when she kissed Granny Isobel when she was a small child: soppy.

'I want us to fuck until we die,' said Jocelyn.

Matters were spiralling out of control and Alyssa knew she needed to be cruel. 'Oh, Jocelyn, I'm so sorry. So sorry. The last thing I ever want to do is hurt you, but no. I just can't do that. I'm just not . . .'

'Why do I get this feeling that you are lying?' Jocelyn brushed Alyssa's face with her hands.

'I'm not, Jocelyn. Promise.'

'You're not. No, of course you're not. I'm such a silly thing, aren't I? It's just that I've been hoping so much. But it's okay. Really. Deep down I've always known you aren't gay. It's just that it's such a pity. It's just such a big, big pity.'

Alyssa stroked her friend's hair gently, which made her curl up like a little child. 'I'm sorry,' she said to her. 'Let's just rest here for a little while.'

While Jocelyn once again lay across the bottom of the bed, and she remained sitting, Alyssa used the opportunity to take in Jocelyn's bedroom. Like everything else about the unexpectedly fragrant woman whose head was on her lap, the room was surprising. The curtains were luxurious, the carpets deep pile, the chairs exotic oriental-looking numbers, and the double bed enormous. She twisted around to look behind her. Most of the wall above the padded headboard was occupied by a large art print. Pictured was a beautiful young woman with blonde hair, wearing a flowing white gown. The image dominated the room. The woman's head was bowed in sorrow, and she was standing in front of a tomb, weeping. One of her sensuous breasts was naked and she was holding a single red rose against it in a bleeding hand. Drops of blood stained the dress and her chest, but the pain from the rose thorns tearing her flesh seemed to be nothing compared with the pain in her heart.

Alyssa felt overcome with grief as the meaning of what she was seeing sank in: the beautiful young woman on the wall was a version of the supermodel Polly Alexander, a woman whom she herself resembled in some way. Which meant that the lover above Jocelyn's bed, the lover who had lost everything, was an idealised version of herself: none other than an Alyssa of another life. Unbelievably, what she was looking at was *herself* in fantasy form—and not only that. She was also looking at the alter ego of the ugly duckling on her lap. She, Alyssa, represented what Jocelyn desperately wanted in her own life. Even more frighteningly, the blood from the lover's hand in the artwork was the exact colour of the rose that was cutting into her flesh: rich and dark.

Black velvet.

Which was impossible.

Yet it was impossible too that Jocelyn could have such a thing in her bedroom. But there it was.

Jocelyn had always wanted . . . *her.*

'The picture . . .'

'Great, isn't it,' said Jocelyn, coming to life. 'It's a modified Victoria Francis artwork. I had it specially altered. At an art shop.'

'Incredible. This is so tragic.'

Jocelyn had truly lost the plot. Alyssa decided not to ask her how long she had had the doctored creation on her wall. It seemed better not to know.

Her lover was reading her mind: 'It's from before your job interview. Crazy, isn't it? Like fate or something. It's like I've always known you.'

Or always wanted to know me.

'Sweet Jesus. I'm so sorry to have disappointed you.'

'You haven't.'

'You know I have.'

'Who says I've given up?'

'Stop it, Jocelyn.'

'Sorry. Okay, I have given up.' She sat up. 'I repent. Happy?'

It was a lie.

7

They sat together in the bedroom, still at the foot of Jocelyn's giant bed. 'How about being a bit more honest with me in the future,' Alyssa suggested.

'What do you mean?'

'Like with that music you played for me earlier. What did you mean by that? What's with the mother/father stuff?'

'It was a test, Alyssa, because I wasn't sure. But I *am* sure now. Oh, you poor, poor darling.' She tried for another kiss, but Alyssa held her back.

'What sort of test? You really must stop playing games with people. Me especially.'

Jocelyn ignored her question about the music. Instead, she tried to find some other part of her to kiss. In desperation, she took hold of one of Alyssa's hands and kissed it feverishly. 'Oh God, just think what great love we could make. Couldn't you change your mind about it just this once to let us see how we go with each other?'

Alyssa closed her legs. 'Sorry, Jocelyn, but you are *not* fucking me.' She could well imagine what the lovemaking would entail. 'So, stop trying to distract me. Instead, why don't you tell me what my reaction to your music made you so certain of?'

Jocelyn was not going to tell her. 'It's nothing. Forget it. I shouldn't have said anything.' She proceeded to attempt to stand up, assisting herself in the process by placing a supporting hand on Alyssa's lap. The hand rested on a place where normally only a lover's hand should ever go. Jocelyn grinned.

Technically, it was sexual assault.

'Sorry, accident. Just seeing if you want to change your mind. No?'

'You've got it. No, I can't.'

'Oh, all right then.' Jocelyn stood up, properly this time. 'I've got a question for you too. What made you think earlier that there was something going on between me and Cy?'

Nothing surprised her anymore when it came to Jocelyn and her mind games. Alyssa stood up too. 'The key. It was the key that first got me thinking.'

'The key? What key?'

'The key to the balcony door of my flat. That time you came to visit me and showed me Cy's dope plants. You *knew* that the key to our balcony door was behind the curtain. How could you possibly have known that—unless you'd been there before with Cy.'

Jocelyn appeared perplexed by the accusation. 'What the hell are you suggesting? That certainly wasn't it. And how am I supposed to know how I knew? I don't even remember anything like that even happening.'

'It sure did.'

'Well then, I must just have known.'

'Shit. And there I was hoping for a better answer.'

'Oh, calm down.'

'Really!'

'I'm off to fix my face. While I'm doing that, I'll think of an answer for you.' She disappeared into the ensuite bathroom and after less than three minutes she re-emerged. Her face looked brighter. 'We'd better get back to the boys. They'll be wondering what's going on. Come.' She took Alyssa by the elbow: 'But first, let me show you this.' She opened the bedroom curtains, which had been closed. 'What do you see?'

Behind the curtains was a glass door leading into a small, enclosed courtyard. There were windows on either side of the door. 'I see a secluded courtyard.'

'Exactly. Which is where I plan to install a hot spa for us to enjoy together after work.'

'You have to start trying to be serious.' Alyssa turned to leave.

'Wait! Look.' Jocelyn pointed to the window ledge nearest the door handle. On it lay a key. She picked it up. 'Voila! See. Force of habit. That's all that business over at your place was about. Habit. Nothing sinister in it at all.'

The explanation seemed plausible.

Force of habit.

Alyssa felt relieved. It seemed Jocelyn might be innocent after all—when it came to Cy. Or was she? What about all the other strange coincidences that were going on? Jocelyn smiled at her, but it was not the smile of a victor. It was a kind smile. It was the smile of someone who genuinely loved her. Alyssa felt ashamed of herself. She no longer knew what to believe. With Jocelyn, fact and fiction were getting harder and harder to separate.

8

Back in the lounge, Cy and Brian were engrossed in a football match on the TV and had barely noticed their absence. Alyssa therefore returned to the kitchen and helped Jocelyn prepare the dessert earlier promised to all.

Jocelyn became all weird again. 'Now, tell me, Alyssa,' she whispered as they scooped out various flavours of ice cream, 'this Brian of Cy's: I assume he's not capable of being *taken* by a woman, right? So, what do you think I need to do? Should I assume he's going to think he's in charge and just go along with things? Is that going to be best?'

'What!'

'I need your advice. Quick, give me the heads up: is he a slap, tickle, and slurp man—you know, face, boobs, and fanny—or is he a back of the hair, female neck and shoulders, submit your ass kind of a guy? I need to know.'

'What the hell are you talking about?'

'Oh please, I give up with you. When are you going to grow up?' She took two bowls. 'Bring the rest. Come.'

The bowls of ice cream were accepted with enthusiasm back down in the lounge.

Fortunately, the football match was just about over, with one side hopelessly behind in the score.

'Wondered what became of us did you?' asked Jocelyn, interrupting their viewing.

'Not really,' said Cy. He got up and switched the TV off. 'We've already lost. Still, it was good for a while. We assumed you two went on a tour of the house or something.'

'We did,' said Alyssa.

'We knew it was some sort of women's business,' said Brian sagely.

'Exactly right, Brian. We've had a nice exploration.' Jocelyn's expression was deadpan.

'Us too,' said Brian. 'Cy's been giving me heaps of information about women. I just sell books about them, but he writes about them.'

Alyssa felt annoyed all over again. 'Who is *them*, Brian?' She was half-yelling. 'You have to stop listening to all kinds of nonsense about women and start thinking for yourself.'

He cringed visibly. 'Jeez, okay then.'

It occurred to her in that moment—as she realised what a weak fool Brian truly was—that Cy might be using him as a ventriloquist's dummy. The idea had never occurred to her before, but now it seemed entirely possible that Cy was using Brian to say things to her that he couldn't bring himself to say. Or had Benjamin Clayton started something in her mind with *his* talk of dishonest people hiding themselves by making the Bible say whatever it was that they *themselves* wanted to say? The bizarre suspicion about Cy seemed suddenly not as far-fetched as she once would have thought.

Jocelyn was far more tolerant of Brian. 'What further information have you received about women, Brian? I'm all ears. Give us your best shot.' She handed him a spoon for his ice cream.

Brian had placed himself in a difficult spot. 'It's not so much Cy's findings as mine,' he assured her. 'Cy just helped me clarify what I meant earlier about psychoanalysis. You know, about "men desiring return and women desiring restitution". Apparently, this isn't regarded as just junk anymore. It's once again one of the hottest theories out there. The whole of sex is now believed to be explainable in just those seven words—no pun intended.' He gave a little titter of a laugh, which made him sound like a girl.

'Men desire return, and women desire restitution?' Jocelyn appeared to give the simplistic summary of the whole of sex some thought. 'Seven words, you say?' She counted them off on her fingers, like another Cy. 'Seven. Mm. You know, perhaps I *am* inclined to agree with you on this one.'

'Good,' said Cy.

'In which case, why don't you give me a demonstration of your new-found skills after dessert, Brian? Perhaps later tonight you could show me how a woman *should* be handled.'

'Gosh.' Brian almost choked on his ice cream. Clearly, he had failed to detect the sarcasm in Jocelyn's words. 'Seriously?'

'Quite seriously.'

'Well, brilliant, then. I'll get a move on with this ice cream.'

They ate their dessert in relative silence. It was getting late, and Jocelyn was giving knowing winks.

It was time for guests other than Brian to head home.

Jocelyn came and whispered in Alyssa's ear: 'Seeing that you won't oblige, I'm going to do Brian instead. I'm going to get him to fuck me until he dies.'

Alyssa flinched. Sadly, it was going to be nothing like that at all.

She felt really, really sorry for Jocelyn.

The last thing she saw before she departed with Cy was the woman who loved her wrapped in Brian's arms and sending her a brave smile and a forlorn kiss. Jocelyn, it seemed, was determined to punish herself. She was even going to put herself at risk of catching a nasty disease. All for her sake.

It was all too sad. Really, it was.

As they walked home, Cy, who had done his best to ignore her for most of the evening, became more talkative.

'That Dr Goronowski chick of yours seems really hot,' he said. 'Maybe there's some hope for Brian after all.'

'Please tell me you are not serious.'

'Oh, I'm serious all right. I think they'll hit it off. They were practically banging each other already by the time we left.'

'What on earth did you say to him while we were away touring the house?'

'I told you. I explained how to handle women.'

'How? Tell me.'

'It's nothing specific. It's for women in general.'

'How!'

'The secret, if you really want to know, lies in a man knowing that a woman is *always* dissatisfied with her lot. In other words, what men need to do is understand that declarations of dissatisfaction by their partner are not worth worrying about too much. That's the key because women are never able to feel fully satisfied. Always, for them, there is something lacking. So, what we men need to do is realise this and understand this and be assured that none of this is *our* doing—it's not the fault of men. The condition of permanent dissatisfaction is an inherent feature of female psychology. What men need to do is sympathise with women and agree with them, and then carry on regardless. It's that simple.'

Carry on regardless.

'Is that so, Mr Freud.'

'Yes, that is so. As I said to Brian, the answer to the female problem, from our perspective, is to never take them too seriously. Let a woman be a woman, but don't make the mistake of letting her drag you into her problems because they are not fixable by you or by anybody else. Treat them with respect, but, as a man, live your own life as a man.'

'You told Brian that!'

'It's obviously worked. For him at least.'

'And you don't see that Jocelyn is just playing with him like she would with a lab rat?'

'No, I don't.'

'God help me.'

'No need to bring God into this.'

Later that night, they argued further, this time about plans for a baby.

His answer remained unchanged.

No way, Jose.

CHAPTER TWENTY-SIX

1

SOME WEEKS LATER, AT four o'clock in the morning, Alyssa was still not asleep. Instead, she was wide awake. She had insomnia, and the attacks of the malady, which she had been experiencing more and more lately, were showing no sign of abating. Even her self-prescribed treatment of making love to Cy at bedtime had become ineffective. As if to prove the point, she and Cy had had sex earlier that evening, yet she was still not asleep.

It had not helped that Cy had once again left her unsatisfied. In the end, he had simply gone ahead and ignored her and pleased himself. While she knew that sex was really not about pleasing someone else and actually about pleasing oneself, and though she knew that the cause of her new inability to climax lay with herself rather than with him, it still felt hard to maintain objectivity and avoid feeling angry. Black thoughts were not the answer, though. She was not able to achieve an orgasm regardless of what anyone did or did not do. She was too tense—too anxious about too many things. She had lost the ability to relax.

Cy was a problem, yes, but it was Gilbert's death that was weighing her down. She had greatly liked Gilbert as a person and had tried her best to be a good therapist during his visits to the cottage. She had honestly believed that she was helping him, but now it seemed that she had been deluding herself the whole time.

The story of my life.

The Gilbert matter was still up in the air. There was still no word from either the psychology board or lawyers, though this was only a matter of time. The police, too, despite the earlier interview, remained mysteriously silent.

She tried to view the problem objectively. Maybe there was a good reason for the lack of activity. Given Gilbert's notorious history with fast cars, maybe a simple road traffic accident was all it was thought to be. The other explanations would still need to be ruled out, though. Not only homicide but also the possibility of suicide by vehicle as had been alleged by an informant. At some point an attempt was going to be made to blame Gilbert's death on *her*. But would that really be the great disaster that she imagined? After all, it was not unheard of for mental health clients to die. The rational part of her brain kept trying to tell her this. However, with Gilbert something more was at work. She was too close to him emotionally. Somehow, she *was* involved. The fact that he had died troubled her more deeply than it should. She felt guilty. She knew she *was* guilty. But why? What bad thing had she done?

Normally, she was not given to feeling very much at all about clients after hours, especially not when trying to sleep, but Gilbert stirred up aspects of her past life—especially memories of the death of her father and of her own car accident. Also, in a strange way, Gilbert's dying caused flashbacks about the traumatic death of her mother too. Death was not something that she had ever been able to deal with adequately. Too many people close to her had died. But not, until now, one of her clients. Had she killed Gilbert without knowing? Had the cottage clinic become her new feeding ground, a new source of victims ripe for harvest?

I just can't deal with this.

The possibility was not as far-fetched as it seemed. If Gilbert really did have childhood post-traumatic stress disorder, as she had begun to suspect towards the end, then she would not have had the capacity to be truly objective in the mutual intersubjective embrace with him. After all, some psychiatrists at Olympic Hospital during her *own* illness had said that she also suffered from C-PTSD, i.e., the same condition. She had not believed this to be true—for good reason—and even today she still had her doubts, but if genuinely true that she really did have C-PTSD, then both she and Gilbert suffered from the same illness and been just two helpless people feeding off each other. She would have had insufficient insight to counsel him to an acceptable standard.

She frowned in concentration because the truth of the matter was far from clear. Her own psychiatric file at Olympic Hospital, which she had read countless times, had mainly described her illness as "Situational psychotic delusions predisposed by organic brain injury and induced by extreme emotional distress". The C-PTSD was only the opinion of some. And besides, none of the labels they used for her had seemed even remotely correct at the time. She was none of that. A brain fade due to a fractured skull she could understand, the rest not.

In post-traumatic stress disorder, including the childhood-related type, the sufferer was supposed to dwell constantly in the past, have a negative worldview, show evidence of issue avoidance, and have flashbacks of memory intrusions with signs of emotional dysregulation. They were also supposed to exhibit self-destructive hypo- or hyper-arousal. None of which applied to her in any serious way as far as she could see. No, something *else* was eating away at her, making her feel like she was about to disintegrate at any moment. As far as she could see, what *was* wrong with her was far simpler than PTSD. All that was wrong with her was that she was a bad person.

She had tried her best to face up to this and had thought that she was making progress. Foolishly, she had even started to believe during the past few years that she had put the past behind her. Yet now, somehow, the past had returned and there had been another death. Gilbert was dead.

The pressure in her head felt unbearable.

No wonder she could not fall asleep.

She felt like screaming.

A few minutes of blessed relief is all that I ask.

2

She needed to escape. A narcotic would do it—and she could get some if she really wanted to—but she knew enough about drug addiction to know that it was nothing but a slow form of suicide. Her body was too good to waste. Besides, there were other things just as effective as drugs in achieving stress relief but not as destructive. Exercise was one such, especially at places like Fabio's ultra-glamorous gym. Also, indulging in wine or chocolate or going on a shopping spree were useful. However, of a more practical use at four in the morning was yet another of the classic forms of self-soothing, namely, fantasy sex with oneself. With this form of escape, satisfaction was guaranteed at any time, even four am.

Already, while worrying about Gilbert in the dark, she had been caressing her breasts unthinkingly, something she now became aware of. The behaviour was a legacy of her teenage years, and it made her smile as soon as she realised what she was doing. It had earned her many a slap in the past from her stepmother, who called it a *filthy habit*. Filthy or not, she kept her hands on her breasts.

Cy was asleep, facing away from her, while outside a large truck rumbled past the apartment leaving the smell of diesel fumes hanging in the sticky air, but otherwise she was alone. It would be getting on to sunrise before much longer.

She thought about the lovemaking with Cy earlier that night. Why, she wondered, had she found it impossible to get any real satisfaction? She had tried everything she knew, but her body had rebelled at every turn. Now, with him out for the count, that was him done for. What was a girl to do?

Bizarrely, the dead Gilbert Rockport who had been occupying her mind, became alive and well again in her imagination. She could see him now as he used to be during his visits to the cottage: charming and desirable. In a flash of black humour, she imagined applying one of his Mistress Veronica's canes to *Cy's* backside. Gilbert's beatings were no joke of course, but she wondered how Cy would handle rather more gentle tingling sensations applied to his tender cheeks—not by Veronica but by *her*.

There was not much point in wondering. She already knew the answer: he would not handle it at all. Cy was a wimp. Besides, it wasn't his thing. He would never allow anyone to do such a thing to him. In fact, she knew he would not even spank *her* even if she asked him to. If she wanted strong medicine, she would not get it from Cy. Cy was a lost cause for that.

She focused instead on imagining a lover who was commanding, someone who would take no nonsense from her and be almost cruel. She needed someone like that at that moment, someone to take over her life and release her—for a short while—from the burden of control. Who could do it for her? Not Cy, because it was beyond him. Brian? No, not Brian because he was too creepy. Jocelyn maybe? Jocelyn could certainly be forceful and commanding. She tried to imagine lesbian sex. All the licking and the sucking. No. Too distasteful with a woman. What then *did* she want—and more to the point, with what fantasy person? She was lying flat on her back, with her head on her pillow, so she flexed her left thigh at the hip to enable her right hand to rest comfortably between her legs. Who to have imaginary sex with and how?

Intriguingly, and seemingly out of nowhere, the mysterious stranger from the gym materialised. Of course! The hunky spunky young surgeon called Mark. He was just the man for her. Over the previous months, she had caught herself thinking about his cock at the oddest times. Which seemed ridiculous because she had never actually seen it or felt it. She could not even be sure that she remembered *him* accurately. So, what cock had she really been thinking about? Was it just her idealised fantasy of one? She did not care.

Such a hot guy.

It was weird how the disappeared Mark from the gym was still able to mess with her head. There were few males who could do that; make her gag for them in absentia. Weird, also, how he had appeared out of nowhere at the beginning of the year, then disappeared into nowhere, then reappeared out of nowhere—all within the huge expanse of the city— only to disappear again. Lately, though, he seemed to have disappeared for good. She had not seen him again at the gym, her imaginings aside, despite continuing to attend there regularly. But not to worry. He was in her bedroom now, and his pants were off.

3

She felt her horny old self returning. No longer did she feel numb below the waist. She recalled the memory of Mark walking across the gym floor at their first encounter, his butt like that of an angel. Even though the night was warm, her body shivered with desire. He would not have things all his way, though, not to begin with. First, he would have to suffer a little for having neglected her. She tried to imagine what it might be like to be Mistress Veronica and have Mark as her victim. She would command him to take off all his clothes and then position his ass for a whipping.

She tried to imagine the expression on his face. She wondered, too, if he would get excited in the same way that she was getting excited. She wished she knew for sure what it might be like. The cruel thoughts did not want to stop there. In her fantasy, she discovered that Mark had beautiful, smooth skin under his clothes—like hers—and a toned body that smelt intoxicating. What would a cruel mistress do next? Tie him down over the punishment bench, of course. Only, unlike Veronica, she would tie Mark face up, on his back. In that way, she would be able to get to know him better and he would still be completely at her mercy. She would not be truly cruel, though. It was not in her nature and never had been. Or was she kidding herself? With Mark helpless, she would be able to find out. First, though, she would inspect him carefully to discover how he responded to her kisses and discover how he tasted. Once he was as excited as she was, she would see if any cruel feelings came over her. She had heard that women often became cruel once their man was excited by them but completely under their power . . .

Would I want to crush his balls?

She imagined sliding her hand around his silky globes and staring into his eyes as she squeezed, but as soon as he began to cry out in pain it made her feel sick rather than horny. She decided she would not want to do that—not squeeze hard, at any rate. She tried squeezing less hard. A gentle squeeze while still looking right into his eyes would not be too bad, she decided. That would not be a case of wanting to hurt him but more a wish to know how he responded when he was at her mercy. That was what would interest her: having Mark at her mercy.

And, if it was safe, she would like to be at *his* mercy too.

With her mind as inflamed as it was, she was not going to need her vibrator.

She was going to ride Mark just the way she usually rode Cy, but this time her steed was going to behave properly. Electric sparks began shooting backwards and forwards between her nipples and her lower belly. She kicked off the sheet that had been covering her lower legs. She had lost all shame. Ever so demurely at first, she began to make rocking movements with her pelvis. Ecstasy grew in ripples, and then in waves that became stronger and higher. In silence, eyes tightly shut, concentrating on her created world, she sailed along, feeling her response starting to rip into her with serious intent. It was all about to happen: a *big* "Big O". Cy was still fast asleep next to her. Everything was as it should be. Tightness was encircling. Desire was clamping the life out of her.

She strained desperately for a climax, cried out for it. But no . . . no . . . yet again, it refused to come.

It was not to be.

She had failed yet again.

·   **4**   ·

Alyssa knew that she was holding herself back. She was cheating herself. She knew what she wanted, but she was afraid to go there.

She felt like either screaming or crying. Yet, even in her frustration she knew what she was going to have to do. If she wanted to climax, she was going to *have* to face up to her true sexual wishes no matter how disgusting and shameful they were. But how could she? Deep down she was so incredibly damaged that nobody would ever want her *that* way, the way she *really* was.

Yet, without that, she was at risk of going mad.

Without her permission, the illicit movie in her head began to play. She had tried over the years to prevent it or disguise it or ignore it, but always it came back, the same sick, disgusting track. For her to climax, it *had* to play.

Done to me. Things that must be done to me. Rough and degrading things. Things that cause me pain. Yet not truly harmful or against my will. That paradox.

She needed strong physical sensations. She needed to feel overpowered. She needed to be monstered. She needed to be made to feel. She needed to fuse "being in control" with "not being in control" in a physical way. Her body was screaming out for it. She needed to be degraded while not being degraded. But how?

So far in her life, it had remained the great unsolvable riddle.

In her secret fantasies, she gladly allowed random men to slam her against walls and unceremoniously fuck her, or grab hold of her from behind and fuck her up her ass. In real life, of course, besides the fact that she would never allow such things to actually happen, they would need to be with her permission and be done by someone she loved and trusted. But that was another story. She glanced at Cy. Unfortunately, he

523

was never going to be doing anything resembling her fantasies. Would *any* real person whom she loved and trusted *ever* be able to see her right?

Her face flushed with embarrassment as—out of desperate need— the required movie went on playing in her head, the movie that she never confessed to, not even to her lovers. In the background of it all, as a psychotherapist, she knew that the shame she was now feeling was ridiculous, but she still felt it.

She was not going to be able to stop it: the sick movie of a bad person. *This is so embarrassing.*

At last, she was getting in touch with her true sexual feelings.

5

Sweet and compliant Mark turned into Alan Summerfield, a man who took no nonsense from anyone, including her. With contemptuous ease, Alan shrugged off the bonds she had pathetically applied to him, stood up, and took command of the situation. He was naked, like Mark, but different, more solid, and he grabbed hold of her and swept her off her feet in arms that felt unfairly strong. Without a word, he stripped her naked too. Then he kissed her, first full on the lips and then everywhere, intimately, and hungrily, not caring as she squirmed. He made no comment at all about her scar. Instead, he appeared eager and more than ready for her. He wanted her just the way she was.

He was going to take her and there were going to be no discussions and no arguments. He was beautiful, but he was scary too because there was no way she could stop him from doing what he was going to do. Physically and mentally, he was too powerful for her. Without asking, he forced her down over her own punishment bench, face down this time, and kissed her neck and said what lovely hair and skin she had. She was glad he had positioned her like that because it meant he could not see her scar. He came and stood in front of her and lifted her head by her hair. She had to suck him until it made him groan. Then, to get his revenge on her for earlier trying to control him, he leant over her shoulders, forearms resting flat on her lower back, and played the bongos on her bare cheeks. At first, it seemed playful, but after a while, the stinging forced her to start clenching and protesting, something that she found deeply humiliating.

As he continued to spank her, he told her that she was the sexiest person alive, but that she had gone too far with him earlier. When she could not take any more punishment, her bottom went limp, whereupon he went behind her, parted her reddened and now submissive cheeks and ran his tongue deep down the centre of her. She could scarcely believe that anyone could do such a thing. Ruthlessly, though, he continued the degrading act with increasing enthusiasm despite her protests and futile attempts at modesty.

Once satisfied that she was completely humiliated, Alan stood up behind her. It seemed impossible to be more embarrassed, so she gave up on her efforts to maintain her dignity and allowed herself to relax. After all, there was nothing Alan did not know about her now. She closed her eyes, confident that he was at last going to have his way with her and that it was going to be just perfect. She became dreamy with anticipation.

Without warning, he jolted her awake, causing her head to rear up on a stiffened neck. Although he was taking her from behind, as expected, it was in a way she had not expected. He was going to fuck her up her ass. Her face and neck blushed red with shame.

'I'm a virgin,' she tried to say—but the words would not come out.

The intensity of it was shocking, causing her to squeal like a little pig. She tried to struggle against him, but her resistance was in vain. He was too determined, too strong, and too eager.

'Aah!' she moaned. There was no way to stop what was happening. There was nothing she could do except try and be as accommodating as possible. She gave up struggling and became passive. In any case, in a perverse way, she wanted it that way anyway; wanted to be tested to the extreme.

Until she could take no more. Until she was screaming.

She was struggling to cope. She was desperate now. It was too much to bear. Her back was arching, her head rearing back. Her mind was flickering. Fully impaled, she could not do or think *anything*. She was in a life and death struggle. A struggle between control and surrender. And all she could do was *be* the disgrace that she really was.

Now, at last, she *was* herself.

6

Already, her body was orgasming, though not yet her mind, where the brakes were still on. Rhythmic ripples were pulsing. She could feel them. Alan would feel them too. Her body was quivering, her skin warm and sweaty, and he, in turn, was breathing heavily. Lost in her secret fantasy world, she was being brutally taken by a man. He was doing what he wanted with her and causing her pain in the process. How was that fair?

The movie changed. Illogically, she was now on her back in the fantasy and Alan had entered her properly, up her cunt. He had power over her, but she had power over him too. He was deeply affected by her and was struggling to resist the seductive wonder of her body. His needs resonated with hers. She might not be able to love properly, but, clearly, neither could he. He *needed* what he was getting out of having sex with her in the way he was. His/her desire went beyond love—beyond reason—and was a triumph of something else: a triumph of inner need. No matter how or why it had happened, there now existed an intimacy between them that went beyond words. Her path to a fusing of thought and deed with a kindred spirit was travelling wordlessly and necessarily through the valley of humiliation, hurt, and control. Though her path did not appeal to all, to some, thankfully, it did.

Properly fucked. She was being properly fucked. Her scalp began to throb over the metal plates in her head, at the places where screws held together the shattered bones of her skull. She always thought of the accident at times like this. Better that she had died. Up until the molestations and the accident, she had believed she would at some stage come to terms with the feelings of worthlessness that had dogged her after the death of her mother, but not after. After the accident, all hope was lost. Deep down, she no longer had the ability to believe in herself or feel good about herself. She was not worth very much at all. It was best that she got fucked with no love involved at all.

She had tried to love people—normal, ordinary people who believed that they were worth something—but had discovered to her dismay that she could not love them. Such people made too many demands on her. She could not trust them with her true emotions. She could not relate to the self-satisfied. Her ability to love normally was lost forever. And, as universally true when it came to sex, only the truth truly satisfied. The *truth*. Her head throbbed as Alan Summerfield roughly pounded into her. Her entire body shook with the impacts. The metal in her head was paining badly now, which meant that her brain was swelling. She was about to come . . .

She tried to look away to the side, unable to face the shame of her response to him, but Alan forced her to look at him. He put his hand behind her head and grabbed a fistful of her hair and held her head so he could see right into her eyes. He was panting and seemed unable to focus his own eyes properly. His voice came to her, ragged: "I just love that look in your eyes when you are so fucked that you don't know what to do with yourself".

He was only interested in satisfying himself.

As if to prove it, he whispered into her ear: "Suck it up, baby. I'm not interested in any of your fucked-up emotions".

The world flickered in and out of focus as she tried to cope with the imagined pressures, deep pressure, pressure up between her hips, unbearable pressures right into her guts. What he was doing to her was too much for anyone to cope with. She was helpless and he was using her to slake his lust. What she had created in fantasy now had control of her. Wild with desire, thoughts now feeling real, the fingers on the centre of her being went for the kill.

Am . . . on . . . fire. Aah . . .

She tipped over the edge of reason and spun away into an abyss. Alan had her and there was nothing she could do about it except give up. He was so hard that she could no longer take him. It was so shocking, so rude, so painful, so dirty, so wonderful, so unstoppable, so exquisite . . . that she no longer had any control over anything at all. Everything was more than she could bear.

In the quiet stillness of her East Hubron flat, Alan Summerfield drove her to madness and her mind shattered into a million pieces. She began to beg for mercy. Miraculously, he too became frantic. He who had subdued and conquered her now became someone whom she controlled. She had turned the world on its head. She had *him*. Alan could no longer control anything, least of all himself. The supposedly great man began to shudder. It was all happening. Somewhere deep inside her. Alan gave her his everything, became *her* Alan. She drew him tight into her and let herself go with him, giving up altogether on existing. Suspended in time, with all sensation transmuted, she became overwhelmed by contractions. Her head exploded, her back stiffened, and her bare buttocks lifted from the sheets. Thrusting her pubic area into the sky like an offering to the gods, she cried out, the cries merging with his in one united vocalisation, unintelligible to others, somewhere between a wail of woe and an exultation of jubilation.

Oh help, oh Cy, oh God!

Then she was growling. After that, she tried to say something, but instead of "Oh God don't stop" there came mewing sounds. Shuddering and immobilised, she mewed and mewed for what seemed like eternity. It was all she could do.

When she finally came to her senses, she found herself on her back on her bed in darkness. Her face and hair were wet with perspiration and the sheet under her bottom was damp. For a while, she stared blankly at the ceiling.

Cy had woken.

'You okay?' he asked.

'Just a bad dream.'

Cy gave a smile and fell back asleep, but not before giving her a conspiratorial wink and saying, half incoherently, that he believed her.

As her mind cleared, she began to feel ashamed of herself. She would never have permitted what had just happened in her head to actually happen in real life. She was not a person for such things. She would never allow any man to humiliate her and control her in that way.

No way. Although one day I might try anal sex.

If she did, though, it would have to be done properly, with the right person, and without infecting herself. For now, that part of her would have to remain a virgin. And, in any case, Cy was one of those people who found the idea disgusting.

Perhaps it is.

Even though at no stage in her fantasy had she ever been face down in the bed, she continued to feel guilty about having imagined herself taken up her ass, roughly or otherwise.

How embarrassing.

She could not deny, though, that it had been a great orgasm.

Why, then, keep her real desires an absolute secret from others? As she fell asleep, Alyssa's final thoughts came in the form of yet more questions: *Why, I wonder, do I always fantasise about control issues and degradation when I have an orgasm? And why, always, the "she/he" confusion?* After all, her real-life sex life was nothing like that.

Thinking about it proved to be of no help. She had no idea why sex had to be such a screwed-up subject.

What she did know, though, was that it all stemmed from her childhood. When something inside her head broke.

PART VII

THE PAST NEVER FORGETS

CHAPTER TWENTY-SEVEN

1

ALYSSA FOUND THE LETTER on Sunday evening when she went downstairs to put the garbage out. As part of her routine, the trip included a check for junk mail in their letterbox in the open ground floor foyer of the old apartment building, with the idea of adding such mail directly to the garbage. There, in their letterbox, she found the unusual item: a sealed letter addressed to her by name in longhand but with no stamp. It had been hand delivered. On a Sunday. There was no mistake. The name of the intended recipient was quite clear: Ms A. Brown.

Her heart began to beat a little faster. The lawyers, it seemed, were onto her at last. She had been wondering why it was taking them so long. Or, possibly, it was from the Psychology Board. She examined the yet unopened letter more closely. It seemed too thin to be anything official. And the handwriting looked familiar. Perplexed, rather than open it immediately or throw it away, she kept it and took it with her when she finally returned upstairs.

Cy was lounging on the sofa watching television, so she sat at their small round dinner table and carefully opened the mysterious envelope. Inside was a single sheet of paper covered in scrawls. With great relief, and then mounting concern of a different sort, she saw immediately who had written the letter: Benjamin Clayton, one of her clients at the Donald Clinic for the mentally troubled. The micrographic, spindly, severely back-sloped writing was clearly his, complete with its deficient upstrokes and downstrokes. She frowned. It was not the fact that he had written her a letter that was the problem. The problem was that Ben Clayton obviously knew where she lived. And that was a very big problem indeed. A shiver of fear ran through her. Clients were not supposed to know her home address—especially not dangerously paranoid ones. This was rule number one for almost every mental health institution in the world, even the Donald Clinic.

How does Ben know where we live?

Quickly, she read what he had sent her:

CONCERNING: ***THE SIN OF HUBRIS***
Evil cannot be good.
It deserves the condemnation
Of the nation.
Depraved you do not see
Instead, you make it be.
You snatch at words
To fill the chasm dread
And soothe the warp
That is your head.
Evil of unconscious motive
Spawns your unholy votive.
Censorships, burnings,
Yes, garrottings too,
These all-too-human sins—
You say that Jesus did it.
*Well, **He never did!***
That is not his name. It is not his name!
No!
Out of the vagina of space,
Regarding the human race,
Speaking ever so nice,
Like a bowl of rice,
Spoke the Cockatrice:
This so hurts
That you must die
As four-and-twenty blackbirds
Baked in a pie.
But you say when the pie is opened
The birds begin to sing.
That is the boost

When we get home to roost.
You say it is the Holy One.
But I say no!
Never.
Never!
THAT is not his name.
Cry, Human Formulation,
Cry, O birds of pie,
Cry.
Cry, cry,
Cry for your goose
Because your goose is surely cooked.
Hallel yu Jah.
Cut them down, O Jabba!
O Jabba, cut the root of our iniquity.
This day, under our hand,
by most high command,
THE LORDS OF SACRIFICE

What the hell?

Alyssa stared at the letter. "The Sin of Hubris". Was Ben referring to pride of Self? Had he judged her guilty of the Devil's sin? Was it some sort of death threat? Whatever the meaning of the letter, it was clear from the jumbled fruitcake of words that Ben was in a deteriorated, paranoid state of mind—that he was dangerously unwell, in fact. She toyed with the sheet of paper, uncertain what to do. She studied it again. Without any doubt, the words were threatening. Yet, who exactly was Ben threatening? "Birds" were about to cry, so it was not necessarily her. Or was she just one of many intended victims? Or was the intended victim none other than Ben himself? She turned the page over. It appeared blank, but on closer inspection there were a few faint words near the top written in pencil and barely legible. They read: "There is a dog exercising in our back yard".

Outside, it was getting dark, so the situation was getting potentially more serious. With someone as physically powerful as Ben showing evidence of relapsing into paranoid psychosis, something needed to be done, and fast. Yet possibly she was overreacting. She had had almost no exposure to clients suffering from schizophrenia during training, so she was uncertain if the letter was truly concerning. After all, Ben was on medication and there was no doubt that he was taking it because nurse Gail Wilson administered it to him by injection every two weeks. Not only that, but his levels were regularly monitored. And, in any case, in the unlikely event of Ben crashing through the locked front door, she had Cy there to protect her.

On a Sunday evening, how much trouble did she need to cause for the staff of Donald Clinic? The last thing she wanted to do was appear hysterical and incompetent. So, she put her head in her hands and thought about it for a while.

2

Alyssa decided, finally, that the situation was serious enough to warrant at least a phone call to Alan Summerfield or Dr Barnes. They would be able to advise her on the best course of action. Clearly, at the very least something more effective than his current medication was required for Ben; also, the source of the practice leak regarding her home address needed to be traced. Ben had been behaving oddly for quite a while and she had long suspected that his delusions and hallucinations were getting the better of him. Perhaps Alan would know why. Hopefully, the deterioration had nothing to do with her counselling. On the other hand, she had had almost no training in counselling psychotic clients ...

Could this all be my fault?

Cy looked up during an advertising break on the TV and finally noticed that she was concerned. 'Hey, what's bothering you there, honey?' he said. 'Is it the power bill again?'

'No. Some psycho who calls himself Jabba has put a letter in our post box.' She brought the note over to Cy to read. 'See what you think of it. I know him well, but I'm a little scared of him. He's incredibly strong, so he's potentially dangerous if he gets out of control.'

Cy scanned through Ben's scribblings. 'Oh, please!' he groaned. '*The Sin of Hubris? Birds in a pie?* What next? Where do these nutcases get these moronic ideas from?' He waved the piece of paper at her. 'You know, actually I agree with your friend here about one thing: God sure is a bum steer. Perhaps it will be best for us all if this Jabba fellow of yours *does* head out tonight and start slaughtering every last religious crank on the planet, sanctimonious sadists that they are.' He grinned, knowing that he had offended her. 'Okay, I know you think differently, but your madman does have a point, you know.'

'This is not funny.'

'Sorry.'

'It's just that I know Ben well. He's not just another religious crank. He's nothing as bad as that. He's just a harmless paranoid schizophrenic who gets upset by certain aspects of organised religion.'

'Judging from his letter, at least he's sane enough to realise the truth about the whole religion business. Clearly, he hates the hypocrisy of it. So, maybe this is what has destabilised him. Has he been in contact with a religious hypocrite lately?'

'No, not that I know of. His parents, though, are regular churchgoers.'

'Well, there you have it then. His brain has been screwed with right from birth. Maybe we should get the government to officially announce tonight that religious certainty is nothing but baloney. Then your client could relax.'

'You are not helping.'

'Just joking.' He handed the note back to her. 'We should probably call the police.'

'No, not them. All the police do in this sort of situation is make things worse. They'll probably just go out and shoot and kill Ben as soon as they see him with one of his knives. This is not the time to get idiots involved. Ben is unwell. He doesn't deserve to die like an animal. In any case, I don't think he's a real danger to anyone yet. Judging from the letter, he is not *completely* insane. I'll give Alan a call and see what he thinks.'

'Whatever you decide.' Cy returned to his television program.

She dialled Alan's emergency number but got a voicemail message instead, which informed her that he was not on call and therefore unavailable. More to the point, he was not in town. The psychiatrist Dr Simon Bristow was on call for the practice for the Sunday.

She spoke over the phone to Simon Bristow about Benjamin Clayton.

'Remind me who he is again, Alyssa. He's not a *noisy*, is he? I can't stand the noisy ones.'

'No, he's not one of the noisy ones. Quite the opposite.'

'I feel better already. Ben, you said. Ben. Is he the one with the scary hairy legs? Built like a country outhouse? Trilby. Short pants?'

'That's him.'

'Good. I remember his details quite well now. Mad as a snake, though he's never done drugs. Father big in the bank. Ben's our *Blade Runner*.'

'I hadn't thought of him that way, Dr Bristow, but yes, that's him. What do you think I should do? Should we get the on-call CAT team onto him tonight?'

'Surely, we don't need to bother Crisis Assessment. Ben's getting his medication by injection, not orally, I know that, and I know Alan has been very strict about the monitoring. Also, given his history, he won't have been taking anything illicit. But thanks for your call. I'll get hold of Gail Wilson and see if she can see him tonight. Failing that, she can see him first thing in the morning.'

'What if that's too late? He sounds dangerous in his letter.'

'And why would that be, do you think? Are you suggesting a tapeworm has suddenly sprung up in his brain?'

'No. Of course not.'

'Well then, relax.'

'Thank you, Dr Bristow. Sorry to have bothered you. It's just that I didn't know what to do. Ben's given me quite a scare. He could have accosted me when I was putting out the rubbish.'

She could hear Dr Bristow laughing over the telephone. 'Don't worry,' he said. 'He won't harm you. Far from it. You'll get used to paranoid schizophrenics after a few years. They are a real hoot. Ben is completely harmless. Well almost, anyway. It's only his parents—or possibly a religious crank—who are likely to send him off pop.'

With that reassuring news, Dr Bristow ended the call.

Alyssa made sure they locked all the doors and windows that night.

She had no wish to encounter any "blade runner".

3

The on-call psychiatrist, Dr Simon Bristow, proved correct about the fact that Benjamin Clayton retained a small potential to "go off pop"—as he had put it—under certain circumstances. What he had unfortunately failed to do—as he outlined to his colleagues later—was inform the counsellor, Alyssa Brown, that her client might define religious hypocrisy in ways not immediately apparent to the untrained. The reason, however, for his not elucidating so basic a fact to Ms A. Brown was that he had—incorrectly, it now transpired—believed that this would be perfectly obvious to any professionally competent mental health worker. Therefore, the horror that subsequently unfolded had nothing at all to do with him.

Early on the Monday morning following Ben's muddled Sunday letter, an event correctly foreseen by Dr Bristow—but nobody else—happened at the Donald Clinic. In the upstairs office of Gail Wilson, Ben Clayton arrived to find his nurse levitating in a corner of the room. Her feet were hovering a good ten centimetres off the ground. They were not on the floor. There was no doubt about it, to quote from his explanation afterwards.

The ability to levitate was available only to the demon possessed, so when Gail Wilson began to glide in his direction, Ben had had no option but to produce his hunting knife to defend himself. Merely presenting his knife, though, did not prove sufficient. The show of force was unable to hold back the gliding. Under the power of Satan, Gail Wilson persisted towards him, placing him in mortal peril. As loudly as possible, in a final attempt to save himself, he quoted commands that began to come to him from the Lords of Sacrifice. Nurse Wilson, however, in keeping with her demonic powers, cackled at him and began to stream his breath away—as only the possessed could do. Deprived of air, he found he could not breathe. Gail Wilson was choking him, choking out his commands. Drawing him towards her.

Then, before his eyes, she transformed into the entrance to Hell. Her lips turned into a giant funnel, red with lipstick, and the suck from them was so powerful that his body got drawn towards her by the vacuum. Her mouth opened to reveal a gigantic cavity full of mincing blades. Still unable to breathe, Ben knew he was going to die. The vacuum pulling him to his doom was too strong and the blades of hell were too sharp.

Not a man to go down without a fight, hallucinating Benjamin Clayton attacked the levitating and satanically transformed Gail Wilson with his *own* blade to save himself. Resorting to a cutting edge was the only known remedy against the *Death Suck*. This was a well-known fact. One had to go blade to blade against Hell or be turned into mincemeat.

There were no other options.

Luckily for Gail—and for everyone at the Donald Clinic—every time Ben went in for the counter-slaughter, knife swinging wildly, his frenzied slashes fell short of their intended target. Gail, who was by now screaming in the corner where she had been trapped, remained unharmed. Instead of finishing her off, Ben's deadly blade plunged repeatedly into his own upper legs. Confused, and enraged with pain, he began bellowing and overturning the furniture. As the fury of his actions increased, blood began to spray all over the room, including over Gail. Ben had inflicted deep wounds on himself and was missing chunks of his own thighs. The Lords had control, but their control, it seemed, was incomplete. Despite blood-soaked furniture being turned into matchwood, terrifying roars, and a flashing blade, Nurse Wilson failed to die.

She was not harmed in the slightest. Not physically.

Alyssa, meanwhile, was in her counselling office at the cottage, busy with client Mary Judd, a compulsive gambler. Before long, the emergency alarms went off.

As Mary Judd was to say later, "all hell broke loose".

While the alarm was still sounding, the cottage telephone began to ring. There was an automated message from Trish, a message to say that there had been a serious security breach and that everyone was in danger. The cottage needed to go into lockdown immediately. There was not a second to spare. Alyssa jumped to her feet and with the help of Mary Judd rushed to bolt the front door and close all the windows and lock the internal doors. Before long, they heard the wail of sirens and through the closed windows they saw concerned figures dashing about in the main building.

Finally, the phone rang again. This time it was Trish in person. 'All sorted,' she said. She sounded breathless. 'Boy, that was something else. Anyway, he's gone. We can return to normal.'

'What do you mean *gone*?' Trish had a habit of being deliberately frustrating. 'What on earth has been going on?'

'That, my dear Alyssa, was your patient Ben Clayton. When he arrived this morning, he thought he was going to be seeing you for an appointment. Instead, I had instructions from Dr Bristow to send him to Gail. And now he's just about gone and killed her.'

'Oh no!'

'Oh yes. It's okay though. Gail's not dead. In fact, she's unharmed. Ben's the one that copped it. Apparently, he kind of attacked himself. With a blade. He's pretty cut up. There's blood absolutely everywhere.'

'This is terrible. I *knew* something like this was . . .' She stopped herself. 'How badly is he hurt?'

'Oh, pretty bad, I'd say. They've rushed him off to the emergency department at the Public to try to save him. From what I could see, he looked just about dead when they put him in the ambulance. There were drips and things everywhere and he wasn't moving, and they were breathing for him.'

'Oh, I am so sorry.'

'Luckily, we had Dr Barnes himself here today. He's such a brick, isn't he? As soon as all the screaming started upstairs, he rushed out of his office with a syringe in his hands and just about flew up the stairs. Must have been powerful stuff because I'm told the injection stopped Ben in his tracks. You should have seen the size of his knife. Oh my God! The police put it in a bag.'

'This is terrible. The police being involved, I mean.'

'Dr Barnes is furious. Gail told me Ben went off crazy the moment she told him that he wouldn't be seeing you this morning. Apparently, he wanted to see only you. Gail says she blames you for the whole thing. That's what I heard her telling Dr Barnes.'

'Gail blames me?'

'I'm afraid so. In fact, I think they all do.'

CHAPTER TWENTY-EIGHT

1

MIDWEEK, ALYSSA HAD NO option but to attend a supervision session with Susan Lindow. It was a regular, pre-scheduled two-weekly visit, but was the last thing she felt like doing given the unfolding dramas at the Donald Clinic. However, supervision sessions were compulsory. She dreaded what awaited. The visit to the fat lady in the little house off Olympic Parade was not going to be much fun at all. The visits there never were.

Part of her told her that this was as it should be—supervision was, after all, work and not play—but she could think of nothing worse than having to spend time in the company of someone who knew all the private details about her past mental collapse and subsequent time at Olympic Hospital as an inpatient. That said, she had enough insight to concede that Susan Lindow was precisely the sort of woman who pressed all her buttons of intolerance. Susan therefore opened a pathway to getting the better of the emotional blind spots she knew she had. After the counselling failures with Gilbert Rockport and Ben Clayton, improvement was obviously needed. Nevertheless, the thought of having to admit to Susan Lindow, of all people, that she suffered from counselling blind spots felt depressing.

What was the point of taking advice from a person she absolutely would not wish to emulate in any way whatsoever? It was not Susan's age, or even her figure, that she baulked at—or even the fact that she was physically unattractive—but rather that she was too smug by half. It was the woman's smugness that she could not stand, the imbecilic self-satisfaction in the face of so little real accomplishment.

Escape, though, was not possible regardless of her philosophical reservations. Alyssa took a seat on the couch in Susan Lindow's converted garage as mandated, and in due course the session with her kicked off as planned.

Given the widely publicised recent events at the Donald Clinic, Susan wanted to gain more clarity about certain issues. 'All the time with you, Alyssa, all I encounter is brambles and thickets. We need to clear a path, the two of us. So, before we go any further, it's your *own* understanding of yourself that I'm interested in today. *Your* idea of what colours you're thinking. Sound reasonable?'

'Knock yourself out.' The purpose of such an invasion, she knew, was to enable Susan to assess her vulnerabilities in relation to non-objective counselling practices and thereby help her to avoid falling into even more unseen pitfalls.

'Good. So, let's go for the jugular, then. What do you—personally—perceive to be your psychological biases and weaknesses? And don't look so alarmed, my dear. I'm not about to eat you. I'm here to help you.'

'I understand.'

Susan obviously didn't think that she did *understand* because she carried on in this vein for quite a while, insisting on mouthing concepts already perfectly obvious. And then, finally, she explained that it was not her role to *treat* any personal issues uncovered.

'That's not my role, my dear.' No. Her role was simply to gain knowledge of a junior colleague's stable and self-declared issues, not make diagnostic judgements. She was not expecting Alyssa to reveal current emotional issues. 'Definitely not. That sort of thing is best kept private from supervision sessions and supervisors. I cannot stress strongly enough that this is not therapy, Alyssa. This is professional guidance. I'm on your side. Unlike in normal counselling, I will always assume that you are being honest with me.'

Yada, yada, yada.

What rank hypocrisy from a woman who had illegally obtained access to her inpatient notes at the Olympic Hospital. 'Thank you, Susan. As I said quite a few minutes ago, all of what you are telling me, I understand perfectly well.'

Susan smiled. 'Remember, if you ever feel in need of active counselling you need to arrange that separately. You could return to Norman Bullock of course. I understand that he was your clinical psychologist when you were having those traumatic-stress psychotic episodes that you were admitted to the Olympic for. Correct?'

'Yes,' said Alyssa, 'he was.' There was no longer any need to keep quiet about such things because with Susan there was no longer any hope of privacy. Which did have its advantages. She might not trust Susan, but she certainly did not fear her.

She recalled their very first supervision session, months earlier, when it slipped out that Susan knew too much about her past. Many times, subsequently, Susan had retold the story of how she had innocently mentioned the name of her new supervisee, Alyssa Brown, to a close friend in the psychiatry department at Olympic Hospital only to have the innocent breach of privacy snowball rather mortifyingly into something quite unexpected. How this "close friend" had then insisted that she see Alyssa Brown's inpatient file, and how—unforgivably—she had done just that. Which always sounded a little too glib because undoubtedly it was just that. Hogwash.

Susan Lindow was nothing but a nosy parker.

Fortunately, though, Susan understood the potential ramifications of her unethical actions and had cooperated when challenged. In the preceding weeks, armed with a signed supervisee consent form, Susan had obtained an authorised official copy of the Olympic Hospital notes and placed them in her supervisor's file. Alyssa's past could now not be divulged to anyone by Susan Lindow. Not without fatal legal consequences.

This had been the best way forward. Sweeping Susan's misdemeanour under the carpet, so to speak, had given some leverage over her. She could have reported Susan to the Psychology Board—with serious consequences for Susan—but hadn't, and this had made Susan grateful to her. It hadn't been kindness on her part, though. There was no upside to coming under the radar of the psychology board, even as a complainant. The less anyone knew about her the better.

Susan's droning voice brought her back into the present.

'Did you get on with Norman Bullock?' she was asking. 'I know a lot of people don't.'

'Norman was excellent. He thought my difficulties were under control and he's discharged me. I haven't needed to see anyone for over three years now.'

'He thought that did he? Under control. Excellent.' Susan Lindow placed a pair of bifocals on her nose and found a place to write. 'Now, where were we?'

'Psychological biases and weaknesses.'

'Ah, yes. That's what we need to address today. As a certified counsellor yourself, I'm sure you have identified some of your biases, the main ones at least. Are you willing to share any of these conclusions with me? It's entirely voluntary, but the more you tell me the more I will be able to assist you to stay on track with your counselling.'

'No problem. We all have our biases and weaknesses. I'd say there are at least six or seven tendencies in my psychological makeup that I'm consciously aware of as problematical. Do you want me to be completely frank, though? Some of them obviously involve my perception of you, so is that really what you want?'

'Be my guest,' said Susan squinting through her bifocals. 'I'm sure I can take it.' She gave what looked like a smirk.

Fat enough for a comedian.

'Okay, then.'

2

'Perhaps we should start with your obvious problem with your stepmother. I assume she has an increased waist circumference. I'm intrigued by the animosity.'

Alyssa had the good grace to blush. She was up against a professional. 'I didn't realise I was that transparent. But, yes, I do struggle with negativity towards the woman I blame for my father's unhappiness in his later life—and yes, she is overweight. It's an issue I am aware of. Diana has always seemed despicable to me. Even now, she's turned herself into an excuse for a human being by becoming pathetic even though she's only fifty-six years old.'

'Why do you think this bothers you? Especially now that you've left home.'

The answer to that was easy: 'Because she's supposed to be a stepmother to me yet is a complete insult to everything that I am. I can't think of any person less like me. When she tried to mother me when I was a young child, she was an utter failure. I really can't forgive her for that. She's an affront to my real mother, who was brilliant.'

Susan glanced at her notes and frowned. 'And will you be like that one day? A brilliant mother, yet someone who abandoned her children?'

Alyssa ignored the sarcasm in Susan's voice. 'Obviously, I won't be making the same mistake. You don't know the half of it anyway. No one does. I remember only good things about her. Like Grace, I'm not totally self-obsessed. With Diana, though, everything is always all about *her*. There's never been any place in her life for me or anyone else. I'm sure you know the type, the kind of person who sucks the air out of a room. That's her exactly. Everything with her is to do with sickness and death—hers, yours, the plants, the insects, the atmosphere, everything. Not to mention her constant pains. She's *always* in pain. Then there's the slow walking. Instead of walking, she shuffles—for no reason other than to irritate and offend. Everything she does is done just to wind others up. There's no end to the negativity. To top it off, she completely neglects herself. To be brutally frank, she's a slob. Physically, she's hopelessly out of condition.'

'You don't approve of her, obviously.'

'No.'

'Would you say she has a controlling, passive-aggressive personality disorder?'

'Exactly that. And throw in a good dose of Munchausen by proxy and some depression.'

'Is she *very* fat?'

Susan knew how to put her on the spot. 'Sort of middling.'

'And is that an insult to you too? Any sort of fat, I mean.'

'No, of course not. I've got nothing against overweight people per se. It's more the "everything about Diana" that I can't stand. She's an insult to everything that I am. And to my father. He was great.'

'I see.' Susan wrote something in her notes, then flipped back a few pages in her copy of the psychiatry department admission file. 'Here in your file. Robert Brown. It says here that he was a chronic alcoholic.' Susan squinted at the text. 'It also mentions, besides some carrying on about his alcohol problem, that *you* were found in the driver's seat of his car when it crashed. That's odd, isn't it? A thirteen-year-old. Doesn't sound very great, does it?'

'Why not? He was still a great dad. That file of mine has most things back to front, exactly as you would expect from a bunch of clowns going through the motions of running a public psychiatry service. They've just copied the police report, which is crap. The truth is, I was found in the front seat *with* my father. There were no seat belts on either of us.' Her heart was thumping, and she knew she had gone red in the face and was almost shouting. 'People are so stupid!'

After the outburst, there was an awkward pause.

Alyssa knew how the "pregnant pause" trap worked in counselling, so even though she had a lot more that she wanted to say, she forced herself to remain silent. Susan Lindow was not a person she would ever trust.

'In that case,' said Susan finally, 'let's move on. What about your extended family, Alyssa? Weren't they of some assistance? Why didn't you approach them for help?'

'My mother Grace was an only child and her father died young from a heart attack. I never knew my grandfather, but my grandmother, Isobel Starke, I did know. I was very fond of her, but Grace's death proved more than she could bear. She got cancer and died shortly after that. My dad's family are all in England, but we could never afford to meet up with them, so we never got to know them and drifted apart. Diana, I think, came straight out of hell because she's never had any family of any sort.'

Susan ignored her comment about Diana. 'So, you had an isolated childhood. Is that what you are saying?'

'Pretty much. But it never bothered me.' She did at least have good memories of Granny Isobel, a cultured and refined woman to her young eyes—who died when she was eight. What remained with her the most about Isobel was how earnestly she had tried to impart religious advice to her in the months before she died.

Promise me, my darling, that from now on you will try to model yourself on Jesus. That is the only way for you to stay safe.

She remembered nodding earnestly at the dying woman in the hospital bed, but she had not really understood at that stage why everyone seemed to think that Jesus was her only hope. She had prayed for at least a year for Grace to be made alive again, but nothing had happened.

'Are you still there, Alyssa?' It was the voice of Susan.

'Yes, I'm listening. Please keep going.'

'The six or seven psychological or personality issues that you mentioned earlier, the issues you are aware of. Let's get back onto those. Just stick to what you are comfortable revealing.'

Alyssa tried to focus. 'Well, as you know, there was my mother's death when I was five and my dad's when I was thirteen, including my own near-death experience and severe head injury, so obviously there are going to be issues. As you'd expect, I've been left with a spectrum of consequences. I've been diagnosed at various times with almost every possibility in psychiatry—virtually all of it complete rubbish—such as hyper-sexuality, for example, which was really what the psychiatrist at the time was suffering from, not me. What I do accept, though, is that I have a lack of self-confidence, low self-esteem, and a compensatory hypercritical personality. Supposedly, this all stems from a childhood chronic post-traumatic stress disorder, although that explanation doesn't make much sense to me, so I don't really believe it. Beyond that, I'd say I'm unable to handle rejection very well for obvious reasons, and then there's this chronic anxiety thing. All in all, though, it seems the only functional limitation that I have is an inability to empathise with older women.'

3

Susan Lindow appeared impressed by her insight into herself. 'Very perceptive, Alyssa. Very perceptive. I note, though, that you make no mention of your episode of psychosis—what they have labelled here in your notes as "post organic brain injury and childhood PTSD-related psychosis involving a fixed delusional state".'

'I prefer not to think about it.'

'So, no delusions currently?'

'No.'

'Mm. Really?'

'Really.'

'Okay then, let's look at your anxiety problem. May I ask what you mean by the word anxiety. To you, what is *anxiety*?'

'You're not serious, are you? I'm a counsellor.'

'Humour me.'

'Anxiety is the normal response to a perceived threat.'

'Very good. There is a threat. That is the essence of it.'

'Yes. So?'

'So, tell me about this threat to you. Who or what is threatening you?'

Alyssa was no fool. She could see where Susan was going with the question. She was after the truth. There was no way she was going to be saying anything further. 'My answer is I don't know.'

'You don't *know*? Really, Alyssa? That is disappointing. Or is it that you don't trust yourself to be truthful? Is that it? Could it be that deep down you blame yourself for the death of both your parents? Could it be that you fear that you may harm those whom you love? Could it be that what is threatening you is that there is a part of you that you feel unable to trust—given your past? These are just concepts that I raise, which you may wish to comment on.'

'As I said, I don't know about any of that.'

'Mm. Grief, then. You know about that, I'm sure. About the unstoppable sadness that comes from being unable to be there for someone you love?'

'I do get sad. Sometimes.'

'Your mother's death was by suicide, wasn't it?'

'No. She died by death. Like in *she died*. A train cut her in half.'

Susan Lindow scratched her head and flipped back another page in the file. 'It says here it was suicide.' She read out the exact words in the psychiatry notes: "Grace Brown committed suicide at the age of thirty-one. She threw herself under a train.".' She looked up. 'When you were five years old.'

'Believe me, that's all wrong. If anyone should know, I should. I was there. You've gone and upset me now.' Her body had begun to tremble violently, but she was unable to stop the movements. While she tried to calm herself, Susan politely looked down at her notes.

Alyssa tried her best to sound normal. 'Sorry. I think my head injury is playing up.'

Susan adopted a kinder tone. 'How *did* your mother die then, Alyssa? If you don't mind me asking?'

'She fell under the train. *Fell*.'

Alyssa could feel the pulses in her neck beating.

'I'm so sorry to hear that. It must have been terrible. Where were you when it happened?'

'Nobody knows the half of it. Nobody knows!' She began shaking even more uncontrollably.

Susan finally had the sense to back off and change the subject. Her tone became one of fake cheerfulness. 'Any other kinks in your makeup, then? Remember, I'm trying to help you. I'm on your side. You only need to list issues that you are willing to share in the interests of enhancing your own counselling objectivity.'

'I understand, Susan.' Alyssa stood up and took a walk around the room to calm herself. Finally, she resumed her seat. 'You are right, Susan. I should have mentioned that breakdown thing of mine when I was at university. The truth is, I don't like to talk about it because I don't really know what happened. It started out as something to do with feeling guilty, that much I do know, but it got way worse than that. Things got out of hand. I'm still confused about a lot of it, and I've never properly understood what happened. I do have some blind spots there. I know I have.'

'Are you able to put what you are saying into more truthful words?' Susan began jabbing at the notes in front of her. 'The reality you claim to know so little about is recorded right here, Alyssa, in your file, which you have read many times.' Susan was relentless. 'Your file records you as requesting—and being sent—full copies of this file on at least four occasions. What *don't you remember*? Do you deny that you broke down into a deluded state and began hallucinating?'

'Yes, I do actually. It wasn't a psychosis. Although I do admit that I don't have a good alternative explanation. It was something out of my control, that's all I know for sure.'

'So, no delusions or hallucinations then?' Susan scribbled in the notes, muttering under her breath. 'Unbelievable.'

'If you knew psychiatrists as well as I do, Susan, you wouldn't believe much from them either.'

Susan was not convinced. 'According to Dr Bullock here—though, sure, he's a clinical psychologist, not a psychiatrist—you were diagnosed as having suffered, due to environmental stress, temporary psychotic decompensation of a chronic fixed delusion related to events in your childhood. While hallucinating about something to do with "evil", you almost succeeded in killing yourself by throwing yourself out of a window on the eleventh floor of the hospital but got pulled back to safety just in time.'

'What's your point?'

'What are you even saying! It says here that you had years of psychotherapy before being successfully re-stabilised and weaned off antipsychotic medication. At final discharge, you were said to be still in possession of your original fixed delusional belief, which is that you are a bad person. What do you think of all that? Any blind spots there, do you think?'

'That whole thing only happened after I dumped my boyfriend. I was young and stupid, and he was in jail. That's all it was. I never swallowed most of my pills anyway, and it's never happened again. I'm fine now. That's as much as needs to be said about it.'

'And the fixed delusions?'

'What about them? There aren't any. A delusion is something that isn't true. I don't believe anything that isn't true.'

Susan leant over and showed her the file. 'You see here? See how it's been recorded as such? "Psychotic delusions. *Chronic*".'

'It's not the truth, believe me. Nobody knows the half of it. But why don't we leave it at that, Susan?'

'What do you mean, *leave* it! *Are* you a bad person, or aren't you?'

'You know full well that it doesn't matter what I *say*. If I said I wasn't bad, you wouldn't be able to know for sure that I wasn't because I might in fact be evil and telling you a lie. The important thing is that *I* know what I am. We've talked about this nonsense as much as I'm prepared to, I think.'

Susan frowned at her. 'Your call, I suppose.' She closed the psychiatric file with an exaggerated sigh of exasperation. 'What do you propose?'

'Why don't we do what I'm here for: discuss some of my cases.'

'Discuss some cases!'

'Yes. Do that.'

Susan Lindow was showing all the signs of becoming a major pain in the ass.

4

Alyssa took the tram home once the supervision session finally ended. It was late already, and the tram was packed, so she had to stand and hold onto an overhead strap. On the way, the tram passed the familiar library of the medical school at Olympic Hospital, so, for a while, she occupied herself with wondering how her super-sexy surgeon Mark was getting on. Later though, as the tram lurched its way east through the centre of the city, the pleasant thoughts about Mark were driven from her mind by a mounting realisation that she needed to stop daydreaming. Susan Lindow was going to be a problem. Once she and Susan had moved on to discussing some of her cases, Susan had been scathing about her management. She was going to have to get rid of Susan Lindow. As soon as possible. And she needed to work out how.

While thinking about alternative supervisors, her phone, which was in her shoulder bag with her work documents, began to vibrate. The sudden interruption startled her.

What the . . .

She let it go through to voicemail. It wouldn't be Trish from work. Technically, she was still at work, so not taking any calls. Trish knew that.

Half an hour later, once out of the tram and walking down Jowlett Street near home, she revisited the call. She half-expected it to have been Susan Lindow trying to deliver a final tirade of castigation, or possibly even Mark at the Olympic trying to say that he had seen her passing by in the tram and was missing her. He didn't have her number, of course, but one could dream. The attempted call had been nothing of that sort, however. It had been from her family doctor, the female GP who didn't like her very much. Which was surprising. She thought it best to return the call without delay. She pressed "dial" as she walked.

'It's about your results, Alyssa,' said the GP. 'There's no need for alarm, but things aren't quite normal.'

'You mean with my Pap test?'

'Yes, the cervical screening test. You will need to see a gynaecologist. Within the next week or two if you can. That part is important.'

'What! I mean, I beg your pardon. What do you mean by "not normal", doctor? Are you saying it's cancer?'

'No, Alyssa, no. It's important we don't jump to conclusions.'

'What's wrong, then?'

'There are some changes in your cells, but it's not clear yet what they mean. A specialist gynaecologist will be the best person to take it further. Is there one you know that you would like to be referred to?'

News that her smear was abnormal was the last thing she had expected, so she found it difficult to think clearly. She felt shocked. Normally, everything in that department was perfect. It was important that she be healthy. 'Gynaecologist?' She had not ever seen a gynaecologist before. She had never needed to.

'Do you have one?'

'No.' She had forgotten all about the Pap test that the GP had performed when she went to get a prescription for anxiety pills. It had simply been an afterthought, a ploy to force the reluctant doctor to see her and give her the script she needed. The screening test had seemed routine and uneventful, hardly uncomfortable at all. Now she had cancer. It really was the last thing she needed.

'Are you still there, Alyssa?'

'Yes. It's just that I'm a bit shocked. You see, normally I'm a really healthy person. Are you quite sure there hasn't been a mix up?'

'Quite sure.'

'What exactly does the report say?'

'It's very technical and hard to explain properly over the phone. The nub of it is that they have found something called severe dysplasia. As far as we can tell, it's not yet cancer. As far as we can tell . . .' The rest of the doctor's words faded into the noise of a passing truck.

Shit!

'I'll go and see a specialist as soon as possible,' said Alyssa loudly, above the truck noise. 'Can you recommend someone?' While she was trying to talk, a vehicle turned in front of her. Unsurprisingly, it had become hard to talk and avoid traffic at the same time. The car hooted at her.

'We use Andrew Jensen,' said the GP above the noise. 'You'll like him, I think. He has rooms near us. I'll do a referral to him if you like, after which you should receive an appointment shortly. Happy with that?'

'Dr Jensen it has to be, then. Okay. Thanks.'

The GP rang off.

Alyssa felt angry. There were no signs of any mischief in her vagina and never had been. Maybe a bit of thrush once or twice, but that was normal. It did not seem possible that she could have "severe dysplasia"—whatever that was—or worse, at her age, without knowing about it. There had to be a mistake. It had to be one giant cock-up.

She paused at the front door of her flat.

What if I can't have children?

How—then—would she be able to face the rest of her life?

When she opened the door, she saw that something even more dreadful had happened.

Cy was gone.

Cy had left her.

CHAPTER TWENTY-NINE

1

WHILE SHE HAD BEEN out fulfilling her professional supervision requirements at Susan Lindow's house on the opposite side of the central city, Cy had moved out.

Alyssa sat on her couch in the empty flat with her head in her hands. Everything seemed unreal. The television set was gone—it had been his. Gone too were Cy's laptop, his Bluetooth soundbar, his headphones, the round table and its two chairs, the bookshelf, and his books. All his things in the bathroom were gone too. And all his clothes.

There was a farewell card on the kitchen bench, a card bought at a two-dollar shop. On the outside of the card was a picture of two toy bears cuddling. On the inside, a note hastily scribbled:

Alyssa, I had to go.
I've been unhappy for a long time now, but I haven't had the guts to face up to you. I need to be myself again. I need to be free.
Please don't take this too hard. This is more about me than it is about you. You have been good to me. So good. Too good. I'm not the man for you. You deserve better.
Soz my Bambi. Forgive me. It's better this way.
All the best.
Adieus, *Simon*

Simon? Soz my Bambi? Sorry? Nothing seemed real. Cy never called himself Simon. He hated the name. And he never called her "Bambi". She read his note twice over in case she had misread it or misunderstood it. It seemed hard to believe. The treachery of it. The weakness of it. The absolute betrayal.

Her body went numb. She left the note on the kitchen benchtop and headed for the window to get some air, but once there, the absence of the round table and Cy's bookshelf and books seemed to make her feel dizzy. The world began to reel, like she was on a ship heading for a giant whirlpool. She felt like she had been punched in the head and had some sort of concussion. She staggered, gripped the window ledge of the open window to steady herself, then almost slipped on a piece of paper on the floor. She kicked at it angrily, but then picked it up because it was from where Cy's bookshelf had once stood. It was one of his many notes to himself and had probably escaped from inside a book when he moved. She read it:

Re the Harold book:

These twelve not myths at all but True Nature of Women

Leave this lot out. Publishers won't touch it

➤   Women believe they are more important to their lover than they really are.

➤   Women's morals: What is mine is mine and what is my man's is mine too.

➤   Women are not people first; they are women first. They like to pretend that human faults like dishonesty, violence, unfaithfulness, and so forth, do not equally apply to them.

➤   Women have only one aim: to get all they can from their man.

➤   Women love their fathers first and deepest and to the end of eternity—not you.

➤   Women struggle to orgasm regularly and reliably during sex with men.

➤   Women are not happy with themselves; they live much of their life by proxy.

➤   Women who fall in love with you are extremely dangerous, so are best avoided.

➤   A woman who falls in love with you will demand your entire life and your soul.

➤   Sexually, women want/need men to shoulder the guilt they feel over what they, as women, do sexually.

➤   Women have silly ideas about the robustness of the male erection.

> ➤ Women have secret sadisms. Their main sadism: "*they* fuck *you*". Ha-ha.

'Bastard!' she screamed, suddenly furious. In a fit of violence, she tore the sheet of paper into shreds. Then, going down on her knees, she feverishly scooped up the contaminating fragments and went and hurled them into the kitchen rubbish bin together with the card from the two-dollar shop, which she first crushed.

'Monster! Fuck you!'

After that, she did not know what to do.

She walked around in the half-empty flat for a while. Then, feeling deflated, she put herself to bed even though it was only six o'clock and she had not eaten anything.

She had a nightmare.

In the nightmare, she was a fairy princess, young and beautiful. The air was light and sunny and the flowers bright. She had magic and she was very happy. And then a bad witch appeared, a witch who wanted to stop her doing what she wanted; a witch who wanted to steal for herself everything that belonged to the fairy princess. And so, it had to be a fight. The witch was very strong, very powerful. And she fought dirty. The fairy princess could only fight fair, but she had her own magic too. In desperation, she did what she knew had to be done: she cast a spell on the witch, one that made the witch feel unloved. It worked. The witch became very sad. She became so sad that she went and sat down beside a train line. Meanwhile, the fairy princess danced in triumph in front of her. This upset the bad witch so much that after a while she stood up to fight again, but when she did so she lost her footing and began to fall. She fell in slow motion, casting many spells to try to save herself as she went down. A large black locomotive was coming, and she knew it. The witch began to scream in terror. She was losing the fight. The fairy princess smiled. She did not put her hand out to save the witch. She could have. But she did not. She let the witch die. The witch fell directly under the train, and it cut her into two pieces. The two parts wriggled for a while, but it was the end for the witch. She was dead. However, instead of now being happy, the fairy princess began to feel very sad at what she had done. She tried to undo her magic but found it could not be undone. Nothing more could be done for the witch. Because of this, the fairy princess had to be severely punished. They took away her magic and told her that she too deserved to die. From that day forward she was transformed into a witch herself—an evil witch. Thereafter, she had to hide from everybody. It was terrible. Everybody hated her. She became the most hated person in the entire world . . .

Alyssa woke gasping for breath. It felt as if someone had been choking her. She sat up in the darkness, bathed in sweat. She hadn't had that nightmare for years.

She felt scared.

She wondered where Cy was. Then she remembered.

He was dead.

It had happened again.

It was going to happen all over again.

Her life was over.

2

Cy wasn't dead, of course. So, there was nothing for it but to continue as if nothing had happened. Alyssa felt certain that Cy would be back soon with his tail between his legs. Most likely, he had acted impulsively—as he so often did—and would not be able to cope without her. It was a tough world out there. Besides, she had no option but to carry on. She could not afford to take more time off work. Not after the disruptions following Gilbert Rockport's death and the further disturbances in relation to the disaster with Ben Clayton. She needed to keep going, keep soldiering on.

The cottage clinic was fully booked. A busy Thursday beckoned.

Even though she had been abandoned by Cy, she was only fifteen minutes late for work in the morning. However, it seemed she was already in trouble over even that trivial failure. Trish phoned her at the cottage shortly after her late arrival and said that Greta wanted to see her. Greta had scheduled a meeting with her for 1330 hours and the venue was Greta's office.

A disciplinary meeting with someone like Greta was the last thing she needed but unfortunately non-attendance was not going to be an option.

Not if she wanted to keep her job. Greta McCreedy, as the Donald's clinical psychologist, was her nominal superior. She needed to placate her. The job at the Donald was the only thing she had left in life.

And so, so much study debt . . .

The morning clinic seemed busier than usual. The clients were difficult, and the late start not helpful. When she arrived at Greta's office for the meeting, she was four minutes late. Once again, she had failed. She was trying her best though. This was surely all a person could be expected to do. After all, she was not Greta's servant. She resented receiving orders via third parties, and she resented being forced to attend meetings during her lunch break. She was a professional person in her own right. Not only that, but she needed proper lunches because she was physically active.

Unlike this dried out old prune in front of me.

Greta looked pointedly at her watch. 'Sit down,' she said rudely. Alyssa dutifully sat on the client side of Greta's desk. Greta leant forwards slightly, elbows on her desk, and peered at her for a while above steepled hands. 'Are you quite settled?'

'Yes, thank you.'

'I'm afraid, Alyssa, that we have a problem.'

'And what's that?'

Fifteen minutes late in the morning too much to bear for you, is it?

She never said it.

'Nurse Gail Wilson. She has made a formal complaint about you to the organisation.'

Alyssa was shocked. 'Gail? What about?' It was the last thing she expected. Gail had taken a week's sick leave after the episode with Ben Clayton, but Alyssa knew she was back at work. She had seen her walking around looking much the same as always: terminally unhappy.

'The complaint has to do with your professional competence, Alyssa. Or should I say, your lack thereof. Gail Wilson asserts that you destabilised Ben Clayton because of an unacceptable degree of counselling incompetence and that you thereby placed her at risk.'

'She can't be serious! I mean, come on. You can't be serious.'

'We have no choice but to take this seriously. And we do. We take all formal complaints seriously.' Greta glared at her. 'It gets worse. You know who Gail's husband is, don't you. Well, together they've been to a lawyer. A really, really expensive one. Dr Barnes has received a civil claim for damages. A very large one. Millions.'

'What a bastard.'

'I'll ask you to withdraw that statement.'

Alyssa felt herself shaking with rage as she struggled to contain herself. 'Of course,' she said finally.

'I'm sure Dr Barnes will be getting in touch with you in due course.'

Alyssa stood up. 'Can I please be sent a copy of the complaint, exactly as worded?'

'Sit down, please.'

'I've got a client scheduled for two o' clock and I haven't had lunch yet.'

'Sit down Alyssa. Clients and lunches can wait. Gail is not the end of the problem we have with you.'

Alyssa felt as though she had been slapped across the face. She did not know how much more of Greta she could take, but she had no choice but to sit down. 'What do you mean "problem with me"?' She could hear the deflation in her own voice.

'Barrister Rockport's law firm has also been in contact with Dr Barnes. The law firm is collaborating with his widow. They have filed notice of intent to sue for damages in the event that suicide is determined to be the cause of his death—which according to them it almost certainly is. You are specifically cited as the person in Dr Barnes's clinic in whom malpractice is suspected. That makes it two very large disasters in a row. Can you see why we have a problem with you?'

Greta was now glaring at her with something akin to satisfaction tugging at her face.

Alyssa meanwhile felt blood draining from her own face She tried to say something sensible, but without success. 'I don't know what to say. I don't think Gilbert Rockport's death was suicide. I mean, it's highly unlikely. Isn't it?'

Greta remained stony faced. Her expression said it all: it was not. When it came to Gilbert Rockport, suicide was far from unlikely.

Oh shit.

'What should I do?'

'We'll wait for the inquest findings. And I'll send you Gail's complaint. Meanwhile, may I politely suggest that you *stop* causing disasters. Take this as your final warning, Alyssa. Another incident and we'll be forced to suspend your employment.'

Alyssa stood up again, this time white with rage. 'It's come to *this*, has it?'

'Believe me, I have no idea what you are talking about. Obtain professional help by all means, but there is no future in adopting a threatening attitude—either with me or with anyone else.'

'Cow!'

'What did you say!'

'Wow. Wow, I appreciate all that you are doing for me.'

'Goodbye, Alyssa. Let's not have any more problems with you.'

3

A few days later Alyssa attended her appointment with the gynaecologist Dr Jensen. She went without a support person seeing that she did not have one. Cy appeared to have disappeared for good. The only other possibility would have been Jocelyn, but she did not yet trust Jocelyn enough to reveal intimate details about herself to her. Besides, it was easier to be alone because she felt disheartened and depressed.

She had found out via Jocelyn, who had found out via Brian, that Cy had shacked up with an artist-come-drug-addict called Rosie Skye, who lived in an outer suburb called Nandedong, which was many kilometres away. Jocelyn had informed her further that Brian was extremely angry about the whole business because Cy had abandoned him too and chucked up his job at the bookshop without notice.

How selfish.

All for some old skank going by the name of Rosie Skye, which was about as ridiculous as Cyrus Beauchamp.

For God's sake!

At least, she thought bitterly, they could do their drugs together.

On the tram to the gynaecologist's rooms, she could not stop thinking about Cy. His walking out on her would not be the end of the matter, she decided. It could not end so swiftly and with such finality. Not with so much brutally. They had meant more to each other than that. What they had had was genuine and not sordid. It was impossible that she could mean so little to another person.

The timing of the medical appointment—right in the middle of the crisis with Cy and in the middle of a working day—could not have been worse. The going absent from work *yet again* had upset Trish. It had once again thrown client bookings at the clinic into chaos. An *entire* afternoon off work was required. Trish was not happy.

'Just do it Trish. It's important. It's a medical appointment and I can't change it or miss it.'

'Appointment for what?'

'None of your business.' Trish was too much of a blabbermouth to be told anything.

'Is it serious?'

'Just make the bloody arrangements.' After that, she had put the phone down.

On the day of the meeting with destiny, after completing her morning clinic but before venturing out to be intimately examined, Alyssa first went home to freshen up. With that done, she at least had no concern about the prospect of needing to remove her pants for the male gynaecologist. If anything, she was a bit of an exhibitionist. She was certainly not ashamed of her parts. With the appointment letter had come an information sheet. Dr Andrew Jensen was going to be looking up her vagina with a microscope. Obviously, one could not get to a cervix without encountering certain other areas of anatomy. Hence the shower and change of underwear.

Abandoned by men but clean.

The bathroom had seemed bare without Cy's things. The whole flat, in fact, had seemed sad and dispirited.

Dr Andrew Jensen, on the other hand, turned out to be much as expected—except for the fact that he was strangely nondescript. He looked to be in his mid to late forties and was of average height and quite slim. He could just as well have been a bank clerk or a minor civil servant. His voice, though, was assured and polished, as though he was used to being in command. His hands looked soft, and he had clean fingernails. There was a young, overweight, and depressed-looking nurse sitting in the corner of the room with him. She was dressed in surgical scrubs and was obviously his assistant and chaperone.

He introduced her briefly. 'With us today is nurse Robin, to give me a hand. Okay with you?'

'Sure.'

He consulted his notes. 'Now, Alyssa, do you understand the implications of your Pap test findings?'

'No. What exactly has been found?'

'The technical term is *CIN III plus*. Which is a little unusual in young women these days and a bit unfortunate too in your case considering that you were vaccinated against the HPV virus at school. I have the records here via your GP.'

'Yes. I remember us all getting vaccinated.'

'Excellent. Now, the unfortunate part is that the vaccination doesn't cover all the viral subtypes. You've been unlucky and picked up something very uncommon.'

'But what? I'm still not sure exactly what it is that I'm supposed to have.'

'Has your GP not explained it to you?'

'Not really. She said you would.' She hoped she did not sound too dumb.

The gynaecologist turned to an illustration card on his desk and placed it in front of her. 'See.' He pointed with a finger. 'A cervix.'

In the diagram, Alyssa could recognise a vagina, a rectum, a bladder, a uterus, and ovaries. She felt quite pleased with her anatomical ability. The cervix was where the gynaecologist's finger was resting—at the top of the vagina.

'What you have,' he continued, 'is a pre-cancer in the skin of your cervix, caused by an oncogenic wart virus. The virus type you have is type thirty-eight.'

It was too technical for her to understand. 'It's not cancer, is it? Or is it?'

He smiled at her. 'It usually never is. But that's why you are here: to find out for sure. The colposcopy and biopsy will clarify the matter. Once we get today's results back, assuming no invasion is found, I'll be able to arrange treatment here at my rooms. Treatment is usually a simple office procedure with an electrical loop. If you do indeed have what we think you have then the abnormality is only skin deep and easy to get rid of. If not . . . well, we'll see.'

Dr Jensen nodded to nurse Robin, who came to life and escorted Alyssa to the examination couch. The nurse closed a curtain around the couch.

'Shoes off, skirt off, undies off,' she barked in a disinterested voice. 'Right off.'

Barefoot and naked from the waist down, Alyssa was placed on her back on the colposcopy couch and then had her legs processed. The nurse lifted them, bent them at the knee, parted them widely, and secured them on behind-knee rests. The top of the bed was raised, leaving her half sitting. Alyssa wondered if this was how women gave birth. A machine on wheels was positioned between her legs.

'Ready,' yelled Robin.

Dr Jensen took up position. 'You've not had warts down here before, have you?' he said pleasantly while inserting a speculum into her vagina.

'No warts,' said Alyssa. 'Not down there. I had some under my feet at school, but they're gone.' Alyssa realised that she was looking at a man who had probably seen over ten thousand vaginas. She wondered what went on in his head. Her own naked vagina did not seem to have any effect on him at all.

He was obviously an expert because he was gentle with what he was doing despite cranking various devices open inside her. He also conversed with her in pleasant tones as he worked.

'Your records show that your last screening test was over five years ago. Is that correct?'

'Yes, I think so. I know I've been a bit remiss. Sorry.'

'Well, at least we know that your first Pap and HPV result was clear. Absolutely normal. Looks like the wart virus is confined to your current smear only.' The gynaecologist began applying a pungent smelling chemical somewhere inside her.

'I thought viruses cured themselves over time,' said Alyssa.

'Oh no,' said Dr Jensen. 'Not the virus type that you have. It stays with you. It's on your results form. Oncogenic. As I said, type 38. That's how you get the pre-cancerous cells. Certain persistent viral subtypes cause it.'

'You mean I got this maybe cancer thing *from* somebody?'

'It's not that simple,' said the gynaecologist from between her legs. 'The HPV virus is very common. Almost everyone has it in some form or other, and with no ill effect—especially in the vaccinated. High grade dysplasia is rare in Astoria these days. You need to be very unlucky to get conversion to pre-cancer—or worse, of course.'

Dr Jensen had completed doing what he had to do. He went back to his desk, after which nurse Robin once again closed the curtains.

'You can get dressed,' she said. Then the nurse whispered in her ear. 'Don't let the doctors lead you astray, Alyssa. This does not mean that you didn't get this virus from someone. You *did*. You got it from a man, and somebody needs to tell you this.'

You got it from a man.

CHAPTER THIRTY

1

ALAN SUMMERFIELD INVITED ALYSSA out for a drink a few days after the visit to the gynaecologist. The news had spread that her boyfriend had dumped her.

The way the invitation happened was that while she was heading to the front door of the Donald clinic one evening, on her way home, Dr Summerfield appeared out of his own office too and caught sight of her passing at the point where the main corridor crossed the side corridor. He had been both surprised and pleased to see her. He had his jacket on and his briefcase was in his hand.

'Alyssa,' he said from a distance. 'What a pleasant surprise. It's always nice to see you. I'm on my way home too. I'm tired of late nights.'

She waited for him to catch up to her, politely pausing between two tall pot plants in the hallway. She knew he wanted to talk to her. She knew too that she was blushing, so she tried to keep herself in a shadow.

Alan Summerfield came right up to her. 'I've been a little concerned about you,' he said kindly. 'Given what's happened.' There was true tenderness in his voice rather than mockery. 'I've noticed that you have been looking rather sad lately. Would you like some company? Why don't the two of us go out for a drink? Are you free? I'd love to have a drink with you.'

'You mean, like now?'

'Sure. Why not. I could do with some exercise, and I know you like walking. Why don't we walk down to the Park Hotel together? I'll buy you a drink and we can have a bit of a chat.'

His offer, though unexpected, did not feel unwelcome. There was something irresistibly attractive about Alan Summerfield. 'Well, okay then. Let's go. I certainly wouldn't mind having a drink with you. There's nobody waiting for me at home—as you know.' She knew the

566

Park Hotel. She had been there before—with Cy—though only once. It was a few minutes' walk away, although in a direction that would take her away from her flat. The hotel commanded a fine view over the Troy gardens and had a pleasant enough lounge bar. Normally though, it was too snobbish for her liking and far too expensive. With Alan, such limitations would not apply.

Alan placed his briefcase into the trunk of his car, which was parked in the street, and then they walked. At the lounge bar he found a quiet corner with a good view and got them a drinks menu.

'Are you sure you don't want to try a cocktail?'

'Too many calories. Wine will do me fine.'

'What about champagne then?'

'Are we celebrating something?'

He winked. 'Of course. Us. That's what we are celebrating. Settled?'

She acquiesced.

He ordered two gasses of outrageously expensive Dom Perignon.

'It's *us* now, is it?'

Again, that smile. 'A man can dream.'

She was still in her work clothes—a fitted above-knee business skirt and rather unglamorous underwear—so it felt odd trying to relax under such circumstances. It felt even odder being out alone with a married man and drinking his expensive champagne. Though she liked Alan and instinctively trusted him, he was starting to make her feel mildly anxious. Socially, she was not in his league. And she was not in the right space mentally or physically to have sex with anyone. Especially not after what Dr Jensen's nurse had said. Who would want to have sex with someone with warts—even if invisible— and possible cancer? It had been foolish of her to lead Alan on and agree to a drink with him. Wendy had warned her repeatedly about her stupid behaviour with men:

You need to stop giving in to temptation.

Easy to say, but not always easy to do. Alan Summerfield was like a magnificent jungle cat; a fabulously male one. Earlier, on the walk to the hotel, side by side, close, she had noticed for the first time how strongly he moved. He was graceful too; easy and supple in the way she imagined panthers were. Beautiful and a bit scary at the same time. It seemed impossible to believe that he was as old as she knew he was. Jocelyn had told her his exact age: fifty-two. Her own father, Bob, would have been fifty-four had he lived, but Alan seemed nothing like a father figure. With him, age seemed to have lost its meaning. He could just as well have been her own age. What she felt for him had nothing at all to do with fathers and everything to do with sexual desire.

Alan desired her too; that much was obvious. Unlike most men of his age—or even most young men these days—he was not mentally castrated. She was his prey, and she could feel it. He wanted her and he was going to try to have her—and somehow that felt flattering.

He spoke again: 'You know, this feels like a special occasion. The first time out for a drink together. Alone, I mean.'

'I agree. It does feel a bit special.'

'Let's drink to that, then. To many more times together. Just the two of us.'

She clinked glasses with him, and they smiled at each other. She realised then that she had not smiled in a long while.

'I know I shouldn't say this, what with our work ties and all,' he said, 'but it's rare these days to come across a genuinely attractive woman. Something seems to have gone wrong with them lately. They've become so assertive, and so hideous—usually both, in fact. You, on the other hand, well, I just can't tell you enough how sexy you are. I hope you don't mind me telling you this?' He looked directly into her eyes the whole time he spoke.

'I'm really not that great, so it is a bit embarrassing.'

'Nonsense. You are wonderful. It's a pity I'm not single and a bit younger. Some women are so uptight, but there's this wonderful way you have of your clothes always seeming about to slide off your body. They don't of course, but everything about you says that you're comfortable with being naked. Easy with it. Good at it. Physically, Alyssa, you are a breath of fresh air, a precious rarity. I'd love for us to be able to go upstairs together.'

You're right, Alan, I am proud of my body—only, just not just at present. Besides, there are all these scars.

He needed to have his aspirations truncated. Though it made her feel bad, she said the appropriate blocking words: 'Me too, Alan, but not today. It's just too soon for anything.'

She was surprised how much it hurt her to be untruthful with him.

Under normal circumstances, she probably *would* have abandoned herself to the spirit of the occasion.

But now was not the time. And she could not tell him why.

He seemed surprised and a little disappointed by her refusal. Defensive, too. Clearly, she had hurt not only herself but him too. 'I know we'd good for each other,' he said. 'But don't worry, I do realise that we can't. Not really. With me married it wouldn't be right. I hope I haven't shocked you.' He studied her face. 'You know, I know I haven't. It won't help you trying to look innocent. We can both read each other a mile away. That's what's so great about this. We can be honest. I can be honest. You have this marvellous gift, Alyssa. You are so easy to talk to. There's nobody else in the world that I can talk to like this. Nothing seems to shock you.'

'Well, if it means anything to you, I confess that I really like being with you too.'

'Now it's my turn to feel embarrassed. I'm just an old man who can't accept getting old.'

'No Alan. You are still hot, believe me.'

'Thank you.'

He put his hand on her knee and they sat close together in the subdued lighting, chatting, drinking champagne, and enjoying the view of the Troy gardens at dusk, with its wall of freshly lighting-up skyscrapers marching along its far side.

Alyssa could feel her pulse beating in her neck. It came from a combination of excitement and anxiety. It felt so nice being wanted. She needed that so badly. Too badly...

'I've been itching to take you to bed ever since I first clapped eyes on you,' said Alan once his drink was finished. 'But, you know, this evening I think I've just called my own bluff. I'm married, and that's so hard to get past. And of course, despite your kind words, I'm far too old for you. Even I can see that.' He smiled ruefully over his empty glass. 'I think I'd be so anxious making love to you that I'd be impotent.'

'I doubt it, Alan. I'm sure you've never been anxious or impotent in your entire life. But I agree, it would be wrong. For Kara's sake.'

And your own.

She had untreated viruses on her cervix, courtesy no doubt of someone called Cy.

Damn him!

Before long, she might not even have a uterus.

'Yes. It would be wrong.' Alan seemed to be trying to convince himself. 'Perhaps in another life. I'd like that.'

'Me too.'

.... 2 ....

Alan took her hand in his. 'You are such an incredible young woman.' He gave her hand a squeeze of affection. 'Let's just enjoy each other's company, shall we? It's wonderful to be able to sit here like this and talk about anything. I've never been able to achieve that with any of my wives, you know. They've all been so psychologically limited, so quick to take offence, so self-centred. I've never been able to be completely honest with any of them.'

'Really?'

'Afraid so. Far too stupid, all of them. And too prudish. It's been quite demoralising.'

'It's funny how life tends to work that way when it comes to partners, isn't it? We instinctively choose people we think will fix our problems, but actually they are our worst enemies.'

'Yes. Kara is an exotic dancer, yet mentally she's a complete prude. You tell me how that works. It took marrying her to find that one out. Same with all my wives. People seem hopelessly confused about sex. Excluding you, of course. Or, at least, I hope so.'

'I'm probably just as confused as everybody else, Alan. There I was thinking that my boyfriend loved me only to find he was bonking someone else behind my back.'

'Is that what happened, is it?'

'Yes. I only found that part out later, of course, after he walked out on me. I found out through Jocelyn.'

'Our Jocelyn?'

'None other. She managed to find out for me because she knows a friend of my ex, the guy Cy used to work for. Apparently, it was going on for about a month before he left—the bonking behind my back.'

'Incredible. At least he had the good grace to leave.'

'I suppose so.'

For a while, they sat in silence.

'Mentioning Jocelyn has reminded me of work,' said Alan after a while. 'I'm really sorry about how you've been dragged into that Ben Clayton business with Gail.'

'Me too. Someone gave Ben my address, you know. He put a note in my letterbox the day before he attacked Gail. He was clearly off his tree even then.'

'Are you telling me he found out where you live? Do you think someone from the Donald told him?'

'Yes.'

'Mm. So, do you think you were his original target?'

'Don't know. I think it's unlikely. I think he was looking for help. Ben and I have always gotten along just fine.'

Alan steepled his fingers in thought. 'Mm. In that case, are you sure he didn't at some stage during his time with you simply follow you home from work one evening? It's a kind of hero worship thing that these people often do. You wouldn't be the first. It's the most likely explanation.'

Followed me home?

'I hadn't thought of that.' If true, it meant that Ben could easily have killed her at any time. Instead, he had tried to kill Gail.

'Stalking behaviour wouldn't surprise me when it comes to Ben. I'm sure he must be sexually frustrated. In my opinion, Greta should never have dumped someone like him onto someone like you in the first place. Why add to the dangers? What is it with you and Greta McCreedy, by the way? It's possible to cut the atmosphere between the two of you with a knife. Greta's never been like this with anyone else before.'

'She hates me. And I think the feeling is mutual. There's something terminally toxic going on between us that neither of us can fathom.'

'Well, maybe I can help you there. You do know that her husband left her a few years ago, don't you?'

'No.'

'Yes. They were an older couple who didn't have any children. One day, just before her sixtieth birthday, her husband up and left her for a woman half his age—an attractive one at that. I know because I knew this woman.

Jocelyn appointed her and she used to work for us as a receptionist. Greta's never gotten over what happened, and she's become very bitter.'

'And to think that nobody told me.' Alyssa felt quite shocked. 'So, since being abandoned by her partner, Greta lives all alone, does she?'

'Yep. The usual sob-story.'

Alyssa remained silent. Her glass was empty.

The usual sob-story.

A curious question came into her mind in the silence, one to ask Alan about. He knew a lot, so maybe he had the answer to this one too. 'Tell me, Alan,' she said, 'on a completely unrelated matter, what do you think about Jesus? Is he real?'

'Jesus?' He seemed taken aback by the change of subject. 'Are you serious? You mean as in . . . Jesus?'

'Yes, that Jesus. Don't worry, I'm not being weird. I'm just trying to clarify something professionally. Our Ben Clayton has been confusing me a lot on the subject. And Jocelyn too because she seems such an amazingly caring person without any reference to Jesus.'

'Yes, Jocelyn is Jewish—you know that much, do you? Me, I'm not religious. And Ben's away with the fairies. So, what was the question again?'

She persisted. She really did want to know what he thought. 'Just tell me if you think he's real. I won't be offended by anything you say.'

He searched her face and his hand returned to her knee. 'You are serious, I can see that. You mean real, as in . . .'

'Yes. Real.'

'Well, of course, no, he's not.' He looked quite certain about it. 'Sorry if that disappoints anyone. Many people think he is, though, and I understand that too. Unfortunately, the Jesus they rely upon for their salvation is not really Jesus at all but something akin to an Obermaaier Jesus. You've read that explanation, I assume? Jesus is merely whatever any person imagines him to be; something between a bar of soap and a reflection of oneself in a mirror. I don't agree with much of Obermaaier, but I think he's on the money here. Why? Because if there were a real Jesus, then surely the people who have met him would at least *try* to be Christ-like too. Know any such people? Case closed.'

The answer, despite being very confident, did not seem to solve anything.

3

Alan took her home to her flat in his car. He insisted on doing so once they got back to the Donald Clinic, saying that as a gentleman he considered it his duty.

He didn't know exactly where in East Hubron she stayed, so she had to direct him. When they parked outside her home, he got out of the car despite her protests. 'I'll see you to the door,' he said. 'It's the least I can do. Besides, it's exciting being in the company of a beautiful young woman. A man can't get enough of it.'

They did not hold hands on the way up the stairs, but somehow, not doing so felt strange and wrong. She wished they could have. When she unlocked her door, her hand was trembling. She turned to face Alan and for a moment they both looked directly into each other's eyes.

Such intelligence and power.

She could not read his gaze further. He was far too superior. She felt something inside her wilt.

'Thank you for taking me out, Alan. You have no idea how much I appreciate it.' She resisted a strong urge to reach out and hug him because she knew that if she did, she would lose control and be blown away.

How much she wanted that: to be blown away . . . to lose herself entirely. And how tempting it was to toss herself to the wind in an act of madness. Yet, she lacked the confidence. She was out of Alan's league, and she knew it. Not to mention the fact that he was a married man.

Alan Summerfield gently took her hand in his. It was the fourth time they had touched that evening. Like her hand on the door key, his hand was trembling too. 'Look after yourself, Alyssa,' he said, in a voice choking with infinite regret. 'Because I think I'm in danger of falling in love with you.' With that, he turned and trotted down the stairs to his fancy car.

Alone in the gloom of her deserted flat, Alyssa burst into tears.

4

A visit to Fabio's gym was always a dependable source of encouragement and emotional support, both of which were in short supply, so, after a light supper of canned tuna and a banana, Alyssa resolutely set out for

Fabio's in the deepening darkness. The gym was a good fifteen minutes away on foot, but she chose to walk rather than take the tram. Walking was a good way to warm up; besides, it was mentally soothing.

As she walked, the feelings of guilt and regret she had been having over her disastrous outing with Alan Summerfield became replaced by thoughts about Cy. She increasingly thought about him with each purposeful stride. She wondered where he was, and if he was happy, and whether he was having second thoughts, and if he was missing her. Before long, to her surprise, she began to struggle to hold back tears again. Being abandoned was starting to feel like too much to cope with. The sheer treachery of it. The cheek of it. After all, she had never been dumped before. Always it had been the other way around. But now, this time, she had been the fool. Or had she? As she walked along, she tried to console herself by telling herself that deep down she had always suspected Cy might be a rotten swine. A bit like her father.

Rotten to the core.

Trouble was that she knew he wasn't. Not really. Only superficially. Her father had been like that too: weak but good. It was all too much to process for now, so she tried to focus on the surroundings instead and get Cy out of her mind. She studied each building as she went past, seeing some seemingly for the first time ever. Closer to the CBD, still attuned to the surroundings, she began to wonder if her imagination was playing tricks on her. She could swear there was a man following her.

Not again!

At first, she tried to ignore the feeling, but it grew stronger to the point where she felt alarmed. Constant suspicions about being followed were not normal. Was it a sign of what was to come? A developing symptom in a return to madness? Worried, she turned suddenly, as if to cross the road, and looked back in the direction she had come.

Nothing.

Just impending psychosis? Or Cy secretly tagging along behind to check on her welfare? A figure in the far distance who could have been Cy disappeared out of sight. If not Cy, then who? Was the secret figure Ben Clayton? After all, he still knew her address. Though he was supposed to be in hospital, what if he had escaped? The hospital was not far away. Anything seemed possible, even the possibility that nobody was following her, and everything was in her head. After all, despite the strong sixth sense suspicions, there was no *evidence* that anything was awry.

It was important that she pull herself together. Determined to get to the gym, she continued walking, even as the looming bulk of Public Hospital shadowed the sky to the right. Ben was almost certainly in there, somewhere deep, in some ward where they had thrown away the key. And Cy was almost certainly far away in Nandedong, in bed with his Rosie-in-the-Sky. It was important to maintain a grip on reality.

That said, Ben Clayton was still very much alive—and obviously very dangerous.

Fortunately for Ben—and for her own career as a counsellor—a vascular surgeon had been able to patch up his severed femoral artery successfully. The last she had heard, Ben was still in the psychiatric secure ward at the Public, held under the power of an Inpatient Treatment Order—or so according to busybody Trish. He was convalescing nicely, and for now the community was safe from him. Unless, of course, a bleeding heart or rank incompetent had let him out by accident. As she well knew—having trained at that exact institution—such events occurred all too often in that ward at that hospital.

To her great relief, she safely reached the heritage-listed, four-storey building near the state parliament where Fabio had his gym on the top floor. At the entrance to the building's main foyer, she flashed her member's key card at the twenty-four-hour card reader and the security door slid open. She slipped into the brightly lit space and watched as the door locked smartly behind her. Then, instead of taking the stairs up the three flights to the top floor as she usually did, she rushed into the safety of an open lift and swiftly closed its door.

5

The lift door opened into bright lights and people: Fabio's famous gym. It was still busy, filled with normal, happy people. A safe and familiar place. She felt her anxiety wane. The gym was where she felt most confident about herself. One of the duty instructors waved at her in greeting. People knew her there and people appreciated her there. They appreciated what she added to the atmosphere: a body to die for.

Fabio, though, was nowhere to be seen. Probably he had taken the evening off to do more fine dining. When he was there, he was a pest, but now, paradoxically, she missed his presence. She missed the familiarity of him. She had developed a perverse fondness for his endless secret game with her. He, at least, was someone who appreciated her. At least physically. Although he did not, of course, know about her scar—unless there really were secret cameras in the women's change room, as was rumoured. Sometimes, knowing Fabio, she did wonder about that.

Fabio may not have been there, but the trainee surgeon, Mark Stanford, certainly was. To her absolute amazement and extreme surprise, she came across him while walking through the weights section of the gym on her way to the water fountain. He was doing bench presses. She did not see him at first, but then he dropped his bar with a deafening crash—sure sign of someone in danger—causing her to spin around. It was him.

Oh my God! Mark!

He was not injured. 'Hi,' he said weakly, struggling into a sitting position on his bench. 'Sorry about that. Overestimating my strength as usual.' He looked embarrassed.

'Hi,' she said, looking down at him. 'Fancy seeing you here. What a surprise. Nice surprise. We really need to stop meeting like this, don't we?'

He stood up. 'I agree. I've been missing you. I mean, it *is* you! Incredible. At this time of the evening. How's it going, Alyssa? See, I even remember your name.'

Good. And what else have you been remembering?

'What brings you to this part of the world after so long?' she asked.

'Reliefs. I'm filling in here at the Public for a few months to cover various peoples' leaves. It's really nice to see you again. I still feel a bit of a banana, though, for thinking you were my student the last time. I hope you've forgiven me.'

'It's okay.'

They stood next to each other for a little while longer, as though they were the best of friends, but she soon realised that they had reached the limits of idle talk. What more could a woman who potentially had cancer growing on her inner bits say to a man she did not really know and who was engaged to be married? She even remembered the nickname she had made up for the fiancée: Beak Face. 'Your girlfriend here too?'

'She is. Ruby.'

'Look after yourself.' Alyssa continued to the water fountain and bent over to drink. She was conscious of Mark's gaze from behind.

She turned. 'See you around.'

'You, too.' He was back to sitting on his bench, but he was watching her instead of exercising. He gave a wave. He seemed lost about what to do next. Forlorn. Nervous in her presence.

Beak Face.

That was their problem.

Alyssa scanned the gym to locate her. She was over at the freestanding area, doing ridiculous things with a two-kilogram dumbbell. She had not been wrong in her initial impressions of the woman: tall, skinny, bad skin, pinched face, oversize nose. What was it that Fabio had once said? Mark's Ruby was a doctor too? Bully for her.

Feeling angry, she did her best to ignore the obviously contented couple and went about executing her own exercise program. She could not help noticing, though, how easily Mark and Ruby chatted to each other from time to time as they did their own programs. When she finally went to the change room for a shower before going home, the two of them were still at it out in the gym hall. She had not felt up to going to them and saying goodbye. No, instead of feeling good after a workout, as she usually did, she felt thoroughly depressed. Did cancer do that to a person? And the prospect of childlessness?

She had a long shower in water pleasantly hot, but when she stepped out of the cubicle to dry herself on the matting, she immediately felt a cold draught of air. She looked for the source, and for a moment she could not believe her eyes. Mark's fiancée Ruby, still in her gym clothes, was now in the change room squatting next to an opened window smoking a cigarette. There were "no smoking" signs everywhere. The gym was fully air-conditioned, so the windows—which in a multi-story building were an obvious safety risk—were never open. She had not known, in fact, that they *could* still open.

She paused in her efforts with her towel and gave a loud cough to indicate her annoyance. The smoker's eyes flicked across to her naked body, froze for a second, then flicked away. She knew the smoker had been amazed by what she had seen, and rightly so. The scar was her only flaw. She knew too that Beak Face had not recognised her. Ruby did not know who she was.

Alyssa moved towards her, making no effort to cover herself. 'Hi. I think we've met before. You're Mark's girlfriend, aren't you? I'm Alyssa.'

The smoker stopped in mid-puff, still crouching. 'You know Mark, do you?'

'I sure do.'

Alyssa came right up close, but Ruby made no effort to stand up. Instead, staring up at her from her squatting position, she said, 'That's nice for you. Well, I'm Ruby.' There was an awkward pause.

'There are smoke alarms,' said Alyssa, unperturbed. 'I think you are going to set them off, even with that window open. There's quite a stiff fine for doing that.'

Ruby stood up and stubbed out her cigarette on the aluminium window frame. 'Shit!' She slammed the window closed and walked past Alyssa, studiously ignoring her, entered a shower cubicle still fully clothed, and closed the door. 'Mark's not my boyfriend,' she announced from inside the cubicle as she began draping items of clothing over the door top. 'He's my fiancé. We're engaged to be married.' She turned on the shower.

'How nice for you.' It was drowned out by the sound of the water.

Have fun with your eating disorder.

Being catty to Mark's fiancée was not going to be the solution to anything and she knew it. To make matters worse, the hands of the clock on the change room wall, a clone of the clock outside in the gym hall, read half past eight. It was going to be completely dark on the way home. The bright lights of the gym had been deceiving and she had not given adequate thought to how she was going to get home safely. Even to get to a tram stop, she was going to have to walk alone in the dark for some distance without Cy, who normally came to collect her.

Oh Cy. My dear, dear Cy, what have you done?

She did not know it was possible to miss anyone so much.

Her anxiety had returned to an even worse level than before, but at least she recognised the feelings. She had had them often enough. Especially in the distant past. She had always coped, though. There was just that one time when she had not coped.

Not coped.

She took the stairs this time down to the foyer, not the lift, but by now she had a bad headache and could only move slowly. The three flights down seemed to take forever.

Once out in the darkness, tightness began to squeeze her chest.

She was in serious trouble.

I think I am going to go mad.

CHAPTER THIRTY-ONE

1

ALYSSA FELT LIKE SHE was living in a vacuum. There were no demands from any law firm—not to her personally—and no further visits from the police, or messages from Dr Jensen the gynaecologist, or updates from Cy. She felt it understandable, therefore—given all that had happened over the past weeks—that she was finding it difficult to concentrate. It felt strangely as though she did not really exist. To top it off, the person sitting in front of her on the cottage consulting room couch was none other than Ellen Goodman, an Ellen who had cranked into top annoying gear and was making it additionally difficult to generate any interest in listening to anything she said.

Ellen was, of course, one of the original "big three" from the infamous Greta McCreedy offload at the beginning of the year. As such, she was a client pre-selected for maximum destructive impact. Greta had certainly chosen her "diabolical three" with care in her determination to destroy the career of a certain incoming young psychologist who was too attractive to be tolerated. Alyssa could just imagine how diligently the ugly old crocodile had scoured the clinic's files to find the "right" clients to accomplish her dark mission. And Alyssa knew, too, that she was not imagining things. After all, Alan Summerfield had confirmed her suspicions recently during their drinks at the hotel.

Greta McCreedy hated her. And exactly as Greta had hoped, Ellen Goodman was succeeding in making her uncertain of her skills and aware of her inadequacies as a counsellor. Ellen had that effect on everyone, of course, but the frightening aspect to the situation—as Alyssa was finally discovering—was that right from the start Greta had somehow known that she was a person who had more difficulty than most in coping with being unappreciated by a client. The fact that she was particularly vulnerable to dis-validation was something that Greta McCreedy had somehow already known prior to her first day at the Donald.

She must have spent an awful amount of time making enquiries with ex-associates at Public Hospital.

What a cow.

And now she had Ellen Goodman to contend with. Trying to relate to Ellen was like trying to get through to stepmother Diana Croft. It was something she was never going to be able to do. As a counsellor, she had little or no empathy with people who deliberately acted as their own worst enemy. It could hardly be said to be unexpected that she was failing to get anywhere with trying to counsel her. There was no way that she was ever going to be the right counsellor for this sort of woman.

No surprise, therefore, that her client *still* suffered from unabated insomnia despite all the visits to the cottage to date. Nothing that she had done for the woman so far had helped in any way. Which was most disheartening—inevitably so. Despite conscientious and resolute efforts to be warm-hearted throughout all the previous sessions with her, Ellen remained resolutely determined to believe that the person counselling her was a hopeless counsellor. In Ellen's book, nothing anyone did was ever going to be good enough, ensuring that a heavy feeling of being a failure always overshadowed any visit from her.

Trying to tell oneself beforehand that the negative effect from Ellen was to be expected in someone with a passive-aggressive personality disorder never seemed to help either. Always, Ellen made her feel a failure, both as a counsellor and a human being.

Today, while Ellen continued to talk away in the background, mournfully reciting yet another of her "sad stories", Alyssa realised—for the first time—that she had finally lost interest in the woman completely. She had tuned out of Ellen's endless miseries for good. There was no point in even trying anymore when it came to people like Mrs Goodman.

The only thing that had ever provoked Ellen out of her defensive routine at the cottage had been the few questions she had once asked her about her sex life.

Alyssa scrolled back on the work tablet on her lap to locate the essence of that conversation:

"Sex? We don't do *that* anymore, for heaven's sake!"

"Sex? Is that *all* that is on your mind!"

There had also been a powerful reaction from Ellen to her question about abortion.

Something about sex upset Ellen greatly. Sex as topic was *verboten* for her.

Which was ridiculous, thought Alyssa, because this was obviously where the source of her insomnia lay. At least, it seemed obvious to her.

Coming to a decision, she interrupted the latest sob-story, which she hadn't been listening to anyway. 'Ellen,' she said, 'how about we pause here and adopt a new approach.'

'What?'

'How about we try honesty. What about that idea? How about we get back to a discussion about your sex life with Steven. We haven't yet made any progress there. It's important, though, because I think that's where a lot of your problems lie. Honestly, I do. In my opinion, there are almost certainly problems going on between you and your husband in that department. So, why don't we at least look at that. How about we leave off on the sob-stories for a change and face up to real life?'

She knew she shouldn't have said that last part.

'Sob-stories! Sex! Well! How *dare* you! Especially after what I've told you about all this before!' Ellen Goodman stood up, suddenly enraged. 'Yes. How dare you!'

She had gone white with anger.

Knocking over the water jug, she stormed out of the consulting room, slamming the front door of the cottage as she went. In the driveway, her aging Mercedes threw up a hail of gravel as she gunned its accelerator and ignominiously fishtailed her way out of the garden into the safety of the streets outside.

It was all too much to cope with. Really, it was.

Things were going from bad to worse.

2

It was Alyssa's turn to be like Ellen Goodman and feel out of her comfort zone. She was back at the gynaecologist's office, about to have an excision under local anaesthetic of the offending patch of skin on her cervix.

Dr Jensen had phoned earlier in the week with the biopsy result. It was relatively good news: a pre-cancerous condition without obvious invasion. So, now she was once more positioned on a surgical couch with her pants off and her legs up in the air. Only the nurse was different.

Just like the previous visit, Alyssa had decided to come alone—even though she had been strongly advised to bring a support person seeing that it was a surgical procedure. The only realistic prospect for a support person was Jocelyn, but after giving the idea some thought, she had decided against asking her. Jocelyn had far more important things to spend her valuable time on. And besides, lesbianism somehow muddied the waters. Jocelyn admired her for her healthy body, and it seemed better to maintain that illusion. She had few enough admirers as it was. Other than Jocelyn, there had been no one else to ask. Her stepmother was essentially housebound, her brothers were completely out of the question in this situation, Cy had disappeared, and Wendy Greene had forbidden further contact. She had not quite realised how few friends she had. Wendy had been right about her inability to trust herself: it seemed that the only relationships she was capable of—and barely so—were sexual ones with men.

Talk about stuffed.

A poor wretch with a shameful sexually transmitted disease. She knew that Dr Jensen had stressed that it *wasn't* a sexually transmitted disease at all—not exactly—but today it felt more suitably depressing and heroic to believe that it was, and that Cy was responsible.

Dr Jensen's nurse this time was an older, uglier, and heavier one—perhaps more senior—and he himself seemed in more of a hurry. He talked mainly to his nurse rather than to her.

'It's CIN III,' he said to the nurse. 'Moderately extensive, although a lot of that's just the HPV. I'll have the medium loop, thanks.' The nurse gave him something and he attached it to an electrical cable coming out of a machine. Alyssa heard a suction machine starting up.

The gynaecologist had earlier injected her with local anaesthetic and assured her that she would feel no pain when he finally cut away the small patch of diseased skin on her cervix. Having to lie there stark naked from the waist down did not trouble her—she was a fine specimen, after all—but Dr Jensen seemed mildly uneasy with her this time. Why? she wondered. Previously, he had seemed completely unaffected by her.

He's not making eye contact with me.

The procedure was not going as well as he had hoped. That seemed to be the problem. He took a long time over it and there was much sucking from his machine. She hoped it wasn't all blood.

Perhaps there was no cure. Perhaps she would never have perfect pink bits ever again. She knew it was unfair, but she cursed Cy under her breath.

What has Cy done *to me!*

'There. Should be okay,' said Dr Jensen, finally. He seemed weary. 'The bleeding is finally under control, I think.'

'Do you think you've got it all?' asked Alyssa, raising her head. The gynaecologist took his time with the answer.

'I think so,' he said carefully. 'I'll let you know when the final path report comes through. If it shows that the margins are truly clear, then I think our worries are over.'

'So, no hysterectomy? I can still have kids?'

The doctor smiled at her. 'Shouldn't be a problem. But let's wait for the final report, shall we, Alyssa? I'll send it to you in a letter, together with information about any follow-up required. The letter may take a while to get to you. Depends on how speedy the pathologist is.' He snapped off his gloves and went off to another patient in another room.

The middle-aged nurse took over proceedings.

'No exercise for three weeks. No tampons. No swimming. And no sex either. Especially that.'

Alyssa assumed she meant three weeks for all, not permanent bans.

The nurse's attitude to sex reminded her of Ellen Goodman's.

Where do they find these people?

Many women, it would seem, ended up as disgruntled old bags. She wondered if this would be her own fate too now that the honeymoon with her body was over.

3

Alyssa took the tram home from the gynaecologist's rooms. As usual, the conveyance was crowded, so, despite the recent surgery, she ended up having to stand the whole way as it swayed and jolted her towards

Jowlett Street, where she would be able to get off. In obedience to the old nurse's warnings about the danger of bleeding after the operation, she held her legs tightly together the whole way. There was no pain, and she was grateful for that.

As she travelled, she could not get Ellen Goodman out of her mind. The hysterical response from the woman and the way she had fled from the cottage the moment she once again mentioned sex to her had been completely unexpected. After all, during the week before, Ellen had been quite openly forthcoming about the abortion she had indeed had when she was young. During that earlier visit—when she had challenged Ellen to deny that she had once had an abortion—she had expected a slap across the face but instead a dam had burst, and a flood of pent-up emotions had been released.

She had been hoping that another dam would burst with a direct challenge to Ellen to reveal her sex life, but no such luck there.

Still, the abortion revelation had been a breakthrough of sorts. How easily a woman's life could be ruined by a male partner, thought Alyssa. Ellen Goodman had indeed had an abortion. And not a straightforward one with manageable consequences, unfortunately, but a life-destroying one. She had fallen pregnant soon after the fateful college dance with Steven, following which Steven had insisted on a termination seeing that they were both still students. The exact date of conception was unknown because, being young and naïve, they had had unprotected sex more than once. Scans were not that good in those days, the doctor miscalculated, and on the day of surgery the fetus turned out to be older than expected.

"He was a little boy. You could see that clearly because he was already fifteen weeks along. We only realised that when we saw him. There were only pieces of him. That's what we saw, pieces. He was taken with a curette, you see. While alive."

It was horrible.

The tram went around a long, sweeping bend and Alyssa found herself forced to cling to an overhead strap for support. She was feeling faint. Was she bleeding? There was nothing on the front of her skirt. She tried to see the back of it in a window refection, but there were too many people in the way. Perhaps it was just hunger. A low blood sugar could make one feel dizzy.

Ellen had had complications after her operation. Because the baby was too big for curettage, a perforation of the womb had occurred, and infection had set in. She got better on antibiotics, but years later, when she and Steven finally had their daughter, the earlier perforation resulted in a rupture of the uterus during labour, one that necessitated seventeen pints of blood and an emergency caesarean section and hysterectomy. Ellen was only twenty-eight. The child was saved, but no more children were possible. Not in those days. Weighed down with guilt over the earlier gruesome abortion death of her son and the subsequent loss of her fertility, Ellen Goodman continued to exist in name alone. Inside, she had died. From then onwards, she was already dead.

Which, according to her, was as good a reason as any to not require sleep.

When Alyssa finally got off the tram for the short walk home to her flat, she discovered that she really was haemorrhaging. She could feel the blood pooling. Fortunately, nothing was yet on her dress or down her legs. Disaster, though, was not far away.

Worse, there was nobody at home to care for her. Nobody would know if she lived or died. Nobody cared in the slightest. Not really.

'Rats.' She hurried along, hoping to make it in time. She had the phone number of Dr Jensen in her bag. She would phone him as soon as she got home.

This is terrible. I'm turning into another Ellen.

CHAPTER THIRTY-TWO

1

THE POLICE REQUIRED MORE information. Alyssa found them sitting in her waiting room at the cottage when she finally got back to work after two days off sick for post-operative haemorrhage. The officers were the same ones as before but encountering them unexpectedly as she entered her sanctuary gave her quite a shock. Trish had arranged it in her absence, without telling her—arranged for the police to interview her in her office. And, no, Trish had not arranged for anyone else from the Donald Clinic to be present in support.

She could hardly tell the police officers to go away.

Damn Trish.

Alyssa felt angry. The police were contaminating her spirit by invading her personal space. After the two days off on emergency sick leave, the bleeding problem was still not fully under control. And she was preoccupied, too, with worries about whether she might need to have a hysterectomy in the future and lose the ability to have children. Dr Jensen had assured her that everything would settle provided she rested—which it had—but now, after the walk to work, she was spotting again. Yet here they were, in her waiting room, police officers.

Staring her in the face.

Before allowing the officers to enter her consulting room, Alyssa phoned Trish and told her in no uncertain terms what she thought of the bad thing she had done. Emotionally, she was in no condition to cope with them.

She knew she was ranting.

'It's a damnable disgrace!' she yelled at Trish. She had expected to find a vase of fresh flowers in her waiting room, not two swaggering fascists. 'How could you do this to me!'

587

Trish could and she had. She had simply followed the orders of the police. It was the same pair whom Alyssa had encountered the previous time. 'Get over it.'

She had no choice but to do exactly that. Once she had composed herself after the meltdown with Trish, Alyssa ushered them into her office: Detective Beta Male and Constable Stretched Tit.

'Good morning, Ms Brown,' said the young man. 'Detective Mortimer. We meet again.' He did not extend a hand or re-introduce the middle-aged uniformed policewoman who was with him. 'We'd like to ask you a few more questions.'

'Does Dr Barnes know you are here?'

'Our visit is officially cleared I can assure you.'

She remained standing, and so did they.

'Well then, what do you want?' She could feel her heart beating violently in her throat. The two officers were triggering ancient memories of something she had almost not survived. She could hear the detective speaking, but he sounded as if he was at the end of a long tube.

'We are seeking further clarification in the matter of the death of Mr Gilbert Rockport QC. Further information has come to hand, which raises further important questions. We are hoping you can be of some assistance to us.'

'In what way?'

'By telling us what we need to know.'

'I've already told you everything that's relevant.'

'Possibly not. You see, we have received the results from Italy regarding the analysis of the stability control computer in Mr Rockport's car. Also, we are now in possession of the report on the analysis of certain paint fragments. What I am about to tell you is, of course, highly confidential. We have found something unexpected.'

There was a pregnant silence while the two police officers stared at her.

She allowed everyone to sit down by taking a seat herself at her desk. 'I don't understand. What is all this supposed to mean?'

'We are hoping you are about to tell us.'

'Really?' She had no idea what they were on about, but she had news for them regardless: Gilbert Rockport QC was her professional client, not her friend or her lover. She was not going to be telling them anything.

'I can't reveal any specific details to you about his visits to me, and you know that.'

The two continued to wait in silence, occasionally staring at her or at parts of her consulting room. After five minutes, they finally seemed to give up.

'So, you have nothing more to say?'

'No.'

'Well, that is most unfortunate, Ms Brown. You see, the stability control computer in a Maserati is like the black box in an aircraft. It records historical data. And it records the data right up to the exact millisecond of impact.'

'*Milli*-second,' repeated the female constable for emphasis.

'So?'

'There is absolutely no evidence that Gilbert Rockport was asleep behind the wheel. In fact, there is no evidence of any loss of control of the vehicle whatsoever.'

'Whatsoever,' repeated the constable. 'And no alcohol or drugs in his system.'

'Yes,' said the detective. He consulted a notebook. 'Just "ibuprofen" and "paracetamol". Harmless painkillers.'

'I still don't understand what you two are getting at. What is all this supposed to mean?' Alyssa was genuinely puzzled.

'It means, Ms Brown,' said Detective Mortimer with extreme gravity, 'that Mr Rockport was at all times making supreme efforts with his steering wheel in the moments before he ended up upside down against the end of a roadside barrier. The exiting of the highway was no accident. We do not yet know the reason why he came off the road, but there appear to be only two possibilities: one, that he had no choice, or two, that he did so by choice. Whatever the case, the going off the road was a deliberate act. A desperate one too, considering the high speed at which he was travelling, which is recorded as near to two hundred kph. In an eighty zone. His accident was no accident, Ms Brown. Mr Rockport died either because he was forced off the road by another vehicle or because he deliberately committed suicide.'

'Which would have required an offending vehicle—if any—to be as powerful as his own,' said the constable.

'Which means that we now have to consider that he may have been murdered,' said the detective, 'by someone in a high-performance vehicle.'

'Murdered!'

'Yes, that. Or maybe he killed himself,' added the policewoman with satisfaction. 'Not long after attending the Donald Clinic to seek help.'

'But first, we are scouring the underworld,' added the male detective. 'We know Mr Rockport had enemies. What man of his stature does not? We have information pointing us in that direction. However, we also have information leading us in the other direction. Therefore, it remains possible that our suspicions about an underworld linkage may be a red herring. Help us put these uncertainties to bed, Ms Brown.' He gave a strange smirk after the word "bed". 'Did Gilbert Rockport have a known reason for wanting to commit suicide? Is suicide plausible? Was he actively suicidal? If anyone knows, you do.'

'Suicide?' Alyssa felt the blood draining out of her face. 'I don't think so.' Her voice shook. 'Honestly, I don't think it was that.'

'Really? We have heard via the grapevine that he may have been a *sicko*.'

'A what!'

'This part is obviously highly confidential too, but we are entrusting it to you as a professional person: we have information to the effect that Mr Rockport may secretly have been some sort of sick pervert. You know, really bad illegal stuff, so bad that either he couldn't live with himself any longer or he knew that his cover had been blown and he more or less had to kill himself. We think you may be able to advise us further on this matter, even if only in general terms.'

She was shocked by their attitude and their ignorance. 'I . . . I can't.'

'We find disgusting men in the strangest of places,' said the policewoman, piping up again. 'Throw away the key, is what I say.'

The two police officials stood up and crowded in front of her. 'Come, what can you tell us, Ms Brown? How much do you *really* know about this whole matter? Tell us now because we *will* find out the truth. Was Gilbert Rockport secretly a disgusting and evil man?'

'Excuse me, but I need air.' Still seated at her desk, Alyssa held her head in her hands. There seemed no hope for humankind. A giant nauseating wave that felt like all the cruel, self-righteous stupidity of the entire world had crashed over her. She wanted to scream to make it go away.

Instead, she said nothing.

'I have nothing further to say on this matter.'

They would never understand.

Nobody will ever understand.

2

Late in the afternoon, Alyssa received a phone call from Box Town Hospital. After a short delay, her stepmother came on the line.

'I need you here, Alyssa,' she said. 'I've been admitted.'

Again.

'Oh dear. Unwell. What sad news.'

Diana Croft, official title Mrs Diana Brown, was nevertheless well enough to talk. 'It's the pain, Alyssa,' she said in a suitably pained voice. 'I'm in pain again. The doctors are doing their best, but they still haven't found the cause. They say that until they do, there is no cure. It seems it's incurable. I don't know what to do.'

Alyssa felt like saying: "Well, for starters perhaps you could simply get over yourself and go home," but she restrained herself. It was not the first time her stepmother had been in Box Town Hospital, and it would not be the last. She kept getting bouts of severe pain in the lower abdomen. Over the years, confusion had grown over the exact diagnosis. Every doctor seemed to give a different answer. Possibilities ranged between diverticular disease of the colon, atypical endometriosis of the pelvis, irritable bowel syndrome, interstitial cystitis of the bladder, adenomyosis, severe constipation, and still more. None of the possibilities appeared correct, however, because no investigation had yet yielded a conclusive result and no treatment had yet stopped the pains from recurring.

The call from the hospital had come to her consulting room at the cottage between client appointments—Trish had arranged it so, she discovered later—which meant that she was expected to talk to her stepmother for a while.

She tried to reassure her.

'You're in good hands, Di. Just listen to what the doctors say and I'm sure you'll be safe.'

'It's all so confusing for me.' Diana's voice sounded small over the phone. 'It would be so helpful to have you here by my side. You know how much I trust you to deal with the doctors and the nurses. Could you come? Please.'

It was the same old story. With Diana, it always came to this. Alyssa's knuckles turned white from the tension in her grip on the phone. She felt trapped, trapped between some bizarre sense of duty and her own needs. However, no matter what was best, there was no way she was going to be able to take more time off work and visit Diana—not with the recent absences. Besides, it wasn't safe for her to go on a long train trip. Dr Jensen had said she should not move around too much until the bleeding stopped completely for at least a week. Yet, Diana knew nothing about that. Unfortunately, she had no idea there was even a problem with her cervix let alone that she was limited by post-surgical complications.

'I'm all tied up here, Di. There's no way I can get off work. I'm sure you'll be fine by yourself.'

'That sounds cold and uncaring.'

Abandoning a lonely old lady was not going to be the answer. 'What about Harry?' Alyssa suggested in desperation. Her youngest brother was a student at the local technical college in Box Town and no longer a child. 'Harry could come and visit you.'

'You know he never does,' said her stepmother. 'I love him to death, but he's given up on me completely.'

And whose fault is that?

'I really can't get away this time. I'm afraid it's going to have to be Harry or nothing.'

'Oh Alyssa, I can't believe you are saying this to your own mother.'

You are not my mother.

There was only one thing for it: 'I'll get hold of Harry for you myself and see what he says. Sorry, but that's the best I can do at the moment. I'll check regularly with the hospital and if there are any major concerns, I'll drop everything and come running. Please try and understand. Speak to you later.' She put the phone down on her stepmother.

There was just so much that one human could cope with. Not only had she not told her stepmother about her own health problems, but she had also not bothered to tell her about Cy leaving. There was no point in telling her anything. Diana was completely self-centred and would offer nothing beyond condemnation. She was the kind of person guaranteed to demoralise anyone who came near, no matter their needs or circumstances.

Maybe she shouldn't have taken the call in the first place because, as always, conversing with her stepmother had made her feel suddenly very tired.

Too tired to think properly.

3

Susan Lindow read her the riot act when she attended some days later for yet another scheduled professional supervision session. The telling-off from her was not unexpected.

'No, Alyssa,' she said. 'No. It's not good enough that you've been given an official warning about patient management by your employers. It is also not acceptable for you to be displaying such a negative attitude towards Greta McCreedy and the police.'

'Things are not as simple as you are trying to make out, Susan.'

They most definitely were not. Earlier in the session, she had outlined to Susan Lindow the unfortunate developments around Gilbert Rockport and Benjamin Clayton, including the involvement of the police and her troubles with Greta, but she had found it hard to convince Susan of her innocence. To complicate matters, Susan had no idea of the real identities of the clients they were discussing, in keeping with the usual supervision requirement for client anonymity. The names Rockport and Clayton—which were widely known in the press—had to become clients G and B, and certain features, such as occupation or location required suppression. Somehow, referring to Gilbert and Ben in this way made it seem like what had happened to them had all been her fault.

'I know it's hard to explain,' said Alyssa, 'but all my instincts at the time assured me that client G was not in the slightest bit suicidal, and that client B needed a psychiatrist. That's what I'm finding confusing.'

'Let me get this straight,' said Susan, 'and let's stick to your dead client to start with, Mr G. Mr G, you say, was a middle-aged man, wealthy and attractive—according to you—and yet in treating him you were relying on your *instincts?* Tell me you are joking.'

'What's wrong with me relying on my instincts?'

'Hooh boy,' said Susan, mopping her brow.

'I'm not a fool Susan,' said Alyssa, bristling. 'Do you seriously think I'm some sort of sucker for the sugar daddy type?'

'With your history, of course you are. Of course, you are. Aren't you?'

'What level do you think I function on?' Susan was making her angry. For all the woman's pontificating, she almost certainly knew nothing about real men. 'Naturally, I find such men attractive,' said Alyssa. 'I'm not repressed. But that doesn't blind me to the issues at hand. I have full awareness.'

'You know the ego defences, no doubt. Projection? Displacement? Reaction formation? Denial?' Susan Lindow emphasised the last one. *Denial.* 'There are many more defences, but why am I mentioning these four to you in particular?'

'You really do take me for an idiot, don't you?'

'You have a lot of anger on board, Alyssa. Can you see that? What about you listen to me for a change. What if I suggest we flip a metaphorical coin here? Let's flip it from male to female. Where will that take us?'

What am I even doing here?

She studied the dowdy form on the counsellor's chair. Today, she looked more than anything like a duck.

'Go on. Flip that coin in your head, Alyssa. Middle-aged man to middle-aged woman.'

Alyssa did as she was told: In her mind, she flipped Gilbert Rockport and Alan Summerfield into Susan Lindow and Greta McCreedy. Admiration turned to disgust. Love turned hate. 'You're freaking me out,' she conceded, finally.

'You can see it now, can't you?' Susan spoke hypnotically: 'Now focus, Alyssa. Focus on that thought stream. Reach down into yourself. Reach even lower. Can you begin to sense those underlying archetypes? Can you make sense of the blurry images that you are starting to see? Who are they? Who is the male and who is the female? What paradigms have you absorbed? Close those eyes, Alyssa. Focus. Delve into your essences.'

This is ridiculous.

She already knew the answers she was supposed to give. She was supposed to say: "My mythical admired older man is my lost father, and my mythical wicked witch is my stepmother." There was only one problem: Susan's hoary standbys did not apply to her. She was a trained professional. It was time to put Susan Lindow in her place. 'Sorry to disappoint, Susan, but these are issues I resolved a long time ago during training. Today, I like men who are attractive, and I dislike women who threaten me. Nothing psychologically messed up there, just pure biology at work. Why are you so resistant to the facts of life, Susan? Me, I don't have that problem. Honestly, I don't.'

'Ah, the youth of today,' muttered Susan, her voice full of disappointment. 'Still clinging tenaciously to your blindnesses. That's okay, dear. Fool yourself. The truth will get to you some day.'

The atmosphere had become a little too tense for comfort, so they moved on to client B, a young male paranoid schizophrenic.

'I had serious concerns about him right from the start,' said Alyssa. She explained how inexperienced she was with counselling clients with this condition and how disappointed she was with the lack of clinical assistance, and how disturbing client B's behaviour had been right from the beginning.

Susan's response was to deliver a boring mini lecture. She droned on about professional boundaries, the rights of counsellors, and how to say a professional *no*. According to her, client B should have been returned to Greta after the first consultation. 'Can you not see it, Alyssa? Can you not see that your pig-headed competitive attitude towards Greta clouded your judgement in the case of client B?'

What complete crap.

Alyssa struggled to keep calm. 'It's Greta who's the problem, Susan, not me. She's an obnoxious cow and someone needs to do something about her.'

'Too simplistic. Try not to be so unfeeling towards people, Alyssa. Try to show more genuine care and kindness. A change in your attitude will pay big dividends in more goodwill towards yourself.'

'Really? Thank you, Susan.'

'Yes. And do try and take my recommendations to heart. I have nothing but your best interests in mind. Honest, I do. You remind me so much of myself when I was your age.'

'Really?'

God spare me.

'Yes. So, how about you start being less harsh in your judgements towards your stepmother? That would be a good place for you to practice being kind to people. Practice makes perfect. You need to persevere with that, even if it's hard for you—very hard. Unkindness is the bug that you are going to have to iron out of your system.'

Alyssa crossed her fingers behind her back. 'Okay, I promise to be kind to my stepmother.'

Her stepmother was already out of hospital despite no kindness from her. The hospital had phoned the day after Diana's admission to inform her of that fact. They'd kicked her out was another word for it.

'Can I go now?'

'Not quite.'

4

Susan Lindow had some advice for Alyssa.

'Whether you like it or not, my dear, you need to listen carefully to what I have to say now. Two things. Firstly, in my opinion things are going to turn out badly for you. There is so much litigation around these days. There will almost certainly be sizeable lawsuits against you—or at least against the Donald Clinic—and you must be prepared for that to happen and not allow it to unsettle you unduly.'

'Do you really think there will be?'

'Yes. But here's the thing: the other point I want to make is that you *must* fight back. If there is one truth that I have learnt in my long career in the health profession, it's that when we are accused, we must fight back. Bad things regularly happen to clients because that's part of life, but when they do, we always feel personally responsible; guilty. Complainants sense this and they feed on it. They can be like dogs going for blood. You need to stand up and fight them. If you don't fight, people are going to walk all over you. Lawyers especially. Legal people tend to be bullies by nature. However, the good news is that like all bullies they tend to lack moral fibre. This means that as soon as they encounter resistance and sense that they may lose money, they will abandon their client and melt away. They have no true morality, just the humbug variety, so they have no courage. Therefore, fight. Everyone my age has been sued at least once, so I know how it goes. And one final tip before you head off: you can never have enough background information on your accuser when it comes to striking back.'

'Background information?'

'Yes. Previously concealed facts. *Information.* My advice to you is that you do as much sleuthing as possible on anyone who comes for your blood. You will have to do that alone, of course, because nobody is going to come and save you or protect you. They won't. You will be abandoned.'

'I'll have the Donald Clinic to assist me, surely.'

'Dream on. If you look like losing, they will drop you like a hot cake. Forget about anybody helping you. If you truly believe that your client G did not commit suicide while under your care, then you need to gather as much evidence as you can under your own steam about his state of mind at the time of his death. If anyone can do it, believe me, you can. Despite our little difficulties, Alyssa, I can see that you are super tough and super-intelligent. Snoop around a little. Speak to those who knew your Mr G. Listen. And same with client B. Find out more. There is always more to an unexpected event. And usually, it's a whole other can of worms.'

Alyssa did not know what to say. Susan Lindow had completely surprised her. Before her eyes, the wonderful woman had morphed from a dowdy duck into a mother hen.

Alyssa had to resist an urge to give Susan a hug. 'Thank you, Susan,' she said instead, softly and warmly.

'Think nothing of it, my dear,' said Susan. 'It's just that I am so sad for you. So sad. You are so emotionally vulnerable, so ripe for abuse. People sense it. They are going to use you. I simply cannot imagine how much it must hurt you every day to have never had a proper mother—or father—and how much this must weaken your ability to resist conditional affection.'

'You think so?'

'Yes. It's so bad that sometimes, when you are gone, I cry.'

5

Less than a week later, on a Monday morning while busy at work, Alyssa received a phone call from Trish to inform her that she needed to attend a meeting in Dr Barnes's office in fifteen minutes' time. First it had been Greta's office, some weeks back, but now it was Dr Barnes's. The last time she had been in the office of the Dog himself was during her job interview the previous year. It sounded serious.

'What's this about, Trish? And what about my next client here at the cottage? She's due in a few minutes.'

'Already cancelled. Don't worry about it.'

'Cancelled? Why the urgency?'

'No idea.'

'You must know, surely.'

'Just be there.' Trish put the phone down.

No idea, my ass.

Alyssa had a pretty good idea what the meeting was going to be about: how to combat the lawsuits relating to Gilbert Rockport and Benjamin Clayton.

She could not have been more wrong.

At first, though, the scene that greeted her when she entered the Dog's office appeared to be in keeping with her prediction: in the centre of the large room, arranged in a semicircle around the familiar centrepiece of Dr Barnes's enormous, politically incorrect hardwood desk, sat Dr Barnes himself, with Alan Summerfield on his right and Greta McCreedy on his left. Just as at the job interview, the ostentatious desk seemed a ludicrously obvious Freudian statement about the state of Donald Barnes's mind. So far though, the scene was nothing she had not expected. The first hint of trouble came from the sombre manner of those arranged in the semicircle. No greeting. No humour. No banter. No invitation to form a collegial circle. Instead, treacherous Trish materialised from a shadow and solemnly ushered her to a solitary straight-backed wooden chair on the client side of the desk. It was a tribunal, and she was the prisoner. No one in the room had any intention of helping her. Her innocence had been betrayed.

Finally, Dr Barnes spoke. 'Thank you for coming Alyssa. And I apologise for the short notice. I have called this special meeting because we face a difficult and somewhat delicate situation. I think it best if this is outlined by our chief clinical psychologist. Greta, please.' Dr Barnes indicated to Greta that she should say her piece.

Alyssa could scarcely believe what was happening. Self-consciously, she tucked her short skirt under her thighs and kept her legs tightly together. She could feel her heart beating fast and it became hard to swallow. They were making her feel like a criminal—and it was deliberate. She was looking at pure sadism, if ever she saw it.

'We've had another complaint about you,' said Greta in her dead voice from the grave. 'It's the third in as many months.' She paused to allow her victim's fear to fill the room, while slowly turning her head to give meaningful looks first to Alan and then to Dr Barnes. 'This time, it's a Mrs Ellen Goodman. She has made a formal complaint to the clinic.'

'This is first I've heard about it,' said Alyssa. She tried to be brave, but her voice came out like a whisper. 'Are you sure there hasn't been some mistake? Ellen and I have been making such good progress recently.' Which wasn't strictly true.

'Oh no, there is no mistake.' Greta waved a piece of paper at her. 'Mrs Goodman says you insisted that she engage in sexual intercourse. She has, accordingly, lodged a claim of abusive counselling practice against the clinic. She and her husband are suing us for three million dollars. She says she has never felt so revolted in her entire life.'

'You can't be serious,' said Alyssa, feeling the anger rise in her. 'I would never insist she did anything. You all know that. And how can any of you possibly take her complaint seriously? How can sex be revolting to a married woman of fifty-three? What nonsense!'

Her outburst was greeted with dead silence. As before, nobody was smiling.

'We take all client complaints extremely seriously,' said Greta. 'In my opinion, it is a perfectly valid complaint. Most women would agree with Mrs Goodman. The lawyers are going to go to town on this.'

'What absolute nonsense.'

'What did you say?' Greta's voice assumed a deadly edge.

'I said I disagree with you.'

Nobody came to her defence, neither Alan nor the Dog.

'As I have outlined to our two senior partners,' said Greta smugly, 'we now have a critical situation on our hands: three potential lawsuits courtesy of a certain Alyssa Brown. First, we have the almost certain suicide of Gilbert Rockport—the most prominent lawyer in town— while under care. At least five million dollars. Probably far more. Then we have the psychotic relapse and murderous rampage of Benjamin Clayton while under care. Gail Wilson has the entire city cathedral praying for her daily. The bishop has been phoning me. And now this!' Greta slammed Ellen Goodman's letter of complaint on the desk with what appeared to be an air of triumph. 'This!'

.... **6** ....

'Do you have anything to say for yourself, Alyssa?' asked Dr Barnes.

'None of any of this is true.'

I don't even believe that Gail is a Christian.

'And that is your genuine belief?'

'Absolutely.'

Dr Barnes turned to Alan. 'What do you think?'

Alan maintained a sombre, deadpan demeanour. 'Your call.'

'Well, I say that all these cases are fraudulent and therefore unacceptable.' He looked thoroughly unamused at having to state what seemed to him perfectly obvious. 'Therefore, we go for the kill. We apply De Glanville and Chikarovski to all bloody three of them.'

Alan looked alarmed. 'Those turds? You think it worth the cost?'

'I do. Rockport is almost certainly going to blow up in our faces. Already he's looking bigger than Ben-Hur. I've heard his wife is working the phones big time.'

'Who told you that?'

'Never you mind, Alan. I'd say we are best to stonewall and attempt extrication. If we bundle all three cases together, we should be able to get a big discount.'

'Mm. Not sure it's what I would advise.' Alan Summerfield looked worried. 'Can't we just fight these cases in the normal way. None of them except Rockport look very solid. We have the insurance. Why waste money?'

'Because we can't allow people to get away with this sort of nonsense, now can we? The malpractice insurers may be happy to be weak suckers but *I'm* not. Besides, using our conventional insurers will give these cases oxygen out in the press. This sort of stuff catches fire. If they do, the downside for the clinic will be too ghastly to contemplate. We may well find the clinic gets ostracised. Wiped. Cancelled.'

600

'Mm.'

'We have no option but to *snuff* this out.' Dr Barnes turned to Trish. 'Take Alan as agreed. Do a letter, please, on all three situations. The usual. And send it to De Glanville and Conmanovski asap.'

'Chikarovski,' said Alan to Trish.

'Whatever,' said Dr Barnes. 'Chikarovski, Check-enough-ski, Charge-enough-ski, Conman-novski, what does it matter? It isn't his real name. The man is an ex-con. And as for you Alyssa, as from this moment you are suspended from all duties. Until further notice.'

'What?'

'It's the standard Chikarovski protocol,' explained Dr Barnes. 'It's nothing personal. They demand it whenever we feel that a situation is so bad that we are forced to resort to them. Have you ever met Martin Chikarovski? No? Well, if you ever do you will understand everything. If anyone can clear up a mess, he can.'

'This is very irregular, Doggy,' said Alan under his breath.

The Dog clarified the situation for Alyssa: 'Martin is not a lawyer. Not anymore. Not in the Ukraine and not here. What Martin does is get results. What he says goes. We get no choice in anything.'

Alan tried to voice his objection. 'I still think this is a mistake, Donald. What's got into you? Think of the cost. I thought we'd already agreed to just leave things be. Just fight it in the normal way. These cases aren't that watertight, and Nikki Rockport has life insurance money to soothe her feathers anyway. Have you lost your mind!'

The Dog was not for turning and appeared angry. 'No. I refuse to see my life's work ruined. Seems I have not become senile soon enough for some people.' He signalled to Greta to wrap up proceedings.

Greta, who was looking confused, smiled for the first time, and launched into her new duty with relish. 'It's for your own good, Alyssa, that you are leaving us,' she said. 'Please clear out your office. We expect you to be gone within the hour. We will let you know what is to become of you within two weeks.'

And that was that.

She was not wanted anymore.

She left the meeting in a state of shock.

7

Her final hour at the Donald Clinic turned into a blur. When Alyssa got back to the cottage, she discovered that Trish had, in advance, made every one of her bookings disappear. Even as she searched for them, the cottage computer suddenly lost connection with the main practice system. Her time there was over. There was nothing for it but to pack her bags. And there was nothing much to take, just her lunch box and her two books. The world seemed to go in slow motion while she carefully fitted them into her bag. Finally, bag over her shoulder, she stood in the middle of her office and took a long look at the space she had grown to love. It was likely the last she would ever see of it, this place where she had hoped to forge a great career. Why had she ever hoped for that? she wondered. Why had she ever believed that she was any good or that she would be able to co-exist with someone like Greta McCreedy?

She closed the front door of the cottage carefully behind her and stood for a while on the porch, close to tears. Not far away was where Gilbert used to park his Maserati and play his boyish games with its powerful engine. Feeling numb, she set off down the garden path in the direction of the back door of the main building, on route to the front exit. She felt unbearably sad as she passed beneath the sheltering canopy of her beautiful tree, so she paused there to stroke its wonderfully touchable trunk. Trish had once mentioned that the tree came from Africa, but that was all she knew about it. And now she would never know anything more. She had not even had the time to discover what kind of tree it was. It was enough to break her heart.

Kicked out of my own garden. Oh dear.

She felt unable to go on. For some reason, breathing became difficult. She was breathing as much as possible, but she was unable to get enough air. Her hands and lips began to feel numb, and the world began to recede around her. Nothing seemed real. Terrified, she staggered out from under the tree. She knew she had to get away. She could not stay at the Donald Clinic a moment longer—not now that she was not wanted. Being unwanted was more than she could bear. She had to escape, or she would die.

The bag over her shoulder felt increasingly heavy as she struggled to the back door. Only there, at the back steps, did she finally realise that she was hyperventilating. She recognised it now. It had happened to her before—at university when she was so unwell. Standing at the foot of the stairs, she fought to control herself. She forced herself to take deep, slow breaths. Finally, feeling stronger, she climbed the three steps, slowly, one at a time, resting on each step. Once inside the building, the corridor swayed around her, but she found that she could make progress down the main corridor towards the front entrance provided she moved slowly and cautiously. When she reached Trish's desk, still treading gingerly, Trish pretended not to see her and busied herself with a patient file. She did not blame Trish for avoiding her. She knew it was better that way. There was just so much pity that a humiliated person could cope with.

Greta McCreedy had somehow seen her coming and was at the entrance to make sure that she left the building.

'Take care Alyssa.'

Alyssa saw for the first time how sick the woman was. Bitterness had eaten away Greta's soul. She felt a strange pity for her. Maybe she should have reached out to her there and then and embraced her in solidarity and confessed to her that she too was a woman betrayed. Instead, she ignored her. She could not stoop that low. Besides, she hated people like Greta.

There is nothing worse in the world than a vindictive woman.

'Goodbye, Alyssa.'

Alyssa did not respond. Instead, she carefully closed the gate behind her. She did not blame Greta for what she had done to her. Greta was a weakling who had given up and gone to the dark side. People like Greta she could flatten with one punch. The person she blamed was Cy. It was Cy who was to blame for everything. Was there anything in the world worse than a weak man? She asked herself this question as she walked unsteadily down the street.

He had ruined everything with his treachery.

Nobody wanted her now.

PART VIII

ONLY THE BRAVE

CHAPTER THIRTY-THREE

1

BACK HOME AT HER FLAT in Alfonso Street, Alyssa found it hard to accept that she had been suspended from employment at the Donald Clinic and that she was in danger of losing her job entirely. The fateful meeting with Dr Donald Barnes, Dr Alan Summerfield, and Greta McCreedy, at the end of which she had been as good as thrown out into the street, now felt like just a bad dream. She felt sure she would soon wake up and find it all to be nothing but a nightmare—with her real life still stretched out happily before her.

However, the dream remained reluctant to end. When she went to bed early that evening, everything continued to occur within the same nightmare of betrayal. She found something in Cy's vacated bedside drawer, an object abandoned by him as obviously worthless. It was a card, a card that she had given to him on Valentine's Day a few months earlier. It burned in her hands like hellfire as she read the words that she herself had written:

> A card cannot express my love.
> What I feel for, you my love,
> Is tucked in my beating heart,
> A heart that beats for you my man
> With a love that is sincere and true,
> A love for you and only you.
> Through thick and thin we've come this far.
> So, on this day celebrating love,
> I pray that onward we will go,
> Hand in hand and heart to heart.

607

Whatever life will throw at us,
Our love is strong, and I am blessed to have you here
To share the journey as we go.
I love you Cy with all my heart.

Her own innocent and foolish words. How he must have laughed at her feeble attempt at writing.

Like the staff at the Donald Clinic, he too had judged her worthless and thrown her away.

On the next day, Tuesday, she looked at her smartphone and saw that the previous Friday's pay slip was for an amount that was less than half the usual amount. Her pay had already been reduced to the basic rate at the end of the previous week. Obviously, this was all still part of the same extremely long and rather horrible dream. Fortunately, in real life it was not possible that what had been done to her pay could really have been done. That would be illegal. Besides, once she accounted for rent, utilities, and automatic loan repayments, there would be less than nothing left.

In the nightmare, she was now being punished in advance.

However, there was nothing to be done about it except get through the apparent day. Clearly, the dream was now all about her being in serious financial trouble. After all, as she realised—even within the nightmare— she had no savings and wasn't going to be getting her old job back any time soon—or *any* job anywhere in fact, certainly not in the field of counselling. Given enough time, she was going to starve. Pretty scary.

Not to worry, though. As in all nightmares, all one needed to do was keep a cool head.

So, for a while, she did just that. She went and washed her face and found it cooled her head just fine. Then she went and busied herself with financial affairs for what felt like many hours. It was all part of some game in which she needed to become financially hyper-efficient. Humming to herself, she cancelled all non-essential outgoings, including debt repayments. Many phone calls were required, and the activity stopped her from thinking too much about anything else at all.

By Wednesday morning, however, it became all too clear that everything was true.

It was not a nightmare. She was never going to wake up to find her old life back. The horror was *really* happening. She was suspended from her job, and she was penniless and abandoned.

Her head felt hot again, but unfortunately this time, even though she repeatedly washed her face, the washing did not help.

Nothing would help.

She was beyond help.

It's all true. I am the worthless piece of shit that I always suspected I was.

A curious numbness now crept over her. She sat motionless on the sofa in the lounge uncertain how to proceed. She could not even watch television because there was no set. She had sold her own television set when Cy moved in because his was bigger. Now, with him and all his things gone, the flat not only felt dead but was barely functional. There was no proper table to eat off and not even a radio.

Nothing. I've got nothing.

In times of emotional distress in the past, she had always had the gym to escape to, but now there was her "condition" to consider. She could not go to the gym. Dr Jensen's ban on physical exertion still had a week to run. Comfort snacking was also not an option because she seemed to have lost her appetite. When she tried to find a book to read, she discovered that Cy had taken them all, even the few that were hers.

What to do? Listen to music on her phone? Music would not help— not her. She went and checked on the bottle of anxiety pills that she had obtained via the prescription from her reluctant GP a while back. The bottle was still in her bedside drawer and—as she well knew—empty. Yes, it was.

Shit!

Just then, a spider appeared. It was large and black, and it watched her from the wall above her bed.

Oh God!

She was scared of spiders. There was no insect spray in the flat either. She had banned such things in her home because of the trauma she experienced as a child from suffocating in the gaseous fumes of stepmother Diana's anti-insect excesses. Alyssa grabbed a T-shirt out of the cupboard and quickly rolled it into a weapon. Then, stretching up, she whacked at the spider. However, as always happened with her and creepy crawlies, she missed. The spider moved sideways with frightening speed and then fell to the floor. Once there, it rushed straight towards her bare feet in muscular leaps. She gave a scream and ran out of the bedroom, slamming the door behind her. She threw the T-shirt onto the floor as quickly as possible to block the space under the door so that the spider could not follow her. She used a bathroom towel too.

Where was Cy when she needed him?

She would have to deal with the spider herself. Later.

She went to the lounge window, to where the bookshelf had once been, and studied the weather outside. It had closed in and there was a steady drizzle. She could hardly go for a walk in such weather. She did not know what to do with herself.

She was still in the pyjamas that she had slipped on against the chill in the air when getting out of bed, but she did not see any point in getting properly dressed. She had washed her face, but not yet *done* her face—or her hair. There seemed no point. She knew she looked a mess, but that no longer seemed of any importance. *Nothing*, in fact, seemed to matter anymore. It seemed pointless exerting oneself over anything.

She tried to cry, but she could not.

She did not seem able to think properly either.

2

What they had said at that Monday meeting did not make any sense to her at all. The attack by Greta—and the obvious collusion of Alan and the Dog—seemed not only completely unreasonable but was impossible to understand. Why, she wondered, had they been so intent on blaming her for Gilbert Rockport's death—the cause of which was yet to be determined—and been so willing to accept the ludicrous accusations regarding Ben Clayton and Ellen Goodman? Maybe it all related to the amount of money involved, but she had expected more from them, especially Alan. Collegiality, at least; respect. Instead, nobody had shown the slightest interest in supporting her. Nobody had seemed to care what became of her. Nobody wanted her.

Obviously, they *knew* about her. About her past. They *knew* that she was a bad person.

The old, negative feelings had returned with renewed power that morning and Alyssa felt scared. Why had she fooled herself earlier into thinking that she could aspire to a normal life? How stupid that had been. How naïve. How could she possibly have believed that she was alright and that everything was going to be okay. The ineradicable rottenness was still there, and once again it had become glaringly obvious.

Nothing was okay, and it never would be.

It was proving difficult to get enough air, so she opened the balcony door to allow a breeze to flow through the flat. The breeze did not help. Of course not. Why did that not surprise her? She was spiralling dangerously close to a stall. She had to do *something*. But what? She did not know what to do. Besides, in her heart, she knew that she had already given up. There was no point in doing anything.

It was already too late. She was going to crash. There was too much power in the bad feelings. The demons of old had well and truly wakened and she had nowhere to run. She could feel their presence increasing. They were coming for her, streaming down from the ceiling. They had force. There was pressure. Something was attacking her from the outside. Outside of her body.

No longer could she control what was happening. The badness in her had become too strong.

She huddled, trembling, on the couch. The ceiling was pressing down, pressing on her upper back. The pressure came down between her shoulder blades, right in the centre. She kept her eyes tightly shut. A giant now had hold of her, a disembodied hand, very large and very strong. It was pushing. It had her by her pyjama top and was pushing her. Streaming down; pushing. It pushed her off the sofa and onto the carpet. She cowered there, but then it began to push her towards the open balcony door. Out. It was trying to get her out onto the balcony. The force was immensely strong. She tried to fight it, but she could feel it winning. It was too strong. It had too much power. She could feel herself losing. A bad person could not be allowed to live. Better for them to go. Better to get them out. Out to where they belonged. Out from high up. Out over the edge.

Like in second year.

Better off dead.

Eleven floors would have done the job, but three would do just as well.

She was off the carpet now, so she huddled on her knees against the far wall of the lounge to try to stay away from the balcony door. Relentlessly, though, the force kept pushing her there. She felt herself moving across the slippery floor. Desperately, she tried to hold onto the coffee table, but it tore from her grasp. She rolled up tightly into a ball, but even that did not help. She began to roll. It was very slow, the movement, but unstoppable, and it was then that she knew she was going to die. If only someone had helped her when she was little . . . It was too late now. 'Help.'

But her voice was too soft to be heard.

Too small.

3

There came a knock on the door. 'Lauren.'

She heard it but could not respond to it.

'Lauren!'

It was Jesus.

'Open this door!'

Except that it was a woman's voice. Jocelyn Goronowski.

'Open the bloody door!' She began hammering on the door. 'I *know* you are in there.'

The evil force that was busy killing her hesitated. *Lauren?* Then it lifted clear away, as though it had evaporated. It would be back later. Alyssa stood up slowly and shook her head. Was she dreaming or was she already dead?

'Stop yelling Jocelyn. I'm coming.'

Carefully, she unlocked the front door and opened it.

She was neither already dead nor dreaming. It was indeed Jocelyn. She was in her work clothes and had obviously come to the flat during her lunch break. 'Hello,' she said cheerfully.

'Jocelyn?'

'Good thing I was patient. Mind if I come in? Shit, you do look terrible. What's up with you?'

'Nothing.'

'Liar.' Jocelyn kissed her forehead. Then she grabbed her head and studied her face. 'You poor, poor thing. I estimate that you are only one step away from death. Even worse, you always have been.'

Alyssa freed her head and looked at the balcony and felt fear. She knew Jocelyn claimed to have poor people skills, but her ability to see through her frightened her.

The psychiatrist closed the front door and the balcony door and then pointed at the couch. 'There. Sit. Now here's the thing. I've seen your file. I know who you really are. Your name is not Alyssa at all. Your name is Lauren.'

It was.

They sat side by side.

'Maybe it is, Jocelyn, but so what? I know this sounds weird, but do you believe in God?'

'God? Where did *he* come from all of a sudden? Besides, I'm Jewish, so what exactly are we talking about here?'

'Just tell me.'

'Okay, okay. The short answer is no. Not literally. God is a mental computation. He exists only in the mind. Does that help? Now, can we get back to what I've discovered about you? Back to who you *really* are.'

'First, just humour me. Did God send you here?'

Jocelyn waved a hand in front of Alyssa's face. 'Hello. Anyone home? What's with the fruit cake act?'

'Did he?'

'What kind of question is that? God is imaginary. That stuff is for deluded crap heads. And can you please stop looking so disappointed?'

She tried to smile. 'What about Jesus, then?'

'You *know* you are asking the wrong person about that one. What's got into you?'

'I don't know. That is my problem.'

Jocelyn studied her. 'You are seriously unwell, aren't you? I can see it in your face.'

'I've been having these strange coincidences. It's . . . well, everything has been very weird lately.'

Jocelyn took her by the hand. 'I promise to try and understand. As far as Jesus goes, if it's any use to you, I've been reliably informed that the reports in the gospels about what he supposedly said and did are mostly just re-imaginings of the ancient texts by his followers once they began to experience him as an ongoing mighty spiritual force years after he died. It was all to do with wishful thinking back then, and it still is today. There, that is all I know about the matter. Can we leave it now?'

Alyssa frowned. 'Thank you for trying, Jocelyn.' She squeezed her hand. 'You know, the weird thing is that nothing anyone says seems to make any difference. He comes. Always, He comes . . .'

'What the hell are you talking about? Who comes?'

Jesus.

She couldn't say it. Not to Jocelyn. The level of concern on her friend's face made her feel ashamed. 'Sorry. It's okay. I've become too emotional, that's all.'

'Don't get yourself hung up over God, Alyssa—or should I say Lauren. First, we need to clear up this gigantic mess over what the hell is going on and who the hell you really are.'

4

Jocelyn Goronowski took charge of the situation. 'We've got to get you through the next few months. So, first we need to focus on your present situation. Lauren.'

Alyssa ignored her friend's determination to call her Lauren. 'How come you know what's been done to me at work? Were you also in the know about that meeting on Monday.'

'Didn't have a clue. But I did find out about it today—which is why I'm here now, during my lunch hour. I've been finding stuff out and Alan had no option but to tell me when I confronted him at morning tea today. That's when I realised it was urgent. You see, I've finally worked everything out. I've finally nailed the truth about you.'

'You mean about the name thing?'

Jocelyn gripped Alyssa's shoulders with excitement. 'Yes. You aren't really Alyssa Brown at all. You are Lauren Truebody. *The* Lauren Truebody. From the Truebody family murder.'

'So?' Alyssa was amazed at how passive and calm she felt as Jocelyn dismantled her life in front of her.

'Is that really all you have to say about it. "So"?'

'Yes.'

'Really. Despite the fact that you are a complete fake who has been lying to everybody?' Jocelyn snapped her fingers in front of Alyssa's face. 'Hey? Hey? Lauren!'

'Stop doing that, Jocelyn. I'm very tired. Very tired of everything. Just do your worst. Tell me what you think you know.'

'I sure will. Your so-called name, Alyssa—that's just a word your people made up for you, isn't it, Lauren? It's supposed to stand for *Truth*, but the irony of it is that you yourself are a complete lie. It must cause endless mirth to those who know.'

'It's not like that at all.'

'I think that's exactly how it is. You had a life before you were Alyssa Brown. You are no Alyssa, you are a Truebody through and through. Go on and admit it: you are *the* Lauren Truebody, the girl who everybody in the country hated.'

Alyssa burst into a flood of tears. 'It was Social Service's idea,' she cried. 'After the trial. We had to be renamed for my protection, so, as some sort of sick joke prompted no doubt by our original surname, they renamed me Truth. They said that one day this might prevent me from causing more harm. Through being called Alyssa, they said, I would find the strength to stop lying when I got older. That's why I'm called Alyssa. To stop me from telling more lies. As some sort of punishment.'

'Then I *am* right. Yes! You *are* my Lauren.' Jocelyn put her arms around her and held her tenderly. 'Oh, you are such a poor, poor thing.'

5

In friendship and kindness now, they sat together on the couch and tried to work out how best to unravel the mess that was Alyssa's life. Confidentially, Jocelyn confessed that she had abused her position as a psychiatrist and accessed forbidden information to accomplish investigations that were both illegal and unethical.

'Technically, I could probably be thrown into jail. I know I could, but my conscience is clear. Let's hope I've gone and done the right thing. I did it out of love for you, Alyssa. Out of concern for your wellbeing. Honest.'

'What wellbeing? You know I have no future. Nothing much matters much anymore.'

'Don't be so negative. A lot may matter once you hear what I have to tell you. Firstly, it really is true that nobody told me about the Monday meeting, or even that you were suspended. I only found out today, and it's already Wednesday, and Alan only told me *where* you were because I insisted. That was at this morning's coffee break. He seemed reluctant to talk and left as soon as he could. Originally, I planned to visit you at a more suitable time, but I've come now while I'm supposed to be at work because I became alarmed when I overheard Alan talking to the Dog about an hour ago. They were in his office, and I wasn't meant to hear what was being said. Okay, I was snooping; I was worried about you. Anyway, what Alan said was that he thought you would probably harm yourself. You wouldn't, would you? Would you?'

'No,' lied Alyssa.

'Exactly. There's no reason to, is there? Not now that I know everything.'

That's what you think.

'No reason, Jocelyn.'

'Excellent. Nevertheless, I had good reason to worry after listening to what Alan was saying to the Dog. He saw you leaving work on Monday after you were suspended and was quite sure that you were extremely unwell—mentally, he was talking about. I know he often watches you from the staff room window. He then said something rather alarming. He told Doggy to "calm down" about the lawsuits because you were "broken" and there was every likelihood that you would be "popping off" fairly soon. Now, why on earth would he say something like *that?*'

'Alan is good at understanding people, obviously.'

He knows a broken monster when he sees one.

'Me, I'm hopeless at that,' said Jocelyn. 'But, yes, Alan reads people like a book. Which is why I started becoming concerned. But then, you see, I heard him say something even more alarming. I heard him tell Dr Barnes a complete and utter lie. He said his conscience was troubling him and that he thought he had grown too close to you. He said it was affecting him. Which I knew immediately was total garbage. He was talking garbage to Donald Barnes.'

'How do you know he was lying? I think he *does* worry about me.'

Jocelyn grabbed her head and looked her in the eye. 'Believe me, Alan doesn't *have* a conscience. Nothing. Zilch. Yes, really. So, when the florid fabrications started up, I just knew he was doing it to cover his tracks and realised that you were in real danger. I knew I had to get to you as soon as possible. No more delay.' Jocelyn studied her earnestly. 'Please don't tell me that you and Alan have been having sex. I just couldn't bear it. Alan is terrible that way.'

'Relax, Jocelyn. Alan and I are not, and never have been, in the sack together.'

'Brilliant.' Jocelyn gave a kiss of approval to her cheek. 'Because of what Alan said, and because of what I have been uncovering about your past since you were last in my bedroom, I just knew that I had to get to you right away. Was I right to come?'

'It's a good thing that you came, Jocelyn. I am grateful. Thank you.' She stroked the back of Jocelyn's hand. 'How's it going with Brian, by the way? Still going strong?'

'Don't mock. We are still on friendly terms, but it's over. Obviously.'

'Obviously.'

'Forget Brian. What I want to know is everything about Lauren Truebody. Everything about the *real* you.'

6

'What do you want to know about Lauren? What *do* you know, anyway? What if you are just bluffing?'

'I'm not.'

'Well then, in that case I'm sure you understand that I'm within my rights to feel angry about your snooping. I mean, *how* did you discover my real name? And who else has been pouring through my records? Who else knows about her? The whole world? Who exactly have you been blabbering to, Jocelyn? Alan and the Dog?'

'*Blabbering*?'

'Gabbing. Jabbering. You know what I mean. As you so magnanimously pointed out, looking me up is illegal. I was a small child.'

'Come on, I'm not a motormouth like Trish. You know you can trust me. We can trust one another, can't we? I've known you since I was sixteen and you were five, even though I've only just confirmed it, and you never knew it. Poor little Lauren. When I was a teenager, the thing

I wanted most in life was to meet you. Ever since Ricky died, I've always wanted to meet you. My Innocent Angel.'

'Your brother Ricky?' She remembered Jocelyn had a schizophrenic brother who hanged himself. 'The one who killed himself?'

'Yes. My Ricky. Shortly after *he* died, your mother died too. Only, in that case you were accused of killing her. I don't know how much you remember because you were so tiny, but you were in all the newspapers in the country. The magazines too, and TV—for weeks on end. It helped me cope with Ricky's passing. Watching what they did to you caused me so much grief that I thought I too would die. The terrible unfairness and cruelty that people showed towards you obsessed me. I felt so guilty on your behalf because everyone hated you. You became the country's Little Monster. Do you remember people calling you that?'

The Little Monster.

'Yes, I remember.' She had barely been able to read at the time, but she remembered.

'I went to your trial every day, even though it was supposedly about your father. You looked so lost and so sweet. All I wanted to do was touch you. I wanted to help you. But, of course, I couldn't. I was only sixteen. I tried to find your house, but after the court case you disappeared.'

'We were given new identities. To protect me.'

'I searched for you every day for almost a year. You almost drove me mad. But after a while I realised that something secret must have happened. I never stopped keeping an eye out for you, though, at the back of my mind. I've had a few embarrassing false starts with wrong people, but then, out of nowhere, you applied for a position at the Donald. Everything came flooding back. When I saw the photograph on your application form, I could not believe my eyes. I knew immediately it was *her*—you—my missing Lauren, my soul sister. Your age was right, you had grown up in the right area, and most importantly, you looked like you *should* look. Even so, I wasn't one hundred per cent certain. I've made some truly bizarre mistakes in the past. I needed to be one hundred per cent sure. And now I am. You *are* my beloved Lauren. All grown up.'

'So, *that's* how I got my job at the Donald,' said Alyssa. 'I've always wondered. I knew I was too inexperienced to have a chance, so I thought it was because Alan and the Dog liked my body.'

'Oh, that they do, they both do. I know for sure because they've said as much in front of me.' Jocelyn winked. 'But, yes, I was the one who got you appointed. I insisted.'

'Even though it was obvious that I would be useless?'

'Nonsense, you're not. Oh, Lauren, I'm so happy!'

Are you fucking crazy?

Alyssa realised once again that she was not the only one who was unwell.

'I so wanted to kiss you when you were a little girl. I was so ugly. I'm still so ugly.'

'You're not.'

'The day before he died, I told Ricky that he was better off dead—me, the only person in the world he trusted. I told him *that*. I even showed him where some rope was in the garage. Can you understand what I'm trying to say to you, Alyssa? Lauren? Now do you understand . . . me?'

'You were a teenager.'

'I still blame myself every day for what happened to him. I know I shouldn't, but I do.'

'My poor Jocelyn.'

'So, you *do* understand? And you *can* see why we had to meet? My sweet little Lauren, my Innocent Angel.'

'I suppose so.'

'It was always meant to be. We have always been meant for each other.'

7

Alyssa had some questions of her own. 'I still don't understand how you managed to confirm that the person you were after was me, Jocelyn. Nobody knows who I really am. No one is supposed to know.'

'I got the answer from Lauren Truebody's police forensic file, dummy. The one you had when you were a child, when the police were trying to charge you with murder. It was sealed after your father escaped conviction in the trial and your family went into protection. Doggy has access to everything on the police system—so use your imagination. Don't worry, he has no idea about you. It's just me who has the interest.'

'As far as I know, unauthorised access to the police database is highly illegal. You are going to be caught, you realise that?'

'Don't worry, I know it's illegal. That's why I resisted doing it for so long, despite my desperate curiosity. But now, with everything looking so bad for you with all these lawsuits, my hand has been forced. I had to do it. For us. Before it's too late. Aren't you impressed that I've gone and done something so brave? Gone and become a criminal for the sake of us?'

There is no "us", Jocelyn.

'You've been really, really silly. You could lose your job.'

'I don't care. I'll be just like you, then. We could join up. Some things are more important.'

'You are giving me a headache.'

'Don't be cross. Alan is partly to blame for what I've done. A week ago, given your troubles with Gilbert and Ben, he suggested that under his authority I have a quick look at the hospital national database to see if you have a psychiatric record. He didn't want to know any details, just whether you'd previously had psychiatric admissions. He said that the lawyers would want to know. Needless to say, I was greatly surprised by what I found.'

'And why *surprised*, exactly?'

'You know why. You never mentioned any of it in your job application.'

'That's entirely my own business, Jocelyn. You and Alan can't just go rummaging through people's health records if you aren't treating them, and you know that. Are you people *all* bent!'

'Relax. We're not the Gestapo. And, in any case, you'll be pleased to know that I saved your ass for you. I told Alan that there was nothing to find. How's *that* for a soulmate. Your university file is easy enough to locate, though, and it's bloody scary. You will need to take more care with your job applications in the future.'

'Okay then. Thank you. I get it.'

'After that eye-opener I simply had to know more about you. So, the next thing I did last week—strictly between you and me—was sneak into the confidential national forensic database. I needed to do so three or four times before I found what I needed, and I only got to that yesterday. It's been tricky, but I got opportunities every time Dr Barnes went away to meetings. Avoiding Trish has been a problem too. As I said, there's a computer in his office with access to the police system. Logins are recorded and monitored of course, but, hey, that's been no big deal. Doggy's getting old and careless, and I've long ago learnt his password. I've done the dirty on him, sure, but it's been for a good cause. I have found you!'

'How exactly?'

'Enter "Lauren Truebody" into the police database, Alyssa, and what do you get? Hello, you get "Alyssa Brown"—though, granted, after an incredibly convoluted process. The records finally informed me that little Lauren was issued with a protected new identity, that of Alyssa Grace Brown. I could not believe my luck.'

'And I can't believe how stupid you have been to do what you have done. All that for what? Besides, I've never seen that file. I didn't even know I had such a thing. Is anything you are saying about me even true?'

'What do you take me for? You were so young at the time. That's why you don't remember much about any of what went on. In fact, I'm sure you remember hardly anything at all with any certainty. You must try to obtain access to that file one day. I'm sure you could apply. From what I have gathered from my sneak peeks, it seems that despite your initial denials the police were convinced that you deliberately killed your mother, so they persisted with an attempt at prosecution. That's why this is so important to me: the fact that you were found not guilty. The fact that you are pure and innocent. That's what I loved and still love about you. Your *innocence*. Oh, Lauren. Oh, my poor angel, my innocent Alyssa.'

Alyssa remembered perfectly well that this was not how things had been. Jocelyn's precarious emotional state had made her delusional. She was making things up to suit her own desperate needs. Lauren Truebody was never the one on trial. One would have to be insane to think that a five-year old child could be on trial for murder It was her father, Robert Truebody, who had been the one on trial. And, based on his little daughter's confession, he had been found innocent.

However, nobody had believed *her* innocent in the matter. People decided to hate her. And for good reason, too. Little monsters were scary. They had the potential to grow into big monsters.

Somehow, Alan Summerfield had understood all this perfectly. He even knew of the alternative fate available to little monsters: they could become broken monsters.

Something was going on behind her back at the Donald Clinic. Alan had not referred to her as broken for no reason. She was being used.

And all the while, here was Jocelyn in her flat, stroking her hair. A Jocelyn who was behaving alarmingly like a psychiatric patient and not a psychiatrist.

8

'Lost your tongue?' Jocelyn peered into Alyssa's eyes with concern.

'Mm. Just thinking. So, does this reading of my childhood file mean that you know *everything* about me?'

'Everything, I'm afraid. Yes, everything. You are not who or what you say you are, or who people think you are. Instead, you are perfectly sweet and innocent and have been highly abused your whole life.'

Without batting an eyelid, Jocelyn checked the time on her phone, then stood up as if to leave. 'I'm going to have to get back to the Donald. From now on, whatever else you may try to say about yourself to me, one thing is for certain: you are not going to be able to be Alyssa Brown. Oh, and heads up for future job applications: officially, according to *both* your files, you are not well—in the head, I mean—and never have been. You are going to have to watch that.'

'Is that all?' Alyssa remained sitting on the couch. 'And what is that supposed to mean? The *both* files bit.'

Jocelyn looked down at her and squirmed a scrap of paper out of one of her pants-suit pockets. 'I brought this along for you. It may be helpful. On it are your file numbers, both.' She squinted at the crumpled note. 'And I've written down the conclusion of the forensic child psychiatrist for you. It says: "there is evidence in this child of extreme self-loathing, self-doubt, distrust, and emotional degradation, causation as yet unknown, probably parental and institutional abuse".'

'What sort of shit is that!'

'The opinion of a child psychiatrist.'

'Really?' She felt quite shocked.

'Yes. I feel just so incredibly sorry for you.'

It was time to get Jocelyn to stop fantasising. 'Won't Doggy know that someone has been on his machine?'

Jocelyn appeared unconcerned. 'I doubt he'll notice anything. Even if he does, all that the old goat will see is that he himself looked up someone called Lauren Truebody. He won't easily make the connection to either you or me and he certainly won't have the persistence required to pursue the matter. If he does ask around, I'll confess it was me and apologise. I'll say it was something urgent for my research project for the conference. It will be fine. I'm a psychiatrist. Don't you worry about me. Concentrate on yourself.'

Jocelyn continued to look at her tenderly. 'All that people like us can do, Alyssa, is limp along behind the emotionally well people and pretend that we are okay, even though we are not okay. Welcome to the club.' She bent down and once again cradled Alyssa's face in two hands, her own face close by. 'Things don't look very hopeful for either of us, do they? But here's the thing.' She sat down next to Alyssa again. 'I have full confidence in you. Fight. Don't let anybody spoil things for you now. Go for it, girl. Do what has to be done.'

Do what has to be done.

'And what is that, exactly?'

Sensing the depth of her uncertainty, Jocelyn whispered into her ear. It was secret, motherly, advice.

'Got it?'

Somewhat taken aback, Alyssa smiled in acquiescence.

'Promise?'

'I promise.'

'Excellent.'

'Thank you.'

Jocelyn really had to get back to work. It was urgent now. 'I'm so sorry to have to leave you, but I really have to go. I've got all these patients waiting for me and there's this bloody conference thing hanging over me too and I'm nowhere with my presentation. It's in less than two weeks now. I need to get cracking.'

'I understand. Don't worry, I'll be fine.'

'I want you to be there. Lecture room five at the Olympic.'

'I will try.'

'Look after yourself, my love.'

'I will. Promise.'

9

Alone once more, Alyssa locked the front door, then went back to the couch. She sat there in silence for a long time.

She felt numb.

Jocelyn had saved her life. Or had it been God? Or Alan?

It seemed too hard to work it out.

Whatever the reason behind Jocelyn's miraculously timed arrival at the flat, she realised after a while that the visit had made her feel better. The previous hallucinations and overwhelming sensations of danger and imminent harm were gone. The visit had strengthened the edges of her mind. Bizarrely, she now felt almost cheerful.

Despite Jocelyn's crazy and doomed love, Jocelyn was the closest thing to a female friend she had ever known. Everything that Jocelyn did or said, though often perplexing or surprising, seemed intended in a good way. Jocelyn was trying to help, and she liked Jocelyn. However, she needed to be careful because without doubt Jocelyn was seriously unwell.

Alyssa knew this now for sure. Even though she had been only five years old at the time of her mother's death, and much of what had happened was a blur, there were some things that she did remember perfectly well. Well enough to know that some of what Jocelyn Goronowski had just been saying to her existed only in Jocelyn's head.

Either her new friend deliberately told lies—which she doubted—or Jocelyn suffered from hallucinations and needed help. Alyssa knew for certain that as a small child she had not been in any courtroom and therefore could *not* have been seen there by a disturbed teenager called Jocelyn Goronowski, a girl fresh from as good as killing her own brother.

Robert Truebody, her father, had been the one on trial for the murder of Grace Truebody, not her. The defence that her father had used, namely that unexpected behaviour by his young daughter, Lauren, was the real cause of his wife's death, had been supported by secret video testimony from the small child, who said that it was *she* who pushed Grace down the hill and caused her to end up under the wheels of the train. The physics involved in the small child's testimony had been problematical, so ultimately it had been decided—by a jury reluctant to blame someone so small—that there must have been some involvement by Grace Truebody herself in the ultimate outcome. Not unexpectedly, Robert Truebody's sensational not guilty verdict had caused widespread outrage, disbelief, and consternation. After all, many of the witnesses on the train had sworn under oath that Grace Truebody was pushed under the train by her estranged *husband* Robert Truebody. A national paroxysm of outrage had followed his acquittal, with salacious vilification conveniently deflected onto the defenceless child. Overnight, Bob's Little Lauren became the nation's Little Monster, her image screaming *evil* on every front page—even though the jury had concluded that she was innocent of the actual death and that the police had been vindictive. According to the verdict, the whole incident had, in reality, been an act of suicide by Grace Truebody.

The Monster, because of her age, had never once so much as set a foot in any courtroom. Innocent-looking children seen by teenage Jocelyn in courtrooms had nothing to do with a young child called Lauren Truebody. As for the ubiquitous media images of the evil child, they would all have been with face pixelated out because of her age. Even back then, there were such laws. So, no. Jocelyn had not seen her before when she was a child. Not in the flesh and not in the media. Jocelyn's "Innocent Angel" existed only in Jocelyn's own head. Jocelyn Goronowski had never met or even seen Little Lauren Truebody.

It was all wishful thinking.

Part of her mental illness.

Jocelyn had no idea who she was really dealing with.

There *was* no Innocent Angel, and Jocelyn knew nothing about the *real* Little Monster.

And nothing about the big one either.

Either Jocelyn took after brother Ricky and was half-mad, or Jocelyn believed that she herself had killed Ricky and suffered from disabling guilt over it, or Jocelyn was an emotional nut job.

Most probably it was all three.

Almost certainly.

Which was going to be a problem.

Why? Because Jocelyn was now in danger. In danger from a young woman who lived in a flat by herself and sat on a couch.

CHAPTER THIRTY-FOUR

1

ALYSSA SPENT THE REST of that Wednesday afternoon deep in thought. In the evening, she ate a good meal of wok-fried tempeh and broccoli, had a shower, and then, while still naked, went into the bedroom and hunted the spider with her towel. This time, the muscular arachnid was no match for her determination, and she managed to smash it into a thousand pieces.

Her bedroom was now a safe place. Normally, she disliked killing innocent creatures, but not now. Now was not the time for wimping out. Not after what Jocelyn had whispered in her ear, not after what Jocelyn said she needed to do: fight. She *would* fight. It was her only option. She would fight them all, every last one of them. There was no other way if she was going to survive . . .

Do what has to be done.

In some ways, Jocelyn Goronowski *was* a genius.

Pleased with her new self, Alyssa climbed into bed and was soon asleep. Bizarrely, she dreamed of making love to Alan Summerfield while being supervised by Susan Lindow. In the dream, it turned out that Susan knew a surprising amount about men.

In the morning, after waking with the sunrise and having breakfast, Alyssa followed Susan Lindow's advice about the need to gather as much information as possible about one's adversaries. Busy and efficient, she checked websites, looked up telephone numbers, and made phone calls.

She discovered that The House of Fantasy catered for both male and female clients and took telephone bookings. Also, a certain Mistress Veronica, expert at corporal punishment, really did exist and was on the staff. What better way to learn more about Gilbert Rockport than to meet Mistress Veronica in person, she thought—especially seeing that according to Dr Kreef's autopsy report, Gilbert was beaten only a few hours before he died.

Determined to make progress, she phoned the BDSM establishment. To her surprise, she was able to secure a session with Veronica that same day. As the remarkably polite receptionist at the other end of the telephone explained, Mistress's morning session—Mistress's only *morning* session—was seldom used. All other sessions were fully booked for the next four days. However, if the lady on the phone urgently needed to be corrected, she could attend at 11 am today.

Today. Which meant in a few hours' time.

Alyssa knew that this would not leave her much time to prepare or to reflect on the rashness of what she was doing, but when she heard further that the establishment was situated only a short tram ride away in North Troy, she decided to proceed regardless of the consequences.

What have I got to lose?

'Book me in.'

'Excellent,' said the well-spoken receptionist.

Alyssa gave her a false name, "Lauren"—which she found amusing considering that it was her real name—and said she would pay in cash. She knew Gilbert had done the same; used a false name and paid in cash. She would go past an auto teller on the way. She had little enough to spare in the way of liquid assets, but she could get the cash off her credit card. The interest sacrifice would be well justified. Like Gilbert, she did not want anyone getting the wrong idea about her should the House of Fantasy's financial records ever become public.

She knew Gilbert had called himself George Roberts when he attended there—which was the same false name that he had used when he first attended at the cottage. It would be the name Veronica knew him by, so she would need to be careful not to use Gilbert's real name when she spoke to Veronica. She needed to remember at all times while she was there that she was researching someone called "George" and not Gilbert Rockport. Hopefully, Veronica was the type who did not watch news programs and hadn't seen too many photos of Gilbert Rockport in them—most of which were unrecognisably pompous anyway—and did not know that client George was dead. It was better for everyone that Gilbert Rockport's reputation not become tarnished unfairly by public knowledge of his need for The House of Fantasy.

'See you at eleven, Ms Lauren.'

Once the arrangements were finalised and the phone call had ended, Alyssa realised that she had not given any serious thought to the practical implications of what she had just arranged—which was extremely foolish of her. Almost certainly, she had just volunteered for some sort of beating or other. Which was the last thing she needed. Especially at such short notice.

Or maybe beatings were better if had that way.

At short notice.

With the clock now ticking, she began to feel more nervous than she thought she would, especially when it dawned on her that to avoid arousing suspicion, she was going to have to attend The House of Fantasy as a genuine client. Mistress Veronica was going to have to be duped in some way into divulging details about client George's state of mind the last time she saw him. After all, there was no way otherwise that Veronica would be willing to have a helpful and pleasant conversation with her about "George" unless Veronica knew the reason for it—which could not be revealed. She was going to have to go in and improvise as she went and try to get Veronica to talk as much as possible. Naturally, while taking care to come across as a client and not as an investigator, she would try to keep any pain that needed to be inflicted in the process to a minimum. There was going to have to be *some* pain though—some punishment—while fishing for information about Gilbert Rockport's state of mind before his death. She could not afford to get caught out as a fake. If the lawyers behind the Rockport lawsuit ever found out that Veronica had been talking to an investigator, they would track her down. It would be yet another nail in her coffin—a very large one.

She reached the street address without difficulty, but it did not seem to be the right place. It was nothing like she had imagined. The site was occupied by what looked like a derelict warehouse. There was no signage, no windows on the street front, and only a single rusted metal door, half concealed in a small recess, which had no information on it and no bell or buzzer. She knocked, but there was no response. After walking up and down the street checking and rechecking the street number and feeling very conspicuous, she made sure that nobody was watching, then attempted a turn of the doorknob on the rusting door.

Imagine if someone who knows me sees me here!

2

She need not have worried. The door to The House of Fantasy opened on well-oiled hinges. Greatly relieved, Alyssa entered and quickly closed the door behind her, conscious of the fact that the hurried act of concealment was what the great Gilbert Rockport had had to resort to on a regular basis. What prize, she wondered, could drive a person to such an undignified routine.

She found herself in a small concrete anteroom, which was completely empty. A single bare electric bulb glared overhead. Ahead was another door, also solid-looking, but this time made of wood. Set in the door at face height was a metal grille, covered on the inside. It reminded her of a prison—not that she had ever been to a prison. A buzzer at the side of the wooden door bore a sign saying, "ring here".

She took a deep breath and pressed the buzzer. While she waited for a response, she began to feel anxious about her clothes. She hoped she had come dressed appropriately and was not about to violate some sort of dress code and make a complete fool of herself. For want of any better idea, she had decided on a conservative look and selected the sober, grey-green pleated below-knee skirt that she usually wore on the rare occasions that she went to church, matched with unadventurous mid-heeled shoes. It had seemed the best way to support the newbie nerd fake identity she was about to assume. The choice of clothes also facilitated her choice of heavy-duty underwear. Best to have as much protection as possible.

An intercom squeaked into life. 'May I help you?'

She spoke into it: 'I have an appointment at eleven. With Mistress Veronica. It's Lauren.' Once again, using her real name as a fake name made her smile.

There was a scuffling sound on the far side of the door and the cover to the metal grill slid open. An older woman's face peered at her. Evidently satisfied, the woman unlocked the door. 'Come on in, my dear.'

The older woman sounded like the receptionist she had spoken to earlier. Alyssa found herself ushered into a tasteful waiting room, which, to her surprise, looked much like her consulting room at the Donald. She was offered a seat on a classic red leather chesterfield sofa, next to which, on an elegant ebony table, stood a crystal vase full of assorted flowers, freshly cut and hauntingly fragrant. Everything seemed so civilised and so cultured that for a few minutes she felt disoriented enough to wonder whether she had come to the right place. She had. In a corner of the room was an old-fashioned easel and a blackboard on which was listed—in breathtakingly skillful white-chalk calligraphy—the available sex workers for the day. That aside, though, and beyond the forbidding street-side façade and heavy doors, The House of Fantasy was a remarkably pleasant place. She wondered why, given her level of education, she had thought it might be otherwise.

'First time?' said the presumed receptionist, sweetly.

Alyssa grinned at her. 'Afraid so.' She hadn't realised her state of bewilderment was that obvious.

I probably look like a rabbit caught in a car's headlights.

Which was how Gilbert Rockport had looked when still a rookie at the cottage.

'I'm Agnes, by the way. Do try to relax. Would you like something to drink? A glass of water?'

'No. Thank you.'

'You'll be in good hands with Mistress Veronica, I can assure you. She's very experienced. And very kind. She won't be long now. I'll leave you to prepare yourself mentally for what's ahead for you.'

'Thank you.'

The cheerful woman calling herself Agnes departed for a nearby office. Alyssa watched her go. Her backside was rather fat. She wondered if she was a recycled prostitute, one who had passed her use-by date and was now otherwise employed. She assumed it was a major problem for prostitutes: the early use-by date.

What to do when nobody wants you anymore?

What indeed.

She studied the names on the blackboard. There were ten in total, Agnes at the top and Veronica near the bottom, with a summary of key attributes next to each. The entry for Agnes read: "Ms Agnes. Owner and manager, The House of Fantasy". That was a surprise. For Veronica, the entry read: "Mistress Veronica 26. Stunning blonde, size D. CP. Does <u>not</u> sub". The "not" was underlined. She presumed CP stood for corporal punishment. Not too much of a surprise there, though she had not realised that Veronica never allowed herself to act as the submissive in a discipline scene—not at work anyway. She knew enough about psychology to know that being a top or a bottom were flip sides of the same psychosexual coin, which meant that Veronica's adherence to a top role probably meant that she had limited emotional resources. After all, a dominant person *could* act as a bottom in a scene. Almost certainly, therefore, Veronica would turn out to be someone who was emotionally extremely vulnerable to being harmed. Pre-judging her from the blackboard, Alyssa felt almost sorry for her.

The other surprising thing about Veronica, besides the large size of her breasts, was that the blackboard seemed to indicate that she did not do penetrative sex. Many of the other women obviously did, Agnes excepted. Two, "Mandy" and "Angel", even had the words "does anal" in their lists of attributes. It shocked her to see women advertising themselves in this way—as though they were sex objects, or animals in a cattle market. It also caused her heart to beat faster. She had entered a world that seemed a long way away from the world she had known in Ocean View.

While she waited for Veronica, she began to hear sounds in the building coming from somewhere in the distance. It sounded like voices. She concentrated, trying to make out what was being said. Then the pitch of the sound changed abruptly. Was it her imagination, or had someone just started screaming? A woman. There seemed to be a woman, somewhere. A woman in pain, screaming…

God!

Her legs began to tremble. To distract herself, she made a nervous last-minute check of the note in her handbag, where she had written Gilbert's fantasy name in case she forgot: "George Roberts". She had to remember to use only this name. Footsteps began to approach. She snapped the bag shut.

Mistress Veronica was at the door, super-intelligent looking and crushingly beautiful. Suddenly she felt afraid. For some reason, she had half-expected a statuesque, muscular, somewhat butch, somewhat dumb

Amazon with boots and a corset, but Mistress Veronica was none of that. Instead, she was enough to break anyone's spirit, hers included. Alyssa felt her heart sink. She realised that she had been foolish enough to place herself at the mercy of an extremely able—and therefore dangerous— person. She could see, straight away, that Veronica was extremely brainy, cruel, and inclined to have an emotional need for power over others.

Or is that all just my imagination?

No. The woman's hard face said it all: a predatory combination of distain and interest. And now, this same Veronica was about to have power over her. Without needing to say it, the woman at the door already declared by her confident pose and air of authority that she was in charge. She would be dealing effectively with whoever the new culprit happened to be, no matter their identity. Humiliation, pain, and degradation would now follow as sure as night followed day.

She's way more intelligent and beautiful than I am.

First, though, would come the fake pleasantries. 'Lauren, is it?' said Veronica, extending a hand. About her own height, she looked clean and well-groomed. 'Gave you a fright, did I? Sorry about that.'

Alyssa shook her hand. For a cruel person, Mistress Veronica had a warm hand. The grip, though, was powerful. She was dressed in a micro-miniskirt, fishnet stockings, suspenders, and stiletto heels, and had black-painted fingernails and was fragrant. She wore a revealing top, and her breasts were indeed as sizeable as the ones promised on the blackboard; quite fabulous. Her hair, too, was fabulous—beautiful long blonde hair with curls.

'You booked for just half an hour. Is that right?'

'Yes,' gulped Alyssa. 'I'm just exploring . . . things.'

'I see. You want a taste. No doubt, you know what we are about?'

'Fantasy?'

'I take it you know what sort—when it comes to me?'

'Err, punishment?'

'Very good, yes. Scenes. I do scenes. We do scenes. People often get confused about that, especially at low quality establishments, but have no fear, we don't get confused here. You tell us what you want, we all behave normally until that scene begins, we conduct the requested scene according to your prior rules, and afterwards, once fully accomplished, we all return to normal.'

'It still sounds pretty scary.'

'It can be. We must be careful what we wish for. But, come, time is short. Let's get you to the dungeon.'

Dungeon!

3

Mistress Veronica proceeded down a long corridor and Alyssa followed. Her hostess walked with supreme confidence in her stilettos, like a cat, her shapely hips swaying in perfect rhythm with her feet, like a metronome, and her bare upper thighs flashing at times between the bottom of her ultra-short skirt and the top of her stockings. Alyssa tried to imagine how a man might feel in her presence; how Gilbert would have felt as he gave himself over to her in the knowledge that what lay before him had the power to make his troubles fly away. Only trouble was that she herself had no need for that sort of thing.

'How can I help you today, Lauren?' said Veronica over her shoulder as they walked. 'There's nothing mentioned in the booking. Usually, if I know in advance, I can dress appropriately.'

'I suppose I really just want to talk,' said Alyssa.

'Talk?'

'If that will be okay. I'll pay the going rate.'

They entered a room marked "Dungeon", and Veronica closed the door. There were two padded bar stools just inside the door and a counter with glasses and a jug of water. The room was large and had a high ceiling with exposed beams. A roped pulley was attached to one of the beams, and on another was an array of large hooks. Against the far wall she could see a display of what looked to her like torture instruments and tucked into the corners of the room were gym horses, benches, and even a bed.

She tried not to stare too much.

'Business first, Lauren. It will be one hundred and fifty dollars. That's our special first-timer's rate for thirty minutes, our minimum. Normally, it's an hour and four to five hundred dollars.'

'I understand. Thank you. Do you want me to pay now?'

'Yes.'

She had been told the rates when she made the booking, so she had come prepared. She paid the money over in cash.

'Do you want a receipt?'

'No,' said Alyssa, a little too loudly.

'Excellent.' Veronica placed the money into tea canister on the counter. 'Well, go ahead, take a seat.'

'Thank you.'

Veronica sat opposite her, with her legs apart. Alyssa noticed with some alarm that she could see right up her dress and that she wore no underwear. No doubt the pose was a force of habit, done to titillate male customers. The last thing she needed, though, was to see between Veronica's legs. She hoped she was clean.

'What would you like to talk about?' asked Veronica. 'You know that with me you can say anything. We have no shame and no secrets here.'

Alyssa almost laughed from sheer nervous energy. She bit her tongue. 'I'm interested in being punished,' she said. 'I've heard you do that sort of thing.'

'Indeed, I do. You are in the right place. You're talking about a hand spanking I presume? Over the knee domestic? Or school? Or do you have something more exotic—more severe, perhaps—in mind?'

'Possibly. Not just hand spanking. Proper corporal punishment. The cane, maybe? I'm interested in severity.' She struggled to keep a straight face. The only experience she had of anything remotely uncomfortable was from her second boyfriend, Aaron. He had tried to put her over his knee a few times and spank her with his bare hand, but she had stopped him each time after only a few smacks. The problem with Aaron had been that he was a frustrated ass fucker. His real intention with smacking her bum had been to try to make her submit it to him. She had not been ready for that, not then.

She blushed.

'The cane would be a bit too harsh for a beginner. Spanking is good, though. I just love spanking,' said Veronica, drawn to her embarrassment. 'Would you like to try it out? Go over my lap? I can do severe, but perhaps something gentle to begin with?'

'No. No. Not that.' Her reply was a little too hasty, but her courage was returning. She had realised, finally, that even though in a fantasy sense she was in Veronica's clutches, nothing would happen without her consent. She had frightened herself needlessly. While the activities at Veronica's place of work might sometimes be extremely painful, such things were optional, and, in that sense, not part of reality. 'I just want to talk. You know, about *being* punished. It might interest me in the future. I have this good male friend of mine who comes here regularly, and he recommended I talk to you. Maybe someday I would want to arrange the *same* thing for myself.'

'Is he a client of mine?'

'Yes. He sees you often. He thinks you are great.'

'And who are we talking about?'

Alyssa took a deep breath, hoping that the bluff would work. 'George Roberts. He swears by you.'

'George? You want the same as George? You surprise me, Lauren. Yes, George and I go back a long way. He's a great guy, incredibly tough.' She peered into Alyssa's eyes with some concern. 'Surely you can't be wanting the same as George?'

Without knowing it, Mistress Veronica had confirmed that Gilbert's accounts of visits there were at the least partly true. Veronica had also just confirmed that she had no idea that George Roberts was in fact Gilbert Rockport, or that he was dead. Elated, Alyssa continued with her deception: 'In fact, that's exactly what I do want. I came to find out if I can get the same as George gets. Not today, of course, but at a future appointment.'

'The same as George?' Mistress Veronica closed her legs. 'Are you serious?'

'Quite.'

'I'm not sure you understand what you are saying, Lauren. How well do you know George? George is a very special case, a real pro.'

'He tells me he can take a lot,' said Alyssa. 'But I think I can too. In fact, I'm sure I can.' She saw a flash of irritation pass across Veronica's face.

'I doubt George has told you the whole truth, Lauren. Normally, I give him fifty of my best strokes without interruption. Believe me, that is not something for the faint-hearted. It's not the same as with the bare hand, my dear.'

'It isn't?' She felt amused at being called "my dear" by someone her own age.

What is it with these people?

'Nooh. Those fifty are with a heavy wooden paddle and a four-foot rattan cane. I don't think you would last even six strokes.'

'Really?'

'Afraid so. Would you like to try? Perhaps just one stroke with my cane? One hard one.' She turned her head towards a rack of canes on the wall. 'I suspect that you are in serious need of some education.'

'One never knows, does one. But tell me this, then: if it's as bad as you are making out, doesn't it upset George? Why does he keep coming back to you?'

Veronica peered at her, uncertain what to make of the conversation. 'George obviously loves it,' she said, finally. 'In fact, he's even told me it's the only thing that makes his life worthwhile. He has his problems. We all have.'

He's got problems all right.

'Me too.'

'I don't think you understand, Lauren. Honestly, I don't think you do.'

'Well, what I *do* know is that George is terribly depressed. We are kind of in a relationship, so I want to understand him better, help him. I was thinking I might get myself punished too, so I can become depressed like him. What I want is I want to be punished until I feel thoroughly depressed, like George.'

'You are a priceless one, aren't you? Sorry to disappoint you, but the George I know has never been depressed in his entire life. He's the happiest, sanest person I've ever met. He has a gold digger of a wife, of course, but that's another story. Last I heard, he's planning to get rid of her.' A sudden thought crossed Veronica's mind: 'Oh shit! You're not *her*, are you?'

'Of course not. And I do know he's married.'

'You scared me for a minute there. But you're too young. His bitch is in her forties.'

'Exactly.'

4

Mistress Veronica looked at a clock on the wall. 'Enough of George. Time is running out. Why don't I just put you over my knee?'

Fat chance.

Alyssa held on to the side of her bar stool with both hands as an insurance. 'Maybe another day.' She smiled sheepishly. 'I just wanted to talk to you about being depressed. I know George a bit, but the real truth is I have a brother who's severely depressed. I want to find out how that feels. I thought that getting a good beating, one like I know George gets here, would be a way of getting myself thoroughly depressed.'

'We *are* talking about the same George, are we? Middle-aged, upper-class gent. Posh accent. Money. Excellent butt. That one?'

'That's my George.'

'In that case, I don't know what you're on about. I saw him here only recently and he never looked happier or left more pleased with himself. Getting a beating won't make you depressed, my dear. It will have the exact opposite effect.'

'You are surely joking.'

'Far from it. I don't think you understand how the mind works. A voluntary beating—as opposed to, say, one in a prison or something—is an absolutely guaranteed cure for depression.' Mistress Veronica leant forwards in her chair and adopted a concerned tone. 'I hope you don't mind me asking,' she said, 'but you're not one of our friends from down the road, are you, Lauren? We're all completely honest here. You're not on any . . . medication, are you?'

Alyssa presumed she was talking about the mental health residential house that she knew was not far away. 'Oh, no. Nothing like that. I just need to know things.'

Mistress Veronica finally seemed to lose her patience. She climbed off her stool. 'Come. Let me show you around in the few minutes we have left.'

'Okay then.'

She paused the tour in front of the cane rack.

Alyssa stared at them in fascination.

'You like them, don't you. Isn't that what you said when you first arrived here?'

'No.'

'No? That's what they all say.' Veronica looked into her eyes. 'It's very common, that fascination. That fear.'

She might fear canes, but Alyssa no longer feared Veronica. She realised that the dominatrix was cheating with her high heels. She was taller than Veronica and almost certainly physically stronger. With the advantage of gym-toned arms, she would have little difficulty putting Veronica over her *own* knee should the need arise.

'Something tells me that you've been a bad girl, Lauren.' Mistress put a hand on Alyssa's back, between her shoulder blades. 'Something tells me you need to be punished.'

'Maybe.'

'It's a beneficial experience, believe me. You'll be forever grateful. Come on, we are right here. Bend over and I'll give you a taste of a cane. I can make it as light or as severe as you wish. You can even leave your pants on if you like, but that kind of defeats the purpose.'

'Pants?'

'Emotionally, you are far better off having them pulled down. Then, once you've been properly punished, I can do a forced orgasm on you, if you like. Generally, my female clients like that.'

'A *forced* orgasm?' asked Alyssa incredulously, remaining standing. 'How do you do that?'

'Easily. I just tie your hands to that hook overhead and then I deploy our electric roller-tip vibrator. It's hanging over there on the wall, see.' She pointed to a device that looked like a large power tool plugged into a wall socket. 'No woman can resist it. Want to try it? It's quite safe. We use sterile disposable roller heads.'

'Err, not today.'

'You need to stop being so shy. You should at least do *something*. Just think of all the money you are wasting.' She ran a hand over Alyssa's bottom. 'This is just such a fabulous butt you have here, Lauren. I'm sure your ass is itching for some action. How about a cane stroke?'

Time was almost up.

What the hell. I've paid a hundred and fifty bucks.

'Well okay, then,' she said, out of sheer curiosity. 'Just one.' She always did wonder what had drawn Gilbert to it so strongly. 'One—or maybe two. Proper strokes. Just to see how it feels. And I'm not taking my pants off.'

She had always wondered about canes. Even before Gilbert.

'That's my girl.' Mistress Veronica took her by the elbow. 'Come with me young lady.' Firmly, she marched Alyssa to an open space in front of what looked like a gym horse from school. 'Put your bum up here for me, up over the horse.'

'Up? There?'

'Yes. It's the perfect place for you. You need to give a little jump to get up, but once you are in position it leaves your feet a few centimetres off the floor, which is the ideal. You'll need to grab onto the horse's legs on the other side to keep yourself in position, and that's ideal too because it keeps your hands out of the way. Come on, up you go. Get that bum up.'

Alyssa positioned herself as instructed, surprised at how easily and unselfconsciously she had fallen under Veronica's thrall.

'Comfortable?'

'I suppose you could say that. It feels weirdly sensual.'

'Your ass up in the air like that, you mean?'

'Yes. The dangling legs, too, I think.'

'Everyone seems to feel horny at this point. From what I've observed, I think it stems from the unique combination of submission and fear of submission that arises in this situation. There's always that conflict, especially in us ladies, and clearly its now being focused for you. Marvellous. Just think how much better it would feel with your pants off, Lauren. Would you like me to pull them down for you? These undies.'

Alyssa nearly jumped off the horse when Veronica placed a hand on her left buttock, over the top of her skirt.

'Calm down, for heaven's sake. No need to panic. I won't touch your undies, then. I'll just get this skirt out of the way of the cane. I'm going to lift it and fold it back. Will *that* be okay for you? Otherwise, it will be in the way.'

'Okay,' she said meekly.

'Nice colour.' Veronica was referring to the skirt. 'Classy. Celadon green?'

'Yes . . . I think so.' She had no idea what celadon green was. Alyssa felt an uncultured fool as Veronica folded the skirt up over her back. She could hardly believe that she was willingly going along with what was happening, but, somehow, the process of being prepared for punishment felt mesmerising. She let herself go with her feelings, even though she knew that to an outside observer it might appear as if she had fallen into the well-known compliance trance that occurred in those under the complete power of another. She had not. Victims of genuine punishment often did, though. But this was not genuine punishment. Even though what Veronica was about to do felt increasingly irresistible and sexual, she remained firmly in command of the situation. Of that, she was certain.

5

'Nice and calm,' murmured Veronica, completing her preparations. Alyssa's skirt was now out of the way and her underwear was exposed. 'I know I keep saying this, Lauren, but what a fabulous butt we have here. Truly.' She stroked it. 'Are you quite sure that these panties should not come down? It seems such a waste not to display your assets.'

'Thank you for the compliment. Maybe in the future, but not today, thanks.'

'As you wish.' Veronica ran a finger up and down the crease in the centre of her bottom. 'Receiving discipline is all about this, you know, about *receiving*. I'm sure that one day you will come to understand what I am saying.'

'How so?'

'Once you are brave enough to go naked you will find out. The level of compliance in the bared bum is the only way to gauge when punishment has become effective.'

'You've lost me there.'

'Resistance needs to be *seen* to have ceased. At its core, discipline is all about that. About ensuring that the culprit has become fully receptive.'

'Receptive?'

'Not so great in the psychology department, are we Lauren? Forget it. Would you like me to take my clothes off for you instead? Some ladies like that.'

Alyssa twisted her head sideways from her bent over position to look directly at Veronica. 'Once again, no thanks. Not today.' She could not imagine anything worse than Veronica prancing about naked.

'Suit yourself. The men like it. With them, of course, I don't expose myself until their hands are tied. I don't tolerate any monkey business.'

'I sure you don't.'

It occurred to Alyssa that they were going well over time. It could only mean that Veronica was getting something out of *her*. Veronica was actually enjoying toying with her and was deliberately keeping her waiting for the cane. Up over the horse, scantily clad bottom in the air, she was completely disempowered, and Veronica was revelling in the emotional discomfort. She tried not to imagine what might be going on beneath Veronica's knicker-free miniskirt. Cruelty was probably literally oozing out of her.

'Nice and ready for a slice or two into these little bum bums, are we, Lauren?' asked Veronica with what seemed like a little too much relish. 'A few minutes draped over a caning horse does wonders in that department.'

'Just go ahead and cane me, please.'

'Very well. You asked for it. In keeping with your request earlier, I'll keep it the same as for George. Which means it'll be the senior rattan and extremely hard.' She selected the correct cane from the rack and began to flex it and whip it in the air as though to get a feel for it. 'Any friend of George is a friend of mine. Are you sure you only want one or two strokes? That sounds pretty feeble to me. Compared to George.'

Feeble?

'Well, okay then. Three. Four at the very most. No more.' She had no idea what made her react to Veronica's insult with such foolish bravado.

Veronica tapped her chosen cane on Alyssa's raised bottom to get her aim. 'Stings a bit, doesn't it, the tapping.'

Alyssa remained silent and gritted her teeth.

Veronica paused. Then she came closer. Alyssa felt her place a hand on each of her cheeks, over her underwear. Heat flowed up between her legs in a most disturbing way. 'Go nice and slack here, Lauren. Try to relax.' She felt herself being gently spread apart. It will be better for you this way. You are holding yourself far too tense.' Her voice seemed filled with kind concern.

'Okay, then. I'll try and be less tense.'

Veronica got back into position and did a few more taps to get her aim.

Tap.

Tap.

Tap.

She spoke. 'Except for George-people such as yourself, we normally get clients well warmed up with some mild stuff before using the cane. It can come as quite a shock otherwise and lead to nasty welts. But I know it's what you want. Some *extreme severity*.'

Before Alyssa could qualify Veronica's assumption, Veronica whipped four extremely savage cane stokes into her backside, the force of the impacts so great that they lifted her cheeks with every stoke. It was fast, expert, and vicious. Before she could even react, there were four searing welts across her buttocks, grouped around the level of her anus. To any eavesdropper outside, the explosion of extreme brutality and the subsequent outburst of loud squealing would have resembled nothing so much as the slaughtering of a pig.

Alyssa heard the incredibly loud whooshing sound of a cane in full flight through the air and the equally loud and sickening sound of flesh being impacted, but it seemed unreal. Then pain struck like a bolt of lightning, followed by a tidal wave of agony. She emitted a high-pitched shriek and reared up off the horse, as though electrocuted. Her hands flew to her bottom and clutched at her cheeks, jerking at them feverishly.

Jerking them apart . . .

'Ow, ow, ow!'

As she struggled to compose herself, she realised that she had been duped by a sadist. She had thought Veronica had been half-joking, thought that she might have some compassion, but that had been a big mistake.

'No, Lauren. No. Get back over the horse!'

6

With her body trembling violently, Alyssa got back into position. The unexpected ferocity and violence of what had just happened had left her bewildered. She wasn't sure if she had had three strokes or four. She felt scared. Her bottom felt like it was on fire, a fire that flamed up between her cheeks and inwards. There was no way she was going to be able to tolerate another stroke. The cotton panties, which had provided her only protection, might just as well not have been there for all the use they had been.

'Poor, poor, Lauren.' With Alyssa dutifully and fearfully back in position, Veronica ran a fingertip over her trembling freshly caned bottom, pausing at the feel of each raised ridge caused by her handiwork. There were four ridges to feel.

She had already had all four strokes.

'Lovely welts, Lauren, even if I say so myself. And nicely quivering cheeks. So much less resistance here now. Pants down and another three or four? I think with that we might even get you *fully* relaxed.'

Alyssa finally came to her senses. 'No.' She jumped off the horse. 'Enough, thanks.'

'Now don't tell me you didn't enjoy that.' Veronica was breathing heavily.

'You caught me there; I'll admit that much.' Even as she talked, the stinging in her bottom remained maddeningly severe and Alyssa found herself needing to rub the area. Veronica watched intently, seemingly drawn to the humiliating spectacle.

'Your face has gone completely white,' said Veronica. 'I hope you are okay.'

Alyssa put a hand on Veronica's shoulder and had a sudden irrational urge to kiss her. Veronica had gone the extra mile for her. Just for her. Crazily, she wanted to embrace the woman—a person who had just whipped her senseless. She understood suddenly—in a revelation—what it was about Veronica that was so special. Gilbert had tried to explain it, but back then she had not understood. Veronica had not merely whipped her. What had happened had not been just *work* for Veronica. Not on this occasion.

No. What had transpired was a profound intimacy so deep that it required reciprocation with at least a hug and a kiss. Veronica had whipped her with a savage intensity that was deeply personal. And in doing so, Veronica had communicated her own weakness and vulnerability in a way that was truly endearing. In the process of overpowering another Self—herself, Alyssa—and achieving control of her, Veronica had revealed the deepest part of her *own* Self and shared her *own* deepest pain. Veronica had gifted her a *knowing*. Breathtaking metacommunication had informed her—Alyssa—that Veronica was suffering too. Veronica was an abused child too. Truly incredibly, the overriding communion in the whipping had been that of sisterly solidarity. Kindness. Love. In the weirdest of ways, they had both psychologically orgasmed *together*.

Veronica and I have something in common.

She fought the urge to embrace.

It was crazy.

Instead, she gave Veronica a warm smile. 'I'll be okay. It was pretty bad, but in a good way. It's not often that someone gets the better of me.' Her body was still shaking.

'I sensed it was what you needed. Loss of control. You'll have welts, of course, but only for a few weeks. Don't worry, they'll fade completely, as will the bruises, and there will be no scars.'

'Thank you. For your kindness.' Alyssa touched Veronica's arm affectionately once again, uncertain how to express what she was feeling. The roller coaster intensity of her emotions had caught her by surprise.

'My pleasure. At least your colour is returning.' Veronica, for her part, remained physically aloof.

'I'd best be on my way.'

'Yes. Your time is well up. Next time book an hour. For you, I'd recommend an eight-of-the-best caning, maybe a twelve—after a decent warm-up—followed by the power vibrator. You have no idea what a rush that will be. Needless to say, it needs to be with those pants of yours well out of the way.'

'Maybe.'

Only joking.

Alyssa adjusted her skirt and left.

CHAPTER THIRTY-FIVE

1

BACK ON THE STREET, Alyssa found it hard to believe that she had gone and done what she had just done.

Talk about emotionally confused and deranged.

Why had she been so foolish as to get herself beaten severely? she wondered. A trivial hand spanking was all that had been required. After all, she had only intended to obtain information about Gilbert, not get herself actually punished. Somehow, Veronica had persuaded her that a proper beating was what she needed; what she deserved. And Veronica had been right. The whipping she had just received was the very least she deserved. There was no way anyone could punish her enough for the badness that was in her.

As she walked to a tram stop, she could still feel four burning ridges across her seat. It was no trivial sensation, and enough to make walking difficult. She realised with dismay that she would not be able to sit down once on the tram. It would be too painful. She would have to stand all the way home.

It's what I deserve.

What had started off as a simple undercover trip to obtain information about Gilbert Rockport's state of mind had run completely out of control. Still, there had been some extremely important findings.

Mistress Veronica *did* exist, and she *had* known Gilbert—though as George Roberts. And Veronica was indeed as wonderful as Gilbert had said. Visits to her did not result in depression or a need to kill oneself. Quite the opposite. Being dealt with by Gilbert's mistress left a person feeling light-hearted, not depressed. There was no way in a thousand years that Gilbert would have killed himself a mere six to twelve hours after such a visit.

Gilbert Rockport had not committed suicide.

No.

Yet, his death had not been an accident either. According to the black box in his car, he had not lost control of the vehicle.

Which meant that there was only one possibility: murder. She knew this now for certain. Gilbert Rockport had been murdered. It was the only possibility. Someone had killed him.

Frightening and sad as that might be, it at least had nothing to do with her. At least not officially or in any way that could possibly be linked to her. Certainly nothing that anyone could prove.

There was no longer any reason for Nikki Rockport to be coming after her.

She now had the ammunition she needed to get Gilbert's gold-digging ball and chain of a wife off her back. Finally, she knew what to do next. She needed to put a stop to the carry-on from Nikki Rockport.

She thought back to the motherly advice that Jocelyn had whispered in her ear the previous day at the flat: "Do what has to be done". In the case of Nikki Rockport, it meant play dirty just like Nikki Rockport. Jocelyn was right about such things. Susan Lindow too. She needed to fight back against those trying to take advantage of her. If she did nothing, Nikki Rockport was going to walk all over her.

The same went for Cy. He needed to come home. She needed to get him to come back to her.

Once back at the flat, Alyssa removed her pants, lifted her skirt, and studied her bottom in the bathroom mirror, stretching her cheeks this way and that. The four raised tram tracks looked worse than she had imagined. She applied hand cream to the area to try to improve the discomfort, but the effort proved in vain. The cream made no difference.

How unfortunate.

Resigned to having to be in discomfort, she put on fresh underwear, took two pain pills, and went in search of lunch. She remained in the grey-green, below-knee, church skirt—which, courtesy of uber-cultured Veronica, she now knew to be *celadon* green. The formal nature of the clothing seemed appropriate for the task ahead.

There were things to do, and time was tight. As a new, hyper-efficient Alyssa, she needed to get to Nandedong and back before dark that day—if she was to keep up with the survival schedule that she had drawn up in her head during the tram ride home. She could not afford to lose momentum. Unfortunately, though, she had forgotten to include time for shopping on her list. That had been a mistake because, as she now discovered, there was hardly any food left in the flat. Cy usually did the shopping while she was at work, and there was no longer a Cy.

She needed to get herself better sorted.

All that was left in the fridge was an almost empty carton of soy milk, while in the freezer there were just three suspect-looking Brussel sprouts, and in the grocery cupboard a single unopened bag of prunes. Also, eight stray unshelled monkey nuts that had escaped the disappeared nuts jar.

Shit!

At least Cy had left the coffee, so she fixed herself a soy latte. Then, because she was hungry, she ate all the sprouts and peanuts and five of the prunes. She did so while standing because it was still too uncomfortable to sit. Veronica had certainly excelled herself.

How stupid can one person get?

At least it had been in a good cause. She had learnt a lot.

Also, the miserable lunch had at least kept her plans for the rest of the day on time.

2

Still feeling confident and resolute, Alyssa conducted a quick online search for Nikki Rockport's phone number. Though Gilbert and Nikki Rockport's private home phone number was not listed for obvious reasons, a certain N.M. Rockport's was—and this person lived in Baronbridge, the swankiest suburb in Hubron. It had to be her: Nikki, the bankrupt gold digger and socialite wife turned grieving litigious widow. Crossing her fingers for luck and taking a deep breath, Alyssa punched in the digits.

A woman's voice answered, a voice with an uncertain and wavering tone, as though wary of the identity of callers. 'Hullo?'

The phone said it was BBR. Berkowitz Berkowitz Rockport. 'Nikki? Is that you?'

'Who is calling?'

Alyssa smiled. Her own phone number was not visible to Nikki because it was a private number due to her position as a counsellor. 'It's Alyssa Brown here, Mrs Rockport. Gilbert's counsellor.' Alyssa was surprised to hear her own voice sounding so strong and clear, and it made her even more sure that what she was about to do was the best way forward.

'Alyssa!' There was a sharp intake of breath, an unmistakable gasp. 'Do you mean Alyssa Brown?'

The woman at the other end was obviously the right Nikki. 'Yes, I do,' she said to her. 'That Alyssa, yes. Hello. Your late husband's therapist. Me.'

'From the Donald Clinic?'

Nikki knew exactly who she was talking to.

There was a pause. 'I'm not sure you are permitted to contact me in this way, Alyssa. In fact, I'm sure you are not.' The voice of the financial incontinent had recovered its composure. 'How dare you! How did you get my number?'

'How do you think, Mrs Rockport? May I hasten to assure you that I greatly respected your husband and may I extend to you my heartfelt condolences. Why I phoned, though, is to tell you that I have been doing all in my power to keep Gilbert's personal issues confidential from the investigating authorities. I'm fully aware of the harm any revelations will cause to his business and his reputation—and of course to you, and to his children.'

'So, is this what you are phoning about? To threaten me with revelations?'

'No. Quite the opposite. To find out if you agree with me that I keep these matters confidential.' Which was an awful lie, of course, and a dirty trick. She was not asking Nikki Rockport for advice about anything. Oh no. What she *was* doing was making Nikki understand the price she was going to pay if she went ahead with her lawsuit—a suit doomed to failure anyway seeing that Gilbert had *not* committed suicide.

Nikki Rockport was obviously not particularly intelligent because she fell for the ruse. 'Oh, Alyssa,' she said, sounding less aggressive, 'your call makes more sense now. I'm pleased you are taking a helpful attitude.'

'Yes, all I want to do is protect the business and the family name from harm. Forgive me if I startled you earlier with my intrusion. I simply thought it best to clear up the confidentially matter as soon as possible.' That was another lie. Then she went for the jugular and mentioned that she knew all about Nikki's financial incontinence; all about her unseemly semi-criminal graspingness—which would need to be dragged out into the open in any court case. 'You see, Gilbert told me an awful lot of things about himself. And, of course, about his relationships—and, of course, about *you*.' She emphasised the last word for Nikki's benefit, surprised that Nikki did not immediately end the call.

Mrs Rockport had swallowed the bait and was now breathing heavily, but she remained on the line. It seemed she needed a question answered before she could terminate contact. The voice became thick with menace. '*All* about *me*? Really? I don't think so.'

'Try me.'

'Are you trying to blackmail me! Just what exactly *has* Alan been saying to you? Do you even *know* Dr Summerfield, Alyssa? Or is your imagination running away with you, you stupid hussy!'

Alan? What has Alan *got to do with all this?*

Alyssa remained dead calm even though she had no idea what Nikki was talking about. 'That's for me to know and you to find out, Nikki.' Though mystified, she realised instinctively that there was one more lie that she could resort to, one that would weaken Nikki even further. 'You see, Nikki,' she said, in her same dead calm voice, 'here's the thing. I know Alan incredibly well. Intimately. Which is going to be an insurmountable problem for you. If it comes to a lawsuit, I am going to have to reveal *everything*, not only about Gilbert and you, but about Alan Summerfield and you, too. So, drop the lawsuit—otherwise *everyone* is going to get harmed, not just me.'

'You are lying, you little cunt!' screamed Nikki Rockport. 'Lying! Don't you ever *dare* phone me again!' The phone went dead.

Alyssa smiled to herself once more.

Dear, dear, I seem to have opened a can of worms.

She was not afraid of any woman. If Nikki was looking to come up against her, Nikki was going to get her teeth knocked out. It had been unexpected, though, to hear her mentioning Alan by name. Alan had never mentioned that he knew Nikki rather more deeply than just as the friend of his wife Kara. Not even at the Monday meeting with Greta and the Dog. She needed to remember to ask him about it the next time she saw him.

3

Alyssa knew that above all she needed to sort out exactly where she stood with Cy. It was unacceptable that he had walked out on her without an explanation. This was not good enough. The least he needed to do was tell her what his problem with her was. Maybe it could be fixed. She needed to at least try to get him back, try to see if anything could be done. Despite their problems, they had been good together. People needed to be loyal to those they loved. She herself had always been loyal. Maybe too loyal. Too scared to let go. After all, there had been a time after she turned thirteen when she had had no one. Nothing at all. No love.

Relationships were hard for her, and a relatively new achievement in her life. So, when they worked, they were precious. They needed to be preserved. In her book, she and Cy needed to be civil to each other and try to patch things up.

Getting Cy to speak to her was difficult because he had disconnected his phone. Fortunately, though, Brian—who said he still felt devastated by the loss of Cy—had tried to be helpful. She had phoned him earlier that morning—before heading off to The House of Fantasy. Though Brian did not know for sure where Cy now worked, he had given her his best estimate of where he probably was. Judging from what one of his bookstore patrons had told him, he believed Cy was now assisting at a newly established second-hand bookstore near the metro station in Nandedong. This was as much as he knew because Cy was no longer speaking to him—or anyone else. And, no, he did not know the name of the bookstore. And no—he had checked—it didn't appear on Google maps, probably because it was new. But he did know other things about Cy, matters that he now felt free to divulge seeing that he no longer considered himself bound by any rule of friendship with Cy.

Did Alyssa know, for example, that Cy had been having sex with Rosie Skye for at least a month before he disappeared?

No, she did not, she had said. Which was not true. She had already heard the bad news via Jocelyn—who had heard about it from the same Brian who now feigned outrage about the matter over the phone but had not thought fit to mention it to her earlier.

Brian assured her over the phone that his heart was broken too. "Which doesn't mean that the two of *us* can't stay friends, does it, Alyssa? Maybe we two could do coffee later?"

"Maybe, Brian." She had said that only to shut him up so she could end the call.

Brian always had sex on the brain, so possibly his assertions that Cy had been having sex with Rosie Skye while still having sex with her amounted to little more than overheating of his one-track imagination. It seemed unlikely that what he had been saying to people lately was literally true. Cy was weak, but she refused to believe that he could be *that* treacherous. To sort the mess out, she was going to have to go to Nandedong in person and find Cy and force him to at least talk to her. She needed the truth. It was not going to be an easy task, but she was up for it.

As Jocelyn had said, she needed to do what had to be done.

She needed to get the Cy situation sorted.

Which meant that she needed to keep moving and stay one step ahead of the despair lurking dangerously close to the surface of her mind. She needed to stay in *fight and action* mode. Her physical self was her strongest suit and therefore her best hope for success.

Willing herself forwards, Alyssa stepped back into her church shoes and headed out on foot towards the nearest metro station, which was situated below the state parliament building at the edge of the CBD. The route to it was similar to the one she regularly followed when going to Fabio's gym and this seemed to fill her with added resolve to go through with the do-or-die mission to Nandedong.

She felt surprisingly strong, the positivity of the day no doubt greatly due to Jocelyn's unexpected arrival and friendship the previous day. Alyssa still felt thankful for that strange coincidence. She could just as well have been walking to her own funeral instead of to the train station.

Best not to think about it.

Not only was she feeling strong, but greatly pleased with herself too. Not everyone would have been so brave as to tackle both Mistress

Veronica and Nikki Rockport head on the way she had—and on the same day, too. The success of those earlier encounters still left her feeling elated.

However, the darkness within her was not far away. She was enough of a psychologist to know that her positive frame of mind was not going to last. The emotional problems that she had were actually very serious. One could not bottle things up forever. One could not live a lie forever. Doing so always had serious consequences, so much so that it was often fatal. That said, there were unfortunately some things that were not survivable when faced up to. Things that one was better off never thinking about again. In those cases, one had to just keep fighting. Keep on struggling to keep it hidden. And to do so, one had to stay brave. She could not afford to slacken off. There was no other way for her. The badness was very, very powerful. Restless.

Time was running out.

She had to get Cy back before it was too late.

Nandedong, where he now lived, was a poor, notoriously crime ridden outer suburb over fifty km away but getting to it was not going to be an obstacle. A suburban metro train would have her there in less than an hour.

4

She ended up standing most of the way despite seats becoming increasingly available as crush loading waned with increasing distance from the city centre. She discovered—by experiment—that she *could* actually sit for short periods of time without too much discomfort, but it remained easier to stand. Little did the other passengers know of the macabre work of art on her backside. Veronica was obviously an expert. Despite the speed and power of the rattan's strokes, the resulting tramline welts were perfectly placed across her seat: central, parallel, ideally spaced, and without any lateral straying off target. Quite amazing, really. She felt almost like showing them off. If anything about corporal punishment could be said to be preferable, it would have to be that it be done by an expert.

According to the map on her phone, the street directly outside the Nandedong station was called Foster Street. How many bookshops could there be in Foster Street, especially near the station? Still standing, she hung onto an overhead strap as the train rushed through the suburbs. She lurched from side to side with the carriage as it made its way and tried to imagine Cy's new life with the improbably named Rosie Skye. Two complete fakes puffing on dope. Maybe, after all, they did deserve each other. As a couple, Cyrus Beauchamp and Rosie Skye had no prospect in the long run of turning out anything other than the mutual sick jokes that they were. It was even possible that Brian was right, and they *had* been having sex behind her back.

Bastards.

The two lovebirds were dirt poor, she decided. Why else would they be living in Nandedong, which was nothing more, really, than a human wasteland? She had never been there, but she knew its reputation. Cy had made a bad choice. Misery was in store for him if he stayed out there. Hopefully, once he saw her again, he would come to his senses.

He had a lot to answer for. To start with, he had given her some sort of horrible disease. Also, because of him—okay, maybe other things too— she had nearly ended it by going off the balcony. Only the miraculous advent of Jocelyn had saved her life. Furthermore, it was now clear that there had been a lot of sneaking around going on from him behind her back. She had every reason to feel hurt and angry. Yes. Although, to be fair, the horrible disease part wasn't definite; that much she *did* know. The HPV virus may just as well have come from Ethan or Aaron. Apparently, the virus was extremely common. In fact, according to Dr Jensen, in the days before vaccination every single person who had sex contracted some or other strain of it. The dysplasia part was just bad luck. The gynaecologist had not wanted her to blame anyone. But she did. In her heart, she blamed Cy.

She blamed him for everything.

She had nearly died on the balcony.

Such a weak person.

Or was that her stepmother speaking?

Only the freakishly fortunate visit from Jocelyn had saved her. What, she wondered, did that say about the nature of existence and the meaning of life? The more she thought about the balcony episode, the more ashamed of herself she felt.

There had been that attempt during sociology too. From the eleventh floor. Unfortunately, it seemed that attempts to get rid of herself by falling to her death from a height were determined to recur. Whatever force it was that was behind the determination that someone needed to die, was going to try again. She was going to fall to her death. Something was going to push her over an edge. And when it finally happened, there would be no random eleventh floor tea lady to save her, and no Jocelyn. She had used up all her miracles.

Which was why she needed to get Cy back. She was much more stable when he was around. Cy's mind was as solid as a rock. She knew nobody else who was as sane as he was. Yet Cy was now behaving just like Diana Croft: doing his best to be harmful to her.

It was all too much, really.

At least Jocelyn cared about her. Loved her, in fact, especially now that Jocelyn had finally managed to confirm to herself that she was dealing with "her Lauren": the innocent angel. The one hated by all as a monster yet pure as snow. *The* Lauren Truebody.

Jocelyn's love for her was doomed, of course, because it was an angel whom Jocelyn loved, not anything real. Jocelyn's Lauren was nothing but a fantasy in Jocelyn's head; nothing but a yearning for her lost girlhood. Innocent angels did not exist. There were no such things, no innocence at all in the real world. An angelic Alyssa/Lauren was a figment of a half-mad woman's imagination.

Alyssa Brown, currently on a train, was far from innocent.

Still, Jocelyn had her uses.

5

Only gradually did Alyssa become aware of his stare. While she had been standing deep in thought, holding onto her overhead strap with one hand, he had been watching her. She realised this now, as he continued to stare at her rudely. The offending pest took the form of an untidy youth with a sullen face sitting in a nearby seat. There were pustules on his face, and he looked in serious need of a shower. Despite his young age, he had the debauched look of a serious substance abuser. She looked away, but when she looked back at him, he was still staring fixedly at her. It was no absent-minded stare; far from it. Predatory. Rude. She knew the type well: the total scumbag. Undoubtedly, there would be more such low life in Nandedong.

The next time she glanced in his direction, he was still staring but now he had his hand on his crotch. As soon as their eyes met, he moved his hand up and down. She knew exactly what lay under his pants. It would be stiff, sure. But it would also be pathetically skinny and somewhat laughable. She made a mental note to keep an eye on him because she sensed he may become dangerous. Nandedong was fast approaching, and it looked increasingly probable that it was his destination too. Possibly there would be police at the train station—there often were on the metro system—but even so they would not be much use in her case. She would not be able to bring herself to trust them to do the right thing by her. However, she was not overly worried. If the scumbag so much as tried to touch her, she would not hesitate to kick him in his balls. It was the only way to deal with such people.

Despite years of counselling, the police were still a mental health issue for her—mainly because she couldn't stand them. Knowing that she should not detest the police did not stop her from detesting the police. The problem with them was that no sooner had her mother Grace died in front of her than they had begun to swarm around her and tell her that she was a bad person. None of them had thought to help a child whose mother was gone. Instead, a policeman came up to her and said she had killed her mother. So, no, she did not like the police.

Robert Truebody uses daughter to murder wife.

It was a long trial. When the jury finally returned a verdict of suicide and not guilty, the police had had no choice but to accept that Grace Truebody may in fact have deliberately rolled under the passing train that killed her, but they did not in their hearts believe it. They had hated Lauren ever since, and she them. What the police believed happened was that at the instigation of Robert Truebody, his daughter Lauren had pushed Grace Truebody to her death. Which was wrong. Her father had had nothing to do with it. He had personally assured her of this afterwards and ever since. And while Bob had never recovered from the loss, he had never stopped loving his daughter. Up until then, her father's love for her had been her only certainty in life, and so it remained. She still felt his love. Without it, she would have nothing. No life. The only problem being that her father had been dead since she was thirteen. Gone from this world since the accident. The one with her in the driver's seat. When a father's love had temporarily failed.

And now Cy had failed her too. Alyssa felt her spirits beginning to wane. The closer the train got to Nandedong, the more destroyed she felt. Soon, the grief of life seemed once again almost too hard to bear.

Meanwhile, the awful youth was still on the train. Cy, in his biblical anti-biblical way, would no doubt have called him a product of unbridled fornication. Probably that was exactly what he was.

Foster Street lay just outside the Nandedong metro train station. With her bag over her shoulder, Alyssa headed in the direction of the shopping area, directed by a helpful sign. According to a diagram on the sign, there were some general shops, some just numbers without names, next to an Indian restaurant called the *Curry Pot*. That looked like a good place to start. She looked behind her. As feared, the unpleasant youth had indeed alighted from the train and was slouching behind her, about fifty metres back. There was no law against that.

Even if there was, it would have made no difference. There was no patrolling police constable anywhere to be seen.

She needed to press on. She would be safe once in a shop. With luck, she would find a second-hand bookstore nearby and Cy would be there, behind the counter—or, if not, she would be able to convince whoever was there to at least give her his phone number. Maybe even his home address. Searching for him in this way was going to be humiliating, but it was worth it. She had to try everything while she still could.

She felt increasingly anxious as she strode along in the gathering late afternoon gloom. It had been silly to come to a place like Nandedong dressed like she was, and she realised this now. She had made herself conspicuous. That aside, she was also still in considerable pain from Veronica, and hungry too. She should at least have eaten more food back at Parliament Station because she was now feeling mildly giddy from lack of it. She glanced over her shoulder once more. The creep tailing her had moved closer. Nandedong was living up to its reputation. Perhaps, she thought despairingly, it would be better if she simply ended things and allowed herself to fall victim to him. She cared frighteningly little about what became of her. After all, for worthless people nothing really mattered.

It was an anxiety attack. That was what it was. She needed to pull herself together. She had her pride in herself to maintain. If she was in danger, she needed to move faster. She glanced over her shoulder yet again to see if she was outpacing the pustular youth. She wasn't. He was taller than she was and walking faster than she could. He was going to catch up to her.

There was nothing she could do.

I'm so tired of having to fight.

6

Ahead was a sign indicating the Curry Pot restaurant, and beyond that a sign reading "Bertie's Bookshop". That had to be the right place. With her heart beating in her throat, Alyssa made for the door. The lewd youth overhauled her as she slowed to enter the shop, and, as he passed her on the sidewalk, he brushed his arm against the side of her chest.

'See you later tonight, baby,' he breathed into her face, finishing with a slurping sound from his mouth.

She almost slapped his slurping face. She should have, but she did not. She had not come to fight anyone. She had come in peace. Besides, she had begun to feel extremely unwell. Instead of slapping faces or kicking balls, she cringed and slunk into the bookshop. Luckily, he did not follow.

There was a woman behind the counter and the shop was brightly lit. She would be safe for a while. She stopped in front of a shelf of books and pretended to examine them while she composed herself and got her bearings within the shop. There seemed to only the one staff member present. No sign of Cy. It was a deadbeat shop. The books were mostly second-hand, and an inordinate number of them seemed to be about the Crimean War for some reason. Her hands would not stop shaking. The potential confrontation with Cy was affecting her more deeply than she had thought it would, and the pain in her rear end and her low blood sugar were not helping. She was real mess.

I'm hardly going to make a good impression, am I?

She wondered where Cy was. She gazed around the shop furtively, trying to locate him. He did not appear to be there. Not only that, but she was the only customer in the shop.

Through a gap between books, she studied the woman behind the till. She appeared to be in her late thirties and was artistically dressed in a somewhat shabby rainbow-striped loose frock covered in sunshine-yellow paint stains. There were flecks of dried paint on the backs of her hands too. Alyssa realised with increasing dismay that it had to be *her*: Cy's new woman. It did not seem fair. It seemed wrong that fate had made it turn out this way. It should have been Cy who was there. Cy's new flame had no business being there. Anyone could see that she was not a book person. In the correct version of fate, Rosie Sky should have been in her studio painting pictures of the sun instead of standing behind a till in a dingy second-hand bookshop. It should have been Cy who was there. Knowing him, he had probably persuaded her to do some of his sessions for him, while he, no doubt, sat in the gullible woman's home taking his ease, tending their cannabis crop, puffing on bongs, and claiming to be thinking deeply. The usual crap.

She tried to work out what best to do next. Part of her still hoped that Cy would miraculously appear out of a side office. Meanwhile, the woman in the rainbow frock steadfastly ignored her presence, which seemed to confirm her unsuitability in her role as book salesperson. Alyssa kept an eye on her. She was vaguely untidy in a Bohemian sense and had the indefinable yet unmistakable air of someone who was short of funds. She was not fat, slim rather—although not particularly well-shaped—and of average height, with long, dark-brown hair. Her breasts were well developed but nothing exceptional. She looked old, older than she probably was, and tired. She was probably malnourished. If the woman was indeed Rosie Skye, there seemed nothing about her that could explain Cy's behaviour.

Why dump me for a creature like that?

From a different angle she was able to see that the woman had no shoes on. She was barefoot—which would be against council health regulations—and, surprise, surprise, had a ring on her big toe and a bell on her ankle. Tattoos too. Some looked like literary quotations. Clearly, despite her age, the woman had the brain of a weeny bopper.

Cy steadfastly failed to materialise. Realistically, she had always known that this might happen, so she *had* thought of a plan B—which was to at least get his address or telephone number. Simple enough in theory, except that she had not planned on finding Rosie Skye in the shop—and certainly not as the only person there. Which meant that matters had become infinitely more complicated. Perhaps, now that she knew the name of the bookshop, she should just leave and phone the shop later in the hope of reaching Cy. Which would mean more delay. Which would be no good.

She was running out of time.

The unkindness of fate seemed to have conspired with everything else that was wrong with her and it lowered her confidence. With a sinking feeling, Alyssa began to suspect that what she was doing was nothing more than making a fool of herself. Cy had never really wanted her. Strangely, she could see that now. Her own pride had blinded her. She was not his type. Their relationship had been one big mistake. The trip to bring him home had been a big mistake. She was all wrong for him. She was no good for him. No good for anyone.

More than likely, her own parents hadn't been right for each other either. Which explained everything. Maybe Grace had been forced to marry Bob. Because of a pregnancy. Because of *her*—because of a product of unbridled fornication. Maybe, after all, this was all she was, all she had ever been, all that hell-child Lauren had ever amounted to. An inconvenience. A nothing.

Standing at the till in front of her was what Cy wanted. What he had always *really* wanted.

'Can I help you?' asked the woman. Her voice was surprisingly deep, like a smoker, and her accent pronounced and uncultured—way worse than her own. The fingernails were chewed and dirty.

With the room threatening to spin around her, Alyssa felt a tiny part of her mind clinging to a hope that the woman talking to her was not Rosie Skye. It felt as if her life hung in the balance.

'Is Cy around?' She asked the question as calmly and as casually as she could.

The woman squinted suspiciously at her. 'I've been watching you. You're *her*, aren't you?' Evidently satisfied with the correctness of her deduction, she became unpleasant. 'I thought so. Hubris Magnus. That's what he calls you. So up yourself.'

'What! I beg your pardon!' Alyssa felt sick in the stomach. In front of her stood the sum of all her fears. This was who Cy had been cheating with. This was who he had been licking everywhere, like he always did. This was whose slime Cy had been covering himself in and then returning home to pass on to her. Her courage failed her. The betrayal by Cy seemed too much to bear.

'No need to look so surprised that I know it's you. You are so obvious you are a joke. Cy warned me you'd turn up. What part of *it's over* don't you understand?'

'I think you two owe me at least a telephone number or an address.'

'You think everything is all about *you*, don't you? Especially, I've heard, when it comes to sex. Well, we've got news for you: leave us alone!'

Alyssa felt the blood draining from her face but said nothing. What could a person say? It was well within her physical ability to reach over and grab a fistful of the obnoxious till assistant's dirty hair and slam her head on the counter to improve her manners, but she did nothing.

'Tell Cy I came for him. Tell him to phone me. Tell him to stop being such a coward.'

'Didn't you hear me? Go on, piss off! Cock shrinker.'

'I. I . . .' She just stood there, as though mortally injured. Her mind seemed unwilling to function. A *cock shrinker* . . . was *that* what she was?

'I won't say this again. Fuck off.' Rosie Skye turned her back and walked into the side office and slammed the door and locked it.

The terrible names: Hubris Magnus; Cock Shrinker. Those were not Rosie's words.

They are Cy's words.

His true opinion of her.

What an utter failure as a human being she clearly was. Nothing but a deluded fool. Until now, she had always hoped that in the world that she had created for herself this was no longer the case.

Wrong.

Alyssa found herself at the shop's entrance. Her body was shaking, but her voice was loud and clear and like ice: 'Tell Cy I've picked up a terrible disease from him.'

She was talking to an empty shop.

There was nothing for it but to head home alone.

How could anyone be this unfair to her?

She did not realise she was crying until she saw people looking at her oddly. But then, when she did stop crying, they still kept looking at her oddly.

All the way home.

CHAPTER THIRTY-SIX

1

THAT NIGHT, IN BED, existence felt too heartbreaking. Alyssa found herself in tears again, the weeping proving impossible to stop. All that she had in life was a very sore bottom and nothing else. She knew she was being immature, but still she sank into a pit of self-pity and used up tissue after tissue. What a fool she was, she told herself. She had spent her time blaming Cy for everything when she herself was the problem. All the while, she had been too proud to admit what a thoroughly bad and worthless person she was.

Grace had not deserved to die.

There was a price to pay for killing one's own mother, and, clearly, she had yet to pay the bill in full. No reconstructed road to happiness lay ahead for her, just endless suffering and misery.

In between the night-time tears, she thought about her real mother. When Grace had died at the age of thirty-one, she herself had been only five years old. Which meant that there was precious little that she could recall with certainty, either about Grace or about the events surrounding her death. She did know, though, that her mother had been beautiful. Of that fact she had definite memories—images that were deeper than subsequent imaginings based on photographs seen later in life. Grace's hair had been long and dark, and she used to make lovely cakes. Grace used to help her dress for kindergarten and used to brush her hair. Grace had been a kind person—of that, too, she felt certain. Yet there were other memories too, memories that jarred with her positive recollections, confusing ones that had to do with much shouting and screaming at their old house in Cloverdale—their home before the move to Ocean View. Or had the screaming and shouting been afterwards, *after* Grace's death? There was no way she could ever know. Had it not been for her father, she would not even have known how Grace had died. Not for sure. He told her afterwards. Later. He had been a witness to it all.

She had murdered her own mother.

That was what he said.

She remembered the train, of course. And the body cut in half. And the blood. And the intestines. That was too gruesome and shocking to ever forget. And she remembered being on the embankment with Grace. Arguing with her. She remembered that too. But not the rest of it.

What she did know at the time, though, was that Grace had not even said goodbye to them before she ran away.

A few months before she died, Grace simply disappeared from their house. One day, she never came home. Their father, Robert—Bob as he was known—was at work. According to what came out later, Grace had left the three of them home alone—herself, Greg, and Harry, who was still a baby—and gone off shopping, never to return. Her father, though, had then acted as if nothing had happened, which had spared them all much anxiety. She remembered taking her cue from him and not worrying too much about the disappearance. "Mum is fine and will be back soon".

Some boys at kindergarten cruelly said that her mother and father were each trying steal her for themselves, but she had not believed a word of it. Instead, she had spent the evenings during those months helping her dad cook for the family. The four of them had been happy as they waited for their mother to return. It was at that time, though, that her father had first begun to get drunk. She remembered that because it was so scary the first few times. He never used to hurt them though. Not back then.

Sometimes, they went out in the car and drove through the streets of Cloverdale looking for their mother. They could never find her. Then, one day, with her brothers at childcare, her father kept her at home, out of kindergarten. He said it was so that she could help him. Once again, he had been drinking too much—she remembered that. He took her—his little Lauren—with him in the car on yet another search of the streets. Alone with him in the car, sitting on his lap, she told her father that she had had a dream that told them where their mother was.

"And where might that be"? Bob had asked.

It was at the place where Grace often took the three children to play after grocery shopping. So, she led her father there—proud little Lauren herself—to the river reserve near the supermarket. It was a nice place: a few acres of grass and trees at the river's edge next to where the railway line cut through the adjacent hill to reach the bridge over the river. It must have been winter because she was cold. They never had enough clothes. She remembered that too.

Grace was there, all right. Not in the fenced park itself but up higher, sitting near the top of the steep edge of the railway cutting before where the grass petered out. It was a place with a good view. They saw her from some distance sitting up there, a lonely figure out in the cold wind.

From that position, from high up, Grace would have been able to look down over the fenced park where her three children once used to play after doing the grocery shopping with her. That was why she was there. Alyssa knew this by now—that Grace must have been missing them—but she suspected that even back then it would have occurred to her that it showed that her mother *did* miss her after all and would be coming back for her.

Bob, though, became very angry when he saw her.

She remembered that too. In real time.

2

She remembered running towards Grace and her father outrunning her. By the time she managed to climb over the fence at the edge of the official park and clamber up the side of the steep embankment of the railway cutting, Bob was already at Grace's side, and they were arguing.

She remembered the shouting. Meanwhile, a train called the Noon Express was coming. She saw it coming. And the wind was freezing cold. When she finally reached her parents, they both looked very sad. Then her father sat down on the grass and started crying—from drinking too much—and little Lauren came and stood by his side. Her mother came towards her with her arms outstretched. All this she remembered with certainty.

The train was almost there, about to pass well below them, but it was making a thundering noise, so it was difficult to hear. Her mother screamed something like "she's mine!" and her father screamed something like "nooooh!"

Then the bad thing happened. Her mother stumbled on the steep slope and put out a hand for her daughter to steady her.

She kind of remembered that, but she wasn't really sure it wasn't something Bob had told her afterwards. Certainly, what happened *after* that, *nobody* knew for sure. Except her father.

She had tried to remember many, many times, but she simply did not know for sure. She could not remember. Next thing, the train was rumbling past below them, full of commuters, and her mother was tumbling down the embankment. Then she was cut into two pieces. She had gone under the wheels of the very last carriage of the train. The train came to a stop and then they said she was dead. They would not allow her to go and talk to her mother.

A lot of people came. Finally, a policeman came and told her that he had spoken to her father and that she was a bad girl.

The newspaper said: "Woman under Wheels of Noon Express. Murder Suspected".

Lauren had done something *very* bad.

Her father told her what it was that she had done wrong: she had thrown her mother under the train. When her mother put out a hand towards her, she had pushed her away so hard that she went tumbling down the steep slope and onto the train track below.

Alyssa shivered in the darkness of her flat at the horror of what she had done.

Her father said afterwards, though, that he forgave her.

And a while later, the court found Robert Truebody innocent of his wife's death after a fine performance by him. He knew, he said during his trial for his wife's murder, that despite the evidence of most of the witnesses on the train that he had pushed his wife to her death, he had not done anything wrong. He knew too, he tearfully said, that his daughter Lauren had not really known what she was doing when *she* pushed her mother down the hill. She was too young to understand the consequence. Both he and his little daughter were completely innocent of murder. This, he had insisted upon.

She wasn't innocent, of course, but that was their special secret.

Trouble was, she could not *remember* doing what she had done.

No matter how often she revisited her memories, she remained certain of only one thing: on a cold day, at noon, in a park, she had killed her own mother.

Which meant that she could not trust herself.

If she was not careful, she was going to end up killing still more people without really knowing what she was doing. After all, by now not only was her mother done away with, but her father too, and Gilbert Rockport, and *herself*—almost. The herself bit was just a matter of time. It required courage, though, so how many *others* were going to get done away with before she got there? Victims, all of them, of someone dangerously sick in the head.

Okay, maybe she was being over-dramatic and wallowing in self-pity. But surely it was justified. She had been left with nothing. She had nobody.

And as for Gilbert Rockport . . . who knew *what* was going on there, *what* she was capable of? What if she had done something weird? It was hard to know what to think.

I can't even trust myself.

She got up and took three pain tablets. Then, finally exhausted, she fell asleep—but not before realising one more truth. She was going to have to do away with Cy. Not literarily, she hoped. Surely not. No, just as in dump him and find a new boyfriend. Someone she could trust.

The matter had suddenly become urgent.

She was going to need to get working on it first thing in the morning.

If she did not find someone to love her, if nobody wanted her, if she wasn't good enough for anyone at all, then she was going to go *seriously* mad.

Being with a man who loved her was her only way she knew to remain functional. It was the only card she had to play in life. With her, there was nothing else. Just a terrifying emptiness. She needed a man who loved her. She needed to find one.

If she failed in that quest, she was going to be as good as dead.

3

It felt strange being back at Public Hospital. It was almost like stepping back in time. She had done much of her training here after graduating, so she knew it well—especially the mental health section. The familiarity of the building was comforting given that so much in her life had changed since she was last there. If she was to take charge of her future—as so eloquently advised by both Jocelyn and Susan Lindow—the visit was well overdue.

The previous night, after all the fretting about Cy and Grace, she had slept unexpectedly well once she finally fell asleep, and she now felt strong again. It was puzzling that this should be the case, given all that had happened, but then who was she to argue with her feelings? The trip earlier that morning to the local convenience store with her credit card to obtain basic food supplies, followed by a good breakfast, had no doubt helped. Amazingly, except for the continuing discomfort in her rear end, she was almost back to her old self. Or so it felt. In fact, it felt better than that. It was almost as though she didn't have a problem in the world and that life was quite pleasant.

Had she tipped over some edge in in her mind? No, she did not think so.

On the contrary, she felt perfectly resolute. She had been putting off the inevitable for too long and she had realised, finally, that this had to stop. The time had come for her to do what had to be done. No more ifs or buts. She needed to claim Mark Stanford as her own.

But first, she had to find him.

From what Mark had said at the gym recently, he was back working at the Public. And, as fate would have it, Ben Clayton was a patient there too—which meant that she had every justification for being there. She could go walking around in the corridors of the hospital with impunity, armed with a perfect excuse: visiting a patient. After all, had not her supervisor advised her to go forth in the name of kindness and demonstrate a better attitude towards others, especially clients? What better way to search for Mark Stanford than to pay a visit to Ben?

She knew, of course, exactly where Ben would be. Walking around aimlessly in the building pretending to look for him would simply be a cover for looking for Mark. Unlike most other people, she could get to Ben Clayton without needing to do any wandering about at all. He would be in the psychiatric secure ward, a place and location she knew perfectly well. By pretending that she was searching for her client, counsellor Alyssa Brown had the ability to penetrate any and every part of the hospital without being unduly challenged by security systems. Mark would not escape her this time.

For all Ben Clayton's faults, she nevertheless quite looked forward to getting to see him again—in a safe environment. Well did she remember how he had once threatened to "rip her head off" at the cottage. She had not seen Ben since the day Gilbert died, when the paranoid schizophrenic had appeared suddenly from behind the pot plants in the foyer of the Donald Clinic and "captured" her as she was fleeing for home after hearing about Gilbert's accident. Ben had been a tough assignment, but, bizarrely, she missed the professional challenge that interacting with him had represented. Since the letter in her letterbox and the associated psychotic breakdown and attack on nurse Gail Wilson, however, she had heard little about Ben. The secure ward was a lonely place. Without a doubt, he would agree to see her. For those stuck in that ghastly place, kindness was always appreciated.

There was more to it than kindness, though. In visiting Ben, she would be able to gather intelligence about Gail Wilson and her lawsuit. As Susan Lindow had so cleverly pointed out, one could not have too much information when it came to those intent on spilling your blood.

She would get Ben to spill the beans on her accuser instead.

Gail Wilson won't know what hit her.

And, as a bonus, she would be able to find out whether Ben presented an ongoing danger to her personally if he ever got released.

4

The hospital was gigantic. As Alyssa journeyed circuitously through the corridors towards her official destination of the psychiatric secure ward—with no sightings yet of Mark—she discovered that the building generated no negative feelings in her. Her own psychiatric admission during university days had not been here but at Olympic Hospital, across town, which was why she had chosen to train at the Public. Her time here as a student had been one of the best parts of her life.

As she got closer to the mental health area, she half-hoped that by chance she would bump into her old mentor, Wendy Greene. It was thanks to Wendy that she had qualified as a counselling psychologist. She may have lost everything, including Cy, but her career—even damaged as it was—remained; that other rock of hers, besides men, upon which to reconstruct her life.

At least she had a qualification. Wendy had been a great blessing.

The location of Benjamin Clayton was exactly as she had predicted: the psychiatric inpatient secure unit. He was still locked up there. At the unit's reception desk, she lied and said that her relationship to Ben was "good friend". To have been truthful and said "former counsellor of Ben currently being sued for three million dollars by a former nurse of Ben" would not have gone down well. Following a brief telephonic enquiry by the administrative clerk, Ben agreed to the visit as predicted. And luckily, the nurse—a trainee as expected—who emerged from behind the locked doors to escort her in was relatively new and did not recognise her.

Alyssa passed successfully through the security checkpoint, which included a scan for concealed drugs and weapons, and was ushered into the small visitor's lounge within the secure unit. The chairs looked hard, so she remained standing. From a legal point of view, the visit was illegal, but—just like Gilbert Rockport when he was alive—she no longer cared about the technical aspects of the law. It was too late for that. What was needed was information and the law was an ass.

Ben was a changed man. The previous nervous, darting look in his eyes was gone, and he now seemed perfectly at peace. 'Miss Alyssa!' he said bashfully, extending a hand in welcome. He appeared extremely glad to see her. Both his legs were still swathed in dressings and a burly male psychiatric nurse accompanied him.

'Hello Ben,' said Alyssa, shaking his hand. 'Long time no see. I thought I would pay you a short visit. I've been worried about you.' Which wasn't really true.

'I'm okay now. Much better.'

'I'm so pleased to hear that. I'd love to have a bit of a catch up with you. Are you happy to sit and chat for a while?'

'Sure. Sure. Take a seat.' Ben turned to the nurse. 'It's fine Dave. I know her well. She's good for me. Promise.'

'So, you're a *friend* of Ben's, are you?' queried nurse Dave, as though doubtful that such a mismatch was possible.

'Oh, yes. Old friends. Good friends.'

Ben nodded vigorously in agreement.

Outvoted, the psychiatric nurse left them to chat. Alyssa then selected the softest of the chairs and sat down.

5

'You look amazingly well,' she said to Ben, who remained standing. She meant it. Ben looked normal, whatever that meant. However, he still used the same overly sweet and pungent deodorant that his mother bought for him. *Homme Support*. It made her smile.

'Thank you for coming,' he said in his strangely formal way. 'I'm really sorry I caused so much of a stir last month. I don't know what came over me. Honestly.'

'I can't help blaming myself partly for that,' said Alyssa.

'Would you like a glass of water? It's paper, unfortunately. The glass.'

'Not right now, thanks. I'm fine. Come, sit. Somehow, I feel I've failed you. I just wanted to tell you how sorry I am for what happened.'

Ben took a seat opposite and grinned. 'Don't blame yourself. I think you did your best to help.'

'Do you? Truthfully?'

'I'm sure of it. I have no doubt it's part of the reason I feel so well now.'

'I'm really glad to hear that. So, no more people levitating?'

He gave an amused smile. 'No. Your feet are on the ground. I feel quite well.'

'Wonderful. Now, Ben, there's another thing I want to ask you about. That letter you sent to me. What was that all about?'

'Oh. That. It's so embarrassing. I can't believe I write stuff like that sometimes.'

'Writing things down can be helpful. What do you think you were trying to say? What did your letter mean?'

He became bashful and appeared hesitant. 'To be honest, I don't really know. Nothing, probably.'

'That letter from you was so amazing I find that hard to believe.' She gave him an encouraging smile. 'Surely it must have meant something.'

'Probably it meant that sometimes I know too much. I think that's what it was. Knowing too much. But not now. I don't want to know anything anymore. Honestly, I don't. I wasn't well at the time.'

'Because you knew too much?'

'Yes, exactly. I'm sorry. Dr Shelton says I shouldn't dwell on such matters. It's better for me to stay on my medication and forget about trying to solve riddles. Asking questions is only going to land me in trouble—I have to follow a new pathway.'

'You've stopped writing?'

'Oh yes, no more writing. It's too scary for me now. It's all very inappropriate. Dr Shelton says I can see that now.'

'As long as you are happy, Ben. You look happy, I must say. Did they change your medication? I suppose they've stopped the zasperidone. That certainly wasn't working, was it.'

'Oh no. I'm still on that. Same as ever. Still the old needle every two weeks. Same high dose. My mum is furious about it, but Dr Shelton says it's for the best.'

'You mean nothing has changed with your medication since you've been here?'

'Nope. Should it have?'

'I don't know. I must confess, though, that I don't know much about medicines. I suppose they must know what they're doing because you look so well. Really, you do.'

'Thanks. Dr Shelton is very strict, but he's okay. I would much prefer having you, though.'

'Why, thank you, Ben.'

Alyssa looked at him again. Though still in short pants because of the bandages on his legs, he had on a stylish sweater and looked confident and relaxed. This was not the same Ben that she had had to contend with all those weeks back. She had never seen him this way.

'I'm afraid I can't offer you any coffee or tea,' said Ben. 'They won't let us handle boiling water. Understandably. So, it's a bit of a boring place. Still, I should be home in a week or two. That's what Dr Shelton says. As soon as my legs are healed.'

'Wonderful.' She did not mean what she said, though. She hoped he was misinformed about his prospects of early release back into the community. She was almost sure he was. One could not go around trying to kill people with a knife.

She had another question for him. 'As a matter of interest, Ben, how did you find my flat? How did you know where to deliver your letter?'

'Oh that.' He became guarded. 'You won't tell Dr Shelton, will you?'

'No, of course not. If anyone can keep a secret, it's me. You know me.'

'It's really embarrassing.'

'You know you can't embarrass me.'

'I followed you.'

'You followed me!'

'I'm really sorry. I know I shouldn't have. I know I did wrong.' He hid his face in his hands like a small child. 'I couldn't help myself. I wanted to help you. I saw how sad you were.'

'So, you followed me home from the Donald?'

'Yes. Only to see what was wrong with you. When I was waiting for my mother to pick me up, I saw you leaving. You looked like you were crying, so I followed you. I got into lots of trouble afterwards because I wasn't in the right place when my mum came.'

'Nobody gave my address to you?'

'No.'

'And since then, you've been following me?'

He covered his eyes again but nodded. 'Not anymore. I'm better now. I know what I did at the church was wrong. Where did you go that day, by the way? You disappeared.' He hesitated. 'You are very sexy, that was my problem. Too sexy for me.' His voice trailed off. 'But that is never an excuse. I understand it now. It is *not* an excuse.'

She felt her face turning pale as he smiled matter-of-factly at her: Ben Jabba Clayton, the intruder at the church. It had been *him*. She was looking at the Fondsdale Street church interloper; the potential rapist whom she had feared. The person she had thought she was imagining.

There was *someone there after all.*

She struggled to think of something to say. 'What do you mean, "where did I go", Ben?'

'I lost you somewhere. I looked out of that office and into the church, but you were already gone.'

He wasn't making much sense. She hadn't gone anywhere during the time he was there. Not only that, but he obviously had no insight into the seriousness of the details he was so blithely revealing to her, so she hesitated to question him further. He would have been quite unwell when it all happened. Capable of anything. The important thing was that he was now under lock and key and looking much better.

She did have a final question for him, though, one which remained greatly relevant for the future. 'Do you think one day, once you are home, you'll want to come back to us at the Donald, Ben?'

'Probably not. Only if I don't have to see Gail again.'

'Is that because you feel guilty that you tried to kill her?'

'No. It's because she's a bad person. She deserved what happened, believe me. It's because of her that I wrote that letter to you. I'm really scared of her. I hope they put her in prison.'

Hello. How interesting.

'Gail? Sent to prison for being too scary?'

'Yes, that is where she belongs. Behind bars.'

'Why on earth would you say that?'

'Because of what she did to me. Kept doing.' His face clouded. 'I've said too much again, haven't I? Dr Shelton says it's a real problem I have. I have to forget about Gail. I can't say any more. You, on the other hand, have never scared me.'

'It's kind of you to say that.'

'I am worried about you, though, Miss Alyssa. You seem different from how I remember you. Why is that?'

'What do you mean, Ben?'

'You're not the usual Miss Alyssa that I know. You're not the same. No. You are a different person.' He studied her. 'You look too . . . how shall I say . . . fragile.'

She nearly laughed. She could imagine Dr Shelton saying exactly the same thing to him earlier. For an inmate in a psychiatric secure unit, Ben certainly did not lack self-confidence. 'Don't you worry about me, Ben. I'm okay.'

'Here's a thing. You see, I don't think you are. Upstairs.' He put a finger on his temple. 'You don't look very well to me at all. In that department. Why is that? Should you see a doctor? You know you can be honest with me. Is something bad happening inside your head? Is that why you are here?'

CHAPTER THIRTY-SEVEN

1

THE VISIT TO BEN Clayton had given Alyssa a headache. She was tired of mad people. There was nothing wrong with *her* that a good strong coffee would not fix. It was time to get one.

As she journeyed back through convoluted corridors towards the main cafeteria near the hospital's official entrance, she mulled over the conversation she had just had with Ben Clayton; the bit about him stalking her. She realised, finally, why, he had failed to find her at the Fondsdale street church—why he had thought that she had already left. He must have glanced into the nave during the time when she was slumped on the floor between the pews—an event she was still trying to process. Whatever its cause, she would then have been invisible to someone at the front of the church.

Which was extremely fortunate because *had* Ben seen her in the church, he would without a doubt have come over to her. And what then? Mentally unstable as he then was, what would he have done? Tried to "make love" to her and killed her incidentally during that addled process? Strangled her when he found it necessary to remove her personhood because of the guilt he was feeling at what he was doing to her i.e., giving free rein to his secret sexual desires with her. Or would he instead have just plain slaughtered her with his knife after catching her red-handed as an apparent religionist in a church? Had she escaped death at the hands of Benjamin Clayton?

And had this been just a matter of luck?

The day had started off well that morning, but everything seemed once again to be becoming too much for her to cope with. She was starting to feel distinctly unwell. Walking had become more difficult. The building seemed to be swaying with her footsteps. It was as though she was not herself anymore. She fought against the feeling. There was nothing wrong with her, she told herself—besides an aching bottom. It was nothing that something to eat would not cure. She needed to get to the cafeteria. If she could just get there, then everything would be all right.

The large eating hall lay just off the hospital's main foyer, and she knew it well from her past life there. The moment she entered she felt much better. Virtually everyone who worked at the giant hospital passed through this refreshment hall at least once a day. Here, she would potentially find Mark. Here, there was hope.

The facility was open to hospital visitors too, which meant that she would be able to stay for as long as she wished without getting into trouble. Midday was not far away, so she could even have lunch here. After that, depending on what happened, she could make further plans to find Mark. There was no rush. No pressure. Anything was going to be better than returning home to an empty flat and misery.

That would be totally pointless.

Therefore, she went and stood in the queue at the food counter.

Why did I ever leave this place?

While she waited, she could not help dwelling further on what Ben Clayton had said, especially the part about her "not looking well". Was it *that* obvious that she was struggling? She doubted it. She looked good physically—of that much she was certain. She had taken considerable trouble with her grooming before heading to the hospital that morning and was smartly dressed in a tailored black pants-suit bottom, black pumps, white top, and light pink cardigan. The mid-heeled formal shoes matched her pants, and though the white top over-emphasised her breasts—according to some—the overall effect was in good taste. She had even, for the first time in many days, put on the silver bracelet that used to belong to her real mother, Grace. Cy's ring, on the other hand—a small sapphire one that he gave her when he first moved in—had remained in her bedside drawer at the flat. In its place on her right hand was the fake diamond ring from her previous boyfriend, Aaron—fake only because he had been a student at the time, like her. Alyssa lifted the hand and smiled.

Fuck Cy.

Aaron may have been a control freak, but at least he had *wanted* her. Now, by herself in a coffee queue, life felt very lonely. Almost unbearably so.

She obtained a large skinny latte and a firm, fresh banana at the counter, then seated herself at a vacant table in a corner with her back to the wall. From there, she had a good view of the goings-on in the eating hall. As a vocational trainee in psychodynamic counselling, she had often sat at that exact same table, mostly with Wendy Greene, drinking endless coffees and analysing and criticising people from a distance. While she sat there, the cafeteria slowly began to fill with hospital staff members once midday passed—just like in the old days. Most of the newcomers were junior nurses and medical students on early lunch break. Everyone looked in a hurry, but she herself was in no hurry.

She sat quietly and observed everyone. The medical students were easy to differentiate from other health care staff; they were the ones with the rather comical air of supercilious superiority. During the time when she worked there, they had regularly amused her. While she ate her banana, she wondered whether Wendy Greene might turn up. If she did, it would be rather embarrassing. Almost certainly, Wendy would have heard about the trouble she was in at the Donald. Wendy would be terribly disappointed, and Wendy had a way of making her opinion clearly known. She tried to imagine what she might say:

> This is so disappointing, Alyssa. We all know you come from hell, but *this*! Is this all that you amount to? Just a child well and truly broken? Just NOTHING!?

Maybe she *was* just a nothing. Just a piece of trash worth nothing. She did not think she could survive any more criticism.

What to do with a broken child?

A tear began to brim. As discretely as possible she brushed it away. She felt ashamed of herself for being so weak. Already she was twenty-six, yet she had nothing and nobody. She was a disgrace. Yes, Cy had betrayed her behind her back, but she had probably deserved it. What a disappointment she was turning out to be.

2

He came to her, as planned.

'We meet yet again!' exclaimed his cheerful voice. 'I *knew* it was you. Even from far away.'

'Oh shit!' She almost spilled her coffee as the voice startled her. 'Sorry. Didn't see you coming.' It was him, Dr Mark Stanford. 'I've been watching the people coming in, but I never saw you enter.'

'You just sit there and watch people?'

'Sometimes. Take a seat if you want. I was half-expecting that you might turn up here in the cafeteria anyway.'

'Don't mind if I do. It's not every day that one gets to have such good company.' He sat down to the left of her, his back against the other wall of the corner. 'Hi, Alyssa.'

'Hi, Mark. Long time no see. Just the two of us, I mean.'

'Yes, afraid so. The other day at the gym wasn't much good, was it. But you know how things are.' He placed a lunchbox filled with a stack of homemade sandwiches on the table. 'I came via the little stairway in the far corner, by the way. For the exercise. That's why you didn't see me.'

'Oh. Yes, I remember it now. The other way in. From the floor above only.'

'Exactly. Anyway, why the long face? And why aren't you at work?'

'I don't have a long face. It's just that you've caught me deep in thought. I've got a few days off work.'

'Here on your days off? Don't tell me you miss *this* place.' He took out a sandwich.

'In some ways, I do, I suppose. The good old Public. There's a whole lot of bullshit going on at the place where I work. The whole private practice thing—I'm sure you know what I mean.'

'Too true, I do. You're at the Donald, aren't you? To me, there seems something immoral about the way that place squeezes so much money out of people. I don't mean that as a personal criticism, by the way.'

'Sure. I felt the same way when I first got there. The clients, though, seem to enjoy wasting their money, which is something I never realised before. What worries me more, now, about deluxe private practice, is the lack of peer accountability. The deluxe side is a bit like the Wild West.

Especially the politics involved.'

'Mm.'

She sipped on her coffee, and he ate his sandwiches. It dawned on her that they were behaving towards each other like old friends even though they hardly knew each other.

'Sorry. Have to eat,' he said between bites. 'Limited time.'

'Don't worry about me.' She studied him as he ate. His fingernails, as he held his food, were clean. So was his hair. Short and clean. 'Are you still covering someone's sick leave?' she asked.

'Not that exactly, though I'm still on the relief rotation. Currently, I'm covering maternity leave for a cardiothoracic resident.'

'What happens if you get sick yourself?'

'I never get sick.'

'Amazing.' She had meant the comment to sound politely sceptical— as in "pull the other one"—but she realised he was being factual: he literally never got sick. Instead, he radiated the same indefinable physical superiority that she often saw in other doctors. The sandwich eater was clearly a medical man: he had the right sort of supreme ability and personal confidence. Without a doubt, he would grow into another Alan Summerfield.

'And what exactly does cardiothoracic mean? Is that heart surgery? You look far too young for that.'

He smiled at her, much like her youngest brother Harry, and it went straight to her heart. 'Yes, it's mostly heart surgery, and yes, I'm pretty junior at that seeing that I'm a general surgery trainee, but the resident I'm covering for is only the look-in resident, not the actual cardiothoracic resident. Mainly, I just assist. And I'm not that young, by the way. I'm thirty-one. More to the point, what are *your* plans? Are you coming back to the Public? To work here?'

'Not at present, no. I'm only here because I came to visit one of my clients. He's in the psych secure unit.'

'Is that why you are looking so strained? From what I've seen of nutcases, I don't know how you mental health people cope.' He had brought a reusable container of coffee with him, and he flipped its lid open with a thumb. 'I almost did psychiatry, you know.' He took a swig of coffee. 'The stuff interests me, but I decided it was all a bit too hopeless. The patients don't ever really get better, do they, and they are all so horribly dependent. Or is that too negative?'

'It's not all doom and gloom, Mark. I mainly do counselling. Mostly I have clients rather than patients, and the people I try to help generally aren't nuts, as you so delightfully put it. A lot depends on what one means by the concept of mental *illness*. Also, on what one means by *better*.'

'Apologies for using "nuts". Not a word I'd ever use in front of someone I didn't instinctively trust not to be weird about things. Must be a good sign. I'm impressed. I never realised you were so together. And so intelligent.'

'Intelligent? Did you think that possibly I was an idiot?'

He smiled. 'I knew you were a psychologist if that's what you mean. I've come across quite a few of your lot in my time at medical school, and I must say it hasn't always been a good experience. You are restoring my faith.'

'That's a good thing, I suppose.'

He gave a friendly smile and offered her a sandwich. It looked like white bread with lettuce and cheese. 'Hungry? Would you like one?'

His teeth were white and perfectly straight, just like Alan Summerfield's. 'No thanks, Mark.' She gestured towards her banana skin. 'I'm okay. Thanks for the offer, anyway.'

'Anytime.'

'What do you think is wrong with psychologists? The clinical sort, I mean. Feel free to be honest. I won't take it personally.'

'You are taking me far too seriously. I was just shooting my mouth off.'

'You started it, so now you are going to have to answer.'

'I've put my foot in it, haven't I?'

'You have.'

'Well, it's the arrogance, I suppose. That's what pisses me off the most about them. Their idea that they know how peoples' minds work when in fact they know nothing of the sort. Some, in fact, seem to know nothing at all. Not you, of course.' He turned to look at her. 'You don't give me that feeling.' He looked directly into her eyes as he said it.

He had stopped eating. Like the first time at Fabio's gym, the world seemed to stop as his eyes locked with hers. She saw herself looking at eternity. The power of life. It flowed. Between them.

'You are just so incredibly beautiful,' he said softly. 'I feel I have to tell you that.'

She felt herself blushing.

'You remind me so much of a song by Van Morrison called *Brown-Eyed Girl*.'

Her eyes weren't brown—but he knew that.

A mobile phone rang in his pocket. 'Oh, oh, it's Ruby. She normally meets me here for lunch, and she's looking for me.'

'You'd better answer, then.'

'I'll go one better.' He stood up and waved.

Alyssa noticed the swipe card clipped to his belt on the right of his crotch. The card displayed his photo ID and read: Dr Mark Stanford MD, Senior Resident, General Surgery. A large, red, semi-transparent number 5 was superimposed over the card. Dr Mark Stanford was for real.

'Ruby has seen us. She's on her way here.' He tried to make polite conversation as they waited for her. 'It was great us seeing you again at Fabio's gym the other day, by the way. Recently, Ruby and I have been back there on days when we can both spare an hour off together. Hard to predict. Ruby mentioned that she met you in the change room.'

'Yes, we met. I probably shocked her, though.'

He looked puzzled. 'Why?'

'I was a bit snappy. Boyfriend problems.'

Her words hung in the air as the atmosphere between them became suddenly pregnant with meaning. Mark attempted to say something: 'I find that hard to believe. You couldn't have a boyfriend problem even if you tried.'

Again, their eyes locked. 'Can so.'

3

Mark's fiancée, Ruby, arrived, complete with engagement ring on her finger and crucifix around her neck, and tossed her bag onto the table. 'Sorry I'm late. Who's this?' Ruby squinted at Alyssa. 'Oh, God. Don't tell me. It's "The Body". It is you, isn't it? From the gym. I might have known!'

'Hi, Ruby,' said Alyssa sweetly.

Mark hastily explained: 'Rubes,' he said, 'let me introduce you. This is Alyssa. From the gym, as you said. She's visiting one of her clients who is a patient in the hospital.'

'So, you have clients, do you?' said Ruby, rudely.

'She's a qualified psychologist,' said Mark.

'I think I should be on my way,' said Alyssa, gathering her things. Despite the crucifix around the neck, Beak Face did not seem to have a very Christian attitude.

'No. Please stay,' said Ruby. 'I know I'm overreacting. It's just that I've been under a lot of strain lately with my thesis.' Ruby sat down next to Mark.

'Yes, stay,' said Mark. 'We'd be quite keen to hear about the psychology world. Ruby is thinking of getting a job in that area.'

'I thought you were a doctor,' said Alyssa.

'Almost one. But that's a PhD, not medical doctor. How did you know?'

'Fabio.'

'Bless him,' said Ruby.

'She's as good as Dr Ruby,' said Mark. 'She's just about got her PhD finalised.'

'I'm at the Sapporo Institute, across the river, at Hubron City University,' explained Ruby. 'It's in biochemistry.'

Alyssa felt herself shrinking in her chair. She knew she could never achieve intellectual brilliance as great as that. Mark too, as a medical trainee, would be brilliant. Compared with them, she was nothing but a silly snotty-nosed little fool. It was time to leave before she became a complete embarrassment. She stood up.

'Ruby here will be done by the end of June,' said Mark, standing too.

'You know it won't be done by June,' she hissed.

'Don't be so negative,' said Mark. He appeared irritated by her.

'What's the thesis on?' asked Alyssa diplomatically.

'Neurotransmitter biochemistry,' said Ruby, who was still seated. She looked despondent. 'I've spent all these years looking at the upregulation mechanisms of GABA—as if that means anything to anybody.'

Alyssa frowned. A PhD in biochemistry sounded like Simon Bristow territory. 'Have you heard of Dr Simon Bristow?' she asked. 'He's one of our psychiatrists at the Donald Clinic and he's apparently a national expert on brain chemistry. I'm sure he'd be a good contact for the future.'

'Dr Bristow?' Ruby looked up. 'Tall guy with fancy specs? Sure, I know him. Everyone does.'

Alyssa had a sudden idea. 'Good. I'll give you his number. It will be on this business card for the Donald Clinic.' She dug in her bag and found one and handed it to Mark, not Ruby.

'Thank you,' he murmured under his breath, then spoke more loudly: 'To be honest, Ruby is not too worried about future employment opportunities here in Hubron. It's more to do with her future prospects in underdeveloped countries.'

Ruby said nothing.

'Why is that?' asked Alyssa, turning back to Mark.

'Because we're off to Africa at the end of June, that's why,' said Ruby with some passion. 'For a whole bloody year.'

'You know I don't have a choice. It's all already arranged.' Mark turned to Alyssa. 'I've been awarded a sponsored fellowship to study advanced surgery in deprived settings. I have no choice but to go if I'm to get my specialist registration completed next year.'

'He could get out of it, he knows he can,' countered Ruby.

It was time to go. Alyssa had no desire to act as referee in the couple's apparent domestic dispute. 'Nice talking to you both,' she said, 'but I really must be off. I hope everything works out.' She made a little side to side wave with her hand. 'See you at the gym.'

She headed for the exit. However, she had good ears, so she caught Beak Face's whining voice when it became raised in the ongoing argument with Mark: 'You *know* I can't finish by the end of June. The bloody *wedding* is in June!' She seemed upset.

Alyssa did not know whether to laugh or cry. Her scheme to "find" Mark had been both a surprising success and an abject failure. She had forgotten all about Ruby. The visit to the hospital had been doomed to failure from the start; nothing but an act of desperation. Even she could see that now. Mark was already taken. She was nothing but an idiot and a loser.

She would have to move on.

But I can't. I just can't.

Diana Croft had been right about her stepdaughter all along: not only was it an idiot but it lacked the ability to take no for an answer.

4

She was in love with Mark, and it felt impossible to give up on the man she loved. She admitted this to herself now; admitted that she loved him. She had loved him from the very moment she first saw him all those months ago. She could not give up on him now. Not ever. To do so would be worse than death.

Therefore, instead of leaving the hospital via the nearby main entrance, Alyssa turned sideways and headed blindly down a long corridor. Then another. Then another. Anything seemed better than facing up to the truth, which was that realistically there was never going to be a Mark for her. She was going to have to resort to online dating sites and beg for affection. But she was in no condition, mentally, to be able to do any such thing. Also, she did not have the emotional toughness needed to dispatch hundreds of frogs. Maybe it would be better, therefore, to seek out Aaron on Facebook and see what he was up to. Or she could get Brian to organise a blind date for her with one of his many male friends. Another option would be for her to become a lesbian. Jocelyn seemed to love her and find her attractive. Maybe she too was a lesbian and didn't know it. She had read about such things. Living with Jocelyn might not be all that bad.

Morning munches . . .

Oh God.

It seemed a real pity that there had to be somebody called Ruby.

A real pity.

She kept walking.

She could not walk around her old hospital forever. Before much longer she was going to get herself arrested by hospital security. That would be all she needed.

Summoning the strength to focus on reality, she worked out where she was in the building and then headed for the hospital exit. When she finally emerged into the sunshine of the broad sidewalk, she was surprised to see Ruby standing under a tree near the kerb, waiting for a bus and smoking a cigarette. She recognised her immediately, even from behind. The skinniness of the rump, the distracted, nervous movements, the flash of blue spectacles, the length of the nose in half-profile: unmistakable. Beak Face it was. The stick insect.

The aspiring bride looked headed for a mental breakdown in her opinion. Maybe, as a psychologist, she should try to help her. Go and talk to her. Maybe. The only trouble was that she was in no mood to deal with emotionally troubled people. Lately, such people just made her feel sick. The only suggestion she would have for Ruby would be that she should jump *under* her bus when it came.

That would solve all problems.

Making sure that Ruby did not see her, Alyssa quietly made her way down the sidewalk in the direction of her flat, sticking close to the side of the hospital building until out of the potential line of sight of the PhD scholar. How sad it would be, she thought, if an accident *were* to happen: if skinny old Beak Face *did* go under her bus one day and end up all cracked up. How unfortunate that would be.

Yeah. Yeah.

Killing people was not the answer.

Enough people had told her that.

So, then, what *was* the answer?

She did not know—and that was the problem.

Strangely enough, out in the autumn sunshine, walking, she began to feel strong again. By the time she got near to home, she knew she was on the mend. During the entire walk, she had not had any symptoms from her gynaecological procedure and the aftermath of Veronica's heartfelt ministrations to her bottom had settled down nicely. Not only that, but her appetite had returned. She was ravenously hungry. She still had her credit card. Time to stop off at the local supermarket and really stock up.

Despite what people had been saying about her not looking well, she had never felt better. She was fine. Absolutely fine.

PART IX

CLARITY COMES

CHAPTER THIRTY-EIGHT

1

PROFESSOR ALAN SUMMERFIELD, Principal Psychiatrist at the Donald Clinic and Alyssa's employer, asked Alyssa out for lunch the day after her failed visit to Public Hospital. He phoned her flat from work at nine am and said that if she agreed, he could pick her up in his car at around one pm. He knew of a place nearby that would not be crowded and where they could get a decent meal and have some privacy.

'What's the occasion, Alan?' asked Alyssa, who was still in bed trying to work out how to keep going after the collapse of all her plans and dreams. Still feeling strangely strong, she had not yet given up hope—probably, she suspected, because she had gone into complete denial. Or maybe because she couldn't face the fact that her stepmother had been right all along, and she was too stupid to understand anything.

The phone call seemed to prove the point. A call from Alan was not something she had expected. And nor was the non-subservient tone she found herself taking with him. 'Last time I saw you, you and Professor Barnes arranged for Greta to suspend me from my job.'

'It's about that, of course. Unofficially, you understand, because there will be all hell to pay from the Dog and his De Glanville and Chikarovski cronies if they find out. Work is not supposed to have any contact with you whatsoever at present, but the truth is I've been worried about you.'

Pull the other one Alan.

He seemed to be a mind reader: 'I know it hasn't seemed like it, but I'm really fond of you, you know. Besides, Jocelyn has had a word to me.'

Which is really why there is this sudden concern.

'Don't let Jocelyn tell you stories,' she said to him. 'There's no need to worry. I'm just fine.'

'We both know you are not.'

After a troubled night, she knew that what he was saying was partly true. Alan probably sensed it in her voice. The insomnia of old had returned overnight and she had been too restless to sleep. Despite feeling strangely well the previous evening and having had a good supper after getting back from the supermarket, she had only drifted off at about four o'clock that morning.

'Hell, Alyssa. Forget everything else. The truth is, I miss your company. I miss you. Isn't that reason enough for us to have lunch together? Is it a deal or what?'

'That's very sweet of you Alan. I'd love to have lunch with you. As long as you understand that I can't pay my way. For obvious reasons.'

'Of course. This one's on me. Thank you. See you at one.'

'I'll be downstairs on the street, at the entrance to the flats.'

'Excellent. I'll book a table. It will be at the Grand Roswind.'

And so, it was arranged. A meetup at yet another nearby hotel. Yet *another* chance for her to do what had to be done.

It was time to wake up.

Time to get my ducks in a row.

Time to finally and actually do what had to be done.

The nonsense that my life is turning into simply cannot be allowed to continue.

Alyssa put her phone back on the bedside table. She had not been to the Grand Roswind before, so she wondered what it would be like. Expensive—that much she did know.

2

Normally, she was an early riser but after the restless night and now the phone call from Alan, Alyssa curled up back under the covers— not to sleep but to think. Besides, she was naked, so she needed to stay warm. She wondered if Alan was expecting sex. Knowing him, he was. It would probably not be too bad—and she would not particularly mind. It would be interesting, if nothing else, because of his advanced age. Different. She had once valued Alan's friendship. Maybe she would be able to restore honesty between them and maybe making love to him was what was required. Maybe it was what she needed to do.

Maybe not.

It did not take her long to come to her senses. This was not a time for weakness or indulgence. As Jocelyn had pointed out earlier, she needed to be strong. Going to bed with Alan needed to be avoided. For many reasons.

Firstly, his intentions towards her were clearly more calculated than he was pretending. He was up to something. Furthermore, according to employment law, he would be abusing her if it did come to sex. Not in reality of course, but technically, yes, because she was a suspended employee of his. And then there was the none-too trivial fact that he was married, and that she even knew his wife, Kara. To complicate the situation further, she was in no condition—emotionally, financially, or physically—to be having sex with anybody. She felt her bottom with her hand. The pain and welts had subsided, but she knew that extensive bruising was still present. Not a good sight to greet a new sex partner, even one as broad minded as no doubt Alan would turn out to be. She had surgical scars, too, that he knew nothing about.

There was a risk, though, that he might go to her head, and she knew it. After all, he was almost irresistibly charming. Despite herself, she might still end up between the sheets with him in an upstairs room at the hotel. Concerned, she sat up in bed and counted on her fingers the number of reasons *not* to have sex with Alan Summerfield at lunchtime. Initially, she got to eight reasons: married, employer, too old, probably a player who was just going to use her, the surgical scars, her bum too embarrassing—how could she possibly explain it—and her pet hate, the risk of disease. There was an eighth reason too: something was going on at the Donald Clinic that she did not yet understand. She was being taken for a fool. Every one of her instincts warned her that lunch with Alan Summerfield at the Grand Roswind Hotel smelled like a trap and was a bad idea. Unless she exercised extreme care, there was every possibility that just like Gilbert Rockport she was going to find herself at the bottom of the Yarradonga River—not physically like him, but in every other way.

While staring at her eighth finger, she realised that there was a ninth reason, too, to not have sex with Alan: she would sense Kara on him. That would be a big turn off.

A bit like being a lesbian.

Agreeing to lunch with Alan had been a mistake. There was no certainty that she would be able to resist his flattery—or possibly his threats. She wiggled her fingers and once again counted off the reasons to resist him. Nine. She needed to remember them. Then she realised that she was channelling Cy. With the fingers.

Shit!

At least with Cy she had learnt the art of making herself "palatable" for sex, the last of the skills—other than anal sex—she had mastered in the art of being competent at enthralling men. Over the years, since age nineteen and her first experiences with boyfriend Ethan, by trial and error, she had steadily learnt what was required to be a good sex partner— beyond what had to her always seemed the obvious basics, such as being scrupulously clean everywhere and adopting an emotional attitude appropriate to one's partner's erotic peccadilloes. Therefore, though she doubted that Alan was orally driven like Cy, it nevertheless seemed a good idea to prepare for even that unlikely possibility. If she did end up being utterly irresponsible and climbed into bed with him, then it was probably best that she at least made a good impression in the process.

With the upcoming encounter finally thought through, she jumped out of bed and into a warm dressing gown. Action time. As part of the required preparation for possible oral sex, she made herself an appropriate breakfast: half an avocado with extra virgin olive oil, juice of a fresh lemon, cracked pepper and sumac, a small handful of activated almonds, a sprinkling of flax seeds, a slice of fresh pineapple, some fresh strawberries, and a slice of fresh watermelon. Soon, she would be the most heavenly creature ever—at least to someone's taste buds.

She thought about Alan as she ate. Clearly, he had thought nothing of sacrificing her to his business interests, yet strangely this did not make her like him any less. The only thing it had done was make her more wary of him. In truth, she felt quite flattered by his interest in her welfare—and by his interest in her as a woman. Bizarrely, in some illogical way, she trusted him in both those areas. She knew a bad man when she saw one, and Alan was not a bad man. He was a selfish and greedy one, though, and extremely intelligent, all of which made him potentially dangerous to her. But, when it came to sex, all his advantages would come to naught. In her experience, all men functioned emotionally at the level of a two-year-old boy when it came to that. If they liked you, they just *had* to *have* you, and if they could not get you, they broke down before your eyes into an almighty tantrum. If push came to shove, she would be able to handle Alan. Of that, she had no doubt whatsoever.

She had been abused once too often.

Thinking about sex in this way, the little movie in her head began to play uninvited:

> Finally, roughly, he pinned her down. He was too strong for her. There was nothing she could do. There was nothing she had to do. She was worthless now, and worthless, he plunged into her and fucked her. He fucked her so bad that her brain seized up. She was nothing but a worthless piece of shit. Great pulse of joy, pure light out of pure darkness. Reborn. And so forever trapped.

Trapped now by Alan Summerfield.

No. There was Mark Stanford to think of. There would be no abuse from Mark. Him, she would be able to control. It was not the time to give up. Not yet. She thought of his leather belt, the belt that held his name tag like the belt of a gun slinger, low across his front.

Just beneath the silver buckle of that belt lay something that she needed more than Alan Summerfield; a something breathtakingly near . . . and yet so far from her grasp. She could not let what she had in Mark slide away. It would not be fair on her. Mark was hers.

Yes, she thought, studying herself in the mirror in the bathroom while naked, she needed what Mark had, but he needed what she had too. He was that kind of man. A proper man. She was at least as beautiful as he was—except for the scar in the front and the bruises at the back. From what she could see, her backside still looked spectacularly horrifying. Yet, she felt incredibly well. Which seemed rather odd for a person so seriously screwed up.

3

She wore her navy-blue pants for the date with Dr Alan Summerfield. There was a sheen to the fabric that seemed to do something to men's brains. She did not have long to wait. A few minutes after one o'clock, he came storming up the street in his magnificent white car and came to a halt next to her. He got out to greet her. He had come straight from work. 'Hello. Good to see you again.' He opened the passenger door for her.

'Hi, Alan.' She got in.

'Sorry I'm a bit late,' he said, getting back behind the wheel. 'I got held up by a yakker. You know the type, I'm sure.' He made movements with his hand: 'Yakkety-yak.'

She knew that type of client very well.

The hotel was near to Fabio's gym and the state parliament, and it was as upmarket as she had suspected. Alan took her to a restaurant inside that was large and business-like. Tables were arranged into alcoves and booths, and Alan had reserved a table for them—one that enabled private conversation. There was an extensive menu to choose from.

'I hope you are hungry,' said Alan. 'I'm starving. Fortunately, we don't have to rush. I've cancelled my two o'clock. I'd rather see you any day instead of some no-hoper.'

'Gee, thanks.' To amuse herself and test Alan's intentions, she had kept a large part of her shirt unbuttoned, exposing her cleavage to him fairly blatantly. While they selected their meals, he pretended not to notice.

She was hungry too, so she chose what Alan was having. Although normally not a great meat eater, preferring vegetables and at most taking fish or chicken in moderation, she did occasionally have a weakness for lamb. Today, she felt weak. The order became two full portions of lazy-cooked pulled lamb shoulder with rosemary on a bed of polenta, with crisp fresh green peas, pomegranate highlights and rich mint jus. To keep things simple, Alyssa also chose the same wine that Alan chose: Otago Pinot Noir from New Zealand. It was the same as the wine Jocelyn had ordered at Umberto Ponti.

Alan and Jocelyn. Interesting collusion.

Alan looked at her, somewhat bemused. 'You don't have to have what I'm having you know. Don't you want to try something else?'

'No, I like it. What made you choose the wine?'

'It may surprise you, but I know a lot about wine.'

'You or Jocelyn?'

He looked taken aback but had the good grace to confess. 'Okay, it was her. I asked her for a few tips.'

'About me?'

'I want us to be friends. So, yes. I know she knows you quite well. We both want what's best for you. I want to try and be helpful you.'

'Well, that's a good thing, I suppose.'

The food arrived and the atmosphere soon became less frosty. Alan clearly enjoyed eating and seemed to genuinely enjoy her company. She enjoyed his company too, and the meal. Despite her reservations about his motives, they seemed to at least have similar physical tastes. Alan was the kind of man she would never tire of.

'How are you bearing up under the strain of being suspended?' he asked.

'Oh, I'm okay, I suppose,' she lied. 'I'm doing my best to be adult about it. I'm still hoping it can all be resolved.' She had no choice but to be polite. Alan was her employer, after all. He and the Dog wielded full power over her fate. She wondered how he would cope with her if she were free to interact with him on an equal footing.

Brilliantly attuned to nuance that he was, Alan Summerfield interrupted her defensive posturing by reaching across the table and placing a hand on hers. 'I'm not here as your boss,' he said. 'I don't want that. I want to be your friend. Jocelyn says she's worried about you. I'm worried about you, too.' He removed his hand again and continued eating. 'When I saw you standing there under the milkwood tree outside your cottage when you left us, when I saw how distressed you were, it really affected me. I realised then how fond of you I had become—how much we all like you and care about your welfare.'

'Is *that* what it is?'

'How do you mean?'

'The tree. Is that what it is? A milkwood tree? I've always wondered.'

He looked mystified. 'You are a strange one, aren't you? You want to know about the tree?'

'Yes. It felt like a friend.'

'I'm pretty sure it's a milkwood tree. Apparently, it's as old as the Donald building itself. The original owner who built the place brought the seedling back with him from Africa after making his money there in diamond mining. Or so the story goes.'

'An African milkwood tree. Imagine that. You know, it always used to whisper to me about things like beauty and love. Or does that sound really cracked to you?'

'Not cracked. Jungian maybe. Perhaps the aroma of the bark or something similar affected you unconsciously. I know what you mean, though. You see what others cannot see. Like me.'

And Ellen, and Gilbert, and Ben.

'Thank you, Alan.'

There was a pause and they both sipped their wine.

'May I ask you another question, Alan? A professional one because in a way it's got to do with Ben Clayton.'

He became wary. 'Not about Gail's case, I hope. You know I can't discuss that.'

'No Alan, I'm not that silly.'

'Then shoot. Sounds serious.'

'Ben has this thing in his head about religious people, as I'm sure you recall. He thinks that they deliberately and wickedly distort the truth to suit themselves. The trouble is, they probably do, so how is a therapist supposed to react? What I mean is, what are we to make of religious people when they are our clients? Is religious belief a disease?'

He almost choked on his drink. 'Didn't we discuss this once before? At the Park Hotel? Something about Jesus?'

'Yes. You explained that he wasn't real. But what I want to know is what to do when clients think this stuff *is* real.'

'As in: are religious people nuts?'

'Exactly. If you don't mind me asking. I know you are not a believer yourself.'

'No. Are you? I don't remember.'

She made it easier for him. 'Not really.'

'Is anyone anymore?'

'Still, I'd value your opinion.'

'Mm. Religion. Religion is a funny beast, Alyssa. It's completely illogical, yet most people in the world refuse to give up on it, so it can hardly be viewed as a disease. I'd view it rather as an inherent component of the immature mind. In that sense, God has almost all people in his power because—for psychological reasons obvious to the educated like you and me but not to uninformed people—the human mind always insists on an "explanation" for everything. Everything we encounter *needs* to have a "meaning". Because of this, once a specific herd mental construct about the unknowable becomes agreed upon, it becomes almost impossible to eradicate. The herd idea is invincible precisely because it isn't real. There are different herd ideas, of course, but in view of the intractable need for meaning, and the omnipresence of certain historically formulated explanations, and the futility of other courses of action, I generally recommend that the various notions of why we are here be tolerated yet completely ignored—unless, of course, attempts are made by such people to *compel* others to agree with their fantasies, in which case strong resistance is essential. That answer your question?'

'Yes and no.' Alan Summerfield was obviously amazingly clever, but she could not help thinking how lucky it had been that Jocelyn had turned up at her flat when she did. And what about the church in Fondsdale Street, where something even more strange had happened? Just like the episode at the gym at the start of the year, time itself had seemed to stop. What if something supernatural had happened in each of these events? How could anyone, she especially, be sure there wasn't something more to existence than Alan thought? What if she had been raped and killed by Ben Clayton in the church and this had then been miraculously *undone*? Or was she confused about such things because of her road accident, where she had died but not died? Or had something supernatural happened *there* too? Was *that* how she had woken up alive? She brushed a sudden tear from her cheek.

'Hey,' said Alan Summerfield with some tenderness, taking her hand. 'What is it, Alyssa? Have I upset you? Please forgive me if I have.'

'No, no. It's not you.' He let her hand go so she could blow her nose. 'What if things are revealed to us? From the other side, as it were? What then?'

Though an experienced psychiatrist, Alan looked taken aback by her question. '*Revealed*? You mean, as in "a tapping on a glass darkened"? That sort of thing?'

'Yes.'

'Easy. Freud resolved that sort of experience a long time ago. Mumbo jumbo is nothing but our unconscious childhood speaking to us. Besides, it's impossible to make sense of what the tapping says. Some hear that it's telling us that God alone determines our fate after death regardless of anyone or anything else, while others hear the exact opposite, namely that what decides our fate is the way we have lived our life. And, of course, there's yet another bunch who claim that *they* hear that our fate after death is not determined by God or our lifestyle at all, but by the opinion of God's agents on earth, the priests. Take your pick. All conceivable possibilities are catered for. The whole business of religion is too silly for words. It's beyond crazy. Like the brain of a one-year-old, religion is absolutely and utterly devoid of logic. It's toxic, too, because then everyone who disagrees with you needs to be eliminated. Why damn all people who are not in your tribe? It's ridiculous because then the other tribes are forced to kill *your* tribe in return. And so it goes, for ever more. Ad nauseum.'

Ad nauseum?

'Religion can be toxic. I see that.'

'Fortunately, today, most properly educated people realise that infallible truth about the unknowable is not possible. This, I would say, is the current position of the emotionally mature section of at least the modern West.'

'He did exist though, didn't he? Does exist . . . Jesus.'

He took her hand again. 'Has someone been bothering you, Alyssa? Is that what this is all about? Jesus freaks? I can come around and see them off if you like. I'd be happy to. You can call on me any time.'

She sighed. 'No, it's okay, Alan. I'm just trying to clarify what's been happening to me over the past few weeks.'

4

Alan Summerfield gave her hand a squeeze. 'I know you've been left high and dry by your partner, Alyssa, and honestly, I don't know how you've managed to cope so far—especially considering what you've told me in the past about the events of your childhood. I had a reasonably happy upbringing and I still have two live parents, yet I still fell apart after my second divorce. Believe me, it was bad enough, but I can't even begin to imagine how shattering it must be to someone like you.'

'Thank you, Alan. It hasn't been very pleasant, I must say.'

'I was unable to work for two months. We're all human, Alyssa.' He let her hand go. 'I had to seek professional help. Even me.'

'Is that when you developed your dislike of cognitive behaviour therapy?'

He frowned, then nodded. 'Yes, I have my reservations. Have they been that obvious?'

'Afraid so, Alan. Everyone knows you don't like CBT. I've long suspected that someone must have used it on you in the past and spooked you.'

'Someone sure did: a fool with unresolved personal issues cloaked in a carapace of pseudointellectual statistics.' He seemed suddenly angry. 'The level of bullshit and arrogance was unbelievable. Talk about a total lack of Self-awareness. That's what I detest most in any so-called therapist: smugness and intolerance. "Therapists" who fly off the handle the moment their prejudices are not pandered to are of no therapeutic use whatsoever to anyone.'

'Sounds like you had a bad time of it.'

'She was supposed to be *helping* me for God's sake. Granted, she didn't know who I really was, but that is no excuse. For obvious reasons, I couldn't tell her I was a professor of clinical psychiatry. That would have been too humiliating.'

Just like Gilbert Rockport's problem.

'I agree it was best to go incognito. At least until you knew where you stood.'

'I can't begin to tell you how bad she was. Critics of our sort of psychodynamic treatment say it's too subjective, but by golly I'd rather have the benevolent intersubjective embrace of transference-focused psychodynamic therapy any day rather than the ice-cold, prescriptive, pseudo-objective fare I received from the CBT crowd. Such is the benefit of hindsight. But enough about me.'

'I've had therapy too, of course,' said Alyssa. 'All kinds, so I know exactly what you mean. No need to try to look surprised—I know you and Jocelyn managed to find out about it. I've had lots of it. Mostly, the therapists have been just plain pathetic.'

'Sorry about that delving into your past, by the way.'

'Bit late for sorry, Alan. Anyway, luckily for me, I finally got to see

Norman Bullock who, as you no doubt know, is a psychodynamic therapist.'

'I know Norman vaguely, from meetings. Not personally. I have heard he is excellent.'

'He is. He's the one who got me functioning again. In fact, I'd say he's the reason I decided to become a counsellor.'

'I'm glad to hear it. In retrospect, I suppose I should have had the sense to go to someone like Norman—or Susan Lindow—when I went off the rails after my divorce, but I knew that going to someone I knew, even vaguely, was never going to work. In fact, I couldn't have gone to Norman anyway seeing that he's a male. How do you break down into sobbing or talk about your sexual issues with another male? Instead, I ended up going to a random female, an unknown-to-me clinical psychologist from the CBT world. Big mistake. As I said before, the average prostitute knows more about psychology than she did. To my dismay, it turned out that she was virulently anti-male yet completely unaware that she was. I don't think she even knew what countertransference is. In the end, I had to unilaterally terminate my visits, not so much because of her ignorance but because of her hostility. She became quite dangerous to me in fact.'

'Let me guess: dangerous as in writing pejorative reports about you without your permission or knowledge? Bad therapists especially love doing that when it involves the opposite sex. I think it gives them orgasms.'

Like Jocelyn, Alan seemed particularly interested in the word "orgasm" but to his credit he did his best to stay on track. 'Exactly. You should see the reports she sent to my family doctor behind my back. They were such vindictive rubbish that they amounted to criminal libel. Luckily, my doctor knows me well and showed them to me. The reports said I was confused and showed evidence of paraphilia. Really? *Confused? Paraphilia?* Completely ridiculous crap. Who in their right mind registers such people as *therapists*? After showing me the letters, my GP tore them up in front of me. The whole experience of seeing a bad therapist did one good thing, though. It made me realise that I had been living a sheltered life in higher academia. Up until then, I had not understood quite how many swaggering idiots there are out there in the real world pretending to be "therapists". I honestly had no idea just how much these clowns fail to understand even the basics of interpersonal interaction. The unconscious

Self—theirs or the client's—is complete news to them. It's so bad out there that the average therapist thinks that whatever they think about a client is literally true and whatever a client says to them is literally true too. What I discovered, to my horror, is that the world has lost its mind.'

One of their minds, anyway. The Un-conscious.

'Too true.' Alan's degree of outrage made her smile. In some way, he reminded her of Cy in his frustration at the stupidity of the world. Cy, no doubt, would have added a quote from a medieval pope, something like: "Heresy is everywhere, and it is increasing". She missed Cy. She turned her attention back to Alan. 'Now I understand why you are so tough on quality control with your courses. I knew there had to be a reason.'

'I'm tough, am I?' He smiled. 'Well, I suppose I do have a duty to weed out those who are no good.'

'I hope you're not including me in the people you don't think are any good. I suppose you are, aren't you, given what's happened.'

His face fell. 'No, no, don't get me wrong, you're not one of them. I didn't mean anything like that. You *are* good, believe me. You've got the good counsellor basics taped. I've seen it all: safe containment of client hostility, countertransference insight, non-judgemental attentive listening, empathetic reflection—*all* that and more. Please let me encourage you to keep going. Some days, in fact, I wish I could come to you as a client myself, even though obviously I can't. You have no idea how many issues I'm having with Kara.'

'Considering what's happened between me and Cy, counselling anybody on relationships with partners would be laughable, wouldn't it? Besides, I don't do clients anymore, in case you've forgotten. I've been suspended. By you.'

.... **5** ....

Alan Summerfield did his best to appear concerned. 'We at the Donald must seem an uncaring bunch to you, Alyssa. I know that. However, we don't mean to be unkind. It's just that we are obliged to follow instructions from above. Your suspension is just a routine precaution. I'm hoping it will sort itself out. We've *all* been sued. I myself have been sued four times already.'

'Really? And how did that turn out?'

'Four zip to me. One was touch and go, but then we discovered De Glanville and Chikarovski, and they got everything back in its box. Cost us a bob, though.'

'At least that's comforting, I suppose. The four zip.'

'I'm sure you are in for a long and happy career with us.'

'I doubt it. Not with my past. You and Jocelyn shouldn't have gone prying into my psych file. I'll always be at a disadvantage now. You people had no right to do that. You know that.'

Alan seemed surprised she knew so much about what he had done. 'I had to do it. For your sake. And at least I made a point of not looking through it myself. I promise you that. Cross my heart.' He gazed into her eyes. 'I value you too much as a person to prey on you in any way. Only Jocelyn has read it. I have no idea what's in your psych file. None at all. And I prefer not to know. Really.'

She studied him, uncertain what to make of him. In his crisp white business shirt and blue-and-gold silk tie, he looked remarkably professional. Not to mention intelligent and physically toned and upmarket. Nice, too. There was no denying that he looked like a kind person. Was he honest? Possibly he was, she decided. Right from the beginning she had always instinctively trusted him. Perhaps, after all, he had not actually read her file himself. 'So, are you saying that you *don't* know how much of a fruit cake I am?'

'I have absolutely no idea. Although I would love to find out. The hard way.'

'You mean like upstairs? In one of the guest rooms?' She laughed, as though making a joke. Except she was not joking.

'Don't tempt me.' He was not joking either.

In silence, they continued eating.

The sexual tension between them was becoming difficult to manage.

'Jocelyn told me that she's read all about me and knows everything about me,' said Alyssa after a while. 'With her, though, I don't mind that. She's a funny old thing, but she has a heart of gold. I owe her a lot. And probably you, too.' It was her turn to place a hand on Alan's. 'The two of you, you and Jocelyn together, somehow managed to save me from doing something very silly recently. Thank you.' She removed her hand again.

He said nothing but looked pleased. 'Yes, I like Jocelyn,' said Alan. 'She has her eye on you; I assume you know that?'

'Yes. But I don't mind. She knows where I draw the line.'

'Sounds reassuring. Anyway, it's through her that I know how stressed you've been since your suspension from work. Donald Barnes and I feel bad about it. We know that making you leave us came at a difficult time for you considering this business with your boyfriend. That still unresolved, is it?'

'Yes. It seems I've seen the last of Cy.'

Alan tried not to look too pleased. 'Getting walked out on is never a good experience, is it? It can really hurt, as I myself know only too well. We all experience it at some stage, though. Even people like Greta. By the way, you should see the old bitter biscuit *now*. Jocelyn filled her in a few days ago about the fact that you were dumped by your partner recently and the news has driven Greta over some sort of edge in her mind. She wasn't well to start with, as you know, but now she's moping around in an inconsolable state. She keeps saying that if only she had *known* that you had been abandoned, she would never have allowed you to be suspended— not that it was her decision. But now she's gone and succumbed to some sort of re-traumatisation related to her own abandonment a while back. Hoo boy, I don't think I will ever understand women.'

'And I will never understand men,' said Alyssa. 'I've tried to talk to Cy, but he won't even let me near him.'

'To be frank, it sounds to me like this Cy was always a bit of a rotter.'

'No, that's the sad part. He isn't. That's why I can't understand what's happened. He's really nice.' She was surprised to find tears welling up in her eyes again, and when Alan appeared not to notice she knew he was doing so out of compassion.

Her heart warmed towards him as they sipped the last of their wine.

6

'So, Alyssa,' asked Alan Summerfield, 'what have you been doing with yourself in your time away from work?'

'You mean, besides trying to find Cy and going almost mad from stress?'

And trying to kill myself and getting myself soundly whipped.

'Yes.' He smiled. 'And by the way, in my professional opinion I'm sure you are not at any real risk of going mad. You are far too sane for that.'

That's what they always say.

She returned his smile but said nothing.

'Don't smile at me like that,' said Alan. 'You'll force me to take you off to bed.'

Instead of responding appropriately—in other words, agreeing to his suggestion—she tried to stall. She acted as though she had not heard the words he had just said, even though she knew she was blushing. So, instead of saying yes or no to his latest suggestion, she answered an earlier question of his, the one about what she had been doing during her time away from work. 'I've been spending my days pulling myself together,' she announced. 'After Jocelyn came to my flat and encouraged me to get a grip, I've been doing just that. Getting a grip. As our Jocelyn said, I don't really have any option but to take a pro-active approach.' Actually, Jocelyn had put things a little differently, but the exact words she had whispered in her ear that day in her flat were hardly repeatable. Certainly not to Alan.

Get out there, girl, and whack them with your pussy yet again.

The *yet again* part was the disturbing part. She shivered as she recalled those exact two words because Jocelyn had meant something sinister with them. After all, Jocelyn had read *all* her files and thought she understood everything. The secretive "yet again" had meant only one thing: Jocelyn believed that young teenage Alyssa Brown had deliberately killed her father to avenge her mother's death. In Jocelyn's mind, Robert Brown had died because a young girl had seduced him into allowing her to drive his car and then deliberately crashed the vehicle to kill him and thereby avenge Grace's death. Jocelyn believed that innocent angel Lauren Truebody/Alyssa Brown had "whacked" her father in this way.

Which was entirely wrong, of course. With that, as with so many other things, Jocelyn had it all wrong. She had not seduced her father, and her father had had nothing to do with the death of Grace. It had not been like that at all.

Bob Truebody/Brown had died for quite different reasons. Bob had died because he could not both drive a car safely and molest a struggling child on his lap at the same time while drunk. He had died because his mind was addled, and his daughter had grown bigger and stronger. He had not died for any other reason. He had not been "whacked" in the way that Jocelyn imagined. Not that way. No.

He had died because of her resistance to him.

Jocelyn and her fantasies.

Alan Summerfield's seductive voice brought her back to the present. 'So, you've been spending your days pulling yourself together? Sounds commendable, but what exactly does that entail?' He sounded mildly amused.

'Well, for starters, I'm trying to gather information on my aggrieved clients,' she said brightly. 'After all, everything that's happened has been very unexpected and I've been left at a disadvantage. All I've ever wanted to do is help people. I've never deliberately set out to harm anyone, so I'm trying to make sense of why everyone seems to be attacking me.'

'You've been investigating?'

'Exactly. Getting information.'

She beamed at him.

7

The sight of Alyssa's top teeth seemed to put Alan Summerfield on edge. 'What sort of "information" are we talking about here, Alyssa? I assume you know how this suing stuff works. If Martin Chikarovski gets wind of anything inappropriate, he'll have a fit. It might invalidate our relatively good fee agreement with him.'

'That's not what Susan Lindow told me. Susan said I should gather as much background information as possible when sued. So, that's what I'm doing.'

'Good grief!'

'Relax, Alan. I've managed to track down one of the last people to see Gilbert Rockport alive. From what I've managed to find out, he definitely was not suicidal. And I mean *definitely.*'

'Oh, oh, oh, why is this giving me a bad feeling? Have you let Donald Barnes know?'

'No.'

'No!'

'It's too sensitive for that. Client confidentiality and all that. Instead, I spoke to Gilbert's wife about it.'

'Oh my God! You spoke to Nikki? How could you do that! That's against all the rules. She's trying to sue us for absolute millions. What have you done!'

Alyssa felt certain, now, that her instincts and suspicions were correct. It was time to do what had to be done. She took a deep breath and made her play: 'Calm down, Alan,' she said. 'Don't get your knickers in a knot. Instead, why don't you tell me why you never told me that you know Nikki socially and why you never told me that you knew Gilbert socially, too.'

She had him trapped off guard and at a weak moment. The blood drained from his face. 'You never asked,' he said, without thinking.

'Crap, and you know it. Do you people all take me for a complete fool? There is too much cloak-and-dagger stuff going on at the Donald.'

He tried to recover the situation: 'Look, I don't really *know* Gilbert. I only knew *of* him—and only through Kara. My wife is a friend of Gilbert's wife, Nikki. Kara gives Nikki dancing lessons. That's how I vaguely know Nikki. Even more vaguely, I knew that her husband was some sort of big shot lawyer, but that's all. There's no cloak-and-dagger stuff going on. Honestly, there isn't.' He looked hurt that she might think such a thing.

'How am I supposed to know what to think?'

He took her hand. 'Okay, okay, look, this Nikki of Gilbert's, yes, I have met her a few times. That's all. Nothing more. She scares me. She's bad news, Alyssa, a complete gold digger. We will never hear the end of her.'

'Gilbert's death had nothing to do with poor counselling on my part, Alan. Nothing to do with me at all. Gilbert was murdered. There is no doubt about that.'

'Murdered?' Alan went completely pale.

'Yes. Nikki won't be suing *me*. Not after what I told her.'

'After what you *told* her! Have you gone completely off your head!'

'Yes and no. Mostly no.' She grinned at him.

He looked alarmed. 'Are you saying you have *evidence* that someone killed Gilbert Rockport? On the Shamon freeway?'

'Yup.'

'And the police? Have you been to the police?'

'The cops? No, why?'

He looked relieved. 'Jeepers, you are scaring me.'

'I've got a mental block against the cops. As you know.'

There was an awkward silence.

'I'll see what Donald Barnes can do,' he said, finally.

'You do that.'

A waiter enquired about dessert.

'Yes,' said Alan. 'We'll have some. We need some. I'll have an affogato. They make good ones here, Alyssa, and serve them in a beautiful glass. Would you like one too? Or feel free to have anything on the menu.'

'That's very generous, Alan. Thank you.' She scanned the menu. The desserts were all far too high in calories. 'You know what,' she said after a while, 'I'll have what Alan's having. A dessert affogato.' Judging from the menu, it contained Frangelico—which was a liqueur—but did not otherwise seem too calorie dense. One could hardly go wrong with fresh vanilla gelato, fresh espresso, and fresh mint leaves. 'Looks like we make a perfect pair, the two of us.'

That made Alan smile. 'Good choice.' He beamed.

He seemed to think he was back on track with her.

Yes, we probably would be good in bed together.

It was just a thought.

8

Alan was speaking again: 'I'm almost too scared to ask, Alyssa, but what *else* have you been up to while roaming around unsupervised?'

She laughed. 'It's not that bad. Mostly, I've just been feeling sorry for myself.' Once again, she thought it best not to mention the visit to Veronica. 'Something else I have done, though, is pay a visit to Ben Clayton.'

'Oh shit. You've visited Ben Clayton!'

'He is my client. Besides, I like him.'

'How's that possible? I mean, how could you possibly have seen him? He's locked away.'

'He's in a secure ward in hospital, sure. However, I know the hospital and the ward very well, so I simply visited him without revealing who I was. He was happy to see me. It's no big deal. The place is very slack.'

'Oh, my God. You do realise, don't you, that he tried to kill you? He'd been thinking of doing so for a while. You were the one he was after, not Gail. I wouldn't advise you to go anywhere *near* him. He could very easily still kill you.'

'It was Gail Wilson he was after, not me.'

'No, you, silly Billy. It was you. You were his target.'

'Says who?'

'Gail. She says he was going to knife you, then rape you. That was aways his fantasy.'

Maybe it was true, but Alyssa stuck with the alternative narrative. One that was better for her. Better for everyone except maybe Gail. 'I don't think so, Alan. Something's not right about that. Ben wouldn't harm me. I think Ben's on the level. I think he's been trying to tell me about something that's going on at the Donald. I think Gail has the whole story twisted on its head.'

'Are you saying you believe a certified madman ahead of Gail Wilson, a psychiatric nurse?'

'Yes.'

'You know what Gail says, don't you? She says you've been unsettling Ben with unprofessional counselling, and that's why he's been wanting to kill again.'

'That is complete rubbish. Besides, he's never killed anyone, not even Gail. Just a pet donkey.'

'Whatever the case, Gail and that annoyingly wealthy husband of hers have gone and found some really serious lawyers. If they get wind of the fact that you've been talking to Ben, we'll be toast. Already, they are demanding millions.'

'Well, Gail shouldn't be suing us. Or having a whole cathedral praying for her. How can you employ a person like that?'

'That approach won't help. You need to cooperate.'

'Well, guess what, Alan. I think there is something unholy going down at the Donald and I am going to find out what it is.'

He looked at her with concern. 'We are concerned about you, Alyssa. Jocelyn, especially. You need to rest and leave things to our Mr Fixits.'

'It's a free country, and I'm not going anywhere without a fight. The only person I haven't got around to investigating yet is Ellen Goodman.

She'll be next, but I'm not yet sure how to approach the problem. I haven't got old women quite figured out. I just don't understand what makes them tick.'

'They tick the same as anybody else, Alyssa. Just leave her to us. Chikarovski will neutralise her. Somehow.'

'How? How does one deal with a merciless hypocrite? How am I supposed to defend myself against people who claim to be insulted by the very concept of sex? I think she's going to have us all beat. So far, she's got me beat.'

'Ellen? Ellen is a nothing. You attach far too much weight to her.' There was a moment of silence while he applied his considerable mind to the matter. 'I've treated her before, you know, so I know her well. The funny thing is, I've just realised something: she couldn't possibly be offended by sex. Ellen Goodman is an old tart. If anyone knows, it's me. She's no prude.'

'She's hardly a tart. She comes across as quite the opposite.'

'Maybe to you, but not to the likes of me. Women can't easily hide their sexual truth from men like me. I think Shakespeare was right. I think she does indeed "protest too much". Brilliant idea. I'll get Martin onto it first thing when I get back. Together, we'll force the tart out of Mrs Goodman.'

'I'd be grateful for your help with this. Thank you.'

'Think nothing of it. After all, we are in this together.'

.... 9 ....

By now they had finished their affogatos. Alyssa held Alan's hand across the table. 'We make a good pair, don't we?' she said. 'In another world, we would be so good together.'

Alan held her other hand in his and gazed into her eyes. He had nice eyes, and they were ablaze with desire.

'It doesn't have to be in another world. I could get a room upstairs. I know I keep saying so, and I know it's completely inappropriate, but I really would love to get to know you better. You are one devastatingly sexy woman. People like you should be illegal.'

So very tempting.

But she knew what she had to do. It was for the good of everyone, herself included. She freed her hands, held them up, and wordlessly began to count her fingers, which looked rather elegant in their nail polish. Alan watched, intrigued, as she managed to get all the way to digit number nine. After that, she spoke. 'You know I'd like nothing more than to go to bed with you right now, Alan, but you know we can't, and there are nine reasons why we can't.'

She showed him the nine fingers. 'These are the nine reasons why we can't let it happen. I won't recite them all, but the ninth one says: "especially not for Kara's sake".' She wiggled the finger in question.

Alyssa watched as the awful realisation begin to cloud Alan's features. She thought she had handled the final push rather well.

He became silent. 'I can't go on without you,' he said finally, in a soft voice. 'I need you too much. You are going to drive me crazy.'

'I am not the first or the last woman you will fancy, Alan. You will get over me.'

'You don't understand. I think I'm half in love with you. I can't stop thinking about you every day.' He looked heartbroken.

She wondered if it was an age thing or just a man thing.

In Alan's case, probably both.

She genuinely liked him, so she felt sorry for him. She opened her mouth and almost said something like "Oh, all right then, let's go upstairs and have a shag", but she maintained the presence of mind to close her mouth again.

'Please,' he said, as earnestly as he could.

'Think of Kara. It wouldn't be right. Let's stay friends. I really enjoyed the meal and your company, Alan. Thank you for that. I can assure you that under different circumstances I'd love to go upstairs with you. I hope you can understand.'

'Pretty please.'

'The answer is no, Alan. Besides, I'm not very well. Mentally, I just can't do it. Sorry.'

It was clear that her rejection was final, and Alan looked suddenly angry. His thwarted desire turned to rage, as was virtually inevitable, probably more so in his case considering that he was so used to getting his own way—and not used to making judgement errors about the psychology of others. He became barely able to remain civil.

'In my opinion—my professional opinion,' he added, for extra spite'—there is nothing wrong with you mentally that getting a good screw wouldn't fix. That's what *you* need. A good screw. Up your ass, in fact.'

Rather than being shocked or offended by his final suggestion, she laughed at him. 'No, Alan, that's what *you* need. Me, I'm a virgin in that department.'

'A what!' He looked flustered.

'You heard me.'

She was laughing, and she knew she shouldn't be laughing in the face of his attempt to be hurtful to her, but she couldn't help it. She wasn't anything even remotely resembling a virgin in any department—certainly not psychologically. Alan Summerfield's proposed diabolical fate for her already happened regularly in her fantasies. But, of course, this was not something to mention in the current circumstances.

'What's so funny?'

'The fact that we are being so truthful with each other. We *are* being truthful with each other, I hope, because trust is a good thing, surely. In particular, I value how honest you have been with me about your relationship with Gilbert's wife.'

'What! How dare you. There's nothing going on between Nikki and me.'

'Is that so. Well then, how about you tell me who it was who really got Gilbert to come to me for counselling? And *why?*'

He swore at her. 'Fuck this! And fuck you, too. It was Nikki. Obviously. You stay *away* from Nikki!'

CHAPTER THIRTY-NINE

1

THE WEATHER BEGAN TO turn as Alyssa made her way back to her flat that afternoon. Against Alan Summerfield's advice, she had declined a lift home with him in his car and insisted on walking home by herself. The gathering cold front seemed a good match for her mood.

She knew she had been right to resist him. She had succumbed to men in the past, but she was not going to succumb this time. Alan had miscalculated. She was not the delicate flower he imagined. Not anymore. She was not going to lie down and die. Not only had he been wrong about that, but he was wrong about other things too. Jesus wasn't dead.

She had seen him in Fondsdale Street.

Felt the power.

A tear ran down her cheek.

Sentiment aside, she was in big trouble. The rejection of Alan's advances meant that whatever she had once had with him was over. It had been with a sinking feeling that she had watched him drive away from the hotel in his beautiful sports car. Their relationship was never going to be the same again. In future, their interactions would be cold and distant, poisoned by hurt and humiliation. The future with him was fatally damaged. An indefinable part of her life was over.

The farther she got from the solid luxury of the Grand Roswind Hotel on her lonely walk home, the more anxious she began to feel. Alan was not a man to be trifled with and the last thing she had needed was to have him turn against her. Yet, she had accepted his invitation to lunch knowing that she was going to do what she did. She had been as polite as possible about it, but it had been cruel. She had needed to do what had to be done, and she had done it. But had it been the wisest of moves?

To have wacked him with my pussy like that.

Wise move or not, it had been her only option. As Jocelyn had pointed out, the world was not a fair place. It certainly wasn't, especially considering that she herself had just gone and used sex—or the prospect of it—to catch a person off guard. It was not a nice thing to have done to Alan. It had been necessary, though, under the circumstances. And it had worked. He had confirmed to her what she had begun to suspect: that almost everyone at the Donald Clinic was lying to her.

They took her for a fool, and they had been doing so since day one.

As she progressed towards her flat, a sickening sense of despondency began to creep over her. What a stupid little failure she was, she thought. Living in her own dream world. No job. No partner. No prospects. Mentally sick. No children. No future.

And now she was getting cold in her flimsy white shirt.

She shivered her way down Alfonso Street. Getting cold served her right, she thought.

It's what a bad person deserves.

By the time she unlocked the front door she was filled with serious doubt about the wisdom of what she had just done to Alan. She had just thrown away her career at the Donald Clinic.

2

As the door to the flat swung open, Alyssa was struck with intense deja vu. It rushed out at her like a hurricane, leaving her mind reeling. Cy.

Cy. He was there. The realisation came instantly, like a slap in the face. There was no doubt about it, about his fragrance: *Authentique* by Maria Rainer. There was even a note for her—though not a card this time—under a glass of water on the kitchen counter, and a small pile of mail from the normally locked downstairs letterbox. Life seemed to have gone into a repeat loop. This had all happened before, including the note from him. She went rapidly from room to room in search of him, but soon realised that he was no longer there. He had come and gone. Undoubtedly, he was no longer there. Not even out on the balcony, the final place she checked.

It seemed he had returned to the flat at a time he knew she would be away at work. Yet, had fate not been so cruel, she would have caught him out. Had she not been out on a lunch date with Alan Summerfield, Cy would have stumbled upon her by surprise. She would have been there—should have been there. Then, he would have discovered how much he had thrown away. She would have had a chance to bring him back to his senses.

Now, it was too late. Far too late.

Love was such a tragic creature.

Next to the little pile of collected post on the kitchen bench, standing in the glass of water that stood on top of the note from Cy, was a single dark red flower. It was not a rose. It was pretty enough, but what it was she did not know—possibly a Chrysanthemum or a Dahlia. She did not know plants. Next to the note was a key.

She unfolded the note and read it:

Hi. Sorry about the intrusion. Popped in to drop off my keys to the front door and letterbox. I thought you might need them. It feels odd being here; it brings back so much. What we had was good. Pity it had to end, but you know I never promised you anything. I do feel sadness, though. The end is always sad. You are a good chick, Alyssa. Never doubt that. Maybe you don't know how to let go and maybe you always need to be in control, but your heart is in the right place. You are ever so brave. I wish you nothing but the best and I will never forget you. Love, Cy.

Her hands trembled as she went and sat on the sofa with the note. There, she read the note again, and then she cried.

She did not know what else to do.

3

Later, she went and looked at the letters Cy had placed on the benchtop. They were just the odd bill and some junk mail. Nothing of importance except for one; a letter from Dr Jensen the gynaecologist.

Her heart began to beat in her throat.

This will be it. The final report from the gynaecologist.

The letter was indeed from her gynaecologist. The doctor's

official letterhead was printed into the A4 sheet of paper and her own identification details were formally set out near the top of the single sheet of paper. At the very bottom were the doctor's signature and qualifications, and in the middle was a paragraph that had obviously been dictated by Dr Jensen himself:

Dear Alyssa,

I trust this letter finds you well after the recent electrical loop excision procedure on your cervix done in my rooms under local anaesthetic. I apologise for the delay in the final report.

As previously explained, the initial impression was one of severe dysplasia (CIN III) fully excised. The pathologist did, however, have some concerns about both the margins and the possibility of microinvasion, so he requested a review at Olympic University. I am now pleased to report, finally, that the expert consensus is that you have been adequately treated. What this means is that you can be regarded as cured. Careful follow-up remains essential, however.

You will receive an appointment for a follow-up assessment in four months, which will provide more certainty.

While looking at the letter, she realised that she was finding it difficult to accept what it was saying. Everything seemed to be going wrong in her life. What did Dr Jensen mean by "concerns" about the findings? And why involve the Olympic Hospital? Clearly, when it came to her future as a woman, there *was* no certainty.

No certainty.

It seemed so terribly unfair.

She felt numb and the flat felt small and cold. She did not know how to make things better. Life seemed hardly worth living.

She decided to have a hot shower and put herself to bed. Although it was only mid-afternoon, that seemed the safest place to be.

4

Alyssa realised that she must have fallen sound asleep because it was dark outside when the ringing of her phone woke her.

It was a phone number and voice she was not familiar with. The caller said his name was Martin Chikarovski.

'Mr Chikarovski?'

'Yes. Is that Ms Alyssa Brown?'

'How did you get my number, Mr Chikarovski? You do realise it's night already?' It was ten pm.

'Never mind that. I'm phoning on important business. Doubtless you are aware that I am acting on the instruction of the Donald Clinic?'

'Yes. I've heard about you.'

'Excellent. Ms Alyssa Brown, I regret to inform you that the principals of the clinic have asked me to issue you with a gagging order.'

'Issue me with a what?'

'A legal instruction to desist from harming their business. I'll get it to you in writing as soon as practicable. You are to stop having contact with any of their clients forthwith.'

'But I'm employed by them.'

'Not any more you aren't. I have also been instructed to inform you that your employment is terminated. As from now.'

'What?'

'The three lawsuits involving you amount to a combined quantum of at least eleven million dollars. Probably three times that by the end. Given your recent behaviour, the business has determined that you are an unsupportable risk. To put the matter bluntly, you're fired.'

'What?'

'The documentation will be couriered to you. That is all for now, Ms Brown.' Without saying another word, Martin Chikarovski ended the call.

CHAPTER FORTY

1

SHE WAS NOT WELL. Alyssa knew she wasn't, but it seemed there was nothing she could do about it. She had no interest in caring about anything anymore.

After the late-night phone call, she got up out of bed as though nothing had happened and made herself some supper. She could not taste the food, but she ate it anyway. Then she went back to bed. A strange thing happened: she did not sleep, but neither did she think about anything.

At some point, sunrise infused the flat with light.

When next she noticed, it was ten am. She got up and drank a glass of skim milk, ate a banana, and went to the bathroom. Outside, the weather looked cold and miserable, and there seemed to be fog in the flat. There was something in the air, a pressure on her skin.

She tried to ignore it and focus on planning for the future. She had been terminated. She needed to try to understand the implications of this concept.

It was going to take some getting used to. She had always been unsure, but now she knew for sure. She *was* a bad person. Very bad. The pressure was back behind her shoulders once more and the insistence of it was beginning to worry her. She was going to get what she deserved: she was going to fall to her death. She just knew it. Death felt heavy in the air.

She had nowhere to run, but she knew she had to get out of the flat immediately. If she stayed there, she would surely die. She would not be lucky twice. She felt close to panic. She needed to phone Jocelyn, but maybe she wasn't allowed to phone Jocelyn. She would not survive if Jocelyn refused to speak to her.

She decided to escape to the gym. Things would be better there. Her body was her strength. Exercise would make her feel better. Fabio liked her. Maybe, once there, she would be able to think better. Maybe she would know what to do once she was there. She grabbed her things and ran out the door.

2

At the gym she did not feel any better, unfortunately.

People's voices seemed too far away. It was as though they were talking down long tubes. She felt very, very unwell. She was finding it difficult to get enough air.

She saw Fabio. And then she saw that Mark and Ruby were also there. Seeing those two was a big surprise. Their attendance was always so unpredictable. So intermittent. And now the two of them were still arguing. It made her feel very sad. Mark deserved better. He deserved so much better. She really liked Mark. She really did. She felt sorry for him. He needed help . . .

She went and tried to talk to Mark, but she did not seem to be able to speak sense. He looked very handsome, and his blue-green eyes sparkled at her, and his clean brown hair looked as tousled as ever. His perfect teeth smiled at her. She was looking at paradise.

Something he was saying got through to her. 'Are you okay, Alyssa?' He seemed concerned.

'I'm fine,' she said. 'Just tired. Very tired, but just fine.'

She wandered away and started exercising.

People were looking at her strangely.

Then she saw Ruby going to the change rooms.

She knew what that woman had in mind, and it wasn't allowed. So, she knew what she had to do about it. She had to do what had to be done.

What had always needed to be done.

Right from the beginning.

Right from the start.

'I think I'll head home now,' she said, but nobody seemed to be listening.

She made her way to the female change room. Her legs were feeling very heavy. Something was pushing down on her again. It had followed her from the flat. It had found her. It was back . . . the pressure.

The *pushing.*

There was no sign of Ruby. The change room was empty.

She stripped off all her clothes, leaving them in a heap on the floor, and stood there, naked.

Something was not right.

There was a strong, cold wind in the room and the clock on the wall was ticking too loudly. A window was open in the far corner. It should have been closed. She felt herself being forced towards it. Her feet began to slide across the floor. She tried to hold on to a laundry basket to stop herself from going, but that proved no use. As she got closer to the corner, she realised that she was going to die after all. The window was too high above the ground, and her body felt too numb to prevent what was going to happen. The force was too strong for her, its power too great.

Closer and closer to the open window she went, and she felt extremely frightened.

So high up.

3

There were two legs at the window, in the way. Two thin, skinny legs sticking out at the bottom of the partially opened sash window in the gym's changeroom. They had to be Ruby's. Of course, they were. Ruby's.

Ruby was in her gym clothes, but her feet were in socks. Very dangerous. Very easy for her feet to slip. She could slip and tip over backwards and tumble down.

It had happened before. The tumbling down. Down, down, we go, and break into two.

She was smoking. Of course, she was. She was sitting on the window ledge with her body out of the window to avoid the smoke detectors. Very clever, she was.

Behind the frosted glass of the sash window, she was invisible. Out there, she could smoke in peace.

Too clever.

Unfortunately for the clever woman, the change room floor was a floor that got cleaned regularly. It was shiny and a little slippery. Accidents could happen. Her hand, though, kept her safe from falling, that left hand of hers that held nice and securely onto the bottom of the window.

But the frosted glass meant that she could not see anyone approaching.

The ticking of the change room clock became louder. Alyssa looked up at it. It read twelve noon; the right time for something bad to happen. Ruby was in a lot of danger. She could plunge three floors to her doom at any moment.

Great danger.

She did not feel at all well.

She reached for Ruby's hand.

One hand to push away and one foot to hook away.

Then that would be that. If Ruby got pushed and lost her grip . . .

If her hand . . .

Ruby could fall.

Ruby *would* fall.

And then Ruby would die.

She was only centimetres away from the hand now, but she could no longer breathe. The burden was too great.

It was killing her.

There had to be a better way.

She sank to her knees and let out a piercing scream.

'Nooooh!'

It was all that she could do. Scream. It was all she had ever done.

She fell down and curled up into a ball on Ruby's feet.

She had not pushed Grace to her death.

Something else had.

Someone else.

Later, they took her away in an ambulance.

CHAPTER FORTY-ONE

1

WHEN THE DRUGS IN her system finally stabilised, Alyssa realised where she was: the psychiatry ward at the Public Hospital. A nurse told her she had been there for more than a week and that it was a Friday.

As if that discovery was not mortifying enough, she learnt that the psychiatrist in charge of her case was a certain Dr Shelton—Ben's psychiatrist.

How utterly embarrassing.

On the positive side, it was not the secure unit. Also, she was back to feeling her normal self. Dr Shelton seemed pleasant enough too, though somewhat faded like most public full-timers, and a bit of a creep. He knew nothing of her connection to Ben.

Once it was reported that she was back in her right mind, the psychiatrist came to see her. Kindly, he explained what had happened. Alyssa had collapsed during an attempt to save Ruby's life. When Ruby—to Ruby's great surprise and shock—felt somebody suddenly clinging firmly and seemingly desperately to her feet, someone incoherent and shaking violently, she had screamed for help. Fabio and then later Dr Mark Stanford, who had been on site, had come rushing to her aid. They found it was her, Alyssa, completely naked and holding onto Ruby's ankles and refusing to let go. Fabio summoned an ambulance on his mobile phone while Dr Stanford freed Ruby. The two men had then stayed there with her—Alyssa—because by now she had become unconscious. Dr Stanford made sure that her airway was kept clear, and Fabio located her clothes and covered her as much as he could.

While they waited for the ambulance, Mark Stanford did his best to determine what was wrong with her. Given her enormous abdominal scar, her non-responsive mental state, and her rapid, thready pulse, he suspected a ruptured ectopic pregnancy. When the ambulance arrived, Dr Stanford arranged to travel with them in the back of the ambulance to assist with resuscitation—something the crew agreed to seeing that their destination was the emergency room at the nearby Public Hospital and Mark worked there as a trainee surgeon. The emergency room investigations soon revealed, though, that she was not pregnant and that she was a psychiatric case, not a surgical one or a medical one. Mark Stanford had then returned to his fiancée at the gym in a tram.

The haematology, biochemistry, and drug toxicology screens were all negative, as were the EKG, abdominal ultrasound, and MRI of the head—though, surprisingly, there was evidence of a metal plate and numerous healed skull fractures on the MRI, and an absent spleen on the ultrasound. Another surprise had been the discovery by a nurse in ER of four purple stripes across the patient's buttocks.

'After all that drama, you turned out to be a plain and simple nut job,' said Dr Shelton. 'What a relief.' Dr Shelton seemed to find the fact quite funny, so she laughed too. 'Your old file from the Olympic is at least a foot thick. The stripes'—he gestured towards his own bottom—'part of all that, I assume?'

She nodded, to keep it simple. 'Sorry. I know I should have saved everyone a lot of time and money and simply told them about the Olympic.'

'Oh no, believe me, you weren't talking. You were so out of it that you did not even know that you were completely naked. Gave them quite a shock when they took the blanket off you in ER, I hear. Wouldn't have minded being there. Ha, ha,' he laughed. 'Only joking. What I *would* say, though, is that you are the most attractive patient I have ever had. Nice to have you here, Alyssa.'

Dr Shelton did not seem very professional to her. 'How long will I be in here?'

He grinned. 'How long is a piece of string?' True to form as a psychiatrist, he gave a wink. Then he moved on to the next patient.

2

A few minutes later, Dr Shelton returned and announced that three psychiatrists had arrived in his office. Professors Barnes and Summerfield, and a Dr Goronowski. They were doing the early morning teaching grand round and wanted to come to her bedside and see her—not as part of the ward round, but personally. He appeared to have no idea that she had once worked for them.

'You don't have to see them, of course. Say no if you want to. They do a regular huge round through the entire unit on Fridays, but none of them are involved in your care.'

Alyssa was dressed in dowdy hospital-issue pyjamas, but other than that there seemed little point in refusing a visit from her old colleagues. They could hardly harm her any further. And Jocelyn was still theoretically her friend. 'It will be okay. Send them in. Just those three. And give me a minute to set myself up in bed.' She felt quite capable of dealing with the professors. Though her ex-employers had rejected her, she felt that, somehow, she was a better person than they were. More importantly, she was no longer in their power. Having as good as destroyed her, there was nothing further they could do to hurt her. She felt almost delirious with her new freedom.

'Do you want me to stay with you and support you?' asked Dr Shelton.

She smiled sweetly at him. 'No, I'll be fine. They won't upset me. Promise.'

While she waited for her visitors, she quickly brushed her hair and then propped herself up neatly in the bed. She made sure that her pyjama top was properly buttoned up. She was not wearing a bra and did not wish to accidentally make a spectacle of herself in front of two old men.

Professors Donald Barnes and Alan Summerfield duly arrived, both impressive in expensive business suits and both bearing appropriately grave demeanours. Trailing behind them came Jocelyn, who looked like nothing so much as a misshapen afterthought. The sight of her old friend immediately warmed her heart. Because it was a Friday, she knew that the two professors were only there because they were busy doing their normal weekly Friday teaching round at the Public. Jocelyn, however, never normally did rounds at any of the public hospitals, so she, at least, was a genuine visitor. Her hair might be wild and her dress formless, but her smile was genuine. She smiled at her friend, a secret smile that only the two of them understood.

The two men no longer frightened her. She knew her rights as a patient from long experience. If the professors tried to be unethical and turn her into a Friday teaching case, she would immediately show them the door. She was past being abused. Jocelyn seemed to understand her concern. Silently, she pointed towards Dr Shelton's office. Alyssa glanced in that direction. A long train of psychiatry trainees and general medical students was waiting there, parked uncomfortably inside the little room.

She need not have worried. The professors were not there for teaching purposes.

'We owe you an apology,' said Professor Donald Barnes. 'We never realised how good you were at your job.'

'Or how bad things were at the Donald Clinic,' said Jocelyn.

'That too.' The Dog gave Jocelyn a stare of disapproval for interrupting him. 'The truth is, Alyssa, irregularities have been exposed. That said, we have moved swiftly to shut them down. Regrettably for Nurse Wilson, she has had to leave our employment. I am pleased to inform you that her complaint against you has been withdrawn. So too the allegations from Mrs Nikki Rockport that you were responsible for the death of her husband. That too has been withdrawn. Mrs Rockport has decided against such a course of action. Martin Chikarovski assures me that there will be no further accusations from that party. And as for the Ellen Goodman situation, let me just say just this: it too has been resolved.'

'What we are trying to say, Alyssa,' said Alan Summerfield, 'is that you are completely in the clear.' He came up close and squeezed her upper arm. 'I hope all this makes you feel better.'

She did not know what to say. Nothing of what was happening seemed real. There was no explanation offered for anything. They seemed to be talking to her as if she were a child. She wondered if being in a mental ward made her appear brain damaged. Dressed in pyjamas and propped up in her hospital bed, she did her best to smile. The people in the room seemed different to how she remembered them. The two men looked predatory, dangerous even, like high functioning psychopaths, Jocelyn, on the other hand, looked sweeter and more vulnerable than before. Something seemed to have changed in her head.

Maybe it was just a lingering effect from her medication, but she doubted it.

Dr Barnes was speaking again. 'Needless to say, Alyssa, your employment has been fully re-instated. We will be happy to have you back just as soon as you are well enough.'

The three made as if to leave. They had people waiting. Hospital rounds had to continue. Jocelyn, meanwhile, stood to one side, examining the medicine chart she had taken from the foot of the bed.

'Thank you for coming to visit,' said Alyssa politely to her visitors. 'And thank you for keeping me up to date with developments. Do you think that Jocelyn could stay for a few minutes?'

'Of course.'

3

Alyssa took Jocelyn to the patient lounge in the psychiatry ward. It was still early in the morning, so there was nobody else there. In the open ward, one was allowed access to boiling water. 'Would you like a cup of tea?' she asked.

'What a jolly good idea.'

She made them both a cup. 'This is really embarrassing for us both, I know. I'm really sorry.'

Jocelyn came over and gave her a hug. 'Don't be silly.'

'I've even managed to miss your presentation at the conference. I feel really bad about that. I know your paper meant a lot to you. How did it go in the end?'

'Stop worrying about me, will you? It went well—they all laughed their heads off, just as you predicted.' Jocelyn smiled and did not appear concerned.

'Oh dear.' She went and sat at a table with her cup of tea. 'Anyway, come sit Jocelyn. Start at the beginning of all this business of me being here. What exactly has happened? And what exactly was the Dog saying back there? Have I really got my job back?'

Jocelyn nodded. 'You're back at the Donald all right. They're all terrified of you now. Didn't you notice? Doggy and Alan are worried sick that *you* are the one that's going to be suing the pants off them now. It's incredibly funny.' Jocelyn's expression became more serious, and she moved her chair closer. 'There are some things that you are simply not going to believe.' She looked around to make sure that she could not be overheard, then spoke in a low voice. 'Gail Wilson has been shagging Ben Clayton. At least him, probably others too.'

'What!'

'Yes. Simon Bristow worked out what was going on—and all because of you! Clever girl.' She slapped Alyssa on the knee. 'You see, when you got suspended, he felt a lot of sympathy for you, and it focused his mind. Simon thinks highly of you, you know. And he likes you, too.'

'Simon Bristow likes me?'

'Yes, Alyssa. He likes you. These things happen. And it doesn't have to be because he wants to have sex with you. It's called liking someone.'

'You are a fine one to speak.'

Jocelyn grinned mischievously. 'Suppose so. Anyway, Simon decided to do a little snooping on your behalf, given Ben's attack on Gail and the lawsuit and all. And what he found was scarcely believable. The first thing that troubled him was a conversation in the staff room that he overheard between Doggy and Alan regarding Gail. According to Simon, Alan told Doggy that you suspected that Ben Clayton was having issues with Gail Wilson. After that, Simon remembered how you had once told him that Ben seemed undermedicated. Being the genius he is, Simon put the two snippets together and came up with the answer to everything. Easy as pi.'

'What? Stop dragging this out.'

'He went and checked Ben's drug levels. And what he found was what he suspected: though the levels *appeared* to be in the therapeutic range, they were fraudulent. Ben's levels were too normal. Simon is no fool when it comes to biochemistry, as you know. He saw immediately that although variance in Ben's drug levels was present in his lab results display—as expected—the distribution of the variance was not mathematically likely. So, he spoke directly to the lab. And guess what?'

'What?'

'The lab's actual results were nothing like the figures appearing on the computer screen under Ben's name. Gail had been making results up and overriding the lab reports with a spreadsheet of her own. Ben's actual levels were too low. In reality, he'd been sub-optimally treated for months on end.'

'Shit, you don't say.'

'Oh yes.'

'But why? Why would Gail do such a strange thing?'

'Patience. After his discovery, Simon went and confronted Gail directly with that exact question. Why? To his surprise, she went to pieces. Apparently, her conscience got the better of her. The rest, as they say, is history.'

'Stop talking in riddles.'

'She's made a full confession. She's been having sex with Ben upstairs in her clinic room on occasions when he's been there to be checked for weapons or have a blood test. The zasperidone was interfering with his performance—as it does—so she resorted to under-dosing him deliberately. Just to keep his pecker up.'

'That is really sick.'

'You haven't heard the half of it.' Jocelyn leant over and whispered in her ear. 'According to Gail's confession, she has also been having sex with Donald Barnes—in *his* office.'

'Please, no.'

'Oh yes. But that can't be repeated, of course. There is no evidence of anything like that. Nobody knows if it's true or if it's just Gail being vindictive.'

'Has Donald Barnes denied it?'

'Yes. Vehemently. I hope he's telling the truth because I don't think he'll ever get over it if Gail's version proves true. Then he'll be in the same league as Ben Clayton. It will finish him, mentally.'

'Personally, I find it hard to believe Gail's version.'

'That's what I thought initially, but the more I think about it the more I have my doubts about the Dog.'

'Why's that?'

'Because of the way I've seen him looking at you, my dear. Behind your back of course, and when he thinks nobody is noticing. He's far from past it when it comes to sex, but I doubt he's getting any of that at home.

We'll probably never know. Donald Barnes is far too clever for anyone.'

'You mean because of his training in forensics?'

'No. Because he's a complete psychopath.'

4

Jocelyn Goronowski had many more juicy stories to tell. The Donald Clinic, it seemed, harboured no end of nasty surprises.

'Talking of sexual secrets, Alyssa, you'll never guess how your Ellen Goodman's been gotten rid of. What *she's* been up to.'

'What's happened there?'

'Martin Chikarovski took the advice given to him by Alan and aggressively searched for a sexual angle of attack against Ellen's lawsuit. As only Martin can do, Martin then soon managed to produce a sworn statement from a seventeen-year-old schoolboy—as well as photographic and audio evidence from a long-range telephoto lens and concealed microphone—to the effect that Ellen's husband propositioned said seventeen-year-old for sex. According to Martin, our litigious Ellen had offered this youth casual employment as a pool cleaner and garden assistant in the full knowledge that her husband, who is gay, was regularly propositioning her domestic hirelings for sex.

'The contention is that Ellen Goodman always knew that her husband was going to proposition whoever she hired, including underage children like the seventeen-year-old. Ellen, for her part, has tried to claim that she was somehow duped and that the underage school student was a plant of Chikarovski's, but the Goodman's are done for. You see, Martin has a private eye in his pocket who's managed to get onto the money trail. The couple pay their employees, of course, but Martin is claiming that the payments are actually for sexual services. Not only that, but the money man found out that the Goodmans are close to bankruptcy. The attempt to sue you seems to have been a last resort on their part. They saw you as an easy target.'

'Mm.' Given what she knew of Ellen Goodman, Alyssa doubted that any of what she was hearing could be true. 'You know, I don't think that any of what Martin Chikarovski has alleged is even vaguely true.'

Jocelyn grinned. 'Does it even matter? He threatened to go to the police with the allegations unless Ellen dropped her lawsuit, and the

Goodmans have done just that. They've given up. They can't fight someone like Martin. They don't have the money. They're history.'

'It is fortunate, I suppose—for us—that Ellen's bitten the dust, but I do feel rather sorry for her.' She genuinely did. It didn't seem fair. Much of what the stupid old woman had done—if anything—would have been motivated by an attempt to preserve her marriage.

Mrs Goodman's insomnia would unfortunately not be ending any time soon. And neither would the endless blame she heaped upon herself for aborting her son.

'As always, Mr Chikarovski has worked wonders.'

'For the Donald, at least,' Alyssa agreed.

But not for Ellen.

Ellen's sadness would never end.

5

Jocelyn stroked Alyssa's arm then stood up. 'Is there anything to eat in this ward? I missed breakfast.'

'In the top cupboard. There are some shortbread biscuits up there for morning tea. It's all the ward has, I'm afraid.'

'They'll do.' Jocelyn reached up and grabbed a handful. 'Want some?' She began to chew hungrily.

'No thanks. Now, come and sit down next to me again, Jocelyn. Enough talk about me. Tell me more about your paper at the conference. You've gone and got me worried for your sake. If everyone laughed at you, why hasn't it upset you?'

She grinned. 'Well, sure, for a moment I thought my star had crashed, but then they went and presented me with a prize for best paper. Flowers and a bottle of wine. Big surprise. I think they meant it as a joke, but, hey, it will look good on my resume. I suspect it was my conclusion that proved the killer. Here, see. It's the stuff you've been telling me all along.' She took her phone out of her pocket, found the file, and read out loud the concluding paragraph of her research presentation about the psychology of orgasms:

In conclusion, we see that achievement of the mental state known as orgasm requires the activation of two main mental operations. The first is a focusing by the subject on the *origins* of the life streams and death streams specific to her or his conscious neurological computations, and the second is a *short-circuiting* of these deep currents by allowing the two forces to touch. "Life" (for the subject) needs to meet "death" (for the subject). *If* the reunification is achieved (possible for only a fraction of a second), then a seismic whole-of-brain discharge of energy occurs (observable on brain MRI images taken during orgasm). The conscious mind then undergoes failure of its home-grown logic circuits and short circuits into a fatal collapse, from which almost instantly it recovers—much like hot reset in a computer. However, during the disruption caused by the deliberately engineered momentary life stream and death stream reunification, the opaque wall normally shielding the Un-conscious space on the other side of mature consciousness—that space we sense as "eternity"—is momentarily breached. The wall "breaks" and the *real* truths of early childhood, which modulate the logic assumptions of every individual's consciousness, escape. Due to the untamed energy of the real truth, which is normally incarcerated within in the Un-conscious, the escape of real truth is experienced in the **conscious** mind as an explosion. In this way, through reunification, the mental state known as orgasm enables the conscious mind to momentarily lay down its greatest burden, namely the burden of its *specific* early splitting. It is the task of orgasm to return one's consciousness of Self to ground zero, as it were—however briefly—by means of a normally illicit re-touching of its base elements and consequent structural disintegration. If the goal is achieved, the mind shatters, after which light enhanced springs from the darkness plumbed.

Ladies and gentlemen, I give it to you that the purpose of orgasm, quite apart from the obvious one of compelling reproductive copulation, is psychological fitness. The purpose of the orgasm is to bolster the structural integrity of the conscious Self.

Jocelyn put her phone back into her pocket. 'Great, isn't it? Especially the bit about light enhanced springing from darkness plumbed. A bit

Shakespearean, don't you think?'

What could any audience have done except laugh?

'Not bad, Jocelyn. I'm really happy it turned out well for you in the end.'

'Thank you. Took long enough to get it sorted, though, didn't it? Are you sure you don't want a biscuit?' She waved one at her. 'I suspect you might need one when I tell you what's been happening over the Gilbert Rockport business.'

'It's okay. I've had breakfast.'

'Don't say I didn't warn you.'

6

Jocelyn chewed as she talked. 'Even now, there is big shit going down over Gilbert.' She rolled her eyes. 'I suspected that something like this might happen. He was too big a fish.'

'Why? What do you mean? Stop holding out on me.'

'I should probably begin at the beginning, shouldn't I? A week ago—considering, you know, that you had just been thrown into a psychiatric ward—I had another look at your Olympic psych file. Before you get all angry with me again, it wasn't the contents of the file that I was after this time—that bit was wrong of me, I know it was. No, this time I just wanted to have a look at the listing of the dates of access. Given what's been happening with you, I had hunch about something, and it turned out I was right. Alan accessed your Olympic Hospital psych file long before I was asked to do so. What I mean is that Alan had *already* read your file *before* I was asked to. Before I had you appointed to the Donald Clinic.'

'Before?'

'Yes. Why is this important, you may ask—besides the obvious fact that it's unethical. Well, because it may explain how you ended up getting given Gilbert Rockport as a client. You see, the cops have been interviewing Alan! Something is going on between him and Nikki Rockport that the rest of us know nothing about. According to Trish, the police want to know from Alan exactly how he relates to Nikki Rockport because she's been seen on CCTV driving his white sportscar on the night Gilbert died. They've taken Alan's car away for forensic analysis. Something to do with a side mirror that's been replaced recently.'

Alyssa felt herself going cold. Had she eaten lunch at a hotel with someone involved in a murder? She clutched at her chest to try to keep away the fear that suddenly rose within her.

Jocelyn noticed her distress. 'It's okay. You're safe here. I keep forgetting that you aren't well. Sorry.'

'I'm sure Alan isn't involved in anything bad,' said Alyssa quietly. 'It will be just the cops being stupid. They should rather be looking into Nikki Rockport's finances. I hate the cops. I'm sure Gilbert's death has nothing at all to do with Alan.'

'I like Alan too, but how can you be so sure? You know what Alan is like with women.'

'I just know.'

Jocelyn studied Alyssa's face intently. 'You just *know*?'

'I know men.'

'Well, I sincerely hope you are right. So, you think a *woman* is to blame?'

'I do. You know I do.' She became quite agitated.

'Of course.'

7

Jocelyn steered away from the subject of Alan Summerfield.

'I was looking at your medication earlier, Alyssa. You are remarkably alert for someone who's supposed to be a zombie.'

'The drugs don't affect me much now. Initially, Dr Shelton loaded me up pretty high because I was in such a bad way, but I seem to have gotten used to them. I suspect that when I came in, they were worried I might kill myself.'

'And will you?'

'No. Not this time around.'

'That's what happened the last time, isn't it? When you were a student and got admitted at the Olympic. I remember the notes in your file said you kept wanting to jump to your death from the top floor.'

'I don't remember much about that. I was pretty bad.'

'And you don't feel like jumping now? Not a jumper?'

'No. I'm better.'

'And are you still a bad person because both your parents died?'

'It's been wrong to think that. I know it now.'

'That's a positive development, I must say, because you've *always* been delusional, right up until this business at the gym. According to your files, you've been delusional since your mother's death, since you were five years old. You've been convinced your whole life that you *deliberately* killed your own mother. Then, of course, later you were left with no option but to kill your own father, which then left you suffering from a determined belief that you were a bad person. No one has ever able to cure you of it—until now, of course. Now that you've gone and cured yourself by freaking out at the gym and forcing the issue—and forcing yourself back onto medication.' She smiled. 'What a girl. What a brave Alyssa you are, my Lauren angel.'

She ignored the allusion to innocent angels, as well as Jocelyn's continued wrong understanding of how she had killed her father. 'I know I've been thinking bad thoughts in the past. I blame the police for that.'

'Now, Alyssa, we've gone through this before, remember? In your flat. From now on, we can't give in to weakness and irrational thoughts. We can't blame others—not even the police. Stay on your medication in future. What does the forensic file on Lauren Truebody say?'

'You know I haven't read it. How am I supposed to know if what you have been telling me is even true?'

'I always tell the truth. Besides, after that business at the gym and taking your medicine, you now *know* what happened, regardless of me or any files. You *do* know because you were there. And you were at the trial too.'

'Do I? Was I? I forget. There's no reason to treat me like I'm slow witted. I'm emotionally unwell, not retarded.'

Jocelyn ignored her. 'Your file says that what happened to your mother was witnessed by at least eleven passengers on the train. It all came out at the trial.'

'So? There were a number of differing accounts. Each witness had a slightly different story. Other than my dad, nobody knows for sure what really happened.'

'They do. The trial verdict, as you know, was that it was suicide. When your mother reached for you, a scream from her estranged husband—your father—caused a distraction, your hands missed, and she fell over backwards on the steep slope. Instead of controlling her fall, she kept rolling and ended up under the wheels of the passing train. Suicide. Even though that was not how many of the witnesses on the train saw the situation unfold—or, granted, how the police wanted to see things—the trial's official verdict was that it was suicide. You did *not* kill your mother. Believe it and get over it.'

'Okay. I'm trying,' said Alyssa, breaking eye contact. 'But always there's this same problem: somewhere deep down inside I've always *known* that it *wasn't* suicide. Besides, some witnesses said that they saw my dad push my mother to her death when she reached for my hand, even though others said it was me who did that. What actually happened, I've never been able to remember exactly. Dad did, though. He saw everything. Away from the court case, he told me what really happened. He saw exactly what happened.'

'Don't say it. You don't have to say it.'

'I do. I pushed her. I killed her deliberately. There, I said it. But the strange thing is that now I don't know if I really did push her after all. That whole business with Ruby . . . it was so weird.' Alyssa suddenly wrapped her arms around Jocelyn. 'I realised with Ruby that I could never kill anybody. Not deliberately. I just couldn't. Hold me please, Jocelyn. I feel very scared. I am so unwell. I love my dad so much, but I think he lied to me. He put the blame for what *he* did onto me. My father loved himself more than he loved me. That's why, in the end, he couldn't live with himself. And my mother was no better either when she lived with us. She abandoned us. They both put their own needs first. Everything those two ever told me was just one big self-serving lie. Oh, Jocelyn, it's all too awful.' She began to cry.

Jocelyn rocked her from side to side. 'There, there, you silly thing.' she said. 'All families are always nothing but one big lie. This is the beauty of medication, isn't it? When you take it, you see the truth for what it is.'

In her friend's arms, Alyssa sobbed her heart out. 'Jocelyn,' she said, in a voice that was barely audible, her blonde head buried deep in her friend's breast, 'I think I've finally learnt something about myself.'

'And what is that my dear?'

'I think I am very dangerous.'

I don't know what is really true and what isn't.

8

Jocelyn had to get back to work. After seeing her off at the entrance to the ward, Alyssa returned to the patient lounge for a further cup of tea. So much had happened in the space of a week that it was hard to process it all. The day's newspaper lay on one of the chairs, still rolled up, and she looked forward to a read and a catch up on the world she had left for eight days.

Before she could do anything more, though, Dr Shelton appeared at the door. He looked terrified. 'Why didn't you tell me, Alyssa, that you work for Professor Barnes?' Donald Barnes was standing next to him.

'Because I wasn't. I was fired. Up until a few minutes ago I was unemployed.' She had no fear of either of the two men. 'What exactly is the problem now? Come for tea?'

Dr Shelton brushed a bead of sweat from his forehead. 'I know this is highly irregular, Alyssa, but would you agree to Professor Barnes having a little chat with you? In private?' Clearly, it wasn't a request, and clearly, she had no option but to agree.

'Here? Now?'

'Yes,' said Dr Shelton. 'I'll put a "do not enter" sign on the door.'

'Mm.' Did she trust Donald Barnes? Absolutely not. Was it possible that he might inject her with something and have her "removed"? Absolutely yes. Therefore, could she overpower him physically provided she remained wary of his movements? Almost certainly, she could. He was skinny and near to seventy. With her, he would end up with his needle in his own neck. She gave the required answer: 'Sure, I'm happy to have a chat. For fifteen minutes, but no more. My head. The medication . . .'

'We both understand,' said Donald Barnes. 'Thank you, Alyssa.' He nodded at Dr Shelton, indicating that he should vanish.

He did.

9

Donald Barnes made himself comfortable on a chair and once privacy precautions were completed, proceeded to tell Alyssa what he thought she needed to know.

'Gilbert Rockport,' he said. 'The link to the Donald Clinic needs to be terminated. That's why I'm here. The whole saga is busy getting completely out of hand even as we speak, and it's still potentially lethal to the clinic. We need to keep the police away from us. Alan feels it expedient, therefore, that we include you in the loop. He has asked me to come and talk to you. For reasons that will become clear, he is unable to approach you himself. However, he assures me that you can be trusted. I hope he is right.'

'What link of Gilbert's to the Donald Clinic are we talking about?' asked Alyssa. 'Gilbert's death wasn't suicide, so there *is* no link. Besides, as you said earlier, Nikki Rockport has withdrawn her lawsuit.'

Dr Barnes studied her face. 'And this is all you know about the matter?'

She hesitated. 'Oh, I get it. You want me to mention that I know that Dr Summerfield has always been a friend of the Rockports? More than a friend to Nikki, in fact? Is that it?'

'Fantastic! Damn, so you *do* know. Alan said you knew. I'd love to know how you found out, because this has turned out to be the clinic's get out of jail card. It has forced Alan to come clean—at least to me. Well done. Single-handedly, you have saved the Donald Clinic from reputational and financial ruin.'

'Steady on, Professor Barnes.' What he was saying did not make much sense. 'Obtaining the information was no big deal. Nikki herself told me. Or rather gave it away inadvertently, I suppose. When I phoned her. Why is this so important?'

Donald Barnes put his finger to his lips. 'Say no more. The less I am told the better. I'm not interested in the details. The main reason I'm here is because I owe you, Alyssa. Also, I think you have a future in mental health. Therefore, I want to tell you a little story in complete confidence— one that in future I will always deny ever having told you. It's assembled only here,' he pointed at his head. 'The truth about Gilbert's death. I have no absolute proof of any of it. All I have is a personally constructed

734

amalgam of Martin Chikarovski's illegally obtained confidential findings and Alan Summerfield's private confessions. I am only going to air this theory once, so please listen carefully.'

She did. She sat well back from Donald Barnes, and all the while watched him carefully, especially his hands, so that he would not be able to surprise her with any sudden moves.

'Nikki Rockport has always spelt trouble when it comes to money,' said Donald Barnes gravely. 'However, Gilbert Rockport always knew this and was no fool. His law firm is owned by a family trust and Nikki was explicitly excluded from it when they married. Quite predictably, Nikki exhausted their domestic marital assets over the years with her lavish spending and was soon floundering in a mountain of debt, including second and third mortgages on their house. Finally, Gilbert started threatening to divorce her, which added to her woes and drove her to thinking of potential solutions. As far as she could see, the only thing that seemed to be holding Gilbert back from offloading her was his preoccupation with some or other intense personal struggle related in some way to his past, which she knew made him feel suicidal at times. Suicide would have its advantages, of course, seeing that Gilbert owned a large life insurance policy taken out when they married, and which covered him for suicide as well. Given the structure of their marriage contract, suicide was financially a far better prospect for Nikki than divorce. Clear so far?'

'Makes sense.'

'Good. Now, according to Martin Chikarovski, Nikki Rockport therefore dreamt up a scheme to save herself from destitution by actively encouraging her troubled husband to kill himself. Immoral, no doubt, but perfectly logical. So, where did it all go wrong? And more importantly, where does Alan fit into all of this? Well, both Alan and Nikki like to play the field, to put it delicately, so Nikki took advantage of this and told Alan about her approaching divorce, all the while pretending to be very wealthy and in store for a multimillion-dollar divorce settlement. She couldn't very well ask Alan to arrange for Gilbert's suicide, but she could ask Alan to help speed up the divorce for her sake—which he then willingly agreed to do. The added carrot for Alan was that this divorce might well end up in his own financial interest should the two lovebirds ever marry each other.

'A plan was duly hatched between the two, and this called for Gilbert to be sent to see a severely substandard female therapist who would, out of their normal prejudice, encourage Gilbert to go ahead and "free" his wife—as would any substandard therapist in that situation. You, of course, were then appointed to the clinic for that specific task: getting Gilbert Rockport to "set his wife free". With the understanding, of course, that you would be severely substandard and prejudiced against men.'

Donald Barnes was looking directly into her eyes as he spoke the cruel words, but his expression did not change, and he did not blink.

Not once.

The Dog had moved beyond the emotion of pity.

10

'It was all arranged by Alan via Jocelyn,' the old man assured her. 'I had nothing to do with any of it, and Jocelyn was just the innocent dupe. It proved to be a catastrophic miscalculation of course—on Alan's part. He got you all wrong. You turned out to be nothing like you were supposed to be. They had no idea who or what they were dealing with.'

'You mean, including Nikki?'

'Oh yes. Big miscalculation on her part too. Even bigger. Hard to have too much sympathy there. Nikki's intention with the so-called bad therapist had nothing at all to do with an optimised divorce and everything to do with getting Gilbert to hurry up and end it all. She double crossed Alan. She played a dangerous game with him by spurring him on to employ a hopelessly bad therapist but not telling him the truth, which was that it was Gilbert's suicide she was after and not divorce.

'It directed Alan down the wrong path, of course, towards the wrong sort of therapist. And then, of course—apart from anything else—you turned out to be a joker in the pack. Nobody expected deadbeat Alyssa Brown to be as intelligent as she turned out to be. That came as a real big surprise to everyone and a shock. Somehow, you had *everyone* fooled— me too—which is incredibly impressive. It seems you are nobody's fool.'

Dr Barnes did not fool her either, so she did not smile at his attempt at flattery. 'Where does Jocelyn fit into all of this?'

'Jocelyn? Well, Jocelyn is the one who got you appointed. Officially, yes, that is so. To cover Alan's tracks. That's all I'll say. How and why? Well, let's not go into all the details. Sufficient to say that Jocelyn is disturbed—unlike you.'

Once again, the vulture eyes never deviated from hers. He did not believe for even a moment that she was mad.

'Okay, maybe a small part of you *could* be mad. That aside, as you have no doubt realised, our Jocelyn is endlessly in search of her own lost innocent girlhood. She's been like this ever since the suicide of her brother. A quite predictable fruitcake for Alan to control. You, on the other hand . . .' His eyes narrowed. 'Everyone's fatal error. Against all expectations, you turned out to be the exact opposite of what was required. In your hands, Gilbert Rockport perked up rather nicely—Nikki Rockport's worst possible nightmare.'

Alan Summerfield's too, especially regarding his plans for a future with a wealthy Nikki.

'Do I need to say any more?'

'Yes, Dr Barnes, you do. What about Alan? What does Martin Chikarovski say about *Alan's* current financial state, and about his degree of involvement in the accident?'

Donald Barnes gave his best impersonation of innocence to date. 'Nothing. Because I told him to stop once he started on that. It is not in my interest to know.'

Alyssa studied the man in her room with fascination. Jocelyn was right. As a clinical specimen, he was the most complete of psychopaths. She had read the relevant chapter about such people in Obermaaier, so she knew exactly what she was up against. There was going to be only one way to survive him. She was going to have to not cause him any trouble.

'I understand,' she said. 'However, as you so kindly pointed out earlier, I'm no fool. Therefore, I have one more question. Gilbert's life insurance policy did not cover death in a car, so why would *Nikki*, of all people, kill him in a car? Surely, she would have known.'

Professor Barnes gave a smile, the first genuine one she had ever seen from him. 'How greatly your brilliance was underestimated.' He chuckled. 'You must be a literary type. Are you that? A literary type?'

She kept her eyes on him, waiting for any sudden blur of movement and the appearance of a syringe. 'No. Not really,' she said warily. While everything that the Dog had said so far could be true, it could just as well be a complete fabrication—with the real truth even more frightening than the one he was trotting out.

'Heard of "the best laid plans of mice and men go oft awry"? That sort of thing? From Robbie Burns.'

What's with psychiatrists and literary quotations?

'What is that supposed to mean?'

'A lot. According to the narrative that Chikarovski has assembled for us, Nikki did *not* know that Gilbert's life policy excluded death in a car. You see, that is a new and relatively recent addition—following one too many traffic violations. Therefore, when the husband's specially arranged counsellor failed to cause the husband to end his life and instead seemed to be making the husband increasingly likely to go through with a divorce, Nikki decided to take matters into her own hands.'

'Says who?'

'Martin Chikarovski.'

'Really.'

'Yes. In desperation, Nikki Rockport personally arranged what was needed, namely the death of Gilbert. Hence the curious car crash. With that accomplished, imagine the horror and consternation when Nikki discovers that there is going to be no payout after all. So then, from this there flows the desperate idea of making a civil claim against the Donald Clinic for wrongful death—the entire Rockport lawsuit saga being in reality nothing but one of crime and attempted extortion.'

Alyssa was finding the story she was being told hard to swallow. 'Really?'

'Real enough.'

'And you say Nikki has now withdrawn the claim? Because why?'

'Because Martin Chikarovski has suggested to her that otherwise he will need to mention his assemblage to the police.'

'Without evidence?'

'Sounds unethical to horse trade in this way, I know, but sometimes, without the proof, it's better for all. Remember, these are desperate times. Whatever the moral of the story, Nikki Rockport has indeed gone and dropped all claims. And we have not gone to the police. We have not only Alan to think of, but also the reputation of the clinic.'

'Is that so? What about thinking about Gilbert?'

'Pointless. Unfortunately for Gilbert, Gilbert is dead. Sad, I agree. However, on the positive side, you and I have resolved all three of the recent lawsuits against the clinic. You have been a true hero. You have given us the key we needed in every case. Well done.'

'But. But . . .'

Donald Barnes stood up to leave. 'Farewell, Alyssa. I sense that in you I have found a kindred spirit, and I don't say that lightly. You'll go far.'

'Surely, we can't just let everyone get away with this?'

'I never said a word and you are mad—officially, anyway.' He paused on his way out and with the tip of his shoe he nudged the rolled-up newspaper lying on one of the chairs. 'As I said, Alyssa, I like you. For your own good, it will be best that you leave matters exactly as they stand. I trust that what I am saying to you is perfectly clear. Goodbye.' With that, he left the room.

11

Near the bottom of the first page of the newspaper, Alyssa found the relevant report:

> Mrs Nikki Rockport, widow of eminent QC Gilbert Rockport, found deceased at her home in tragic circumstance. Foul play not suspected.

She was shocked by what she saw. Clearly, there were people related to the Donald clinic who were seriously dangerous. But, instead of collapsing into a panic at the sight of the news article, she surprised herself by standing up and calmly making herself another cup of tea. That done, she sat down again and took a sip. It seemed her medication was still enabling her to see things clearly. She needed to use the opportunity she had just been given and think fast and well. While she still had the chance.

It was going to be necessary, she concluded, that she accepted things as they were if she wanted to avoid the same fate as Nikki Rockport. If she got any nearer to the truth, it would result in her own death. Some truths one could not grasp without one's death being the consequence.

Delivery of this exact message had been the purpose of the visit from the Donald Clinic.

And the same applied to her past life, she now realised. Her approach to that had to change too. If she continued to insist upon extracting the truth out of those who had controlled what she had been required to believe while under their power, she was not going to last much longer. She was going to become collateral damage; be forced to remove herself from the world. The recent events at the gym had been proof enough of that.

So, what to do? She was going to need to create her *own* little world; create her own special place of safety; do what had to be done to survive. This was going to be the only way forward.

She needed to believe that there was love somewhere, despite all the evil in her past. After all, her father had not been *all* bad. Or was she confusing him with herself? Or with Alan Summerfield?

She needed to stop dwelling in the past and start living again. Which would mean allowing everyone to get away with whatever they had done— which still felt impossible to do. And yet it was what she was going to have to do; the price she was going to have to pay. In return for being allowed to go on living, she was going to have to continue to feel guilty forevermore for not confronting the evil surrounding her. Guilty even though she was innocent. Guilty as hell. That burden.

Like Gilbert and his struggles with pain, Ben and his feelings of constant threat, and Ellen with her constant sadness, she was going to have to continue to struggle with her own special form of torment: guilt.

But at least she now had insight into her problem. Quite calmly, sitting all alone in the psychiatric inpatient tea lounge, Alyssa saw that for her there was going to be no other way. To preserve the myth that she had ever been loved by anyone, she needed to persevere with her sacrificial delusion that the dreadful things that had happened to her mother and to her father had been caused by her and by nobody else.

Donald Barnes was right. To have a future, she needed to leave past matters as they stood. For her own good.

CHAPTER FORTY-TWO

1

ON SATURDAY MORNING, with Alyssa back home at her flat, the call came.

The getting home had been the easy part. As soon as Professor Barnes left the hospital the previous day, Alyssa asked Dr Shelton to discharge her. He said he was strongly opposed to the idea, but she had insisted, knowing that he could not legally refuse to comply with her request seeing that she was not in the secure unit. He had protested, but she had ignored his protests.

'I've never felt better,' she assured him. 'And anyway, as you now know, I work in this field, so I'm pretty clued up about the warning signs. At the slightest concern I'll come rushing back. And not only that, but the medication is working wonders.'

Dr Shelton had a bad feeling about the whole business. 'Given your training, Alyssa,' he said gravely, 'I'm sure you realise that the last person in the world we expect to have insight into their condition is a patient in a psychiatric ward.'

'And as *you* well know, Dr Shelton, there's nothing much wrong with me in the first place and I'm much better now.'

After that, it was just a matter of completing the paperwork. An intern was sent to process her. With the approach of weekend, it was common for hospitals to shed as much load as possible, so the junior doctor—a vacuous youth who talked too much yet believed he was overworked— unquestioningly filled in the discharge paperwork. He arranged for her to be given three bottles of pills to take home and gave her a date for a follow-up appointment at an outpatient clinic. She knew what the pills were for: one lot was for agitated psychotic delusions, one lot for depression, and the final bottle was for anxiety—vorazepam. Once home, she flushed the contents of all three bottles down the toilet.

She had no need of medication anymore. Not after all that had happened. Not after Professor Donald Barnes. And not now that she had finally come to understand herself. Besides, back in the psych ward she had not been swallowing any of her pills for the last three days anyway. It was a trick she had learnt in her previous life, during her months as an inpatient at Olympic Hospital. If anyone knew how to conceal a pill under the tongue, she did. A visit to a toilet cubicle after medicine rounds completed the simple strategy. She doubted there was much medication left in her system.

Which was how it needed to be, seeing that there was no longer anything wrong with her.

'Hello Mark,' she said, answering the phone call. She knew it was him even before he spoke. 'What a surprise. How nice of you to phone. How did you get my number?' That too, she already knew.

He sounded nervous. 'You gave me your business card, remember?'

'Oh yes. That.' At the cafeteria at the Public.

'I used it to phone your work yesterday and someone there called Trish kindly gave me your mobile number. But only because you had already given me your business card, she said.'

'That's our Trish through and through.'

'She told me that you were much better, but thought you were still in hospital. You're out of hospital, aren't you? I couldn't find you on the inpatient lists.'

'Yes, I'm at home. I got home yesterday afternoon, thank you, Mark.'

'I thought I should ring and see how you are. I'm off call today, luckily, so I've been thinking about you. You've had us all worried back at the gym. How are things?'

'Definitely much better.'

'If you don't mind me asking, have they managed to work out what caused your collapse? We don't often see such an event in a young person other than in epilepsy—speaking professionally, of course; as a doctor. What did it turn out to be in the end? It wasn't something cardiac that I missed, was it?'

She smiled. 'No. I know you are doing cardiac surgery, but sorry to disappoint. It was nothing as serious as that.' She stalled while she thought of something plausible to say: 'Nice to hear your voice again, by the way. Yes, as I said, it was nothing much. It turned out to be just a bad case of low blood sugar. From missing breakfast, probably. I've learnt my lesson. It won't happen again.'

But then why keep me in for eight days?

'That's a big relief. I'm sorry I wasn't able to work it out at the time. Not much of a doctor, am I?'

'Nonsense. I'm very grateful for all the help you gave me. I'm told you even came to the hospital with me in the ambulance.'

'It was the least I could do. The ER doctors took over from there, of course.'

'Thank you for your efforts, anyway. So, what are you and Ruby up to today, Mark? What do you two do on an off day?'

'I'm at a bit of a loose end, actually.'

'And why is that?'

'Ruby and I have split up.'

'Oh, my goodness. You don't say. Now, that *is* a big surprise. I'm sorry to hear it. What happened?'

'Don't really know,' he sighed, 'but I suppose that in the end it was probably inevitable. I know she's been stressed out lately, but there's been more to it than that. She's been unbearable for the last year or two. The last straw for me was when she went ballistic after I went to the hospital in the ambulance with you. She hasn't stopped ranting on about it ever since. I've always known she has trust issues, but I never realised just how bad they were until now. She keeps accusing me of being so obsessed with you that I've been seeing you behind her back—which we both know is ridiculous. So, I've decided to take a break from her.'

'Sounds like the wisest course to me.'

'I think so, too. She's turned into someone I don't even know anymore. It's like she's this incredible prude. You know, like Queen Victoria or something. Her attitude really got to me when you were out for the count on the change room floor, and I was trying to discover what was wrong with you and she kept saying that she was finding the whole business disgusting. I mean, what is that supposed to mean? What did she expect in a female change room? She said she could see treachery in my eyes. I've decided I'm not prepared to put up with such nonsense any longer.'

'Sounds sad, but that's women for you, Mark. There's no knowing what they'll get up to next. Here's an idea that may cheer you up, though. Cheer us both up, in fact. I'm planning to go out this morning for a bit of fresh air after being cooped up in the hospital for so long, so why don't we meet somewhere for coffee? That way you won't be too lonely, and I'll be able to fill you in on my hospital adventures. Besides, it would be great to see you again. You were very kind to me.'

'Sounds good, but what about your other half? I don't think you've told me his name. The guy you were having boyfriend problems with that time at the hospital cafeteria. I don't see him being too keen on me tagging along. I don't want to cause any trouble.'

'Actually, Mark, my partner is out of town at the moment, so the timing could not be more perfect. Like you, I'm at a loose end. It would be nice to have your company.'

'Great. Perfect. I'd love to catch up with you then.'

The matter was agreed: coffee at the Troy Gardens pavilion at 11.30 am.

The venue was her suggestion. The coffee shop lay in the heart of the sizeable public park and was popular. She liked it there, especially seeing that getting there involved a walk through the gardens.

2

Following the phone call from Mark Stanford, Alyssa made herself a good breakfast of muesli, orange juice, and coffee, and followed this with a long shower. In the shower, she felt her strength returning. Her mind felt clear again and her spirit resolute. It was time to put the past behind her and start a new chapter in her life. While she rinsed herself, she sang a song. It was from a nursery rhyme, from when she was a small child:

> *One, Two. Buckle my shoe*
> *Three. Four. Open the door*

Outside, the sun was out, and the clouds had cleared. Even so, the air was crisp following the recent cold snap. She placed potential items to wear for a trip to the park in a row on her bed. From it, in the end, she chose a pair of skimpy white French-lace knickers and matching bra, a plain T-shirt in pastel pink, a pair of well-fitting three-quarter-length jeans, and her brown lambswool jumper. She liked the jumper because of the way its colour contrasted with her hair and her skin tone—and because of the way it tapered to emphasise both her bust and the trimness of her waistline.

Not to mention that the jumper stopped just short of her butt. While checking its fit in the mirror, while still otherwise naked, she could not help noticing that the bruises across her cheeks were still there. Although no longer painful, they were still alarmingly visible and likely to persist for at least a few more weeks. They were unlikely to spook Mark, though, if he got to see her naked within that timeframe because he had already seen her naked body. He would already have seen the huge abdominal scar and the heavily bruised butt. Despite which, he still seemed hooked on her. Possibly, he was even attracted to the fact that she was not an entirely well person.

For her feet, she selected her trusty ankle boots. They had been expensive to buy because they were supposedly a copy of Manolo Blahnik originals, but she liked them whatever the truth of the matter. Not only were they refined and feminine but also comfortable to walk in and sexy too. Cy's Brian had assured her of this last part: "drop-dead-sexy" had been his assessment.

Makeup done, hair sorted, and perfume applied, she put on Grace's silver bracelet, together with a pair of silver stud earrings and the gold neck chain from Ethan—innocent Ethan, her first love. He had given her the chain all those years back in Ocean View and it had probably cost him everything he had. She still felt bad about the way she later abandoned him simply to suit herself. Wearing his gift seemed a good way to remind herself of the need to be a better person.

She looked at herself in the mirror with approval. It was time to believe that the dark days were over. Time to believe in herself again. As Jocelyn had wisely pointed out, there was no option in life but to do what had to be done. And what had to be done was that she had to obtain Mark. There was a high probability that she would succeed, she told herself. She hadn't lost her knack. Look how easy it had been for her to induce Alan Summerfield to tell her what she needed to know about Nikki Rockport.

Like Alan, Mark needs what I have.

Coffee in the gardens would be all that was required.

I can do this.

Despite the bruises, she set out bravely on her date with destiny.

During the walk along Alfonso Street towards the top end of the Troy Gardens, she found herself feeling increasingly nervous. The anxiety did not seem related to uncertainty about how Mark would respond to her—although that was undoubtedly part of it—but more to a fear that she might become emotionally or mentally unstable without warning. Lately, she had been capable of doing the strangest things. The recent weeks had been evidence enough of that. And even now, though the Donald Clinic lay outside the far end of the gardens, to its left, down near the river, the prospect of heading in that general direction once in the park felt strangely unsettling. Working at the Donald had come close to destroying her. If ever a competition for unsupportive workplaces were held, the clinic would take first prize with ease. That much she did at least now know.

She entered the park via its main gate at the top end, where a statue known as the Nature God was situated. She was well ahead of time, but this was deliberate because she had left the flat early to allow for a relaxing walk along the many pathways in the gardens before going to the coffee shop. She needed that—a good, calming walk—because already her heart was beating in her throat.

As always, the enormous park's extensive lawns were beautifully green. Dotted everywhere were large specimen trees and small clumps of forest, while paved pathways crisscrossed in all directions. Towards the centre of the park, before one reached the coffee shop, the trees became denser and the pathways more hidden. From her position at the entrance gate, the restaurant was invisible behind all the trees. To the right of the park stood the wall of skyscrapers belonging to the CBD, to its left, leafy old East Hubron, and at its bottom end, far away, the Yarradonga river.

Alyssa headed along a familiar path leading to a dense growth of trees. Walking always made her feel a stronger person. She wanted everything to be perfect.

As she wound her way through the trees, the relative isolation made her think unexpectedly of Ben Clayton.

Jabba, the horticulturalist.

She remembered that he used to work part-time in council parks.

Alone among the trees would not be a good place to encounter the likes of him. After all, the most predictable thing about the insane was that they were not only unpredictable but also frighteningly persistent. What if Ben had been accidentally released from the secure ward? Or had escaped. And was back stalking her?

A bird chuckled loudly in a tree and made her jump.

Shit!

She walked faster, making for an open part of the park. In the trees above, birds continued to shriek angrily at her.

Psychotic people could be dangerous.

3

'Boo!' said a voice, and a hand simultaneously touched her shoulder from behind.

She just about jumped out of her skin.

It was Mark Stanford. He had seen her in the distance from behind and silently caught up with her.

'Hi,' he said, 'I seem to have given you a real fright. Sorry about that.'

She grinned with relief at the sight of him. 'Hi. Yes, you gave me real scare there, Mark. I never heard you coming. You must walk really softly—and fast. How come you were so sure it was me, from behind?'

It was his turn to grin. 'Your shape in those jeans. Even from a distance I knew it was you. And I mean that in the nicest possible way.'

He had recognised her by her bum. 'I see. That's a good thing, I hope,' she said sweetly. Yet again, she found herself struck by his reassuring openness and confidence in himself. 'You're a bit early.'

'So are you, I see.'

'I was just going for a walk in the park. To get some exercise.' She could not help noticing that they were dressed in a similar way. He had on a pair of black jeans, leather boots and a rib-knitted navy-blue zip-through jumper. Unlike Ben Clayton, he smelt good. Reassuringly good.

Not insane.

'Mind if I go for a walk with you before we meet officially at the pavilion?' He sounded slightly anxious. 'I could do with some exercise too. Work's been stressing me to the max.'

'I'd love to. Why don't we go around in a long semicircle to the pavilion? We can take in some sunshine along the way.'

'Brilliant idea.'

And so, they walked together, side by side.

'So, tell me, why were you so jumpy?' he asked.

'That. Oh nothing. The birds probably. You know, the tree chucklers. I thought one might attack me.'

'The kookaburras? We have a lot of those in Euticha. They won't harm you. The magpies might, but not at this this time of year.'

'Is that where you're from? Euticha? I knew it had to be somewhere small. From your accent.'

He smiled. 'Speaking about yourself, are you? Yes. It's pretty small, but yup, that's where I grew up. It's right on the river, so at least we had a lot of fun swimming and boating. My folks and my sisters are all still up there.'

'I've never been there. Imagine that. Kookaburras in Euticha.'

'We have everything there.'

'Sisters too. I wish I had a sister. I've only got brothers.'

'And I've only got sisters. Two. I'm in the middle. The only boy. Difficult for me sometimes.'

Sisters can be like that.

'Do you do a lot of operations?' she asked a while later, as they walked along in the pleasant sunlight, passing at times through dapples of shade.

'That would be an understatement.'

'That's amazing. Don't you sometimes lose your nerve?'

'I'm not sure what you mean. Surgery doesn't work like that. You can't lose your nerve unless you don't know what you are doing. But that's another matter entirely—not knowing what you are doing. Which, I suppose, is why I lost my nerve when you collapsed in the gym change room. Do you know that you just about scared me to death?' They were passing through a shady area of the garden, and he stopped her.

She turned to face him. 'It was that bad, was it?'

'Seeing you collapsed on the ground was the scariest thing I've ever faced—which doesn't make any sense to me. I see collapsed people every day, many of whom die in front of me, and normally it doesn't unsettle me in the least. But with you it was entirely different. The situation wasn't helped, of course, by the fact that I couldn't work out what was going on with you. In the end, I foolishly concluded that it had to be something surgical like a ruptured ectopic pregnancy. I don't know why I became so flustered. In my line of work, it's not unusual to not know what's wrong at first. Being unsure never usually affects me. Not emotionally. Not like it did with you.'

'Sorry about that, Mark. Although, I'm glad too.' She took his hand and before he could react to that, she had a question for him: 'What made you think I had an ectopic pregnancy?'

He blushed. 'Your scar. I thought there might be . . .' He stopped in an apparent attempt to avoid saying anything hurtful or revealing how much of her he had seen.

'Might be what? Internal damage?'

'Adhesions. Post-operative scar tissue can cause ectopic pregnancy. But it wasn't that, I know. ER told me later that your pregnancy test was negative. They told me just as I was leaving.'

'So, the scar worried you, did it?'

'No, of course not. It's a beautiful scar. I was surprised to see it, though—such a large one, I mean. What happened there?'

'Car accident when I was a child. I almost died. My dad was killed.'

'Oh, I am sorry. At least you seem to have recovered very well, I must say.'

'Yes. Physically, I'm fine.'

'That's good to hear. When I was called to see you at the gym, you were completely incoherent. Nobody could get any sense out of you. I knew it would take imaging and labs to sort you out, so I got Fabio to call an ambulance.'

'You doctors crack me up. "Imaging and labs". Sounds impressive.'

'It's the only way, especially if a patient is mentally out of it. I honestly thought you might die. And for some reason, that really upset me.' He placed a hand on her arm.

4

At that point, the garden seemed to claim them for its own. The narrow, paved pathway on which they had paused seemed to hold them there, closely encircled by trees and shrubs and embraced by air suffused with the heady smell of fresh vegetation. Mark reached down and took her free hand in his. 'You feel very special to me,' he said shyly.

She pulled him gently forwards and hugged him. 'Thank you for coming to save me,' she whispered.

'It was the least I could do. I'm just so glad I was there.'

They resumed their walk, now hand in hand and side by side, as though it was the most natural thing in the world. His hand felt warm and soft. She was holding his hand, yet he was holding her hand. She had never experienced such a feeling.

'You are going to do my head in,' she said at last.

'Same here,' said Mark, rather illogically.

'I haven't been able to get over you since the first time I saw you.'

He turned his head. 'Seriously?'

'Seriously. I've always kind of wished you never had a fiancée. Sounds a terrible thing to say, I know, but it's the truth.'

Mark stopped walking and looked at her with interest. 'Us together here is like some sort of fairytale, isn't it?'

'It is a bit, isn't it?'

Meet the wicked witch.

'Well then, I may as well confess that you have had much the same effect on me. I haven't been able to get you out of my mind. Not since the very first time I saw you at the gym. Remember that? When you blocked my way to my keys?'

'Sure do.'

'And then later, I almost dropped a weight on my head because I got so distracted by you. At first, I thought it was just a sex thing—you know how it is. After all, you really are incredibly sexy, as I'm sure you know. But it isn't just that.'

She was amused by the flustered masculinity in his eyes. 'Thank you,' she said. 'You're not so bad yourself, you know. But I am pleased you agree it's not just a sex thing between us.'

'No, it's not, is it. I've finally come to realise this. There is something truly magical going on between us.'

'Well, that's a good thing, isn't it, Mark?'

'Would be if you didn't have a boyfriend—if we weren't both tied up elsewhere.'

'Looks like we may be in luck, there, at least from my point of view. You won't believe this, Mark, but I dumped Cy a few weeks back. He's history.'

'Wow,' he whispered, as his mind absorbed the implications of what she had just said.

They resumed their walk once more, this time in silence, heading now in the direction of the coffee shop.

It was time for more honesty on her part, Alyssa decided. 'That low blood sugar story I gave you over the phone, Mark,' she said, 'it wasn't really true. You probably know anyway. It's not what was wrong with me at the gym.'

'Don't let it worry you. I've no right to know, so you don't need to tell me more. I'm just pleased that you seem so well now.'

'I do want to tell you. In my own words. You know I'm a psychologist, right? Well, a counsellor, really. A psychotherapist. Well—and this is hard for me to say—the truth is I've had psychological issues of my own in the past. That's why I took up psychology in the first place. It's been nothing serious—not schizophrenia or endogenous depression or anything like that—but I still don't like to own up to it. I still find myself trying to make excuses. But, with you, Mark, there's no point. I want us to be honest with each other. That collapse of mine at the gym—that wasn't a medical thing. It was purely psychological. The whole episode was some sort of out-of-control dysregulation event related to a severe post-traumatic stress disorder. Up until that moment, I had always tried to deny that I had the condition, but there's no point anymore. The bizarre behaviour in the gym has forced me to face up to the truth about myself. I've had a really traumatic childhood, one that has really badly screwed with my mind.'

'It's very brave of you to tell me.'

She looked down at the ground. 'I don't feel very brave. I feel like a fool for having to confess that I have severe PTSD and just don't seem to be able to get over it.'

'Well, don't feel a fool. I understand these things.'

5

It was then that she saw her tree—or at least one that looked identical to the one outside the cottage at the Donald—and had a sudden idea.

'Do you mind if we stop for a few minutes at that tree, Mark?' The tree was some distance from the path and among a dense clump of unrelated specimen trees. It was the only one of its kind there. She pointed it out. 'There's one just like that at my work. I suspect we may be able to get in under its branches and find a place to sit. Want to give it a go?'

He looked amused but willing. 'Sounds interesting. Lead the way. I like trees.'

The tree was larger than the one at the clinic, probably even older, but undoubtedly of the same sort. In this one, the drooping branches came even closer to the ground, but once she and Mark squeezed past them, they reached an enclosed space big enough for four or five adults. There was no evidence that others had been there. It was their own secret place, one that she had produced.

A magic bubble.

Those words, from Gilbert Rockport, now became clear. It was what her tree represented: her own special place. Her own little world. Their own little world. Like the tree at work, its trunk was wonderfully touchable too.

Mark became enthusiastic. 'Look,' he said, testing a low branch. 'We can sit here.'

She came and sat next to him, an arm around his waist for support.

'How did you know about this place?' he asked, looking impressed.

'Instinct. Great, isn't it? Reminds me of when I was a child.' As she said it, she recalled for the first time that there had been a similar tree near her original family house in Cloverdale—before the tragedy with Grace and the move to Ocean View. She had played under it with her brothers, and they had believed it was an enchanted castle. They had been happy there.

His arm was around her shoulder. 'You are very sweet. Bringing me to this and being honest with me and all.' He turned his head and looked into her eyes. 'I think I need to be *truly* honest with you too, Alyssa.'

She blinked at him. 'In what way?'

'About that gym collapse thing. As you know, I went with you in the ambulance when they took you to the ER, but there's more to it than that. It's not in the regulations. They only allowed it because I insisted, and because they knew I was a doctor at Public Hospital, which was where they were headed anyway. I didn't want to let go of you. Everyone was a bit freaked out at that stage because you were completely naked. When we got to the ER, the staff were grateful for the bit of info I was able to give them, but obviously I wasn't permitted to be involved in your care after that. Nevertheless, I *did* learn some things. What I'm trying to say—trying to confess, I suppose—is that I couldn't help seeing part of your file as it came up on the screens in ER. I saw only the first page, though, because I turned away as soon as I realised what I was looking at. I knew I had no business seeing any part of your file, not even the first page. I wasn't even supposed to be there. And I saw your bruises too.'

She looked into his eyes not with fear but with interest. 'What did you think of it all?'

'Well, I was relieved, I suppose. It explained everything; the fact that you had a psych file—that you were a psych case. Can you forgive me?'

'It's better that you know. How much did you see?' She smiled at him. 'In my psych file, I mean.'

He looked apologetic. 'Nothing, really. Honestly, just the first page. I couldn't *not* see your diagnosis, though. It was right there. It came up on the screen, just below your name.'

'Under what name?'

'Your name. Alyssa Brown. Why?'

She laughed in relief. 'Oh, nothing. That's my psych file all right. I wouldn't worry about it. It's old history. Apparently, I'm too hard to understand anyway. It seems that so far only one person has ever even begun to understand what's going on in my head—and she's not even listed in the file.'

'And who's that? If you don't mind me asking.'

'My colleague and dear friend at work, the psychiatrist Dr Jocelyn Goronowski. She assures me that there's nothing seriously wrong with me. It's just a PTSD thing related to the deaths of my parents when I was young.'

'Sounds like you need protecting.' The branch swayed as he moved closer to her. 'Now I'm even more in danger of falling in love with you. What am I to do?'

'It's Ruby, isn't it, that's the problem for us.'

'Yes. I wish I knew what to do about Ruby. She's gone and booked the church and the reception and everything.'

'I could give you some professional advice. Unbiased advice.'

'And what is that?'

'You need to do what your heart is telling you to do.'

He placed a finger on the tip of her nose. 'And you are not being biased?'

She held his gaze without blinking. 'No.'

'Ruby's parents will kill me.'

'You can't live somebody else's life, Mark. You have to live your own life.'

'It's not that simple. The church will have a fit too.'

'It *is* that simple, Mark. Believe me, I *know*. In this life, you need to do what has to be done. If you don't, you will end up wasting your life.'

He studied her face. 'You mean it's in Ruby's best interest too, in the long run, don't you?' He frowned, as if trying to work out whether to take the advice. He took a deep breath. 'What the hell, Alyssa. Let's do what we must do.' He slid off the branch, lifted her to her feet, and embraced her. 'I think this deserves a kiss. May I?'

She nodded. The power of his arms left her breathless.

They kissed. Normally, she did not particularly like being kissed on her mouth, but his kiss was everything that she had been missing, everything that she had really wanted. It spoke of the uncomplicated masculinity of his soul. Something profound happened in that magic bubble: vindication of everything she had ever believed. It had been such a long wait; so much aloneness. Now, finally she had triumphed.

Mark Stanford was what she wanted: a real man. He had a real man's lust, too. He was hard for her. He wanted her.

With his kiss had come no invasion of her spirit. Instead, there was tenderness, respect, concern, joy. Purity. She knew they would never again be apart. He was the One. And she knew he knew it too. What they had was predestined. Being together had been inevitable from the beginning. They had always been meant for each other.

It was like it had once been with her father in the days when he was still her father—even though Mark was nothing like her father. Like before all the badness.

'I want to go to Africa with you,' she said, finally.

He seemed suddenly concerned. 'That would be wonderful, thank you, but what about your job here? It wouldn't be right.'

'I'm happy to go anywhere with you.'

'No. Better if I change my plans. For you, I would.'

'No,' said Alyssa. 'I need to get away from the Donald Clinic. I know you want to further your career and I want to help you. I would love to help you.'

He kissed her again. 'Agreed then,' he said. 'I already have accommodation for two pre-arranged. Let's go to Africa together. I'd like nothing more.'

6

The surrounding branches of their tree appeared to add their own embrace. 'It feels so right being here with you, Mark,' said Alyssa.

He held her.

'I wish we could stay here together forever.'

'Me too.'

After a while, he had a question: 'I wonder what sort of tree this is.' He studied it. 'It's no ordinary tree. It must be something unusual. Clearly, it's not a conifer, or an oak, or a eucalyptus, or a pepper tree—but then again, I know nothing about plants.'

'I'm almost certain it's some sort of milkwood tree.'

Mark went in search of its nameplate at the base of the trunk. All the specimen trees in the park were labelled with a small brass plaque. On his hands and knees, he found it. 'Here it is: "Milkwood". You are right. That's amazing. How did you know?'

'Someone from work told me.'

A someone called Alan Summerfield, a man who had been happy to arrange a scheme whereby Gilbert Rockport would be encouraged to get divorced by a specially appointed hopeless therapist—a woman, one who would most likely fail to cope at a place like the Donald Clinic in the longer run, suffer career failure, and thereafter disappear. Not only that, but when the hopeless therapist's client unexpectedly went and committed what appeared to be suicide instead of getting divorced, he thought he could sit back and watch the hopeless therapist commit suicide too. All of it in pursuit of his own selfish schemes—until his feelings for her got the better of him. Or was she again confusing Alan Summerfield with her father?

'I think it should be called a love tree,' said Mark. He kissed her again. This time he had his hands on her bottom. 'This overseas trip of mine,' he said finally, 'I'm going to cancel it. It was never the right thing to do professionally. It was just a way to get away from Ruby. I've got plenty of opportunities right here in Hubron. It will be for the best. For us both.'

'If you are sure,' she said. 'Then I can stay friends with Jocelyn and get a job at the Public, and we could live at my flat if you need to move out of yours.'

Once again, she was getting her own way.

Am I another Donald Barnes?

She needed to be a better person than that. A kinder one. 'Honestly, Mark, I really don't mind going off to Africa with you,' she said. 'I need to try to be a kinder person.'

Then she realised that they were sitting under an African tree.

We've already done Africa.

'I'm sure it's the right decision to stay,' he said. 'Here is best.'

'Okay. As long as you are sure.' She let the new reality swirl through her mind. 'Staying would be good too. Then I'll be able to tell Professor Barnes to get me a new job away from his clinic. I'll tell him to make it at Public Hospital.'

'*Tell* him?'

She grinned at the irony of it. 'Yes. He will do what I say. For this once.'

Mark took the decision that they had just made to stay on in Hubron in his stride. 'It all sounds perfectly brilliant. There is just one thing that I don't understand, though.' He looked into her eyes with a perplexed expression: 'Why do you want to be a kinder person, Alyssa? You so obviously are one as it is. I can't imagine you as anything but kind.'

'You can't?'

'No. You are too sweet.'

'Don't be fooled. I've had a difficult childhood and my past troubles me. Sometimes, I don't know if I can trust myself. You mustn't forget what happened to me at the gym.'

'And you mustn't forget that I'm a doctor. I'm not entirely ignorant about mental health, you know. Psychological issues don't alarm me—provided, of course, that I'm made aware of them.' He smiled.

'Thank you.' She took his hand.

'I've even read one or two books by Freud,' he announced.

'Good. Then I hope you realise that according to current views he can be quite wrong at times. Also, even when he is correct, what he is saying is usually completely misunderstood by the general reader.'

'Really?'

'Afraid so. Freud and therapists like him are deep but they are also very technical. The other problem is that according to modern understanding they are quite wrong in their belief that they can fully know the metaphysical Self psychology of clients, or that it is *they* who cure their clients. Modern psychotherapists have realised that a Self can only be diagnosed and cured by itself—no therapist can do this *for* you. Benevolent guidance, support, and encouragement from the Self of a therapist, though still essential, is all that can be offered.'

'The Self needs to cure itself?'

'Yes. There is no other way.'

'I just love it when you sound like a psychology textbook.'

'The trouble with me is that I am still a work in progress.'

'Mm. A challenge, then.' He grinned. 'I'm sure I'll cope. I know people, and I know that as a person you are just great.'

'That is so sweet.'

He appeared to realise something for the first time. 'That psych file of yours: it is a bit weird, isn't it? Why *is* that? Have you seen what it says? I'm sure you must have.'

'Why, specifically, do you think it's *weird*?'

'Remember, I only saw the first page, but it was perplexing—to me, at least. Under "diagnosis", it said: "The client suffers from a chronic fixed delusion that she is a bad person." What is *that* supposed to mean?'

'That workers in mental health are confused, Mark. As usual.'

'Confused? In what way? They are saying, aren't they, that they believe that you are actually a good person and not the bad person you claim to be. Do you think they are *wrong* about that?'

'Yes, Mark.'

'Mm. So, are you saying that you are *not* deluded about it and that you really *are* a bad person. Is that it?'

'Yes, Mark.'

He appeared puzzled. 'But if you *did* happen to be truly deluded, then how would you be able to know for certain that your opinion about yourself was correct?'

Somewhere, a clock began to chime the hour of twelve noon.

'You don't get it, do you, Mark?'

After that, she remained silent. What could she say? Even she—a psychologist—had not understood the intricacies of her own mind until after the collapse at the gym. Fortunately, that event, and the admission to hospital and visit from Donald Barnes, had, at last, enabled her to understand that she had not actually killed anyone, despite her fears. No. Her father, in the past, and now, more recently Nikki Rockport—or, heaven forbid, Alan Summerfield too—had been to blame for *all* of the deaths. And, yes, these people had arranged to have their crimes attributed to her. They had done so either in the knowledge that as the victim of deception at an early age, she had nowhere to hide and no way to defend herself or done so in the incorrect belief that she would understand nothing about psychology. Yet, despite all this, now, miraculously, she was innocent. None of the deaths had been the result of anything that she herself had done, and she was not a bad person in that way at all. No need for guilt.

But this was where things became weird. She *was* still bad. The new understanding of the past had done nothing to remove the feeling that she was a bad person. She was bad, through and through.

She knew now why she felt like she did, but how could she explain it to Mark, or to anyone? How could she make them understand that she had no choice but to view the past in a certain way if she wished to remain alive? Who but she herself could understand that according to the plans of the bad people in her life, she too should have been among the dead by now? The expectation from these people had been that in the end she would simply cease to be a problem; that she would commit suicide or in some or other way finish herself off and rid the world of her sorry presence. More to the point, after the death of Gilbert Rockport, Alan Summerfield's Donald Clinic had undoubtedly *planned* for her to have the same fate as the one arrived at by Nikki Rockport. Yet this had not happened; she was not dead. And she knew why.

After fleeing from the psychiatric ward yesterday, she had worked it all out: how it was that she had been allowed to escape; how it was that she was still alive. The brilliance of her analytical insight took her breath away once again, even now in the park. She was alive only because she was a bad person. It was this that had confused her adversaries and would continue to confuse others. People fatally failed to understand this one thing about her; that she habitually took upon herself some of the badness of those who sought to harm her. By accepting that she was bad, she had the ability to bring any goodness present in such people to the fore. From her only caregiver in childhood, her bad father, she had learnt in this tragic way to extract sufficient goodness to cause herself to be loved by him—as a bad person. And this love had been just enough for her to maintain the will to live. And this same quality in her, this apparent badness, had compelled Alan Summerfield to love her too. He had tried to resist, but he had fallen in love with her in the end. Just like with her father, she had engendered enough love in him for him to make the effort to save her. Obtaining love from men always required that some part of her be bad. With her, it would be forever so. There was always a price to pay for being damaged goods; for having one's childhood permanently screwed up; for being a worthless piece of trash. Too late now, as an adult, to rewire such deep circuitry. Feeling that she was somehow a bad person would always accompany any attempt that she made to feel loved. And feeling loved was, of course, necessary. Without love, one could not maintain a will to live.

But how did any of this apply to her and Mark? How was it that she was feeling love for him? How was it that she was *still* bad, even in the presence of a good man like him? She knew the answer, of course, and it was time that she lived up to her name and spelled it out. It was time to be a truth teller. Time for her to confess the truth—even if only to herself. And the truth of it all was this: badness had played a central role in her acquisition of Mark. Obtaining him for herself had *always* been her intention—whether he liked it or not. Right from the very beginning she had been working on it, even though she had not been truthful about it until now, not even to herself. Mark was always going to be hers, and nothing was ever going to stand in her way. Not Cy. Not Ruby. Not Alan Summerfield. Not Jocelyn. Not even Mark. If ever there was a monster to contend with in life, it was human needfulness. And she was needful.

Yes, her plots to get Mark had been mostly unconscious—until now—but this was no excuse. Badness had played a part for sure. She had obtained what she wanted regardless of others. She was a bad person. And that was the truth because it *had* to be the truth. Because, if it was the truth, then she had found a way to feel loved and had succeeded in breaking the cycle of death; that cycle of feeling comfortable only in the company of men who were going to abuse her.

Mark was her breakthrough. With him, she could stay alive by acknowledging the bad in herself while clinging to him for strength. She wanted to stay alive for Mark's sake, and with him, this was going to be possible. She would be safe with Mark—and he with her—because he would love her unconditionally. Her burden of past guilt would steadily wane. While the burden of the past would always be there, the beast within was finally under control.

'You *are* actually deluded? Is that it?' asked Mark.

'No Mark, I am not deluded.'

'What, then?'

'Everyone else is.'

I am a bad person, Mark. The only person around here who is not deluded about this is me.

He laughed, but then he embraced her with genuine tenderness. He kissed her sweetly, then whispered into her ear. 'You are so amazingly transparent, Alyssa. I can see that your mind is working overtime to try to justify how you are feeling, but, you know, with me there is no need. You are *not* a bad person. You are just lovely, and I just love you. Emotionally, you are so fragile. You are so vulnerable that you are in danger of breaking my heart.'

Tears of undeserved healing streamed from her eyes as he held her in his arms.

He really did love her.

'You are not alone anymore,' he said. 'Together, we will get through this.'

THE END

ENDNOTE

Readers are advised that the whereabouts of Professor Jorken Obermaaier are currently unknown. All attempts to contact him since his departure last month on a major overseas lecture tour to a foreign power have been fruitless. Despite extensive efforts, the professor has yet to be found. Realistically, given the current hostile and irrational state of the world, he may never be found. To add to our sense of alarm, copies of his famous and disturbing textbook *Beyond Freud; Practice of Validated Transference-focused Psychodynamic Therapy* have begun to disappear from bookshelves.

Perhaps, therefore, it is fitting to conclude with an extract from the great professor's rapidly disappearing *magnum opus* before it is too late, a piece concerning the nature of the Un-conscious mind of the human:

> For the past twenty-eight hundred years, humanity has been advised to *Know thy Self.* Yet, Self-knowledge remains poor. People still do not know *why* they do things. People remain unpredictable and cruel. People remain dangerous to themselves and to others. How are we to make progress?
>
> Could it be that we have been wrong all along? Have we managed to fool ourselves? Even though it seems obvious from personal experience that a mental Self exists in every person, what if the Self we claim to *know* is of little relevance to reality? What if there exists within us all ANOTHER Self, a secret Self, a "state of being" that is hidden from us; a force that works against our ability to be rational and humane?
>
> *Is* there, for example, a persistence of the unseen Self of early childhood? And *are* we—all of us—possessed of this unknown, *secret* Self? Given the past twenty-eight hundred years of ongoing human misery and slaughter despite the advice from the Oracle of Delphi, surely this possibility deserves serious consideration.

Are we victims of Self-deception? Upon honest reflection, can anyone today seriously believe that any Self-stated *motive* is ever wholly true? Does anyone *really* know why he or she does or believes anything? Or do hidden forces lead us by the nose?

Could it be that every Self is affected by a degree of unawareness; that there is a veil in the mind; that the Self exists in TWO parts, one conscious and the other Un-conscious—in keeping with *Higher Order* theories of consciousness, where "consciousness" is nothing but a *created* neurological depiction of those aspects of what can be sensed that seem useful for personal survival—as decided Un-consciously.

I say this is not only possible but highly probable. Having personally interacted with many clients, it seems obvious that there is indeed an Un-conscious early component to the conscious mind and that this difficult-to-access Un-conscious mind is true mind and not part of either our readily accessible subconscious repetitive mind or our non-declarative vegetative brain—contrary to what is claimed by neurophysiologists who talk instead in endless circles about the *Hard Problem* in consciousness and stare themselves blind against *qualia* (i.e., why and how "it" *feels* like x to "me").

What, then, necessarily lies on the underside of a metaphysical Self to give it the base rules required for operation in any environment? What prevails in that *Un*, within our darkness? Could it be that lurking within us all is a self-centred, cruel, and irrational infant? And, if so, are all the precious "truths" we consciously proclaim as adults, especially those about ourselves, merely delusions stemming from our own hubris? If there *is* an early childhood *Un*-consciousness to us all, then surely the *real* truth is that the mind of almost everyone we encounter is but a scrambled mess. And if what lies in our darkness should happen to be nothing but a *broken* child, then surely, in such as these, we are especially *not* who or what we say we are. Yet, whether our child be broken or whole, of one thing we may be certain: we are, all of us, owners of another name.

Jorken Obermaaier, Beyond Freud, *21ˢᵗ century CE*

There is a problem with "The Truth". The problem with the truth is that it has more than one name. O "Adult", what is *your* other name? What has grown out of *your* darkness? And how wary do we need to be of *You*?

763

GLOSSARY

Alyssa: (1) Currently unpopular female name meaning *Truth*. (2) Name of a fragrant flower, *Sweet Alyssum*; sometimes used as a remedy for madness and known then as *Madwort*.

Countertransference: The feelings of a "therapist" towards a client that derive from the therapist's *own* unconscious mind; technically, those parts of the therapist's *own* Self that via unconscious mechanisms the therapist genuinely believes belong instead to the client. The problem applies to everyone else too.

Delusion: A delusion is any sincerely held *belief* that is inconsistent with or not based upon objective reality. Seen in all people.

Gnomon: (*One that knows*). (1) Literally, the time-determining piece on a sundial. (2) Figuratively, in this novel, the entity in the Un-conscious mind that points to when a true perception was lost.

Meaning: What do words *mean*? Words mean what you choose them to mean. Really, they do. (If in doubt, consult Lewis Carroll and Ludwig Wittgenstein).

Time: A function of movement in space that is perceived by the human mind after a certain age and called time. Not perceptible in early childhood, also not by adults during times of close synchronicity with the Un-conscious.

Truth: Indefinable. Dependent on the nature of reality, which is currently unknown despite various overconfident assertions to the contrary. All that can be said about *Truth* is that it has more than one name.

Un-conscious: As used in this book, the Un-conscious is the foundational part of the *aware* mind that we are not conscious of. The term does not refer to a non-aware neurological state of the brain, as in the normal English language sense, but instead denotes a necessary component in a Self-aware metaphysical mind assembly. Note that the Un-conscious part of the aware mind cannot normally be accessed and is not the same as the easily accessed "subconscious mind" of popular use, which seeks to trivialise the influence of the mind's innate dark certainties about "truths".

*Ewin Genghis endeavours to write informative fiction
that explores the deeper meaning of things.*

The author has interacted closely with many people in a career as a biological scientist. Familiarity with the truth of peoples' lives has led to a realisation that we often express views to others that are greatly hypocritical. The phenomenon is explored in literary form, with the author focusing on the main areas of interpersonal dishonesty: sexual truth, the spoken word, religious practice, and philosophical certainty.

A survivor of many of life's challenges, Ewin Genghis is married and currently lives in Australia.

www.ingramcontent.com/pod-product-compliance
Lightning Source LLC
Chambersburg PA
CBHW060720190726
48285CB00001B/4